PHOTOGRAPHS OF OCTOBER

Photographs of OCTOBER

David Slatt,
Congratulations on your
new release!!
From one horror writer
to another—keep at it! The
world needs our writing more
than ever now. Wishing you
abundant joy & success,
M.K. D
1/6/21

BY M.K. DEPPNER

This is a work of fiction. Any references to historical incidents, historical figures, or places are used fictitiously. Other names, characters, places, and events are products of the author's imagination, and any resemblance to actual persons, living or dead, events, or locales is entirely coincidental.

First paperback edition May 2020

Book Design by Danna Mathias
Edited by David Cathcart
Magpie Press Design by Brian Cartwright

ISBN 978-1-7345602-0-6 (paperback)
ISBN 978-1-7345602-1-3 (hardbound)
ISBN 978-1-7345602-2-0 (ebook)

Published by Magpie Press
www.mkdeppner.com

For my family and their unwavering,
lifelong encouragement

Do not let anyone lead you astray.
The one who does what is right is righteous,
just as he is righteous.
The one who does what is sinful is of the devil,
because the devil has been sinning from the beginning.
1 John 3:7–8

"—a wicked little town. Indeed, its character is so clearly and egregiously bad that one might conclude, were the evidence in these later times positive of its possibility, that it was marked for special Providential punishment."
– a letter that appeared in the *Washington Evening Star*, January 1, 1878.

"If a man knows anything, he ought to die with it in him."
–Outlaw Sam Bass, 1878

I

Thursday, October 1st

"The traveling photographer for the festival backed out. We'd like you to take his place," Dr. Cahara said casually as Olivia slid an eight-by-ten into the developing tray.

Great. Olivia's stomach cramped, but she pretended she didn't feel it. She set the timer and sent Dr. Cahara a look that the other woman likely couldn't see in the dim light of the darkroom. "We?"

Olivia was surprised that the breeze from her colleague's heavy sigh didn't reach her from across the room. "He texted me on Monday. Texted! Coward. I met with city council on Tuesday. They want landscapes from around the area. Ten or a dozen. You can handle that."

"I sense stipulations." The timer went off, and Olivia peeked over the side of the tray. Just two more seconds. "Traditional?"

"That'd be nice."

"How much?" She'd done enough favors for the university as a graduate student.

"I'm not really asking," Dr. Cahara said.

"You already know I can't tell you no, Cecelia. How much?" Olivia repeated.

Dr. Cahara said nothing, but Olivia felt her stare. "Ten grand," the woman said finally.

"Christ!" Olivia whipped her print out of the tray—the two-second mark having come and gone. She tossed the ruined print and her gloves into the trash.

But ten grand. With that kind of money she could put a down payment on the house on Sunset Avenue. Olivia's mind spun up and down the list of responsibilities the job would entail. She'd spend over a thousand on paper, chemicals, and film—all expedited, of course, but B&H was good with quick orders. She'd also pull some all-nighters and gain five pounds from stress eating, but she'd been through worse. Maybe it would be OK. And B&H did have a roll of photo paper taller than she was.

"You know what would wow them?" Olivia asked.

"That's up to you," Dr. Cahara replied. "You've worked large scale for longer than anyone else here. I know eight-by-tens won't impress them though."

They wouldn't. "They were really going to pay him ten thousand dollars to come here? Tell them to donate to the university while they're at it. The ventilation system in here sucks, though not literally."

Dr. Cahara was already at the darkroom's interior door. Olivia could only see the outline of the woman's hair in the available light as a dark floating halo. "I talked them into giving you more. I want a print by the end of the day tomorrow though. The largest the printer can handle. Traditional if you're feeling froggy." There was no room for argument.

"When do they want them on the walls?" Olivia conjured images of the Flint Hills in her head. The area offered no shortage of scenic views ready to be captured. If the weather was good, she might be able to get half the shots she needed in one day.

"A week before the showing."

That was on the thirtieth. She had an artist show card on the fridge for the traveling photographer already. Rolling into town and hanging nature prints was apparently too difficult. Or he'd decided Warren wasn't worth it.

"That's, like, three weeks away," Olivia stated. She hadn't meant to sound whiny, but there it was.

"Maybe you'll disappear too, and then you won't have to worry about it at all," Dr. Cahara joked.

"Yeah, ha-ha," Olivia tried to joke back. The comment hit her strangely. "Maybe then my art would be worth something."

Dr. Cahara had a good laugh at that as she exited the darkroom. Olivia still wasn't sure she thought it was funny.

The string of disappearances had already led to announcements that increased security would be present at the festival, but October threw the town off kilter every year anyway. And Olivia hadn't known anything to get in the way of the annual Harvest Festival. One Halloween the sleet had been so bad the city had to run their ice trucks and scrape the streets with snowplows to make sure the festivities went on. To Olivia, that was almost more disturbing.

She'd lived twenty minutes outside of town for most of her life and had been relatively secluded from the hysteria, though her last few years teaching at the university and living in town had made her Octobers inconvenient. She preferred to spend the weekend of the festival at her mother's home outside of town, safely away from the noise and the crowds.

It looked like this year would be different though. Ten grand, she reminded herself. What an absurd amount of money. What they requested was just as ridiculous.

Back out in the open studio, her phone buzzed on the long table that was littered with her most recent printing project. Mother. Again. The mail hadn't appeared for the day, she was deathly ill, or Olivia was late getting the lawn mowed that week. Lots of little emergencies. Olivia had to get outside before the sun set though. She silenced the call and started packing her equipment.

An hour later she dragged herself outside with her large-format camera and some sketches in tow. The beginnings of what would be twelve roughly drawn landscapes looked back at her as she sat in her SUV. She had parked off the side of the road near a deer trail that followed a path of least resistance up the hill to the cliffs. She'd been there the day before with her digital just messing around, but now she had a purpose. If she could realize these photographs in under a month and get them up at the gallery, the house on Sunset was as good as hers.

She got her digital and a light meter out of the back of the vehicle. It would be more efficient to take some backups while she waited for the perfect light. Her set of prints from the previous day was off the table—a distinct horse-like figure in almost every shot. The fact she had missed it proved how careless she had gotten, how far removed she was from taking her art seriously.

At the top of the hill that looked out over the valley, the spread of reds, yellows, and golds of the turning trees caught the fading sunlight in a thousand different directions. Each tree down the side of the cliffs and into the valley below was different from its neighbor.

Olivia had always thought the cliffs held their own sort of beauty. They weren't vast or deep, but they had an artistic darkness about them. They held shadows that shifted and changed every moment just beyond her field of vision. Olivia liked the mystery behind it, especially in the fall when the cool air felled the leaves and sent a sharp chill through the once-warm breezes of summer.

Color seeped from the landscape, heading toward the tones of grey, black, and white that appeared just before the sun winked out of existence. It was the time when the world was only a photograph, when what the eye saw and what would come out in a black-and-white photograph were one and the same.

Olivia stared out at the approaching shadows as she set up her tripod and camera and watched them move through the leaves and branches of the trees. The setting sun always played tricks on the human eye as the light shifted and bent. She kept her eyes on the shadows in the cliffs beyond, waiting for whatever spirits lurked among them to show their laughing faces. She checked her light meter again, then slipped under the dark cloth. Now the world belonged to her through the glass before her, and the world outside the light-blocking cloth fell away.

She opened and closed her hands, stretching between shots. They had felt oddly cramped and cold over the past few days. Her fingertips had turned white the other day too. If she didn't get used to the extra work quickly, she'd have to find someone who did hand massages. She couldn't allow anything to slow her down.

2

5:45 P.M., THURSDAY, OCTOBER 1ST

SIMON MONROE HAD JUST FINISHED READING THOMPSON'S new biography on the booming days of Warren in the late 1800s, and he finished with more questions than when he started. He'd almost quit reading halfway through at the painting of the "good" Mayor William Monroe. The man famously worked his staff to death. There were unsubstantiated claims that he'd had his hands in all manner of unsavory enterprises, and he was a douchebag. Perhaps most famous was his reported involvement in the murder of his wife and another well-known member of the community prior to his own suspicious death.

His scrupulous, frugal governing of the town was likely the single biggest contributor to its flourishing and the reason it was still around, but if that was the tradeoff for being a giant dick, Dr. Simon Monroe wouldn't have minded if Warren had passed into history, and he were working in one of the state's other university towns instead. It was hard to compete with the haunted city of Atchison, but a headless horseman and one intense haunting had been enough to keep people in Warren entertained for over a century now. It made for a good story and supported their tourism industry if applied in the right doses, or so city council seemed to think.

Simon pushed back in his chair and stared at the bookshelf on the opposite wall that housed dozens more books on Warren's somewhat unsavory past. *Warren: The Heydays, Warren's Victorian* (an attempt in the 1970s at a lighter look at Warren's booming years, which came off a little flat in Simon's opinion); *Warren: A Critical Eye; Warren: You're the Best; Warren: It Couldn't Have Actually Been that Bad; Warren: We'll Justify Anything Because We Live There,* and so on. All he was missing was *Warren: A Christmas Special,* but he had a feeling that was out there too.

Thompson's vision of Mayor William Monroe was more gleaming than most, and Simon was interested to see where the man had found some of his information. Fifteen years earlier, a few residents still had second-hand knowledge of the events, but now they were all dead, and the story had taken on mythic proportions.

The headache crept up on Simon, as did the shrinking of his vision as he continued to stare idly at the

books across from his desk. He dug his hands into his hair as the pain scaled up from a dull throb to an escalating alarm in his brain.

Someone knocked on his door. Fucking open office hours. He wouldn't be having them from four to six ever again. Steeling himself as best he could, he called out for whoever it was to come in. The door opened, but no one entered.

Simon stood and went to the door, his usually slow temper about to boil over. But no one was there except a hot breeze that smelled like smoke off the prairie. Heat crawled over him, up his arms, behind his eyes. Despite the heat, all the hair on his arms and neck stood up, and goose bumps broke out all over his body.

The way flames will creep over the burning frame of a house, consuming it before your eyes.

He stumbled back into his office. Sinus pressure, or maybe it was allergies, coupled with the stress of mid semester. A migraine. Smoke from the fire out at the Tallgrass Reserve had gotten to him. Maybe he was allergic.

Pain slithered from his temples behind his eyes, and the dark tunnel feathered across his vision until he thought he might thrash his head against his desk. He scrambled in the top drawer of his desk for the Excedrin and popped three into his mouth. This was normal for some people, right?

Ten minutes later he was still panting as the pain started to subside, and then it was gone. He looked at the clock. Six on the dot. The air would be good for his head on the walk home.

Dizziness nearly overcame him when he stood, and there was a brief burst of light behind his eyes but no more pain. If it was like this tomorrow, he would go to urgent care. Poor university insurance and all. Maybe it was low blood pressure. He was almost forty. That wasn't unheard of.

Then the dizziness was gone too. He shook his head, but nothing seemed wrong. Did Excedrin work that fast?

Assuming the headache stayed away for the evening, he was ready to go home and work on his speech. Pandering address, more like. Warren took itself so seriously that it almost seemed satirical, and the more he curated his portion of the opening words to the area's historical tastes, the more city council approved. He'd have to stop by the historical society at some point and talk to Don to see what he thought about it all, but that was a week or two away.

He was halfway home by the time he realized he'd forgotten his notes and his light jacket. He was forgetful, especially at this time of year. The festival always seemed a bit frenzied, the way animals rushed in for feeding time on the ranch when fodder in the pastures was sparse, and the energy was palpable. Midwest Warren overloaded on the cornstalks and pumpkins as much as any New England town might. It felt old enough that none of it was out of place.

But somehow it was all unsettlingly genuine, right down to the children's reenactments of the death of the town's mayor and his wife. His cousin had come one year and left mid-performance, either unable to stomach the subject or unable to watch it performed by fifth graders. Perhaps Simon was numb to it now, or he'd just taken to seeing it as satire after so long.

He wandered up the sidewalk to his home and felt happier again. The scrolling woodwork around the porch, the dark wood siding that contrasted with the white around the sides, the gables in the front, and the two stained-glass windows on either side of the door—one in flowers and the other in art deco geometrics, changed sometime in the 1920s, no doubt—it all relaxed him. Old-world charm. Bits of history cobbled together until it felt nostalgic.

But something was wrong with the house. Simon didn't feel he was particularly in tune with the world around him, but Shep didn't greet him in the window next to the door, like usual, and it seemed he'd left the front hall light on. Unusual for him.

He scaled the steps and tested the front door—locked. That was a good sign. Feeling paranoid though, he went around back, through the wooden gate, still heavy and hidden under the honeysuckle he'd let get out of control. Nothing looked amiss there, and the back door was locked. No broken windows on the French doors, and no tears in the patio screen, but still no Shep at the door.

He let himself in from the back, something sure to get the dog's attention, but there was no sound of skittering claws on the hardwood floors. He called Shep's name as he walked through the house. Nothing was knocked over, and all the books seemed to be in their rightful places, but his heartbeat still climbed up his throat. Shep always came when called.

When he reached the living room, he was relieved to see the dog sitting on the couch.

"Shep, you idiot, there you are. Come here."

But the dog wouldn't move. He sat on the middle cushion with his head turned to his left, staring into space.

"Shep? Look back!" Simon said, resorting to the first herding command that came to mind, but the dog didn't even flinch. He was riveted, looking at nothing.

"Shep, look back!" Simon commanded again, walking toward the dog. The sharp smell of urine greeted him as he neared the couch. Still the black, white, and brown dog sat looking into space, frozen. Too much eye; that's what the old-fashioned herders called it. When the dog would be entranced and staring at the objects to be herded, ignoring its handler completely. Shep might be ending his days in comfort, but he had been a fine herding dog in his youth and not prone to losing his confidence.

What was wrong with his dog? Simon reached out to touch the air next to Shep, where he was looking, and his hand bumped something solid, warm, invisible, almost like bumping into someone's shoulder as he walked past.

And then Shep was all motion, a deep growl breaking the silence as he leapt toward where Simon's hand was, teeth and gums bared.

Simon jerked his hand backwards and fell on his ass as he attempted to get away from the ball of fur and fury. Shep landed on the cushion and then cartwheeled off the couch, sliding into the nearest bookcase. He was up in an instant, growling at face level not halfway across the room from his master.

"Shep! That'll do!" Simon cried in a last attempt to get the dog's attention, holding his hand close to his chest even though the dog had not bitten it. What had he imagined he had touched?

One ear perked toward Simon. "That'll do!" Simon commanded again, hoping the fear he felt wasn't permeating the air around him. Everyone knew dogs could smell fear. But why the hell should he fear his dog whom he'd raised since he was a tiny puppy and hadn't taken hold of anything else unless commanded to do so?

"That'll do!" Simon yelled again, and this time the dog relaxed and slunk over to Simon.

Simon flinched and stood quickly, still wary of the dog and its odd behavior. He reeked of urine, but Simon was relieved when Shep pressed himself against Simon's leg and looked up at him, awaiting his next command.

"Are you OK?" he asked the dog, who whined in response. "Do I need to call Dennis?"

There was a giant piss stain on the center couch cushion, along with a smear of shit. How had Shep sat there until he pissed himself? Simon needed to get him into the bath and clean the couch, but his legs felt like they were about to give out.

Simon went into the bathroom and sat on the toilet, his insides churning. Shep slid in after him, shoulders hunched and tail between his legs. Where the white met the black on his neck, his hair stood on end, on alert even though he was acting submissive.

Simon groaned as his belly cramped. "I'm so sorry, pup."

The dog sat his urine-soaked ass on Simon's feet, but Simon couldn't think straight due to the seizing in his belly. Nervous stomach. Something he'd gotten from his mother. His lactose intolerance came courtesy his father.

When he could finally get up without worrying he was going to shit himself, he started the walk-in shower and stripped down. Shep following him in without a peep and let Simon scrub him down. Small blessings for a laid-back dog. Most of the time anyway.

After his shower and Shep's scrub and dry, Simon peeked into the living room. Nothing there. He could have written it off as a complete fantasy if not for the giant wet blotch on the couch. How long had Shep sat there, staring at nothing? Maybe the dog had had a seizure, or a tumor was pressing on some spot in his brain. God, Simon hoped not. But that didn't explain bumping into something—or someone—who was invisible. He wiped his hand on his jeans. It wasn't right, whatever it was.

His headache had returned. Not surprising after the scare. Shep was finally curled up in his nest of blankets in the corner opposite the couch, clearly and thoroughly pooped and not interested in helping his master clean the couch.

Simon scrubbed until his fingers smelled more like urine than the cushion. It was late, and he was starving and restless.

He washed his hands under hot water until they were red and raw. It reminded him of the cold winters as a kid out in the freezing air while his grandfather tended the animals. He was still thinking about how raw his hands felt when he fell asleep in his recliner before he'd even had a chance to fix dinner. Sleep carried him away, but dreams about whatever he might've touched kept the sleep from being restful.

3

GATHERING THE BONES WAS THE MOST DIFFICULT PART. NOT that there weren't plenty around, but Warren of the twenty-first century presented a few more obstacles than it had in the nineteenth. There were blessedly few cameras around, though it was unlikely any of them would spot him at this point.

The skull of the beast had been remarkably easy to locate. Still at the bottom of the canyon with assorted other pieces. Skull, femur from a hind leg. All it took was a little poking around in the brush. Remarkable what years of legends could do to keep a place untouched by humans. An old handkerchief rested there too, and he stared at it for some time before pocketing it. How it hadn't disintegrated with time was curious, but so was his return.

The dust had been disturbed near where he'd found the old beast's bones. It could have just been an animal snuffling about, but if he was back, there was a chance his old friend was around somewhere too. And just as well. Must have one with the other. Symmetry. Balance in the universe and all that.

Austin would have a fit if he saw what was being done to the bones of his old steed. Let him.

The other pieces had been a more difficult, but anything could be had with money these days, or a little searching and time. He'd obtained the owl's skull, ribcage, and ear feathers with patience and a night spent in the loft of a barn outside of town. The heart of a bull was also easy, though he wished he could have stuck around for the rancher's reaction the next morning. He'd only taken a moment to press his hands inside the dying animal's chest, to feel its heart beating wildly in panic before he'd torn it out and painted the creature's stall with its warm blood. A little redecorating. No big thing.

It was remarkable to be in a body again when he could worm his way in. There had been no struggle, as he'd expected, but the human was so connected to his past that slipping in when the man was engrossed in looking for *her* or dreaming about the past, well, it was almost too easy. It was nice to come and go as he pleased though, to sail away on the wind and hunt around for the lovely ladies with *her* scent. Not that he could do much more than smell them out when he wasn't in his willing carrier, but it was nice to have that option.

He wasn't certain what had brought him back. He'd served an infinitesimal time on the rack for what he'd done, and he still had eons to go, but something had brought him back to the surface, to that place with all the warm living souls he'd almost forgotten about. Humans disturbed old things all the time though without realizing it. Plowing the land, digging foundations, scraping the earth for roads. Perhaps they had disturbed his bones in the quest for progress he had been part of not so long ago.

At least no one had summoned him. Or if they had, he wasn't tied to one place. He did retrieve a rib, just for kicks, and he took a moment to pay respects to his remains before he was ousted from the place. That was a little odd, disconcerting. An out-of-body experience, as it were.

Finding the herbs was shockingly easy. He could get just about anything anywhere nowadays, but there was a great little voodoo herb shop in town run by a nice lady who had been very helpful. How long would he have searched a century ago for all that? Lucky little fiend he was. The sinew was donated by a deer unlucky enough to be passing by on his way to the cliffs. Then he hid the little bundle out of the way and put the key where he could find it. Insurance, just in case things got out of hand later on.

Warren at midnight in early October was delicious, but how was he going to enjoy it if he kept wondering about all the particulars of his return? He detected a snap of decay in the air but not much yet. The traditional cool weather of October was still coming a little late that year. Many people were still awake, what with electric lights in all the houses and down all the streets, but a few were sleeping soundly. He knew exactly who they were and where they would be. It was so hard to choose just one at a time though, and he'd made a bit of a mistake taking the first three so close together. Order was important. Mayhem was fine on occasion and kept him in business, but consistent orderliness made the havoc that much sweeter. It would also ensure he could stay hidden.

Who?

He decided.

He knew he should have steered his host home, to the dark warmth that was waiting for him, but he couldn't, not on such a night. That night was important. Moving with the wind, he went through town on foot, only another person out for a late-night walk, someone who could not sleep on such a cool night, when the trees were beginning to rustle.

Ah, the beginning of decay, a putrid rotting to senses so sensitive, senses that had not smelled the world until that year, that month, that day. The rotting wasn't like a corpse. No, he knew the distinct way a corpse smelled, how the earth and the small crawling things and the flesh all melted together after the essence had fled the body. The rotting was new, like a scent that brought change and coolness into the world. It was like that every year, but he had waited patiently for this year

Now he was at the residence of one of the thirteen. Earlier, when she had been out and all those in her home had been away, he had unlatched two of several windows in the front room. He found them still unlocked and pushed one open effortlessly, assuring himself that no one was still awake and that the place was silent before he slid inside and listened again.

He moved through the dark as part of the house and made his way down the hall to the first door on the right. She'd left it open, silly girl, because she thought she was safe from everything there. But she had no fancy alarm system, no dog, no tricks to keep intruders from walking in and doing what they wanted. Not that any human security system would have kept him out anyway. A pity her boyfriend hadn't stayed the night. Otherwise she might have been safe. At least for the time being.

The bed was close to the door, and she slept soundly, her back to him as she faced the open window. She looked so peaceful, so much like the other girls who didn't know they were related, that they could all trace their bloodlines back to *her*. Fine brunette hair and pale skin gleamed in the light from her bedside lamp, which she had forgotten to turn off before she fell into slumber.

He pulled his handkerchief from his pocket and squeezed it in his fist, then moved to the bed. He paused to align his steady breathing with her slow pulse. Then he moved in to press the cloth over the girl's mouth and nose. He reveled in the struggle when she awoke. Her grey eyes were wide with fright, and she tried to scream, batting uselessly at his arms.

In that moment just before she fell unconscious, he saw the recognition in her eyes. It wasn't recognition for the man he was but for the man he once was. Old memory, scent memory, ancestral memory didn't die.

She was conformation that it lingered. Then her eyes rolled back in her head, and she relaxed.

The first had been quick and tasty, as this one would be. Really, he had been greedy to go after them so quickly, but with the spell he assumed only lasting so long, a demon had to act fast. Snap them up, crunch their bones. Thirteen in all, saving the best for last. Or not, depending on his mood.

He hefted the woman over his shoulder, carrying her out of her comfortable home. Heavy meat. He'd had some trouble finding the best of them, truth be told. *She* was hiding. Or *he* was hiding her. Cloaking her somehow. He wasn't sure, but there was the tang of something else in the air that concealed her. His nose was good though. She wouldn't stay hidden forever.

4

Friday, October 2nd

Olivia woke before dawn again, unable to sleep. It had started even before she'd learned she was working the impossible deadline for the Harvest Festival, but the looming event seemed to make the restless sleep that much worse. How long could she stay awake and still function? Didn't truckers take No-Doz, so they could make long-haul trips? She felt she'd read that somewhere.

That morning she'd woken up from a nightmare that clung to the fringes of her memory. She couldn't remember specifics, but it seemed to obscure her vision, like dust on a print. She stared at the film of dust on the window, visible in the light of the approaching dawn. It had not rained enough lately, and the window sported spots across its parched surface. She moved her tongue around her dry mouth and reached for the water bottle next to her bed.

Her head cleared somewhat on the walk through campus. She liked to park in a less-used lot on the far side. Everyone else seemed to be in a funk that morning too, and the usual chatter that surrounded her on the stroll wasn't present.

She pulled her shawl closely around her and picked up her pace. It was one of those odd October mornings where it couldn't decide whether it was summer or fall. A cool humidity left pockets of mist in the evergreens on either side of the wide walks into campus. She would get into the classroom, and all would be well.

And really, she should enjoy fall. It was supposed to be a transitory time, a time of great change, and it seemed like all the world loved it—pumpkin spice everything and fuzzy boots and all that. But all it ever meant to her was that there was still half the semester left to go and another entire semester until summer break. She couldn't argue with the breathtaking scenery though. Warren boasted great old trees in every shade of autumn that a tourist with a digital camera could handle.

The bell hadn't rung by the time she reached her classroom, but her students were buzzing louder than usual; either that or her quiet walk into campus had left her feeling off. She sat in a chair at the front and pretended not to listen, scanning through a stack of papers as if she were making sure they were correct. She had just about sorted out their chattering when one of the students addressed her.

"Professor?"

She looked up. Many eyes were on her, but the voice came from Diana, a junior in the art department. "Yes?"

"Did you hear? There was another disappearance." Diana pulled a newspaper out of her backpack to show her the headline.

"Oh?" Olivia pushed her reading glasses farther up her nose and put down the papers she was looking at. How many was it now?

Diana pushed the newspaper toward her. "When we first saw her picture, we thought it was you. I mean, until we saw the name. You're usually here so early, you know."

Olivia scrutinized the color photo on the front page of the *Warren Herald.* They weren't wrong about a resemblance. They had the same brown hair, the same deep-grey eyes, and the same facial shape. But her nose certainly didn't look like *that*, nor did her hairline. Olivia could see how her students thought it was their early morning professor at first glance. Almost out of their 8:30 bright-and-early class. Were they disappointed or relieved? That wasn't a productive line of thinking. And who at the *Herald* had decided that sensationalism was back in style? It seemed an odd thing to report on with so much else going on in the world.

"That's bizarre," she commented quietly, squinting to see the picture and the subsequent article more clearly.

The missing girl was twenty-one-year-old Lynne Jacobs, an undergraduate majoring in the social sciences with a focus on pre-law. She'd had roommates, a boyfriend, and a slew of friends, but none of them had been there that night. Pre-meditation. Window unlocked during the day. Suspects were being sought for questioning, and so on and so forth. Olivia pursed her lips as she read further, eyes scanning the notices at the bottom of the article stating that if readers knew something about the crime or had seen something suspicious, they were to call such and such number and that their information would be kept confidential. The police were considering a curfew and suggested that those out and about finish their business and get home by 9:00 p.m. in the meantime. Seemed a little fast for them to be reporting on it, but Warren was sleepy. Nothing much happened around there, so reporters were probably hungry for the story. Perhaps that was the only cause for the article's sensational nature.

The bell rang, and Olivia handed the newspaper back to Diana. She forced the strange misfortune of the girl who resembled her so much out of her mind. She would have to grab a copy of the paper later and dissect the article when she got home. Surely she wasn't related to the girl. She would know something like that. But people saw their doppelgangers all the time.

She launched into a lecture on photography in the late 1800s, relying heavily on her detailed lesson plan for the day. She tried to shift her perspective; it wouldn't do to have resting bitch face all day.

To lessen the pain of sitting in a classroom for an hour at 8:30 in the morning, she brought in relevant objects as often as possible and let the students experiment with them. That day she'd brought in a working box camera from the late 1800s for her students to take photographs with. ("Carefully, please!" she reminded them.) Still life today and into the studio for portraits in a week or two, provided their initial work went smoothly.

While she helped another group with their still-life setup, someone behind called out to her. "Miss? Miss Weatherford?" they inquired again before she could tear herself away from the group she was with.

"Norwich," she corrected automatically as she turned to see which male student had gotten her (not difficult) name wrong. The voice was unfamiliar. Probably someone who didn't show up to class regularly. However, everyone either had their heads down concentrating on settings for the camera or were talking with their group members.

"Did someone need me?" Olivia asked.

Silence and twenty-six heads shaking.

"No one?"

They shook their heads again and returned to their work.

As Olivia promised to take the film to her studio and develop them for her students to see during the next class, the odd feeling that someone needed her—wrong name or not—persisted.

The bell rang, and Olivia's students filed out, some waving to her and others walking out in a sleepy haze. She didn't blame them; all she wanted to do was go back home and sleep for the rest of the day. But it was Friday, and for that Olivia was grateful. She hoped whoever had had a question had gotten it answered. It needled at her.

Her weekend was about to be busier than the five-day school week. She would get Dr. Cahara her print before the end of the day. She would need to spend a morning in the darkroom developing her students' photographs from class and a few more of her own that needed a chemical bath to reveal their secrets. And then hopefully she could take a drive out to the prairie reserve and photograph the view from there, so long as there was no wind or rain.

She quickly rearranged desks and stacked up her papers and notes, prepared to leave and see what was happening in the photography department. Escape from one building to the next and outside for as short a time as possible. Climate control was one of the world's greatest inventions.

The half-hour bell rang out from the campus's tower bell a few moments after the bell inside the building, the sound carrying throughout the campus. Olivia looked out the window at the grey sky that soared high above the second-story classroom. She wondered if it was going to rain. They needed rain even if that would keep her from getting the shots she needed. Everything felt dry. Her eyes drifted down to the semi-empty grassy area outside the building. Only a few students still moved toward their classes.

Then, right in her line of sight next to one of the large maples that towered over the building, she saw a figure in black. The figure stood still, facing the humanities building. Olivia got the disturbing feeling that the figure, tall and broad shouldered, was staring at her. It was impossible, of course. He was probably standing there smoking a cigarette and admiring the architecture, but she still didn't like it.

Creeping paranoia sent her pulse racing. She couldn't see his face, didn't know who he was. His head was obscured by a branch of the tree whose branches reached right up to the windows of her classroom.

Olivia stuffed her things into her bag and grabbed the box camera. Then she bolted out the door and down the stairs, heading for the doors opposite the side with the figure in black. As she barreled outside, she ran right into the tall figure and yelped.

"Olivia Norwich, what a surprise!"

Recognizing the voice, Olivia apologized profusely and extracted herself from the arms of the figure in black (black suit and coat, though it wasn't quite *that* cold outside).

"Oh, Dr. Monroe, I'm sorry! I was in such a hurry to get out of the classroom that I didn't see anyone on the stairs!" She was out of breath and felt silly. He was handsome but harmless, married to his work like she and so many others in the art and history departments were. That he made her a little weak in the knees was not something she needed to pursue.

Dr. Monroe dropped his hands, which had reflexively grabbed her arms to steady her. His grip was strong even with the black leather gloves he was wearing. His strength surprised her. What had she expected out of a history professor? Some of them probably went to the gym too.

He had already apologized for frightening her and had moved on to another topic. Olivia tried to catch up.

"You know, Olivia, we need to talk about the history of this town sometime. I know you have photographs from some of the older families stashed away in your department's archives. You should study them. The history here is amazing. And please," he smiled, "call me Simon."

So old fashioned. Steadfast. Being on a first-name basis with Dr. Monroe wasn't that high on her priority list. She had way too much going on. But the flush crept up her neck and face before she could stop it. She was staring, objectifying. God, she had to extract herself from the conversation before she said something she might regret. "Thank you, Dr. Monroe, but I really need to get to my studio. I'm running on a pretty tight schedule today."

Either he didn't hear her, or he knew she was lying because he kept talking. Sort of lying. She had lots of things to do, but she was flying by the seat of her pants.

"I heard you're working on an exhibit for the festival. Congrats. They don't ask that of people lightly." His smile was genuine, as were his congratulations.

Olivia felt herself thaw. Why was she so damn uptight and paranoid? The man was just trying to be nice. She could at least give him the time of day. And she thought he knew Dr. Cahara. Maybe he would be a good contact to have. "Yeah. Yes, I am, thank you. Scrambling to finish even though I've just gotten started. I'm just kind of winging the direction I'm taking. They're vague about what they want and didn't exactly give me a reasonable deadline."

Dr. Monroe rolled his eyes, a gesture that made him look younger and more attractive, much to Olivia's dismay. "That's the way they are. I've given the opening and closing addresses for a while now, and they're always vague about what they want until the day of. Then they try to change everything."

"Oh, please don't tell me that," Olivia said, laughing. "If they ask for new prints, they'll have to postpone the festival for a week."

Dr. Monroe's easy laugh filled her. It was the kind of laugh that made her think he had a good sense of humor. "Well, we both know they certainly wouldn't do that. Let me know if you have any questions about the festival or if you're wondering what they might be looking for. I'm glad to help."

Olivia felt the tension that had been developing between her shoulder blades ease a little. "Thank you. Really. I appreciate it."

"Of course," he replied and then turned to go. She couldn't pass over the potential lifeline or at least someone to share the misery with her. And to be honest, she probably needed the help.

"Actually, I do have questions," she said, and he stopped to look back at her. God, those eyes. The flush returned. "A lot. I think I'm in over my head with it. This isn't your first rodeo with them, as it were, so yeah . . . yes, I could use the help."

They exchanged numbers and emails, and Dr. Monroe shook her hand. Professional, polite, courteous. Nothing like what she'd heard.

"I'll let you get back to work. Please give my regards to Dr. Cahara, and have a wonderful day." He dipped his head in a half nod, half bow and then disappeared up the stairs.

Olivia hurried down the flight of stairs, glancing back to see if Dr. Monroe was standing there, staring at her as he had been staring at the building just a few minutes earlier. He wasn't. She just saw the tails of his coat disappear around the corner at the top of the stairs. After their pleasant encounter, she felt bad for being creeped out when she caught him staring. He had probably been deep in thought, looking at the building or staring off into space. There was the paranoia again.

They had politely stayed out of each other's way for at least eight years now, though she had taught off and on down the hall from his office for at least four of those years. Had they ever even had a full conversation? A hello here and there? A "How are things in your department?" A brief lecture on how she should look into the history of something or other? (Right, like she had time for that.)

She had watched him at various faculty functions, seen him move through rooms and through crowds of people with the ease of someone who enjoyed being around others. Olivia kept to the outside of the room, glass of wine in hand, more than happy to watch people from a distance. He had caught her . . . studying him on more than one occasion, and she'd always looked away after the little jolt his gaze gave her. She'd never meant to stare. It was just that his form drew her eyes whenever she let her guard down and let her eyes wander. She'd not done much in the way of portraiture photography, but he would be an excellent subject.

Of course, she'd also heard he was obsessed with his work, that he had no social life, that he didn't attend many department functions, and so on. Dedication to work didn't bother her. She'd be obsessed with her own project for the next three and a half weeks. And dammit, she was grateful that someone else knew what she was going through. She was thirty-five years old, for God's sake. It was time she learned to ask for help.

By the time she arrived at the steps of the Schneider Arts & Sciences building through the long breezeway that connected the other arts and sciences building to it, she was over the day already. The last thing she wanted to do was develop more film or make contact sheets or fuck with masks if the ventilation was on the fritz. But she needed to quit being whiny if she was going to get anything done.

Olivia dragged out her most recent contact print and looked over the images with a small magnifier. Nothing. No horse. She hadn't wanted to ask Dr. Cahara if she thought strict landscapes were in order because she was afraid of the answer. No challenge was too small for that woman. Better to make sure any farm animals or wildlife stayed out of it.

She pulled the scanned images up on the computer and zoomed in on the sections where the horse had appeared in the eight-by-ten.

Northing.

A tiny horse on the prairie that appeared between developing and printing. It didn't make sense.

Olivia selected an image to print, was more careless than she cared to admit with her adjustments, then waited while the large printer warmed up. Once it whirred to life and started churning out the large print, she wandered back downstairs to the newsstand by the front doors of the building, bought a paper, and then ambled back up.

She stared at the girl on the front page as she walked. Maybe she was a cousin. Mother might know, but then again, Mother might be in a mood.

Olivia set the paper aside with one final look at the picture, then went inside the first door to the darkroom and let her eyes adjust in the dim light. Once the door behind her was firmly closed, she slipped inside the inner door into darkness. She did a quick recon to make sure no one had left anything light sensitive out, firmly closing several packets of paper. She reminded herself to chastise the graduate students when she saw them next. She could have really fucked up their next visit to the darkroom, and they knew better. After a second trip around the room checking the enlargers and the long counters on the far end, she thought it was safe to turn on the overhead. She hadn't tripped over anything on her way around, so that was promising.

She blinked in the florescent light as it warmed up.

Suddenly, she was in a basement somewhere. The floor was earthen. She could smell the dust of it, the old musky odor. Something watched from nearby, but she wasn't frightened of it. What had she heard her mother say, buried somewhere in her childhood? Something that had been floating through her mind on repeat lately. Oh, yes. *My dear, if you wake and see a man standing at the foot of your bed, be not afraid. He is your guardian angel.*

She touched her face, and she was back in the darkroom again. Sleeping on her feet, not in her bed. She needed a nap. She scanned the room. A few drawers at the long counter had been shaken open at some point, but that was it. She slid them all shut and then pawed through the stash of photographic paper. The largest they had was sixteen-by-twenty-ish. Dr. Cahara would have to be happy with that. She flipped the overhead light off and headed out of the room to get the rest of her supplies.

At the printer, her heart did a little jog. There was the horse again. Larger . . . and closer. That was impossible.

Olivia grabbed her eight-by-ten. Same horse, different location. Like it had been grazing and moved between the earlier print and the later one. Its magnificent details were no doubt thanks to the large-format camera. No matter that it hadn't been in that position when she'd taken the photograph.

She no longer felt froggy.

5

October 2, 1895

Austin thought about his mother and how her boots had flown from her body after the accident. How tightly had they been laced? He had never seen his mother's feet without boots or stockings, and he couldn't stop staring at them, tiny and bare and white, peeking out from under her skirts. And her boots, somehow flung to the middle of the road.

The ghost of his mother had stood in the doorway to the barn before he left for Texas the first time. She was prim in the dress she had been wearing when her buggy and was blindsided by another buggy coming around from a side street. She wore no boots, and her feet were clean, though the lace on her hem was two inches deep in mud. Her boots had flown off her tiny feet when the wheels of the vehicle had taken her to the ground. They had never caught the driver, though the carriage itself was found abandoned blocks away at the end of the town. There were no signs of the driver or any identifying placards. Austin had an idea, but he wasn't about to start rumors regarding any of the Monroes. He didn't need more trouble with them.

When he was nearly to her, she turned her head and disappeared, as she always did. Austin had become used to her presence and the feeling of warmth when he passed through where she had been standing. She was his sentinel, he supposed, and he had grown used to her being there over the years. The horror when he had first seen her, the shock, the tears, the cursing of the devil for the reminder, that had all faded with time. He would miss her when she moved on from whatever she needed to accomplish. At least that was what the traveling gypsy had said when they stood together in the yard and stared at the wispy figure waiting in the doorway to the barn. The gypsy woman stared long, and Austin's mother returned the stare with equal measure, not disappearing until whatever silent conversation she was having with the dark-haired woman was finished.

"If she ever speaks to you, listen," was all the woman said after a long silence. She wouldn't accept any payment for the visit except his promise that he would listen and a small portion of grain. She didn't say if she had spoken to Austin's mother or not. For some things of this world and not, it was best to know less.

Sometimes Evelyn seemed as fragile to him, as if she would disappear if he reached out to her. But she wasn't. Despite the haunted feeling that surrounded her and the shadows that followed her, she was strong and good. If he could get himself in with Gates down in Texas and bring the wire back up into Kansas and Colorado, he'd be set. Evelyn's family couldn't object.

Gates seemed to agree with his string of thoughts. The heat was not so oppressive that day, though it tasted of storms. It had a different tang to it from Kansas. He would be glad to get on the train and head back north.

"I need you up there in Kansas, Hearth. You've got connections to Nebraska, Missouri, and Colorado. Texas and Oklahoma finally like me pretty well, but you've got a way with the folks there in your corner of the

Midwest, and the Colorado flatlands sure will benefit from miles of wire. We'll have to send in posts there, but that shouldn't be a problem."

Austin turned the edges of his hat around and around. "I had a thought about that."

Gates leaned back in his chair. "I'm listening."

"You're a big bug in the business. I'm certain you've seen the limestone posts up north and to the Nebraska border. Out by Dodge too. The posts are heavy, but there will be no need to haul lumber there. Mine the limestone out west, and it'll stay out west. No transportation costs for lumber or the chance it'll rot on the way. I can't expound upon its advantages enough, and it will cost you less than your wood fence here in the long haul. No rot and no splitting. That fence'll stand for a hundred years or more with the limestone."

"I've seen them," Gates replied, "and some customers have ordered wire with the intention of using it with limestone posts. I'm attracted to the idea of not shipping thousands of wood posts out west just to hear of them rotting on the way or within a few years of being installed." He paused, perhaps gauging Austin's thoughts. "Some might suggest that wood makes the posts more profitable. What do you make of that?"

Austin shook his head. "That wouldn't sit right with the Gates name, I imagine."

"Right you are."

Austin held his breath, hoping for more good news.

"If you can get me some convincing numbers, that might be what we need to do out that way. Lower maintenance makes for a happier customer."

"Yes. Thank you. You know my family's been small time in cattle for a long time, but this really helped my father make it. He got me set up pretty nicely before he left."

Gates extended his hand to Austin. "Happy to help as much as I'm happy for the business. You just need a woman to keep the dust out of your place now, Hearth."

Austin wisely kept his mouth shut about Evelyn, but Gates eyed him all the same. "If you've got someone you're sweet on, wait no longer. I can't tell you how long you'll be away with this work. Farmers and ranchers out west are hungry to keep their cattle restrained and their crops untouched. Land laws are changing."

"I don't think I ought to lay my bets on any of that, sir. It seems like all the good women are taken or smart enough to stay well away."

Gates laughed good-naturedly. "You'd better find someone before you're so old that bitterness sets in. Roaming the plains will kill a man sooner than later. And I don't mean the natives."

"But don't you want—"

"Of course I want your skills, Hearth. But you'll make your way in just a few years here, and then you'll likely have enough to settle down nicely back home, take just a week or two a year to make it to the fairs and such. You'll have loyal clients by then and not so much need to travel."

"I have time to think on it?"

"Not long, but the train runs this way regularly now, and I'm sure you'll have your answer before it's come this way a half dozen more times."

They shook hands again, and Austin took his leave. He picked up his bag from the hotel and headed slowly to the station with his horse, Evan. He watched a motor car sputter down the street before it finally coughed, and its passengers were evicted from its cage in a cloud of dark smoke. What a waste of time and material. And the loss of life. Rail would take a man as far as he needed to go, and if he needed to go farther, he needed to take company with him anyhow. He patted Evan and traded the commotion in the street for the welcome noise of the train station.

The train ride home was uneventful and left Austin with far too much time to think. He compulsively checked on Evan in one of the back cars at each stop and didn't find as much joy in the terrain as he usually did. Indian country. Unspoiled except for the steel tracks cutting through the landscape.

At the Tulsa stop, he got out and stretched his legs again. Walking up and down the passenger car was fine, but it was no substitute for moving his legs on ground that wasn't rocking beneath him. The station was subdued. There was noise from the nearby Harvey's, and the engine gave off a great amount of steam, but it was welcome after the bustle of the large city.

He slapped the dust from his hat and gave Evan a final check before he headed back to the passenger car, gazing out at the plains as he did. Not far from the tracks was a fence. When he paused for a closer look, he saw the telltale barbs along its length. Gates was a good man, and his men did fine work.

Back in his car, he watched the barbed-wire fence as it started and stopped until near the Kansas border. Could he sell the railroad and the farmers enough fence to make it the rest of the way back through Kansas? He thought he could.

He took one last look at the rails heading off into the distance behind him when he led Evan off the train in Junction City. He thought about it the rest of the way home, settling back into the rhythm of his companion beneath him.

The next morning, he was doubting his gift for Evelyn, but she would be expecting him, so he set off anyway.

The day was warm and still felt like summer, though not as warm as Texas had been. Soon the cold winter winds would sweep across the prairie, and his walks with Evelyn would shorten for a time.

She was waiting for him under the old cottonwood, as usual. He hugged her hard when he dismounted. Lord, she smelled good. Texas and stale train cars were poor substitutes for Kansas and this beautiful woman. Their conversation continued as if he had not been gone for two months. He wondered if they would continue the same when he was gone for longer stretches.

"Do we need to go hunting for more specimens today?" he asked once they were installed on the front porch of the Weatherford home.

"Yes! Oh, please!" Evelyn shot up from her seat, nearly upsetting the fine little table. "Let me get my basket and scissors."

She emerged from the house moments later in her worn boots, her skirt hitched. As they stepped off the porch into the sun, Mrs. Weatherford came sailing out of the house, hat in hand, dog and youngest Weatherford child running in her wake. Evelyn, who could not be mollified by her mother, let the woman fuss and cluck and tuck strands of hair under her hat until she was satisfied.

"You'll be as brown as an Indian before the year is up," she chided.

"I suppose then you'll send me to work in the garden, Mother," Evelyn said, grinning.

"Hmph!" Her mother playfully pinched her daughter's side. "She knows my words too well, this one. She'll not find it so funny when she's out there baking under the sun!"

She turned to Austin, who offered her a warm smile. He no longer had anyone to cluck at him at home, so he enjoyed Mrs. Weatherford's pecking. "Now you listen here," she began. "You keep her safe, and don't let her out of your sight. And she's not to be getting sunburned. Just because I trusted you before doesn't mean I must today."

So it was every day he visited. He supposed Mrs. Weatherford saw him as a son of sorts. They still insisted he come around often, not halting in their invitations even after the requisite year had passed since his parents' death. It had been a natural progression with which he felt at ease until the day he realized he might someday have to speak to them both about taking Evelyn for his wife. For all their warmth, he was not certain how they would react to such a proposal, though he had felt so certain while in Texas.

At least October was cooperating with their out-of-door plans. If they could spend the day together, and Austin could get away from business at the house, they did. It meant the world to him that Evelyn's mother and father trusted them implicitly. And that day was rather special.

They had ridden together on Evan to their favorite spot above the estate in the prairie hills, enjoying the sun and the cooling air. Evelyn sat proper behind him, hanging onto the little leather strap Austin had put there especially for her.

"I brought you a little something," Austin said.

Evelyn touched his arm. "You know you don't have to. Seeing you is enough."

Austin smiled and slowed Evan. "But you're so fun to spoil."

"Can you see me rolling my eyes?"

When he turned to look at her, her grey eyes were mirthful and happy. He laughed and brought Evan to a halt. He let Evelyn down and then dismounted himself. He reached for something in one of the horse's saddlebags. "Evelyn Weatherford rolling her eyes? What would your mother say?"

It was Evelyn's turn to laugh. "Nothing good certainly."

She stood by quietly, her hands clasped as Austin handed her a small rectangle covered in brown paper. Her eyes gleamed as she looked at it. "May I open it now?"

"Please do."

She felt him watching her, probably wondering if she would like the small thing he had found for her. She always did. Sometimes it was something she hadn't known she had needed, and sometimes it was just a lovely gift, but they were always meaningful and wonderful. The journal that was meant especially for pressing flowers and plants was her favorite. It wasn't a very heavy package. What could it be? A strange book, perhaps? Carefully, she peeled back the paper. She stared at the leather case that gleamed up at her, so new. Then she looked up at Austin, emotion pricking at her eyes. "Is this what I think it is?"

"Open it. I almost couldn't resist looking at it myself."

Handing the wrapping back to Austin, she opened the case and slid out the black leather-clad camera within, feeling its fine weight in her hands. "I've seen these in Harper's, and Cynthia has one in town, but Father says we can function just fine without such an indulgence."

"I thought you might enjoy it. Each roll of film has twelve exposures, and they'll print the pictures up for you." Austin watched as Evelyn touched the leather of the camera and the little brass turning key on the outside. His heart swelled with the joy on her face when she looked up at him.

"Thank you. This is wonderful. I've always wanted to try my hand at this when I heard these were around. I'll be able to do so much more with the flowers now. Get their shapes and angles just right. Pressing them changes that, you know." She stood on her tiptoes to press a warm kiss to Austin's cheek, feeling the smooth warmth of his skin against her cool lips.

Her happiness warmed him through. "What will you take a picture of first? Surely your wildflowers."

The smile that spread across Evelyn's face was radiant. "No! You and your gallant steed, of course. Do you know how to work it? We can start now!"

That little word stuck somewhere in his heart, and he was lost to her. Evelyn pulled the blanket from where it was rolled behind Evan's saddle and set it on the ground. She bade Austin sit with her, outside the circle of her dark riding habit. Together they fiddled with the camera in the late-afternoon light, learning how it worked and reading to each other from the manual that came with it.

True to her word, the first photograph Evelyn took was one of Austin next to Evan. Then Evelyn wove a crown of wildflowers from the bouquet Austin had given her, and he took a photograph of her wearing it.

"Oh, how indulgent!" Evelyn laughed. Then she set the camera down on the blanket and took his hands in hers. "Thank you so much. I can't remember the last time I laughed so much and with someone so enjoyable."

He squeezed her hands, feeling her slim, fine fingers curled into his palms. She was so tiny, a wisp. He wanted to speak, to make this *the* moment, but it was not the time. He felt it as surely as he felt when the temperatures dipped low enough to freeze the cattle's noses shut in the winter.

Little Evelyn removed one hand from his and cupped the side of his face, her grey eyes full of concern. "You're suddenly so serious. What's wrong?"

Austin committed that touch to memory, then took her hand in his again. "Not a thing. I merely wish this afternoon would never end."

Evelyn laughed lightheartedly. "Then it shall not! Here, help me with this flower chain. I want to make one for Evan."

She was an autumn storm. Dark, grey, and brooding one moment, light and joyful the next. He wanted her to retain that childlike nature forever. She was naïve, but she had a way of looking at the world that he knew could be spoiled by the dark things lurking on the prairie and beyond.

He would not hold her too tightly though. If he held her too tightly she would be gone like fog with the sunrise. So, he set to helping her with her sweet daisy chain and hoped his fortune would visit him sooner rather than later.

6

October 1, 2003

Austin didn't know what stirred the memory, but he stirred again, somewhere beyond the veil. He had drifted for a while, his solace the music of her voice singing through him. He felt her, as he had felt her when she was alive. She was nearby but many, many nights' journey away. Across the vast prairie of time. He still felt their tether though, heart to heart.

But something had disturbed him. Several things. The first had been the hint of her perfume, floating in from God knew where. The scent of her was unmistakable. It stirred his senses in a way nothing else had in the many years of restless half slumber. She was a wispy thing in his mind now, but he would see her again.

He felt the drumming over the earth above him. That part of him still lay immobile, waiting to be discovered. Sometimes it was like thunder, and he knew that any beast that could make so much noise would be a force to be reckoned with. Other times it was the earth itself, waiting for the time it chose to spit him out.

She must be in danger. That thought was enough to make his sluggish essence wake more with each passing moment. He would find the strength to return; he must, and this time he would make certain she was safe.

He spent most of his time sitting under a honey locust tree near the old canyon crossing. The bridge came and went intermittently, as did his memory. But the thought of her roused him. Could she be in danger after all this time?

He leaned back against the tree and for the first time in many years was poked by a long thorn that the tree offered so readily. The pain stirred him to his feet.

"Evelyn?" he asked the nothing that kept him company.

He was met by an answering breeze in the cottonwoods in a place that knew no wind. He watched the trees sway, absorbing the sight, then turned and walked toward town.

7

Saturday, October 3rd

Olivia rolled over to look at the clock. 7:00 a.m. Great. She'd overslept. And here she'd thought she could get a better night's sleep at her apartment.

She pulled a pillow over her head and dozed for a few minutes, searching for the will to get out of bed. The struggle was real. Black-and-white images, random memories, thoughts that had been plaguing her lately drifted through her semi-conscious mind.

She saw scenes in black and white: the town when it was founded, though she had never seen those archived photographs before. But it was all jumbled together with the present. There was Gessler's in black and white, a woman in a high-necked blouse with a tiny waist accentuated by the belt of her long skirt exiting the door, and a Lexus parked out front. Jumbled. Dr. Monroe walking down the dusty main street in his black suit and black coat, saying how he wished to live in that time. What would it be like to run her hands through his perfectly coiffed hair?

Then came the photographs from the day before. The dark horse. Olivia saw the animal raise its head in a moving photograph and call out a silent neigh that she felt rather than heard. It felt old, grainy, like the picture. Dr. Cahara had liked the sixteen-by-twenty off the printer but was stuck on traditional. She had said nothing about the horse, and Olivia didn't push it. She shut her mouth after she promised traditional prints.

Olivia awoke some time later, the memories of her photographs still fresh in her mind, and hurried to get ready for the day, so she could head out of town to take more photographs. She'd have four cartridges for her field camera. Eight chances to get at least one shot for the show.

Outside, the day seemed cloudy but cheerful. When she opened the window to check the temperature, she was pleasantly surprised. It felt like it was going to be warm. God bless Kansas sometimes. Perfect photography weather in October. It would probably be snowing by the end of the day.

Coffee in hand, she went down the hall to wake Ann. She poked her head into Ann's room and was met by an almost overwhelming odor of fabric softener and air freshener. Ann was awake, lying in bed and grading papers or marking up her own; Olivia couldn't tell which. She raised her eyebrows at Olivia.

"You ready to pay up?" Olivia asked.

Ann groaned. "Not really."

Olivia threw a pair of socks at her roommate. "You owe me for helping you grade all those history tests two weeks ago."

Ann threw the socks back at Olivia. "What's the torture?"

"Come with me to the preserve? I need to shoot for a few hours."

Ann cracked a smile and tossed her stack of papers on the floor. "Oh, that's not so bad. Sure. I'll get ready."

Back in her room, Olivia opened her closet and stared at all the work-out clothes she had amassed during her time with Nathan. It'd been a year since their breakup, but she'd kept wearing the stuff she'd bought when she was with him. Shoulder-baring tanks and tight shirts and a dozen pairs of shorts. The bright hues and crisscrossing straps looked foreign now. It had happened over time, the decline of the workout ponytails and hours spent at the gym, but she had gone a few times just the previous week, hadn't she? She ran her hands over the fabrics. For all their dry-touch, sweat-wicking properties, they felt rough, grimy, like sweaty workouts that ended with her and Nathan arguing because he thought she wasn't working out hard enough or long enough, which she probably wasn't.

Pushing the shirts aside, she looked at the sweaters at the back of her closet. Soft cottons in greys and faded burgundy and olive green were much more soothing on the eyes.

But have you no skirts, Olivia?

The thought was odd. She'd never worn skirts. They were either too cumbersome or too revealing for being outside with a camera. But there was a nice thrift store in Junction City.

When she returned to the straps and stretch clothing at the front of the closet, something like anger came over her. How many thousands of dollars had she spent, and for what?

She reached for the first shirt and snapped it off the hanger, tossing it onto the floor behind her. It felt good to do that, to let out her frustration. Several more shirts followed until she was grabbing workout clothes with both hands and casting them to the floor around her. The hot-pink one with the open back, the low-cut black tank tops, the spandex and spandex and spandex until she was out of breath and half the hangers in the closet were either askew or on the floor with the clothes. She kicked a soft storage cube over, and neon compression socks rolled across the part of the floor wasn't covered in clothes.

Satisfied and sweaty, she pulled a faded burgundy sweater and skinnies from their position at the front of the closet and finished getting ready, kicking several pairs of socks on her way out the door for good measure.

Out with the old, in with the new.

An hour later they were driving out of town into the rolling hills and waving grasses. The prairie had already begun to brown as the nights and days turned cooler. As Olivia drove she mentioned her strange dreams to Ann. She didn't mention her clothes though. It was too weird. The compulsive tearing them from the closet had left her feeling triumphant but a little hollow inside.

"You're asking a PhD in history about dream interpretation. I thought you didn't believe that dreams meant anything. P.S., they don't. Plus, I think you're avoiding talking about other things." Ann opened her second soda of the day and took a long drink.

"Yeah, I know, but I wanted to hear what you had to say about them. And there's some history in there. And P.S., I still don't wanna talk about that."

Olivia turned off the highway toward the grassland preserve. No one would disturb them there, and no random animals would show up in the photographs. At least she hoped not. Their conversation turned briefly to the good weather and their luck that it was such a nice day. No wind or cloud cover. Perfect, really.

"So," Ann began after Olivia had parked the car and begun unloading the camera equipment, "you really want to know what I think?"

"Of course I do." Olivia grunted as she fought with her camera bag and Ann stood by, casually directing.

"I think you're probably stressed about the festival."

Olivia shot Ann a look. "No fucking kidding, Sherlock."

"Well? What more do you want from me?"

Olivia slammed the hatch for her SUV. "I don't know. I just feel like I'm going slightly crazy already, and I haven't even gotten three good shots for the show. I need ten. Preferably a dozen."

Ann shrugged again. It had to be her favorite gesture. "I don't know what to tell you. Get your shit done, and quit worrying? You'll figure it out? Do a bunch of coke, and pull a few all-nighters?"

Olivia huffed. That didn't help. "If you had Lortabs, I might take you up on the offer. They'd at least mellow me out. Did you know Dr. Monroe offered to help me with my work for the show?"

"Oh, did he?" That seemed to pique Ann's interest.

"Yeah. I might actually see what he's going to talk about for the opening speech, see if I can tie in to it somehow."

Ann helped Olivia unpack and set up her field camera. Olivia could do it by herself, but it was nice to have someone around who could carry the bag with the cartridges and extra pieces. They wandered away from the car toward the various trailheads the preserve offered, pausing for Olivia to stare out at the landscape.

"Not a bad idea. The guy's smart as hell, you know. He goes to the department functions but I haven't seen him at the pub crawls. Probably too social for him. He knows his history though, especially in this area."

Olivia thought about meeting Dr. Monroe on the stairs. His perfectly pressed coat, the musky smell of a man close to her. She licked her lips and pushed the thoughts away. Fantasy was where he needed to stay. "I think I've been wrong about him. We both have, maybe."

Ann laughed and choked on her soda. "Just wait until he starts talking about Warren's ghosts and the headless horseman all the fucking time. Come tell me you were wrong about him then."

"Ghosts and a headless horseman? He doesn't seem that juvenile to me. I know they say Atchison is haunted. I didn't realize Warren was too." Olivia turned slightly to snap a few more photographs with her digital, liking the views that she was getting of the hills through the lens. The slight breeze was cooperating, blowing the grasses around just perfectly, and Olivia was confident she had caught their grace in the few photographs that she'd taken. Between the digital (only as a backup, of course) and her field camera, she hoped she had a shot for the showing.

"Didn't you grow up here? It's what the festival revolves around."

"No, I went to Riley. Mom's house is in Warren but not Warren schools."

"Oh, yeah, that's right. You weren't a Warren Horseman."

"How do *you* know so much about it?"

"I exist here. You'd have to be blind and deaf not to know about it."

"Thanks, bitch," Olivia said. "So?"

"Well, he loves talking about how the headless horseman was real and that he was the lover of Warren's mayor's wife in like . . . nineteen hundred. He's written books about it, but a lot of the evidence is circumstantial. I'm sick of hearing him talk about it. It drives the rest of the professors crazy too, but he's such a great teacher, and he's got such a passion for what he does that no one's ever going to fire him. As a matter of fact, they can't. He's tenured." Ann pulled a cigarette from her back pocket and lit it.

"Mmm . . . tenure." Olivia moved a few steps away and knelt to take more shots of the scene before her, scanning the landscape for any out-of-place objects before she took the picture. "You're not allowed to smoke on the preserve."

"God, will you ever have some fun? I'll put the butt in my pocket. I suppose you would've told the natives they couldn't smoke their peyote here either."

"Peyote is native to—"

"Shut up," Ann replied.

Olivia rolled her eyes. "I thought the headless horseman was some Hessian soldier's ghost in a New England town. Or a townsperson in disguise. Some dudebro who wanted the girl's hand, so Crane couldn't have her."

"I see you're up on your great American literature, Ichabod."

"Fuck you. Really, though."

Ann looked flustered. "I don't know. If you really want to know, ask Dr. Monroe. I can't believe half of it. Ghosts and murders and murdering ghosts and evil that I can't wrap my head around."

"I want to hear it from you. Ghost story. Headless horseman. It's October. How appropriate. PhD in history me."

"That's not what I studied. But do you want the short version or the Dr. Monroe version?"

Olivia rolled her eyes. "The short version. Let's take the short loop trail, and you can tell me on the way."

Ann hopped down from her perch atop a pile of crumbling limestone posts. "God, if I knew I'd have to exercise, I wouldn't have come."

Olivia laughed. "I hate it too. I'll walk slowly. You don't even have to be my pack mule this time. You're getting off easy after those stupid tests."

Olivia set off down the gravel trail, camera and tripod in tow. Ann crunched along beside her. "Sooo, Warren was founded in the mid-eighteen hundreds," Ann began. "Water nearby, good land, beautiful vistas. Basically, the story of every single town on the prairie at the time. Close to the railroad, fertile land, wealthy assholes with money who could bring in other wealthy assholes. In the Dr. Monroe version, he says the remaining natives told us the land was cursed because, you know, it makes for a good story."

Olivia stopped when some clouds obscured the sun. The light was nice. She quickly set up her tripod and attached the camera. The trees to the south and the hills to the east showed the landscape of the area well. It wouldn't be a perfect shot, but it was a good place to start. She wasn't sure which direction exactly, but her family's home shouldn't be much out of eyeshot from where they were standing. She still heard Mother telling her not to wander too far from the house, practically screeching it on some occasions, so her guess would be as good as anyone else's which way home was.

Olivia disappeared under the cloth to see her view. "I'm listening."

Ann kicked at the gravel in the path. "You know he wants to fuck you, right?"

Being under the light-blocking cloth saved Olivia from having to explain the heat that rose in her face at the statement. A brief flash of fantasy played out in her head. Dr. Monroe tearing off her shirt, her skirt. Dr.

Monroe pushing her down onto her bed. Rough. Forceful. It didn't mesh well with the exceedingly polite conversation they'd had the day before.

"Well," she muttered, "I've wanted worse men."

"Nathan was the best yet."

Only Ann could get away with a comment like that. Olivia stayed tight-lipped under the cloth, still in her Dr. Monroe fantasy. Maybe it wouldn't be so bad to let a polite guy—man—onto the scene.

Thankfully, Ann moved on when Olivia didn't participate in her poking. "So, time marched on, the town flourished, the people here did well for themselves in trade or on the land or old wealth settled here to retire for the quiet and the views. And then there was a scandal."

Olivia reappeared from under the cloth once she felt her flush subside. She got the cartridges back in the bag Ann was carrying, detached her camera, grabbed the tripod, and they moved on, trudging uphill. The day was cool, and the prairie grasses swayed gently in the breeze. So far the weather was cooperating for long exposures. "Of soap opera proportions?"

"Yes. The town's mayor wanted to marry one of the prettiest girls in town. Go figure. So, he did, but there were rumors that she had been in deep with another big name in the area. Before and after the marriage. Our good mayor eventually got wind of the affair, of course."

"And then?"

Ann toed at the gravel path, "There was a huge fight, and he beheaded the man. Then a few weeks later, he hung his wife in the front foyer."

Olivia touched her neck. "That escalated quickly. Jesus."

Ann nodded as she lit another cigarette. "You wanted the short version. Fucked up, right? And I have to hear Dr. Monroe's theories all the time. Nothing like a little century-old drama to liven up your day."

"So, why have I never heard about all this?"

"I don't know. Haven't you been to the festival? They're obsessed with it."

"No. Mom always needs me on the weekends."

Ann shrugged. "The town records from that time are vague or missing, but there are enough stories passed down and bits of evidence to suggest there's at least something to the tale. Legend. Whatever. They all ended up dead pretty young. We know that much."

"I've yet to hear about a ghost."

"That's the best part. Pretty much all the 'eyewitness' accounts match up on this. Between the time when the lover was beheaded and the wife was hanged, there was a span of about three weeks where Mr. Mayor's kin started dying mysteriously. I mean, like, a dozen people or more. The town thought the wrath of God was upon them or something. And there were rumors of a headless man riding a black horse through town. There's unsubstantiated oral tales from the few natives who still lived in the area about this headless horseman that started at the same time."

The hairs on Olivia's arms stood up. "The lover. He wanted revenge."

"Big time. Long story short, it made Mr. Mayor go crazy. His wife and kids were gone. He died himself shortly after."

Olivia was enthralled. "Who killed the children?"

Ann was grim but in the thralls of storytelling. "The 'ghost,' apparently. Their bodies were never recovered. They were likely dumped in a pond or burned or tossed into a limestone quarry. The coroner's report—well, what went for one at the time—said it looked like the mayor had been dragged behind a horse for a great distance at a high speed. How's that for spooky?"

"Fuck me. That's really what happened?" Olivia shook herself. The creepy-crawly feeling wouldn't go away.

"Supposedly. I'm sure it's been embellished over time. Happy Halloween."

"Yeah, no doubt." Olivia framed up her next shot and looked out over the distant rolling hills and the myriad varieties of trees. No doubt her ancestors had brought over the seeds or saplings, little pieces of home. She'd lived outside of town forever, but it wasn't a different planet. Even her parents had lived in the area their whole lives. Surely they knew about it all. Why hadn't she heard all this before? Surely she had. Had any of that taken place in the prairie hills just outside of town? Either way, she hoped her shots were emotive enough for the people at the gallery.

"Earth to Olivia. What's going on?"

Olivia quit fidgeting with the camera and focused on taking the shot. "Nothing. Just thinking. Want to grab some lunch at the Bakehouse on the way back into town?"

By the time they made it to the Bakehouse, it was almost 1:00, and Olivia was beginning to seriously doubt that she'd be able to finish the ten or twelve photographs by the end of the month. She had to try to get the prints done the traditional way. She had a lot of leftover chemical from the summer classes, so as long as she could find a place with a large enough wall, it would work. Aside from that, she was seriously considering getting her head evaluated with all the shit she felt she should have known but had somehow missed despite three decades of living in the area.

Ann stuffed her face with a prosciutto-and-cheese baguette. "Did you get what you needed today?"

"I think so." Olivia rubbed her eyes. Between her allergies and the interrupted sleep the night before, she was beat. She couldn't remember the last time she'd been so tired, and Ann's story had left her stomach tied up in strange knots of anxiety. "I'll at least make a contact sheet and a few test strips tonight."

"Good times. There's a poetry reading at the new gallery tonight. Want to come with me?"

Olivia eyed Ann suspiciously over her turkey on wheat. "The words 'poetry reading' just came out of your mouth."

"Shut up. The new gallery had a bunch of old local paintings restored, and I want to see them. Don't care about the poetry."

"Yeah, I don't really care about either of those things. Sorry, but I'm surprised you didn't work on the paintings. You know how to do that stuff, right?"

Ann pouted. "They sent them out of town. No idea why, but they were apparently keen on 'having it done right.' Total BS. The paintings aren't even that old."

"How old are they?" Olivia didn't even know why she was asking. "Old" in the painting world meant nothing to her.

"Late nineteenth century. They couldn't have been in bad shape. Everyone fucking keeps everything around here anyway, and everything I've ever seen come out of storage or a dugout is in great condition. Whatever. They'll travel to the school gallery for the festival if you don't see them tonight. But, you know, free booze."

Olivia waffled on her decision to go to the gallery that evening. The contact sheet had turned out nicely, and she was halfway through a small handful of test strips that looked promising. Maybe she could squeeze out an eight-by-ten just for fun if she liked any of the test strips. But she was exhausted, and something had been niggling at the back of her mind ever since Ann had told her about the town's history that morning. With everything going on though, she couldn't figure out what it was.

She checked her phone again. Still nothing from Mom. It made her nervous when she went a few hours without hearing from her. After the trouble with the microwave a month ago, Olivia was still wary about not hearing from her all the time. She'd started staying at the apartment again more though, which was good for both of them. Her mother grew hostile with twenty-four-hour care, and it took Olivia more patience than she thought she had to bear it. Legal guardianship was a delicate balance that she hadn't been warned about.

She slid her third print into the chemical bath and moved it around with a pair of tongs, watching the solution slosh back and forth and the image ghost into being. The sound of the running water for the final rinse was soothing, and she let her mind drift while she waited for the timer.

The harvest festival was three and a half weeks away. She needed at least ten more good shots. If she had fifteen, she was guaranteed at least ten, hopefully twelve selections that would pass Dr. Cahara's scrutiny. She had tentatively said the first shot with the horse could stay, though she hadn't said a word about the horse, and Olivia wasn't about to bring it up. It wasn't that noticeable, even when the photograph was blown up, so maybe Dr. Cahara hadn't noticed it. If she could replace it with something better, she would.

Had she heard something about what Ann had told her? Maybe something when she was a kid. Something about ghosts. About old Warren. Or maybe not. She'd grown up pretty isolated outside of town, and she spent grades K through twelve at the little Riley County rural school. She had vague memories of going to a carnival in the fall growing up, but that could have been in Ridgehurst. She'd certainly had friends growing up, but with her mother the way she'd been back then, Olivia had spent most of her time at the house. There was plenty to get into there.

She tossed the test prints onto one of the wire drying racks. They could dry overnight, and she'd flatten them the following day, if need be. From what she could tell, the tonal range was amazing, and the eight-by-tens she managed to squeeze in looked great. She'd pick the best, scan in the negatives, and see how they looked on a screen (horrible, most likely, and they'd lose their wonderful depth). But everything tomorrow. She mentally kicked herself. She still had to come up with test questions and samples, so her students could study. She rubbed her eyes. Now the gallery, if she decided to go. Hopefully, Ann had enough energy for both of them.

The drive home was a bit hazy. It was early October, so it was getting dark by 7:30, and the remaining light threw strange shadows across the old limestone buildings on campus and the main street adjacent. No students walked across campus or on the sidewalks beyond. They took their weekends seriously.

As she pulled up to the first of five annoying stoplights that stood between her and home, Olivia rolled down her windows in the hope that the cool breeze would revive her. Early fallen leaves skittered across the intersection. Their dead conversations with the concrete gave her shivers. A shift in the air sent leaves colliding with her car, and a few sailed in through the open windows.

Warren really was a pretty town, especially in the fall. Quaint Victorian houses, the limestone buildings on campus, and the cobbled streets. They blended almost seamlessly with the more modern construction. Always with one eye turned to the past, all new construction, especially in the oldest parts of town, adhered to a rigorous set of stipulations, so there was no competition with the historic buildings.

Most of the businesses on Main Street had put their artfully arranged straw bales, corn, and pumpkins outside by late August or early September. Warren certainly did fall—Halloween—right. And why? Had she really been in that much of a bubble her entire life not to know a smidge about the town's history? She wasn't a scary story junkie, a connoisseur of horror, so if it had slipped in one ear and out the other, it wasn't that surprising.

As Main Street and the historic homes faded behind her, Warren gave way to a few more modern-looking apartment complexes, mostly full of college students and teachers. She'd hung around after graduate school, as had quite a few of her graduating class. She saw them from time to time, the other art students, at the library or at the Bakehouse. She'd socialized with them a little in graduate school but hadn't made any close friends. She wasn't sure why. She looked a certain way in her workout attire and topknot for sure, but if they hadn't drifted her way for those reasons, she didn't want anything to do with them anyway. Her MFA with distinction certificate hung proudly in her room, and that was all the validation she needed. Macro shots of leaves and twigs, ladies and gentlemen.

Her thoughts drifted further out, thinking vaguely about how she was going to set up her prints in the gallery. They would have to be large, fill each long wall. If Warren didn't pull any punches for the festival, as she had heard they didn't, then she wasn't going to pull any for her part of it. They had a printer large enough for the job if she couldn't get the traditional prints done in time, and she'd ordered the biggest roll of photo paper she'd ever seen. *You're welcome, B&H. Please, take all my money.*

Her phone rang just as she was pulling into the apartment complex. Olivia looked at it and sighed, then answered. It was like she had summoned her. "Hello, Mother."

"Why don't you ever have time for me?"

Olivia braced herself, letting the sigh linger. "Mom, you said you were really busy this week. I just didn't want to bother you."

"Well, you know I'm very lonely here at the house all by myself most of the time. You never come out and see me. And you haven't been calling me back."

"It's not like you come out here and see me," she bit back, regretting it immediately.

"You know I can't leave the house much! How could you say something like that?"

Olivia knew she shouldn't engage, that her mother was goading her, but she was too tired not to rise to the bait. "It's not my fault you can't leave the house, Mother. You can always ask to leave."

"Of course it's your fault. It's your fault I'm this way." Over and over the same ruts, like infinite tree rings or the fantastic bright circles caught on film that some people mistook for spirits.

"Are you calling me just to make me feel bad?"

"Of course not. I have something for you. I've found the most exciting things in the old storage dugout."

"What did you find?" She wanted to tell her mother that wasn't the way to get things to happen, like she might with a child, but that would only make her angry. Olivia pulled into a parking spot but left her car running, her seatbelt on. She would take the old paintings gallery show over a tense evening with her mother, but the former option had just sailed out the window.

"You have to come see. Lots of old stuff. Some photographs. Books, journals. Behind all those half-finished projects of your father's."

Olivia hadn't heard her mother so excited and lucid in a while. Then again, it could all be a ploy to get her out to the house. "Oh, really? I thought most of what ended up in there was junk."

"Oh no, not at all. I think it all has some purpose left. Just maybe not for us. But I think you'll want to see it. I saw the photographs and thought you must come see them."

Olivia backed out of her parking spot and headed north. "I'll come out. Give me ten or fifteen to get there. I'll paw through the photographs, see what's there."

"You still do the photo thing, right?"

Maybe not so lucid. Add it to the list of things she needed to ask the counselor and the doctor and the psychiatrist that month.

They said goodbye and hung up. Olivia eyed the Red Bull she'd bought on impulse at the photog department that evening. What the hell. She cracked it open and took a drink. It was going to be a long evening. If she only spent ten minutes at the house, she could be back in time for most of whatever was going on at the gallery.

At the north end of town, she turned west onto K-15, and Warren fell away. Not that Warren was a big town, but the university swelled its population by tens of thousands during the school year, and she could see the light from the town even a few miles outside of it. The wheat fields and grazing land were a welcome sight as she took the familiar two-lane highway back to her mom's house. Ancient limestone fenceposts were ghostly sentinels flitting by in the moonlight, rhythmic and familiar. Some of the tension in her eased. The short drive had always been a soothing one, leaving behind all the bullshit in town that was stressing her out.

She saw the porch light on the house before she saw anything else, even before the lone streetlight at the end of their long drive. Between the porch light and the safety light on the detached garage, it illuminated the front of the mid-century modern in a way that had always seemed welcoming to her. The land had been in her family for quite a while, though the house had changed significantly over the years. She'd heard her mother say there had been a fire at some point, and the house had to be rebuilt entirely.

As she rolled up the drive, the stars winked at her through the mature trees that lined either side. She sighed and relaxed for the first time in the last few days. The property, with its expansive lawn and big old trees and rolling prairie beyond, eased whatever tension had been brewing in her. Warren was suffocating sometimes, though she loved the town dearly. Hell, the house had been suffocating as she was growing up, never leaving the front yard. Now that she was older, she could appreciate its distance from town and neighbors.

Going inside through the unlocked front door, Olivia stared at the black-and-white photograph in the hall by the entryway that welcomed her every time she came in. She had another print of it at her apartment and another one at her studio. She had been eight, and the family was on a trip to the limestone formations in western Kansas. They had someone else at the scenic viewpoint snap the photo, and Olivia was still impressed at how well it turned out. It had originally been a color print, but when Olivia dug it and its corresponding negative out of the photo box that it had been stuffed in for Lord knew how many years, she fell in love with it. Her parents had their arms around each other. They looked happy.

In the months after that photograph was taken, her mother's health declined. High fevers that the emergency room couldn't explain came on suddenly, followed by seizures that left her weak and unable to care for herself for days afterward. Finally came the deterioration of her mental health. Depression subsisted between wild mood swings and delirium. Olivia and her father became full-time caretakers. Their world went from adventures around Kansas—hiking, sightseeing. and camping on the weekends—to spending all their time at home, taking care of Olivia's mother.

Her father started building model planes in the basement. Olivia picked up an old camera and basically crawled inside it for the next ten years. Her father left when she was thirteen, and she didn't blame him. She hadn't heard from him since. But there was a pervasive *Ha-ha, I've lasted longer here than you* schtick that she couldn't shake.

Olivia remembered crawling into the back of her walk-in closet when her mother had an episode and anything handy would start flying. Her dad ran damage control. There under the T-shirts and jeans and curled up next to her sandals and boots, she had a buffer to muffle the shouting. In the closet, she sifted through the boxes of old photographs that her parents had collected over the years of their adventures and memories. They had no photographs of other relatives, but that didn't strike Olivia then. In all the turmoil, it was the comfort of seeing familiar faces that kept her going. Of course, she wondered about it when she was older.

The scenic overlook photograph seemed significant. A turning point. She would often look at it and study her mother's face, seeking any clue that would signal what was going to happen. But she saw nothing.

Sally greeted her with a prim look and a wagging back end. Olivia took a moment to love on her mom's Yorkie, then headed down the hall to the kitchen at the back of the house. Her mother was there, setting an old milk crate on the kitchen table.

"Hello!" Olivia called.

Her mother spun around, her brown hair a mess pinned to her head, as usual. "Oh, there you are! Good to see you. Here, look here, I've found such great stuff." Happiness and chatter. Olivia wasn't going to hold her breath that it would stay that way.

Her mother bustled around the wooden crate while Olivia did a quick check of her mom's pill minder. She'd taken everything that week—or at least had the wherewithal to empty each day's slot. While her mother's back was turned, she slid a few Valiums into her pocket from the extra bottle she kept on top of the fridge for emergencies. They might've been in her mother's name, but Olivia was certain she panicked more on her mother's behalf than her mother ever did.

Olivia rearranged the pillbox and peered into the box on the table, unsure whether she should just dive into the contents or look for spiders and mice first. The box was a jumble of papers, photographs, books, and bits and bobbles that were falling apart. "Why were you digging around the dugout?"

Her mother lifted a handful of photographs out of the box and began shuffling through them. "Oh, I want to try cleaning it out. I don't know why I bother though. We'll never even scratch the surface."

Olivia snorted in agreement. The dugout—remnants of the mostly underground dwelling the first inhabitants of the house must have lived in while their home was being built, then turned into a root cellar and finally storage in the modern day—was a large cave-like structure in the backyard. It housed God only knew what. Olivia didn't want to go near the place, photographs or no.

"I'm just glad it was you and not me," Olivia said. "That place gives me the creeps."

"It's clean! Cluttered but clean. And I've never seen a snake or a mouse in there. Maybe they know not to go in there."

"Whatever. Still creepy." Olivia took the handful of photographs that her mother offered her. Some of the photographs had water damage, and some had mold, which she could take care of carefully with some diluted bleach. But mostly they were just old, fading, and foxing.

They were from an old Brownie, and whoever had sent the film off to be developed had asked for the nicer backing and paper. A few of the photographs were of people, and some were of animals. A few were landscape shots, some better than others. The operator had been practicing. Wealthy for sure.

Her mother pulled a stack of books and what looked like magazines out of the box and handed them to Olivia. "What about these? I don't have my glasses. You take them."

Olivia flipped open the covers of the first few books and magazines. Names she didn't recognize, though there was Lippincott's print version of *The Picture of Dorian Gray*, which might be worth a fortune if it was old enough. Olivia knew nothing about books unless it was about the paper they were printed on, but it could be quite the find, even if she just kept it for herself.

She peered into the box. No more surprises. Just some ribbon, buttons, a little trinket box that was empty, and a long-empty perfume bottle. "What should I do with all this? Some of it really needs to be put into protective covers or something, so it won't deteriorate anymore. I guess I'll take it home and sort through it. I don't know."

Her mother hummed while she flipped through a magazine, off in her own world again. Olivia reached into her purse for her phone. Ann might know. She answered just as Olivia was about to give up and leave a voicemail.

"I'm not going to make it to the showing," Olivia said. She heard people talking and laughing in the background. The gallery.

"Kind of figured. You always ditch me."

"I don't either. My mother called."

"Oh, God." Then she hollered to someone in the background.

Olivia chuckled. "Yeah, not bad this time. But still, she had me drive all the way out here for a box of old stuff."

"Old stuff?"

"Yeah, hoarder shit or something. Old-ass photographs, some books, baubles." She opened the cover of one of the books, only to discover that it was a journal. She was greeted by the smell of stale perfume. It was familiar and made the hairs on her arms rise. Roses, lavender, and earthy undertones. Spring scents. It tickled a distant memory. She tasted dirt in her mouth. Standing on the front lawn when she was younger, looking out over the native grasses with the breeze in her face, waiting for something that never came. Always waiting for something. The inside cover had "E.H." in a pretty scrawl in the top-left corner, but that was it.

"Olivia?" Ann asked.

She took a deep breath, the feeling lingering. Her scalp tingled with whatever scent memory the perfume had triggered. "Yeah, I'm here. Sorry. I don't know what to do with all this."

"Well, I'm drinking heavily over here already, so I'm not gonna be much help. Bring the crap home, or better yet, go see Dr. Monroe. He works with stuff like that all the time. He'll know what to do."

Olivia groaned. "Really? That's your suggestion? You don't want it?"

Ann laughed. "Fuck no. I have enough going on right now. And are we in high school? Put on your big-girl panties, and go talk to him. He was here at the showing for, like, two seconds, then went back to his office. Probably because you weren't here."

"Shut the fuck up."

Ann laughed, and they said their goodbyes.

After she hung up, Olivia flipped through the journal, curious.

> 21 April 1897
>
> He produced a small basket covered with a lace handkerchief. It was so delicate and beautiful that I almost didn't want to touch it, so pure and white it seemed. When I lifted the cloth, I nearly felt faint, and that is no small feat. Such lovely little things were inside. Sweet-smelling soaps and three tiny bottles of perfume. And makeup! Mother had forbidden it when we were young girls, but as a woman, shouldn't I have my own say in what I do or wear or put on my face? At least to experiment a little. I know Mother is the reason I have such clear skin, but many of the fashionable ladies are wearing some subtle color on their faces

> now. There was a tiny pencil for the eyebrows, and I tried hard to conceal my excitement. We W—'s have such thin eyebrows, and I have seen how artfully M. M—'s sister uses a pencil. I must learn too. Surely Lady A— will show me sometime when I'm in her company again.
>
> Today was lovely and full of such sweetness that I cannot help but feel happy. A position where I could be so comfortable and could raise up my family name, as he suggested. I never thought it possible, and with a man so generous. He spoils me.

The next entry was more disjointed, perhaps written in fits and starts or late at night.

> 25 April 1897
>
> I have not heard from M. M— for four days now. It is the longest duration of time since he has come to call. Perhaps he has lost interest? Maggie saw him in town two days ago.
>
> I received a letter from A— today. His adventures take him so far from here. I worry for him and his safe return. He does not come around like he used to. I wonder if I shall die of boredom in this house before I hear from either again. Mother trusts me to do nothing by myself. And if she could trust me to do less than nothing, she would find a way!
>
> Tomorrow I'll ask Maggie if she has heard any news of M. M—. Tomorrow.

Olivia felt like she was snooping through someone's underwear drawer. A woman had once confided in this book. Olivia ran her fingers over the page, sensing the writer's worry. How old was she when she wrote those words? The pages were thin, but the paper was fine. Olivia could appreciate fine paper in her line of work. Whatever scent the journal had been drowned in filled the room again.

Warren had a similar smell every autumn—dirt and leaves and cool winds and sometimes warm rains that hung in the air long after the shower had left. Olivia recalled Halloweens as a kid where freezing rain had kept them inside all evening, listening to the rain on the second-story roof while she watched the cottonwoods whip around in the deepening darkness. It hadn't been eerie at the time, just disappointing to be stuck inside.

Had the woman lived in Olivia's home once upon a time? It had been rebuilt a long time ago, Olivia had heard. Or perhaps whomever had owned the house before her parents had collected things, or the journal was from their family.

With everything that had happened to and with her mother, Olivia had no idea who her grandparents were or if they were still around. She had vague memories of an elderly gentleman and the astringent smell of a nursing home but nothing concrete.

Olivia got her mother set up on the couch with HGTV and a cup of peppermint tea. The woman was off in her own world by then, which was always a relief after the emotional guilt trips. Olivia scooted out of the house as quickly as she could and headed back toward the lights of Warren. She didn't want to stay at her mother's house that night. Maybe the following weekend.

At 9:30, campus was thinning out, but the library was bright and busy as Olivia walked by on her way to Dr. Monroe's office. She'd called him on her way over, professional. "I've found some historical documents, some photographs and some other papers, would you be willing to take a look for me?" He'd sounded flustered, like he'd been in the middle of something. She apologized, then was mad at herself for apologizing. He was quick to apologize himself and invited her to his office. Oh, this was going to go well.

The halls in the art building were hushed. She wandered through the first floor, pausing at the large foyer in the middle of the hall. Outside the windows, it was deep night, and she walked to the door to peer out. The lights of the quad seemed far away, fuzzy yellow orbs floating in the mist. She pressed her hand to the glass, felt its ridges. The panes on the doors and windows to the building were foggy too.

A scent reached her. Not oil but something similar. Gas?

Kerosene. The word floated through her mind as if it had been whispered by a soft female voice.

Olivia sauntered back to the center of the hall before the stairs, looking around. Why would that smell be there? Students used all sorts of things in art projects, but kerosene? She looked up at the old chandelier above her. The light was muted but didn't flicker. Why would it?

Odd. She pulled her hands inside the sleeves of her sweater, readjusted her grip on the box of junk, and headed up the stairs. At the third floor, she slipped into the hall. Her hall that semester.

A light was on down the hall, spilling onto the floor from under the door. The kerosene smell was stronger there.

William Monroe.

No, Simon.

Olivia shuffled down the hall, her heart rate accelerating with every stride. She paused at his door and looked in. He was sitting at his desk staring at the door. Expectant. His gaze met hers.

His office was just like she expected it to be, though she hadn't even thought about it. It was cozy. Floor-to-ceiling bookcases were full of she could only imagine what. Histories of the town? But that was all she could suppose. She really knew nothing about him. She caught titles at random as she scanned the room. Then she set the box on his desk. "Thanks for seeing me tonight. I can just leave this and go if—"

"Please, stay." He gestured to a little French press and kettle that sat on an antique silver platter. Odd, but maybe he was more hipster than she thought. "Can I get you some coffee or tea? I know it's late."

"Um, tea?" She'd never been interested in hot tea before, but the quaint kettle in his office made her feel like a cozy cup of tea was just what she needed. A large chair by his desk looked perfect for curling up in too. She was herself jealous of his large, inviting office. Hers was so sparse. She wouldn't mind a return visit.

"Something without caffeine?" he asked. "Lavender chamomile?"

"Perfect, thank you." She accepted a delicate cup from him that she suspected was porcelain. It shouldn't surprise her though, she mused. The man was a history buff. He probably had a house full of cool old things. The warmth of the cup in her hands was wonderful. He stared down at her cup for a moment, murmured to himself about something being odd, then set to making his coffee.

Any awkwardness that she'd felt about coming over (all probably invented in her head) disappeared as they chatted idly for a few minutes and sipped their drinks. She watched the lines in his face when he smiled and suspected dimples were hidden under the neatly trimmed and styled beard. Jesus, he was handsome, and it wasn't just his looks. There was something about how easy she felt around him, something she hadn't noticed before.

He held her gaze for a few moments. She couldn't read what his earth-brown eyes were trying to convey, if anything, but she found it was easy to return his open gaze with her own. What was he reading in her face?

"Shall we get to it?" he asked finally.

Olivia set her lovely cup down where she didn't think she would knock it over. She felt better, like how she had felt on her drive out of Warren and into the open country. There was no love lost between her and nature, but she felt herself leaving the stress behind in much the same way. When had that happened after the rush of the last few days?

They took the box over to a larger table on the opposite side of the room and stood shoulder to shoulder to go through the items together. Whatever flustered tension was in him when they were on the phone was gone. His presence was calm and steady, and they fell into an easy rhythm sorting through the contents of the box, arms and hands brushing casually. Why had she ever been so skittish around him? She felt disarmed, in a good way.

"These photographs are in poor condition. More foxing than not on some of them." Dr. Monroe carefully unstuck one photograph from another. "I hate to say it, but some may not even be worth keeping."

That was painful to hear. "I know. I just wanted to go through all of it to make sure there wasn't anything important."

Dr. Monroe paused on a photograph of a woman in a white frock. Her features were washed out, but that didn't diminish her beauty. She wore a wide ribbon belt around her tiny waist, and a hat twice her width sat tilted on her head. She stood on the downslope of a hill.

Olivia turned the photograph over. No name or date. "Too bad," she said.

"May I see that?" Simon asked.

Olivia handed it to him and watched as he scrutinized the photo. Ms. Professor of Photography paying less attention than the historian. She felt herself flush. "What do you see?"

Dr. Monroe seemed to come back to himself. "Just trying to understand the details here, when the photograph was taken. Any guesses?"

Olivia took in the woman's dress, the halo of hair that peeked from under her large hat, her tiny waist, and her small bustled skirt. Those things were less telling for Olivia than the yellowed photographic paper and its stiff backing, the fancy artwork from the developer on the back and a scrolling italic that proclaimed: "The negative of this photograph is preserved for future orders at reduced rates."

"Late eighteen nineties, nineteen hundred? Brownie era. A popular camera of the time."

A hum from Dr. Monroe. "Yes, that's when I would pin it as well. Dewey's was handling much of the portraiture photography at the turn of the century. You would know the camera style much better than I."

"There was a journal too," Olivia said.

She handed him the bound pages from her bag and felt a pang of possessiveness even though she wasn't handing it over for good. She felt like she had first rights to everything in the box, but those things needed be shared with someone who might know more about them.

Dr. Monroe opened the front cover, and Olivia could have sworn she heard him hold his breath. He stared at the opening page with the initials "E.H." The perfume from the pages, which Olivia thought would have faded after she had opened the journal, was more potent than ever. She felt the prickle of scent memory at the back of her mind once again. Something about the open prairie, then a small frightening room. A tingle ran across her scalp.

"Uh, sir?" Olivia cleared her throat quietly, breaking the spell of quiet. The formal term had come to her lips unbidden. Did he know who the initials belonged to?

When he looked at her, he was smiling, but his eyes seemed different. "I'm sorry. I was lost in the moment. You said you found all these things at your home?"

"My childhood home, yes. In an old dugout. I have no idea if it's from our family or not. Do the initials look familiar at all?"

Dr. Monroe raised an eyebrow at her. "You don't know any of your family's history? I'd have to peruse it in order to know. I have no idea at the moment."

Olivia shrugged. Something had changed the tenor of the room. The ease she had felt had a bite to it now, and she felt guilty at his statement. It took her a moment to realize she didn't want to disappoint this person she was just getting to know. "Just never had a desire to know about my family tree, I guess."

"You know what that does to me, right? You saying that to someone like me?" He laughed.

Someone like him. A history nerd? The phrase sounded peculiar. But it was late, and Olivia laughed too. Overanalyzing again.

"I'll have to dig more then. Maybe when I'm done with this festival project. It's really stressing me out," she admitted. It felt good to say it to someone who understood. "Would you like to keep this stuff for a day or two? I don't know what to do with it."

"If I may. I'll return everything to you shortly, especially the journal. Museums are fine things, my dear, but I believe families should keep their treasures close. Have you read through it yet?"

"No. I just kind of flipped through it." Feeling cold, she reached for her jacket, which was draped over a chair next to her.

When she turned around, she found herself nearly nose to nose with Dr. Monroe. The sudden closeness sent her body into excited shivers. It was where her recent fantasies began. If she could just taste his lips, just once, she would know.

Dr. Monroe's eyes looked like they had a red tint to them, but when she blinked, it was just his brown, gold-flecked eyes looking back at her. Surely a reflection from something in the room. Too close. She was too close to some edge.

She leaned back slowly, the perfume from the journal thick in the air, in her throat. "I'm sorry, it's late. I'll get out of your hair."

Dr. Monroe cleared his throat. The tips of his ears were red. Was he a little embarrassed by his actions? Or was he as aroused as she was?

"My apologies. I shouldn't keep you so late. I'll keep these things just for a day or two and let you know when you can come pick them up."

Olivia backed though the door, eyes flicking back up to Dr. Monroe's. She licked her lips involuntarily. "Yes. Goodnight."

He kept his eyes on hers. "Goodnight."

Olivia all but ran out of the building to her car. The cool air and the darkness were welcoming. There she could hide from whatever mess she had almost gotten herself into.

"Christ," she cursed and pulled her phone from her purse. Guilt and shame washed over her as she hurriedly checked her phone, looking for missed calls or a string of unanswered texts, but there was nothing from her mother. It would be Olivia's fault if her mother had set the house on fire again, but the fire department would have called.

The guilt followed her home and into bed. Tomorrow she would call her mom and make sure everything was OK.

8

Sunday, October 4th

Olivia dreamed about the women who had disappeared.

They weren't pleasant dreams. In her dreams, they were dead.

Her imagination had never been terribly inventive. She'd had the standard nightmares produced by anxiety or stress. Falling dreams. Dreams about her fears. Fire. Tornadoes. Standing naked in front of a crowd at a gallery showing of her photographs. But nothing on this scale. Her brain had concocted some serious shit.

The five dead women stood in a lineup in a jail. It was old, old Warren, likely brought on by the photos she'd found. Their bodies were contorted into strange zombie-like positions. One had a broken neck, her head lying on her shoulder as if it belonged there, a pet parrot staring out at the world, glassy eyed. Their clothes were torn and covered in dry blood. The one on the far end showed serious signs of decay. But they stood still for the lineup. Dr. Monroe was there, looking a bit younger, maybe taller, more slender, and clean faced, but there he was, standing before the women with his hand on his chin, studying them.

Then he looked at Olivia with those same red-tinged earth-brown eyes she had thought she'd seen for a moment earlier that night. They seared straight inside her with his preternatural gaze. "What about you, Evie dear? Which one do you think looks most like you?"

She tried to reply, but something was tight around her neck. She clawed at it. It felt soft, like a scarf, but it pulled tighter.

The Dr. Monroe look-alike smiled. "Oh, you want to look like them too?"

Olivia tried to say no, but the soft fabric around her neck was too tight. Her vision greyed at the periphery. Panic. She clawed harder at her neck, her fingernails tearing her delicate skin. She scratched and scratched, but the fabric only tightened.

She awoke with a start in the middle of the night. Noise outside. Ann. Upstairs neighbor, her sleepy brain processed. Nothing around her neck. The blankets were mussed, so she pulled them up around her shoulders and rolled onto her side. *Cold in the room. Freezing, really. Turn the heat on tomorrow night. Moon is bright. Lots of shadows.*

Big shadows.

Big hulking shadows shaped like a person.

She opened her eyes wider and turned cautiously to her right, peeking over her shoulder. Someone was standing at the foot of her bed. Her pulse went from the soft beat of sleep to hammering in her ears so loudly she couldn't hear anything else. Unless the person spoke. Or jumped in her bed. Or raped her. Or worse. Thoughts of all the women who bore a striking resemblance to her flashed through her animal brain. Oh God, she was next.

Then her mother's voice, lucid: *If you should wake, and there is a man standing at the end of your bed, be not afraid. He is your guardian angel.*

Olivia didn't dare more, but her eyes watched carefully, took in every detail. The man (she assumed it was a man) was tall as fuck. Over six feet as far as she could tell, though anything looked gigantic from her position, cowering under the covers. The light from the moon didn't give much away, but it looked like he wore a black hooded cloak with the hood pulled close around his face. Or no, not quite. No, he didn't have a hood. He simply had no head. The cloak stopped where there would be a neck on any normal person. In the dark she could tell no more.

Olivia ventured to lick her lips and swallow the saliva that had collected in her mouth. This was a joke or a nightmare. Yes, she was still asleep, just moving from one nightmare to the next. Could you wake yourself from a nightmare? She would have to look that up.

The figure didn't move though. Didn't say "Boo!" and make her piss herself. Just stood there watching her—or whatever a headless figure might do.

If you should wake, and there is a man standing at the end of your bed, be not afraid. He is your guardian angel.

Should she say something? It was possible she didn't have a voice anymore. But if this was nothing more than a nightmare, what would it hurt?

She swallowed again. Her mouth was dry. "Hello?" she whispered.

She was flooded with a feeling of warmth and love that brought a wetness to her eyes. Her sight blurred, and the figure disappeared. The fear that had been there only moments before was stilled, and she loosened her death grip on the blankets. The earthy smell of the prairie filled the room. Earth. Dust. Falling leaves. Autumn wind. The wind, the wind, the wind. It brought something with it.

Evelyn. I have missed you, missed you, my heart.

When another flood of some deep emotion she had no name for coursed through her, Olivia felt her eyelids shut, and she fell back to sleep, dreamless and undisturbed.

She woke at her alarm with a vague sense that she had dreamed, but she couldn't remember it clearly. Some nightmare about someone in her room.

Just a dream.

She didn't feel quite as tired as she had. Even the vague nightmare feeling wasn't keeping a strong hold on her. She stretched, then froze. What day was it? She needed those questions done by Monday.

Sunday.

Shit.

Sundays were supposed to be for laundry, grading, and cramming in as much relaxation as possible before the work week started again. She wasn't going to get to the laundry that day. She had at least enough clothes to last her though the week, so no big deal there. She would have to get to it during the week or the next weekend though. That was OK. Schedules could change temporarily while she was working on the photo project. She could be spontaneous for a month.

Ann had grabbed a newspaper when she was out at whatever absurd time she got up to run, and another face stared at Olivia from the front page. She stirred the half-and-half and sugar into her coffee as she scanned the article. Warren certainly wasn't shying away from covering the sensation. It was disturbing and strange. Maybe she did have cousins in the area.

She grabbed the stack of newspapers that Ann brought in daily and took them to the table, setting them all out, so she could see the faces of the women before her. From their twenties to their late forties, whether their picture was smiling or not, they all looked nearly the same. Surely that was just a weird coincidence.

Olivia wasn't sure why she hadn't noticed that so many people in town had the brown hair and grey eyes that were featured on the cover of the newspapers so much recently. It wasn't that they all looked vaguely similar; no, the women looked eerily the same. And Olivia fit the mold precisely. Fine brunette hair prone to waves. Small grey eyes. Fair skin that freckled if she spent too long in the sun. But if her family had been in the area for a while, then it made sense, she guessed.

Once she noticed it though, it was impossible to un-notice it. The clerk at the gas station—a male—with short wavy brown hair, but his eyes were dark grey instead of light grey. The older woman at the recycling center whose white hair was surely once brown, her face dotted with fine freckles, the palest grey eyes. Everywhere. She saw them everywhere.

She brought it up to Ann when she swaggered into the kitchen a few minutes later. Ann eyed her over her soda can while Olivia's second cup of coffee was brewing. "You know that between brown-haired people and people with black hair, you're looking at, like, eighty-five to ninety percent of the world's population, right?"

Olivia's stomach dropped. "You're telling me I'm imagining things."

Ann shrugged. "I didn't say that."

"You implied it."

Ann shrugged again. "I don't know what to tell you. The disappearances are weird, especially now that there's been a few of them, but to think you're connected to it? Isn't that a little, like, I don't know . . ."

"Don't say it," Olivia said, bristling. "It's not like that at all. I just thought they all had an uncanny resemblance is all, and I fit the bill too."

"It's a little paranoid," Ann said.

"I don't think it is."

"Whatever." Ann went back down the hall.

Olivia sat at the table in the uncomfortable silence that ensued. Should she even show Ann the new photographs? Suddenly, she didn't feel comfortable bringing up the rest of what she thought either. Anxiety. Stress. That was all.

She rooted around in the pocket of her jeans (same pair from yesterday, but they weren't *visibly* dirty) and popped one of the emergency Valiums into her mouth. As shitty as she felt, it didn't matter that it wasn't her mother's emergency.

9

SIMON NEEDED HIS COFFEE BEFORE HE COULD THINK ABOUT the rest of the day. Who was he kidding? He needed coffee before he could even think about putting pants on or looking out the window. He stumbled into the kitchen, pressed the switch on the electric kettle, and watched the clock on the stove.

It was 4:30 a.m. Absurd. No decent human being ever had to get up that early. And this fucking headache. Simon rubbed his temples. The pain came and went so irregularly that he almost wondered if they were separate issues. Tension one day, stress the next. And the terrifying night with Shep had been enough excitement for awhile. The dog was up with him and quiet but alert. Simon had avoided that corner of the living room with the couch on principle.

And the . . . thing he'd touched? It was either the growing tumor in his head or a spirit, something supernatural. He could live with the latter. His home was old, built in the 1880s during a prosperous boom in the town. It had belonged to a cousin of Evelyn Weatherford, Samuel Buckner and family. He could admit that he had a small obsession with the Weatherford/Monroe lore. And who wouldn't? What with how fascinatingly everything had evolved—or devolved, depending on one's perspective.

So, his favorite historical moments were fraught with ghosts, and nothing had given him a reason to believe anything else. He would just avoid the area for a bit longer. Long enough for the cushion to dry and the smell of Lysol to dissipate.

It had been good to see Miss Norwich the night before. Unexpected but lovely. He thought of her flushed and rushing into his office late on a Saturday evening. He wouldn't pretend that he didn't find her attractive. Long brunette hair, haunting grey eyes, and enough confidence to make any giggling, insecure freshman seem like a child. She looked like all the women who had deep ties to Warren through the distant Weatherfords, though she certainly set herself apart. He'd had enough masturbatory fantasies about her over the years that they'd worked together.

But he knew better. Something about her told him he ought to steer clear, whether personal or professional. The way she had skirted his presence in the past told him she felt that same inexplicable force.

Lately though it had been harder not to look at her, to think of her. It was surely just her proximity, that they were both working on a bit for the festival. And the ebb and flow of unrequited feelings. Or so his male ego tried to tell him. He grunted a laugh at that. "Control yourself, Monroe."

The box of mementos. He rubbed his face again. He must have been overtired the night before. What had he told her that he would do with everything? Had he looked through everything? It was alarming how much he needed more sleep. He remembered the photographs though and the shock at seeing Evelyn Weatherford in altogether different attitudes after so many years of seeing the same pictures and running over the same theories and stories. He'd go through the box again more carefully when he got to his office and then get the journal back to Olivia as quickly as possible. It was hers, after all, but something about it . . .

The initials had been wrong, but if the journal belonged to Evelyn, well, that could cause a sensation in town. Imagine if the legend had proof to back it up.

But that was all speculation. He would need to read the journal first, to see if it was legitimate. Not that he suspected it wasn't, but he had seen a few fake antiques come through over the years. Some out-of-towners who wanted a piece of the legend. He had some other handwriting samples to which he could compare it. If it was real, it could be a wealth of information about what had happened during those few turbulent years at the turn of the century.

The photographs were unmistakably of Evelyn and her family. Those alone would be a welcome addition to the historical society's collection, if Olivia didn't want to keep them.

While exciting, it was altogether unsurprising considering where Olivia lived. He walked out to the estate's land every few years, but if he had known that anything had survived the fire, he would've been knocking down their door years earlier to get at those bits of history.

If Olivia even knew the fraction of the history behind her homestead, she should count herself a lucky woman. He would ask her again if she had looked into her family tree. He had taken the liberty of doing so, just for fun. Westford and Norwich. Nothing much on either side, though the families had been around Warren since about 1920, when her home was rebuilt.

It made sense. Typical "coming to America for a better chance at life" story, he suspected, with money to build a new home. He was a little disappointed. Considering Olivia's looks, he would have pinned her as a direct descendent. Would have thought the same of himself if he hadn't checked. No matter what all the historical records said, he had always suspected that somehow one of them had survived.

The sharp pain in his head returned, and he fell back against the kitchen counter, nearly upsetting the kettle. He grabbed blindly for the Excedrin and shoved three of them in his mouth and stuck his face under the faucet. The lukewarm water tasted metallic. He swallowed it and the pills quickly. Then he slid to the floor as his vision darkened.

He stirred. She was near him again. He moved slowly, still becoming aware of his arms and legs and the rest of his body but beginning to feel them for the first time in many years. Somehow, he had come to it. He could see, hear, could find any place that he needed, and he could sense her everywhere. The bloodline still ran true through the centuries, and he smiled inwardly at the thought. That bloodline was his too. If he could scent her and the rest of them out, then he could rest.

The air smelled of decaying leaves, a smell so familiar that it pierced his heart. This was the time that he knew and remembered so well. Now that he was out in the air again, he knew it must be time for the end of all things, then the end of his injustice.

And her.

She was there in her many forms, and he knew he had to find her before it was too late. The old anger flared up again, the anger that he had failed her, the anger for every slight he had put away until he could no longer.

It was like Simon was having nightmares while he was awake. Granted, he probably should lay off the sauce because it was likely exacerbating the headache and the strange, what, hallucinations? But it felt like he was falling asleep briefly wherever he was, still vaguely aware of his surroundings but no longer in control, like during a dream or a nightmare.

The sharp pain subsided, but his head still tingled. He'd never felt pain like that before. He stood at the sink, gasping for breath, waiting for the dizziness to subside. The world stilled. Or just tension. Surely it was just mid-semester tension he was feeling.

Getting up at 4:30 would have to stop. Fall break and the Harvest Festival were a few weeks away. He could make it through. Teaching for midterms and the actual testing would take two of those weeks, and he could easily recycle lesson plans from the previous semester and tests from at least five years earlier. But the opening speech for the festival? He scrubbed his beard with his hands, not caring that he'd have to fix it later. Fuck if he knew what to say for it. He'd given it in the past. "Our great town has such a rich history, blah, blah, blah . . ." But this year? He was at a loss.

It was time for something more . . . poignant.

He got ready in a daze, half praying to whoever was listening that his head wouldn't explode, filtering through the past years' speeches in his head. He'd spoken about particular decades in the past. During the recession, he'd given the speech on how the town had handled the Great Depression, how so many residents had come together to develop businesses that were still successful . The Sawyer house was still open, as was Gessler's and the public library, which was still run by the same family. No one could say that Warren didn't honor its past.

Except . . .

Was it going to be cold outside? No idea. Simon threw on a coat. He'd take it off if it was too heavy.

On the drive to campus, he chewed on the idea that was budding in his mind for his speech and how it might tie in with whatever Miss Norwich was up to.

He pulled out his phone and thumbed through his contacts. If he went to the library, he could have the entire journal scanned into digital format in an hour or so. Maybe less. A digital copy would be beneficial and would allow Olivia her possession back more quickly. And he could see her again. He wanted to. Badly. First though, the library.

He called the vet on his way. It was early, but before or after hours, the line transferred to Dennis or his wife's cell. The phone rang half a dozen times, then the line transferred, and it rang three more times before Dennis answered. "Warren Rural Vet. This is Dennis."

"Hey, Doc, it's Simon Monroe."

There was a grunt on the other end. "You know better than to call outside of office hours. What's wrong with Shep?"

The man's gruffness didn't deter Simon. "I think he's had a stroke or something."

Another grunt. He heard Dennis' wife asking whose animal needed help so early. "This just happen? He breathing?"

"Uh . . . it's been two, three days ago now. I'm sorry, I should've called sooner."

"Really sounds like an emergency. He must be breathing still. What are his symptoms? Both sides working OK? He walking in circles or falling over on one side? Head caught in a tilt?"

The heavy sarcasm wasn't lost on Simon. Shep had danced on his hind legs for a piece of toast just that morning, eyes sparkling as only a herding dog's could. For an old damn dog, Shep remained spry.

"Um, no, he seems to be fine now."

"Then I can't help you."

Simon heard Regina say something in the background. Dennis hemmed at whatever it was.

"Regina will put a note in his file in case something happens again. Only call me if he gets worse." Then he hung up.

Simon let the guilt and shame needle at his insides the rest of the way to campus. It was going to be one of those days.

10

Sunday

Olivia scrutinized the contact print under the safe-light in the darkroom. No sign of anything strange. Again. She'd have to adjust a few things when she made her prints, but the negatives and the contact print looked fantastic. Again. And no horse in it either. Again.

She could find a wall and see what damage she could do with the large print. The long wall in the darkroom would work.

She moved the shit sitting there and put her enlarger in the middle of the room. She could have done the sixteen-by-twenty at a table, but she needed to practice how it would be for the larger prints.

The first roll of paper would arrive later that day. Almost as wide as she was tall and one hundred feet long. The paper was a creamy not quite white that she couldn't wait to get into the darkroom. The feeling that she was an artist bloomed in her again. Jesus, she hadn't felt that way since graduate school.

She grinned several hours later when she slid the sixteen-by-twenty through the chemical baths. She would have to roll larger prints through each bath, but that was part of the excitement. Something new, different. She leaned eagerly over the trays to watch as the image appeared before her eyes. The faint outlines of the grasses and hills appeared, their details still hidden, and she felt the rush of accomplishment she experienced every time she completed a set of prints. She leaned farther forward, and when the timer run out and emitted its pitiful *ding,* she pulled the photograph out and moved it to the stop bath, then the rinse. Afterward, she hung it up to dry and then slid more photographs into the chemical baths.

She paused for a moment while the new prints soaked and stepped over to the drying photograph to see how it had turned out.

Her heart skipped several beats. She grabbed her chest when it flip-flopped back to beating. There was a horse again. It was no dark spot that could be confused for a shadow or a mistake in the film itself.

It wasn't the same horse as the first time though. It looked sick, emaciated, like a wet towel hung over a skeleton. She was no expert on the skeletal anatomy of a horse, but she thought she could be now. Curious, she touched the wet print, then recoiled. She could have sworn the horse's ribs were protruding off the page.

"No, no, no," she whispered.

She moved to the student photographs she had printed from her Alternatives Processes class. They'd taken traditional thirty-five-millimeter black-and-whites, and someone had dropped out before developing their roll. It was a perfect opportunity to see if she simply needed a new camera. Obviously, she didn't.

While still not more than a few inches long in an eight-by-ten photograph, the distinct features of a horse were visible, down to the mane and tail moving in the breeze. The horse's hide looked wet and shrunken over its poor body. And the eyes . . .

Olivia dropped the one photograph that she had picked up, frightened by the pinpoints of white light that served as the animal's eyes. While spots usually meant dust on the film, it was no mistake caused by forgetting to dust everything. The horse's eyes were white. Devilishly spooky. As she watched in the red safelight, the horse changed, skin bunching up over its spine as if it was stretching, head turning at strange angles. Its knees knocked together, unable to support its own weight.

Prints were still sitting in the chemical baths, and the timer had gone off long ago.

Olivia rushed away from the horrifying image to the developing trays, her stomach turning over as she fished out the prints with a pair of tongs. She had let them go too long, but in every picture, the pinpoints of white that formed the horse's eyes, whiter even than the paper they were printed on, remained like someone peering at her though a portal, a door to somewhere that she didn't know.

She dropped the print onto the floor and reached for her cell phone. She had to hear another human's voice. But when she opened her contacts, she didn't know who to call. She didn't want to bother Ann after she'd taken up half her day. Calling Dr. Monroe was out of the question, and anything she told her mother would likely rile her up.

Olivia swallowed the nervous bile rising in her throat and put her phone away. She could handle this on her own, but she couldn't look at the photographs for now.

After she had fished everything out of the solutions, she walked away from the trays, which she could clean up later when she was good and ready. She didn't look at the remaining photograph on the floor.

She wandered back out to the adjoining room through the two sets of light-limiting doors, grateful to be back in sunlight and out of the spooky red-lit developing room. Things seemed less creepy. It was irresponsible of her to leave the darkroom full of her mess like that, but the likelihood that anyone would be in there that day was low. And screw them if they did; this was stressing her out.

She needed time to cool down, to think. Maybe she could come up with a reasonable explanation for the strange horse in her photographs—dust, someone tampering with her film, something.

The joy of making art dwindled with the fear of what the next photograph would bring.

She fiddled with the chair next to her with her foot, pushing it away slowly as she looked over her sketches for the twelve photographs. She had vague ideas, but she needed exact subjects. *Start with what you know. OK.* She knew the buildings on campus. She knew some of the historical sites around town but was more familiar with the trees and landscapes that peppered those sites. Her home had history, but that was outside the city limits. Her name though . . .

An idea seized her. Her name. Norwich. She hadn't been down there in years, but the limited-access archives downstairs might have historic photographs that could generate some more subject matter. If anything of good quality was there, she could do a side by side in the gallery. But that would be cheating, wouldn't it? Finding a subject from someone else's photograph?

She kicked the chair next to her more violently than she intended, and it tipped over. An apology to the inanimate object fell from her lips, and she rushed to pick it up.

Perhaps she could find out who the journal belonged to down there. E.H. and 1897? There couldn't be that many people back then in Warren with those initials. And a little diversion, a little harmless Nancy Drewing, might do her some good. She would find some ideas for subjects for her remaining photographs. And she could compare the photographs she had found in the dugout with what she found in the archives. A digital database would be helpful, but where the hell would the department get the funding for that? When she imagined Dr. Cahara handing the scanning reins over to an undergraduate or a first-year graduate student, she understood why nothing had happened.

Ah, the archives.

She shoved her loose notebooks and pens and her phone back into her bag and headed down the stairs toward Cecelia's office. She knocked on her superior's door and faintly heard someone telling her to come in. Stepping inside, she greeted her boss and friend. She procured access to the archives—along with an ancient-looking skeleton key and large flashlight—without any fuss.

Following Cecelia's directions, she found room "008 Archive" easily enough. No one else was down in the basement. At one point it had housed offices, but the electricity tended to go on the fritz, since it was so damn old, like 1880 or something. The offices were eventually moved to other buildings, and the basement had become permanent storage to the photography department's messes and clutter that they didn't want to deal with. And, Olivia concluded, photographers were the only ones who could handle the frequent power outages since they were in the dark all the time anyway.

Olivia unlocked the first door with good sealing sides that kept dust and light from entering the storage area. She did the same with the second much less modern-looking door, wiggling the skeleton key around in the lock until it gave.

She hated thinking about losing those pieces of the past. Of losing the past at all. The photographs that survived were integral to telling the story of that time. Clothing, other artifacts, paintings, whatever, could only tell so much of the past. A photograph was indelible proof of that moment. Photographs had always been doctored, but even the doctoring and the layers of truth underneath told a story that could not be falsified. The world would not have known so much about the Civil War, about its brutality, about the awful horror of war itself, without those first field photographers who took snapshots of the battlegrounds. Before that, war was more distant, the drawings and woodcuttings of battle not as poignant. But now the world could see what horrors befell those in the field. It was amazing, and frightening, to know that photography had begun such a thing.

The smell of paper and chemicals and a general basement smell, the smell of being underground, greeted her like a strong perfume in a small room. It was heady, as if the smell of her studio had been left to ferment for a century.

Feeling along the wall to her right, she finally found a light switch and flipped it on. Olivia stood in the doorway as the lights warmed up, listening to the hum of the dehumidifiers on the other side of the room.

The photo storage was as she remembered it. Rows upon rows of banker boxes were lined up neatly on tall shelves, waiting quietly to be opened. Olivia could barely see the far end of the room.

She inched into the room. She had forgotten how old the rest of it looked. Stone and mortar walls. Hard-packed dirt floors covered with rubber mats. Unfinished indeed. The place was a nightmare of cataloging and improper storage. Surely it had just gotten away from Dr. Cahara. She knew better than to let those pieces of history rot in boxes down there.

In some decidedly eerie areas, Olivia had to turn on her flashlight to see what was there. Shelves and small nooks had been dug out of the earthen walls and then made solid with stonework. It was beautiful in a macabre way.

Other sections of the room were in a state of unfinished disrepair. A pile of stones sat in one far corner, and the earth showed through the wall. At another part of the wall, some of the stones had fallen out, as if someone were either tearing down the wall to destroy it or maybe get at something that they thought was there. It wasn't frightening at all. It was just history, and it gave the old, dank room a lot of . . . character.

The shelves weren't organized how Olivia would have done it, but she wasn't in charge. She walked backward in time, scanning the names on the boxes. One unassuming box in the 1940s–1960s section was labeled "Norwich," as was a box in the 1970s–1980s section. She set the boxes on the floor and flipped open the lid of the first one.

The box from the '70s-'80s held photographs of her parent's house and its grounds but nothing else. Nothing interesting. No people, not even in the background. She sighed heavily at it and moved on. The earliest box had a handful of photographs in protective sleeves. A woman who must have been Olivia's grandmother in a veil and wedding dress, smiling as she cut into a large cake. Portraits of the same woman and a man, surely her grandfather. She didn't remember them at all. Who were they? Were they still alive?

She touched the feathered edges of the photographs and fell through her memories, straining for anything. The vague recollection of an elderly man that she'd always carried around, but that was it.

If they were still alive, they hadn't even come around when her mother had been in the worst of it during Olivia's college years. The state of the house, the smell, it still lingered with her, as had everything that transpired: the sad realization that her mother could no longer take care of herself, the lawyers, the fighting, the silence, but finally, acceptance. Most days, anyway.

She'd been her mother's legal guardian for over a decade, but she'd never gotten over how angry she'd felt being so alone in it. Even during the legal proceedings, no one stepped forward. Her lawyer had promised she'd sent off letters and tried to establish communication with several supposed relatives, but nothing ever materialized.

Frustrated, Olivia shoved the pictures back into the box and put both boxes back onto their shelves. The archives disappointed her. What had she been expecting though? To see her great-great-grandparents standing in front of the house? Pictures of her mother before she lost her shit? That was probably all hoarded away in the house somewhere.

She perused the aisles again and felt vaguely impressed by the number of boxes going back into the 1800s. Old Germanic names like Vogt and

Hearth mingled with the more American Wilson and Smith. Then the musty smell and strange, dark corners and the irritation that came with her mother's memory started to get to her, so she left.

When she got back upstairs, she felt like she'd been in alone in another world where time moved at odd intervals. She checked her phone out of habit. There was a text from Dr. Monroe.

It surprised her that he texted at all. He seemed so old fashioned; he might as well send her a letter. That wouldn't have surprised her in the least. But this text seemed appropriate.

> Good afternoon, Olivia. Are you busy? I didn't want to interrupt your work with a phone call if you were.

Well, wasn't that nice. Now she could text him back and say she wasn't busy. Or just fucking call him like a normal human being.

Gritting her teeth, she hit the call button. She was thirty-five, for God's sake, and she'd made phone calls to people she admired before. Stupid. And the night before had just been a moment; that was all. She was, once again, overanalyzing. Human beings had moments with each other all the time. She and Simon—Dr. Monroe—were no exception to that rule.

Once he answered, she relaxed into the conversation. His voice was nice over the phone and calmed her. He said she could come pick up the journal, he'd feel bad having it longer, it was hers, and so on and so forth. Considering the night before, she asked if he could leave it in her box in the faculty room. He didn't miss a beat, saying he would put it and the other "articles" there right after he got off the phone.

Feeling like she had dodged a bullet, Olivia was about to say goodbye with a heaping spoonful of relief when Dr. Monroe politely asked if her schedule would allow her to meet him for dinner the following night to discuss the festival. It was already October 4, after all.

Dinner with Dr. Monroe? But it wasn't like that. It was just to get together and talk about the festival. She could get past their "moment," and he would too. They decided on 5:30 at the mom-and-pop at the corner of Berkley and Roosevelt, which neither of them could remember the name of. Olivia couldn't remember the last time she'd been there, but she recalled it was good. Comfort food. Something she could use at the moment.

When Olivia hung up, she found she was already looking forward to it. There was that edge again. But it was OK, really. Tomorrow she would make her first mural print (whatever oddness was happening with the horse would *not* be there, surely), and she could lose the awful feeling of anxiety and nervousness that was following her around.

11

Midnight

He'd found the next one already. It was too easy. They couldn't be bothered to leave this cursed town, even after all this time. How did they not notice? How could thirteen people in one town who looked so alike and share a common ancestor not know that others existed? Had that devil of a man covered the family's tracks so well? It didn't seem possible, and like quite a lot of work for someone who had died rather abruptly. Once the other—what was he down to, ten?—were finished, then he could rest and let his ancestors rest peacefully as well. Or stick around and spread a little mayhem.

The phone rang, startling him out of his musings, and he frowned, looking at the device as it kept ringing. Technology. Instant communication. The telephones of his time weren't so cloying. He hit the "ignore" button, grabbed his coat and bag, and headed out the door. He whistled as he went—"Blue River Valley." It would be another glorious night for a walk in the dark.

The disappearances in town had provoked some talk, and of course women were being more careful. It was always the intimate partners who were brought in first once the possibility that the girl had just left town was ruled out. Better for him that way. Better to throw off the trail to a body for as long as possible. (William hadn't been keen on him consuming the flesh. He'd called it barbaric or something similar. He wanted to argue that all he was doing was making sure good meat didn't go to waste. William was the barbaric one. But he didn't argue. It wasn't like this would take long in the scheme of things.)

But the concept that someone could just leave town without being noticed was strange to both of them, that it didn't provoke more than casual inquiries with relatives. Even for all their technology, it seemed there were too many of them now to keep tabs on everyone who lived there.

If it were still *his* town, he would've made certain he knew each of their faces and names and what they did for a living. Everything he had done, everything he would do, it was all a favor for the town, which still held his heart. He would admit that to anyone who asked. Warren was still his at its core. It bore his name everywhere, and it would *in perpetuum*. As it was, he could at least rid them of its pollution.

That night the incarnation of the woman who haunted his hours was with her husband. They slept as the tower on the college campus called out midnight, but he knew she frequently got up in the middle of the night to smoke outside. He waited, ready.

There she was, at 12:45, in her sheer robe and bare feet, not a care in the world. She looked left and right before she stepped outside, but he was only a shadow to her, a part of the side of the house or the bushes that surrounded the patio. The woman, with the cascading brown hair and piercing gray eyes that were so prized and desired, looked so much like *her* that he had to stop himself from leaping out from his cover, blotting out those eyes, and ripping out that hair until she looked nothing like *her*.

He remembered how she had looked on their wedding day. Such a sweet, naïve thing. She had chosen yellow for her dress (he had approved of pale yellow or pink because it would look good next to his complexion), and she looked like a perfect little flower, ready to be plucked from the prairie. Lace gathered at her neck and wrists covered her skin, which had seen far too much sun. With time indoors though, that would change.

He watched as the copycat took long draws from her cigarette. Face upturned, she watched the pale moon behind the clouds. He saw in her form and face that she knew that fall had arrived, bringing the cooler air and the turning leaves. Her figure relaxed visibly as she stared up at the sky, thinking she was all alone in the world. She was at her most vulnerable, and he knew he should strike.

When he was close enough, her smell reached him. The smoke could not mask the woman, could not mask that faint scent of *her* that he caught every time he looked at them.

With a quick, quiet leap, he tackled the woman to the ground. He pressed his hands around her neck as she tried to call out. Her eyes rolled around when she realized there was no escape. She resisted, putting out her cigarette on his arm, but it was nothing he could not handle. It would not save her.

He saw in her eyes as he pinned her to the ground that she recognized him, knew him from seeing him before, perhaps now but perhaps even longer ago, sometime in the past that had been buried until that moment. That moment only though, because a moment later, she passed out. Slipping through the shadows, he carried her to his SUV and drove away toward the cliffs at the edge of town.

When he reached the cliffs, he parked so close to the edge that it thrilled him. Another two strides and he could be at the bottom, along with everything else. The drop was nearly sheer, broken occasionally by large boulders and trees that had fought to live on the side of the cliffs. Thankfully, the area hadn't been bothered in a long time. Long enough that he felt comfortable stashing his treasure there. For the moment.

Climbing out of his SUV, he opened the back and pulled out the unconscious woman. She was light. A feather, as the others had been.

"Dearest Evelyn," he whispered, "here's another one for you. Why don't you come out and show yourself, if you have it in you to be worried about the rest of them?"

With that he set the woman at the edge and rolled her off. He listened intently as she hit rocks and trees on her way down, startling her into consciousness. There was a single, long, drawn-out scream before she hit the bottom far below, and then everything was silent.

He smiled, already thinking about the next one. They were so easy to track down. Much easier than *she* had been. But soon her brown hair and grey eyes would be eradicated, and then he could rest in peace.

The papers the next day reported a missing woman of average height and slender build, long brown hair, and grey eyes. The details were hazy in print.

Rumors around town and on campus were much more exciting. They went something like, "Her husband said she had gotten up in the middle of the night to go outside and smoke a cigarette, as she often did, and she never returned." He thought that perhaps she had gone on a walk, but he was suspicious because she hadn't left a note to let him know where she was going. He had waited until morning anyway before he called the police, and by then he was frantic. Of course, the officials had to keep him for questioning because he had waited all night to call her in as missing. Idiot.

After the next one, surely the connection would be drawn. He hadn't meant to kill them. Not at first. Just taking them out to the cliffs was thrilling enough. And if he jogged a person's memory hard enough, and in just the right way, they remembered things from long ago. He would shake them, and they would say, "William, please, I'm so sorry! Please let me make it up to you!" They would confess and apologize and be properly remorseful.

That had been enough until William reminded him why they were there. Then there was bloodshed and that awful business. The man had a *serious* taste for grudges. But that was fine. For the moment.

12

October 1897

THEY HAD WANDERED WITH EVAN FOR THE BETTER PART OF the morning, through the hills and prairie of the Weatherford estate. If they wandered far enough, they would come upon the wire fence that separated Austin's ranch from the Weatherford lands.

Evelyn dismounted at one point and walked at Evan's head, catching tall stalks of grass and feeding them to the horse.

When she remounted, Austin grabbing her forearm and pulling her up even as she lifted herself by one stirrup, Evan carried them both without complaint, moving along one of their previous paths through the prairie grasses that he knew so well. A mutual understanding and trust existed between master and horse. If Austin called upon him to pick up the pace, Evan would obey willingly and happily.

The trio saw the man from some way off. He was riding a horse and pulling a smaller pony or donkey behind him laden with an odd contraption that Austin recognized from an advertisement in town and from rumors he had heard. Evan tensed slightly, his ears pricking forward in interest. The great horse lifted his nose into the wind and took a deep breath, trying to identify the animals ahead of them. Austin patted the horse's neck reassuringly and felt Evelyn shift behind him, leaning so close to Austin that he could smell her, a combination of a wealthy, rose-scented home and the outdoors that she loved so much.

"It's been awhile since I've been out this way," Evelyn murmured, watching the man with as much interest as Austin. "Isn't this the road that eventually leads into town? Who do you think he is?"

"A photographer. A traveling one."

"I didn't think they came this far." Evelyn squinted to see the man, who had noticed them and turned his horse and pony toward them. He waved, and Evelyn waved back.

"Some people still can't afford their own cameras, you know. They're still too extravagant an expense for many."

Evelyn tensed at his words, wondering if he meant himself. "I'm sorry, I didn't mean—"

"No, I wasn't speaking of me. I have no everyday use for a camera. Otherwise I would own one. Perhaps later when I'm spending more of my own time here. For now I can hire Gerald and his sons for portraits and photographs."

Evan nickered out a greeting to the other animals, who responded in kind. Evelyn felt the rumbling vibration from Evan's call through her legs. "I think we should have one taken."

"Of what?" Austin wished he could turn to see what was happening on Evelyn's face but decided against it. She wasn't just playing a game with him, was she?

"Of us. And Evan. This is a moment that I would like very much to remember."

"A photograph, Evelyn. It's permanent. Real."

"I know. The Monroes have a camera in their home. When they sent the first one off for them to make the pictures, it was like magic. I know it's science, but the things that we photographed, they were so clear and crisp and frozen forever. If I had one of us, Austin, I would carry it with me, so I would always have you near me." Evelyn laid her hand on his arm

"Evelyn . . ."

"Please? I don't ever want to forget our walks, should they ever cease."

It was the most she had ever said about their time together—the long walks and the ambling conversations. Where did he stand? Was he simply a friend and guardian to her, as he was in the eyes of her parents? Someone who wasn't a threat? His name might not carry the same weight as the Weatherfords or the Monroes, but he was certain his financial status was approximate. Still, it didn't bring him the credit he knew he deserved, and the rocks and tumbling weeds didn't care once they were out beyond the sight of town.

The traveling photographer called out a "Hallo!" as he approached and took off his hat to bow from atop his horse. He looked weather-beaten and dusty, but he had an honest smile on his face that Austin liked. He had seen enough hardworking men on his trips up and down the railroad between Kansas and Texas. Enough of the dishonest kind too that had him always at the ready. Rope, knife, or gun, he was prepared.

"Good afternoon, sir and madam! I saw you riding and thought you might be interested in a photograph of your lovely walk. You have a fine horse there, if you don't mind my appreciation."

Austin chuckled as he ruffled Evan's mane. "A fine horse indeed. And yes, Evelyn thought a photograph would be a good way to remember the day."

Evelyn gave Austin a shy smile, "Oh, he makes it sound as if I were the only one who wanted a photograph! But if you have the time, I think it would be lovely."

The photographer stuffed his hat back on his head and slid off his horse to begin unloading his camera and tripod from the shaggy pony. "I can do that, ma'am. The rest of my crew is back in town having their supper, which is where I'll be heading after I do business with you folks and a few others. I can bring back your photographs tomorrow around this time if it be convenient for you, or you may pick them up from the hotel, where I'm having sittings all week."

"William Prettyman?" Austin asked.

The man looked surprised. "Yes, but call me Bill. How did you know?"

Austin nodded to the north. "I heard your name in Iowa when I was there selling wire this June. Said you were traveling and taking photographs, documenting this part of the country."

Prettyman laughed. "Well, my little part of the country. Oklahoma is more my place. I want to put together a book someday, you know? Of photographs from this part of the country. It's not been done."

"Well, we support your cause," Evelyn replied in her musical way.

Austin smiled. It warmed him to hear of the causes Evelyn chose. "I'll pick them up tomorrow," he said.

Evelyn wasn't so certain she wanted her mother to know she was having a photograph of herself and Austin taken. Would Mother care, or would she think nothing of it? Evelyn didn't know.

"Alright," she said.

"Fine, fine," Bill said. "And you may pay me now or after. If you want to be assured that you have a quality photograph though, if I may be conceited for a moment here, I do take a wonderful photograph. And the camera is of my own patent, so I can guarantee you will be satisfied with your result."

Austin nodded, "I'm happy to pay you half now and half when I pick up the finished product. And two photographs will suffice, if you have the supplies for two."

"Yes on both counts," Mr. Prettyman replied and shook hands with Austin on the deal.

The man had his camera out several moments later and was setting it on the tripod. "Now, will you want to be atop your horse, or do you only want yourself and your wife in the photograph?"

There was a moment of silence as Evelyn and Austin processed his words. Evelyn felt a lump rise in her throat. What if? What if they could take such walks every day out on Austin's land? She would love that without question. She was about to open her mouth to tell Mr. Prettyman that she was sorry, but Austin was merely her friend, but Austin was quicker.

"No, we'd like to stay with Evan here. He is well trained and can stand still for the duration of the photograph." Austin turned to smile at Evelyn, whose face was unreadable. He took a chance. "Wouldn't you say so, Evelyn dear?"

Evelyn found her voice, though it was nearly a whisper. "I would say so."

"Wonderful!" Prettyman moved his tripod, so he was positioned to capture the Evan, Austin, and Evelyn in the photograph. "Now, if you two could look toward me, but don't look right on at the camera. Yes, yes, perfect. Now, this will only take a moment. Hold still, please!"

He departed not long after with half his pay and a promise to see Austin the following day. Austin and Evelyn continued their walk in silence until Evelyn could stand it no longer.

"Why did you not correct the man?"

Austin had been waiting for that question. "It prevented questions or speculations."

"Perhaps that is true, but you didn't hesitate." Evelyn was now keenly aware of the man riding in front of her. She had thought of the marriage question before but not when she was in such proximity to him. Even for the cool day, she could feel his warmth. That it could be inappropriate was a new thought.

He was her truest friend, steadfast and loyal. She had hung on his arm and held his hand for as long as she'd been allowed out of the house on her walks. She had run with his cattle in his fields, had traipsed through dark thickets looking for rare flora with him, unbeknownst to her mother. Her trust in him was implicit.

"It was a natural response," Austin murmured after a time. "How would you have had me reply?"

Evelyn didn't speak for some minutes, feeling a flush creeping over her at the thoughts that ran like wild buffalo over the prairie hillsides. "I don't know," she admitted finally.

They were still east of the estate, deep in the prairie hills, but drawing nearer to where they had tethered Evelyn's palomino. Evelyn always preferred to sit with Austin atop Evan.

Austin decided to drop the strained vein of conversation for the time being. "Do you have enough mementos of us for the moment, my dear Evelyn?"

"Never. I could never capture enough of our moments."

He said nothing for a few seconds, feeling Evan's strong muscles as he carried them across the prairie. "Why are you so serious? I meant it only in jest."

Evelyn wound her arms around Austin and rested her head on his back, as intimate a gesture as she dared. "Can a moment last forever? I mean, truly, can it? Isn't that what a photograph does? It takes a wink of God's eye and makes it forever. Immortalized. Our memories, they change, but a photograph, it cannot change."

What deep thoughts from such a tiny woman. He placed one hand over hers, which had curled around to rest on his chest. Could she feel how fiercely his heart was beating? He hardly knew what to say. "Why do you need to make every moment immortal, my dear?"

She hugged him hard, and when she spoke, it was against his coat. He could feel the cadence of her voice as he heard it. Never had she been so forward, so intimate with him. "Because we are not. Because the world has become so busy. Because when I grow old and cannot remember, I want to remember through a photograph."

He thought he heard a strangled sob from her. They were still far out in the hills, though he could see the estate in the distance, a tiny box in the valley below. He stopped Evan on a swell overlooking the valley and gently bade his companion dismount before he did. She turned away from him, hiding her face in her hands.

She was haunted and sad and beautiful with the wind trying to carry off her long hair and her dusky blue dress. He had not seen her in so much blue before. Or perhaps she was just a part of the wind herself, to be carried off like the fog upon feeling the rays of the morning sun.

Austin reached for her, gentle with the wild thing before him. She was certainly not one to swoon, but she collapsed against his chest and sobbed, fisting her hands in his dark coat. There she stayed while Austin soothed her with his hands in her hair, shushing and humming as he had to the orphaned pups he had found that summer.

"Tell me what bothers you so," he asked quietly once her sobs had abated.

She laughed amidst her tears. "Sometimes I feel so old, like my life is just about at its close. There's a darkness around me."

"Even when you're with me?"

She looked up at him, and he saw the smile that he so enjoyed seeing on her face. "Not so much with you, no. You keep it at bay."

He offered his handkerchief to her, and she wiped her eyes and dabbed at her little nose. He wished he could pull her into his lap and hold her close. Impossible fantasy, he knew, and even her closeness to him now was somewhere they should not be lingering, though neither moved away from the embrace.

"You are young yet," he said with a smile, earning another from her. "At ten years your senior, I should be the one worrying about death knocking at my door."

"Oh, shush!" She laughed. "You're so young. You and Evan both. I should not think either of you shall grow old. Time will not touch you."

The hairs on Austin's arms rose and fell. What she said sounded like prophecy, but it was surely only his experience with his mother's ghost that made him leery of such talk.

They stilled, lingering, listening. The wind moved the prairie grasses around them, whipped up from around the sides of the hills saying, *It's coming, it's coming, it's coming.*

"Do you hear that?" she asked finally.

"Yes," he murmured. "The wind says strange things up here if one listens too hard. I imagine that is why the natives left."

Evelyn still clung to him, laying her head on his chest and looking out at some distant point on the horizon, or perhaps back toward the house and estate. "What do you think it means?"

Austin dared to press his lips to her hair, letting the impulse of the moment take him. She smelled like the autumn wind. "I don't know. Have you heard the wind often up here on your walks?"

"Sometimes. Never so clearly."

Evelyn shivered against him. "Let's go back. I don't like the feeling I have here. It's too much like dread, and I want you to be safe and away from it."

13

Monday, October 5th

Olivia shut the journal and felt as if she wanted to talk a walk out on the prairie, as the author of the journal had, walking beside a man she confessed to be her best friend. What was that like? She had never had a male best friend, and all her girlfriends had come and gone with school or careers. Ann had stuck by her since freshman year, but now they were so busy that it had been ages since they had done anything together. Something about the woman in the journal and the way she described her relationship with the man touched her, like a romantic movie. Who would be there for her when loneliness came knocking?

Her seat in the quad was a quiet one. It was a warm cloudy day with the promise of rain later, so no shoots for her that evening. But she could go look at the gallery walls in person. They'd given her a list of dimensions and locations, but that didn't give her the visual she needed. She could print a handful of eight-by-tens from the cartridges she had and hang them in her spots at the gallery to see the effect.

She stood and stretched. Everything was stiff; likely all the time stuffed in the darkroom or sitting there reading a dead woman's journal like she had nothing better to do. Time slipped away while she planned and did nothing.

The gallery was at the edge of campus, a large modern building that had been dedicated just five years prior. Olivia enjoyed the large walls and all the natural light that the gallery boasted, and she had seen her photographs in the gallery a few times over the few years it had been open.

The coordinator was someone Olivia had worked with throughout her time on campus. Margaret Weninger was half as old as her name made her sound and delightfully eccentric. Olivia let Margaret guide her around the gallery and show her which walls would be hers, as if she had never been there before. All long walls well suited for her landscapes. Only two vertical, as she had requested. Being so locked in gave her anxiety that she didn't have time for. She had to make it work.

As Margaret showed Olivia around, Olivia noticed several paintings that were already on display throughout the gallery. She couldn't quite get a good glimpse of them from where her photographs would be.

"What are those?" Ah, probably the ones from the gallery part she hadn't gone to. She'd been losing track of time with Dr. Monroe instead. The thoughts that accompanied *that* thought weren't unpleasant.

Margaret waved a hand toward the paintings. "They wanted history. This is part of the series of paintings that were restored here recently. Several of the paintings were done by a young woman who lived in Warren in the late nineteenth century. They will be on display here for the Harvest Festival before they're taken to the library."

Olivia could at least see the ornate frames of the paintings from where she stood. Wealthy. Painted by a woman who had nothing else to do, most likely. "Would it be OK if I took a look around at everything?"

"Of course. I'll leave you to it. There isn't much here yet though. Your photographs will make up the main portion of the showing, as you know." Olivia wished she could share Margaret's excitement.

"Yes, thank you," Olivia said, and then she was left alone with her thoughts and the blank walls. They were waiting for her to fill them. With such a huge showing, she should have been elated. But each time she'd gotten excited about a print, something had fucked it up. She wondered if she should call animal control and tell them an emaciated horse was wandering around just outside of town.

She knew she should feel grateful that the city had given her so much money. Or would. She'd received a check in the mail courtesy the City of Warren, KS, the day after she'd been volun-told by Cecelia about the project. Two grand, just sitting in her mother's mailbox. She'd have to ask when she'd receive the rest of it. She'd neglected to do that when she signed the papers. Stupid. The compensation was way more than she ever expected though. She needed to leave it at that.

Olivia wandered up to the restored paintings and was surprised when she liked them. She liked that they were more realistic. Most of the scenes depicted brilliant sunsets over the prairie. There was one sunrise over snowy wheat fields. A black horse grazed in the distance. The painting made her skin prickle. In such a painting, an animal was acceptable. No one would want a sick animal in the shots for her showing.

She moved away from it to a scene that caught her eye. Another sunset, lots of trees. Olivia moved closer to see the brushstrokes that made up the painting. Backing up, she took the painting in from a distance. She held the breath she had just taken.

It was a painting of the cliffs at sunset.

The cliffs ran for several miles on the north side of the college campus and out into open country, a natural formation made by glaciers during the last ice age or something. Their edges were well marked. Some points had barbed-wire fencing to protect people from being idiots. It was closer to her mom's house than Warren proper was to the cliffs.

But it was one of the few viewpoints that was unobstructed by human buildings or fences. It had been painted on the top of a hill that looked over the bluffs and the thousands of trees crammed around it. The sun set beyond the hills in the distance.

She knew exactly where the painting had been done because it was the exact spot she had taken the first set of pictures for the gallery showing. She had been on that hill multiple times before. She didn't know how long it had been a place with no fences or other buildings in view, but it was a strange coincidence. How disappointingly unoriginal she was. Someone else had been appreciating that view for more than a century.

The painting had no identifying placard, so she moved on. She skimmed over the other paintings and then went to stand in front of a large painting of a young woman in a white gown. The girl seemed so young, but then so did many younger wealthy people in that day, Olivia supposed.

On a table behind the girl was one of the first generations of Brownie cameras. It had been important enough to her that she wanted it in the painting. And to think of all the girls in the present who took pictures with laundry all over their bedroom floors, their beds unmade, not caring who saw all the shit left out in their rooms. In the 1890s, anyone could tell what was important to someone by what objects they chose to present in paintings. She supposed it might be nice to live in a time when what she did was appreciated. But she would have no vote, so she supposed she ought to stay right where she was.

Behind the Brownie was a stack of books, including a light-brown volume that looked suspiciously familiar. But no. So much was still leather bound back then that her imagination was just messing with her. And that she had been looking at Brownie photographs just the other day . . . all just a coincidence.

Nonetheless, the weird feeling that someone was watching her crept back in, starting at the base of her spine and crawling over the top of her head. For a moment she felt outside of her own body, looking at the gallery walls from behind her. Did she really look like that? Her hair looked awful.

Back at the front of the gallery, she asked Margaret if she knew anything about the paintings.

"The historical society brought those paintings here and are due to come in this week to fill in relevant details for every painting they brought." Margaret pulled her ledger out with a roll of her eyes. "Can you believe Marilyn makes us do this by hand still? It'll take a miracle to get Warren out of the dark ages. OK, here is it. It's one of the Weatherford girls. They all painted, and sets of their works often travel around the state now."

"And the girl in the white dress?" Olivia asked. "The painting?"

Margaret stared at the page, searching. "Evelyn Weatherford."

Olivia hummed around the name. It slipped into her mind with the smoothness of new silver-coated paper, tickling her brain in places that she didn't know could produce sensation. She thanked Margaret and then left for her studio, dragging the weird out-of-body feeling behind her with the name, *Evelyn Weatherford.*

Horse or not, she had to print something. Anything. Maybe the darkroom would soothe her. She really needed to check in with the grad students and with Sam and Viola. If she was going to be monopolizing the darkroom like she'd been doing, she was going to get in their way eventually.

She got the printer going for a few larger digital tests while she readied everything else for the traditional print. Besides the awful horse, she was pleased with how the medium-sized print had turned out. Dr. Cahara had suspiciously stayed out of her way, and Olivia wondered if the woman had been peeking in on her work when she wasn't around.

If the first print or two took too long, she'd go digital. She cringed. The tonal range of a printer was nothing compared to traditional printing with silver paper. Any potential buyers who came to the showing would be able to see that. But she couldn't think about that. She just needed to get it done. No thinking about the horse. No thinking about Simon. Just the print.

Once in the zone, she felt more herself, focused and present. The eight-by-tens were such a breeze. She had to make one large print. Just one.

She dragged the giant roll of paper into the darkroom and set to preparing for the mural print. She'd never done one quite that large, but she was confident she'd be able to master it.

She cut the paper to the size she needed. Fifty-six inches wide and as long as she was tall. It was cumbersome, but the feeling that she was doing something with her artist hands after so many semesters of not doing so made her giddy.

She tripled checked her trays and got the water running in the wash area. If she were careful, she could roll the print through the working chem and roll it through rinse and everything. Once the paper was up on the wall (that was a challenge, but she managed it on her own, checked it carefully with a little laser level and everything), she loaded up the negative and got the enlarger ready to go. She had her test strip and eight-by-ten with notes on timing and settings. Moment of truth.

Not a sound and not a breath after she turned on the enlarger and projected her photograph onto the paper on the wall. Time slowed. The scene before her on the wall was so beautiful. The cliffs, the hill, the wave upon wave of trees below them, and the sun setting brilliantly through the clouds. How many people had found that spot over the years? How many had seen such a beautiful sight in autumn?

At least one, over a century ago.

And it wasn't even in color. The tonal range of a black-and-white photograph, when done correctly, was transfixing. And the depth of field in a few of the shots she'd gotten . . . . She was proud of herself, proud to be an artist.

Strangely, she felt something that she'd never felt before: pride for her small connection to Warren. Something about the city drew people in. Maybe that was why she had stayed. She'd received a few job offers from Kansas City and Wichita and even a few from as far away as Dallas and Denver, but she loved it there. Little town with no opportunities and the same faces every day. It was a town that wasn't stuck, but it was firmly fixed.

She stood and watched the seconds tick by, holding her breath until she switched the enlarger off. The hairs on her neck lifted when a puff of warm air drifted over her neck and shoulders. It was like a warm breath, not a breeze. She spun around, but nothing was there. The feeling lingered that something—someone—had just breathed on her. Her heart rate accelerated as she looked around the dim room. No one could hide in there; not really. There weren't any good spots. It might as well be an open room.

The timer went off, and she had to ignore the creeping feeling. Every second was precious now. She began to unmount the undeveloped photograph from the wall. After a brief struggle that left her frustrated and wet around the eyes, she got the paper off the wall and to the developing troughs without damaging it.

She dropped into the zone and managed to get the print rolled through each bath, though she almost forgot her gloves. She rinsed the print with a great sense of anticipation. She grew more excited as she caught glimpses of the scene. It would be perfect; she just knew it.

She drew the dripping paper from the final rinse and rushed it back over to the setup along the long wall. Her arms ached as she clipped the photograph to the line she'd put up. Then she stood back for a moment before she wiped it down with a paper towel.

Goodness, it looks as if I'm standing there.

She paused. What a strange thought. She *had* been standing there.

She slid a paper towel down the print as she scrutinized it. It was breathtaking. Every beautiful turning tree in the near distance in the photograph was a different grey tone, and so was each leaf. And the depth in the photo. She couldn't believe it. And for it to be so large. God bless that four-by-five negative.

After she got most of the water from the print, she weighted the bottom corners and got out her humidifier. Let it dry a little more slowly overnight, so it wouldn't crimp and curl. Finally satisfied with her setup, she stood back to examine the print.How could she go back to strictly digital after this?

She wanted to holler for anyone who was in the department to come look, but at the same time, she wanted to stand there by herself and watch the image as it dried. She couldn't wait to take it out into the light in the other room. In the darkroom it was dim, illuminated only by the safelight far up on the wall. It was best to let it dry there overnight though. She didn't have a drying rack large enough for the print out there.

The sensation that someone was watching her was gone, but she checked anyway, looking under the large sink and in one corner of the room where an old drafting table had been pushed. Nothing.

Out in the too-bright studio, the digital print lay on the printer looking inconspicuous. The image was impressive, but her stomach clenched when she saw that the horse on it looked larger. If it was in the picture, it was in the picture. For it to get larger was just a trick of the light, or a trick of the print being larger. But the horse wasn't larger, she reminder herself. *Closer.*

Tomorrow she would make it her backup print. Tomorrow. Tomorrow. Tomorrow. She was wasting time, and dinner with Simon was a terrible idea.

Ghosts and magically appearing horses. She stuffed the digital prints into her portfolio and slid the flattened eight-by-ten traditional in carefully next to them. Then she peeked into the darkroom to take one last look at the photograph. She wasn't afraid, she told herself, but she still scooted out of the darkroom quicker than normal, then out to the open studio room to make her way back home.

Traffic was light, so when she breezed through the stoplight at Clay and Sunset, it didn't *really* matter. She felt a brief flush at her carelessness, and then her brain carried her thoughts away again.

She changed her clothes three times when she got home. It was unheard of. Nerves weren't her thing. Getting anxious about an assignment, stressing herself out, sure. But nerves? Over a boy? Absurd. She was a grown woman. But she'd finally settled, and Ann had thankfully kept herself out in the living room, away from her anxiety.

Olivia checked herself in the mirror one more time. Formal gown over the tight-laced corset, airy cotton, long sleeves, no gloves. Those were too old fashioned. She would stay warm. She shook her head out of the daydream. Airy high-waisted skirt with tights, thin sweater tucked into the skirt. Yes, she would stay warm enough. It was still early enough in the month that it was nice out. And she felt good. Feminine.

Girlish. The word drifted through her head. She'd been looking at too many old photographs.

She grabbed her purse, shouldered her small portfolio and headed for the door. "I'm going to dinner."

"By yourself?" Olivia felt Ann's eyes mirroring the question.

"With Dr. Monroe. He's helping me with my shittastic portion of the festival."

Ann hummed around her soda. "Good luck. You'll be back before nine, right?"

"Sure," she replied, only half listening. Olivia was relieved that Ann hadn't given her any grief about going to dinner with Dr. Monroe like she had expected, had been bracing for. What really mattered was whether he saw the horse or not.

14

SIMON'S DECISION TO GET OUT OF THE FAMILY SHEEP BUSINESS wasn't exactly a difficult one. They were in Ohio, worlds away, and Simon was back in Kansas. His great-grandfather had raised sheep and cattle there at the turn of the century, before drought and a woman took him to Ohio. They had loaded up their few prized possessions—a hand-carved clock from the forests back home, a trunk of quilts, some silver, and two wooden chairs that now sat in his library—and made the journey with their infant son to where his great-grandmother's family lived. Ohio was lush, they promised, and there was still so much opportunity, but it was closer to the great cities, and goods were more easily gotten. The plains were dusty and dangerous, and life was back breaking.

Life was hard no matter the year, Simon supposed. He preferred the mental work of teaching to the physical demands on a ranch any day. He looked down at his soft stomach. Yes, the food was better here too, but he still fit into his cardigans and sweaters, in any case.

That day he felt different though. Shoved in the bottom of his chest of drawers was an old pair of grey jeans, softened with age and wear. He slipped them on and was pleased they still fit, though definitely more snugly around his belly. He dug around the back of the closet for a dark flannel button-up. Ah, yes, there. The one with the pearl snaps that had been a size too large back then. Now, where were the boots? Those were sure to fit still.

He stepped back and looked at himself in the mirror. It had been Ohio since he'd worn anything like it, an altogether different time. No question he would fit in to the weather-beaten cow town turned university town. He needed to top it off with a cowboy hat to fit in perfectly, but that had never been his style. Not that it couldn't be, he supposed. He slid a hand through his hair and decided a hat might not be such a good idea. He was proud of his hair. He'd been let off much easier than most men in his family.

Simon shook his head as his vision shifted around the edges. He didn't have time for another migraine. And what the hell was he wearing? He looked down and examined the outfit, then looked back up to the mirror. Was he sleepwalking and changing his clothes now?

Well, whatever. It fit fine, and his ass crack wasn't showing. That was good enough. He would have to take the chance that Miss Norwich didn't think his outfit strange because he was about to be late. Odd for him. He was usually so punctual.

They both arrived at 5:25. Olivia came up the sidewalk just as Simon was parking. The smile on her face when she saw him exit his car seared straight through him. Every time he saw her, he thought she was a little more stunning, more interesting. That night she was all smiles and light of gait, toting her portfolio and a bag that screamed photographer.

She was working so hard; it moved him. They exchanged pleasantries. Simon held the door open for her, and they blew into the restaurant together with the wind and the leaves. Despite the wind, Olivia had left her hair down, and it was a sexy mess around her face that she tried to smooth. It made him smile.

On a whim, he extended an elbow as they walked to their table, and she took it without hesitation, though her eyes scrutinized him. *What's your intention?* He felt them ask. He didn't have an answer for her.

But he did like the way her hand fit in the crook of his elbow. Warm and secure. Stable. He liked her. He let her sit before he did, feeling the pull of something bygone as he took his own chair. History repeating. Or perhaps it was just the season, just the way the cobbled street and gas lamps turned electric outside the windows invited the past. Warren embraced its Victorian years with an aggressive zeal.

They ordered, and then Olivia looked around. "I haven't been in here in so long. I'd forgotten how nice the view is."

Simon had to agree—about his view of the outside and of her. "It is. When were you last here?"

She hummed and set her elbow on the table, resting her chin in her hand. "Undergrad maybe? I was kind of a recluse during grad school. Didn't socialize much. I'm regretting that now."

"Oh?" Simon wanted to ask why. He had seen her with Ann Vogts at many of the Art and History department functions. The pair ghosted around the edges of the groups until Ann had had enough wine to mingle. Olivia sometimes did eventually, but usually she hung around the framed photographs and art at whichever professor's home they'd landed in. He didn't remember her speaking to anyone except Ann.

"I mean, I'd show up, then I'd canter off to work on another project in the studio or help my mom. I was so busy I didn't think I needed people. One of those things you don't learn until you're older, I guess."

Their food arrived, and Simon watched Olivia nibble her way around her club sandwich as he ate his potato-and-leek soup. Halfway in, she slid the tomatoes off and picked at the dark crust.

"You were there with Ann Vogts though."

Olivia nodded. "That's right. You know her pretty well. Does she drive you as crazy as she does me?"

Simon laughed.

"I'm kidding," Olivia said, laughing too. "She's a gem, especially for putting up with me for so long."

Simon could have sworn her laughter briefly changed her into someone else completely, a woman he'd seen only in pictures. Hair up in a soft halo, lace at her neck. It stopped his laughter short and drew a strange look from Olivia. He scrambled to recover.

"I don't see anything to put up with from my end," he said. "And Ann's a staple in the department. She puts in the work with the rest of us."

The mirth hadn't left Olivia's face despite what he thought he had seen. "I always saw you and was intimidated. You've been here so long, and you're such a big name in the department. I just . . . I don't know . . ."

Simon hadn't realized she'd looked at him that way. "Would you believe me if I said I've been intimidated too?"

She cast a sideways glance at him. "No. You're the hotshot history professor here. Rumored department head. I'm just—"

"An artist and respected professor of photography?"

He saw her start to roll her eyes, then stop herself. "In Kansas, sure. I haven't thought about much except teaching and paying the bills for a few years though. My mom needs a lot of help at the house. Big old house, you know."

"Maybe this showing is an opportunity then. A chance to get back to your photography roots?"

Olivia smiled but said nothing.

When the waitress came by to fill their waters and take their plates, Simon asked Olivia if she wanted coffee. She lit up. "Yes, please. I'll probably be up all night developing. Some caffeine would do me good."

They both stared out the window while their first cup of after-dinner coffee cooled. That they had both wanted the coffee after their meal touched him, reminded him of his mom. Simon was about to seize the conversation when Olivia spoke.

"I brought something with me. Some of the photographs. I know what you mean about the showing being an opportunity. I feel like it could be too. But there's something wrong with these prints. The photographs."

Her voice sounded a little strangled, and Simon noticed her grip on her leather-bound portfolio was white knuckled. "What's wrong with them?"

She laughed nervously. "I'll just show you. I think, anyway." She extracted a handful of eight-by-tens from her portfolio. They were curled a little at the edges, he noticed. She had to take her work seriously to develop her own film and print her own photographs. He didn't know much about photography except what he had picked up by studying Warren's more infamous bits of history in the 1890s and early 1900s. When she had said photographs for the festival, he had assumed digital.

He saw her hesitate before she scooted closer to him and shifted the folio, so it was between them. He didn't want her to be wary around him.

"Um, so this is what I've got so far. Dr. Cahara and the committee want landscapes for the showing, but I can't give them that if this keeps showing up in my photographs. I've lost a week on it already. I should be printing and mounting by now."

Simon reached for the photos. "May I?" She nodded, and he sifted through the several dozen photographs in her folio, images so crisp they almost hurt his eyes. Blown up large on the wall for the festival, they would be impressive indeed.

He recognized some of the landscapes—the prairie reserve was a popular place for many—but others he pondered for quite a while. They were familiar in a way that made his mind tingle with vague memories, half grasped, like the moment the brain begins to form an idea, but the body falls asleep. Simply put, the images were beautiful and haunting, if landscapes could seem haunted.

"What's wrong with them?"

He saw her face fall, and she looked away, a curtain of hair obscuring his view of her. "Umm . . ." was all she said.

Simon scrutinized the photographs again, wondering what could be wrong with such lovely pictures. They were soothing, something pleasing to the eye about the lines and shapes she caught in each frame. In several of the photographs, a horse grazed in the distance.

He sifted through the remainder of them, tried to study them for details as he might an historical photo or document. At the last one, he stopped. A horse was in the final photograph. It seemed to be the focus of the shot. It stood in front of a copse of trees, its head turned toward the camera. It was an odd subject in the midst of the landscapes, and its trappings looked less than modern. The familiar feeling crept over him again, but this time a shiver came with it, a cold hand at the base of his skull. Then a distant voice shouted a string of profanities.

A gust of wind blew the door to the diner open, distracting him. The moment was gone. His head felt emptier, like when his ears finally unclogged in the mountains after being at altitude for a day or so.

"This one is worse," Olivia whispered and handed him another print, tipping it so it was shielded from anyone else's view.

The shock of the photograph hit him unexpectedly. He didn't know what he was looking at except that it was horse shaped. The first coherent thoughts were *malnourished, starved, deformed at birth*, but that wasn't right either. It was a freakshow where more disturbing details presented themselves to him the longer he stared at the photograph. What fur the animal had was spread over its dark skin in mottled chunks that looked matted and tangled, like it had tried to shed its winter coat and failed. Its mane and tail looked lusher than they ought for the rest of it to be so emaciated. Its eyes bulged. Or its face was misshapen. Its jaw was oversized, like the sheep he'd seen with abscesses under their chins that gave them a tough, square-jawed appearance.

Simon had to look away from it. Olivia was white when he looked back at her.

"You saw this?"

"No," Olivia whispered. "It wasn't there when I took the photograph."

Their waitress came by to refill their coffees, and they both quieted. Olivia set an arm over the emaciated horse.

Simon almost shouted at her not to touch it, but he saw the waitress's eyes drag over the photographs. He studied her for a moment. Same brown hair and grey eyes. Older though, maybe mid-forties. Was that a flicker of recognition when she saw the photographs? Olivia either didn't notice or didn't say anything because she was zoned into concealing the horse.

"Those are beautiful," the waitress said.

Olivia's head popped up. "I'm sorry?"

"Those landscapes. They're beautiful. I like that black-and-white stuff." The woman set down her carafe and motioned to the photographs. "May I look at one?"

"Uh . . . sure." Olivia handed her the photograph.

The woman pointed at it, left of center where part of the horse obscured the trees behind it. "These details . . . wow. It's almost like I could touch the trees if I wanted to."

Olivia opened her mouth, then shut it quickly. Simon felt like he was holding his breath. Why had the waitress said nothing about the horse?

"These are amazing," the woman continued. "Do you sell prints?"

Olivia cleared her throat. Her pale skin was flushed. "I hadn't planned on running prints for this series, but I can certainly run a few." She dug in her bag and extended a card to the woman. She had composed herself, found her professional side. He admired that. "Here's my information. I have a showing of these at the end of the month at the gallery on campus during all the other festival activities. I'll have a few prints available there."

The woman handed the photograph back to Olivia and slid the card into her apron. "Thank you! I'll be sure to go see it. I just love those landscapes, those trees. So much like that Anise Adamson," she gushed. "Can I get you two anything else?"

"We'll have coffee for a bit longer, thank you," Simon said, and the woman left them to themselves again.

Simon looked down at the scattering of photographs before him, concentrating on the normal-looking horse. "You'll make a name for yourself with these seeing as it appears other folks don't notice the horse."

"Ansel Adams," Olivia snorted, then shook her head. "She must have seen it; it's right there." The look she turned on him didn't make him feel any better.

"You really didn't see anything when you were out there?"

"No. And nothing in my contact prints either. It appears after I enlarge, often during the drying process."

"I've seen strange things in my studies, but this is . . . ." His voice trailed off. What was it? Horrifying? Sickening? He'd seen plenty of sheep get themselves into binds breaking legs or necks when they got lost, becoming emaciated by illness or disease, but this was . . . unnatural.

"Anything like this?"

"Yes. No. Odd things. Not like this, but . . . my house is haunted," he blurted. He hadn't meant to confess that, but he felt a little less in control than he had a moment earlier. More nervous, really. It was strange that the waitress hadn't mentioned the horse, had seemed to see right through it.

"Really?"

"A story for another time, I suppose." The thought of Shep's incident didn't make him keen on telling the story any longer, as if speaking about it might bring on another episode.

Olivia stared at the photographs. "What does it mean? What does your haunting mean?" The look she gave him, the wide doe eyes, caught him off guard.

"I don't know. I don't know that it means anything. This is a bit more, uh, in your face?"

Olivia scooped the photographs toward her and turned them upside down. "It scares me," she whispered.

He remembered the harrowing moment of running to the bathroom before he felt like he was going to shit himself after what had happened with Shep. "I understand," he replied.

When the check arrived, Simon took it before Olivia could argue or ask to split it. He saw her purse her lips, which tickled him. She didn't argue though.

"Do you know the name Weatherford?" Olivia asked after the waitress left with his money. "Or Hearth or Monroe? I was down in the archives looking for photographs of my family, and those names took up most of the space down there. And at the gallery, there are some paintings done by a Weatherford girl or girls. I can't remember exactly."

Surely his heart had just stopped. He chose his words carefully. "They were among the oldest families in the area around the turn of the century when Warren saw its most explosive growth. Affluent. Going places, as it were. The most famous Monroe was Warren's mayor at the turn of the century. A Weatherford girl was his wife. Surely you've heard the stories."

"No, I haven't. Except some stories from Ann. I grew up around here. I mean, around Warren but outside of it. I took K through twelve in Riley because it was a smidge closer to our house. My mom thought Warren was weird. Are you related to that Monroe?"

Simon was stuck on her having no knowledge of Warren's sordid past. The town had a goddamn festival every year to commemorate it. The journal she'd given him was almost certainly Evelyn's. "You'd think, but no. I've never been able to find a connection. So, you've never gone to the festival?"

Olivia shrugged, her fine brown hair cascading over her shoulders and arms. She looked . . . God, she looked like a ghost. He could've sworn she had a tan a few days ago when they'd met in the stairwell. Now she was porcelain pale. Surely it was just the lighting, and the flash of her as someone else was his overtired brain.

"I was too busy with school, and then I was too busy with family," she said. "I don't know. It always seemed like a good time to be away from town. I enjoy the concerts in the summer at the big park, but the festival always felt different. Too frenzied for me."

"'Frenzied' is a word for it," Simon remarked. He recalled the year that someone protested the portion of the festival that celebrated the prosperous Monroe years. It was strange how time twisted everyone's memory of events, how people ignored the truth, even when it presented itself with facts and historical documents.

The girl was escorted out of the event—the reenactments—and Simon didn't see her again. It was the same reason he had published the less-than-savory histories under a pseudonym. People around there sometimes got . . . uptight about their version of history.

"Do you think you'll want to go to some of it this year since you're part of it?" he asked. Idiot. He'd lost all his swagger since he stopped seeing Bridgette.

Olivia smiled. She wasn't stupid. "I suppose I'll have to. I'd be happy to let you show me around the best of it. You seem to be in the know."

Lust roared up to meet his previously collected thoughts. Idiot was an understatement. "Of course. I'd enjoy that."

The haunted look left Olivia's face. It pleased him. He watched her pack up her things with hands that were more confident than they had been a few minutes earlier. Somehow, that pleased him too.

She looked outside, then back at him, her grey eyes watching him closely. "Do you mind taking me to campus? I walked here, but I'm not feeling so keen on being out and about anymore. I mean, it's not you, it's just these photographs and...."

"No, no, I get it. Of course," he said.

When they reached his car, he held the passenger door for her, and she slipped into the front seat as if she'd been riding in his car for years. She arranged her portfolio and bag at her feet, and he felt the trust implicit in her actions.

The drive to campus was comfortably quiet as he watched the road and she watched the trees. Everything he tried to say sounded trite in his head. He wanted to bring up the Weatherfords again, but that was tricky on its own. So, he stayed silent, as did she.

When he parked, the words tumbled out before he could stop them. "Would you like me to walk you up? Will you need a ride home?"

You should not. We are a dangerous man to be hanging around, Miss Olivia. The odd thought flitted through his mind and was gone, but it left him with an uneasy taste in his mouth. Surely that was just the coming dark, the wind that whipped up around them.

Olivia looked as if she had heard the thought too. That was impossible, but her eyes looked wary. She didn't hesitate with her answer though. "Yes, I'd like that. Ann can come get me later though. Thank you."

He escorted her up the stairwell to the Schneider building, and they paused outside the door. Leaves carried up by the wind rustled at their feet. Olivia looked beautiful in her skirt, which danced in the wind. How could she not be related to that woman he had studied for so long? Wouldn't it be fitting for them to meet again on better terms?

She gave him another one of her unreadable looks. "That was wonderful, thank you. I'm feeling better about the series, but the horse bothers me. If it's a . . . ghost or a sign or whatever, how do I know others can't see it? Why am I seeing it?"

He reached for her hand, and she met him halfway with her cool fingers. There was that thought again, that he wanted to devour her, when the moment before he wanted to be so tender. If he were wise, he would leave. "Do you really want to know why?"

"Well, yeah," she said. "Of course."

He knew he should tell her what he knew, or suspected he knew at least. The headache that had nearly evaporated during their meal came raging back. Something must have crossed over his face because Olivia touched his arm with her other hand. "Simon? Are you alright?"

Another taste of the woman, and he would know for certain if she was the one. Just one little taste. He wouldn't even nibble. *Pinky promises!* he said to Simon. What a fight that soul had. Feisty. *But we can't have you telling her everything you know. No, that would spoil the fun.*

"Yes, I'm sorry," he said. Had he lost a few seconds there? "Been working on a migraine these last few days, and it hits me out of nowhere sometimes. Nothing to worry about."

She smiled. "Thank you again."

Just a little mayhem. He pushed her back against the old limestone building and set his lips on hers. Her exhale sounded like a plea, though he wasn't going to take no for an answer. He knew she wanted it though as he felt her arch against him and into the kiss. Searing, she was, right to the core.

He lingered there for a moment, tasting her, feeding on their lust until *Simon* made him pull away. That would have to stop. "I'm sorry, I . . ."

Olivia, flushed and gorgeous, took a few deep breaths, still clinging to him. "No, don't be sorry. Thank you. I . . . I should be going though. More negatives to go through. Prints to make." The question "What's happening?" seemed to evaporate in the density of their lust.

He said his goodbyes as politely as he could manage, wrestling with Simon all the while. (It took an awful lot of energy to keep the man from knowing he was being led around, but then again, sometimes he seemed to like it. It worked out conveniently for them both.) Then he excused himself and headed down the stairs, licking his lips. It surely wasn't as nice looking in this form, but it had to suffice. In any case, he knew for certain that she was the tastiest of them all.

15

Tuesday, October 6th

Olivia stared at the moon, which was still bright outside the window. Her sleep had been disjointed, and strange dreams about walking the prairie, walking through town, and walking through campus had left her with anxiety that settled in her stomach.

The photographs, the terrifying horse, her moment with Simon, it all seemed mixed together. She wanted him but didn't want him. It was less maddening than her project though and much more pleasurable.

Reaching over the side of the bed, she felt around for the journal and then turned on the lamp on her bedside table. The next entry was dated October 7th. Just a day later and over a century earlier. The thought spooked her.

> He asked, and I would have said yes. Would. Would. Would. He has been my closest friend for so many years

> that I didn't see it. I feel I can confide everything in him. Surely he knows. Surely I do not need to say. I think my family should be happy for me, should he ask. I think. He is to be away for such a good part of the spring, I do not know what I'll do in his absence. There will be no traipsing for me, only catching up on my sketches and my studies.

Olivia reread the entry. It was clear the woman wanted someone to ask for her hand in marriage. Olivia sighed. If only the woman knew how much time she was wasting. Nathan had asked, but at the time she was consumed with graduate school and making sure her mother was no longer a danger to herself or anyone else, so the answer was no. He had been gone within a week of that.

It felt cold in the room, so she pulled the blankets up around her and then flipped to the next page. It wasn't dated, and something was scrawled in the margin next to another entry.

> I fear to move lest I should wake him. He does not like to be disturbed from slumber. I lie so still, like a board. My body aches.

An image rose in her mind of a sneering face contorted in rage, eyes ringed red and glowing in the dark. She felt its warm breath on her face, and the smell of decay reached her a moment later. A sweetness in the smell stuck in her throat and squeezed. A heavy presence was on top of her, smothering her. She shut the journal and tossed it away. The heavy feeling disappeared.

"Jesus." She rubbed her arms and looked around the dark room. Nothing but shadows, stacks of prints, and mountains of clothes and camera equipment. "Jesus," she said again and eyed the journal warily. She scrubbed at her face, but all she could smell was the strong perfume from the pages of the old book. It wasn't right.

Crawling out of bed, she skirted the journal and rooted around on the floor for clothes. She hadn't gotten to laundry the day before, like she'd needed to. She'd meant to hang everything in her wardrobe—closet—afterward too. Maybe she could get to it on Thursday. But Thursday she would likely be printing. Maybe she could stretch it another week. Or buy another pack of underwear if it came down to it.

Her phone vibrated twice on her side table. If a student had found her number again somehow, she'd be pissed. The grad students liked to give theirs out willy nilly to students. But for her, the fewer ways they could contact her, the better. She finished pulling on her jeans and pushed her head into a sweater that didn't smell like she'd worn it more than once, then grabbed her phone.

Oh, dear.

> I'm sorry if it's early, but I know you keep odd hours like I do. Wanted to see if you had some time to meet up later today or this week to talk about the festival more. We didn't really . . . get to it yesterday.

She could just give him the journal. She eyed it, the image of the horrifying face still seared into her mind. She could just hand it over and never see it again. It was way too close to Halloween, a holiday that she decidedly didn't like.

She stuffed her phone in her bag and decided to give up on anything resembling relaxation. Better to just get to campus and get to work. Horse or not, she had to keep printing. Keep taking photographs. Keep printing. Keep moving forward.

Anxiety clawed through her stomach as she stared at the image on the screen in her studio not long afterwards. The normal horse, a tiny figure in the small digital image, somehow the only thing she could look at.

She chewed the dry bits on her left thumb until she tasted blood as she clicked "Print" with her other hand. Moment of truth. What a waste of money and paper if the print wasn't perfect.

Racing over to the printer, she watched as the image came out, scanning the nearly four-foot-wide print for any errors she could have missed. She should've had someone there to help her. What was she thinking not having someone around to help her wrangle the giant print?

Because of the horse. Surely someone would see it and wonder. Simon saw it. Surely someone else would see it. It couldn't just be her and him.

Simon.

In the truest cliché fashion, she fixated on the kiss from the evening before. The heat of it, the strange way something just outside her reach said, *No,* while the rest of her said, *Oh, yes.* The way his hands had squeezed her ribcage and pulled her to him—large hands that she wanted to feel everywhere. It made her want to do reckless things. She still hadn't responded to his text from earlier, but it wasn't a question of whether she wanted to.

Gnaw, gnaw, gnaw went her anxiety.

She got a cart under the print and was able to transfer it to the large production table without damaging it. She needed to get the behemoth mounted and vertical before it started collecting dust. If it turned out, she could wait to print the others. But not too long. Timing was everything. Time was everything. If she ran out of time, everyone would be disappointed, and she wouldn't get paid.

Mostly it was the thought of disappointing people that worried her. Simon the most. He probably already had his speech planned. She'd forgotten to ask him about it. She'd been so wrapped up in the photographs, and in him, that she'd forgotten. Today. Today she would check in.

As she centered and adjusted the print, the horse in the photograph began to gallop across the scene. Olivia watched, captivated. It was like a black-and-white movie where a horse ran through the grass along part of the cliffs. The scene began to move too. A jerk and a shift, and the horse moved out of the frame and away, farther onto the landscape. But that was impossible. The corner of a limestone building appeared on the edge of the photograph, and the horse slid to a halt, tossing its head. Finally, she managed to look away. She was out of breath, as if she had been the one running.

When she looked again, the horse was still there, tossing its head and neighing silently. Olivia squeezed her eyes shut. She was imagining things. *Not real, not real, not real.*

The horse was still when she opened them, and the photograph was as it should be, save the horse in the middle of it. No limestone structure.

She kept an eye trained on it as she measured her foam board backing, her legs jelly and her hands sticky with sweat. Her heart couldn't stop fluttering.

The sense of unease stayed with her even when she arrived back at her apartment that evening. Her mother hadn't called that day—a welcome but unusual event. Olivia needed to get out to the house, make sure everything was alright.

Perhaps a walk would calm her. She wasn't a walker, but when her mother's panic attacks had gotten worse, her therapist had suggested exercise. It seemed to work for her mother for a time, until she started leaving the treadmill to wander out onto the back acreage.

The night was damp and cool, and she regretted not having a windbreaker instead of a sweater—hell, it had gotten up to seventy-five that day—but she'd chosen to go adventuring out of the apartment that late, and she wasn't going back until she was good and tired.

The desire to be reckless with Simon swelled in her again. She swore the last time she was around him that he smelled exactly like the damn journal. Earthy, musky, like the prairie in autumn. It made her check her hair and put on lip gloss, the kind that drew attention but not too much. It made her feel feminine. Wanted.

Girlish, a voice within her said again. What an odd word.

She pulled her shawl closer around her body. It was beginning to feel like fall, like a turning of the seasons. The streetlights caught the just-turning trees in their pale white circles of light. The humidity or mist, she could not tell which, made everything hazy. No cars came up the hill. Everything was hushed except for her footsteps.

Someone stood on the edge of the sidewalk close to the stand of trees at the bottom of the hill, a small wooded area between one housing addition and the park.

She moved to cross the street, but when she turned her head from the street to eye the figure again, nothing was there. She rubbed her eyes. It was late, misting. Perhaps she had imagined it. Instead of crossing, she made her way straight past the wooded area before the park, undeterred.

The wood was nearly to her back when the hairs on her neck prickled. She turned, and her stomach fell. The person stood on the sidewalk twenty feet behind her. He must have hidden in the woods when she'd seen him a minute earlier, but she'd heard no sound. No crunching leaves or breaking twigs. Nothing.

Shit. Fucking stupid. Out alone so late with what was going on in town. She knew about the curfew. Like an idiot, she'd left the house not thinking about the fucking disappearances, and now look at what she'd gotten herself into. She stood rooted in place, adrenaline pumping as she stared at the still figure, partially obscured by the arc of the streetlight he was standing behind.

Tall. Black trench coat. No. Long black coat. Black frock? Coat. What? No, that wasn't possible. He was tall, six feet at least, but something wasn't right. She couldn't see his face. She squinted into the light, and more adrenaline surged through her. She couldn't see his face because it wasn't there. No head, only shoulders.

And then it did something very odd.

It spoke.

"Hello, Miss Olivia."

The chill that went through her must have frozen her to the spot. Fucking fight or flight or freeze, she couldn't have gone anywhere if she wanted to. The breeze shifted to the south, and the smell of the prairie and the scent of the journal filled her. She must've accidentally gotten some of the perfume on her. It followed her everywhere. Somewhere was the sound of shuffling, and in her mind she saw a horse coming toward her from a distance.

No, no, this must be a Halloween prank. It was October, for God's sake.

The sliver of something familiar prickled from the roots of her hair down to her legs. The horse. It looked like the one in her photographs.

She shut her eyes and tried to take a deep breath, as if it would stop the image of the horse in her head. Hallucinations from lack of sleep. Stress. She would open her eyes, and nothing would be there, just like in the studio.

But when she opened her eyes, the figure was still there. He hadn't moved closer though, for which Olivia was grateful. Somehow she found her voice. "Is this a Halloween prank? I'll call the police if it is. You can't do that to people."

"Halloween?" The tall man paused. "Ah, All Hallow's Eve. It seemed so, but I imagine that would be the proper time for all this."

"What?" She felt dumb. Why weren't any cars driving by? It was a goddamn college town. *Someone* had to be awake and moving around.

"What year is it?"

Olivia didn't have a response for the inquiry as she pondered how she was going to get around the hulking prankster. She launched herself out into the street, intending to make an arc around the person and head back up the hill toward the apartment. He could be fast, but he was wearing some sort of costume and surely couldn't catch her before she was in sight of people again.

She had just stepped onto the sidewalk, catching a glimpse of the figure behind her, only just slowly turning to watch her, when a man appeared in front of her. *Appeared.* She hit him full on and then fell backwards toward the dirt next the sidewalk.

The man caught her outstretched arms as she hit the ground, hauling her back to her feet just as she was starting to feel the pain of the fall.

"I'm so sorry. I didn't mean to startle you."

Olivia couldn't answer. His hand was still on her forearm, and her head whirred with images but no personal memories to connect to them. Wide expanses of prairie played behind her eyes, endless lengths of barbed-wire fences and lowing cattle and golden-brown eyes in a face she felt she should recognize.

When she did answer, she didn't feel herself. "It's no matter. You're here now."

"Evelyn?" the man asked. The prairie musk was intoxicating. Did it drift that far into town even when there was nearly no breeze?

Olivia finally found her feet and stepped back. She stood, shaking and hot in front of whoever it was. "No. Olivia. Who are you?" *What are you?* flitted through her mind as she stared up at the man. The collar of his cloak was upturned, but nothing rested above it, though the air shimmered where his head should be.

Olivia had to look away. It was disorienting.

The man leaned down slightly, and Olivia took another step back, still uneasy. "Do you not remember me?"

A bubble of anger seeped through the mire of fear and wariness. "Bullshit. Take your costume off. I want to see you."

"It's not a costume. I need to speak with you, but you are forever around others. I apologize for the intrusion. This is not how I wanted to approach you."

The anger surfaced, and Olivia reached out and flattened a hand against the man's chest. The second she felt his beating heart press back against her hand through the soft woven fabric of his shirt, she pulled away.

Her brief anger was quickly replaced by horrified curiosity. When she was eight, she had happened across a dead opossum being consumed by thousands of ants. They had swarmed over the body so quickly and so violently that she could hear them. Their collective chewing and grinding of the dead animal was impossible to forget. The ants devoured the opossum's eyeball in a matter of minutes, and when Olivia poked the creature with a stick, the swarm scattered toward her briefly, a whiplash of anger toward whatever had disturbed them.

That was finally enough for Olivia, and she had run hollering back to the house and stayed inside the rest of the day. It was a miracle she didn't have nightmares afterward.

"You're real," she sputtered.

"Yes," the man said, matter of fact.

"You have no head."

"Unfortunately." The voice was gentler this time.

"How is that possible?"

"I understand you must not trust me." He held out his hand, as if Olivia reaching out to shake it and say "How do you do?" was the most logical idea in the world.

Olivia had to force down the insane giggle that bubbled up in her throat. Had she been roofied? Was she having a reaction to the Valium? It seemed too crazy even for that.

"I don't know what's going on," she choked out.

"How could you not?"

He stretched his hand closer to her, turning it palm up as someone might with a wary animal. Olivia hesitated, then reached out to touch him. Fuck it. If this month was going to kill her, she was all in.

And then she was in a bright field somewhere, on a path infrequently traveled, and she was herself but not. Looking down, she saw deep-green flannel, felt the cinch of a corset when she took a breath. Before her stood a man, tall, perhaps handsome if she could make out his face. He was handing her something, a leather-bound book. No, a journal. *The* journal!

The man might have been speaking, but all she could hear was the roar of the wind. It was ferocious and whipped her fine hair into a mess around her face. Things with sharp wings lived in the wind and turned the moment dark and sour.

When she opened her eyes, the scene lingered a moment, and bright flashes of the field danced in front of her eyes as they adjusted to the darkness. She released the man's hand.

"You gave the journal as a gift to someone. E. H. Those are her initials. I can't figure out who she is though."

"Evelyn, yes."

Her brain was on overload. It was too much all at once. All the stress of the last few days, the festival, the photographs, her mother, Simon. It was all too much. Her breath hitched in her throat, and she felt like she couldn't breathe. When the figure reached out to steady her, she jerked her arm back, stumbling away from him.

"I have to go." She turned from the man and walked as quickly as she could manage back up the hill toward her apartment. When she heard him follow, her head spun dizzily. She had never fainted, but she imagined that was how it began. She took deep breaths, tried to keep the feeling at bay.

"Please, don't follow me," she called back at him.

He took one more step toward her, then stopped. "I need your help, Miss." His voice sounded as hazy as the thick mist that muted and muffled the world around them.

"I have too much going on. I can't do this. I can't." With that, she ran and stumbled the rest of the way up the hill and cut between two apartment buildings. Each time she looked back, he was standing there on the sidewalk, still in the haze. But she knew that he could appear in front of her if he wished. She hoped he didn't.

Olivia hurried up the stairs to her apartment, trying to be quiet. She still didn't see him following. After she threw the deadbolt behind her, she slid a chair under the doorknob. Not like that would do anything, but the sight of it made her feel better.

Frantic, she raced into her room, shut the door as quietly as her fear would let her, and turned on the lamp on her nightstand. Soft white light flooded the room. But she was alone. Just a jumble of clothes, camera equipment, and teaching materials. She started to relax. Perhaps it had all been a waking nightmare.

She slid under the covers with her clothes and shoes still on. She didn't know if she should call the police or a priest.

She wasn't sure how long her brain ran wild, concocting one theory after another, each one crazier than the last. It settled slowly as exhaustion took over. Something he had said stuck though. *Evelyn.* He had called her Evelyn.

Evelyn. Evelyn. Evelyn.

The name ran through her head like an oddly soothing prayer. The man hadn't hurt her, her tired brain argued, and perhaps he was even trying to help her.

Evelyn. Evelyn. Evelyn.

It reminded her of the game Bloody Mary that she had played at a friend's birthday party when she was younger. She had stood with a group of eight or ten other fourteen-year-olds in front of a mirror in the birthday girl's parents' bathroom, the light off. They chanted "Bloody Mary, Bloody Mary" while they giggled. Someone in the group hissed for them to get serious, or it wouldn't work.

The dark bathroom quieted.

On the cusp of young adulthood, with one foot still planted in childish fantasy, they chanted again. "Bloody Mary, Bloody Mary, Bloody Mary."

For how long, Olivia didn't know. They grew still, became one entity wishing for the same result.

Then a face, silvery and ghostlike, had rushed at them in the mirror. The woman's hair streamed behind her as she hurtled toward them, mouth open in a silent "O." Olivia had felt it was looking straight at her with its dead eyes. It had a message for her. It said some things are better left alone. Some things are better left dead.

She and the rest of the girls ran screaming from the bathroom and into the light.

What would she summon at age thirty-five with this new name and no fucks to give?

Evelyn. Evelyn. Evelyn.

A soft voice answered her. *Hello, Olivia.*

She felt like she was being dragged down into a warm, dark pit. Sleep, yes, just sleep. This was no Bloody Mary. "Hello?" she replied.

Olivia, you're so tired. Do you want to sleep?

"Yes," Olivia murmured. The dark void breathed on her, warm and humid. The great lungs of the universe sighed and yawned.

Olivia, may I come in?

What a strange question. But the pit was so warm, so inviting. It was sleep coming. The Sandman. Sandwoman. She laughed. It sounded far off.

"Of course you can come in, silly. I'm ready for bed."

The indigo darkness rushed up at her, made her body feel heavy, so heavy, and so far away. She let go of waking and let herself sink into it.

16

SIMON HAD DEBATED ALL MORNING ABOUT TELLING SOMEONE about the mental breakdown he was flirting with. He should have been grading Early American history papers about the French and Indian War, but it seemed unimportant if he were going to perish of a stroke or an aneurysm or actually lose himself to a possession of some sort. He wasn't sure which was worse. The list of reasonable people he knew was long. The list of people who might also think there was something supernatural happening to him was much shorter.

Old man Fullbright hated talk of the supernatural, even for his position at the historical society and his insistence that someone was consistently vandalizing the Monroe house. Simon thought about calling Dennis for just long enough that he realized he was in trouble. Calling the crotchety old man at the historical society to speculate about spirits was one thing. Calling his dog's veterinarian to talk about ghosts was something else entirely.

The closest thing he had to any family in Warren was Mrs. Hedgepeth down at the little spice and tea shop on Main. His mom had known her from her college days and had told him to stop by and check on her as often as he could. Simon thought about her occasionally, wondering if he should drop by and say hello. He hadn't been able to bring himself to go by though, not since Mom. He was getting more sensitive as he got older.

Whatever it was, he found himself taking the short path on the south side of campus that would dump him out close to Main. Hedgepeth Herbs and Spices closed in thirty minutes, but he wouldn't be there long.

Mrs. Hedgepeth was measuring out something that smelled deliciously and delicately floral when he walked in. It teased at his memory, bringing the dull ache of his recent headaches down a notch. Pleasant side effects of herbs. He might have to get some of whatever that was.

"Well, if it isn't the younger Monroe," Kathy said when she looked up from her scales. "I wasn't sure I would ever see you again, and now here you are twice in a week."

The younger Monroe? Who was the elder? His grandfather? But it had been the early twentieth century since his family had been there. Before her time, even. A thrill went through him. "I haven't been here in a year and a half."

"Before the other day, yes," Kathy smiled at him. "Did you finish the project you were working on?"

The woman was confused. Clearly. Simon looked her over. Mid-seventies, grey hair kept short, loose slacks and a conservative top, clear eyes. She didn't look like someone easily confused, and she hadn't been in all the time he'd known her. She was usually sharp. What project?

"I . . . not quite, I suppose," he floundered. "I need some tea today." The new layout of the store tickled another memory that sent his headache up a notch. Yes, something was wrong. She must have confused him with someone else. That had to be it. "Uh, do you have any of the lavender chamomile?"

Some women liked tea, and some thought it made him a little fruity. That turned on a percentage of that group in ways he still didn't understand.

Kathy turned toward the teas and waved him along. "Yes, always. Still one of our most popular herbals. You not drinking caffeine? I have lots of other herbals you might like just as well."

The scents in the tea aisle started to calm him. Yes, she was clearly just confusing him with someone who looked like him. "No, but a friend likes it."

Something about the look she gave him was piercing. Not the soft knowing old lady look he'd expected from such a comment. "You have a miss then?"

A miss. Miss Norwich. *Miss Weatherford.* The name crawled over him with a force he didn't expect. It sharpened his headache to a needle prick behind his right eye, a guttural laugh between his ears just after toned it down.

"No," he said slowly, willing himself to act normal. "Not quite."

Kathy's face softened. "Well, then you'll have to keep stock in the tea she likes and see what happens, yes?"

He wasn't sure if he'd ever felt so awkward even when his mother asked him in high school if he'd started having sex yet. There was something pointed and piercing about Kathy's questions and expressions. It wasn't any of her business.

He fingered the bag of lavender chamomile, feeling the bits and pieces within. Just a nosy, confused lady. That made him feel better. Better than thinking that maybe he had a tumor pressing on his brainstem causing hallucinations, nightmares, blackouts, and inspiring odd behavior in his dog.

"Do you have anything for nightmares?" he asked suddenly.

"If it's a medical problem, I have to encourage you to go to the doctor. I'm not a physician. Did you already use all the valerian root you purchased last time?"

There was that thrill again, adrenaline ready to flood his system. Every second blasted holes in his assertion about her confusion. "Almost," he lied. "Just want to try upping the dose a bit."

Mrs. Hedgepeth apparently didn't think this was an abnormal response. She hummed her way around the store, then made her way back to the front counter with a bag of what looked like dirty, dried-out shoelaces. She held it out for him. "Grind it up like I told you last time. No more than double the dose and for no longer than another week or so. If the nightmares intensify, stop using it. This is more about helping you sleep deeply and not remember your dreams than anything."

He assured her that he would stop if anything got worse. After he had paid and avoided much more awkwardness, he paused at the door. "I don't remember, did I pay with my card last time?"

"Oh, I think so. Don't take much cash anymore, you know."

Finally, a fucking light. "Thank you."

He couldn't get to a computer quickly enough. Securing the tea in his jacket, he half jogged back to campus, making lurching progress with the return of the pesky headache. He had to stop and walk about every minute. He wasn't twenty anymore. He gave in and walked when the library was in sight. He was sweaty and out of breath.

If there was a charge on his card, he would do something. Maybe someone who looked similar had stolen his identity. That was possible. He would cancel the card, get a new one.

A group of students passed him on the way in the door, talking loudly to compensate for the quiet time they'd just spent in the library, no doubt. One of the girls turned her grey eyes on him. "Oh, William!" His headache turned up to ten. An involuntary moan left him, but the group was no longer paying attention to him and probably hadn't been in the first place.

Pressing his fingers into his temples, he apologized and slid inside the building. The group still didn't seem to notice. And the girl who had said . . . what was it now? She kept walking, chatting with her friends as if nothing had happened.

William. The name slithered through his skull, much like the pain of the headache.

In a daze, he found a computer on the third floor. It was in an isolated area where he could lose it in peace.

He pecked out his login and password, his fingers not functioning properly. The slithering feeling was still there. There was the charge: $62.71 at Kathy's little tea and spice place from October 2. Christ, what had he bought?

He stared at it, willed his brain to understand. He closed his eyes a few times as if maybe it wouldn't be there when he opened them. But there it was every time. What did it mean? What was he supposed to do now? He only had university insurance, and he sure as hell wasn't going to go get a CAT scan or whatever they did for these kinds of things. He didn't have that kind of money.

So, what? He printed off the pages and headed back outside. He needed to get back to his office. His next lecture was in thirty minutes, and he wasn't prepared. What a fucking month it was turning out to be.

He couldn't concentrate before class. He paced his office. Strange charges from a tea shop didn't reconcile with preparing to teach early American history. They were incompatible.

Benjamin Franklin wouldn't have put up with this bullshit; Simon knew that for sure.

17

7:45 A.M., WEDNESDAY, OCTOBER 7TH

OLIVIA CHECKED HER BACK SEAT COMPULSIVELY A DOZEN times before she got into her car. She'd also checked behind the shower curtain before she sat down to pee. Hell, she'd been checking the fridge and the pantry too.

What did he want?

She took Porter Street on the way into campus to avoid Laramie and went the long way around on Main. Everyone was walking to class like nothing strange was happening. Oblivious.

The large limestone home at the end of Main caught her eye again. The thought that it might photograph well put a pin-sized dent in her anxiety. The second story might be perfect for some wide shots of the surrounding landscape. It seemed to be the tallest building in the immediate area. Odd she hadn't noticed that before.

But Main was old, and many of the storefronts were original, if that had anything to do with it. It blended in or something.

She turned to peer up at the home once more as she drove by. Dark windows gazed back, the wrought-iron chains on the stone posts out front swinging in the wind. Being near Halloween, everything seemed spookier. No doubt the house would be charming a month and a half later with a Christmas wreath in every window and a blanket of snow on the roof and lawn.

With a few minutes to spare before she got to campus, she turned her car around and parked across the street under a large maple to survey the potential subject. It wasn't a landscape, as most landscapes went, but Cecelia and her committee hadn't been too specific.

A large black plaque on the front limestone pillar of the home denoted it "The Monroe House: Est. 1886." It had nice symmetrical lines that she could argue either way for inclusion in her set. Or was she just getting desperate to complete the project?

When she got to campus, she Googled the house on her phone. It had its own page on the historical society's website. She had just pulled it up as she hurried up the stairs into the photography department—and right into someone.

The previous night's misadventure came flooding back—the solid wall of man with no head and her abject fear as she fell toward the ground. *Freeze, run, freeze, run*, her brain said. Her phone and the armful of prints fell from her grip and scattered on the stairs around them. She knew better than to store and carry prints that way, but she'd been in a such a goddamn hurry that the poor decision to put them into folders had been born of a desire to save time.

The scent of the person was familiar, as were his arms, which gripped hers.

"Simon!" The fear drained, but her adrenaline was still up, ready to run at a moment's notice.

"God, I'm sorry. I wasn't watching where I was going. Are you alright?"

For fuck's sake, no, she wasn't alright. Could she tell him that? She knelt down and ducked her head as she scrambled to gather the photographs before the wind could grab them or the concrete scratch them.

Simon knelt with her and reached over to still her with a hand on her wrist. "Are you alright?"

She calmed. His grip on her wrist was firm but steadying, and it brought her back to herself. His voice demanded an answer without being controlling. That was novel. Her head cleared. Fear of the Halloween figure dissipated. She hadn't realized how out of it she'd felt. "I'm fine. I mean, from running into you. This month is just catching up to me."

He squeezed her wrist comfortingly, then let go. "I understand. You don't have to explain anything to me."

She couldn't look in his eyes any longer, or she would do something she might enjoy again. "Thank you. Thank you. I mean that."

They turned to gather the photographs, and she felt Simon's gaze linger on them. He hadn't seen the prints yet. The closest photos of the horse. "Where did you take these?"

Olivia's anxiety stutter-stepped back to life. Demon horse or spirit or cruel joke, she still didn't know. But ghosts couldn't hurt her, right? They could only give her secondhand madness, herding her off a proverbial cliff in her mind while her loved ones thought she needed to be medicated.

The horse must have heard her because it turned to look at her from the photograph at the top of the pile, which Simon tossed back to the ground. "Jesus Christ!"

Olivia couldn't look away. "You saw it move too?"

Simon wiped his hands on his coat.

Mesmerized, that was that word. Couldn't she make her fear go away by facing it? But the longer she looked, the more she felt something was wrong. The horse was wrong. So was the scene. Desiccated, ribs protruding, something dripping from its mouth. It looked like it wanted to get at her.

"I don't understand any of it," she whispered, sliding the photograph into a folder. Something akin to terror gripped her as she watched the horse cram itself as far to one side of the photograph as it could, like it could *see* her.

How many photographs featuring the horse did she have lying around her apartment? Her mom's house? Her studio? Her office? It could be watching her nearly all the time.

She smashed the folders into her large shoulder bag, trying to hold onto whatever calm she'd been given by Simon's touch. It had looked at her. It had seen her, and now that it knew where she was, it could come to campus and drag her away screaming whenever it wanted.

Simon stood with her as the thoughts reeled through her head. Something changed in the air around them. Olivia pressed her shoulder to Simon's as she watched the trees next to the limestone photography building dance in the wind. Odd that she didn't love nature much seeing as she photographed so many landscapes.

Ruts. Old ruts that we run over and over again, drawing the same lines year after year, comfortable in our self-made boxes.

Simon was calming in a way that was . . . comforting. And sexual. Even just pressed against his shoulder, staring at the wind dancing in the trees, she felt a deep pull to him. It'd been so long since she'd had sex. Maybe she was just being an idiot woman, following her vagina wherever it led.

Simon's hand slid up her back, and she felt a light tug on her low ponytail. It sent a wild shiver to the places she'd begun musing over.

His hand fell away a moment later. "I'm sorry. I didn't ask."

She bumped against his shoulder, feeling familiar. Perhaps they were going crazy together. "No, I like it. Please."

He tugged once more, harder, before he dropped his hand. The heat that hit her was welcome, almost expected.

"Do you want to talk about it?" he asked.

She laughed. How long had she wished anyone—her mentors, her mother, Ann—would ask that question? Ann was wrapped up in PhD work and teaching. Olivia had no social life. Her mother could barely keep herself together, especially after her last adventure getting lost two counties over, abandoning her car, and walking halfway back before the police found her. Olivia's love life was nonexistent.

"I guess, yes. I need to get a print done this morning but maybe later? Dinner or drinks or something?"

"I'll phone you."

The old-fashioned phrase didn't seem strange coming from him. That's just how he was. "Please. Thank you."

Olivia tripped up the stairs and barely made it inside without wiping out again. She needed to focus.

The rest of the morning melded into a blur of darkroom chemicals and trying not to see the ever-larger steed in every printed photograph. When would it stop, or would it?

Staring down at the magnified images, she kept waiting for the horse to appear in the film or in a contact sheet, but it never did. With every moment that passed as she scrutinized the film or test sheets, she waited for it. Maybe she should develop and print some of the rolls she hadn't gotten to before the project, see if it was there too.

She watched the next print with as much anticipation as the first, but she was almost more concerned about the horse than the quality of the print. She held her breath as if that would help her keep the roll moving through the chemical baths at a steady pace. She hardly had time to get the print hung up to dry before she had to run to her next teaching duty.

Her classes troubled her too. Her students seemed fine with entertaining conspiracy theories about the disappearances, and she couldn't help but listen. She wanted to join in. She wanted to say, *Have you seen how alike they all are? Have you seen how much I look like them? Do you know something I don't? What have you heard from your friends, your roommates, your other classmates?*

But they had said as much in whispers after the first time her earliest class had mentioned it. She'd caught them watching her closely. She imagined what they were talking about. *When will our teacher be next? When will we receive an email from the university telling us not to come to class anymore? When can we say, "We knew her. She was our teacher"?*

It had started to grate on her, their stares. She knew they were thinking she was next. And who would it be? The headless prankster? The fucking horse? Or her own fool self, leaving the house alone at night again?

More conspiracy, more anxiety.

"Miz Norwich?"

The voice brought her out of whatever place she'd been drifting, thinking about the women. "Hmm?"

It was Sarah. Good, wholesome Sarah. "Do you want our homework?"

Olivia looked at the clock above the classroom door. It was fifteen minutes into class already, and the hum of conspiracy conversation was just starting to die down. A second earlier she could have sworn it was still five minutes until class officially started. She wouldn't be able to finish half of her lesson plan now. She flipped to the lesson plans she would have left for a substitute. Easy stuff for her, boring for the students. Thank God for contingency plans.

"Yes, thank you, Sarah." She raised her voice above the murmur, "Everyone, please pass your homework forward. We'll be working in your textbook today."

She had a hard time looking at the photographs on page ninety-five. It seemed like every time she glanced at them, she might see the horse, come to her through some other means. It would eventually. She knew that as surely as she knew her own breakdown was coming.

18

October 1896

Someone settled an elbow on Evelyn's shoulder and startled her out of her trance. She laughed when she saw it was only her brother, a head and a half taller and stately, just like Father. They stood and watched the prairie grasses bend and sway on the other side of the road from their manicured lawn. The post chains swung gaily in the breeze, clinking sweetly every so often.

"Father let you out of the study for some fresh air finally?"

Ethan turned his grey eyes on her, smiled, and ruffled her hair. She defended herself with a pinch at his side, and the two were breathless with laughter in moments.

Ethan straightened and smoothed his jacket, checked his watch, then slid it back into his pocket. Evelyn adored how seriously he took his courses and Father's tutelage. Ethan would surely take over Father's more important work soon. "He did, if you can imagine. Since he's not been feeling well, he's doubled down on the books."

She didn't like to be reminded of Father's weakening heart. "Will you go to Kansas City soon?"

"And Wichita. Father says he'll open a second office for me within two years wherever there's more need."

Evelyn clasped Ethan's elbow and rested her head on his arm. "I'm forever jealous of your being at the university. The visits with Austin are simply a tease."

Her brother squeezed her arm against him gently. "I hardly understand your fascination with it. One slogs in on a muddy track, sits and learns enough legal jargon to flood the Blue River, then slogs back home on the same rutted path. Farmers go there to learn about their cattle and their wheat. You would stick out like a sore thumb."

"They have allowed women for decades, and learning domestic economy is practical here. Mother shouldn't care that I can learn about my plants alongside the domestics." Evelyn felt like the squeaky wheel.

"You know what she'll say to that."

Evelyn huffed. "'I'm just keeping you safe, Evelyn Rose. Think of what I went through to keep my girls safe.' Lord have mercy. I'm kept so safe, I'll hang myself from boredom."

"She'll come around eventually."

"I won't hold my breath."

Ethan chuckled. "I didn't know he was coming in today. You have a knack for knowing, little sister."

Evelyn turned her gray eyes away from her brother and studied the outline of the figure riding toward them through the fields that led to the Weatherford estate. The only person who would ride so slowly to reach their home a mile outside of town would be Austin, slow and steady Austin on his great beauty of a horse.

"I knew this morning when I woke."

Ethan was about to speak when a great clamor on the porch stole their attention. Their sister, frail and willowy, crashed onto the porch with her white frock and pale eyes, looking like a younger version of their mother.

"Sissy!" she called. "Mother's made us lunch! She said we could eat outside if you wanted to speak with Austin."

Evelyn had to smile. Only twelve and speaking so much like their mother already. Evette would grow up to be just like her, all proper manners and outdated mannerisms, but that was the quaint wonder that was their mother. The only difference was that Esther was a plump woman, and twelve-year-old Evette was still so small. Evelyn worried for her. The wind might snap her in twain.

Evelyn smiled. "Mother saw him, did she?"

"She said she saw you standing on the lawn looking moonstruck and sent me to tell you that Maggie will set up the table and tea for us now." Evette squinted and shielded her eyes, looking in the direction that her older sister had been. "How can you even see him? I see nothing but a blur."

Evelyn turned back toward the fields, seeing the distant figure still moving closer. Even from that distance, Evelyn thought she could see Austin shifting in the saddle and Evan flicking his tail at the late-autumn flies. The two were a beautiful contrast to the gold-and-brown fall foliage around them, a ship sailing into harbor.

What things had he seen on his travels west? She longed to ask him all the questions that wanted to pour forth from her mind. The sky, the prairie, it was her home, but it was enough for her to hear about his travels, to fold them away in her heart.

"Evelyn Weatherford, have you got cotton in your ears?" a voice called across the lawn. "Ethan, tell your sister to mind!"

Ethan laughed, and Evelyn startled out of her thoughts. Mother was thin on patience today. "I'm sorry, Mother. I was lost in my thoughts."

"I worry you're going to catch your death out here in this air, daughter. You forget yourself when you stare out into those fields." Esther waved her hands at Maggie, who was bringing the tea out for the two girls, "Yes, yes, please just set it on the table. My girls can pour their own tea. It's good for them, wouldn't you agree? They need to keep their hands busy, or I fear they'll lose their heads. I remember how I was when I was their age, and my idle hands found me far more trouble than I needed."

Capable of pouring their own tea but not much else. New York had turned their mother from a daring debutante into a worried creature. According to Ethan, at least. He remembered their aunt in New York the best and spoke of her and their mother's outgoing secondhand life with all the relish a good mystery could offer. Evelyn ate up the stories of lavish parties and women in their great bustled dresses made by the finest designers New York could offer. That world seemed as foreign as warmth in the Kansas winters did now.

"Evelyn, dear, come up to the porch and sit, or your feet will blister. I can't have my eldest daughter ragged and windblown all the time. What would everyone think?"

"Yes, Mother." With a smile and a glance over her shoulder to confirm that Austin was indeed getting much closer to the Weatherford estate, she walked up to the large white porch where Evette was already sampling the biscuits that Maggie had prepared. Ethan stole a biscuit from under Evette's nose, earning a swat from her.

Esther ushered her daughter into a chair and busied herself with rearranging Evelyn's hair, trying to pin back all the pieces that had escaped in the breeze. "What will Austin think of your untidiness? I'm certain he knows a well-kept woman from an unkempt one. I don't understand why you can't take better care of your appearance. You must think of the rest of the family."

"I would keep my appearance neater if I were spending my time on campus. Austin cares not." Evelyn winced as her mother stabbed her with a pin and wondered if her scalp would survive the onslaught. It would have been better to say her piece after her mother had finished with her hair, she mused. Evette giggled nearby, unable to contain her mirth at her older sister's expense.

"Of course he cares. I won't hear another word. Evelyn must wear her hair up because it is indecent to do otherwise, and Evette, I expect you to do the same." Esther made a vicious stab with a hairpin, making her eldest daughter's eyes water.

"Ouch! Mother!"

"Though it is not your fault that your hair does not get pinned when Evelyn is standing in the yard all day watching for her friend instead of tending to her younger sisters. Maggie has enough to do without worrying about my girls' hair." She licked her thumb and wiped a smear of dust from Evelyn's forehead and shook her head before returning to the house.

Evette was nearly in tears with laughter. Evelyn's ears burned. "I'm their sister, not their tutor, Mother." Her voice was lost again in Evette's gaiety.

And then there was Austin. Evelyn watched him tether Evan at the edge of the manicured lawn. She envied him, getting up and going whenever he wanted and with such a loyal companion at his side.

He stopped to talk with Ethan first. The pair shook hands and shared good-natured greetings. It warmed Evelyn to see how well they liked each other. She couldn't hear much of their conversation, but she gathered they wanted to sit down soon and swap business talk. Ethan knew the paper and the legal end of the business, and Austin knew the numbers, how to make sales, and hard work. She wasn't inclined to business or numbers, but it seemed the two worked well together.

Ethan finally took his leave back into the house, and Austin approached the porch. Even in his traveling clothes, he was a fine figure, and his golden eyes shone with happiness. She rushed off the porch to meet him halfway.

"Ladies, good afternoon. I trust I'm not disturbing you."

"Of course not," Evelyn said. She wanted to throw her arms around him in a hug but dared not in front of her sister, who wouldn't stop nattering about it until Evelyn was in trouble with Mother again.

Austin smiled at Evette. "Are you tormenting your sister again, Evette?"

The young girl rolled her eyes. "She deserves it."

"Can I tell you a secret?"

Evette lit up. "Yes!"

"One day you'll be best friends with your sister, though it does not seem it now."

Evette scrunched up her face. "You're wrong. I'm certain I detest no one more."

Esther was on the porch in a second, having heard every word of the conversation, likely listening from just inside the door. "Evette Mary Weatherford! That is no way to speak to polite company! Come to tea!"

Evette obeyed their mother with a sulk and stomping feet.

When they were alone on the lawn, and Evette was out of earshot, Evelyn tipped her head to look up at Austin. "She is annoying."

Austin laughed. "Of course she is; she's your younger sister. That's what they're made to do."

Evelyn rolled her eyes at him, but it was good natured. "Yes, I suppose you're right."

"I saw you from a mile off today; the day is so clear."

"I'm surprised you didn't see me from ten. I'm in such blinding white today."

They approached Evan, and Evelyn patted him and straightened the horse's mane against his neck. She received a whoosh of appreciation from the beast.

Austin bit his tongue for all the words he might say regarding her beauty in the white ensemble all the Weatherford girls sported. Evelyn always seemed to find a way to add color to her person. That day it was in the form of a lavender belt and the flower-in-amber brooch he had brought her from Texas.

She eyed him. "I knew you would soon arrive. It's the reason I'm dressed for walking today, so you don't have to wait on me."

"I sent no post ahead of me."

"I know."

The silence that rose was not uncomfortable, but it was questioning.

Austin held his arm out for her, and she accepted. She could feel his warmth through his wool coat. "Are you not warm in that?" The man felt as if he were on fire. Evelyn was warm even in her thick cotton dress.

"I'm prepared for colder weather. October tends to be quite cooler than this, and I find myself wanting it. Are you not cold in that?" They moved away from the house slowly, falling into a comfortable stride together.

"You ask an improper question, sir. A woman always knows what she is doing at every moment. To say I'm ill prepared does not bode well for your knowledge of women." She gave Austin a smile when she saw him flush.

Austin stammered. "I'm sorry. I . . ."

"No, no! I jest!" Evelyn squeezed his arm lightly, glad when he smiled in return.

"Thank goodness. I miss your jests while on the road, dear Evelyn."

"So now I'm 'dear Evelyn'?" She moved her hand from his arm to loosen some of the wild locks of her hair, which had already tried to escape from the Esther's vicious pinning. Austin would not mind.

He watched her fight with her wild hair. "You tease me. You said a week ago in your letter that you preferred to be called 'dear Evelyn,' so I merely complimented you. And do you not detest being so formal in front of your family?"

"It is what they expect of me," Evelyn stated. When they were out of sight of the house and heading toward the fields, she let Austin take her hand, entwining her fingers with his. It was natural, easy. "Mother saw what was happening in New York and knew she needed to move elsewhere before she found herself in ruin."

"And what do you think of that?"

Evelyn turned her smart eyes on Austin. "I think one can find ruin anywhere if one wants to find it badly enough."

Austin hummed his accord. "I imagine you haven't said so much to your mother?"

"Heavens, no. Can you think what she would do to me? I should never leave the house again."

"It's a miracle she lets you out with me."

"You have bewitched her. She thinks you pure of heart and intention." Evelyn smiled.

"I'm a man, fallible."

"I've yet to see a flaw in your character, my friend. Save perhaps that you are away too often, and it disturbs my walks."

Austin didn't know what to say to such high praise. Nor did he understand it.

A breeze from the north told him that autumn would not linger long that year, though many of the leaves hadn't fallen yet. The breeze rustled through the tall grasses of the field as they walked through them, following the paths of the deer and the rabbits. Evelyn caught the tall heads of the grasses as they walked, creating a brown-and-gold bouquet that seemed to perfectly represent the day in Austin's eyes. The sky, full of large white clouds with deep-grey undersides, let only the slightest amount of blue through and even less sunlight.

Evelyn looked up to the sky and then stopped for a moment, holding Austin back and making him pause. "Have you ever seen a sky so like the autumn?"

Austin observed the sky again, trying to understand the grey-eyed woman's words. "Does autumn have a certain sky?"

"Spring, summer, and winter do too, but autumn . . . autumn has a certain sky that draws on all the others and surpasses them all. You see that white and grey and blue up there? That all three of them are together in the same place? It's like us down here. So different but in the same place at once and seeming to fit together, even for the difference. And the sumac here on the prairie begins to turn until by the time the winter sky comes, the prairie is afire with red." Evelyn held her hands up to the sky for a moment, and the clouds and limited blue peered through her fingers.

Austin had noticed something when Evelyn's eyes were turned up to the sky, and her profile was to him. In that moment, she wanted to share that piece of time with him, the secret knowledge of the sky that she possessed. He had thought that for all his wonderings about Evelyn Weatherford, he would have already given her his heart, but he felt it slip away from him as he watched the northerly wind muss her hair, her lashes cover her grey eyes when she closed them against the wind, and the way her pale skin, colored with the walk and the breeze and perhaps a while too long spent out of doors on a sunny day, shone with the conviction of her thoughts.

It was Evelyn's turn to watch him as he stared up at the sky, trying to hide whatever he had been thinking. She had seen something there that she wanted to see again. Did he think of her? She felt her palms sweat against his, so unladylike, but the direction of her thoughts wouldn't stop. They had walked that way many times before. Why was this time different?

But he was married to his prairie, she felt. Hitched to the work that took him away on long treks west and south to Oklahoma and Texas.

Together, they watched a young hawk throw himself feet first into a nearby thicket full of doughbirds, which were either very early or very late to the prairie. The birds chattered at the hawk, who was just out of reach. Yet he still flapped up into the air, then dropped straight down onto the thicket, determined to nab his prize.

Evelyn cleared her throat and her mind. "Many do not take the time to look at the sky except when it is threatening. It is exciting then, to be certain, but so much better to enjoy it when I know that others are not, and I can have the sky for myself."

She walked on again, tugging Austin along with her. He stayed close, keeping his arm against hers.

"You speak much more now than around your family." The breeze managed to pull a lock of hair from Esther's pinning, and it twirled in the breeze, dancing and reaching out behind her. Austin longed to see her hair down. He wondered how much different she would look but decided he didn't care. It was Evelyn still, as it would always be.

Evelyn grabbed another stalk of grass for her bouquet. "I imagine I must. At least some. I have a question," Evelyn ventured, dropping pieces of her bouquet back to the earth.

"I'll attempt an answer."

"What were you thinking earlier?" Her eyes met his, grey as the underside of the clouds, the winter.

"Earlier? I was thinking about the sky," he said lightly.

"I don't believe you. What were you thinking? You must tell me." She stopped and bent to pick clinging plants from the hem of her dress. Austin watched her break off the head and a leaf from the plant and stick it in her pocket. He knew she would take it home to sketch and color it later.

"They were thoughts that would not interest you, I'm sure." His heart thudded uneasily in his chest. Would she laugh at him? Surely not. But he felt caught now.

"Now, you know I would not be asking if I thought that they would not interest me. Don't stall." She took his hands in hers and stared at them, willing them to speak in his stead.

"Evelyn . . . I . . ."

"Yes?" Her eyes were wide with interest.

"Evelyn Weatherford, would you marry me?"

Evelyn didn't respond for a few moments, merely stared up at the man before her. Somehow his words hadn't shocked her at all. It was so easy to see it all now and to see her own infatuation with him. No, not just infatuation. They had spent those silly days already in their innocent youth. Now she saw conversation by a warm fire while the snow built up outside the door, her hands sometimes wrist deep in dough as a means to pass the time. She saw his smile, which would never change, though his hair would grow white and curl. She wanted to be part of that, now and then and in between.

"Austin . . ." She was bursting to simply say "yes" and be done with it. How many years had they danced around the question? There would be so much to work out, but they could, she knew. He wouldn't be gone from home so much soon. And they had been such close friends for so long, could talk about anything it seemed, save their emotions surrounding each other. They could convince her mother and father. They could make it work. Once she was in his home, she could attend college classes as she pleased.

"I mean it in the sense in which I say it. I could not ask, you know. Your mother would not allow it."

A stone settled in Evelyn's gut. "Oh. I . . ."

Whatever emotion churned inside her must have presented itself on her face because Austin tripped over her words again. "I have made a misstep," he said.

"No, not at all," she replied. Her hand in the bouquet had stilled. "Only you hadn't given me the chance to answer."

It was Austin's turn to feel the nerves of the moment. He had not expected, even in the slightest, for her to throw herself at his feet, but he had not expected such coolness either. Had he said something wrong?

"My apologies. I should not have said anything."

Evelyn's ensuing laugh seemed rather sad. "You have thought yourself out of it now, and I'm tired. Shall we go back to the house? The wind has turned to the east. It's strange."

Austin didn't know what to say. "Yes, let's."

Evelyn took his hand and twined her fingers into his, and they started back toward Evan. But Evelyn's usual light gait with him was slower, more measured, and he didn't know what to say.

19

Olivia was quiet that evening when she and Simon sat next to each other on the small couch at the back of the café. She had stacked her photographs on the table in front of them, and she watched the ice melting in her drink from her spot curled up on the cushion. Simon put his arm around her as she leaned closer. Their moment in his office, outside the art department . . . her apartment. He didn't know what to make of them.

She didn't speak for a time, and he didn't want to bring up the elephant in the room that was currently watching them from the topmost photograph, dripping what could only be saliva from its mouth, so he began. "Where have you traveled? The Rocky Mountains, in true Ansel Adams form?"

"Nowhere. I've not left the state."

Simon stared at her for a beat, unsure what to say. She looked so worldly, spoke so well, and knew so much. That was his impression, anyway. And he'd seen the way she watched from around the edges of faculty gatherings, careful not to engage.

"Really?"

She shrugged and pulled her cardigan closer around her body. Had he said something wrong? She was behaving differently. Back straight and knees pressed together, she looked so proper, relaxed but prim. It was not quite Olivia. It was not the woman he had run into outside her building. It was not the shy, timid woman in his office.

"Really," she said finally. "I don't know, I guess I just didn't feel the need to leave. And my mom . . . my mom has issues. She doesn't travel. I went to St. Mary's in Bailey, you know. Briefly. For photography. That's close to the state line."

She smiled at her own joke, and his heart twisted in his chest. He wanted to please her, to make her smile again. "I'm sure you crossed it at some point during your stay there."

Her smile widened briefly before she turned her gaze away and sipped her Italian soda, ice half melted. Strawberry and vanilla. His heart sank and then burgeoned. Perhaps she was just worried about her workload.

"Tell me about St. Mary's."

Olivia sifted through the photographs she had brought, hovering over the photos as if she were casting a spell. He watched them too, wary of the horse that snapped at them like a rabid dog. He was about to repeat himself, thinking she hadn't heard him, when she spoke.

"They taught me more than I would have learned here, but it was not home. I only attended for a semester and a half. I like it here. That's why I came back for my MFA."

"I like it here too," he said.

She traced the hazy equine figure in one of the photographs. The normal horse. Simon felt a chill as he watched.

"There's something about this town, you know," she said. "Something that draws people back. Or makes people stay. I'm not sure which."

Her voice had taken on a different lilt, and when he turned to look at her, her outfit was different. Skirts cascaded over her knees to the floor.

The lace of a ruffle at her shoulder tickled his hand. The hairs on that arm stood up. He had to choke out his next words. "Why do you say that?"

"Well, aren't many people here descendants of those who founded the town? Have you seen how many people here have grey eyes and fine brown hair? Like mine?"

There was a hush over the café. No one had stopped speaking, but he could no longer hear the traffic outside. Perhaps she knew something that he didn't. "But you're not . . ."

She seemed to snap out of a stupor and looked at him with her sharp grey eyes. "Right. I checked with my mom. We have no relations here."

It seemed odd. As if she were disappointed. He said as much. That got a laugh. It set him at ease.

"Maybe a little?" she said. "It seems like I ought to be, I guess, for how I look, for what I'm learning."

He wanted to bring up Evelyn and how Olivia looked just like her. Surely that was what she was insinuating. But he danced around it again. Another missed opportunity. He could push her toward the message boards though. "Well, the historical society can only tell you so much, you know. I've found some help on that genealogical message board site as well as the library on campus. They've got quite an impressive amount of cannon fodder for thought."

"Thank you. I'll have to look there. What about you? Surely you have relations here."

He shook his head. "Nope. It dead ends around the turn of the century when my rancher relations moved back to Ohio. And don't think that I haven't searched thoroughly. I imagine my great-grandparents came here as immigrants. Farmers, ranchers, and the paper trail just didn't follow them. Or they changed their name, or it was misspelled along the way. That's common."

She slid a photograph toward him. "And what do you think about these? What should I think of them?"

He didn't know. Kudos to Olivia for going to the lengths she had to try and find an explanation that would sit well with her. But it just wasn't there. He didn't even want to touch the thing after that day's incident.

"What do you think?" he asked, holding her gaze for a moment. They were almost alone in the cafe, save for a few college students in the opposite corner of the room, headphones on and studying intently. The barista was nowhere to be found, and the hush was still over them.

The question seemed to catch Olivia off guard. "Me? Well, if something isn't wrong with my camera, and it isn't a trick of the light, then I guess it's a ghost. Or a demon."

Simon studied the normal horse again. Its trappings were clearly in focus in Oliva's more recent pictures, the feathering on its hooves unmoving despite the wind on the day the photograph was taken. He had seen the horse somewhere but could not place it. The idea he'd had about it the other day had vanished, as had other things when he tried to connect the dots that he was sure were there. He thought for certain he'd woken in the night and written something on the pad of paper next to his bed, but the next morning, the notepad was blank.

Olivia covered the horse with her hand. "I feel like I'm going crazy, but you see it too." She didn't mention her late-night hallucinatory walk. That was on another level. She tried to change the subject. "I'm running out of ideas for photographs. I did preliminary sketches, but nothing is speaking to me right now."

The horse appeared around the edge of her hand, tossing its head and moving just outside the frame. It made her stomach clench. She looked away. "I don't know if it's me or the distractions."

Simon didn't blame her. The weird shit with the horse made him uneasy. "Some of the buildings off Main Street have a nice view of the spread of town from the higher stories."

Olivia felt something she couldn't place when he said that. He couldn't read her mind, but that the same thought had been on hers so recently was . . . odd, like everything else lately. "I was by the Monroe house this morning. It seems like the best vantage point for a few shots. Do you know anything about it? Same last name and all."

That got a chuckle from him. "Just from histories of the town. No relation, as I've said. I tried looking and came up with bunk. William Monroe, the town's most popular or most infamous mayor, depending on who you talk to, lived there for most of his life."

"Until his *untimely* death."

The emphasis on "untimely" hit his ears in a strange way. It almost felt like anger. It was true though. The man's death had been untimely. Dragged down the street by a horse untimely. He felt a pang of anger radiating from somewhere deep within him. It made him tense. "So, you've learned a bit about him."

A slight shrug of her slim shoulders. "A bit. It seems mostly unsavory."

"That's one word for it."

A comfortable silence ensued. Simon watched as Olivia hugged herself and shivered. It was getting late, and despite wanting to stay out all night with her, she seemed off. He wanted her to be well, he realized, perhaps like a brother but also as more. They had time for all that later, after the stress of the festival was behind them.

"Should we go?" he asked.

She looked like she had gone away somewhere in her head. "Yes, I probably should. I'm sorry; I'm no fun tonight."

"Is anything on your mind?" he asked as they packed up their things and headed for the door.

It was her turn to laugh. "Everything. I don't even know where to start."

He hummed his agreement.

They both froze when they stepped outside and turned toward the intersection that bordered campus. A man stood at the corner, but he wasn't waiting at the crosswalk. He was facing them, standing still, watching.

Simon could see right through him to the curb, street, and shrubs beyond, the hazy blue of the man's outline disconcerting and impossible to focus on.

He was dressed for riding; Simon could tell that much. Tall boots over somewhat loose pants, button-up shirt tucked in, though the tails hung out. He wore a hat that would have shielded his eyes from the bright sun in eastern Colorado while he rode fences. Waves of hair poked out from under it. Simon couldn't tell for certain, but he'd bet every picture he'd ever seen that the man had about a week's worth of stubble on his face.

At that thought, Simon felt a chill deep inside, as if he'd internalized his headache, down in his gut. He knew that man. Not personally, but he felt like he should somehow for all the intimate details he knew about him. From every picture he'd ever looked at and every historical account he'd ever read, he had no doubt as to the man's identity.

Austin Hearth.

Something within him snarled from the same place that the headache came from. Outside of historical studies, he didn't find himself particularly observational, but now there wasn't much doubt in his mind that he was sharing space with something that wasn't him.

Olivia tugged on his sleeve like a little girl. "Oh my God, Simon," she whispered. "Do you see him? Do you see him?"

Of course he did. But whatever snarled in him rose up and reached for his neck, grasped his vocal cords and spoke with its own voice instead. "See what?"

The look on Olivia's face was awful, and he tried to wrestle with the . . . thing . . . inside him. But it was like wrestling with air, and the most wrestling he'd ever done was in bed with his last two girlfriends. But in that moment, there was nothing physical for him to grasp.

"See him? See the man there at the corner?"

The thing inside felt something that swelled in him, but Simon felt it in only a secondary way. He had no analogy for it. But the thing was enraged, so angry that it came at Simon in waves of heat and darkness. His vision swam as he stared at Austin, a hazy form not twenty feet from them, dark specks moving like floaters in front of his eyes.

His body moved without his permission, looking around and down the street. "I don't see anyone, sweetie. Maybe it was just a runner out for a jog? I'm sorry I missed him."

Not me, not me, not me! he tried to scream.

"Oh," Olivia replied.

Simon felt his heart clench in fear. He watched her squeeze her eyes shut and turn away, then look back briefly. God, she looked scared. He wanted to reach for her, but he was frozen inside himself.

Goddammit! Let me go!

But all he felt was the rage, which crept over him in waves that felt like the chills of illness. No words, just raw feeling, and it was directed toward the man—toward Austin—who stood at the corner, still and watching.

"I need to go," Olivia said, staring anywhere but at the figure, who seemed unable to move.

"I'll walk you to your car," he heard himself saying.

Don't you dare hurt her!

She licked her lips and finally looked back to where Austin was standing. "OK."

She kept looking behind her on the walk into campus. Simon wished he could too, but someone else was doing the walking and the talking. What did the thing want?

The secondary rage he sensed with him grew during the walk into something that almost had a taste. It was like blood, like he was sucking on a penny. He felt his vision filling with the dark eye floaters as the coppery feeling intensified. Then the feeling evaporated, his vision cleared, and he felt alone once more.

The sound of hooves on concrete reached him as they approached her car in the parking lot. Simon snapped his gaze to Olivia, who looked up at him with grey eyes that were unreadable in the darkness. There was no question that they both heard it.

"Would you like to come home with me?" Was it him asking that now? He couldn't be certain, but he wanted it. Yes, he did. He also wanted her to be safe.

"Yes, please. Tonight was . . . strange." She turned around quickly. The sound of hooves had stopped. "I don't mean with you. Just the vibe of it, I guess. It scared me. Maybe it's just the season."

Maybe it was.

Maybe it is, growled the thing inside him, but when he felt around for it again, it was gone, and only he was in his head, agreeing that yes, yes, it was just the season for it.

20

THE HOUSE WAS LIT ON THE PORCH, BUT OLIVIA DIDN'T SEE it, not really. She felt drunk, the kind where she only cared about finding a soft, warm place to land. Screw where it is. It was on the trendy side of campus, of course, and she fixated on the moths careening around the porch light, watching them as they bumped into each other and the light. In true hipster form, she felt like the moths, bumping around in the dark, just trying to find the light. She scoffed at the thought, and Simon asked her if she was OK.

"Yes," she whispered, for she felt something watching them still. "Just feeling like a teenager again."

Simon chuckled quietly, and the sound tickled another long-gone memory that came and went with the slivers of light in the dark rooms they passed.

Olivia felt her feet on the carpeted hallway, the walls on either side of her, but she couldn't tell what was on the walls. They passed framed work that she touched with the careful edges of her fingers, but she only had eyes for him, for where he was leading her.

They stripped each other in the darkness, light from a neighbor's back porch their only illumination. She sensed a bed, a dresser, clothes on the floor with her sandal-clad feet. The bed seemed old-fashioned, and she grabbed one of the posts while she unstrapped her sandals.

His mouth found hers, half teeth the way people are when they are wanting and not thinking of anything else.

"I want your hands on my throat," she said. The safety after the fear made her want him.

"I don't want to hurt you, but I want to hurt you," he replied. She felt a warm hand snake up her torso, around her neck.

"I want you to hurt me and make love to me after," she rejoined, grasping his hand and making it squeeze her neck until she felt dizzy, power and no power.

She had never wanted like this before, to let go, to give in to the temptation that had been consuming her. But there was something about him. She wanted him, wanted to see the animal in him. Maybe it was the fear she had just felt, the terror at seeing the man on the corner. The thought surfaced that perhaps he had seen it too, and then it was gone in the passion that enveloped her.

Somewhere in her tired mind something quiet cried out for her to stop. The voice wasn't hers. It was a pretty voice though, and she had heard it somewhere before. But Olivia didn't want to stop. She wanted his hands and mouth all over her now that she was inside and safe and away from whatever was trying to get her.

The voice still warned.

"Shush," she murmured.

"Hmm?" Simon surfaced to ask.

"Nothing," she said, and took his face in her hands as he ran his fingers down her neck. "Just quieting my mind."

And for awhile, it was quiet.

21

Spring 1897

Evelyn hadn't known a time when she was so bored. Would Austin *ever* return? She wanted out of the house.

Her father called her into his study one spring afternoon when she wished more than anything that she could be out collecting early spring flowers and seeing what new rarities the prairie would divulge. She huffed and sat down in a chair across from him, only just catching herself from slouching and grumping for the duration of the meeting. She didn't want to be chastised.

"I have asked for the good Mayor Monroe to come out and visit you," her father began.

Evelyn sat and stared at him. What he proposed didn't make sense. Why would the mayor want to come out and see her? She hardly went to town, and the only times they did, she spent it spitefully, wishing she could be going to the university campus instead. Thomas P. Jones'

Stationery and Books was lovely and supplied her with all the colors and sketchbooks she could want, but she longed to keep walking, to take the turns that would lead her to the campus.

"He's been asking to see you for quite some time."

"Me?" Evelyn asked. "Why me?"

"Because you're my daughter. Because you're beautiful. Because you would make a good wife."

"Father." Oh, there was the purpose. It didn't seem right. She felt too young. What was a good wife? Any imagining she had done was about Austin in the privacy of her bedroom with her journal. A life with him had seemed promising, if difficult.

"Yes?" Father was smoking his pipe, relaxing at midday. Evelyn longed to be outside. A picnic with the other families in the area, a boat ride, playing hoops on the Vogt's flat lawn, anything. It was still too cold for all that though.

"I find that I don't much care for him already, if those are the things in which he is interested." Evelyn retorted.

"Evelyn, you know I wouldn't make an unsuitable suggestion. I respect your thoughts on the matter, but this is ideal. You may be nearly eighteen, but you are young yet, and I still know what is best for you."

Evelyn rolled her eyes. She knew she shouldn't, but all anyone could talk about lately was the wonderful Mayor Monroe. Fine state in which to be a mayor, Kansas was.

"Please, my dear, give him a chance?"

Evelyn heaved a huge sigh. "Fine. I'll meet him for tea. Or whatever infernal idea he and you have invented." Mother could chastise her later when Father told her of the eye rolling and sighing. She didn't care. She couldn't put into words how Father's decision and the upcoming meeting made her feel, but uncomfortable was part of it.

The days leading up to their meeting were quiet and uneventful. It was always too quiet when Austin was away. Mother wouldn't let her wander far from sight, though if Mother was napping, Evelyn would take a short stroll up the hills to the south and see if she could see smoke from chimneys that way. Austin was that way, and he always rode in from the southwest.

One day she ventured as far as the fence where she had met him what seemed a lifetime ago. She picked at the barbs on the wire with her fingers, pressing the points into her perpetually cold fingertips until she could feel the barb or until blood came, whichever was first. Making the blood come eased the pain of waiting for Austin, like air being let out of a balloon that was too full.

It was selfish of her to want him around all the time; he must work. But he had been gone too much lately. She liked that he enjoyed his work even if it took him away from home too often. Father didn't completely approve for some reason, and she thought it must have to do with the nature of Austin's work. He was doing the work with his own hands. She gathered her father wanted Austin to be running his own crew of people who would do the work for him or sit behind a desk like her father did. Be a lawyer, a banker, or sell land from an office. But what was wrong with making a living by working with his hands? She had seen Austin's home. It was polished and clean and ready to receive the best company. He had enough. If that didn't mean he was suited for her company, she worried what this Mr. Monroe could give her that Austin could not.

She was sitting properly in the front parlor ready to receive Mr. Monroe when Austin arrived unexpectedly. His trips were so much longer now, so much more frequent, that she began to lose track of when he would return.

She stood to welcome him, and he pulled her into a crushing hug, one that felt so good that she could only melt into his arms. He smelled like he always did: the prairie and all things earthen. Their walks always left her windswept and smelling like him. It was a treasure, and she longed to keep the scent forever. She would hate not to see him so much if she married and moved to town. The thought of it made her stomach turn over.

"I bring back air all the way from Dodge City and on west into Colorado. Can you smell the snow on me? It was still packing the roads there."

Evelyn laughed. "You smell like you always do: like the prairie. I can't get enough of it."

"Then come for a walk with me?" he asked. "I have only just gotten back, and I need to tend to my home soon, but I wanted to see how you were first."

She watched his eyes. He was always smiling, always making her laugh.

"Oh, you know, I've been here pining away for you," she joked. "Put on my tether until you come home."

"I'm surprised. I don't know a woman better equipped for walks alone than you."

"I suppose," Evelyn replied wryly. "I don't know what Mother would do if I pushed courses at the college again. She might opt to bring the entire college here instead of letting me walk on my own. 'It's dangerous out there, Evelyn Rose!'" she said mockingly. "'You'll find your ruin!' My goodness, Mother!"

A commotion at the front door silenced whatever Austin tried to say in reply, and Evelyn stiffened. Her day would soon be spoiled; she was sure of it. She was glad the curtain hid them from view.

Austin touched her arm gently. "Are you expecting company? I do have affairs at the house to attend to and can come back."

Evelyn listened to the group shuffle through the hall toward them. She had an urge to run in the opposite direction or to pull the curtains on the parlor and hide behind them, but she wasn't a child; she could stand up to whomever they might bring to see her.

"Mother and Father are expecting company for me." She bit her tongue, wanting to add *And I could not care less.* She needed to act like an adult sometime and not just when Austin was around.

"Then I'll head home. I'll call perhaps tomorrow?"

"Please do," Evelyn said.

He had just taken his dusty coat toward the hall when her family entered the room. She felt like she was on display, everyone watching her. There was an awkward moment when Father briefly introduced Mr. Monroe to Austin, but the pair didn't shake hands before Austin took his leave. Evelyn felt wholly alone when he disappeared from view. She could battle for herself though.

She watched the man from the other side of the room. Appearances were pleasing, she supposed. He was pleasantly proportioned. A bit shorter than Austin, who was just the right height to be her dancing partner when the occasion called. If this man knew how, she supposed he would be fine as well.

Austin was broader in the chest than this man too but not in any way that made her feel she needed to discount him. His face was clean-shaven, but she didn't have much of an opinion on that. Austin's traveling beard amused her though.

It was his eyes that surprised her. He held her stare for much longer than she could, and she shifted her eyes to the windows to watch Austin riding away on Evan. Her heart lurched, and she wondered if she needed to sit down and have some tea.

Introductions were made, and Evelyn was pleased with the warmth in his touch and how clever his eyes looked when he said her name.

"Miss Evelyn." He gave her an old-fashioned kiss on the hand. "It is my great pleasure to meet you. Mayor William Monroe at your beck and call."

She felt so girlish that she nearly giggled. That was new. She could be fanciful with Austin but never girlish. William Monroe was certainly charming. "It is a pleasure to meet you too. Thank you for coming all this way."

"Again, my pleasure." He had a clever way of smiling that made her feel like it was just for her. There was no lewd winking or anything of the sort, but it felt like he was already sharing a secret that was just for her. She enjoyed it. A lot.

The room cleared, and they were allowed to sit together for a time. Maggie sat in the far corner, mending.

"Mr. Monroe—"

"William, please." There was that smile again, the one that was only for her.

"Tell me what town is like. As I do not live there, I do not know what the bustle is like day to day."

"How far away have you been?"

"Nowhere. I have stayed here. There has been no need to leave."

Another smile, this one a little slower. "I hardly think you are not worldly, Miss Evelyn. Your father speaks highly of your accomplishments."

"Oh, does he? He does not approve of my wanting to go to college, but I suppose the other things do not bother him so."

William's eyebrows went up at her words. "College? Why would you want to? Are you an Elizabeth Blackwell?"

Evelyn flushed. "Oh, no. I'm not so technically inclined. I want to learn though. I have hobbies, ideas I want to contribute. I have done fascinating studies of the plant life in this area. Besides, the college offers cooking and baking classes too."

"I admire that, even if it is silly. If you came to live in town with me, you wouldn't have any need of those skills. I have a full staff who takes care of the domestic."

"Oh." The little sound escaped her. He was forward. It wasn't unwelcome though. Being able to speak one's mind was important, and being heard was the other part of it. And Mr. Monroe seemed to have that in spades.

"You are beautiful," Mr. Monroe said, turning his sky-blue eyes on her again. It seemed like such a strange thing to say at that moment. But again, it wasn't unwelcome. Neither was his presence in general.

She didn't consider herself a beautiful woman. She was interested in makeup but didn't apply it with any frequency or skill. Her face was mostly clear, save the smattering of freckles over her nose. She did have brown skin left over from the summer though. Her walks with Austin had become so frequent the season before and the weather over the winter so mild that they had continued their walks well into December and the first part of January.

Her hair was unruly on the best of days. It was fine and wavy, but there was a lot of it. Mother lost her mind every time they tried to put it up; it just would not cooperate.

"Thank you," she said.

"You're welcome." William produced a small box and handed it to her.

"What's this?"

"Just something small that I thought you might enjoy. Go on, open it."

She carefully pulled the ribbon and peeked inside the box. Then she sat and stared at it for a moment. "This is . . ." She couldn't put into words what she was seeing. Her first reaction was anger, then surprise at her anger. She turned to face the stranger who sat next to her, trying to school her features. She felt hot, and she knew if she opened her mouth, something untoward would fall out. Instead, she stared at the little frilly piece of paper that invited her to Lucy's to have a dress made, courtesy of the Monroe Estate. Mr. Monroe was all smiles, and it put a dent in her anger.

"I want you to have a rational dress," he said, as if it was the simplest gift in the world. "I do not want anyone saying that I'm with a boisterous girl. You are not a boisterous or immoral girl are you, Miss?"

Again, her anger flared, but he was sitting there smiling so nicely. Perhaps he truly meant well.

"Certainly not. Is something wrong with what I wear?" she asked cautiously.

He laughed easily, and smile lines told her that he laughed often. "Not at all! No, truly. It's just that I like a certain style, and I would enjoy it if we were matching when we went out together. If you accept, that is."

She softened and turned the request over in her head. Never had she heard of such a thing. Matching dress? It was silly.

He began talking again before she could reply. "I know that tea gowns are the 'thing' for you ladies by midday in the home, but I'm not on board with them. I prefer a defined waist, and all ladies of your stature and class should wear pale blue. It is very becoming."

Evelyn saw Maggie watching her from the corner of the room, chin lifted and a look of concern intended for Evelyn. Evelyn smiled at her; there was surely nothing to worry over. Everything she had heard about Mr. Monroe painted a glowing portrait. And Father wouldn't have let him in the house if he didn't think well of him. Surely he was just nervous and overexcited about their potential friendship. Showing his wealth was no crime. And she was flattered. She hadn't considered herself one to enjoy being doted upon, but the prospect of a new dress was exciting. Fashion hadn't concerned her overmuch since Mother took care of everything, but she did like looking at *Atlantic* or *Harper's* and seeing what other ladies might be wearing around. For a man to enjoy those things . . . well, it did take all kinds to make the world go around.

"I'm flattered," she said finally. "It's such a large gift. I don't know how I could accept it. I must talk to my father first."

There was that smile again, touching his blue eyes and then her heart. "I already have."

More surprise. He had gotten approval for a gift that he didn't even know if she would want? Strange as it was, he must only want to please her.

"Alright then. I suppose we will have it arranged."

"Yes, please do. I would love to take you on strolls through town. There is always something new to see."

He looked so excited, like a puppy. She had never dealt with what she would consider a true suitor before. Perhaps this is how they acted. Austin . . . Well, she could not even compare them, if she had to look at him that way.

When he took his leave, Evelyn took to her room and sat on her bed. She set the gift box beside her and took out her journal. She hadn't formed an opinion of Mr. Monroe save for his generosity, so where should she begin?

22

11:00 P.M., FRIDAY, OCTOBER 8TH

IT WAS SO HARD TO STAY AWAY FROM HER NOW THAT HE KNEW. He had to give kudos to Simon Monroe, distant doppelganger, for figuring out so much so quickly. That man had an *insatiable* need to know. It was fascinating, really. He was a digger, just like his ancestor.

He would have liked to get ahold of the original journal the night before, but there was still time for that. He'd gotten the worst bits out of it at least, put them away for the moment. He couldn't bring himself to destroy them. William wanted to, but there were pieces of himself in that journal, of all of them. He worried it was somehow integral to their presence there. William was more about shoot from the hip, ask questions later, a bygone relic of the American West. *He* was more concerned about the big picture.

Patience hadn't ever been part of his framework though. But the more of *her* he could find, the better. She didn't need to be running off with

Austin again any more than she already had. Best keep her frightened of him if he could.

He was a little mad at himself for putting so much effort into scaring this one rather than going about his business. But she was awfully pretty, and he could stay the more vengeful William for as long as he wanted. Besides, he enjoyed Warren. Brimstone burned out the nostrils after awhile.

They irked him though. Every version of her had some of that haughtiness that he'd worked so hard to stifle in his Evelyn. If she could just stop and let it all go, let everything unfold as it was meant, then this would all be so much easier.

Purpose was something he'd been mulling over the last few days. He'd tried to get back into his crypt from whence he came, but since the initial oust, he wasn't allowed back in. Iron and sanctity and all that. Couldn't even fly over the damn thing to get a view from up there. And the potential violent expulsion from his host if he tried to go in there was something he wanted to avoid. If poor Simon went in there and got a clear head, he might never come back out.

So, he settled for lurking outside the fence. There was a fair bit of heat from the iron fence that kept him even farther away, but at certain angles, he could catch a glimpse of his handsome plot.

Well, what used to be his plot. He couldn't *really* claim ownership of it. It was William's, truth be told. But he was at least half William, so he supposed that gave him half a claim to it. See? It all worked out.

The outside of the crypt needed to be polished, which was a bit maddening seeing as he couldn't get to it. The limestone had blackened around the sides and edges, but it still stood tall and strong at the back center of the cemetery.

All the waiting gave him too much time to think. He had anger issues. Even mostly mild-tempered Simon Monroe had probably figured that out. It just seemed like no one could do anything the way he wanted it done. Ever. Not quickly enough or efficiently enough or simply not at all. How could it never occur to people that there was more than one way to get some things done?

The more he saw of this "modern" world, the more it disgusted him. It was exciting on some levels, but everyone was so dispassionate. They couldn't discipline their children or their wife without the authorities getting involved. And someone was always watching. He hadn't had to be so damned careful in the past. No wonder everyone on the street had their scent tainted with the astringency of medicine.

Being close to her when Simon wasn't being a baby was thrilling. He hadn't had enough time to follow her around yet—unfinished business with the others and all—but she was untouched by so much of that. Find her a dress, and she might pass for Evelyn herself. Sort of. She would have to lose the attitude first.

It made him think back on their initial courtship. He'd known what he wanted even then. She'd been *almost* perfect. Almost. Malleable, young, and smart. Not clever but smart. If not for her stubbornness, she would have been perfect. And Austin. But even when he was gone, her stubbornness made it impossible for their happiness to bloom. Why couldn't she have tried a little harder?

If she had *tried*, he wouldn't have had to go through all the trouble with Austin. If she had *tried*, he wouldn't have died. If she had *tried*, their children wouldn't have been shipped off to who knew where. If she had just *tried*, this entire mess could have been avoided.

There was the anger again, rising steadily in him, the early summer sun, ready to scorch the prairie. It felt righteous. *He* shouldn't have always had to do all the work. Marriages didn't work like that. But she didn't do anything, and they fell apart.

He could put the anger to good use. One was living near him. He bet if he put it on a map it would show them radiating out from Monroe's current home, spinning out, spokes from the center of a wagon wheel. There was no time for fun of that sort, but it was a pleasant thought.

And it wasn't that he *wanted* to do this. Really, it was dirty, awful work, but someone had to be held accountable, and the sins of the mother—the sins of the father—became the sins of the child. There wasn't any good in any of them being in the world any longer.

And if he could have a little *fun* while he was at it, well, then it would be all worth it. Getting the unsurprisingly unathletic Simon Monroe back on a horse had been less comical than he had anticipated. He was disappointed, then unnerved by it. He didn't suppose the man had ever been on a horse, but perhaps he had. He took to it remarkably well either way. Simon was so in tune with the beast, he almost believed he was back again. Almost.

He was pleased with the cloak too. A little mining in Simon's brain and puttering through a website that peddled historically accurate costumes got him a headless getup that fit perfectly. It seemed anything could be got with extra money and a fee for expediting the product. Keeping the last of them away from Austin was paramount, as was hiding Simon's face from the public.

He was owed this, dammit. He'd been an asshole, but he hadn't deserved to die as he did. And he hadn't deserved a wife who went out of her way to disrespect him. He'd gotten enough grief from his own father and the end of a belt too. And he'd never raised a hand to Evelyn, not even when he'd found her sporting. However many times.

Good and angry now, he stalked back to the house to plan his evening.

It was disturbing how many Evelyns were walking around Warren. Absolutely disturbing. He had counted thirteen in total, and he was down to about seven or eight. He couldn't quite remember. They were starting to blur together. It was important to get all of them though. Of that much he was certain.

He had a little surprise planned for the loveliest of them all, of course. Blood was important, and hers was the purest, if pure was the word to use. The rest were stumbling around in the world doing nothing with their lives. If anything, he was doing the world a favor by removing them from society. They were excess, fluff. Within a year or two, everyone would forget they had even been there

None of them had children. Surprise! And save Little Miss, none of them were going anywhere with their lives. All of them were racing toward an untimely end. He had seen it; he should know. The places he had been. The things he had seen. And he knew! He knew where they were heading! Some chose the bottle, others would choose the gun, and some would perish in untimely accidents. All he was doing was putting them out of their misery before they could suffer any longer.

But her.

Oh, she.

Little Miss was headed toward something that all the others weren't. She moved in circles that would take her to him, and he was willing to wait for her. A few days, a week, two weeks, it was nothing compared to the time he had already waited. She would help him end it all. She would help him rest easily and not on that rack where he had been spending so much painful time. He didn't deserve to be there.

He was annoyingly shut out from Simon at times when he ached to be around. He would work on that because it wasn't something he wanted to keep going. He needed twenty-four-seven access.

Her predictable schedule had become less so. He'd been casually dropping by as Simon to see how she was doing, but she wasn't at her studio the last time he'd gone, and when he'd tried to bump into her following her normally scheduled teaching time, her classroom had been curiously empty.

Simon worried over her, which was more of a distraction than he wanted. He tried to tell the man that he needn't worry over such a woman, but he was drowned out by the saccharine sentiments that followed. Honestly, the man was so smitten it was embarrassing.

That didn't mean he wasn't jealous.

23

1890

Evelyn should have been too young to be so far from home. But there she was, clambering under the barbed wire, catching her hat on it and gracefully recovering. Technically, she was trespassing, but the sight of a young lady traipsing through the prairie hills as if she owned them was endearing.

"Are you lost?" Austin asked from his perch atop Evan. But it was clear that she wasn't. The young lady was armed with a basket of coloring pencils and paper and more than a few wildflowers.

"Only a little," the girl admitted, raising her head to look at the rider. "I like your horse; he's strong. What's his name?"

"Evan."

She nodded. "Good."

"Where do you live, faerie?"

He thought he saw her smile. "I'm Evelyn Weatherford, and I live beyond those hills." She pointed back behind her to the east.

Of course she was. Weatherford Senior was a friend of his father's.

"Who are you?" she asked pointedly.

"Austin Hearth. My father knows your father."

She looked at him from under her hat with cool grey eyes that struck him as both soft and smart. There was no girlish fear in her face. He liked that.

"I have heard the name Hearth," she replied.

"What are you doing out here by yourself? Have you lost your horse too?"

Her laugh was loud and happy. "No! I walked here. I collect wildflowers. For scientific study."

He thought for a moment that she was jesting, but the seriousness of her face and the tools in her basket told him otherwise. Ladies these days had all manner of hobbies and occupations. "Well, you have stumbled onto my fath—*my* property. But you are welcome to go collecting flowers here if you wish."

She turned to look at the fence behind her with its knotty wood posts trailing off in either direction as far as they could see. "That. Is it yours? I have never seen so long a fence. It isn't going to keep the coyotes out."

"But it will keep my cattle in."

She hummed at that statement, as if assimilating it. "Thank you for letting me on your property. I hadn't thought I was trespassing. I'm just looking for a certain flower, and I know these prairie grasses must yield it to me eventually."

From his vantage point, he could see the surrounding grasses and flowers quite easily, certainly better than she could wading through them, picking her way carefully around limestone outcroppings and prairie dog holes.

"What does it look like?" he asked.

She held her hands up, one above the other. "It would be about this tall. They call it Pitcher sage for the man who discovered it. The flowers are deep blue. They look like a slender pitcher being poured, with the lower petals sticking out more than the top. They grow in a cluster. The leaves are thin and about this long. There is white too, but it is rare."

Austin let her description form a picture in his head. "I have seen that. The cattle eat it. I can show you where it grows on my land."

Her smile shocked him. "Oh, truly? Yes, show me, please!"

"What of a chaperone?" He was nearly twenty-four. He knew what it would look like should he not inquire and speak to the lady's parents. He was no fool even for the generally genial relationship all the families had in the area.

He saw the flush creep up her before she spoke. "She could not keep up."

"Oh?"

When she turned her grey eyes on him, they were more somber. "That is a lie. I left her behind too."

"Then go home today. I know the flower will be there tomorrow. I'll call on your family, explain my purpose, and bring your chaperone with us."

She looked disappointed. "You will make certain the cattle do not eat it all before tomorrow?"

"Of course."

The smile returned, and she thanked him.

He was nervous the next day, but his father's friend put him at ease. They were allowed to go with a chaperone to his land. Miss Weatherford rode a pretty grey pony that was pokey but picked her way carefully over the prairie. The chaperone, a young woman named Maggie, came along on a palomino that wanted the group to move along more quickly, but Maggie controlled the animal well.

He led them to where he had last seen the plant that Miss Weatherford had described, and her horse hadn't nearly stopped when she made joyful noise and leapt from its back.

"Mr. Hearth! These are the white ones! They are exceedingly rare! Thank you!" She was a whirl of motion, grabbing her sketchbook, setting up her little stool, choosing the right pencils for the job.

Austin was not a little bewildered by her passion. Who would have thought—plants? Not him, surely, but then again, he was getting into the wire and barb trade. It was becoming widely known, but his father had told him of many people who knew nothing of it. His father had made sales right up until the day he died. Then Austin took over.

Miss Weatherford's passion interested him, and it became a way to pass the time and keep an eye on his cattle, especially during the seasons when thieves were thick on the prairie.

She came out always with Maggie at first (who would find the shadiest spot to sit with whatever chore she came with and let Miss Weatherford ride all over the Hearth property), but it wasn't more than two seasons before Mr. and Mrs. Weatherford allowed him to take her out alone. They likely shouldn't have, not with the way many got during the hot summers when everyone gathered in what shade they could find and cooled off in the river or creeks when they ran. But whether it was the will of the man or the will of God, Austin felt he should keep his intentions pure until such a time as he could ask Weatherford Senior for the girl's hand. The thought made him so nervous he couldn't have unbuckled his trousers had he wanted to.

Time drifted, and they drifted together. He thought about their friendship often and often found himself thinking about it when he was doing inane tasks. Riding long fences, hoofing it out to some remote ranch on business, when he made camp out under the stars in the places that were not quite prairie and not quite desert and not yet mountains. She was always there with him, bidding him look closer at the landscape, to look harder at the things that most would miss. When he could not carry them, he made poor sketches of the flowers and plants he saw and brought them back for her.

And he was always looking for flowers to bring back for her records, telling her where and when he had picked them. She taught him that those things were important. Sometimes she had requests and sent him looking for specific flowers that she had read about when he was in Texas, Oklahoma, or Colorado.

He had known her nearly five years when, one season, the cattle began to fall ill one by one. It was Evelyn who suggested it might be some of the plants they were eating, not an infection that was catching. He had balked at it initially but gave in to her desire to follow the cattle for an afternoon on her horse and watch them. She seemed to find joy in the ride and never complained about being hot or tired under the intense sun.

After many afternoons of watching where the cattle roamed, little Evelyn came bounding up to him through the cropped short grazing grasses, scaring up grasshoppers and bees in her wake. She had left her horse behind in her excitement, and her skirts caught on the grasses and burrs as she ran.

"I found it!" she exclaimed.

Her pretty face was red with the sun and the exertion, her brown hair spilling from its pinning. She looked a lady and a wild thing all at once, and it was one moment of many that endeared her to him. When had she grown into a woman from the girl he had met at his fence those years ago?

She stopped at Evan's nose and pulled at the great horse's bridle. Evan snorted and eagerly followed where Evelyn led, for she often hid sugar in her pockets for him.

Austin stopped Evan with a laugh. "Come, there's no need for you to run in such an ensemble. Here, lend me your hand. Evan can carry us both."

"Oh," was all Evelyn could say, looking up at Austin as if for the first time, her grey eyes searching his. But she only stared a moment before she took Austin's hand, stuck a foot under Austin's in the stirrup, and boosted herself up behind him. Her riding habit pressed against him, and he wondered how she hadn't yet died of heat. The summer had been intense, punctuated by a day of rain every several weeks. It was a wonder anything had grown at all out there that could hurt his animals.

Evelyn pointed toward where they needed to go, and she held onto the side of Evan's saddle as they went. He took it easy so as not to upset her seat behind the saddle, but Evan carried her as gracefully as if he only had one rider. Austin was proud of him, Friesian blood or no.

She brought him to a small depression where some water had collected and allowed much green vegetation to grow. It was quite a large area considering the dryness of the summer, so it was no wonder the cattle went there to eat.

Evelyn slid down from Evan's back and made a half-hearted attempt to shoo the cattle away from the area. Austin whistled in the dog and had him take the cattle away.

Once he had dismounted, Evelyn grabbed his hand and pulled him toward the intense greenery. "Here," she said, pointing. "This is field pennycress. I have read that it is very poisonous to livestock. There is so much of it here, it's no wonder they have fallen ill and died. You must remove this."

Her authoritative tone tickled him. "Yes, and I shall."

Evelyn let out a little huff, as if she were expecting something else. "Oh, good."

He smiled at her. "Thank you, Miss Weatherford. You understand this saves me a good deal of time and money and perhaps has saved all the animals that graze here. Thank you very much."

Her grey eyes filled with tears. "Oh, thank you. I didn't know if you would believe me, but I have read up on these very plants, and I was hoping . . ."

"Miss Weatherford?"

She laughed, finding herself. "Evelyn, please. Yes?"

"Evelyn. Thank you. May I call on you for all matters concerning these things from now on?"

He wasn't certain he had seen such happiness in someone's eyes before. Her polite affirmation was tinged with what he hoped was a genuine desire to continue seeing him too.

24

Noon, Friday, October 9th

The good feelings left behind from the night with Simon didn't last. The stress of everything came crashing down on Olivia as soon as she left his front porch.

She had no right to be doing all this Nancy Drew-ing, falling behind on her lesson plans and her grading. She wasn't falling behind on the photographs yet, but she'd been letting other things fall off the edge—department meetings, grocery shopping, laundry. The list grew every day. Had she missed her mentor meeting with Dr. Thornock? She needed to check her email soon. She was days behind.

The apartment felt confining, and she was out of coffee. She stared at the contents of the fridge. Last week's skinny chicken enchiladas and the beginnings of a science experiment on some strawberries. Shriveled grapes. Dried carrots. Ann ate out most of the time, but Olivia was surprised to see that more of her stuff wasn't in there. What had Ann been up to all week? Olivia couldn't even remember seeing her.

She knew from her mother that anxiety could have physical side effects, but how she'd been feeling off the last week or so was different. It was like if she shifted too quickly, she could see things that weren't there. And not just things. Places.

At her mom's house, the walk from the living room to her bedroom became an event. A wall appeared where the hallway had been moments before. The first time, she'd stopped. But when she could walk right through it, she tried her best to ignore it, not to look at the new room that had appeared around her. She caught an old-fashioned bed in her periphery, a dressing table with a mirror, an armoire.

Tall curtains appeared at the entrances to the front room, the den. Stairs leading up appeared before her in the foyer. Ornate dark wood railings sailed upward to a hazy second floor. Anything she looked at too closely became crisper than the real world, so she stopped trying to register what she was seeing. Then her mother would putter through the scene, and she would be able to see through it to reality again.

Some psychiatrist along the way had told her mother that one way to move past a hallucination was to ignore them. They weren't seeing that psychiatrist any longer, but Olivia was willing to try anything. And no, she was not becoming her mother. This was all temporary. Stress induced. Never mind that ignoring the hallucination didn't make it go away.

The store felt surreal, like she'd never been there before. She stared at the bananas for a full minute before she remembered what they were. Was seventy-nine cents per pound a good deal? She had forgotten. But then everything seemed expensive. How on earth could they charge $1.49 per pound for apples? She grabbed the greenest ones and then headed over to the oranges and stared at them too. They tickled something in her brain. She saw herself sitting in what looked like her parents' living room. A large Christmas tree was in her peripheral vision, covered in shiny glass baubles and popcorn strings. They had never decorated their trees that way. But she was looking down now, pulling a large orange from the toe of her Christmas stocking and exclaiming with excitement. It was followed by a red apple and more cries of happiness from herself and other female voices. Then she was back in the store, still staring at the oranges.

Sleeping on her feet and dreaming; that was all. Lack of sleep, exhaustion.

Everything was jumbled up in her brain. It must all be connected though, this Weatherford-Hearth-Monroe business. She'd never been particularly good at puzzles, and it made her think about the board game Clue and how her mother had tried to get her to play it all the time when she was younger. More frustrating than fun, she'd walked away on more than one occasion with her mother insisting, *Don't you want to know who did it?* No, she didn't particularly care. It was hard to care when her mother had appeared not to care for so long. It made her detached, or something like that.

The journal sent her into daydreams too, to a place from whence she didn't want to wake.

She wanted to tell Simon what was going on but had waffled for so long that she never ended up mentioning it. With midterms coming up, she needed to get everyone their homework back, so they could study. She still had to write the test too. How did Cecelia think she could manage such a workload? She jotted down a few potential test questions in her teaching planner and then paused as her mind wandered. She needed to reschedule the appointment to get her mother's anti-anxiety meds adjusted again. Another plateau.

"Focus," she muttered to herself and tried to look at her planner again, reading and re-reading the questions, but her eyes kept wandering to her folio and the photographs that peeked out at her.

Cecelia hadn't mentioned the horse in any of the photographs, not even the latest ones. Olivia held back a laugh. The most recent photograph was half obscured by the horse.

And the journal. She grabbed it from its place on her nightstand and opened to a random entry.

August 19, 1899

Home alone again. Alone with the staff, I mean. It is the seventeenth day. Mr. Monroe goes away on business in the morning and returns after I'm in bed. He stays to ensure I have eaten a proper breakfast, so I'm sated for the day, then departs.

I suppose he must be overworked and has no time for relaxation, as he is irritable. I suggested visiting Eva or Evette for the duration of his work but was met with remarks of my exaggeration and excessive request making. I'll hitherto abandon such requests.

I have not spoken to any other ladies about this as Mr. Monroe does not encourage them to come by. It seems he dissuades them, but that must also be my imagination. However, I believe the other ladies I have spoken to in the past saw their families often and were invited to their husband's home frequently. Being the eldest daughter in my home, I cannot comment on personal experience with my own sisters, but I feel as if a sister should be allowed to visit her sisters or vice versa.

Olivia flipped to the end of the journal. Someone had torn out the rest of the pages. It looked like fifty or so pages, and the final cliffhanger entry didn't sound like there was nothing left to tell.

She wished she had read through the entire thing before lending it to Simon. He wouldn't have tampered with it, but still. The only other person who would've seen the journal was her mother, but there was no way she would have poked about in something like this; it wasn't like her. Perhaps someone long ago had done it. Or maybe the author herself. She wished she knew what the rest of the journal said.

If everything she had seen was real, there was no question it was Evelyn's journal. Simon would know, but she was a big girl. She knew how to do research on her own.

Her mother had either turned off her cell phone, or she'd let it die again, so Olivia dialed her landline and waited impatiently as the line rang. Her mother kept unplugging the answering machine because she thought someone was recording her through it. Now the line rang forever when her mother got at the machine without Olivia knowing. Her mother was there. She was just taking her sweet time getting to the phone.

"Hello?"

"Hi, Mom."

"I walked all the way to the phone for you. It kept ringing. I was napping."

Olivia gritted her teeth. "I'm sorry, Mom."

"How are you?"

"I'm fine," Olivia said through clenched teeth. She was the adult. No, they were both adults. She wasn't supposed to think of her mother as a child.

"Mom, when you found that journal in the dugout, did you go through it before you gave it to me?"

"What journal?"

That was a lie. Her mother's voice always went up and got sing song-y when she was lying. It had become second nature for Olivia to listen for the telltale tics. "You know what I'm talking about."

"What does it matter? It's not like it's your journal that I was snooping around in."

"Just . . . please. It's important. Were there any pages missing when you went through it?"

Her mother didn't say anything for a long time. Olivia started to wonder if her mother had fallen asleep or covertly hung up. Finally, she spoke. "Yep. Definitely pages missing when I saw it."

"And you didn't see any other pages in the dugout? No stack of papers or anything?"

"Nope. Didn't see any papers."

"OK, thank you, Mother."

"What else do you need?"

She was so sensitive. Olivia gritted her teeth again. "Do you know who owned the house before us? Like way before us in the eighteen hundreds?"

More silence. It was unlike her mother to be silent for more than five seconds usually. She loved to hear herself talk.

"Was it someone named Evelyn?"

"Oh, no. No. No Evelyns owned the home at all." Not a lie.

"Well, do you know who did?"

"I don't know. I really don't." Olivia heard a little hum at the end of that one. Her mother's voice was pitched so high. Lie. Why in the world should she lie about such a thing? It seemed so inconsequential. Stupid, even.

"Well, I'm sorry to bug you, Mother. I'll let you go now. I'll be out around seven with dinner."

"Oh, thank goodness. I'm very tired and need to get back to my nap. Bye-bye."

Olivia sat on her bed with her phone and the journal in her lap. She'd definitely be spending the night at the house. Her mother was frustrating at best and infuriating at the moment. She didn't need the games or manipulations. She just wanted answers.

25

Whatever was looking back at Simon from the mirror wasn't him. When he first saw the gauntness in his cheeks, the odd haunted look he'd only seen in his grandfather on his mother's side right before he'd passed, he didn't look in the mirror anymore. Brushing his beard, conditioning it, could be done without staring at himself and wondering when he would kill someone because he'd fallen asleep behind the wheel.

He hadn't slept in days—or at least that's how he felt. The blackouts were happening more frequently, but he'd found that the less he slept, the more aware he was of the missing time. Not that it made much sense, but he would take it.

He had tried writing down dates and times when he would wake up from an episode, but that notepad mysteriously disappeared a few days after the page from his notepad on the nightstand. How was he supposed to trick someone or something that watched nearly his every move? But did they, really? There were times that his head felt more . . . empty. But what of it? Could he hide things from himself during that time and expect to find them later? The notepad had been in the bathroom, a private place but not that private if he were sharing space with . . . something else most of the time.

Whatever the thing was, it was having a good laugh at his expense, he supposed. He hadn't felt anything like the rage he'd felt roiling around inside him the other night outside the Daily Brew, but he could swear the thing was happy most of the time. Ecstatic, even.

When his head felt empty, he thought about the ghostly appearance of Austin Hearth on the corner of Sedalia and Brown.

Scanning his shelves, he pulled down the well-worn copy of *Warren: The Infamous Years* and flipped through the sections with photographs. He knew there was at least one . . . there it was. A man stood next to a spool of barbed wire, hand out to lean casually on it. He looked like many other men of the time who had made their money on the prairie and found themselves in the lower echelons of the upper class with their money alone: a little windburned, a little bewildered, and not a little tired.

The man had supposedly been beheaded, but his body (and head) were never found. Most assumed he'd just left town for work after perhaps or perhaps not killing his ex-lover and her children. Then he'd died out west somewhere, but his employer, the giant "Bet a Million" Gates, hadn't heard that Austin would be out that way, and Austin never collected the money Gates owed him. There were certainly enough people around who believed he had killed Evelyn and her children that he might not have wanted to risk it, and William Monroe perpetuated the story until he died.

Warren's very own ghost story.

What a hard life it would have been at the turn of the century. So much new technology to integrate, the old ways clashing with the new. Not that it was much different in the twenty-first century. Simon wasn't even forty, but when he'd been asked to run the department's LiveJournal account, he'd frozen. A blog? Promoting the account by posting daily? He found someone else to run it in a hurry.

When had he started to sound like his grandfather?

The shock of recognition had been overpowered by the rage, but the feeling had lingered. Looking at picture after picture of the man for years did not a thing for seeing someone in person. As a ghost!

He wasn't sure what he thought more—that he was lucky to be witnessing this moment in history or terrified that something was clearly going on in Warren. What had stirred up the old soul—or souls?

For all he knew, Austin wasn't the only one back for a haunt. What about Evelyn or the infamous William? And why? Olivia's find might be a coincidence, but it might not.

It had been one hundred years since their three deaths. Time of year was important, but what made the current year any more special than a century of time passing between those events and now? He was stumped. If the other world had a timeline of which he was unaware, he supposed he wouldn't care if he got close enough to ask. He had much more pressing questions.

He was about to jot down some notes for himself but then stopped. Whatever was in him might find out, but if he found out what or who was in him, then perhaps that would help. He could get some answers.

Logging onto the message boards was likely too risky though. Whatever angry thing was inside him, it had gotten angry when it saw Austin, so the turn of the century would be where he could start.

He grabbed several more books from the shelf and spread them out. He needed to see the timeline without writing it down, to think things through without appearing to be *looking* things through, so he opened four of the books to pages on the earliest history of Warren. The fifth book he pushed slightly out of the way and casually flipped through the pages until he was just past the photograph of Austin Hearth.

1854. Land hungry. Immigrants. Indian territory.

He flicked his eyes over to the other book.

Who hated Austin Hearth?

William Monroe, of course. William Monroe Senior too, but this didn't seem like his style. Eccentricity was lost on that old man, but William the Younger . . . one only needed look at his interior decorating style in his home on the quiet end of Main Street to know that perhaps he had been a marble or two short toward the end. Others surely had—farmers, ranchers, the natives he'd dealt with during his time out west. But none like William Monroe III.

He opened the digital copy of Evelyn's journal on his laptop. It offered an incredible glimpse into Warren's past and brought one of its most popular ladies to life more fully. The journal ended rather abruptly during what most considered that era's most turbulent time, but that was to be expected. Disappointing but expected.

How much had Evelyn been privy to? It was no great secret that William Monroe tried to keep her out of the public eye toward the end—postpartum depression or an infection or bad water had robbed her of her faculties. According to William, in any case. Evelyn Monroe wasn't seen much in public after she started having children.

He wondered what other treasures Oliva's dugout might have in store. *That* thought stretched out his trousers. Then he was ruminating on their night together. Her porcelain body against his pasty one. And the way she'd begged for his hands on her.

He rubbed a hand over his pants and stretched his legs. Had to concentrate. They'd been texting back and forth since, dancing around each other. She had mentioned him kissing her at her apartment, something about it being good, but he didn't remember that moment.

That it hadn't been *him* doing that was an issue. A bigger one than simply blacking out and wandering the town. Bigger than wandering around abducting strangers. This was the woman he liked. Rather intensely.

He'd almost fired off a message to Bridgette to ask her how in the hell he'd gotten *her,* so he could have some help with Olivia. But he already knew what she would say. Something along the lines of, "If she's already fucked you, and she's still texting you, she likes you."

He smiled. He'd have to tell her about that. She'd laugh, he'd check on her and her family, and all would be well.

He closed the lid of his laptop. The journal insinuated that not all was right in the Monroe household. He wasn't surprised. It wasn't helping him in his search though. He grabbed a few more books off his shelves, did more scanning, then set about planning how to catch the ghost of William Monroe III.

26

Saturday, October 10th

The trouble with time was that it moved too quickly. Olivia moved four reminders out on her phone and felt the familiar ball of anxiety tighten in her stomach. She could cancel her dentist appointment and the one for her mom's Yorkie. It was just vaccinations. Lots of things that could wait until November. That was what she kept telling herself anyway.

She could handle the rest of October. Then three weeks later, Thanksgiving break would be in sight, and she would have a few days of nothing. A few days to recuperate. A few days to process everything. A few days to stay in bed and pretend the world outside wasn't conspiring to make her incapable of finishing her project. And forget about driving down Laramie Street anymore, let alone walking.

It took some doing to leave the apartment though. She'd finally gotten up the courage to call the historical society and get permission to shoot at the old Monroe house on Main Street, but thinking about actually leaving the apartment for it was another story altogether.

She loaded up two cartridges and checked the rest of her equipment, then thought better of it and loaded the other cartridges into her camera bag. Suppose the view was exceptional. Suppose she was able to get another shot that would work. At the rate she was going, she could still make the deadline with traditional printing. That was cocky thinking though, so she slung her digital over her shoulder. She could get a few good ones there too. Just in case.

Leonard Fullbright, the old man from the historical society, was happy to help her once she described what she was trying to accomplish. Running through the steps made her feel better about leaving the apartment. Not much but a little.

What would be out there for her? Giant headless men? More ghosts? She didn't want to run into any of it. Not again. The images rose in her head, and she felt the shaking begin involuntarily. What could she do to protect herself from it all? Anything?

Staring at her loaded equipment, she had to think of Nathan. Laying out her equipment was still somewhat anxiety inducing after him, and he'd been gone for over a year.

"Why did you leave your stuff all over the counter? We need to fix dinner."

"I'm sorry, I just needed to look it all over."

"Why the fuck do you always leave your fucking stuff everywhere, Olivia? I'm sick of it."

It hadn't always been like that. But they needled around each other's edges until they were both worn thin from it. All the nagging and snide comments had become commonplace, and he simply couldn't understand how much her mother needed her. Needed anyone. Someone.

Olivia reminded herself that she had chosen that role. She slipped around the edges of the memory and concentrated on taking an inventory of everything she was bringing along. She wouldn't have much time to get the shots she thought she might want, and she needed to be prepared.

It helped some to think about Simon, she concluded as she loaded her SUV up at around 5:00. They'd been texting, continuing conversations when they could, not missing a beat. She wanted to like him more than she let herself.

She still hadn't told him what had happened, but fuck, she hadn't had time to process it yet. She would see him soon though, and she would know then whether she could tell him or not. Horses appearing in photographs and headless ghosts appearing on sidewalks late at night were two different things entirely. The man—ghost—had known her name. Just thinking about it gave her a chill.

"*Just continue on, business as usual,*" the counselor had said (regarding her mother's episodes, but this seemed like a perfectly reasonable parallel situation). "*The more she can have a stable household and a sense of normalcy, not a sense that something's wrong with her, the better chance you'll have more days that are better. Routine is your friend.*"

It worked most of the time at least.

When she pulled up at the Monroe house, the old limestone building looked less charming than before. The wind kicked up yellow leaves that were already trying to settle on the green lawn. The old steel posts and chains that ran up the walkway swung in the breeze, and the impressive door—a large wooden creation that looked more medieval than Victorian—beckoned. *Come in, come in. It's such a lovely time. We're all still here, you know, and we haven't seen you in oh so long.*

She glanced behind her. Nothing there but her car and the street beyond. Beyond that, some cedar trees and old cottonwoods. A few other older historic homes in the distance. A small open field and more cedars. The wind whispered through the trees and tall grasses. It was months past time to cut the hay. But the feeling that she had heard something persisted. Anxiety. She could handle it.

Mr. Fullbright arrived a few minutes later as she was studying the outside of the home. It looked like a large rectangle, rectangular windows at regular intervals along each level, more institutional than homely and definitely not like the grand Victorian houses that she was used to seeing in other parts of town. But it still had all the charming limestone details that she had seen on any number of buildings in Warren.

She counted at least five chimneys from where she stood on the front walk. She imagined there had to be more and then wondered what it would have been like to live in a time without a regular heating system. Relying on wood and coal and new technology to survive the winters. It sounded like cold hallways and huddling by a warm fire while the Kansas wind whipped around the house. It was a romantic thought.

The old man stepped up beside her, elastic suspenders taut over his belly. He was shorter than her, and she was by no means tall. "She's lovely, isn't she?"

Olivia hadn't heard of houses being called "she," but Mr. Fullbright looked to be about eighty with the eyebrows to prove it. She wasn't going to argue with him about it.

"Yes, she is."

"Leonard Fullbright." He held out his gnarled hand.

"Olivia Norwich," she replied, shaking it gently.

He regarded her with the sternness that only comes with age. "You'll be photographing landscapes, you said?"

"Yes, for the festival." She gestured to the west. "I imagine the view from upstairs is quite nice."

"That it is. Come inside. I have a few things to attend to on the grounds while you walk around."

He ushered her inside and briefly pointed out a few things that Olivia hardly took note of. He reminded her to be careful, to touch things gently or not at all. She felt immediately transported from the moment she walked inside the home. She thanked Mr. Fullbright when he excused himself to go walk the grounds, then let herself be alone with the large house.

Black-and-white marble traveled the length of the floor to meet with walls papered with dark grey damask wallpaper. Rooms to the right and left were roped off, so the general public didn't trample the expensive rugs or run into the antique furniture. A chandelier in the foyer threw pale light into the room with the late-afternoon sun. Its prisms were of irregular shapes that made tiny rainbows and spots of light dance erratically when the front door shut. It wasn't foreboding, but it was certainly dark.

She took another step into the foyer, and something skirted across her vision upstairs. She looked up just in time to catch the retreating skirts of a woman, the loud thumping of footsteps, then a scream. Olivia squeezed her eyes shut for a moment. Runaway imagination in an old house.

She ascended the stairs. The curved staircase was familiar. Perhaps it was just the oldness of it. Every historic home seemed to run together after awhile, but that didn't seem quite right either. She ran her hand over the smooth hardwood of the ornate railing. It reminded her of the hallucinations from her mother's house. The ones she'd been trying so hard to ignore. She whipped her hand from the rail and gripped the straps for her photo equipment instead.

Rows of doors ran down each hallway on the second and third floors. She kept going up until she reached what she thought must be the door to the attic on the fourth floor. If she was right, there would be a cool-looking window at the west end that she had seen from the street. She hadn't exactly told Mr. Fullbright that she was going up there, but he'd said she could use the entire house, which included the attic.

It reminded her of her parents' home just a few miles away. Her own room had been in the attic, converted maybe sometime in the 1950s into a functioning bedroom. Even the door was similar. Dark solid wood with a brass knob.

The door was wedged shut (rather poorly) with a few pieces of wood, which she removed. It probably popped open with a draft, like hers had. The door caught on the top stair, but she was able to slide past the frame with her equipment.

A window at the far end of the attic was clean and bright. A few pieces of furniture sat on the old wood floor, along with museum displays and holiday decorations. Christmas at the Monroe house was probably a big deal. She counted at least five large boxes of garland, and dozens of wreaths with bright red ribbons sat in plastic-covered sacks on the other side of the room. The image in her head was so lovely that she felt nostalgic for a time and place she'd never seen.

She had to drag a chair over to the window, so she could see out of it, but the view was as promising as she'd hoped. The window looked to the south and west but more south, and the cut of the hexagonal window with wagon-wheel spokes made for an interesting frame.

She set up her equipment at the right height for the tall window. A ladder would have been nice, but there were chairs, and her tripod extended enough that she would manage. She was about to take the first photograph from under the dark cloth when the niggling horror of the deadline brought everything else bubbling up, and her brain began one of its new favorite loops. She sat in the chair and put her head between her knees, something she had seen her mother do more than a few times in her childhood. Maybe it would help.

If you hadn't been out so late with Simon this never would have happened. If you weren't so forgetful, you wouldn't have forgotten your keys. If you'd just stuck with your timeline, you wouldn't be scrambling right now. If you hadn't given in to the stress, you wouldn't be hallucinating right now.

Another part of her brain was more compassionate, but the anxiety always managed to steamroll it. *Cut yourself some slack. This is an impossible deadline. And most artists need to go a little crazy to make their best work. Just don't be thinking about cutting off your ear anytime soon.*

She scoffed. Sometimes she still had a sense of humor. She stood and took a deep breath, then remounted the chair and readied her camera. The wagon-wheel window would make for some semi-unique photographs. She got some nice clear shots of the window itself, then focused on the landscape beyond.

What seemed to be only a stone's throw from up there was surely much farther by road. There on the fourth floor, she was even above many of the mature trees that populated the area. The grey tones would be lovely with all the turning trees. And far in the distance, she saw a bend in the Kansas River as it wended through the Flint Hills. She loved it there. Perhaps that was why she never left. Still musing on that, she took a few dozen digital shots for good measure.

Having what she needed from that area, she broke down the large-format camera setup, wandered down a level, and sauntered down the hall. She had seen a window from the front lawn that looked south over the main thoroughfare that might provide a nice view. Which room was it?

Childhood memories ghosted across her eyes. Picking apart a camera in the alcove on the second floor. Pulling old newspapers from the basement walls and trying to decipher the English that was almost a foreign language to a child.

She touched doorknobs as she went, trailed her hand down the papered walls. Felt the lush rugs worn slowly over time beneath her feet. Something resonated with her.

At the third door from the stairs, she stopped. This was it.

> *This home is so grand. I'm in awe. I cannot wait to put my own touches on it.*

As soon as she pushed the door open, a wave of perfume hit her. It was the journal, only tenfold. The air in the room carried a stale, metallic taste, as if the room hadn't been opened since the original inhabitants had left. But that was impossible. It was more like she was trespassing on some ghost's private moment.

The room was sparse but large. That was unexpected. What had she expected? A plethora of personal belongings in a museum?

There was a four-poster bed, nightstands, a few trunks, a little powdering station with a stool, a wardrobe, and a large full-length mirror that had aged poorly.

Something about the room made her feel like she was trespassing.

She went over to the window and looked out. Warren below was sleepy in the dying light of the day. No cars were on the dusty road, though there had been traffic as she had headed that way not long ago. A few maple branches almost reached the window, but her view of the city was almost unobstructed. The bell tower and other limestone structures were in sight. A bonus.

Structures weren't usually part of her sets, but this was for Warren, the town, and its limestone was as much a part of the town as the views of the Flint Hills. Limestone mined from the landscape made the buildings part of the landscape. They nearly grew out of it.

One of these shots is going to be good, she mused as she set up her equipment and loaded the cartridges. The turning leaves of the maples and cottonwoods, the setting sun, the bell tower, the lattice work on the old window . . . it was Warren epitomized. They sure loved their history.

She took some digital shots for good measure, but she felt certain she wouldn't need them. The traditional shots felt good. Really good.

Grinning, she broke down her equipment and put the cartridges snugly away in her bag. Maybe she could call in a substitute for the week. If she had two or three solid days to work in the darkroom, she could get so much done. But it was what it was. She had responsibilities, and if she wanted good teacher evaluations, she needed to show up. It probably wouldn't do shit to get her closer to tenure track, but she needed all the good juju in the department that she could get.

She could develop that night and print test strips the next day after she taught. If she had one good image, she would be happy. Two and she might pee herself with excitement. And there wouldn't be a horse in them. There just wouldn't. Power of positive thinking and all that. A giggle rose up in her, and it was a good ten seconds before she could stifle it. Positive thinking, yes. Positive thinking and mild insanity. She giggled again.

She took another look around the room, as if someone might have heard her. No one was there, but she saw something on the powder table that she had missed. It looked almost identical to the journal her mother had found in the dugout. And a gold necklace with a pendant. Curious, she reached out to grab the leather-bound book.

Just as she was opening the cover, she was pushed backward several steps by an invisible force. Her fingers and body tingled as if she'd touched an electric fence. The initials "E. H." were seared into her mind.

What the fuck?

"Evelyn," a voice said. A familiar voice.

She felt her body tense and her voice answer, but she hadn't moved. Or had she? She tried to raise her hand to her mouth, but she couldn't move it.

"Hello, William."

It wasn't her voice, but it was. It was a little higher, more musical, and it came from her mouth. *What's going on?* she tried to ask, but she could only think it. And when she tried to turn her head to the right to see what was moving over there, she couldn't. She was stuck looking forward, the way her head was pointed. Anxiety and adrenaline flooded her, but she still stood rooted. Paralyzed.

What's going on?

"Please don't shout. It hurts my head," her new musical voice said.

Had she lost her mind? The adrenaline rushed through her body. She could feel it, but it was as if another part of her couldn't feel it at all. The awful anxiety from the night before had gone, like turning off a light switch.

Had she finally split personalities from all the stress? Oh, God. She felt like she was running in circles in her own head, chasing a tail she would never catch.

"Olivia, please settle," the musical voice said again. "Please, I'm only trying to help you."

Bullshit. You're part of me. You're me, I'm ignoring you or pushing you out, whatever. I'm not my mother!

"Of course you're not," the musical voice soothed.

Something moved just outside of her vision.

Jesus Christ, what was that? Look at that, look at that. Look at that. What is it?

Finally, her vision swung that way but far too slowly for her. She wanted to recoil from it, but she couldn't.

Oh, what is that?

"Hush," the musical voice said.

It looked like a man crouched on all fours. But it wasn't quite a man. Its back was too muscular, too gargoyle-like, and it was covered in what looked like tar or black mud or thick oil. Olivia felt her stomach roil; the acid from the other night still hadn't settled. She screamed for herself to turn and run, but she didn't. She stood there calmly like it was just a normal day.

The thing lifted its head and sniffed the air with a nose that was flatter and wider than normal. Nothing about the thing looked normal. Even the humanoid features were somewhat . . . off. The nose was too wide, the eyes too small, the ears too large. Perhaps it had been a man once.

It opened its mouth and took a deep breath, sniffing harder. Olivia distantly felt her stomach turn again. Those teeth. The same rows of white razors that she had seen in flashes in her nightmares.

"You don't smell right," it said.

Astute, she thought. *You don't look right.*

But instead she, someone, said, "You cannot touch her while I'm here."

The thing scowled, and Olivia realized it must have been smiling before. Its face contorted horribly when it frowned. The urge to run was overwhelming, but she had no control over her limbs. Is this what it was like to have another personality? Or was something else going on?

She let go for a moment, tried to relax. Someone else was driving. She couldn't be crazy. Someone was sharing her body with her.

"I could eat you anyway," the thing said. "You would still be tasty."

"But it's not what you came here for," the musical voice replied. Olivia heard the prairie wind in the voice. But that was absurd.

The gargoyle thing chuckled and wiped a string of drool from the corner of its mouth with the back of one clawed hand. "True. Yes, yes, I know. Must do this the right way and all."

Somewhere, a phone rang. Everyone in the room paused to listen. It sounded like an old-fashioned phone. Then Olivia felt her head empty—a curious, dizzying sensation. Then she was alone. The corner where the thing had sat was empty. The phone kept ringing.

Again, she tried to move, and this time she fell forward, colliding with one of the tall bedposts, nearly losing her grip on her tripod. She pressed her face into the wood, felt her tears spill down the spiral carvings. She heard his voice over and over again, saying she deserved him and was lucky to have him and why couldn't she just be like Viola Thompson or the Schneider women and on and on and on. Why couldn't she just try harder, and why couldn't she just do this and this and this a little differently? Then he would be pleased, and oh God, his lectures went on forever, and he wouldn't stop.

With a cry, she stumbled away from the bed and out of the room, moving awkwardly with her equipment. She headed toward the sound of the ringing phone. Anything to get her out of that room. Half tripping and half sliding, she made her way down the stairs toward the main level, equipment bouncing dangerously off the wall and spindles of the stairs as she ran. The ringing grew louder.

The stairs spat her out in the black-and-white-and-grey foyer. A phone was on the wall. It looked like the original model. Olivia stood in front of it, breathless, and stared as it rang incessantly. No one else rushed to answer it, so Olivia picked up the handset and held it to her ear.

"Hello?"

The line crackled for a moment, and she heard the wind against the other person's microphone. "Miss Olivia, you must get out of the house." A male voice, concerned. Another familiar voice.

"Who is this?" She heard a noise in the house somewhere. Probably just the wind.

"Olivia, please listen. You must leave that house immediately. You are not safe there."

"What do you mean? Who is this?" Another noise. A thump. A little louder. Olivia turned and looked around. Still just the wind?

Oh no.

At the top of the stairs crouched the thing, the gargoyle, watching her. Her mouth hung open as she stared at it. This time it had the squashed face of a bulldog. Almost. It didn't break its stillness or its intense stare. A warning from a wild animal. She realized how exposed she was.

"Olivia!" the man on the other end of the line called.

She dropped the receiver and bolted for the door, slowed only slightly by the equipment over her shoulders. The thing started crawling down the stairs toward her, and for a moment she imagined it was Simon there instead, walking down the stairs toward her. But it wasn't Simon. This man was clean shaven and wearing a dark suit, a man with hard eyes. Then it was the thing again scrambling across the marble toward her, claws sliding on the slick floor.

Olivia covered the last few steps to the door, opened it, and threw herself onto the porch, slamming the door behind her. It shook the wooden porch and the glass on either side of the door. She ran down the steps and stopped on the walk.

Nothing followed her out. Nothing even slammed into the door or turned the knob. She was left alone on the walk with the wind hissing through the cottonwoods and maples.

Her legs felt weak, the Jell-O of a dream state, and her mouth was dry. She watched the house, frantically scanning the windows. Her bladder felt full, and she squeezed her legs together as she caught her breath. Nothing appeared at the windows either.

What could she do if the thing did reappear? Blind it with her flash? She felt vulnerable on the front walk, unable to see if anything was watching her.

"I trust you got what you needed?"

Olivia gasped and swung around, but it was just Mr. Fullbright.

"I trust you got what you needed?" he repeated. "And left everything as you found it?" He jingled the keys at his belt. Did he know what lived in the house?

Her face was bright red, surely. "Yes," she managed to squeak out. "I didn't touch anything." She heard her voice lilt up at the end. Lie.

"Well, I'll just lock up then until later. We've been doing a bit of deep cleaning, and she won't be open to the public until Saturday."

Olivia had to stop herself from saying something or running away screaming as she watched him walk up the front steps, open the door to peek inside, then close the door and lock it.

"Thank you again," she whispered hoarsely. How was she supposed to sound normal after that?

But Mr. Fullbright didn't seem to notice. He was either being courteous and ignoring her meltdown, or he was just a nice, oblivious old man. "Certainly, young lady. Anytime you need something, just let us know. We have a few other homes here around Warren, you know. But there's a lot of old buildings here."

Olivia thanked him and then drove home as quickly as she could without getting pulled over. Ann's car was there, thank God.

When she got inside, she tried to act like a normal person, hurrying to her room and shutting the door. Having someone else in the apartment alleviated some of her anxiety, though Simon had been around when the ghost had appeared at the Daily Brew. But he hadn't seen it. Or said he didn't see it. There was no reason for him to lie to her.

Olivia pulled her knees up to her chest and looked around her room. She'd checked everything before she'd gotten into bed. The door was locked, the blinds drawn. Nothing was in the closet, and nothing was under the bed or under her desk. Nothing in the corners of the room.

Her thoughts drifted to Mr. Fullbright and the historical society. Maybe he had records of all the town's population and ancestry. It was a long shot, but as obsessed as they were with this time of the year and everything that happened, it wouldn't surprise her if they did have records of, well, everything.

If her parents' house were as old as she thought it was, then they should have a record of that too. Someone in town would. There were registries for historical buildings, weren't there? She didn't want to count on her mother being any help.

An image of the thing from the Monroe house slithered into her thoughts as she spun around ideas. She tried to push it away, but it was stubbornly fixed in her memory, grinning at her from the corner of the bedroom in the Monroe house. Was it connected too?

Jesus, it was all so much. How was she supposed to leave the damn house and be safe? If she were even safe there. Or was it a good ghost? Or a person? Could ghosts be good? The horse had been chilling enough, coming to life from her photographs.

She got on her laptop and searched "Evelyn" and "City of Warren, KS." The usual suspects popped up—white pages results for people named Evelyn, the city's website with names omitted from the search, and results for "did you mean Evan?"

She wished she could have peeked inside the leather-bound book in the bedroom at the Monroe house. It looked exactly like the journal she held now. Who had lived in the Monroe house besides the Monroes? E. H., of course.

She typed in "Evelyn Monroe" and "City of Warren, KS." Narrower results this time. She scrolled past the uninteresting links until she reached something promising: a message board on an ancestry website titled "What Really Happened: The Mystery of Evelyn Monroe." It smelled like a conspiracy. Perfect.

She spent the next two hours reading page after page of threads of Warren conspiracies. Dear God, the people there were crazy. The website had a forum dedicated to possible theories regarding the death of Mayor William Monroe and the murder/suicide of his wife, Evelyn Weatherford-Monroe. Anyone could log on and add to the questions about who and what and when and why. Those questions were interspersed between threads looking for Civil War relatives and relatives in Warren during the Antebellum period. She hadn't known the area had so much history, let alone how many people were interested in it.

In 1903. These people were worried about events that had happened over a hundred years ago. And not just worried. Obsessed. Fan favorites seemed to include a ghostly reappearance by scorned lover Austin Hearth. There was that name again.

Other theories included stories from the natives who were pushed off the land and a larger conspiracy involving most of the town. Some voices sounded like trolls, but others made sense, asked logical questions. But really, who cared? Clearly, she did, or she wouldn't have gotten sucked into it.

She scrolled down to the bottom of the page where a moderator with the initials S. J. M. had quieted some of the less on-topic posts.

Oh, surely not.

It surely wasn't Simon. But Ann had said he was obsessed with the town's history.

Olivia scanned the page. The most recent post was from about six months earlier. OK, so maybe the thread was semi-defunct. She could ask him about it sometime. The moderator posts did seem rather sensible, and he was a historian, so it was all fine.

She paused. Why was she trying to justify everything to herself?

So, Evelyn Monroe had died suspiciously. Other threads seemed to be centered on the death of the mayor and the lover, Austin Hearth. Or maybe she hadn't died suspiciously. Maybe she had just been depressed and hanged herself, and that was that. Olivia couldn't imagine being that far gone, but then again, she couldn't have imagined herself this far gone either. What a sad life it must have been.

She kept mining. Somewhere in there, there had to be clues, something to tell her what was going on in Warren. Something to help her get a handle on her sanity.

27

He woke up and tried to roll over onto his side, but his back, legs, and arms screamed in agony. Surely he wasn't getting sick. It didn't feel like body aches. It felt like he'd fucking worked out for two hours the day before. He hadn't had such sore muscles since his days slinging straw bales. Or since the previous week when the co-habitation began. It was worrisome. What had he been up to the previous night? Participating in some underground powerlifting club?

He finally sat up and swung his legs over the side of the bed. On the floor between his bed and the dresser were shoes and socks. Boots and stockings, to be precise. He stared at them blankly for a moment before leaning down to touch the socks. Wool, and he was prepared to bet a lot of money that they were hand-knitted too. The boots were made of soft, supple black leather, and they might've been hiding at the back of his closet, but that was doubtful. They belonged in a museum.

He dropped the sock and skirted the objects to peer around the rest of his bedroom. Fuck, his back hurt. Whatever he had been up to, it was heavier than hurling straw bales. He sat down again, this time at the end of the bed.

Shep's collar jingled, and Simon saw the dog's snout peek around the side of the doorframe to the bedroom. He whistled for him to come, but Shep only stuck his nose in a hair farther, his one green eye looking at Simon warily.

"It's just me, man." Simon whistled again.

The dog slunk into the bedroom, as if he were coming up silently on a group of sheep, his gaze locked on Simon. The hairs on Simon's neck stood up.

"Come on, it's just me," he said again.

Shep got close enough to sniff Simon's toes, decided his human was who he appeared to be, and plopped down on Simon's feet, smiling and panting as only a sheepdog can do.

Simon reached out to pet the dog, the hairs on his neck still settling back against his skin. Shep's behavior, while concerning, was also reassuring. So help him, if the thing did anything to his dog, he would find a way to get back at it.

But how was he supposed to catch something that knew what was going on in his brain at all times? Or did it know? If it suspected he knew, it didn't say anything.

"Hello?" he asked. Nothing. Of course.

He stood and wandered into the kitchen, so he could let Shep out to do his business. Some dirt and grass was by the door. He stared at it for a long moment. It was unusual, considering his yard was dry, and he always wiped Shep's paws when he came inside. Another mystery. Add it to the list.

On the table were the folded papers he'd crammed into his pocket a few days before. He snagged them and sat down at the table to pore over them. He had been so fixated on the charge at the tea shop that he hadn't thought to look over the rest of the charges. Somewhere in there might be boots and socks. Unless they'd been stolen from a museum. Both seemed equally likely.

Approximately eight thousand transactions at the bagel shop on campus: normal. Student union: normal. The tea shop: normal but abnormal. He flipped to the third page and scanned the transactions from September. A $695.99 charge on September 14.

He felt like he'd had the wind knocked out of him.

His first thought was to jump on the phone with his credit card company. There was no way he'd blown hundreds on some craft website. Either someone had stolen his card, or the thing that had stolen his body had. And after the boots, he was pretty sure he knew which it was.

He stumbled back to his bedroom to find his credit card and call the number listed on the back. After a maddening ten minutes, he finally got a lady named Lisa.

"I need to dispute some charges on my credit card."

After answering the requisite questions about this grandmother's maiden name (Winthrop), the street he grew up on (W. 51st Avenue), and his first pet's name (Goldie—aptly), he asked about the charge.

"I didn't make this purchase."

Lisa took nearly a century to type God only knew what into her computer. His palms were sweating, and an urgent shit was imminent.

"Can you give me the reference number as it appears on your statement?"

He did, silently cursing Lisa and her endless typing.

Then she gave him some startling information. "We have your signature on file at 1411 South Sunset receiving delivery on October first."

Something like indigestion clawed down Simon's throat and straight to his nervous bowels. "You do?"

"Yes. I'm very sorry, but we will likely be unable to credit you those charges if you signed for it, unless you find that the signatures don't match. Then you'll need a different department. Are you sure you don't need to just return the item instead? That can be done through the online store where the purchase was made."

Simon tuned her out. What a fucking idiot he was. Of course he had signed for the goddamn thing. Whoever was cohabitating with him was pretending to be him at least part of the time.

After promising to watch his email for a PDF of the signature, he thanked Lisa and got off the phone. No fucking help.

He looked at the statement again. There, a partial name of the store. MasqueHist. He pulled up the website on his computer Masque Historique. He clicked on it, fearing the worst.

"Custom Designs!" the store exclaimed. "Historically accurate clothing, shoes, and accessories for your next reenactment, stage production, museum display, or party! Now taking rush orders for Halloween!"

Well, that explained the boots and stockings, but he had a feeling it wasn't just turn-of-the-century boots and hand-knit socks that were hiding out there waiting for him to stumble over. He scrolled through the store for a minute before leaning back in the chair. Then, thinking twice, he got back on his computer, closed the page, and deleted his internet history. Not just useful for porn, as it turned out. Whoever was living with him couldn't know what he was finding out. If he was hiding anything from it. Couldn't be too careful.

He went back into his room and confronted the shoes and socks. There they were, still lying where he or someone had taken them off. They looked innocent from across the room, hanging out on the floor by his bed like they belonged there. They belonged there for someone but not him.

A baseball bat was leaning by the bedroom door. He grabbed it and advanced on the suspicious accoutrements. It wasn't like they were going to jump up at him, but he'd seen enough horror movies not to leave anything to chance.

Once he got close enough, he poked the boots with the bat. They toppled over like any other pair of boots might in a similar situation.

"Jesus, man, quit being stupid," he admonished himself, bending down to grab the footwear.

Suddenly, he was no longer in his home. He was in a stable somewhere, but he wasn't moving his own body. When he looked down, the boots from his bedroom floor were on his feet. They were newer but still soft and supple and recently polished.

Then he was looking up. A horse stood before him, a foal, really, and he was manhandling the animal, pulling it toward where a saddled horse was waiting. A nervous-looking freckled boy stood at the door of the stable, looking out.

"Boy, are we clear?" he asked with his new voice.

"Yes, sir," the boy replied, looking left and right outside the stable doors. It was early morning, before dawn, and a fine mist was coming in through the doors. Simon could feel it on his face, could feel the coarse rope under his hand, could feel the resistance of the foal he pulled behind him.

Though not particularly observant, he noticed everything in hyper detail, the edges of his vision hazy.

He mounted another horse and tied the tether from the young horse to his pommel. He hadn't ridden a horse in years, and the sensation was at once foreign and familiar.

The surrounding environment was obscured by the fog or mist, but he could tell he was on a ranch somewhere. Those sights and sounds were familiar enough. He felt like he had on his grandfather's ranch. Almost. There was the issue that he wasn't doing the steering.

The earth was soft beneath his horse's hooves, and each step commingled with other hoofprints there. The soft dirt, the fog, it all muted the sounds around him.

The young horse let out a plaintive sound. He responded with a sharp whack from a crop that he carried.

When he began to ride, his body left him behind, riding away on the horse down the misty driveway. Simon was left, bodyless, staring at the back of a man on horseback who looked strikingly like him. He had seen the back and profile of that man in pictures a thousand times through the years, but seeing the man in person? Well, that put things into an entirely different perspective.

William Monroe.

At the thought, the man turned and smiled. Razor teeth greeted Simon, and he was flung back into his room, his ass hitting the floor hard enough to hurt. He sat there, stunned, even when Shep ran up to him and started licking his face as if he'd truly been gone from the house.

28

Fall 1897

It was cold that October day, but Austin saw Evelyn in her summer frock standing at the edge of the autumn-toned prairie, just at the tree line, waiting. She would've had to take the muddy cattle path to emerge where she stood. The hairs on his arms rose. The longer he looked at her figure, the more he thought she was only an apparition. When he rushed outside, the phantom was gone, but there were hoofbeats on the drive, and he ran to meet them.

She was at his gate on her palomino gelding, loose hair all about her like a cloud, her gelding's legs covered in mud to his belly. She wore her dark winter habit, but her appearance was hasty—no white frock like her warning phantom. She must have traipsed through the gullies to take the shortest route to him. He felt a brief flash of anger. She could have been killed at that time of year by sudden swells in the creeks and unsuspecting deep mud. At the very least, she could spoil her poor horse, who had already carried her on adventures that his old legs ought not to any longer.

He would have to find her a stronger animal—male or female—that was better suited for her long jaunts in the prairie hills full of rabbit holes and hidden, slippery limestone shelves.

Evelyn looked so frantic that he could not bring himself to chastise her. It could wait.

She spilled like water from the saddle and into his arms after he let them into the gate. "Austin! There's been an accident! Please, you must come! Father didn't want me riding out to you, but I had to! You will know what to do!"

A prickle of superstition crawled up Austin's arms. "What's happened?"

He grabbed Evan, and Evelyn told him on their way. No road was in good shape after the rain they had the last month, though he urged them to take the drier, higher roads. The corn was fairly rotting in the fields. As she told her story, Austin felt more dread come over him by the moment.

Ethan had been working on the roof looking for leaks when he slipped on the wet shingles. He had been on one of the peaks of the house, near a chimney. Otto had been on the roof with him, carrying the tools and shingles. Evelyn and her sisters laughed as Ethan pretended to be a tight-rope walker, wobbling with every step. How hard they had laughed. Then he became serious at his work, coming down the roof to where Otto had located the leak.

And then he slipped.

She recounted watching him fall, somersaulting down the roof, striking stone and wood every second of the way down. First his head on the roof, then his legs on the chimney, then his head on the side of another chimney. Their laughter hardly had time to turn to gasps.

Ethan did not even scream. His mouth made a great big "O" as he tumbled.

He struck the walk before their feet, his body twisted and turned as only a contortionist might. But his mouth still bore the great "O" shape, as if he meant to make a noise but never did.

Austin heard the story in bursts and starts as Evelyn urged her gelding into a hard canter. He had tried to pull her up, but the heat in her eyes stayed him. There was no reason to hold her up. Horse be damned, they needed to get there quickly, to call the doctor. They needed more time. The weight of it was oppressive.

Weatherford senior's heart attack and subsequent retirement the previous winter had elicited a promising rise in Ethan's character. Austin was proud of the young man. He had treated Austin with respect and had trusted him, something Austin did not take for granted. They had spoken often of going into business together once Ethan set up his practice, and Austin was hard pressed to find someone in the area who knew more about the law of the Plains' states than either Weatherford.

A blast of wind nearly sent him toppling off Evan's back, and he put up his arm to shield his face, the cold air bringing tears to his eyes. Autumn was leaving in haste. The day was an angry one, and the sun shone only weakly through the clouds.

When they reached the long drive, it was clear something was amiss. Though it was a chilly day, no one was outside with the animals or tending the exterior of the house. To see the usually busy estate so empty was a bad omen.

The dark stain and bits of flesh and bone on the front walk was more unsettling.

He had the feeling of being drawn into the past, and Austin saw his mother and father's accident again in horrible clarity. Their mangled bodies. The blood. His mother's boots flung from her small feet.

At the door, Austin felt the tension in the house, and the dark woodwork seemed darker still. Death often did that to a household. But Ethan wasn't dead, he reminded himself.

Evelyn let out a sob from where she stood in the doorway. Beyond her, Austin heard other riders coming up the drive. Hopefully the doctor.

Austin shushed her and guided her gently inside. "I'm here now. Is there staff to spare? A cup of tea and some soup would do you good. You are frozen, my dear."

"Yes, I . . ."

There was a knock at the open door, and William Monroe bowed his way in, taking off his hat as he did. He oozed charm and disarming personality. Austin tensed at the sight of the man. There was no love lost between their families, but it was no secret that Monroe had been courting Evelyn since the spring. It was to be expected, but it didn't sit right.

Austin's father had told him a story once about a bidding war he got into with the late Mr. Monroe at an auction in Kansas City. Monroe Senior, William Monroe's grandfather, reached his limit, and Austin's father secured the beautiful Fresian mare whose strong lines would eventually yield Evan. The act had so enraged Monroe Senior that, in front of a crowd, he challenged Hearth Senior to provide proof of the funds he planned to use to pay for the animal. His father had walked away before the man could become more provoked, but the damage was done.

Not long after, William's father put in a bid for sheriff and ran a campaign that looked to regulate horse breeding in the area and control how some of the land was used. Austin's father promptly rebuilt his stable just over Monroe's line of jurisdiction, overseen by Jonathan Weatherford's superior legal knowledge.

For all that, Austin had steered well clear of William Monroe III, keeping his paperwork and estate in line. He didn't need more trouble than the prairie already offered.

"My dear Evelyn, how are you doing?" William asked. "How is your family?"

Austin bristled at the man's presence but gave him a cursory nod anyway. So many thought the man charming and fun and a joy to be around—he certainly was always surrounded by people and giggling women—but Austin didn't see the appeal. Simpering and throwing oneself at a man didn't appeal to him.

Evelyn rushed to greet him at the door, twining her arm around Monroe's. Austin was surprised at the jealousy that suddenly reared up within him. His Evelyn! What had happened since he had been away? Where was the woman who had ridden her palomino over rock and stream to seek his help?

"I have asked William to help us. He had been stopping by so often that I sent for him and the doctor when the accident happened." Evelyn's sentiment didn't sound sincere. Nor did her gesture of her little white arm twined around the mayor's. Was she trying to make Austin feel poorly for being away so long? That didn't seem like the kind of thought that would enter Evelyn's mind.

He was lost for words, and the welcome he usually felt at the Weatherfords' home dissipated.

The presence of this man turned Evelyn into another woman. There she stood, looking girlish and flirtatious when she had just been worried and ready to turn her cares over to him.

But there, a tremble. Perhaps it was the newness of this Mr. Monroe that gave Evelyn an air of composure. It didn't matter. Austin felt out of place, and anger was growing in him. Toward Monroe. Toward himself.

If only he had been there. If only he could have been the one there and not William. Why had he thought that being away for a month, two, three at a time was the best route for his future? He clenched and unclenched his hands at his sides, then took a steadying breath and tried to put his anger aside.

They went as a trio into the room at the back of the house near the door, where Ethan lay. The only Weatherford son lay on a great pallet of blankets and was covered with a dark sheet up to his chin. Blood was everywhere. The boy's legs were clearly mangled and perhaps his middle too.

Maggie held a soaked towel to his head. Austin had seen enough carnage when a train struck a deer or a bison or wayward cattle, but this sight hurt him. The Weatherfords were family, as far as he was concerned, and losing Ethan would devastate them. Ethan was pale enough that Austin wasn't certain the boy would make it until the doctor arrived.

It transported Austin. He saw his mother lying there, her boots flung from her little feet, her middle turned in a manner that the human body should not have been capable. But this time she began to move, pulling her broken body from the floor, wayward limbs and all, and shuffled toward Austin.

"My son," she said, her voice garbled.

He closed his eyes and tried to take a deep breath. This wasn't real. Then she was touching him, reaching for a hug from her son. He squeezed his eyes shut harder, smelled the stink of death that was already upon her. It hadn't taken more than moments for the flies to set upon the bodies before Austin arrived to see her lying in the street.

"My son," she said again. "My son, you must take her away from this. You are out of time."

Someone brushed past him, and the vision ended, but he was shaken. Two apparitions in one day didn't bode well. The gypsy woman's words from years past floated up and seized him in a cold terror. But what could he do if Evelyn didn't want to go? The terror and anger mingled together, settling within him like a stone.

He prayed as he watched Ethan's shallow breathing become hitched. The doctor arrived to see to him, but Austin knew what the news would be. He feared for the Weatherfords.

29

3:30 A.M., SUNDAY, OCTOBER 11TH

THE LAST FEW DAYS HAD BEEN WARM ENOUGH THAT THE COLD morning brought the fog up. Olivia hadn't thought it was so dense when she'd looked out her window at the floodlight in her mom's front yard, but when she came out, it took her a few moments to figure out how to get to her car.

Sunrise was still several hours away, and the drive into town was slow, but no one else was out, and she knew the way nearly with her eyes closed. But once she got on Sedalia in Warren proper, she couldn't even see the Lewis Street sign from her first turn. Judging distances wasn't her forte, but she couldn't see far past her headlights.

The radio sputtered as she drove, and the Doors were interrupted by something that sounded like a news talk show. ". . . on matters of business," a man's voice said. Signals getting crossed in the fog.

The Doors came back briefly, then: "Evelyn? Evelyn, I know you're there. Can you hear me? Please turn around."

The hair on her arms rose at the voice. The one who had called her on the phone. The one she'd heard in the middle of the night. The one who had warned her out of the Monroe house. Austin.

". . . eternal damnation and a lifetime of shame," the deeper male voice crept back. ". . . keep her contained . . . the best . . ."

"Evelyn? Evelyn? I'll see you soon, Evelyn." The other voice was barely audible over the static. Then Savage Garden was playing, and everything felt normal again. Except for her white-knuckled grip on the steering wheel. She let out the breath she'd been holding and slowed her car. The drive was harrowing enough.

The second voice had sounded familiar too but only in a way that went creeping down the back of her spine and slithering through her insides, like she'd inhaled too many darkroom chemicals and needed fresh air.

She felt unsettled when she went into the department. It could have just been the time of day—she was never in the darkroom so early. But this way, she could get a full print going that might be somewhat dry by the time she was finished teaching for the day. It wasn't like lying in bed tossing and turning the rest of the night was going to do her any good.

She stood in the front hall and listened to the silence. Sounds presented themselves the longer she stood there. Suppose a ghost or a zombie woman from her nightmares was waiting for her at the end of the tiled hallway? What would that sound like? Shuffling? Somewhere, a faucet dripped. Not surprising, considering how the university never gave them money for anything, even if it was just sending a janitor to investigate. She scurried to her studio.

She shook as she set the cartridges out in the dark. Cold, she was cold, even in the temperature-controlled room. Her half-numb fingers felt slimy, but she hadn't touched any chemicals yet.

She felt around the edges of the film for the notch as she unloaded each piece. Turned everything the right way, set herself up so the process went more smoothly. Six minutes with timed agitation in a 1:47 solution. The gentle sloshing sounds soothed her.

It was 4:15. She had time to kill before the negatives were dry. She got her equipment set up and then decided to take a jaunt down to the archives. She had to know for certain who she was dealing with.

Cold and near silence greeted her in the old room. The dehumidifiers needed to be dumped. They sat quietly in their respective corners of the room. The only sound was the odd drip of water and what felt like the walls themselves breathing.

She stalked the aisles of boxes, reading off the labels like an incantation. She would find answers there.

"Nineteen thirty, nineteen ten," she murmured, scanning the labels that had been meticulously placed, so they were visible as she passed by the shelves and rows of boxes. The handwriting, she realized, was that of none other than Dr. Cecelia Cahara. It was a miracle that the precious time capsules were even in semi-protective boxes, though the whole affair seemed rather stinky to Olivia. She was comfortable down there among the photographs, but an odd knot of unease pervaded as she moved through time in the form of cardboard boxes. She certainly wasn't going to poke around in the Norwich boxes again. That had been a waste of time.

As she went further back in time, the shelves, especially before 1910 or so, were populated with more boxes than she'd expected. It was impressive for a time when cameras were expensive and still somewhat bulky and inconvenient.

"Nineteen hundred," she mumbled. There was a lot of history in Warren. How much more was ferreted away in people's homes? In dugouts like her parents'?

She finally found the section that housed photographs from the 1890s. The shelves were packed from top to bottom. Five or six rows were full of boxes containing the images caught on camera from the 1890s. The beginning of the era of the disposable camera. The Brownie. The Folding Pocket Kodak. It was a treasure trove of information about the past.

Two names stood out from the boxes: Monroe and Weatherford. They made up the vast majority of the real estate in the late 1800s unit. Only one small box was labeled "Hearth," which surprised her. As much as she had been hearing the name lately, it seemed like it should hold a more prominent place.

Hands shaking with excitement, she grabbed the Hearth box and sat down on the floor to look at its contents. Lifting the carton's lid, she peered eagerly inside. She felt the same pang of disappointment she'd felt when she'd looked inside the Norwich box a few days earlier. Not much was there. But there were a few things, and she needed to explore all avenues.

Before she pulled anything out, she put on her cotton gloves. It didn't matter how resilient the photograph was or how meaningless it might be; she still wore cotton gloves. But she almost needn't have bothered with the Hearth photos. They were covered in protective plastic, and a handful were half burned. So that was why there weren't many of them.

What was there wasn't very helpful. One family portrait showed mother, father, and Austin. Several others were of what she supposed was their house, a pretty white farmhouse in the trees, land sprawling around it. There were several photographs of cattle and a handful more of close-ups—mostly blurry—of barbed-wire fences.

Olivia studied the family portrait for a moment. Austin looked younger than the . . . apparition on the corner outside the Daily Brew. Staring at it made her nervous. What if the ghost showed up while she was in the basement of the archives, alone?

She tried to shove the thought away as she carefully arranged the photographs back in the box and then stood to look for a box from the latter part of the century that carried the name "Weatherford." She found the Weatherford box, carried it back to where the Hearth box sat, and pulled it down to the floor with her, opening the box with a curiosity that thrilled her.

The photographs from the Weatherford family showed that the family was well off. Their home and estate seemed grand indeed. Olivia was quite attracted to the place. The house looked friendly and welcoming, though it still had the dark Victorian look of many homes of the era, and she'd worked with enough black-and-white photographs to tell that the large trees surrounding it were full of late-summer leaves.

There were photographs of a stern-looking older gentleman and his wife, a plump, happy-looking woman who had a smile that reached to her eyes. In several of the photographs were three girls and one boy. One girl was quite young, probably six or seven, one about ten, and the eldest probably fifteen or sixteen and looking so grown up. She could have been married the next summer for all Olivia knew. She had been seeing the girl's face everywhere. The boy looked older than all the girls, perhaps twenty.

She turned the photograph over. Someone's scrawl on the back read: "The Weatherford family: Esther and Jonathan Weatherford, their daughters, Evelyn, Eva, and Evette and son, Ethan."

Olivia snorted. It was 2003, and traumatizing one's children with same-letter first names still hadn't gone out of style.

The next set of photographs were disturbing but fascinating, and she'd casually flipped past them before she realized what they were. The boy from the pictures, Ethan, lay on a bed dressed in a suit jacket, hands clasped over his chest. He was covered in a blanket up to his abdomen. He might have been sleeping, but Olivia knew differently. Someone had scrawled "D: 11 October 1897" onto the lower-right corner of the photograph.

The boy was dead.

Victorians, in their fascination with death, took photographs of their beloved after they passed. They often sat in positions they would have taken in life, though sleeping was also popular.

Olivia flipped the photograph over. November 3, 1897. Dewey's had taken the photograph, like the ones from the dugout. The developer's stamp was just below the date stamp, and Olivia traced her finger over the long-dried ink, over the ornate flowers and designs on the back of the photograph. She pressed the cabinet card to her nose and inhaled, closing her eyes. Old paper, old chemicals.

She flipped the photograph over. The boy no longer lay in the bed in the photograph. The blankets were thrown back as if he had simply decided to get out of bed and walk away. Olivia's stomach dropped.

When she flipped it front to back again, he reappeared. That didn't settle her uneasy feeling any.

She looked around, feeling someone watching her. Ethan.

"No one down here but you," she murmured to herself. She repeated it half a dozen times, trying to calm her pulse. *No one here but you.* What a great mantra.

She put the photograph back in its place, quickly losing interest now that the photographs were betraying her too.

Still, there was no E. H. The journal was Evelyn's; there was no doubt about that now. Between the half-recognizable photographs from her family's dugout, the journal, and Olivia's digging, she was certain. Perhaps someone had written on the cover in later years, or it symbolized something she didn't understand.

She stared at a portrait of Evelyn Weatherford. She was a willowy, pretty woman, and the softly colored portrait made her look becoming in her hat and lacy white blouse. She had a pin on the high collar of her blouse, and like so many things lately, it looked familiar.

The memory of the Monroe house reared up with excellent timing. She was relaxed and unprepared, and her heart rate shot up. Yes, there on the powder table was a pendant that might have once been a pin. What had it looked like? Olivia got a cold chill from the thought. Had she been trespassing on Evelyn Monroe's personal space?

The Monroe cartons yielded the most interesting photographs. Clearly wealthy, the batch of photographs showed off their possessions—an early car, furniture in a room that looked *very* familiar, (there went that tickling memory of the Monroe house again—gah), and several dozen photographs of horses, many of which looked strikingly similar to the horse in her own photographs.

No one down here but you.

She quickly shuffled the completely normal and not moving photographs of horses back into the stack and went for the ones with people in them instead. If they moved, she was giving up for the day. There were various portraits of lots of Monroes, some sitting together, some alone. The family looked huge.

A few photographs in, she recognized the clean-shaven Simon-looking fellow from the stairs at the Monroe house. The poke at her blood pressure was unwelcome, but she pushed on.

The back of the photograph said it was William Monroe, age twenty-nine, Mayor of Warren. Well, if he were haunting his own house, that made sense, but what was the gargoyle thing?

It felt like something was watching her. Maybe it was the gargoyle thing, come around for another scare. Perhaps it was Ethan, young and dead at the turn of the century.

Her palms started sweating through the cotton gloves.

No one down here but you.

She didn't believe it this time.

As quickly and as quietly as she could, she packed up the photographs, shoved them onto their shelves, and booked it back upstairs. Now she had a few answers, exponentially more questions, and was about to have another panic attack. She popped a Valium.

Her work was punctuated by anxiety so severe that she finally took another Valium and sat back, willing it to work in the next five minutes. The incident at the Monroe house played on a loop in her head, and she tried to accept the horse when it appeared in the large print, galloping from one end to the other. This time the trees were swaying too.

The process should have brought her joy, but it wasn't like she was used to. But she *had* gotten another print done despite the intrusive horse hallucination. That was the important thing.

With the Valium kicking in, she could look at the print and be proud of it. She liked the knobby and mostly dead tree near where she had taken the first photograph of the trees across the canyon. It had character, and it turned out well in print. If only the horse would stop running in front of it and making the photograph move along down the edge of the canyon.

Unable to stand the movement any longer, she turned away from her drying print and headed toward the building's exit. The Valium was tapering off more quickly than she wanted, but she made it through the print without completely losing it, so she was grateful for that. Now she just had to get ready for the rest of the day.

The world was silent and foggy when she stepped outside. She shouldn't have been the only one on campus, but it certainly felt like it. The humid air was cloying, closing in on her. Fog shifted between her and the building even though she stood only feet from the door.

She was about to descend the stairs when a hand touched her arm. Jerking away, she was about to run when she saw the translucent figure of the man from Daily Brew. The one in the photographs below their feet, forgotten by time and obscured from memory. Only now he wasn't so translucent.

Austin Hearth.

She stepped back a few paces, unsure whether she should run back in the building or into the fog. "What do you want?"

"Please, you must come with me, or he'll see you."

That voice.

Her body froze as the jumble of events of the last few days fell into place in her mind. The voice on the telephone. On the radio.

She watched distantly as she took his hand, and he led her quickly down the stairs and around the side of the building, under cover of the tall shrubs there. A faintness buzzed around her head.

She was about to open her mouth when the man—Austin—touched her arm again and pointed toward the parking lot. This time she felt the warmth of his hand, and her head felt light and hummed like the bees in summer wildflowers. No, like the florescent bulbs in her studio. But the image of the wildflowers lingered longer. She saw her hands reaching down into the prairie grass, touching some pale pink flowers that grew there. The man next to her didn't seem to notice.

She shook her head to clear it and looked where he was pointing. Nearly muffled by the fog, she heard the same plodding hoofbeats that she had heard just a few nights before. The immediate anxiety was overwhelming. The fog was unnervingly thick, and she couldn't see what she heard as the sound bounced around. Where was it?

Her tongue felt thick and dry when she could finally speak. "Can it see us?"

"I imagine not here."

"What is it? Who is it? Someone else like you?"

"No. No, that man is mostly flesh and blood."

"Who then?"

"A what, really. The spirit of a man who long ago gave in to the darker parts of this world."

They watched quietly as a figure on a black horse emerged from the fog close to the curb, not ten feet from them. It was the horse from her photographs, the one that could not be real.

The horse was unable to stand still, just like in the photographs. Its head and neck click, click, clicked and turned at a horrible angle even though its legs stood still. Its flesh hung like wet carpet over its protruding bones. The man atop him seemed to be looking for something, but he had no head, Olivia didn't know how that was possible. Was this the man from her walk, or was she standing next to him? Uncertainty bloomed in her.

"I thought that was you," Olivia said, trying to keep her voice low.

The man gave her a sharp look, and Olivia hoped he was just concentrating. The obscured face was starting to make her feel nauseous.

"Why would you think that?"

Olivia shrugged. "I can see you now. I couldn't the other night. Are there two of you?"

"No, of course not."

"So, you're telling me I saw things?" It was like Ann all over again.

"No! It would seem there's an impostor parading around as me."

"Why would someone do that?"

The look Austin gave her seemed pained. Up close, she could feel his warmth. It was unnerving and comforting at the same time.

She took a stab in the dark. "So, why didn't you have a head the other night? When you . . . introduced yourself?"

"I'm sorry for that," Austin said quietly, still watching the movement in the parking lot. "It seems my strength here grows by the day, and I was still very weak then. I thought you would know something of me, would be able to help me as I came back to help you."

"Help me? Why in the world would I need help?" As soon as she said the words, she wished she hadn't. She *did* need help, and it wasn't wrong of her to ask for it or accept it. It wasn't like he was pushing it on her either. "I'm sorry," she said and then was quiet.

Austin didn't reply, and she was glad for that. She felt awkward enough standing next to this half ghost, wondering what in the world he expected from her. Help him? How? The questions she had for him bubbled up with her anxiety, one after another.

She turned her attention back to the parking lot and dipped behind the shrub, which seemed like poor cover. Could the man next to her offer any kind of protection from the thing out there, waiting for her? Sitting in the shrubs until the thing left didn't seem like a very good plan. Would he disappear when the sun came up? When someone else came by? Someone was always on campus, so the feeling of extreme isolation was unusual.

"Come," Austin said, breaking the silence. "Would you like me to escort you home? I don't think he plans on leaving until either you make an appearance or the sun rises. Others seeing him would not bode well for his disguise."

Olivia listened to the rhythmic hoofbeats in the distance. "How am I supposed to get back here later?"

The man in front of her wavered and solidified, and Olivia felt disoriented as she watched it happen. It was like he was underwater half the time, his form not truly there. His head would fade from his shoulders, only to reappear seconds later. The neck of his cloak still stood though in a comical rendition of all the cartoons and TV shows about the headless horseman. And now there were two. How wonderful.

"It is not safe for you to be out right now."

The statement sparked some anger in her, despite the fear and confusion he caused. "Listen. I don't know you, and I have to be back on this campus later. I work here. Doesn't this thing sleep or do anything else except stalk me?"

"I imagine he has other items on his agenda, yes."

At least the man was patient with her surly attitude, but where was his sense of urgency? She wanted to be far from the thing and its wrong horse. Far from everything if she could. "Fine. Take me home. I don't want to be here any longer."

"Come then," the man said and held out his hand for hers.

Olivia stared but didn't take his hand. If she had offended him, he gave no sign. He turned and headed into the fog, away from the parking lot.

She followed him around the south side of the building, keeping her shoulder close against the limestone as he did. The early morning smelled like dirt and cool air, and the fog was so thick that she couldn't even see the trees off the side of the building. They had to be only feet away, but it was impossible to tell.

Now she had a chance to observe the person she was with more readily. If she wasn't crazy, and that thought still hadn't left her mind, this man was back from the dead after how many years? A hundred or so?

His black coat swept out behind him, brushing her feet and ankles as they walked. He had soft leather riding boots over his pants and a tucked-in long-sleeve shirt. His clothing was mostly unremarkable, and he looked like he was from an old western. Not that she'd seen more than what Turner Classic Movies offered, but he looked quintessentially western, like something on the cover of one of her mother's romance novels.

He wore no hat, but his hair was fabulous enough for the twenty-first century, so she forgave him. It fell in short waves over his neck. In the half dark, she couldn't tell if it was black or brown, but she could see how much darker his neck was than the rest of him.

She watched it, wondering what had kept him out of doors so much. It started to tickle some daydream. Or perhaps daydreams were memories in some other world, some other time. He swayed in front of her, his back to her, so she saw his windburned, sunburned neck. No, he was riding a horse. They were. She could feel the horse sway beneath her as they rode, a gentle rocking, like a boat, or what she supposed a boat felt like. The prairie stretched out before them like the ocean. Cicadas buzzed in the distance, their throbbing hum a familiar rhythm, comforting.

But she had never been in a boat, never seen the ocean, never ridden a horse. Ever since Simon had asked about where she had been, the thought had spiraled out through her memories, echoing through her life. Where had she been? What had she done? The lists were short.

They hadn't taken trips when she was a kid, not the vacation kind, anyway. The trips had been to Wichita or Kansas City for her mother's treatment. Such small circles in such a wide world. Small circles around her home. Around Warren. Within the state of Kansas.

When they came around the corner of the building, Olivia heard a whuffling and a shuffling, and for a moment she was overcome with anxiety. The feeling had become familiar lately. It started with a twitch in her fingers that led to sweating palms and a desire to abandon the situation. She wasn't surprised when she saw the animal, which stared at her with big brown eyes that might've looked sweet in other circumstances.

The horse was familiar. It turned its head toward her, and she knew. It was the other horse in her photographs. But there it was in real life, watching her. Its eyes weren't white like in the photographs, but that didn't matter. It had gone from being a thing she could almost push from her mind to being real in one fell swoop.

It was difficult to swallow. Her throat felt thick. She didn't know this man, didn't know if he was the one who was pretending. She stopped her forward progress, then took a slow step backward. The man was occupied with his horse, who watched her with the same intense gaze that it had on photo paper. She felt like she was watching an old western, seeing the ghostly figure checking his ghost horse's saddle in a bank of fog that slid by in thick wisps and tendrils—bizarre fog behavior by any standards.

The horse watched her as she slid her hand into her pocket—good, her keys were there, safe. Ready. He really was beautiful, if terrifying. His long mane fell in waves nearly to his knees, and soft hair fell from his ankles around his hooves. If this was an old western, the horse didn't quite fit. He seemed too soft, too gentle.

Olivia took a deep breath, fisted her key in her hand, then turned and sprinted toward the parking lot. She didn't look back to see if Austin and his horse were following. She crashed through the shrubs she had hidden behind, coming up on them even before she could see them.

The fog disoriented her, and she slammed into the back of a pickup truck in the parking lot hard enough to send a jarring wave of pain up her back. She felt like she might be sick. Had the other headless horseman heard her?

Turning down the row away from the backs of the few cars that had appeared since she'd gotten to campus, she hurried on, trying to find her vehicle.

The headless man and his beast appeared out of the fog in front of her. She could only stop herself by putting her hands out and bracing against the emaciated horse's chest. It screamed at her and sent its head rushing down, mouth open to bite. Oliva screamed and jerked her hands away, as much from fear of being bitten as from the heat the horse was giving off. Her hands felt scorched.

She tried to backpedal, but the man atop the horse, towering above her and much more frightening up close, urged his steed nearer to her. The horse foamed at the mouth and snapped at her in a manner that she was certain real horses did not.

The man on the horse was huge. He was dressed in a similar fashion to the other man who shouted the name "Evelyn" frantically, somewhere behind her. He wore all black, though his long leather gloves looked new, shiny, almost like a Wal-Mart special. She fixated on them.

She heard his hands tighten on the reins, and he jerked the horse's head toward her.

"There she is," a voice crooned, and the tingle of its familiarity ran through her. The other voice on the radio. The gargoyle thing.

"Come here, little Evelyn. I want a closer look at you." The headless man beckoned to her, holding out a hand as if to offer assistance.

Olivia turned to run, but the man and his horse were much faster. The demonic beast spun to cut off her escape. She smelled its putrid breath and felt a faintness creep over her. She had been holding her breath.

The man—or demon, whatever he was—grabbed at her, catching several strands of her hair instead. The pain was intense; she'd never had hair ripped from her head like that. It sent a shock through her entire body.

"Give me your hand, little Evelyn. Don't make this difficult on both of us."

She tried once more to get around the animal as Austin appeared atop the massive photograph horse. Relief flooded her when the hellish creature took a step back, and Austin's horse slid between her and the other pair.

"Leave her be," Austin commanded. Austin's horse backed up against Olivia, pressing his hip into her shoulder as if he was pushing her backwards, away from the other creature. He was warm, his fur soft. It confused the terror in her. Was he real or a ghost?

The other man laughed. "What an ignorant statement, Mr. Hearth. Should we have another duel about it?"

The creature lunged at Austin's mount, and the great horse sidestepped deftly away from the thing, bumping Olivia farther back away from it, always staying in between them.

"William, I needn't give you another warning."

When she looked up, Austin was raising a pistol, his horse still, focused. The gun looked older than him even, a heavy thing with an ornate wood handle. Even though she expected it, the gunshot shook her. The shot hit the demonic beast in one shoulder, and it opened its mouth in a scream, but she couldn't hear it. The fist-size hole in the thing's shoulder flapped open to reveal what looked like bats fluttering around its chest cavity.

Her ears rang, and her stomach lurched. The vibrations of the horses' hooves rattled her when all she could hear was ringing. Something warm brushed her—Austin or his horse, she could not tell—and terror at being trampled, terror at being shot overcame her.

She ran as the two riders clashed, black-gloved fists raised, demonic horse lunging in, teeth bared. She skidded on the loose asphalt in the parking lot when she took a hard turn toward her car. Surely someone had heard that. Surely someone would come investigate the gunshot that had just exploded the silence on campus.

The sound faded when she reached her car, but she could still hear hooves on the pavement. She managed to get into her car and start it before the crying began. She sped through the fog toward home in a haze of tears and fear.

The scene played through her head for the rest of the morning. The trampling hooves, the shouting, the gunshot. It all swirled together like heated mercury for a daguerreotype, like hyposulphite of soda. Austin Hearth, on horseback in between rows of cars, was old enough to have existed with them.

She couldn't get out of the loop.

Totally crazy.

Not crazy.

Hadn't Simon seen some of it? Surely he had actually seen the man—Austin—on the corner when they left the café. Surely he had and just didn't want to sound crazy too. She dialed his number, tried to come up with an excuse for why she was calling him, then hung up at the second ring.

She had to go back to campus. She remembered her lunch and phone charger when she was halfway there, but fuck it; she was late, and there were vending machines. The thought of her phone dying was enough to cause a panic attack though. The computer store in the student union building surely had a charging cable. Or Cecelia did. Someone.

Would the events continue? The fog was still thick when the sun began to come out, and the streets were crowded with cars and students heading to early classes. Still, she looked around, expecting to see either one of the two horseback riders plaguing her.

What had happened to Austin and his horse? The terror at nearly being caught between the two horses shot through her again. Something turned in her belly. Hallucination or not, the man had tried to protect her. She wanted to know he was OK.

Her anxiety almost sent her to another parking lot, away from where the incident had happened that morning. Bile that tasted like black coffee and wine rose up in her throat as she pulled into a parking spot far too close to the spot for her liking.

The memory of it appeared behind her eyes, bookended with a flashbulb of light. Its intensity shocked her, and she could hear the clattering of hooves again, feel the hot bodies of the horses around her, above her. She made her hands into fists and tried to calm the images. Another Valium. She could take another one when she got inside.

If it had happened, wouldn't there be damage to the asphalt? She could prove once and for all that she was simply having hallucinations induced by the stress of the project.

Steeling herself, she hoisted her portfolio and camera bags over her shoulder and headed toward the end of the parking lot. She was so single minded that she almost walked into two cars backing out of their spots. They didn't seem to matter anymore. With century-old horses running around, cars didn't seem very interesting.

The crawling bile leapt into her throat when she saw clods of torn asphalt under a silver Pontiac. Terror rising again, she knelt down to look under the vehicles around it.

Pieces of asphalt were everywhere and extended toward the Schneider building. Hoofprints were visible in the dust of potholes.

"Excuse me?"

Olivia popped up. The apparent owner of the Pontiac that Olivia was peering underneath stood shaking her Sigma Tau keyring.

"Can I help you?"

"I'm sorry," Olivia stuttered. "Just thought I dropped something . . . thought it rolled under your car. I'm sorry. I'll wait until you back out."

"Whatever." The brunette got into her car, and Olivia moved a few cars over, pretending she was back at her own vehicle.

As soon as the girl left, Olivia rushed to look at the spot before another car could snag it.

Hoofprints. Pulled-up asphalt. The turmoil flashbulbed, and again she rushed away from the scene. Something whispered for her to take a photograph of the pavement, but she shoved the thought away. A photograph was too permanent, and photography was betraying her anyway. She trusted it less than her own eyes.

She had lingered too long, so she had to rush to her first class of the day, stumbling into the classroom a few minutes after the bell rang. A few students looked up when she entered, but most of them were occupied, talking.

As she rushed to get everything set up, she realized she hadn't brushed her hair that day. And was she in her clothes from the day before? She brushed a hand down her wrinkled shirt. Was she still wearing makeup? God, she probably looked a mess, but she could do this. She had to.

30

Summer 1897

Austin was at Anderson's Staple and Fancy Grocery picking up some extras for around the house. Being a bachelor had its charms, but he was ready for a woman to be in charge. His housekeeper did a fine job, but when it came to odds and ends, he wanted to hand it over to someone more naturally inclined toward details.

As he made his selections, he saw William Monroe outside looking Evan up and down. He didn't blame the man. Evan was an impressive horse, born of his father's best mare bred with one of only three registered Friesian stallions and the only in the States. He carried as pure a bloodline as one could ask for.

His father had bred the mare out of a longing for a well-rounded horse to carry himself and his son on their excursions, so the Hearths could present themselves well along the way. A man and his horse could be dusty from the road, but first impressions were everything, and a strong but elegant horse could catch eyes in a way other animals could not. And his father had a weakness for the Friesian breed, a point of pride and nostalgia for his home country.

He watched the man get close to Evan's face, looking at his clear eyes and nose, no doubt, but he didn't touch the horse. After another minute or two of inspecting the animal, who appeared to be wholly ignoring the man, William walked off, and Austin continued with his errand.

"I'll pay you ten thousand dollars for both horses."

The voice made the hair on his neck rise. He imagined his father in similar shoes being hassled over his land, over his own horse. It wasn't the first offer William had made, but it was certainly the largest.

"My answer is still no." His response was curt, but he was finished dealing with the man, who didn't understand the meaning of the word.

"You waste a lot of talent in the stallion. He was bred for far grander deeds than being a pack mule. His feathers are covered in mud. A fine horse ought to be well groomed at all times."

The neat core of anger that Austin kept reined in cracked at Monroe's words. The man sounded so genial, so willing to strike a deal that Austin was almost angry at himself for being angry with the man. But the man's demeanor—and his father's warning—was all he needed to keep his guard up.

"Sir, I need to ask you to cease provoking me. This discussion has no further path."

Monroe barked out a laugh. "Me? Provoke you? The only person without sense here and who continues to make this conversation difficult is you, sir."

It would have sounded logical if it weren't so terribly wrong. The man had surely made his fortune on the backs of such statements. If he hadn't made Austin's skin crawl on so many occasions, Austin might have simply put off the sensation as jealousy.

"What would convince you to finally leave this matter be entirely?"

"Only your acquiescence. I'm no chiseler. I'm good on the deal."

"I cannot agree to it at your asking price." There. William Monroe was wealthy, but Austin knew the value of his animal. The Friesian breed might have been in decline elsewhere in the world, but in Kansas Evan and his stock were worth more than gold.

William smiled in such a genuine way that Austin was momentarily terrified. What was going to come out of the man's mouth next?

"Austin Hearth, those are the most logical words I've ever heard from your lips regarding this matter." William settled a hand on his shoulder, and Austin felt the conversation was about to change. Something in the air had changed, as had something in William's eyes. They almost looked red.

Austin didn't know what to say, but William saved him the trouble by speaking first, clapping him on the back as if they were old friends. "I tell you, horses and women are a fine business, Austin. The finer the filly, the younger she ought to be snapped up. Wouldn't you agree?"

Austin's anger flared again. He had kept the filly's presence closely guarded, but it wasn't surprising that William had heard about it. Many came to Austin's property on errands. Deliveries had to be made, and people talked, of course. And if he meant Evelyn . . . . Austin opened his mouth to reply, but William had one more punch left in him. "And your little hoyden." The quiet words dripped from William Monroe's lips.

The anger that ripped through Austin was nearly uncontainable. That Evelyn enjoyed being out of doors didn't seem so progressive any longer, and Monroe's tone was laced with condescension.

His mother. His father. His horses. His Evelyn. The man had everything, and yet he wanted everything of Austin's.

"She is not—"

"But she is," William said. "But she is a good girl still, I see, as do you. The difference between us is that I can make a proper lady of her. Get those boots out of the mud, as it were."

Austin froze. A warning in Monroe's red eyes mirrored a warning from his own heart.

He barely got out of Anderson's without becoming outwardly enraged at William, who was all genial smiles and shaking hands as he took his leave. He watched the man pat Evan on the rump as he walked past, earning a flick of the ears and tail from the animal. Across the street, William's father watched from the walk in front of the sheriff's office.

Austin felt the place he was caught between, but what was there to do about it, save keep his hands clear of the entire business?

Two months later, he returned from Colorado to discover the filly had disappeared from his stables. He'd sent messages back checking on the animals, and all had appeared well until the day he was meant to return home.

Upon his arrival, his farmhand, Jordan, informed him that at some point during the day—perhaps when the young man was out checking the cattle on the grazing lands—someone had broken into her stall and removed the animal.

At first, Austin had made a frantic search of the land, grabbing one of his sorrel geldings and riding him more recklessly than he ought over prairie dog holes and dips and swells of the grazing pastures. The horse was foaming when he returned to the barn, and his regret over riding the horse too hard only just touched the anger he felt.

The filly hadn't gotten out. Austin had little doubt as to who had taken the animal, but how to prove it? The filly had yet to be weaned from her mother and would need to be hand reared. She wasn't registered yet—his fault. She was too young to be judged for breed qualities, and if she were at the Monroe estate now, well, he would certainly never see her again.

He had not sired out Evan to make money. Someday he would need a new horse, and he could not imagine trusting his person to anyone save Evan's bloodline. The filly had been a surprise but not an unwelcome one.

Evelyn would need a horse herself someday as well, and the foal would have been the perfect opportunity to provide that for her.

And now? Well, he could go to the police, but Monroe the Older *was* the police. Austin had a better chance of selling barbed wire to the president of the United States than getting his horse back.

No, he would rather wait and see what happened. His anger was controlled for now, but he wasn't going to be a pleasant man to the good mayor forever if he kept overstepping himself.

All the same, he went down to the sheriff's office and filed a report about the theft. William Monroe the Senior watched Austin from his chair not far from the front desk where Mayor Monroe's younger brother smiled as he filled out the report for Austin.

"And you said you hadn't registered the filly yet?"

"No. She was too young to be judged."

"Do you have photographs of the animal?"

A ray of hope. "Yes, I do." He produced a photograph. "I'll have to claim this again at a later date."

"There is no way of telling when this photograph was taken."

"The filly was only born this summer. She is young still. I can have anyone on my estate attest to that."

Younger Monroe smiled up at him, and Austin expected those eyes to be red, as William's had been lately. "We'll keep this for now. Send it around, see if anyone's seen her."

He thanked the men but felt no hope that he would even see the photograph again, let alone the horse.

31

Monday, October 12th

The historical society was a nondescript brick building a block off Main Street, tucked between a residential neighborhood and someone's attempt at a lawn-mowing company. Thankfully, it was still open when Olivia arrived. She went inside, taking in everything as she went. She wasn't particularly excited about running into the proprietor after what had happened at the Monroe house, but she wanted a firmer grasp on reality, and it seemed as good a place as any to find some answers.

There were many enlarged photographs and large paintings with gaudy frames and miniatures of the town through the years. Glass cases full of railroad and farming memorabilia littered the space. Roped-off areas held antique furniture and farm implements and a thousand other items that would have taken a full day to explore. The last time she had been inside an historical society was in Riley during elementary school, and if she hadn't been at the historical society for a purpose, she would've been just as bored as she was back then.

Mr. Fullbright welcomed Olivia in out of the chilly air and asked if she had any questions that he could answer. Olivia wanted to ask him what was going on in the Monroe house and if he'd had any trouble with a gargoyle thing and phone calls on telephones that she was quite sure were no longer connected. Instead she asked if there were any portraits or photographs of a Miss Evelyn Weatherford, also known as Mrs. Evelyn Monroe. The man's eyes lit up as he looked at Olivia's face and then back toward another room that housed more antiques.

"Yes, yes, we do, Miss. You aren't one of those ghost hunters, are you? You're shooting me straight that you're photographing the town and such?"

"Yes, of course," she replied quickly to his sharp gaze. Ghost hunters. She wished she had that much time on her hands.

Olivia followed Mr. Fullbright as he shuffled forward, stooped over a cane. He had been standing tall and walking fine just a few days prior. An image of the man going into the Monroe house and finding the creature rose in her mind. She imagined him tussling with the thing, fighting it to get out the front door. Had he seen it? Perhaps she should say something.

Somewhere a recording of a piano played a tune that tickled the daydreams she'd been having, and the anxiety about the old man and the demon dissolved. The music soothed her.

"History is an amazing teacher," Mr. Fullbright said. "I've been fascinated with it ever since I was a little boy. Wouldn't have thought I'd be here running this place, but it's nice to be surrounded by all this history. Yes, here we are now." The old man stopped and pointed at the wall. "There you are. This is the best painting of anyone here over the years, and my wife will vouch for that."

Olivia looked to where he was pointing and felt the color drain from her face. Before her was a larger-than-life-size painting of a young woman standing next to a plush green chair. She wore voluminous white skirts that flowed gracefully to the floor. Her pale neck was encased in the lace of her high-necked blouse.

What Olivia noticed most though was her face. Her oval eyes had irises of chiseled steel. Her nose was small and pointed, her cheeks flushed with a dab of rose. Her brown hair was up in a do that turned her hair into a halo about her head. It told Oliva more than the black-and-whites that she had been filtering through over the last several days. Olivia might as well have been looking into a mirror. A younger, slenderer mirror but a mirror nonetheless.

Fine hairs fell across Evelyn's face, and she looked as if she had just finished laughing. Her left hand rested on the arm of a chair, but her right hand rested on her chest, just above her heart. She had indeed just finished laughing, Olivia decided. If Ann had worked on this painting, she'd either kept her mouth shut about the resemblance or was oblivious to it.

The painting did tell her in more explicit terms what the photographs of the woman hinted at. Why was that? Was it simply that this was life size, a nearly exact portrait done by a talented artist? Or was this where black-and-white failed? She touted black-and-white photography's ability to convey emotion better than any other medium, but here, in color before her, she could have argued for the opposite. She couldn't reconcile that.

After several long minutes of silence, the old man finally spoke. "You look very much like her."

Olivia tried to work up some saliva for her dry mouth. "Uh . . . right."

The man looked over at her, "Were it not impossible, I would say you were related to Miss Evelyn."

"Hmm." Words were difficult. Olivia stared at the painting, willing it to tell her something. "Um, my last name is Norwich. Maybe the Weatherford name turned into it through marriage."

The man shook his head. "No. The Weatherford name died around the turn of the century. There is no direct relation living."

"Oh. Well." She looked around and moved to a glass case beneath the portrait. The more she stared at the painting, the dizzier she felt, as if she were looking out from the portrait and at it at the same time. It was the same feeling in the room at the Monroe house, the feeling that she was no longer in control of her own body.

Olivia grasped for a question to ask the old man, caught somewhere in the loss-of-control feeling. "I live in an old home outside of Warren—close to mile marker seventy-four where it's still technically Lewis Street."

"Are you on the east side of the road? A few large cottonwood trees in the front? Bits of old posts and chain and limestone walls left by the road?"

"I think so." Directions were not her forte, but she vaguely remembered balancing on old chains strung between posts as a kid, down close to the road where the flaking limestone border offered hours of destructive childish entertainment.

Mr. Fullbright hemmed. "That's the old Weatherford land. The house burned down in 1903 after all the great flooding and disasters of that year. Come, here's a picture of what the house used to look like. Burned all the way down, it did. Couldn't even save the limestone walls."

There was the buzzing again. She lived where that woman lived? Olivia's stomach turned as she followed him. "Did they rebuild the house?"

"Not immediately, no. I couldn't say when it was from memory. The land was sold. Here we are."

Olivia looked at the large photograph of the house, and the same pervasive feeling of looking at and out at the same time lingered.

The house was impressive. It boasted a large limestone front with what looked like a castle's turrets on either side. Other outbuildings flanked the house on either side. A wide set of stone stairs led up the middle of the yard, stacked limestone fences on either side. That tickled the childhood memory even harder. Yes, that was where she lived.

"So, the house burned down? What about everything else? None of that is there now."

Mr. Fullbright turned a hard eye on her. "Well, I imagine they bulldozed it, young lady."

Thank you, Sherlock. Olivia bit her tongue. It was interesting and helpful but not in any way that moved her forward in understanding what had happened.

"Warren struggled for a bit after that," he continued, easing into what sounded like a speech he probably gave to guests on tours of the museum.

Olivia wasn't going to let him get away with glazing over her questions. If she had to bait him, so be it. "It struggled because of the house fire?"

Mr. Fullbright gave her another look. "The Weatherfords were among the wealthiest inhabitants of Warren, and they perished in the fire, only to turn up in New York a decade later, according to some. The Monroes, the family who founded the town, were driven out by the disasters. Several other wealthy but unsavory individuals also abandoned Warren. Warren struggled because its benefactors left. Were it not for the college, Warren might have disappeared completely."

Left or were murdered? She had come for more of the Halloween story business, so why was she surprised by the casual nature of his explanation? She didn't want to mention the dugout. She felt possessive of the knowledge of its existence. But she did want to poke one more time, just to see. "I don't believe in ghosts myself—"

Yes, you do, that musical voice interjected.

"—but the Monroe house did feel kind of weird. Guess that's just the season." The voice in her head from the Monroe house could shut the hell up.

That seemed to sufficiently wind up old Mr. Fullbright to get him talking more. "That's what I've been telling my wife for years. We get ghost hunters around here regularly, especially around Halloween. The anniversary, you know. I usually turn them away, the young ones. Had one through two years ago who was more professional—as professional as that bunch can be. Only one who didn't come out raving that they'd felt something, but anyone who gets high on enough drugs will feel anything.

I tell them all they're wasting their time, digging around in holes that might have snakes in them."

Olivia wondered if the man had lost his train of thought. She wasn't going to ask about the anniversary because she knew for sure now.

"In any case," he continued, "perhaps they did. I get funny feelings in the house now and again. It's a big, old, empty place. Not surprising it feels full of the past. But you're right too. Maybe it's just the season."

An idea was forming. A grasp at straws, really, but she didn't have any other options. "Could you get me in touch with any of them?"

"Who? The ghost hunters?"

None of your business. "Just looking for more photographs, more history. That's all."

His suspicious look turned friendly once again. "Mmmm, one of them might be of use to you. I don't like the others, but they leave their cards here all the time."

Olivia followed Mr. Fullbright to the souvenir counter at the front of the building and took the business card he extended to her. "Colton Munroe," it read, "Investigating (Paranormal) History Since 2003," followed by a phone number and email address. Munroe. Monroe. Was he related to Simon, or were there just that many unrelated Monroes and Munroes around Warren?

She thanked Mr. Fullbright and headed back into the cold to her car. She'd forgotten about all the groceries in the front seat. How long had she been in there? An hour? Surely they were fine. Her vision wavered, and beside her the seat turned from the interior of her car to a plush velvet cushion. She was rocked slowly side to side, as if on a boat. Distantly, she heard the sound of crunching gravel and the soft voice in her head saying, *I miss him so. You must tell him hello from me.*

Then it was her car again, and her head was empty.

She pulled the business card from her pocket and called the number on it with nervous fingers. It didn't get through half a ring before someone picked up.

"Colin Munroe receiving. What can I do for you?"

The line crackled. Olivia pulled it away from her face to see if she had service. She did. "Hello, my name is Olivia, I—"

"Evelyn?"

The hairs on her arms stood up.

"Yes?" she asked, her mouth dry.

"I'm sorry, did you say Evelyn or Olivia? I can't hear you very well." The voiced touched the familiar creepy-crawly place within her like the voices on the radio, in the Monroe house, goddamn everywhere these last few weeks.

"Um," she began, ignoring the Olivia/Evelyn question. "I don't know where to start, but I'd like your opinion on something. You're interested in the . . . supernatural events of the last century in Warren, right?"

He paused long enough that she was about to ask if he was still there.

"Who is this? I know you from somewhere. Is this Jennifer? I swear to God, Jen, if you're fucking with me, I'm blocking you on this number too."

"No," Olivia said. I'm—"

Miss Evelyn Weatherford

"—Olivia Norwich. I live on the old Weatherford property." That sounded strange coming from her mouth. What had she wanted to say? *This is Miss Evelyn Weatherford. What stories have you to tell?*

"Oh, sorry." He didn't sound very sorry.

"Listen, I don't have much time. You're knowledgeable on the . . . stuff that Warren went through, right? The ghost stuff?" The musical voice kept tickling the inside of her brain, like a shiver on the inside.

"Yes."

Olivia waited for more, but he was silent.

"I live on the old Weatherford property."

"I see."

"Some strange things have been happening lately."

"Congratulations."

Olivia felt the pinch of frustration again. This guy was an asshole. "I got your business card from Mr. Fullbright at the Warren Historical Society. He said you were good."

A laugh. "What did he say I was good at?"

Olivia couldn't tell if he was being sarcastic. "He said you weren't like the other . . . um . . . ghost hunters."

Another laugh, this one definitely sarcastic. "Well, that's as good an endorsement as any. Where and when do you want to meet to tell me about these 'strange things'?"

She felt like he was laughing at her or toying with her. Why had Mr. Fullbright given her this guy's business card if he was just going to treat her like an idiot?

"I'm sorry, but it sounds like I'm wasting your time. Thanks anyway, Mr. Monroe."

She heard him saying "It's MUN-roe" as she hung up.

What an asshole. Her phone buzzed. It looked like the number she had just called. She debated just sending him to voicemail, but she was feeling desperate.

"Change of heart?" she asked.

"You could say that. Meet me Friday at the old cemetery on Sunset Boulevard. Seven a.m." He hung up.

Olivia sighed and set her phone back in her lap. This seemed like more trouble than it was worth.

32

Late Winter, 1897 - Spring 1898

William Monroe courted Evelyn in a flurry of dances and public meetings and dinners with her family. She had never been so spoiled, so overwhelmed with notes and gifts and words of affection. Her wardrobe was full of new dresses that matched William's clothes in some way—a lush red-and-black velvet set that kept her warm during the harsh winter, mint-green skirts wonderfully beaded and embroidered to match his spring looks, and hats and gloves to go with anything and everything. He sent messages the morning before a large gathering, so she would know which ensemble to wear. Eva and Evette helped her into them, barring even Maggie from the room, so they could touch and admire the pieces and laugh with their sister as they pretended to be her assistants.

Since Ethan's death, she hadn't had a moment to think, let alone grieve for him. It seemed that as soon as he was in the hard winter ground, William had taken it upon himself to occupy her every waking minute. It had helped, she supposed, by keeping her mind away from worrying about her family. She hadn't seen Austin since the funeral, hadn't heard a word. That wasn't unusual when the mail was delayed by heavy snows, but as hollowed out as she felt without her brother, she felt hollower still with Austin's absence.

By the spring, William was still showering her with baskets of presents, and she had a difficult time keeping up with everything he sent. Father rarely came out of his study, and Mother became quiet. Some days William visited to see how the family was holding up, often sitting for long hours in Father's study, talking business.

Only Eva and Evette didn't seem to be so affected by grief, continuing their lessons and musical instruments uninterrupted. Evelyn longed for their company when she was out with William, wishing to simply sit with their laughter and chatter. She missed Austin too. So much had happened that she no longer knew where he was, south or west. She hadn't had time to pore over her botanical encyclopedias either, so she might ask him to bring back a plant or two for her. Despite the happiness that the notes and articles of affection from William should have brought her, a haze seemed to have settled over her world.

It was a warm day in late March, and she wanted more than anything to be walking, to see what the winter had left behind, but William was over, speaking to her father, and he preferred that she stay home when he visited. She sat looking over several sketches of new flowers she had yet to identify from the previous autumn. They looked like a kind of rose by their leaf and petal shapes, but she wasn't certain. They were from her last walk with Austin, and she kept coming back to how it sounded when he walked through the grasses next to her, how she could feel Evan's careful plod with them and the unique sound his horseshoes made when he stepped on limestone or flint.

She pressed the point of one pencil into the thick part of her thumb and tried to dim the memory. She pressed harder until she felt it break the skin.

William startled her out of her circular thoughts with a hand on her shoulder. The pencil she wielded fell to the floor, and she covered her sketches with her hands reflexively, protecting them. Her thumb throbbed.

"My goodness, you are immersed!" William smiled down at her.

She relaxed and returned his smile. "Yes. I'm having trouble identifying these flowers. I must have been lost in thought about it."

William reached for the pencil on the floor, then pushed her hands aside to look at her work. "You need new pencils. I'll make certain you have better colors by the end of the week."

Evelyn flushed and looked over her sketches. Was something wrong with their quality? Surely not. He only wanted her to have the best tools, and he could afford them.

"Thank you," she said finally.

William sat in the chair next to her table and took the hand with the injured thumb in his own. The smile that was only hers bloomed on his face. "I asked your father for your hand."

An ache bloomed in her gut, and her heart beat faster. Father hadn't said anything to her yet, hadn't asked if she approved. Did she?

He must have seen the confusion on her face. "I'm an old-fashioned man, Miss Evelyn. Don't you value family and your family in particular?"

"Well, of course I do. I just—"

"Then you will see it is sensible that we marry. It will provide for you now that you are in danger of becoming a burden here."

Evelyn felt her heart twist. Her father had never said she was a burden, nor had he even hinted at it. She felt nothing but welcome in her own home for as long as she wanted. Not that she had ever thought of it the way William put it, but still, she didn't want to be a burden.

"I'm so grateful for your help with my family, William. You have no idea how . . ."

He stilled her with a hand on her forearm and a gentle smile. "Please, don't think anything of it."

Evelyn flushed. He was handsome and so good to her and her family. "Thank you. I . . ."

Something red glinted in William's eyes, and his mouth hardened. "I said it's nothing. Think nothing of it."

"Oh, forgive me," Evelyn said, taken aback, but William was all smiles again. The remark had thrown her off balance.

"I want a wife," William continued. "And I would like you to be her."

She wished she had someone to talk to. Her thoughts were seeds in a gale. What would it mean to marry this man? All she could think was that he had the money to send her to the college courses she wished to take, and she would have the free time in which to attend them. She could continue her research, perhaps publish a paper or a book in time. Even though he had called it silly once, he surely would not care once they were married. And he had already said he would buy her fine pencils. She would uphold the Monroe name as a proper lady in all matters, including her collegiate education and in publications. The thoughts finally stirred enough excitement in her that she surged to her feet. "Yes! Yes, I'll marry you, William Monroe."

He smiled and took her by the elbow to lead her back to her father's study, so they could give him the good news.

THEIR ENGAGEMENT WAS A TORNADO OF PUBLIC EVENTS AND gaiety. William introduced her to his friends in town, and they had dinner with a new friend or relation nearly every night. He took her to the dance hall sometimes twice a week, though they never stayed late, and he always had her home before Mother or Father would worry.

Evelyn tried to keep his vast number of friends and relations straight. She also tried to understand *exactly* what William did for a living. He had his fingers in so many different ventures that it was impossible to pin down any one trade. His father had founded the town, selling lots to anyone who could put up the money, and she supposed William was in the thick of that too, being mayor, but he never seemed to be down at the land office. Perhaps he was when he wasn't with her, but he was with her so often that she hadn't much time for anything else.

33

Tuesday, October 13th

He wanted a wife. The arcane thought followed Simon around. It was an annoying and stupid thought that he couldn't get out of his head. He had had enough women for the sake of having a woman that he knew what he wanted—or thought he did.

He liked Olivia. More than he cared to admit, especially when he'd gotten a few fingers too deep into the scotch on a Thursday evening. Or tonight, for that matter. He'd been invited to the weekly poker game by what went for the good old boys' club, a group of professors whose tweed should have gone out of style in the 1970s but had lately come back into style. Unfortunately, his increasing anxiety about the current state of his mental health (and the current state of his no longer single personality) kept him in with the scotch. He was teetering on the edge of something dangerous by drinking so much during the week, but he didn't care.

He did care about Olivia though and whatever was living with him. Olivia in her spandex workout gear and little crop tops, which had given way to gauzier more feminine skirts and cardigans. They'd skirted around each other for what, seven, eight years? Longer? That had been more than enough time for him to admire her, but she was different now. So was he. This season was changing both of them.

He had watched her with her various boyfriends at faculty functions—the beefy and the lean—all workout-aholics, all with that bit of the devil in their eye once they got a few drinks in them. He'd seen it before, but he hadn't seen her out and about with anyone in a year or so. He knew in the way that something was cohabitating with him that his circle was coming closer to Olivia's. Or maybe that was all about him arriving at forty and panicking that he hadn't done enough with his life.

"That's not it," he said to Shep, who came briefly out of his sleep to gaze at Simon with half-lidded eyes, then conked back out.

"Some help you are," Simon said. This time Shep didn't raise his head. What could a dog do in a man's world except eat what he was given and lay loyally at his master's feet until it was time for walkies, rabbit chasing, or sheep herding?

Bridgette had been good for him, or so he kept telling himself. He was the one who had decided to leave Ohio and return to Kansas. He was the one who had broken up with her after six years and moved to the middle of nowhere.

Bridgette was soft and kind and nice and everything he had thought he wanted in a woman. Hell, she'd lived right down the road from his grandparents' farm for the majority of his post-pubescent life. He'd been a jackass teenager when they'd met, but she wanted to date him for some reason still unknown to him. It couldn't have been his awkward frame or awkward socializing skills or his awkward tendency to spout historical facts in completely inappropriate situations.

But she had been the one who suggested he go to college. She had been the one who pushed him to funnel his love for history into something more productive.

And study he did. He blew the local community college's sparse history courses out of the water, and Bridgette followed him to the state university as he chased a double major and then his master's.

Then he found Warren.

It had been an accident, really. Bridgette was helping him clean out his parents' old house. Also at her insistence—he had no desire to go through their things after they passed. He'd done the bare minimum, then pretended to forget about the rest. All those old bones lying around the basement and the attic and every closet, just waiting to ambush him with times less fraught with stress.

She'd discovered the trunk and called for him to come up to the insufferably hot attic. He was sweating the moment he stuck his head into the space.

Glory be, his big-breasted, red-headed girlfriend was leaning over and digging in a trunk that looked older than Moses. Some things were seared into a man's mind forever.

He peered at her through the dust she had stirred up. "What'd you find? It's hot as fuck up here."

She gave him a little wiggle of her eyebrows that went straight to his crotch. "You keep talking like that and we'll really be sweating."

It was his turn to roll his eyes. "Dammit, woman. What did you find?"

He didn't need to ask. For some reason as he looked over at the aged trunk from his position on the ladder, he knew. It was a traveling trunk, a common one during the turn of the century and a bit after. Very common in the Midwest and the plains.

His grandparents had been forthcoming about the family tree, but something had never quite sat right with him about it. It wasn't that their dates didn't line up. No, that all worked out. But he'd never been able to find any information about it all himself. Those were still the budding days of things like Ancestry.com and national or international databases that were easily accessible to laypeople or professionals. His research had begun with phone calls and library visits. Family histories were an infinite puzzle, and to say he enjoyed that kind of puzzle was an understatement. His own puzzle most of all. And the trunk was part of it.

He and Bridgette spent the rest of that afternoon looking at bits and pieces of a life on the prairie that had taken his great-grandparents with his infant grandfather deep into Ohio's sheep country. They found a lot of moth-eaten clothing and some pieces that might be salvageable. Shifts for a child or baby, handkerchiefs, some silver, books and letters, and so much paper. Some of it was deteriorating quite impressively, but not all of it.

He sat down in the sweltering attic and began to meticulously go through every piece of it. He forgot about Bridgette, who left at some point to get food, which he didn't eat.

What was left of the legible paper trail told the story of a family moving slowly from Kansas back to the north and east. He found tickets for items pawned in Missouri, Illinois, Indiana, and Ohio. There had been a good amount of silver at one point, that much was clear, and enough left when they got to Ohio to buy land, farm implements, and a few animals. What he had mistaken for dirt and rocks at the bottom of the trunk turned out to be seeds of all kinds. The same name kept popping up as he delved through it all: Warren, Kansas.

When he finally came down later that evening, dehydrated and exhausted, all he knew was that he was going to Warren, and nothing was going to stop him. He broke up with Bridgette, packed his bags, and left within a month of the discovery.

He got his transcripts transferred, got set up at the university there, and went to work. It was as if they had been waiting for him. He slid into their history program without so much as a hiccup, then worked his way through the PhD process, put in the time, blood, and sweat, and became a tenured professor almost before he could believe it had happened. It had been so smooth, so seamless, that he almost didn't notice how much time had passed. That fall had marked the passing of his eighteenth year in Warren.

And what had he found of his family since he had been there? Nothing. Nothing remarkable. He felt like he was chasing something that was always just out of reach. But then again, that could be the "forty feeling" creeping up on him.

Bridgette had been astoundingly understanding about the ordeal. He'd seen on Facebook that she'd had her second kid not long ago. Nice conservative husband in a nice conservative home back in Ohio. She liked his pictures of historical finds in Warren, and he liked her pictures of the kids. It scared him a little to think about where he could have ended up if he hadn't gone to Warren.

A twinge behind his eyes didn't feel right. "Bat signal," he muttered, then looked down at Shep. "I guess I'll see you later, pup. Please don't bite me if I smell different in a minute."

Then the pain and rage washed over him like a vengeful sleep.

34

March 13, 1898

Evelyn had never seen so many pleats or so many yards of lace dyed the same pale yellow as her dress. Evette had turned six shades of red and purple with laughter before she finally declared that her sister looked like a churn full of butter. Evelyn had turned a corresponding shade of red, which clashed with her attire.

Eva was much more reserved about it, saying she looked like a wildflower. Evelyn tucked the compliment away, grateful for any words from her shyest sister.

Her mother took her hands, tears in her eyes. "Look at my daughter. You're such a beautiful bride. And such a man for a husband. I'm proud of you."

"Thank you, Mother," Evelyn replied. She took her hands back and curled her cold fingers into her palms, pressing her fingernails into the flesh, willing it to warm. William had said no gloves, so she wore no gloves.

There was a quiet knock on the door, and the photographer entered.

She stood still while Mother and the photographer arranged her dress, handed her the bouquet of roses, and set the garland on her head. The cloth backdrop behind her smelled strongly of linseed oil, but she stood there quietly while her eyes watered, and her mother and sisters arranged her artfully.

Evelyn thought she might request the roses be colored pale pink if they tinted the photographs. The red roses paired horribly with her yellow dress, but it was as William wanted, and it would be such a silly thing to argue about.

When it came time for the event, her father met her in the narthex. Evelyn didn't know what to say, so she told him she loved him, and he kissed her forehead. She felt like a child again; she wasn't ready.

Time blurred. She hardly remembered walking down the aisle. So many faces she didn't recognize.

Her stomach knotted as she stood listening to Pastor Byers. She locked and unlocked her knees and felt a rush when she caught herself nearly fainting. The stiff yellow lace at her neck itched. How slowly time moved that afternoon in the hot church! It was not at all like she had imagined it would be.

She stared at the wooden carving of Christ on the cross. He bore his pain silently, as she did. Then her eyes flitted to the man next to her. He was somber in his suit, but seeing her slight movement, he flashed her a private smile. His blue eyes sparkled with intelligence. She softened, smiled back.

How much like a child she acted, wanting her own way! Mother and Father would not lead her astray, though she did think her mother's nerves and nervous worries were rather too much. And William knew so much more of the world than she. He would raise her already elevated situation.

Evelyn was resolved as she turned back to face Pastor Byers. She would make the best of this new situation.

35

Late Spring 1898

Evelyn was headed to her desk in the informal parlor when William grabbed her elbow. She jumped; she hadn't heard him approach. He pulled her into an embrace that she was too startled to return.

He laughed. "You ought to greet me with more warmth than that, wife."

"I'm sorry. You startled me."

"Oh, love," he chided. "Off in your own head again? You should always expect me."

"Yes, I suppose I should. I'm sorry."

He smiled and looked from her feet to the journal in her hands. "Were you planning on going out later? You need not wear those boots in the house. I bought you soft shoes for that purpose."

"I thought I might see what Jones had today. Evette said in her last letter they had a new shipment of books and stationery."

Something changed in William's eyes. They looked darker somehow, more intense. "My dear, I don't want you to leave the house. And Jones's place is a ticket office. I don't want any unsavories accosting you."

Evelyn balked. "Not leave the house? That's absurd!" She had been coming and going during the first few weeks of her married life at William's home, decorating with his approval, and going for short walks in between.

But William remained cool. "These are dangerous times, Evelyn. I want you safe."

"I had thought us safer than ever. What has changed?" That was why her mother had pushed the move there in the first place. She had heard Ethan say so time and again.

William smiled and squeezed her arms. She was caught in an embrace that felt too close, though he was her husband. "Oh, my dear. You do not see the world as I do. The horrible things I see nearly every day. I wouldn't want anything to happen to you."

Evelyn looked outside at the spring day. She wanted to be out in it, at least in the garden, but she longed for the prairie; her legs ached for it. In town she only had faraway glimpses of it—from the window in their room and from the tall window in the attic that she needed a chair to see out of. "This is only temporary?"

Another squeeze. "Of course! I'm certain times will change soon. I only want you safe, dearest wife."

"All right," she replied hesitantly.

William held her at arm's length and looked into her eyes, as if examining her. His grip felt too tight, but it was only her imagination. "You know how lucky we are to be together, right? How lucky you are to be with me?"

"Well, yes, certainly. I never dreamed that—"

"I can't imagine what would have happened to you if I hadn't found you. Your family was struggling, and I came along at just the right moment."

Something about his words was off, but surely that was only her ear. He had been nothing but good to her. "I suppose. Thank you."

She didn't know what else to say, and she felt more confused than anything. What had he saved her from? Being a spinster? Being Austin's wife?

That thought bloomed roses on her cheeks. Austin and her prairie home had been on her mind obsessively since she had moved to town. She dreamt of the prairie and her long walks on it. She dreamt of the smell of it and the taste of it. But if she was safer in town, then she must banish such thoughts from her head. She ought to count herself lucky. She had the finest of everything she could want. She hadn't been able to formulate how to ask about the college and courses yet, but she would.

William must have taken her flush for modesty or faintness, for he slid his hands gently down her arms to take her hands. "And you must be kept safe if you are carrying my child. It will be a boy, I'm certain."

Evelyn looked away and traced her eyes across the black-and-white tiles beneath her feet. She didn't know when or how to tell him that her monthly had come again, like clockwork. She didn't want to disappoint him, not when he was so happy.

"I hope for the same," she said.

"And how are you eating?" he asked.

No one had ever asked her that, nor had she given it much thought. She ate when she was hungry. She enjoyed her tea and pastries daily. "Well, I suppose," she replied.

"I have noticed you indulge during tea quite frequently."

She felt herself redden. "I didn't think it such an indulgence. I've been accustomed to taking my tea in a similar manner my entire life."

William gave her the smile that always filled her with relief. "I only want what is best for you, my dear. Will you take only tea today and no pastries?"

Her face was still red from, what, shame? She didn't want to disappoint her new husband. "Yes, of course."

"Thank you." He smiled and kissed her and then said his goodbyes before he left for the day.

His brand of concern confused her, as had his concern over her clothing when she moved in. Each day of the week dictated a certain form of dress, and she learned quickly not to misstep, or he might ignore her for the rest of the day, even when presented with a direct question or statement.

She wanted to enjoy the day though, and she hadn't seen Austin since her wedding. Town might not be safe, to William's reckoning, but she knew the prairie well. And surely her best friend would have some kind words for her. She ignored the seed of doubt that sprouted in her stomach. Surely he would.

She left out the kitchen door, not thinking about much other than getting to Austin's house. She soon realized that the outfit William had chosen for her that day was too cumbersome for walking in the squashy spring prairie. The skirts were absurdly full, and the boots, which had appeared as if they would be suitable for walking, soon proved not to be. But she was determined.

It was late in the morning by the time she reached the woods at the edge of Austin's property, coming up the cattle path that led through the stand of trees.

As she watched the smoke rise from the chimney, she knew Austin was somewhere around tending to his land. Evelyn wanted to stop, to turn and run. She felt the doubt again. There was no earthly reason why Austin would show her friendship after she had shunned him and married William. But he had never asked! At least not beyond a hypothetical.

Guilt and pride welled in her throat, but she trekked on, fighting the nausea that also threatened. He had to forgive her. After all they had done for each other, all the hope they had stored up together, he still had to be her friend. In her mind still was the warm fire winter after winter, watching the grey in his hair turn to white and her hands in his, becoming soft and wrinkled as time went on. She felt she was only play acting at being married, that it would not always be so.

She was without energy by the time she reached the kitchen door. She could already feel the blisters on her heels and toes. It had been too long since she had walked like that, and tears of frustration welled in her eyes.

Austin himself opened the door. Evelyn felt her hope dwindle at his stoic presence. She had gone too far.

"Evelyn."

"Will you invite me in?"

His eyes studied her. She had never known his eyes to be so without love for her. "You know I cannot. Evelyn, you hurt me."

"He is not good to me." The words felt bitter in her mouth.

"And how would you characterize your treatment of our friendship?"

She felt heat crawl up her neck and face. Going there had been a mistake. Why had she thought he would welcome her? She had not thought of their friendship, so why should she expect him to think of it now?

"I cannot help you, Evelyn Monroe. You made your choice, and now you must make the most of it. I know that is why you chose him, to make the most of your life. And now you can, with his wealth and his name and his children. You should be thankful." Austin summoned Patrick over. "Bring me Evan. I must take this lady home."

Fear licked at her insides as she turned away from Austin and stumbled down the steps.

"Do not trouble yourself with me then. I'll walk back, just as I came."

"I'll take you, Evelyn." His voice was gentler than she deserved. "Which way did you come?"

"The prairie way, through the cattle pasture."

"Unnoticed?"

"Unnoticed." She felt so small. Where was the man who had loved her drawings, had brought her back plants and flowers and seeds? Where was her prairie guardian?

He bade Evelyn climb atop Evan, which she did awkwardly—something else she was no longer used to. Evan turned his neck to see his other passenger and laid his ears back when he saw Evelyn.

"Easy, Evan. We're taking her home." The horse settled, and Austin eased him toward the Monroe estate. He kept his distance as respectful as he might to the woman who rode before him.

Evelyn didn't say a word on their journey back, merely pulled the hood of her cloak farther over her face. William would return, and she would make certain she was arranged in the front parlor at the piano or sketching at her desk. She didn't want to do either of those activities at the moment though.

Austin took them through the previous year's prairie grasses, and Evelyn saw from her perch that tiny new grasses were beginning to grow. The prairie had awoken early that year. She wanted to say so to Austin but didn't. He didn't want to know.

She wanted to exclaim that *Clematis fremontii* was emerging. Oh, just there! And there! Some of the plant's interesting seed heads had survived from the previous season. And there was devil's claw, a plant that brought no good omen, but could she jump down for a moment to take a specimen? But she did not. Could not, she realized with a shiver that seared her insides. She no longer had the freedom to do what she wanted. What she loved. She curled her hands inside her shawl to keep herself from pointing at the next half dozen plants she wanted to stop and examine.

The long drive up to the back of the estate appeared quicker than she expected. Had she dozed off atop Evan?

Austin had risked much even bringing her to the back door of her home, risked letting others in town see them together. That was enough. "I'm leaving you here. I trust you can find the rest of the way without difficulty."

Without a word, Evelyn let herself down from Evan's high shoulders. Without looking back, she made the walk up to the kitchen door, her face burning. At the door, she turned to see if Austin had watched her go, but no one was in the lane. Something twisted in her belly; he had gone already.

Once inside, Evelyn moved slowly about the quiet house, wondering where all the servants were, where the normal noises of a large home were. With sisters younger than herself, their home had always been full of laughter, singing, and music.

William decorated in dark greys, blues, and coal black. It was not as cheery as her home or as welcoming as Austin's. The chairs were stiff and unused, and the wallpaper stared back at her. The white-and-black marble in the foyer gleamed, though Evelyn gasped when she looked over the second-floor railing to the floor below.

A great pool of dark blood spread across the glossy surface. She gasped, transfixed by the sudden appearance of something so ghastly.

She was about to holler for someone, but the house staff walked through it as if it wasn't there. Evelyn came slowly down the stairs, not letting the apparition out of her sight.

She skirted the pool of blood, which looked like a red mirror. She didn't think it a coincidence that it had appeared when her monthly had come again. It grew with the fear that William would not think she was a good wife.

Before, her eyes had only seen wealth and potential opportunity. As she wandered from room to room, it seemed as if all the signs she had missed before were apparent. There were no books, no means for her to escape. William's study was a picture of neatness, the epitome of cleanliness. Before, she had seen the organization and a man who kept his business in order. He had courted her much the same way, following the protocol that was expected, bringing her trinkets and complimenting her and paying respectful visits to her family. He had so much charisma, so much charm, was always surrounded by so many people. Others loved him, spoke adoringly of him.

The house was so large that she found herself lost. There were no windows in the hall she stood in, only portraits of generations gone. They all bore the same shifting brown eyes of William Monroe and watched her down the hallway. She had no doubt they had all been like him.

And she, who was she? What became of the women who turned to ghosts in the shadow of their husbands, their fathers?

Evelyn was sitting at her vanity when William arrived home, unable to bring herself to be in the front parlor. She idly brushed her hair and stared into the mirror, looking for something there, searching Austin's hard eyes in her mind for a glimmer of the love he once had for her. She jumped when she saw William in the doorway, his frame filling her vision.

"Wife. You missed tea this afternoon with Lily Schneider. I expected to see you there."

Terror ran through her. She didn't want to displease him, and she didn't want him to know where she had been. "I was not told."

"You were not told? I'm not sure I believe that." He was behind her at the vanity, one hand resting on her shoulder.

Evelyn tried not to tense. William had never so much as raised a hand to her, but she didn't know what kind of a misstep this was to him. When had the Lady Schneider invited her for tea? She had not seen another lady in months.

William squeezed her shoulder, just to the point that it was uncomfortable. "It is no matter. I forgive you this . . . indiscretion."

She barely got out a thank-you before William squeezed her shoulder again and was gone from their room. The word settled hard somewhere deep inside her, and she rubbed her shoulder, which was hot and achy.

36

Olivia awoke with tears on her face and her mouth dry from crying out in the night. Why had Austin done that? Who would save Evelyn? The nightmare still played in her mind, lingered on the fringes of her consciousness. She had been reading Evelyn's journal too much, digging too far into the past. But on the nights that her mother needed her at the house, she wasn't going to say no. It didn't seem to matter to her brain that it was no longer the Weatherford home. The hallucinations and dreams were more intense there.

It was still dark out. She had not been asleep very long, and the bed beside her was cold. Why did she feel as if someone had been there, suffocating her?

Olivia crawled out of the damp sheets and went to the bathroom, cringing in the bright light. She was herself now when she was awake. Red crying streaks feathered under her eyes and on her temple, and deep marks trailed up her arms. When she looked down at herself, the marks were no longer there. She touched her arms cautiously, feeling for pain, but there was none. But she felt the curious presence in her mind, reminding her that some part of her at least thought those marks were real.

"Sleepy. I'm just sleepy," she said. A charm. The mirror agreed because nothing was there when she looked back. No burst capillaries from hard crying, no swelling, no Evelyn Monroe from her nightmares trying to get out.

Evelyn was not a happy woman during her marriage, and she had kept a journal. And the missing pages were, what? What did they say that someone had felt the need to tear them out?

Olivia wandered out into the quiet hall. Her body was tired, but her mind was not. She hoped she hadn't woken her mother with her cries. Daughter drama was the last thing her mother needed. The house was hushed though, and it didn't seem like her mother was awake. Olivia didn't want to go back to sleep, and a cup of peppermint tea sounded better by the moment. Becoming a tea person must be part of getting older—she had never liked it before. Simon's love of tea was contagious, it seemed.

She padded downstairs in her socks, going slowly over the familiar terrain of old wooden stairs to carpeted hall to the kitchen's wood floor. Her mom's cow clock ticked quietly over the sink as Olivia filled the electric kettle. Ever since her mother had begun boiling kettles dry, forgetting she had put water on for tea, the swap to an electric kettle that switched off after it was forgotten about was a safer choice.

The back porch light threw enough light into the kitchen that she was able to set herself up with a cup of hot water and a tea bag without turning on a light. The nightmare had receded, but the feeling it left was like going over a long-forgotten memory. It was soft around the edges but still strong enough that she could smell the perfume on the vanity before her.

Evelyn Monroe. William Monroe. Evelyn Weatherford. Austin Hearth. The names ran through her mind like a whispered spell, the cottonwoods out back a chorus binding it. She wasn't certain what it all meant, but learning that her home site was once the place where Evelyn

Monroe walked made her feel the woman's presence even if nothing was there.

And Austin.

She took her tea to the couch by the window and sat in a patch of moonlight that came through the trees in the front yard. It threw dancing shadows across her lap and the floor.

There was a soft knock at the front door, unobtrusive enough that it didn't terrify her, but it was two in the morning. Still, it seemed . . . expected. The nightmare should have left her feeling on edge, but it hadn't, and she went to the window in the front parlor almost in a dream state, pulling the lace curtains back to peer onto the porch.

The shock at seeing who was there was replaced almost immediately by a sense of relief and longing. So, he was safe.

She lingered at the window for a moment, watched the wind catch the trees harder than it caught the man's long cloak. Out of time. He was there, but he was living out of time. The notion came and went, and she found herself at the front door before she knew she had moved at all. She saw herself unlock and open it. The October breeze pressed against her, spinning itself around her. It smelled like prairie and smoke, horse and man. Austin stood there, tall and all man, but he was not imposing as he had been. Perhaps it was the shared presence in her mind or the feeling that she was only dreaming, and this dream was preferable to dreaming of an absent husband.

Olivia surprised herself by speaking first. "I learned today that this house was rebuilt. It burned down in 1903."

He nodded. "Yes, it did."

"Is it much different than you remember?"

He looked from the porch to the front door, and Olivia caught the scent of smoke again, stronger this time. She shivered.

"Much. The home I remember was built of limestone, but the porch was this size and held a little white table just over there for the ladies to have their tea in the shade. The land remains the same though, and one inhabitant, it seems, has not left."

Evelyn.

Austin spoke the name, though his lips did not move.

"Would you like to come in?" Dream Olivia needn't be scared of anything.

"Please," Austin said and followed her into the front parlor.

Olivia reclaimed her spot on the couch in the moonlight and was relieved when Austin took the chair a modest distance from her but close enough that they could still converse quietly. If she wanted, she could reach out and touch his sleeve, which looked dusty.

"Can I . . ." She stopped herself.

He smiled. "You were going to ask if I wanted tea."

"Yes, I'm sorry."

"Not to worry. Old habits are hard to change."

They sat in silence and watched each other. Olivia sipped her warm tea and eased further into the dream feeling. It felt like she was sitting with an old friend, like when Ann had been gone to visit her family in Pennsylvania and then came back, and they needed to catch up. Except . . . more.

She studied his face in the blue moonlight. It was far clearer than it had been even when she had met him at the art department.

Austin broke the silence. "I heard your cries from the road."

Olivia froze, the teacup at her lips. Not dreaming. "You did?"

"Yes. I was out riding, feeling the old places. I heard your nightmare, heard you moving about the house, and I wanted to see you again, on more even ground."

Olivia looked at the clock on the mantel. "It's two in the morning."

"Is the time important?"

"Oh. Well, no, I suppose not. I was awake."

They watched each other again for a time. Olivia expected to feel tension at some point but didn't.

"Why are you . . . back?" It didn't seem like the right word, but it would have to do.

"Because he's back."

She assumed he meant the headless rider, whom he had called an imposter. "Why is he back?"

"Because I am."

The circular notion did not sit well with her. "Who came back first?"

"I don't know." Austin shifted in his chair, and Olivia thought his form shivered, like a hologram in a sci-fi movie.

"More things move in the night than just us, Miss," Austin said into Olivia's frustrated silence.

For some reason it brought to mind the headless man at the foot of her bed and the gargoyle thing at the Monroe house. Had the headless man been Austin or the imposter? She didn't want to know. It terrified her in a way that even her mother's psychotic episodes hadn't. Those could be controlled, dimmed, with Valium, Klonopin. This had no dimmer switch, no easily poppable pill to calm the noise. Valium didn't even make a dent in this terror.

"And the only way out is through." The statement came unbidden, from somewhere in her she hadn't wanted to explore.

Austin looked at her with his head tilted slightly, like a puppy. He looked as endearing as one, she thought, when he wasn't battling a nightmare horse. "Yes. Yes, I suppose it's the only way."

Olivia moved cautiously, reaching out to touch Austin's dusty sleeve. He watched her, unmoving.

She pressed the fabric between her thumb and forefingers. It was soft and warm. It looked like the cloak of a man who took care of his possessions but who also enjoyed comfort and familiarity. And it felt real. That was the most important part.

She felt Austin's eyes on her as she trailed her fingers up the forearm of his cloak, listening to the sound it made under her fingers. Not dreaming. Not crazy.

Her fingers ventured back to the cuff of his cloak. There was a cufflink there in the shape of a gold horseshoe.

"For Evan," Austin said huskily.

Olivia hummed her assent, still lost in absorbing that she wasn't dreaming. The horseshoe felt solid under her fingers and still cool from Austin's ride there.

She paused when she reached the edge of his cuff. She would touch him, or she wouldn't. Those were her only two choices.

She did, breath held.

And he felt like a man. Any other man. She could feel the little hairs on the top of his hands, the rough skin of his knuckles. He was warm, and she could swear she felt a heartbeat under her fingers.

Images played through her head. They were jumbled, out of focus, but his hands were in all of them.

Olivia looked up at him, tears threatening. A feeling that accompanied those images came from the same place she could hear the voice inside her. It was a feeling she'd chased her entire adult life but felt closed off from with each relationship that didn't work.

"Are you real? A ghost? I don't understand."

Austin looked back at her, and the place with the musical voice ached for him in a way Olivia herself had never ached for another person in her life. It was foreign and overwhelming, but she wanted to dive headfirst into it, be consumed by it.

"Aren't we all ghosts, Miss Olivia? Are we not all pale versions of our ancestors, moving through life and trying to become?"

"I don't know my ancestors."

"I think you do," Austin replied, taking her hand.

The images came faster then. One after the other, she felt and saw and heard a torrent of places and people. Austin was there and the man called Mr. Monroe and two girls who looked like her who giggled and laughed as they played the piano while she watched. She saw an older boy too but only for a moment before she saw his face, grey and cold, being placed in a coffin. The photographs of the dead boy reared up. Ethan. Gone before his prime. She saw her hands before her, pressing points of barbed wire into the meat of her fingers, her palms. She felt the pain of it as clear as day.

Austin squeezed her hand, then released it, and the flood abated. She stared at him for another long, quiet moment.

"I want to help you," she stated. It seemed such a simple wish in the hush and calm of the night.

He smiled sadly at her. "I want to protect you from what has come, to finish what was started. And I want to rest easily. But not until you and she are safe."

Olivia nodded and took her mug of tea again; she didn't know what to do with her hands. She wanted and didn't want the images back. When they flooded her, she felt no anxiety, only peace, even for the sadness of some of the things she saw. When the owner of the lovely voice inside her felt something, Olivia wanted to let her drive again. But most of all, she was grateful for the help that he offered.

"Thank you," she said, then stood. Austin stood with her. Old fashioned but not unexpected. "I need to go to bed now."

"Yes, you do," Austin said. "I'll see myself out."

There was the ghostliness, if she could accept it. She thanked Austin again and padded back through the house and up the stairs. The dream state lingered, but for the moment, she felt at peace with everything.

Once in her room, she looked outside into the moonlit yard and saw the retreating figure of a man on horseback riding away from the house. He looked dark blue in the moonlight, but the horse's fur caught the silver of the moon on its back and tail.

Olivia watched them until they disappeared into the night prairie. Sound memories of the way the brown grasses kissed a horse's legs and a man's feet in stirrups when the wind still filled her ears. A desperate urge to photograph the moment rushed through her. She hugged herself, felt the soft cotton of an old-fashioned nightgown against her skin as she crawled into bed. She didn't fight it. It felt good.

Her sleep was punctuated by snippets of conversation from the voice in her head. The woman told her that she was there for good, that she was there to see things through, that she was there for Austin. Olivia told her that everything sounded fine, just fine, and then her sleep was dreamless.

37

Wednesday, October 14th

The events of the night before were so dreamlike that Olivia almost discounted them. But her mug had been where she left it by the couch in the front room, one of Austin's horseshoe cufflinks sitting next to it. Olivia picked it up and put it in her pocket. Real. Not crazy.

The musical voice was quiet that morning, but Olivia was OK with that. Thinking about it in the morning when the spell of the night had worn off made her see it differently. She didn't want it to be like the Monroe house again, where she had no control. Had she accidentally acquired a ghost when she went into that house? Could one catch spirits like one caught a cold? Was it like a virus that needed to run its course?

She finished another print that day, and this time no horse greeted her in it. She had not developed the film from the Monroe house yet though. That was still too close. Perhaps the horse was gone now that she had seen him in real life.

When she wrapped up at the studio, she decided she needed to get into the dugout to see what was buried in the back. If the journal had been there, there was no telling what other treasures it held.

The phone rang a dozen times before her mother answered. A hurriedness to her voice put Olivia on edge. They had had a good evening together the day before, and when Olivia had left for campus that morning, her mother was in quiet but good spirits. It was almost impossible to know what had set her off, but Olivia would bet money she hadn't taken her meds yet that morning. Olivia would have to check the pill minder when she got there that afternoon.

"What? I'm busy." It sounded like another episode was imminent. Olivia hated to aggravate her mother even more, but this was too important to go unasked.

"I just have a few questions"

"Someday you're just not going to come home, and you won't take care of me, and no one will be here anymore. Someday it will happen; you'll see." The line crackled, and Olivia thought that if the connection went dead, she wouldn't be unhappy. Her mother's episodes often led to days or weeks of unhappiness and depression. But as much as she wanted to disconnect and get away from them, she would have to stay out there on weeknights if necessary to make sure her mother didn't drive off without her GPS tracker or start another fire with the damn stove.

"Mom, sit down and have some tea. Do some knitting. It would be nice to have a scarf this winter. You're so good at knitting." It was true, and the constant repetition of the stitches helped her mother with her other fixations, calmed them somewhat. Nothing had ever gone completely away, and medication could only do so much, but at least she functioned better now.

"Yes, I could do that. I'll knit you a scarf. Did you want to ask me something? The weather was awful today. So rainy. So grey. I wish the sun would come out. Do you know how long the sun has been away, Olivia? It feels like forever."

Olivia took a deep breath and held it for a few moments, then let it out slowly and prepared herself for the inevitable outburst. "It will be sunny tomorrow, Mom. And . . . I know Evelyn Weatherford lived on our land. Why didn't you want to talk to me about it the other day?"

Silence on the other end of the phone. Olivia nearly hung up but checked her phone and saw that the call had not been disconnected. Her mother was just sitting on the other end of the line, not speaking. After listening for a moment, her heart starting to crawl up the back of her throat, Olivia opened her mouth to say something, but her mother's voice returned.

"Where did you hear that name, young lady?" Her mother's voice was angry, with more than a touch of fear. "Tell me where you heard it."

Olivia's stomach churned. Why was she so nervous? "I was in the archives at work. I saw some photos, just came across them, really. I did some research. They were of Evelyn Weatherford and Austin Hearth. Do you know those names?"

Olivia's mom let out a rush of air. "Who told you to talk to me? Why should I know anything? I only know what I've heard. Why? Do you think I know something? Do you think I have all the answers?"

"Relax. I'm not trying to harass you or anything. I'm just curious." Olivia opened the envelope she had put some of the photographs in, dropping them onto her lap and sifting through them. The faces looked back at her, trying to tell her their story. What were they hiding? What awful secret had torn them apart?

"I don't know anything." There was that pitch again at the end.

"Mom, please. I need to know."

"Why? Why do you need to know? Did someone make you ask me? I won't talk to anyone else."

"It's just me. I'm worried. I think . . . well, I don't know." Could she really be related to the woman in the photographs? The resemblance was close, though the focus was never great on the old photographs no matter how still they held the camera. They had the same figure, the same high cheekbones and arch of their eyebrows. If they were related, Olivia would have to do a lot of digging.

"I shouldn't be talking to you about this at all. It will stir up old things. Do you know what happens when you stir up the old dust, daughter? Do you know?" Her mother's tone had changed, become chillier. Olivia looked up, feeling someone watching her. No one was there, but the feeling lingered.

"What do you mean by 'old dust'?"

Her mother's voice dropped to a whisper. "The dead. The dead. Don't you know they listen? They're hearing us right now, listening to our conversation. They watch us all the time to make sure we're not overstepping our boundaries. Haven't you listened? Don't you hear?"

This was not her rational mother speaking, but she had heard. And saw. Olivia tried to speak and found that her mouth had gone dry. She tried to clear her throat, but her voice was still rough when she spoke. "Mom, are you OK?"

"Evelyn Weatherford had lots of babies. They're still living here."

"She did? But am I related to her? Mom, please tell me. Is she my great-great-aunt or a cousin or something? She looks just like me." The photographs sitting in her lap watched her quietly, though she felt they were bursting with secrets and information that she could unlock with just a few answers from her mother. Her mother would have told her if she were related to someone like that though, wouldn't she? Unless it really wasn't relevant, though Olivia thought it had to be.

There was silence on the other end, though Olivia could hear her mother breathing heavily a few moments later. Things could get dangerous, and quickly. "Mom, listen, just forget I asked. I'll do some research at the library or something."

"No, no, you asked. You asked me about Evelyn Weatherford. Evelyn Monroe. *Evelyn Hearth.*" The last part came out in a hiss.

Olivia stopped breathing. E. H. Evelyn Hearth. "Did you say Evelyn Hearth? Like, Austin and Evelyn Hearth?"

"No, no I didn't." Pitched high. Lie. Frenzy had taken over her mother, who continued before Olivia could get another word in. "You need to watch out, daughter. Someone is looking for you. Someone is still looking for Evelyn. I know it's true. It has to be . . ."

"Mom, can you . . ." Olivia tried to interject, but her mother had hung up on her.

She stopped short of throwing her phone across the room in frustration.

Evelyn Hearth.

Idiot. That's what Olivia was. Evelyn might have read *Wuthering Heights* and thought it a fine idea to copy. Or maybe it was what normal girls did when they liked a boy, play at using what would be their married initials.

She turned over her thoughts on the drive out to her mother's house. *(The Weatherford estate*, something whispered within her.)

Evelyn Hearth.

But Evelyn Weatherford had married William Monroe. She was never Evelyn Hearth. The Monroe name followed her into the grave.

Olivia compulsively reached up behind herself to turn on the dome light for the back seat. Though it was simply a grey late afternoon, the light illuminated the entire back seat and floor. She checked it quickly. Nothing there. But she didn't feel alone anymore, even on the quiet rural drive.

When she arrived at the house, her mother gave her the cold shoulder. Olivia could feel her stare from across the kitchen as she set up a mug of tea. The woman said nothing, just snatched the tea and scone that Olivia offered her. She would check her mother's pill minder later. Now wasn't a good time.

In the den next to where her mother was set up with her knitting and her tea, a mess of books torn from the shelves caught Olivia's eye.

“What the fuck, Mom?” she muttered as she scooped the books into a manageable pile. She paused before she shut the cover of the first encyclopedia. The inscription read: “To Everly, Happy 5th Birthday! Love, Nana and Pop Pop.

“Mom?” Olivia called. “Who’s Everly?”

No sound from the other room except the TV.

“Mom, I know you heard me!”

“Oh, I picked those up at a garage sale years ago. Saw that too. Don’t know who she is.” Her voice pitched high. Lie.

Olivia was about to challenge her mother when she saw paper sticking out of at least five other volumes. She snatched at the various pieces, some of which turned out to be envelopes, and hoped her mother didn’t appear suddenly. Whatever it was, someone had hidden it, and her mother had wanted her to find it. (Or Evelyn, another part of her mind suggested.) The paper went into the large pocket on the side of her camera bag for later perusal.

Still nothing from her mother on the other side of the wall. She stuffed the books back on the shelf as quickly as she could and then headed outside. If her mother wouldn’t give her answers, she would have to figure it out on her own.

The dugout was in what could have been called their backyard at one point, close enough to the house that she could still see the lights from the kitchen but far enough away that she had to pick her way through scrubby trees and underbrush. She had steered clear of it as a child—if not for fear of being crushed by the unsound structure then for the fear her mother’s shrill warnings about it instilled in her. She grabbed a flashlight on the way out the back door.

From the front it didn’t look too bad. Old, clearly, but not falling apart like she remembered it. Childhood memories had a way of twisting sometimes though. Happy times felt happiest and scary bits felt scariest.

The limestone archway was worn with time, but every stone was in place. What she assumed was the original glass was still on the two windows on either side of the archway. Had the Weatherfords really built it to live in before they moved into the grand house she had seen in the photograph? It seemed wrong for people who must have been so wealthy to live in such a tiny shelter for so long. She couldn't fathom it.

The more she stared at the outside of the dugout, the more she felt like she was walking through a fairy door. That wasn't something she had thought about even in childhood. There was too much going on with her mother for playing fantasy. She had to feed herself or not eat. She wondered sometimes if things would have been easier or harder on her mother if she hadn't had Olivia.

Scrubby prairie bushes had grown up over the top of the dugout, and the closer she moved toward the door, the less she could see of the house. Even the sound of the wind disappeared once she was just inside the doorway.

The dugout might have been charming on the outside, but it was gross inside. There wasn't a better word for it. As her eyes adjusted to the dim light, it appeared she was standing in something that was part storage shed, part rat house, and part junk trap.

From where she stood, she saw a jumble of ancient bicycles. They leaned against an earthen wall to her right, mixed with a rotting wood table and piles of leaves that might house something still living. She hoped it wasn't a skunk or a possum. She could live without running into either of those creatures again. Impossible on the prairie, but she could hope.

Newspapers were everywhere and from nearly every year imaginable. She reached down for a handful and caught 1946, 1974, and 1988 all in the same grab. She carefully extracted a brittle 1934 paper and set it on the ledge of the window to her left. If she looked at everything, she would be in there for a month and never emerge.

She scooped up books as she went, trying to pile them up, but there was so much stuff everywhere. It was a hoarder's dream. Had her mother gathered things for the box just by walking in and taking an armful?

It seemed to go on forever, and the humidity of the day disappeared the farther she went. The depth was a trick of the light, and she was grateful for the lack of humidity. But when she looked behind her, the doorway seemed rather far, like standing at the end of a fun house tunnel.

She turned around and kept going. What appeared to be a long hallway led back somewhere, likely to another room. She turned on the flashlight, trying to see what she was stepping on and around. The crunchy bits were hard to ignore, but mice and rats probably died in there all the time. Just mice and rats. She could handle those.

Something that sounded like glass crunched under her foot. Sifting through the good inch of fine dust and silt, she discovered an ancient framed photograph. It was Austin and Evelyn sitting atop the horse she had seen with Austin in the fog and with Austin on the prairie the other night. She had broken the glass with her careless footstep, but the photograph was still intact. She dumped the glass toward the far side of the earthen hallway and inspected the picture. They were on the prairie on a day that didn't move their clothes or the horse's tail very much. Good photography weather for the time. Olivia imagined a traveling photographer had taken the picture, judging by the odd location.

Traveling photographers had once been very popular, and a few had even put together photo books of the Midwest. The most prominent one she knew of worked mostly in Oklahoma, but it didn't surprise her that he or one of his comrades had headed north in search of clients. She flipped the picture over. William S. Prettyman's name graced the back. So, she was right.

A noise farther back in the dugout made her jerk her head up and shine her light that direction. Thoughts of the gargoyle thing at the Monroe house featured prominently in her imagination.

"Who's there?" she called.

Just more rustling.

Reaching down, she grabbed a piece of wood that might've belonged to a piece of furniture. She tossed it toward the noise, into the dark. She heard a rapid succession of squeaking sounds, more rustling, then quiet.

Only mice.

On edge, she shuffled through the deepening pile of leaves, dirt, and debris. She was determined to reach the back of the dugout. Something was back there for her; she knew it. There was no longer any light from the front of the dugout, due to the sun setting or because she was so far back in it, she didn't know.

At the end of the hall was a room, cool and dry. She could only just see the far wall with her flashlight. The junk and stuff was piled high, but there were fewer leaves. It was more of a storage situation, and it looked like someone had recently disturbed the piles.

It was the likeliest spot where her mother had been, but when had she been out there? Guilt hit Olivia. She was her mother's legal guardian. It scared her to think her mother had been out there unattended, seconds away from hurting herself every five steps.

An old trunk in the corner grabbed her attention, and she waded toward it through bits of furniture and a large wheel from what may have been an early bicycle.

Penny farthing, the voice deep in her brain offered.

"I don't want you here right now," she said. Something about inviting an invisible someone else into that place scared her more than being there alone.

After the cloud of dust dissipated from opening the trunk, she examined its contents. A clutter of photographs, books, and paper looked up at her. One of the trunk's sides was collapsed, and if there wasn't mice damage, Olivia would be surprised.

She pulled up a stool that still looked somewhat sturdy and started sifting. Everything made her stomach clench up in emotions that she could not name. Perhaps they belonged to the voice.

She found photographs of Austin and his horse. They were outside by a barn. The horse's coat gleamed, its mane and tail brushed and moving slightly in the wind.

Olivia fell in love with photography again right there sitting in the dugout with a bunch of old, musty photographs in her lap. The emotion that was captured in the photographs held no flame to anything else.

There he was again with his horse, sitting astride the giant animal with his riding gear and a long black cloak that was guarding against flying snow that partially obscured the photograph and affected the camera's focus. An unspoken accord existed between the two that Olivia could feel coming off the photo paper despite the clarity issue.

She took another handful of photographs from the box and sifted through them. More photographs of Austin and Evelyn. The picture was taken during the fall as the pair sat outside on the porch of what appeared to be the Weatherford home, immortalized there and at the historical society before flames took it.

Evelyn was elegant in her white dress and overcoat, a cup of tea in her graceful hands. She sat next to Austin, who smiled at something Olivia imagined the woman said. The pair seemed to be enjoying themselves on the porch, which one of the figures had been standing on the night before. And the other figure? Her ghost voice was quiet.

She flipped the photograph over with some trepidation. "Sissy," she read slowly, "and Mr. Hearth. Taken with Sissy's camera on May tenth, eighteen ninety-seven."

She recalled the photographs of the Weatherford girls in the basement of the art department. What had happened to them? Maybe she could ask Colton at their meeting. For being the proprietor of the historical society, Mr. Fullbright didn't seem very forthcoming. The photograph had everyone accounted for when she turned it back over.

A flash of the previous night's images came back to her. Two girls giggling at a piano while she watched. There had been a sketchbook in her hands, a drawing of a plant being worked on. It was not colored in yet. She goaded her sisters—yes, her sisters!—into playing a lively tune, something that would keep them all laughing. The ache for the images came back, and Olivia knew then, without a doubt, that it belonged to the voice inside her.

What of it was true, and what was legend? What was fabricated because it made a good story? Did it matter? Who had stuffed these things in there before the fire? Or were they already there?

More answers begot more questions.

Somewhere far off, she heard someone call her name. She thought it was her musically voiced inhabitant, but after a moment, she recognized her mother.

"I'm in the dugout!" she called back. She felt like she was disturbing something. "I'm sorry," she whispered to whatever was there. She thought she heard a *Hmm . . .* in response, but surely it was just the wind at the front of the dugout.

Her mother called her name again, and Olivia reached into the trunk and grabbed an armful of papers and books. She put it all into a wooden crate and then set the stack of photographs close to the top, sandwiched inside a book cover to keep them somewhat safe.

Hide it, the voice whispered. *Keep it safe.*

Olivia grabbed a molding blanket to cover the top of the crate, obeying the voice without another thought.

Regardless of what Simon was busy with, he had to know what was going on, and she wanted to know his version of events. It seemed more than a few versions existed, but they had to diverge from some common intersection. They all had to have true threads.

"Daughter!" her mother admonished when Olivia emerged from the dugout. Even the twilight seemed too bright, and Olivia squinted in the dying light.

"I'm sorry, Mom. I didn't think you knew I was out here."

"Don't you think I can feel when someone is going through my things!"

Her things?

"Mom, it's just some old junk. I want to go through it."

Her mother tried to peer into the box, but the blanket prevented her. It felt odd to hide something from her mother, but Olivia was glad she had listened to the voice.

"Fine," her mother finally conceded.

Olivia managed to escape from the house, but something from the dugout had followed her. The musical voice was louder now, and she saw a haze around her vision. She texted Simon to see if he could meet with her, but texting was difficult—she struggled with it.

She moved through the fog that clouded her vision. Driving by the gym, she saw that the practice fields and tennis courts were no longer there, nor was the parking lot or the cars. A lone horseback rider made his way down the dusty road toward the limestone building, which looked much newer. Wooden structures lined the road around it.

Campus was worse. The fog in her mind was denser. She finally found the parking lot, but the engineering building wasn't where it ought to be near that lot. Olivia put her head down and hurried onto campus. She knew the buildings would still be there.

"Simon," she said as she entered his office. He lifted his head. There was that look again, the one where his eyes looked darker. She hesitated. "I want to know everything you know about the Weatherfords. And the Monroes." She didn't mention the Hearths. She wanted to keep her secret for the moment. She wanted to keep the box in her car a secret too.

"What do you know so far?" he asked. It didn't surprise her that he knew she had been digging. She could tell he had been digging too. At what she wasn't certain.

"Enough to see how convoluted everything is. No one I ask can give me a straight answer, and I want a straight answer." She curled up in the chair by the window but still close enough to reach out and touch him if she wanted. Close like Austin the other night. The memory of his warm touch was strange and pulled on strings that were connected to the musical voice in her head. She tucked her legs under herself, and her long skirts pooled around her to the floor. The corset was loose but still made her sit up straighter. Simon looked at her in silence. Did he see it too? It was still unclear what was only her imagination.

"What I know is likely convoluted too, you know," he said finally. "By something I've contacted too."

She watched Simon's eyes carefully. All brown. "Do you think it'll ever leave?"

"I don't know."

The feeling that a corset was digging into her sides made her sit up straighter again, and she forgot exactly what she meant to ask him. Something about what he meant about the *something I've contacted too.* "You've researched the history more than anyone though," Olivia said. "Surely you know something."

Simon scrubbed at his beard and over his eyes. He looked exhausted. She reached out and placed her hand on his knee. He ran his fingers over hers. The owner of the musical voice recoiled inside her, and Olivia winced at the sharp pain it brought on just over her right eye. Dear God, maybe it *was* a tumor.

"Where should I start?" Simon asked.

"The beginning maybe? I don't know how far back that goes."

Simon left her hand to reach for his French press. "Coffee?"

"Tea, please. You know what I like."

He raised an eyebrow at her, then poured himself coffee, got Olivia's tea going, and launched into the story.

"The Weatherford family is among the oldest in the area. Evelyn Weatherford's father was the first lawyer in town and held a kind of dual position with Monroe the Senior, who founded the town with his father. He was replaced by William Monroe upon retirement near the turn of the century. He was the wealthiest man out here, just ahead of the Weatherfords. That is the briefest of brief summaries of where this all began."

"What were they doing in Podunk Warren? There wasn't anything out here then, was there?" Olivia held the delicate teacup and saucer in her lap. It would turn back into an earthenware mug at any moment, certainly.

Simon watched the teacup himself. It was a little better to know that someone else saw her delusions. Or pretended to. She needed to ask him about the other night. He must have seen.

"Not much, but land was booming, and the wealthy out here could have more at a lower price. Meaning they wanted to be out in the middle of nowhere." Simon grabbed a book from the shelf behind him and opened it to a bookmarked page. He showed it to her. "This is Evelyn Weatherford, with whom it seems you have become well-acquainted."

There was the haunting Evelyn, who looked just like her. "We could be twins."

"Mmm . . . hmm," Simon assented, dragging his eyes over her. It set an instant fire between her legs, and she wanted to let him have her right there. They watched each other, gauging each other's gaze back and forth.

Olivia forced herself to calm down. "Concentrate," she whispered to Simon, and the grin he returned sent her into pleasurable shivers.

"She was the oldest of the Weatherford daughters and as hauntingly beautiful as you," Simon began. "A certain Austin Hearth set his designs on her. They had known each other since they were children, but she was from the Weatherford family, and while he found himself careening into the upper class, it wasn't the upper class that the 'upper class' really considered upper class, if you know what I mean. It was the turn of the century though, and they might've had a chance."

"I know she married William Monroe."

"Yes, that happened later on. Evelyn and Austin grew closer, and when you would have expected a marriage proposal, there was none. And then there was tragedy, as there often was around those kinds of places at that time. Without antibiotics, so many things killed so many people who otherwise would have lived. Evelyn lost her only brother to an infection caused by an accident or maybe just the accident; it's hard to know for certain. But during that tumultuous time, our Mr. Monroe swooped in to 'help' her and her family."

"Ah, opportunity."

"Yes, that." Simon was in his element now. "Mr. Hearth got jealous, and who wouldn't? He had done well for himself, but no one could compete against the good Mr. Monroe, his wealth, and his family. Here Mr. Hearth had been friends with the lovely Evelyn for many years, and all it took to sweep her away was one good deed and a little charm."

Olivia thought about all the photographs of Austin and Evelyn she had come across in her digging. And the photograph of Ethan Weatherford. Was he down there in the archives waiting for her? She pressed her thumbnail into her index finger and tried to concentrate on that instead.

"So, Monroe and Evelyn were married," Simon continued. "The wedding was huge, as you would expect, and Monroe was the perfect doting newlywed. Evelyn is full Mona Lisa in all the photographs from the wedding though. I can't say whether she was happy or not. You'd have to ask her."

Olivia felt a jolt at that. "You know," she breathed.

Simon studied her with eyes which looked darker. "I had a guess. And your shifting outfit is, well, rather a tell."

Evelyn was silent on the matter. Either listening or elsewhere, Olivia didn't know. The flowing skirts were back though, so she couldn't be far. Olivia adjusted them over her knees and felt the petticoats slide between her thighs. Soft leather boots were laced halfway up her calves. Lace cascaded over her wrists and hands. But she felt sore, tired. The purple and blue of a bruise was feathered over one hand, appearing, then fading.

Simon said nothing more about her changing appearance and continued the story. "The details are hazy after that. No one knows for certain what was going on in the Monroe household, whether it was happy or not. But at some point, Evelyn began seeing Mr. Hearth."

"The journal . . ." Olivia began.

Simon flinched. "Yes. It's quite clear to me now how unhappy it was. I don't know if that was a product of Evelyn beginning to see Mr. Hearth or if those . . . things were happening already. I can't say."

Anger rose in Olivia. It was clear to her that Monroe had mistreated Evelyn from the beginning and that she loved Austin and wanted an escape through him. And here Simon was almost defending Monroe, or at least not condemning him. She lifted her chin. "So, then what?"

"So, it went on for years, and William and Evelyn had children. Monroe discovered the affair a few years into things and was rightfully angry. He confronted Mr. Hearth on multiple occasions, and their meetings got uglier as time passed." Simon paused and pressed his fingers to his temples. "I'm sorry, these tension headaches are getting worse. Migraines. Whatever they are."

Olivia reached out a hand to touch his shoulder and then paused. Had the mood of the room just changed? But it seemed just like Simon still, reaching into his desk for some Excedrin. She ran her fingers over his shoulder, soothing. "I've been stressed lately too." Understatement.

Simon laughed, then took the pills with the last of his coffee and poured another cup, adding a few sugar cubes. "Astute observation. Where was I? Ah, yes. The ugly part. Monroe challenged Mr. Hearth to a duel in September of 1903, very old fashioned even for the time, but we're in Bumfuck, Kansas. The purpose of the duel, you know, was to kill, but when shots were fired, Mr. Hearth—on purpose or because he was a bad shot; we don't know—only hit Monroe in the shoulder. Monroe missed completely. Enraged, Monroe left the gunfight, forfeiting, and Mr. Hearth headed back home.

"Monroe did not see a doctor to have the bullet removed. We think he knew it would kill him eventually. But not long after, in a rage, Monroe went and retrieved an axe, a shotgun, and his wife. There were enough people in town that they asked questions. You see, Monroe had not been so quiet about everything that was going on. Monroe shamed Evelyn publicly for her adultery, and an angry mob formed. Monroe, for whatever reason, called them off and wanted to deal with the issue himself. It was *personal* at that point, and Monroe was out for revenge."

Simon sipped his coffee, and Olivia felt his eyes on her over the cup. Were his eyes red tinged, or was that just a trick of the light? Yes, the tenor had changed, and the voice in her head set off an alarm.

This is not your man looking back at you! It took William too!

Olivia was in the far corner of Simon's office, hopelessly blocked from the door if she needed to run. She tried to return his stare with a little smile. Something disarming. "Tell me what happened next."

Simon smiled, and she had no doubt that it was no longer him. "I think you know, love, but we're telling a story, and you're being an awfully good listener."

Olivia curled up farther back in the chair. Simon was too close for comfort, just an arm's reach away. *Danger!* the soft voice in her head cried. She tried to remain calm, to keep her face composed, but the feeling that she was trapped made the animal in her ready to run. "I'd like to hear you tell the rest, please," she said softly.

A softer smile spread across the person who was not Simon. "So polite. You may certainly hear the end of the story, sweet girl. It's perfect for bedtime. And we'll keep the pronouns consistent for the sake of the story, but this is where I got quite involved. Forgive me if I slip up.

"Monroe hunted Mr. Hearth down at the canyon crossing, and this shot, this shot was quite good. He seriously maimed the man and knocked him from his horse, who was awfully protective. Awfully. Austin tried to hide Evelyn but not well. We scooped her up from her hidey hole while Austin was God knows where tending to the holes in his body. Then Monroe, axe, shotgun, and woman in tow, rode out to find where Austin got to with those buckshot wounds. He found him ambling down the road toward his house on his gallant steed. Evelyn tried to shout a warning, but Monroe shoved her off the horse instead, raised his shotgun, and fired at the not-so-distant rider.

"I was a little reckless with that shot; let's be honest. But when you're *that mad*, well, it's hard to concentrate. Austin and his horse were a little maimed by the shot but not much. It was rather a long shot, but then we saw Austin struggling to decide whether he should come try to save his woman or run for the hills with the bleeding he had going on. Monroe settled that by riding after him, Austin turned tail and rode up a hill. Evelyn was safe on the road, but she followed. She had to know what would happen.

"We ended up at the cliffs. Your stomping ground, little lady."

"How do you . . . "

"How do I know where you live?" he asked. "I don't have time for stupid questions. So, Austin had one knee to the ground, slowly bleeding to death by the time Evelyn came running up the hill, looking frightened, dusty, and beautiful. And you know what happened next, darling?"

Olivia had been holding her breath. She let it out and drew a shaky one. "Yes," she whispered.

Not Simon's eyes glimmered. "You know, it takes more than one swing to take off another man's head, even for the extra strength William had found in me. Miss Evelyn came running up just before the first swing. Oh, the look in their eyes, to see each other like that for the final time. Miss Olivia, it was divine."

Olivia looked away as bile rose in her throat. The story, true or not, struck her somewhere vulnerable. When she looked back, Not Simon watched at her with a strange look on his face. He watched her for another moment, maybe reading her; she couldn't tell, but she couldn't keep the emotion from her face.

He cleared his throat. "Beheaded, yes. And kicked his body over the edge. Did you know his horse went down there after him? Such loyalty."

She imagined the magnificent animal tumbling down the cliffs. To go after its owner to certain death, that was devotion. She shivered. But in those few moments before certain death? She couldn't think about it.

When she looked back at Simon, his eyes were brown again. When had that happened? She still felt wary, but the animal urge to run had gone with the man's red eyes.

"Pardon me," he said. "It appears that time has gotten away from me."

Olivia wondered if bolting for the door was an option again. The skirts looked to be gone for now, as did the delicate teacup. But it was only a matter of time before they returned, she thought with some trepidation. And likely only a matter of time before Not Simon returned, and not in so good of a mood. Even for all that, she wanted to know what happened.

"It's OK," she said. "You can keep going."

"Where did I leave off?" She heard another question in his voice, but she wasn't ready to answer it.

"Um . . ." Olivia was chilled. Where had Simon stopped and Not Simon begun? "Um, William discovered the affair."

Simon cleared his throat and continued. "Again, we don't know for certain what happened, but legend goes something like this. After Monroe killed Mr. Hearth, Mr. Hearth's spirit didn't rest easily, and Evelyn was once again caught in the crosshairs of Monroe's rage."

"He hadn't forgiven her for what she had done."

"And would never. The children . . . disappeared, for lack of a better word. Without a trace. We assume they were killed too. It left Evelyn heartbroken, as you can imagine. This began only days after Mr. Hearth's death. And then the tale takes a supernatural twist."

There it was. Olivia's stomach twisted in anticipation.

"Monroe had many cousins and close family living in town. Two cousins who went out for a ride one morning never returned. Their horses were found wandering near the cliffs. The fog was blamed initially. Spooked the horses.

"Then another cousin disappeared, only to reappear a day later, raving. He said he had been walking, and a headless figure on horseback chased him to the cliffs. He made it away by, supposedly, climbing a tree. A little comical, but he was found hanging from the same tree a week later. Joke was on him, I suppose.

"Monroe's brother, it is said, met the headless figure on a bridge at the edge of town. They got into a gunfight, and Monroe's brother was shot in the heart. He died claiming he was killed by a headless man carrying an unusual antique gun and an axe.

"Every living relative of Monroe's, as far as we know, was killed during the month of October 1903 or perished suspiciously. You want to talk about a town that felt terrorized? The reports of the time are absolutely sensational, and even the more rational explanations for the deaths seem absurd.

"And finally, the last were Monroe's mother, father, and a sister. But a few days before Halloween, legend has it that a headless rider overtook their carriage, killed the driver, and drove the horses, slathered and sweating, down the town's main thoroughfare to the outskirts of town, right over the cliff where he himself had been killed."

Olivia unclenched her hands. She had gotten caught up in the excitement of the story. "This all happened?"

"They all died then, yes. What is legend and what is factual, well, that's been a matter of some debate for the last century. Warren's most prized cold cases. We have no record of what Evelyn was doing during that time, or Monroe himself, but I'm sure they were understandably frightened." Simon looked agitated. "I expected the journal to fill in those gaps, but it didn't."

"What happened to Evelyn and Monroe? And the journal? Someone took pages from it."

"Well, according to the legend, on the final day of the month, Mr. Hearth rode up the Monroe's drive late in the evening. Some say dusk, some say midnight, some even say the middle of the day. Several accounts say he was there to save Evelyn. Others say he was simply there to kill Monroe. But Austin did not know that Evelyn had been discovered hanging from the chandelier in the foyer and was already in the ground."

Olivia put a hand to her neck. She had admired the chandelier in the entryway of the Monroe house. "I can't believe Evelyn would do such a thing. She wanted to see Austin more than anything."

"I can't say I understand it either. I had hoped the journal would illuminate that, but it seems someone either didn't want the world to know, or Evelyn tore the pages out herself before she died. It seems her death—whether suicide or murder—will always be a cold case. No justice for her or William Monroe."

Olivia could understand that, but she wasn't so sure it was Evelyn who had taken the pages out. That was just a feeling though. She had nothing to back it up.

"Or Austin Hearth," Olivia added.

Simon gave her a strange look before he continued without commenting on her addition. "There was a brief skirmish between Monroe and Mr. Hearth, but who can battle a vengeful ghost and win? There are at least one hundred accounts of what ensued, but the doctor who looked at Monroe after they found him at the edge of the cliffs the next day noted that it looked as if the man had been dragged for a long distance. They found bits of him along the way, down the main thoroughfare, through town, and out to the cliffs. There might have been photographs at one time because his death was a sensation, but I haven't seen any."

She kept holding her breath. "What of this is even true?" But she knew. At least some of it. Either latently or from the someone who was whispering in her ear.

Evelyn.

The thought of the voice twisted her insides. Surely the woman was only back to help her.

"Some. All. It's impossible to know. Records were destroyed, and the Weatherford home went up in flames, Evelyn's children perished. We assumed the family name had died out, and why should we have thought otherwise? Someone writes a new book on it every decade or so when interest piques again and speculates a little more, but hardly anyone can agree on anything."

"So, what do we do now? I mean . . ."

Simon shook his head and shut the book on his desk. "I have no idea. Of the things we don't know though, the top of the list is where Mr. Hearth's body was interred. People looked for it in the canyon, but nothing was ever found. People get interested now and again and go poking around, but no one's found anything."

She hadn't gotten that far. She was still trying to wrap her head around what she was learning about Evelyn and the Weatherford family. And Austin. A flush rose in her at the thought of him sitting in the chair next to her, how his skin felt beneath her fingers. It was too real for her to believe he was a ghost.

But then the little hairs on her neck rose. Was he back for truly good purposes, or had Mr. Hearth returned to kill the descendants because they actually *were* Evelyn and Monroe's children? Was he back for that kind of vengeance? To put things to rest once and for all? The idea frightened her.

It seemed at odds with what she was learning of him through Evelyn's journal and from the ghost himself. She needed to be more careful. Maybe the paranoia was good after all. A little wariness might save her from an unfortunate end.

"Will you come home with me tonight?" Simon asked suddenly, interrupting her vortex of thoughts.

"Uh," was all Olivia could say at first. He had stilled the storm in her head, and not for the first time. What if Simon's other side appeared? Was there something that triggered him, or did he just come when he felt like it? She wasn't sure she wanted to take that chance. But then again, she wanted to. Wanted him.

Simon lived within walking distance from campus in one of the historic homes in which many of the professors on campus invested. Olivia realized it was only a few blocks from the house she'd had her eye on.

She clutched his arm, and they spoke in hushed tones about Warren's long dead as they walked. The night huddled around them, and Olivia thought she saw glimpses of a figure on horseback that was always just far enough ahead or just far enough behind that she couldn't be certain.

"Where do you think his head is? Have you ever gone looking for it?" Olivia whispered as they took the hill up College Heights Street.

"I did in the first years I moved here. The canyon, the old Monroe house and estate, various buildings on campus, even out to some of the sites William surveyed for other towns."

"And you didn't find anything?"

"Nothing but dust and dark shadows."

Olivia shivered.

As they turned onto Sunset a block from Simon's house, they passed a patrol car parked at the curb. With the window rolled down, Olivia could hear the radio chatter. The officer inside watched as they walked by. She could see his eyes over his steaming cup of coffee. For whatever reason, she didn't feel safer for his presence. The supernatural didn't care for the laws of the land. Simon didn't seem to notice him.

She remembered the outside of Simon's home but could not remember the inside from her first venture there. That had been more one-night stand material. This was nearing *Call your father; I'm dating your daughter* land.

Even in the dark, Olivia could see the ivy crawling over the house's limestone front. A few leaves from the mature trees out front had already created a fine carpet over the old stone walk. It reminded her of the Monroe house, but only its limestone front. The home seemed inviting and warm. The front door was painted a welcoming red, and there were half-hearted attempts at planters on either side of the door on the porch. They were badly wilted, but she suspected Simon kept them watered just enough to keep them from dying. It made her smile.

A black-and-white dog met them at the door. He barked happily, his back end wagging. Where had he been the last time?

"Shep, shush," Simon admonished, but he play wrestled with the dog for a moment before he sheepishly introduced Olivia to him. The curious hound sniffed at her for a moment before turning to Simon for more pats.

Books were everywhere in his house, just like his office. *His office must truly be an extension of his self,* she thought. She also thought about her studio, how she had to share it with others, so there wasn't much of herself there. And her apartment, also shared with someone else. Were there even bits of herself there? Her room was plain, basic, clean. She hadn't done anything to her office on campus either. On Simon's walls were paintings and other pieces of artwork. Houseplants cascaded through each room.

Unbidden tears sprang to Olivia's eyes. She wanted a place like that. Desperately. She had never even hung up the photographs she'd taken.

Simon excused himself for a moment to let Shep out, and Olivia followed him into the kitchen. A set of French doors stood open onto what looked like a covered porch or sunroom.

The pile of dishes and pots in the sink was endearing. The space was clean, if cluttered, and there were more books in the kitchen too. A bookshelf ran along the ceiling, housing more books on, what else, history, and a few cookbooks at an easily accessible end.

Simon came back in. "I'll have to go retrieve him in a few minutes. I don't want him soaked. It's started raining."

"Oh, please. I don't mind at all. I think I could spend hours admiring your home. There's so much to see. How long have you been here?"

His smile warmed her. "About thirteen years. Can I get you some wine?"

"Tea? If you don't mind. I've got to be up early tomorrow."

The mood in the room changed slightly, but Olivia still felt at ease. This was just Simon.

She watched as he went through the motions of pulling a tin toward him on the kitchen counter and measuring out the tea into a sachet. She moved closer, drawn in by the practice that was unusual but familiar to her. Her mother's electric kettle and premade bags of tea from the grocery store seemed worlds away.

She leaned against Simon. He smelled like whatever he conditioned his beard with. Something woodsy. "My mom drinks tea, but not like that."

Simon laughed softly. "I realize this is kinda pretentious, but my mom liked her tea this way. It's a good way to keep her memory alive."

"I'm sorry." Olivia took the mug offered to her. She watched it, expecting it to shift again to the fine china as it had in Simon's office, but it didn't.

"Me too. You're lucky yours is still around."

"Some days." The words slipped out before Olivia could stop them.

Simon sent her a questioning glance.

"She has a lot of issues." She was glad when he didn't push.

Olivia was sipping on the tea and getting sleepier each second by the time Simon got the dog in and took him to his kennel. Then he offered his hand to her. "Come with me?"

Mug in hand, she let him lead her upstairs. His master suite looked like it had been remodeled at some point in the house's history. Such old homes often had small rooms when they were originally built, but modern homeowners wanted larger, more spacious rooms, especially when it came to their bedrooms. So, they knocked down walls and moved things around and made the space their own.

"I feel the history here."

"Yes. The house was built in the 1860s."

"Wow," Olivia breathed, reaching out to press a hand to the wall nearest her. It hadn't seemed so old the first time she had been there. She tried to imagine what it looked like when it was new, but all that crept into her mind at first was the Monroe house. That spiked her anxiety, so she tried to remember her own room at home instead.

There. She imagined old quilts piled on the bed and porcelain pitchers and basins by bedsides, old four-poster beds with curtains. But no, that wasn't her room, was it? It seemed too old, and the ghost memory blended with something newer: a television, a Walkman lying on the bed. She shook herself from the memories.

Tears threatened the more she looked around. Simon's house felt so cozy, so lived in. She felt him staring at her. He took her hand and squeezed. "What's wrong?"

It was just Simon. God, she felt something for him, but it was all caught up within her, tangled up in something she didn't have a name for.

"Your home is so lovely," she said instead of what was lingering on the tip of her tongue. She wanted to be there. It felt safe for the moment.

And there was that spark.

She found herself kissing him. When had she set down her mug? The scent of cedarwood—yes, that was what he used on his beard—pulled her in.

Please, Olivia, her new voice said. *Please, you must take a different path. This one will only end in sadness.*

But why should she listen to that voice now when she had no idea what the rest of her life had been worth?

"I need you," she hummed in Simon's ear, ignoring the voice. That was as close as she could come.

"Olivia." It sounded like a plea.

"Please." Olivia put her hands behind her back, and Simon reached around to grab them and pull them both to the bed, where he pinned her beneath him.

"Yes, please," Olivia sighed. She wanted to give up control, to let him take over. She was so tired of doing everything.

Simon stretched her hands above her head and pushed her shirt and bra up with him, trapping her hands further. He was quick to graze his teeth across her sensitive skin, nibbling here and there and biting so hard that she cried out. But it made her anxiety disappear.

When she cried out again, he nibbled up to her earlobe. "Are you alright?"

"Yes, please, more," tumbled from her lips.

She lost herself in the next few hours of the night. She fully existed in her corporeal form, feeling pleasurable wave after pleasurable wave. The pain licked at her in a way she'd never known until him. Her skin was red and tingling, her wrists sore from his weight on them. And she didn't want it to stop. She wanted him to destroy her slowly. In those moments, she thought he could kill her, and she would have happily died for him, so great was her pleasure.

It was like he released the pressure that had built up over the last two weeks. She felt drunk on the feeling. She awoke the next morning beside him feeling empty of anxiety.

It will not last, the musical voice intoned. *You know what he is.*

"I do?" she asked.

Simon shifted at her voice. She hadn't meant to speak aloud. At the voice's words, she lay back down and thought about what that might mean.

"The red eyes?" she whispered.

Yes. You have seen it too many times now. I saw it too. He is no different from William, on the inside.

"That can't be true." Anxiety swept over her again.

Please don't make the same mistakes I did. Please, Miss Olivia.

Evelyn. It really was Evelyn.

38

Thursday, October 15th

The next morning was a blur of color behind the chatter between her ears. Simon fed her toast and tea before she left for apartment to get ready for the day, but the whispered warnings from Evelyn (Evelyn!) spoiled the moment. Could Simon be harboring part of this mystery too? Evelyn thought so. Olivia wasn't so sure, but the incessant whisper of doubt wore away at her.

She had gotten halfway into a print that day and then lost her concentration because Evelyn was so chattery.

Austin bought me a camera, you know, but I had no idea so much went into making the pictures. Do you sell these? Do you make your living this way?

Olivia stopped her adjustments when the timer went off. "I make a living teaching. I used to sell my prints. They never did well. I'm considering selling these."

Evelyn seemed mature in her journal, but that was only one perspective of a person. The woman asked the kind of endless questions that only a young mind undeterred by the busyness around her could ask. Olivia had to remind herself that the woman had died when she was only twenty-three. Did people mature after death, wherever they went?

She had forgotten to switch off the enlarger when the timer sounded. A few frustrated tears got out before she got it under control and tossed the entire ruined print in the garbage.

"Please, you have to leave me alone when I'm working," Olivia said to the empty darkroom. Evelyn was silent. Olivia hoped that was assent.

After the ruined print fiasco, she got in her car and drove aimlessly. She could hear the crowd at one of the university stadiums half a mile down the street, so she went the other way, toward the south end of town. There were fewer cars there and more winding residential roads through the mature trees. Leaves gathered in the gutters and flowed over the curb. Big reddish-brown maple leaves that Olivia knew would crunch if she walked over them. But she drove on and scattered them from the curb as she passed. It looked more like evening than early afternoon with the overcast sky and the nip in the air.

Mr. Fullbright was ambling around with a duster when she came in, the historical society's only patron. Museums had always weirded her out. The photographs were great, but seeing a long-deceased person's belongings on display was eerie and intrusive at best. Not that she had any right to think that with all the antique cameras she had owned and handled over the years or with all the junk her mother had pulled out of the dugout. But still.

Mr. Fullbright looked up when she shuffled into the main receiving room. "You're back again, young lady. What can I help you with?"

Olivia was glad that he seemed to be in a better mood. "Uh, I just wanted to take a walk around, if that's OK. I didn't really get to look much the other day."

"Please, take your time. I'm just doing a little cleaning. I'll be around if you have any questions."

Olivia thanked him and began a slow swing around the building, looking for anything connected to the turn of the century. She avoided the section that seemed devoted to the Weatherfords. She wasn't ready for another out-of-body experience. Evelyn was silent, but Olivia had the feeling that she was listening.

She hadn't paid much attention to the farm implements on her first trip there, but this time she lingered over them, trying to understand what that world had been like and why such wealthy families would go out onto the prairie to live their lives. It seemed like going out into the desert and hoping to make a living there. She didn't understand it. It seemed too hard, too isolated from everything. It was all relative, she supposed. She'd chosen to be her mother's guardian.

Her circling brought her closer to the area devoted to the Weatherfords, but their name was sprinkled throughout the facility. One display featured a quilt that was supposedly to stitched by Esther Weatherford and the Quilting Circle Ladies, dated 1899. Others were less prominently featured.

A lot of information was threaded throughout the museum about the family that founded the town: the Monroes. William Monroe Senior brought his money and his boys onto the prairie, later bringing his wife and daughter once a house had been built to their liking. Monroe's money brought the train to town. Olivia didn't see anything about what the man had been doing *before* he decided to drop everything and go out onto the prairie, but that hardly seemed to matter to the residents of Warren. What was important was what he had done for them.

William Monroe Senior was credited with the bulk of Warren's founding, but Jonathan Weatherford helped grow and sustain it with his legal prowess. The head figures of the families seemed to run in the same circles, but Olivia got the feeling they didn't interact with each other very often.

The Monroes went about things one way, the Weatherfords another. They didn't often meet in the middle, but it seemed they got along fine when the occasion called for it.

Olivia looked all over the museum for a reference to Hearth and didn't see it. Mr. Fullbright found her contemplating an old limestone post wrapped with wire. The placard said, "Limestone became a popular material during the late 19th century in Warren in lieu of wooden posts for fencing. It lasted longer and was stronger. Barbed wire also came into use in Warren around this time. Today we could not imagine driving by a cattle field and not seeing a barbed-wire fence running alongside the road to keep the cattle in, but in the latter days of the 19th century, it was a new invention."

Olivia harrumphed quietly to herself.

"Is there anything I can help you with today?"

Olivia came out of the thought she was having about not seeing Austin's name anywhere. "Uh, I'm researching my family tree still, my ancestors. My mother's side specifically. They're the ones who've been around the longest I think."

"And you have nowhere to start? What is your mother's maiden name? I thought we went over all of this the other day."

She ignored his comment. "Westford."

"Westford, you say? With an O-R-D? That's not a common name around here and not that old either. When did you say your family arrived in this area?"

"I thought they had been around for a long time, maybe the mid-eighteen hundreds, but I'm not sure." She was a poor liar. Simon would be disappointed in her sleuthing. Not that her mother had been any real help though.

"You know, most people don't come in here anymore. They use the internet now. Seems to get them results a little faster than we can."

Olivia thought about the black hole she'd found on the internet regarding the names she put in. "I understand. I didn't find anything on the internet."

The man showed her the name "Westford" in his register. "Here. Westford pops up in 1904. No, I'm sorry, that's a different spelling. It starts in 1920 and then continues on until today. You, I imagine, through your mother."

"Where else can I go for information?"

"Well, the library will have most of the microfilm. We have a selection here, but if you're looking for newspapers, the campus library is the best place to go."

Of course it would be. She should have thought of that. It seemed the university had a wealth of information to offer that she had never used. *Way to go, Olivia.*

"You're living on the old Weatherford land, yes?"

"Yes."

The old man sighed. Olivia could tell she was asking him too many questions. "The turn of the century, that first decade in Warren, was hard on the town. Many people left, and the town was in danger of falling apart, returning to the prairie. The university saved it."

Either they tiptoed around what happened, or they had conspiracies about it.

Olivia felt nervous but angry. "Why isn't Austin Hearth's name mentioned anywhere in this museum?"

"Oh, you're one of those." Mr. Fullbright pulled full old man status and set his mouth in as much of a line as his fat bottom lip would allow.

"One of those what?"

"The Austin Hearth Club. It's mostly women, as I gather."

Olivia almost laughed. A club? A fan club? It wasn't like the forums were *that* exactly, if that's what he was talking about. "I haven't heard of any such thing."

Mr. Fullbright looked like he wasn't going to believe another word from her mouth.

"I've just been researching the history of the town. I got the impression he was important."

Mr. Fullbright's white eyebrows shot up. "That depends on who you ask. But if you'll excuse me, I need to go get my lunch. Actually, we're closed for the day. Goodbye."

With that he ushered her out of the building, shut the door behind her, and turned the "Open" sign over to "Closed" in the window on the front door.

Olivia stood outside in stunned silence and stared at the sign until it stopped moving. Then she raced to her car to get back to campus, texting Simon on the way. She had to tell him about what happened. Evelyn's warning be damned, this was getting interesting.

He had just returned to his office when she arrived, flushed and laughing. It was all she could do in the moment. Simon looked caught off guard at her hysterical appearance. Good. Let him be. She had enjoyed herself with him, and she wasn't going to let Evelyn Weatherford get between them if she could help it.

Olivia settled in with the cup of tea that Simon somehow already had brewing for her. She could take things in stride. She patted herself on the back. "So, I was at the historical society talking to Mr. Fullbright, right? I mentioned Austin Hearth and how it's kind of strange there's, like, zero mention of him at the historical society. I mean, they have a fucking limestone post wrapped in barbed wire, and they talk about how important it was to developing Warren, *but they completely omit how it got there*. I mean, the guy helped bring Warren up, and they can't even mention him. Please tell me you've heard about this."

Simon sat heavily in his desk chair. "I didn't realize you were spending so much time there. I could have saved you the trouble."

Olivia tucked her feet up into the chair with her. "Why's that?"

"They hate Hearth. It doesn't matter if the man contributed more to the area than the Weatherfords did. As far as they're concerned, he murdered half the town. That's an exaggeration, but you know what I mean."

"What do you think of him?"

Simon shrugged. "Can't say I'm a fan. Ghost or not, he committed horrific acts and then fled the scene. I don't know though. There's a lot that doesn't add up. I hit a lot of dead ends in my research. I teach a class on it, you know."

She wasn't surprised in the slightest. "And you teach that Austin did these things while alive."

"It's open ended mostly. To be honest, it's a great way to see if there's more to it out there, buried in someone's basement, or some new theory from a young, eager mind."

"Using your students to further your own research . . . I like it." Olivia laughed and clinked her teacup to Simon's coffee mug.

He laughed with her, then suddenly stopped and stood up. Olivia's mirth left her instantly. He didn't look good. "Are you OK?"

He leaned on his desk and grabbed his head. Olivia moved to help him, but he held out his other hand to stop her. "Please go. I don't think you're safe."

She watched his eyes shift colors. Warm brown to red, then back to brown for just a moment. Evelyn, who had been blessedly silent for quite awhile, spoke up. *Oh, it is just the same. You must leave, you must leave. He is not in his right mind.*

The pain from the sudden surge of emotion from Evelyn was only just tolerable. Was Simon feeling something similar? She reached over and squeezed his hand. "Simon. I'll see you soon."

Red, brown, pale red, deep red, brown. "Thank you. I'm so sorry."

Olivia backed out of the room and shut the door.

During her walk to the library after she left his office, she felt as if she were being watched. Sure enough, a quick glance at the history building confirmed her suspicions. Simon stood at his window, looking taller than normal. A hat appeared on his head. He tipped it to her. Decidedly Not Simon. Not the Simon she had been learning to know anyway.

She hurried on, looking back occasionally to see if anyone was following her.

If Not Simon was the thing in the headless getup riding the freakish horse, she was an idiot for spending so much time alone with him.

The women who disappeared look just like you, the voice whispered.

No, he absolutely wasn't doing that. Absolutely not. That had to be someone else. But he was a Monroe, and there was a Monroe in the past. Austin had returned. So had Evelyn. Why was it a stretch to believe that William Monroe had returned too?

Olivia's stomach turned over. She looked back over her shoulder again. It was impossible to see if anyone was following her in the throngs of students and teachers who walked the sidewalks toward or from their early afternoon classes.

She took refuge in the library and followed the signs for the reading rooms down into the basement. Once there, she was pointed down another level for microfilm, sound rooms, and assisted archive retrieval.

Surprise, surprise, the microfilm and microfiche were in the basement, but it was bright and cheery down there, and the smell of coffee and pastries wafted through the mostly empty study area. Only a few students were at the tables and overstuffed chairs between the tall bookshelves. A few of them were asleep. God, she didn't miss that time in her life.

The help desk in the basement wasn't quiet. Carts of books needing to be shelved rolled by her. Someone was getting help with a map at least twice as tall as she was, and somewhere at least two phone lines were ringing. The guy who came over to help her looked frazzled.

"Hi, if you're looking for food, it's not here. The bagel place is out the doors and down the hall to the right." He turned to go before Olivia called him back.

"Um . . . I need access to the microfilm or microfiche machines. Whichever. Or both. I'm not sure."

The guy rooted around in a drawer under the help desk and fished out a set of keys and a sign-in sheet. "I need your ID and for you to sign in and out of the room. It's over by the sound room at the far end of the basement." He tipped his head to his right.

Olivia produced her school ID, but when she went to sign her name, she paused. Someone familiar had been in the microfilm room, and not just once. The sheet was old, going back a few years, and it was peppered with other names, but it was largely dominated by Simon Monroe's. His signature lately looked much more elaborate. He had signed into the room the previous day, arriving at noon and leaving by 2:30.

She wanted to say something about it, but she didn't know what, so she kept her mouth shut. That was something she would have to think about. He had said something about digging. They both were, and in all the same holes.

She took the keys offered by "I'm Carl if you need anything" and tried to not run all the way to the room. Once safely inside, she shut and locked the door. If someone wanted in, they could knock. She didn't want any accidental visitors.

Taking in the room, she noticed a painting of, who else, Evelyn Weatherford. Granted, it was among the hundred crammed onto the walls, but it was creepy nonetheless. Had they run out of room elsewhere?

Then there were shelves upon shelves of boxes of microfiches and rolls of microfilm. Another aspect of photography that she had declined to get involved with. Dr. Cahara was famous for calling her up and offering her part-time photography deals for the university (hello, festival project) that offered little to no pay but were beneficial to the university. The microfilm was one that Olivia had declined. That road would have taken her nowhere except good karma. The festival photography might actually earn her some money from prints if she was lucky.

Her phone rang, startling her. Simon's office number. Oh, God. Terror seized her. She ignored the call. Moments later, it rang again. She ignored the call again. It happened twice more before he finally stopped calling. She knew it wasn't really Simon. And Not Simon didn't have anything to say that could benefit her.

Her hands shook as she loaded the first reel. She checked that the door was locked before she started going through the microfiches.

Olivia spent an agonizing next few hours going through microfiches until her eyes burned. What was it they said about staring at a screen? People blinked ten times less or something? She'd go blind at this rate.

The photographs on the microfiche were blurry. Surprise.

"Thank God you didn't take that job, girlfriend," she muttered.

The papers weren't helpful. Austin's death wasn't published, but the sale of his estate sure was.

> Burned structures part of estate's current state. Unknown head of cattle on grazing pastures. Horses sold as lot to Monroe family to be resold at auction. Recommended use for land: grazing. Suitable sites for home and/or outbuildings. Land will not be split.

HOW NICE OF THE MONROE FAMILY TO TAKE AUSTIN'S HORSes after his death. If he had come back and killed them all, Olivia wasn't sure she blamed him. Talk about hitting a man when he was down.

The missing animal posts in the newspapers were interesting and prolific. Missing cattle, missing horses, missing herding dogs. There were applications from bachelors seeking a wife, widows and widowers seeking another partner. Crops were good, crops were bad, there was not enough rain, too much rain, and on and on.

The film was mind numbing. Wind, rewind, wind, wind, wind, rewind. Scads of what must've just been loose paper, the result of dozens of dugouts, basements, and attics. It blurred together.

Finally, something that she almost zoomed past. She rewound. A record dating to 1906. An application to a small boarding school out in the rural area outside Warren. It was for a girl, age five, named Everly Westford.

Olivia kicked back in her chair to think about the find. The painting of Evelyn Weatherford in the room was watching her.

Olivia glared back. "Boo," she said.

It wouldn't have surprised her if the painting had replied in kind.

She felt a weird twist in her stomach. Suppose Simon had found this obscure tidbit, hidden away? It wouldn't have bothered him. Westford wasn't the name he was looking for. But she was. Sort of. If it was the Westfords of her family, it was a start. She took a picture of the screen with her phone before shutting everything down.

She'd had enough for one day, but she didn't want to take any chances that something or someone was out there trying to figure out what was going on before she did and for far less charitable reasons. She checked the lock on the door, then set the reel that she wanted back on the shelf next to its box. She closed the box and re-shelved it out of order on a shelf across the way. If any more interesting tidbits were there, she would be the next to see it.

She gathered her things and slid the reel inside the large inner pocket in her coat. This was temporary. She would return it when this was all over. She wasn't sure when that would be, but she had a feeling she would have to see it through. It would be safe at her mom's house in the dugout, where it was cool and dry and dark.

Olivia left the library, certain someone would come running after her any moment. No one did. It was almost too easy to sign out, say everything was great, and leave.

As she headed toward the parking lot, the photographs were in the back of her mind as she ticked off her to-do list. Evan had returned to the prints, nearly life size, and only those so intimately connected to the past could see them. His presence was annoying but not as anxiety producing as the nightmare horse. What would the public say when they saw them? Would anyone be left by then to see them for what they really were? Under two weeks to hang them in the gallery, and Dr. Cahara called sometimes three times a day for updates. *I'm busy chasing ghosts, Cecelia. I'll get to the photographs when I can.*

Her mother's vehicle was sitting in the driveway when Olivia pulled up. She always felt on edge when her mother said she was going somewhere. But her mother was mentally ill, not elderly, and Olivia had no power to stop her if she chose to go somewhere. It was when she wound up in the hospital a county away because she ran out of gas and stayed outside all night and Olivia was unable to locate her that there was a problem. She had contemplated one of those silver medical alert bracelets, but her mother would probably just take it off the first chance she got. She wasn't a prisoner, though she told Olivia she felt like one almost daily.

Olivia came cautiously into the living room. She was starting to form some conjectures. She didn't expect her mom to cooperate, but she could try.

"Mother?"

Her mother was crocheting. Pot holders. At least a dozen of them were stacked at her feet already, and she was hard at work on another one. She would have to take them to the craft fair next year. Her mother leaned down, tucking herself into her work.

"Mother, I know you can hear me."

The older woman started humming. It struck Olivia that it was the tune she had heard during her first visit to the historical society. It solidified her growing knowledge. Olivia was determined to go on with her question. She had to know. "Mother, was our name changed somewhere along the way?"

Her mother seemed to enjoy the question. "Oh no, you've always been Olivia. From the moment you were born, Olivia was the name I wanted for you."

The well of patience that she could usually call on for her mother ran dry. "Westford, Mother. The name Westford runs in our family. Did it use to be Weatherford or something else? Monroe? Hearth? Did someone change it?"

He mother's head snapped up. The look on her face was ferocious. "Don't you ever say those names in this house, young lady."

"Do you have any idea what's happening in Warren right now?"

The lucidity in her mother's eyes was rather unnerving. "Whatever it is, it's none of our business."

Olivia wanted to stamp her foot, scream, something. "It *is* our business. Literally! Tell me, we changed our name somewhere along the way, didn't we?"

With that her mother went away, curling back in on herself, focusing on the last few stitches of the potholder in her hand. "I think you know the answer to that already," she mumbled.

"Don't you go away on me, please. I have to know."

Her mother was quiet for a moment. Olivia pressed on. "Who owned the house before us?"

"No one. It has been in the Westford family since it was built."

"Then who owned it before it was rebuilt? Before the fire?"

Her mother crocheted quickly. Olivia had to give her props for not missing a stitch. It appeared that her mother was well and truly done with the conversation though, and Olivia didn't blame her. Whatever their family was or had been, it hadn't escaped them just by changing their name.

So, where to go? Where to look? How could there be any evidence if the evidence had been destroyed? Or had there been any in the first place? What did she have to go on except a striking resemblance and a hunch?

Westford. Weatherford. Munroe. Monroe.

When would it have been changed? And why? Did she need to know, or could she go with her gut? No, she needed to know. She had to find a conclusion to this string of disruptions, or she was really going to lose her mind.

There had to be something in the box of stuff from the dugout. She would go back in there if she needed to, and at least once more to put the reel in there for safekeeping. Something about the room at the back of the dugout was attractive. Quiet. Dark. Away from everything. It was nearly a darkroom, without the possibility of interruptions.

Olivia left her mother in her own world and took the box up to her room. She carefully dumped the contents onto the large rag rug at the foot of her bed. If it had all once been organized and then been disturbed by wind, animals, or both, that was a shame. Some of the paper was too faded to read, but other bits were still legible. The books were in amazing condition considering how some of the other stuff looked. The room had been dry though and cool enough.

She found lots of receipts from the 1920s. Timber, nails, paint, varnish—there was no shortage of paper about the rebuilding of the house. Not that she thought Mr. Fullbright had lied, but it was nice to see it confirmed. Her mother wasn't exactly a reliable source either. Olivia set those papers aside and sifted for earlier bits. Those had been there too.

She paused at the photographs again. Seeing Evelyn and Austin together was sad after the story Simon had told the day before. Evelyn hadn't trusted Simon though, so Olivia wasn't sure if he was to be believed after all. *She* believed him, but it was strange feeling someone else's feelings on the matter as if they were her own.

They looked happy in the handful of photographs that Olivia had recovered. Evelyn laughed with a hand on her straw hat while Austin leaned back in a chair. Olivia saw something of their front porch in the Weatherfords' wide wooden porch that looked perfect for hanging out.

The photograph where they both sat atop Evan appeared more somber, but that was likely partly due to the different printing style of that photograph. Olivia could see the telltale signs of traveling photographer portraiture, and it felt like a guilty pleasure to be touching the piece with her bare fingers. She knew she shouldn't, but she couldn't resist. Like when she had watched that Hallmark special eight times over the last Christmas season and bawled every single time.

She lifted the photograph to her face and inhaled deeply. It smelled old. Earth, prairie, photo paper, developing chemicals. She had an absurd desire to eat the photograph, to stuff it in her mouth and let it become part of her.

But it already is, something whispered to her.

She stared at the woman printed on the paper. Yes, the resemblance was there. But if Mr. Fullbright and Simon hadn't both said something, she might've tried to discount it. Anything could look like anything if one stared at it hard enough, looked for similarities long enough.

She set the photograph down carefully with the others. "Happy Life at the Weatherford Home in the 1890s" could be the title of the stack.

Several of the books had "E. W." written in curlicues on the inside cover identical to the "E" in "E. H." on the journal she had. It wasn't a stretch to see that "E. W." turned to "E. M." wanted to be "E. H." It could have been from any of the Weatherford girls, but the more she touched the old covers, spines, and pages, the more she felt she was touching Evelyn's books. Her counterpart and likely the owner of the books was silent though. It must have been nice to sit back and pretend she couldn't hear anything. Or maybe she wasn't there at all. Olivia still wasn't sure how this was supposed to work. At the moment, it annoyed her.

She flipped through one of the old books and was surprised when she saw something tucked inside. She carefully opened the preserved paper and scanned it. "D. W. Musical Instruments and Lessons," it proclaimed, "ordered by Evette Vogt for the daughter of Maggie Vogt. Half term to begin Dec. 29th, '06, and end April 26th, '07. Half term to continue May 11th and end August 15th. Piano album, 5 cents."

"Wasn't Evette your younger sister?" Olivia asked. The name Maggie tickled something. She had heard that name in her reading too. But why had Evelyn's younger sister bought piano lessons for Maggie's daughter? Olivia had gotten a clear sense that the woman was a spinster.

That was well after the Weatherford fire but before the house had been rebuilt, so why was it in their dugout? Maggie still worked for the Weatherfords when the fire happened, as far as Olivia could tell, but suddenly she had at least one school-age child in 1906, and Evelyn's sister footed the bill for piano lessons and boarding school?

She wasn't sure where she had read that. Maybe on the forums the other day. She had a hard time believing she was picking up information from her fellow body dweller like some freakish radio signal.

An odd feeling crawled over Olivia, and she realized Evelyn was shivering, but it came through her own skin, like her nerves fired from far away. Her fingers were cold; so cold they looked white.

"Do you know what's going on here?" she asked Evelyn as she poked at her fingers, which had grown numb. More strange sensations.

Evelyn was silent. It would be annoying if she were quiet only when it suited her. Did everyone who became a ghost become insufferable after death?

I don't know, Evelyn said finally. Her voice was quiet, tired, even.

"Why don't you know?"

It would have happened after I died.

Great. "Speculate for me."

I cannot.

Olivia sighed loudly, folded the paper, and set it back in its place as a bookmark in *Pilgrim's Progress*, then flipped through the rest of the book. More treasures. This time, an envelope. "Marguerite Humboldt Boarding," it read in a formal script on the outside.

She stopped and stared at the paper she had pulled from the envelope. It was identical to the one she had seen at the library earlier. Almost. She couldn't get her phone out fast enough to look at the picture she had taken.

There.

The child's last name had been changed. How, when, and where, she had no idea, but there in italic script was the name "Sarah Esther Weatherford Monroe" where "Everly Westford" had been penned in identical script on the one at the library.

Oh, my child, a soft, sad voice said from somewhere within her.

The hair on Olivia's arms stood up. "At least one of your children survived," she whispered.

She took a picture of the new find and then sat and stared at it, trying to process the implications. When she couldn't, she rifled through some books she had grabbed on her way out of the library—general Warren histories and several more focused on the boom in the 1890s. The books mentioned Austin in a matter-of-fact way that helped her understand Warren better. The Weatherford, Monroe, and Hearth families had all been integral to the early success of a town on the prairie that had a better chance of returning to the prairie than making it at the time.

So what?

She set down the book and wandered outside toward the dugout. It didn't look that bad once she brought a floodlight in and checked out the room. And it wasn't nearly as far back as she had imagined on her initial trip inside. But it was ideal for darkroom activities, should she choose to go that route.

After she stored the reel away at the back of the dugout and moved a few things out of the space, she sat on the old bench under a cottonwood tree near the dugout entrance and soaked up the last rays of sunshine with several of the books on history and photography. The day had been cool, but cold air mixed with the warmer daytime air as evening came on.

Austin appeared on Evan as the sun headed toward the horizon, and Olivia's mother had already headed to bed. Olivia had seen him coming from around the front of the house, a ship sailing into port. It was strange to feel Evelyn's heart burgeoning at the sight. It was so powerful that Olivia could not help but feel something too. Or perhaps she was feeling it all on her own. She was not certain, especially after her find. Was she Evelyn or Evelyn's child? Or was she neither?

Austin dismounted and let Evan wander. Olivia watched the horse nose and tear at the early fall prairie grasses at the edge of their lawn. It fascinated her. Was he really eating, or was the motion so ingrained that he would do it regardless? She wanted to say something to Austin, but she was enjoying his silent presence on the bench next to her too much. He took off his gloves and began applying a pot of salve to his cracked knuckles while Olivia kept reading. Like the grass-eating ghost horse, it fascinated her.

"The world repeats itself," Austin said, breaking the silence.

"What?" Olivia looked up from her reading trance.

"The world repeats itself," Austin he said. "I see it in you too."

If there was one good thing about sharing space with Evelyn, it was that the woman helped temper the times that Olivia wanted to say something sarcastic because someone was being cryptic. And here she had been so relaxed.

Hush, girl. It's all right.

Olivia calmed. "How is the world repeating itself?"

Austin stood and placed a hand on the dugout entrance. Olivia was surprised when bits of dust and limestone fell where he touched, just as it would have if she had touched it.

"I feel I have not changed from then," he said.

"That doesn't sound like a bad thing."

Austin guffawed. "Perhaps. Perhaps not. I was very angry then. I still am."

Olivia thought about the day in the parking lot with the impostor. How big Austin had seemed then. She thought she would have been crushed by him and his horse as they wheeled around her. He had been angry but not toward her. Powerful was a better word.

"Do you think you're here to use that anger for . . . for good? I don't know how all that works."

Austin smiled. "I don't know either. I'll not argue with the powers that be though. I'm here to do what I can, protect whom I can. Be a friend."

That felt good to hear. In the silence that followed, Olivia fell back into looking over the books before her.

"Have you ever considered putting together a photobook?"

"Pardon?" Olivia surfaced briefly, her mind spinning over how the families were connected. Her brain finally caught up. "Oh. Well. Yes, I have. They had photobooks back then?"

Austin's smile was slow and easy, and she could tell he was about to confirm her silly question, but he didn't make her feel like it was silly. She liked that.

"Yes, they did," he said. "And I suspect you knew that buried somewhere here."

He touched the side of her head. She couldn't remember being touched that way. It was a tender gesture.

"I did, yes. Everything that has . . . happened . . . has forced me to recall large amounts of information about a subject that I love but had not focused on in quite some time." She wanted to tell him of the photographs she had found, but was that some sort of a violation of ghost code? She had no idea. She could keep them to herself for the moment.

"So," Olivia began, "what do *I* have to do? This is so chaotic. I've been involuntarily invited into this situation, and I'm at a loss."

"I'm a ghost, not a fortune teller."

"Well, surely you have an idea."

Austin looked thoughtful. "There is much unfinished business, yes. Evelyn was not where I was after death. And in death I could not rest because my body had been purposely separated from my head. I believe Monroe desecrated my remains or something terrible, for I have not rested easily these last hundred odd years."

"Your head needs to be put with your body? Where are you buried?"

It was the first time Austin looked shocked, and it was comical. "You don't know?"

"Know what?"

"Monroe hid my head and my body. I was never given a proper burial. Those two physical parts of me have been separated for a long time. I have wandered in a grey area of his creation ever since."

"Do you have any idea where he might have put your head?" Olivia asked. What an absurd conversation.

Austin looked deep in thought for a moment. "No. There are many places he could've hidden it. I didn't know the man well, save for his public figure and the one that Evelyn reported to me. He and I had a few run-ins, and we never took a liking to each other. Competing affections, you know."

"Where did he spend his time? Do you know?"

"Goodness, Miss Olivia. That was a long time ago."

She put a hand over his. "I'm sorry. I can go pick up a biography or something."

Austin took her hand and twined their fingers together. The gesture was familiar and soothing. "No, just give me a few minutes. Remembering takes much longer now, and I'm out of practice."

Austin stopped and turned abruptly, looking off toward the south. Olivia thought that was the way toward Warren.

"It seems we have a visitor," Austin said, keeping an eye to the south as he whistled for Evan.

Olivia looked to where he had indicated, and her heart sank. How did he know where she lived?

There on a hill not so distant, illuminated by the last light that touched only the tops of the hills, was the impostor. He sat in a manner that Olivia imagined was smugly on his nightmare horse, watching. Even from a distance she could see the jerky motion with which the horse moved its head. She wasn't sure what scared her more, the man or the horse.

"Austin," Olivia said. "I'm frightened." There was a lilt to her voice. Evelyn.

Austin strode to her and took her hands, pulled her to her feet. "Get yourself inside. I'll keep an eye on him."

"Is it . . ."

He squeezed her hands. She could feel how warm they were through the soft leather gloves. It seemed the abrupt movement back in time when he touched her was slowing. Now the memories came creeping up on her, as if they were her own. She remembered him taking her hands and spreading salve on them. On cuts in her palms. The scene was fraught with emotion. Restrained love.

"I'll keep you safe," Austin said. "You don't need saving; I know that, but I know this foe better than you. I'll keep you safe."

Olivia nodded, and Austin swung into the saddle. The distant rider was not so distant now, and she could see the swish of the thing's tail and the large headless man much more clearly. Olivia felt vulnerable standing there on the lawn like a moonstruck girl. Time to get inside.

She had the best view from the upstairs bathroom. She knelt on the counter next to the sink, so she could see better. The tiled countertop hurt her knees, but she didn't care. If she had thought she didn't have enough heart-pounding excitement in her life before, she had more than enough now.

Austin and the headless impostor clashed at the top of a nearby prairie swell hard enough that Olivia winced. They moved like twin shadows in the deepening twilight, sometimes disappearing against the purple hills.

Evan wheeled around, then came charging back, lowered his head, and, at the last second, made a slight turn and slammed his great chest into the side of the nightmare horse and rider. The horse and rider stumbled to the side, and the imposter grabbed his leg, yanking his steed off course. Surely that would have crushed a living man's leg. It couldn't have been Simon but a ghost or a spirit instead, like Austin.

She could hear no sounds from her vantage point, but if it didn't draw attention from neighboring properties, she would be surprised. Their battle was like a violent but graceful dance, and Olivia held her breath with each new move, wondering who would emerge victorious.

After another round of circling and chasing, Austin and Evan instigating, the other rider turned tail and headed back toward Warren. Olivia did hear one far-off holler from Austin, a sound that took her back to county fair days and cowboys whooping while they roped cattle. Then they were gone from sight.

Olivia waited long minutes to see if they reappeared, but they didn't. Twice now Austin had stood between her and something she didn't know how to handle. And he had not answered her question. Perhaps Evelyn knew.

She slid down from the counter. Her knees ached from the irregular tile. Her stomach lurched once as she hoped Austin was alright and a second time when she thought that either way, she would someday meet the imposter alone. That day there would be no one to stand between her and certain terror.

39

Spring 1899

In the days after her walk, there hadn't been much to do except think about what had happened with Austin. Evelyn wrapped her feet in strips of an old dress that William didn't approve of. She appreciated that he wanted her to have all new things, but it was a comfort to have her old clothing. William didn't agree. Her feet healed, grew soft again.

William had brought in a new mirror that winter—an old, dark, gothic-looking thing. She wanted to ask where he had gotten it but was afraid of the answer. It looked like she imagined the old world looked in the time of the Dark Ages and before.

For a time she avoided the mirror, but she was attracted to the antique quality of the gaudy frame and the glass. William was obsessed with it because of its size and for how little he had paid for it.

One spring day she finally gave in to using the mirror and sat down in front of it to brush her hair. But the longer she stared in the mirror, the more she was uncertain it was her face she was looking at. The glass had an odd quality of contorting her features when she sat so close. She had not noticed it when she stood a distance away to arrange her dresses.

She stared hard into the mirror, looking at a face that she didn't recognize. The harder she stared, the more she felt as if she were staring at a stranger. Then the face shifted, became masculine, became William. It contorted horribly, sneered, became dark and ghastly, like a golem. It opened its mouth and revealed horrible, sharp teeth, and Evelyn was certain it was about to speak.

Dear God in heaven! Evelyn shrieked and threw her hands at the mirror. Her hands hit the glass hard enough that it shattered, and pieces rained down on her. Goodness, she didn't know she had been sitting so close to it. She was still sitting there, stunned, when Alyssa rushed into the room.

"Missus, are you hurt?"

Evelyn shook glass from her dress and tried to back up from the shards. In her rush, shards of glass slipped into her palms, and she cried out. Blood welled up from her palms and her blue fingers. It spilled onto her pale peach dress and onto her stomach and her lap, and she couldn't stop it.

"There oughtn't be so much blood!" she cried.

Alyssa was trying to navigate the glass, so she could get to her. "Missus, there isn't that much blood. I understand your fright, but it will be all right."

When Evelyn looked again, there was blood but not nearly as much. And the glass poked out where someone could easily pull it out with tweezers and steady fingers.

Her shock evolved into panic. What would William say when he heard? What would he do?

Not a minute after Alyssa came into the room, William rushed in. Evelyn could have sworn he had a smirk on his face. All she could think of was the horrible golem face in the mirror that had looked like him but wasn't.

"That's enough, Alyssa. I'll take it from here."

"But sir, all the glass! I cannot—"

"I said I'll take it from here, girl. Get out."

Alyssa dropped the small broom and dustpan and ran out of the room. The group of other ladies and staff who had gathered at the door scattered with her. Their hushed whispers still reached Evelyn, who could hear them worrying after her, but William had eyes only for Evelyn.

William strode over to where she sat, tall and imposing. He crunched over the glass, sending more shards flying. Evelyn flinched when he reached her and leaned down toward her. She squeezed her eyes shut.

"What was that?"

"I'm sorry?" Evelyn opened her eyes as William hooked his arms under hers and hauled her to her feet, lifting her like a child away from the glass.

"I thought . . . I thought . . ." She could not finish the thought.

"You thought what?"

Evelyn felt embarrassed. "I don't want to say. Please forget I said anything."

"No, I want to hear what you have to say."

The flush crept up, unwarranted. "I thought you might strike me," she said.

William's face flushed as well, and Evelyn felt she was in great danger. Her insides twisted.

"Why would you think that? I would *never* do something of that sort. What kind of man do you think I am?" William had fisted a hand into the high collar of Evelyn's dress to help drag her unceremoniously to her feet.

Evelyn shrank from him and flinched, his hands so close to her face. His words said he would not strike her, but his tight fists and threatening posture said otherwise. "I'm so sorry. I was only worried about your reaction, and you ran in here so quickly."

William pulled her away from the glass and brushed her dress down with a cloth from her vanity. "I'm appalled that you could have such a thought."

"I'm sorry." Evelyn was shaking and wanted to put her hot face in her hands, but the bits of glass poked out still. She awkwardly held her hands before her, like a beggar.

"Are you really? You don't sound very sorry."

She held out her maimed hands to him, quivering, unable to find the right words. "I am. I'm so sorry. Please forget I said anything."

"You must be somewhat dense, Evelyn, to say such things."

"I . . . no. No. It's just . . . my hands, the glass. I was so frightened, so shocked. I'm so sorry."

William snatched one of her hands and chided her when she cried out. "Shut your mouth. It's only a bit of glass. Get a hold of yourself."

"Yes, sir," Evelyn murmured through the tears that ran down her hot cheeks.

William picked the glass out of her palms. He was gentle with that part. She didn't know any longer when he would be gentle or when his demeanor would become harsh. She had been trying to do everything he asked, but it always seemed that she did something wrong or not to his liking.

That included not giving him a child.

She didn't want to say she could depend on her cycle to come at such regular intervals that she could count the months by it. His anger had grown with each month when he demanded a report of her monthly, and she could only say it had come again.

After he had pulled the glass from her hands, he instructed her to clean the glass up from the floor piece by piece. The mirror and its elaborate frame disappeared for a few days after that. Evelyn's hands seeped. Alyssa changed the bandages and tried to get Evelyn to talk to her. Evelyn sat in silence, exhausted by the experience.

In the days afterward, Evelyn could not rise from bed in the morning. William chased her from bed by 8:30 if she hadn't risen by then, and fear drove her out after that. She did very much want to please him, but his desires changed by the minute sometimes and without her knowing.

As she lay there, she thought about choices and how they had such far-reaching fingers. She had accepted that she had made a poor decision, and her shame at her poor decision—the poorest of her life—was hers to bear.

She had not accepted that her dreams were out of reach though. And she had not accepted that Austin was gone from her life. She would try to make amends as best as she could with him, but she had to wait until William went away on work again.

She still had not ascertained precisely what kept him away for so long each time, but she gathered from meetings with his father that it was about land out west. Surveying land for another town, perhaps. Another Warren on the prairie that the railroad would come to because of its excellent location.

The day he left, she saddled her beautiful mare. Her arms were not as strong as they used to be, and she struggled with the saddle. Ebony stood patiently for her, the horse's deep, wise eyes watching her would-be rider with interest. Not far away, Alyssa's sister and one of the stable hands watched her. Evelyn listened to their half-whispered conversation.

"Mister Monroe says she's mad," the boy whispered. "He said she should not be allowed to leave."

"Oh, I hardly believe that. Sis says she's lovely. Quiet, but . . ." Then they realized that Evelyn was watching and shut their mouths.

Evelyn felt her face grow hot. The girl clouted the boy's ear firmly, then offered to help Evelyn saddle the mare. The boy hollered at her and got back to work polishing the saddle that was in his lap. The stable smelled of leather, polish, and horse. It was comforting.

"Oh, please. I'm not as strong as I used to be."

The tall, gangly girl did so, keeping one eye on Evelyn. "Are you not allowed to leave?"

Evelyn's heart beat rapidly. "William said it is not safe for me out there. Beyond the estate, I mean."

The girl rolled her eyes. "Then why does he let us leave? Oh, right, we're disposable." The word sounded huge in the girl's mouth as she tried to get her lips around it.

"That's an unkind thing to say."

That earned another eye roll. "It's the truth. I'm happy I'm in town at least. Working the farms was bad. Too hot or too cold. Too windy, too rainy, too many grasshoppers. And the mice aren't nearly so bad here as there. They get in the flour sometimes, but that's to be expected."

Evelyn reached under Ebony to grab the girth and stroked the horse patiently until the mare let out the breath she had been holding. Then Evelyn tightened the girth. The girl noticed.

"Mister Monroe doesn't even know that trick. You a rider?"

Evelyn smiled. Oh, the memories that brought back. "I used to be."

"Here in Warren?" The girl teased Ebony's mouth open for the bit. The horse, still young, gave her a hard time until she tickled her ears. Then she took the bit without a fuss.

Evelyn checked Ebony's trappings, happy with the adjustments the girl had made. "Outside of Warren. Out on the prairie."

That got the boy's attention. "There's Indians out there."

Evelyn got a foot up in Ebony's stirrup and hefted herself on the mare's back. She definitely was not as strong as she used to be. "None that I've seen."

"That's 'cause they hide in the grass, and you cain't see them."

Evelyn patted the camera strapped across her body. "If I see one, I'll take a picture for you."

The boy harrumphed and went back to polishing the saddle.

"I can trust you not to say a word?" Evelyn tried to gauge the girl's loyalties. It wasn't something she had ever needed to think about.

The girl shrugged. "I dunno . . ."

"Would you like a new scarf for the winter, new shoes? Anything of the like. I'm happy to get it for you."

That lit up the girl. Evelyn saw the boy's attention pique as well.

"New shoes," the girl said with a smile.

"I could use new gloves," the boy said. "Leather. Good ones."

"I can do that. Thank you both." She had to trust they would not say anything. Her stomach clenched hard anyway.

With the negotiation done, Evelyn eased her horse out of the stable and into the side yard. They were in town, but town ended abruptly at the woods and the prairie. She could take the long route by the university and over the canyon bridge, the smaller wooden one down the way. The larger one would have far too much traffic.

She skirted behind businesses and stayed on the soft-packed dirt and behind the little berms as much as she could before she reached the more heavily treed areas.

She didn't feel nerves for long before she was out on the open prairie. For once it was a nearly calm day. There was no such thing as a perfectly calm day on the prairie, for the prairie lived and breathed. Deep within its swells, it had lungs that always rustled the grass, even if just a hair. The stillest she had seen it was before the great storms that sent tornadoes careening across its vastness. Seeing them from a distance, feeling their roar, was humbling and awesome.

Ebony stamped her little hooves in the grass. Evelyn had never taken her so far out before. They had gone out to town with William but rarely. It was enough for Evelyn to feel the strength and agility that her pretty mare possessed. For all of William's defects, he had won her heart with Ebony when she was a filly.

The horse nosed at the prairie grasses, ripping them while Evelyn stared out over the hills. She was finally far enough away from town that she could relax, become one with her prairie again. The sun was warm, and the breeze was saying farewell to winter. The trees had just budded out, and the air sang with such sweetness that Evelyn felt her heart swell. That was always how she knew her birthday was near. That would be the day that Austin became her friend again.

Evelyn urged Ebony slowly down the hill. As much as she wanted to linger, she didn't want to be away for too long. She didn't want to test William's patience. Besides, her hands already hurt from holding the reins so tightly. The cuts from the glass were not healing well, and she worried about infection.

She came around the back way again, thinking she would need to guide Ebony around the prairie dog holes and limestone outcroppings, but the mare was even more agile than Evelyn had given her credit for. The only horse she had seen take to the prairie more gracefully was Evan. Even though the cattle trail that wound through the scrubby old trees was full of ruts and places even a sturdy horse could trip or break a leg, Ebony took it all in stride.

Evelyn emerged from the woods and stared at the house in the distance for a moment. Suppose Austin had company and could not receive her? But no. She knew he didn't. Whatever innate part of Ebony knew how to set her hooves carefully in the cattle-dug ruts of the trail, Evelyn knew that Austin could receive her at that time on that day.

Austin was waiting for her at the first pasture gate closest to the stables. No one else was in sight. Evelyn knew better than to believe that just because she could see no one that no one was watching. She dismounted and led Ebony toward Austin. She saw a look of disbelief on Austin's face as she walked toward him. She wanted to know why, but she knew better than to start the conversation that way.

Austin started it for her. "I didn't invite you here."

His coolness stung, and she felt the small buoy of hope that she had stored away on her ride over begin to sink. "I thought—"

"No," Austin said. "You thought wrongly. Don't you understand that you can't be here? Do you understand what he would do if he knew you were here? It would bring terror on both of us."

Yes, she had thought of that. But William was miles upon miles away looking at land. "It's safe," she said as she tethered Ebony.

Austin shook his head. "I don't want you hurt. You need to leave. You cannot come here again."

Evelyn felt her hope crumble. It was too much to bear, and the words came tumbling out over each other before she could stop them. "I'm sorry. I didn't know what I wanted!"

Austin looked pained at the confession. "Evelyn, we're too old for that. It was time to make a decision."

She squeezed the fence where she had hitched Ebony until her fingers were white. "And I chose poorly! How could I have known then? But I know now. I know now."

Austin sighed. "You were only eighteen, and the world is different now. You are trapped, as so many others your age are. Forced into responsibilities for which you are too young. I see it now with others on my travels. Women go to college, delay their lives as wives to learn more about the wide world first. How can that be anything but smart? I only wish you had been afforded that same opportunity."

"And yet you would've had me as your wife then! Before!"

Austin didn't rise to the bait. "I spoke to your parents. I wanted to wait until you were twenty, in college. Your father . . . no. William was an opportunity for you, and I understand that. But—"

"What about my father?" Evelyn asked.

"I'll say nothing ill of your father," Austin replied. "We will settle it at he thought it time for you to be wed, and William was agreeable as well. That he also thought you were agreeable seemed a large part in those proceedings."

Evelyn put her face in her hands and wept. "I felt stuck. I forced myself to make a decision."

Austin set a hand on her shoulder, but it felt like her brother when he was about to tell her something wise and somber. It didn't feel like a man who wanted her in the way a man could want a woman. It tore her heart, at once missing Ethan and missing the man she'd taken for granted, treated so poorly she didn't even know where to begin mending the hurt.

"I understand now why you did it," Austin said. "But that doesn't mean I don't feel hurt by it."

"I know. I know!" Evelyn turned her face from him.

"I'm sorry, Evelyn."

She nodded, feeling whatever wrenched her heart twist again. She wiped her eyes gingerly and prepared to head back into town with her shame.

"What happened to your hands?"

Evelyn wasn't ready for the question. She turned back to Austin, then dropped her hands behind her back. "Nothing."

Something dark was in Austin's eyes that she had not seen before. "Did he hurt you?"

"No!" Evelyn insisted while her insides churned at the lie. William hadn't laid a hand on her, and he wouldn't. He could say what he wanted with his words and say he never hurt her. Not once.

Austin reached out gently and took her hands from behind her back. He removed the wrappings so carefully it brought tears to Evelyn's eyes. William had not been so gentle.

"How did this happen?"

"It was an accident. With a mirror." Perhaps at one time she could have told Austin of the thing she saw, the thing that she was certain was not human, but now she was afraid. Not of Austin but of Austin not being there if something else happened.

Austin peeled back the soaked bandages. His face was unreadable as he examined the cuts. He clearly didn't believe her when she said William hadn't done anything.

"These cuts are infected. Have they not been treated?"

"Only with hot water and fresh bandages. William said that was all they needed. I told him of several prairie herbs that would speed healing, but he said there wasn't room for that witchcraft in his house."

Austin remained tightlipped, but Evelyn could tell he wanted to say something about William's comment.

"Go on, say it," she whispered.

"He's an ignorant fool." Austin's eyes were fiery.

"He is a very calculated man in other ways," Evelyn replied, feeling the knot in her stomach when she said it. In some strange way, she feared William would know she had spoken of him. "Please let us abandon the subject for now. I don't like the way the wind blows when we speak of him."

Austin nodded. "I agree. Let's get something on your hands. And then you must go."

The clenching feeling again, this time in her heart. She assented.

The next hour that they spent searching the early spring prairie for herbs was the best hour in her recent memory. Austin was still standoffish and cool, but he wasn't nearly so cold as he had been when last she saw him.

She didn't press against him as she once had when they went rooting around on the prairie. She was afraid that touching him would break the spell that had allowed them the time together.

The prairie was kind to them, and they began to talk, haltingly, as they once had. Evelyn didn't see such beauty in the sky, but the prairie still held magic for her. She felt Austin watch her as she knelt to inspect the little plants close to the ground, still hiding deep in the previous year's grasses for fear of a late cold snap.

Herbs found, Austin took her into the bustling house. The staff watched, and some said hello to Evelyn. Evelyn no longer recognized all their faces. Austin's home had grown, and signs of his good fortune were everywhere. There was a new addition on the south of the house that Evelyn longed to explore, and fine furniture filled the space.

They went into the room off the kitchen, which was warm and lit with a welcoming fire. Austin pulled a jar from a shelf and bade Evelyn sit at the small table there. She did, and Austin applied a poultice of the herbs they had found, followed by a salve, then clean bandages.

"What is that?" Evelyn asked. The salve soothed her hands in a way nothing else had yet.

"I came across it on my travels. I use it for my face and hands when they become chapped and my feet when they blister and on any cuts I get along the way. I can never escape at least a few snaps from the barb and wire, you know." The easy smile that he gave her seared right through her. How different he was from William. Tears threatened again. The moment was nearing its end; she could feel it.

"Thank you."

When he walked her outside, they stood at the fence and watched Evan and Ebony. Ebony had escaped her tether, and she and Evan chased each other up and down the fence. The sun tried to find its way out from behind clouds building in the south. A breeze had picked up.

"There will be storms tonight," Austin said, though his eyes didn't leave the two horses, who were now nose to nose. Ebony let out a squeal, kicked up her heels, and ran off again.

"You think?" Evelyn could not help but admire how fine the two horses looked together. They had to be the same breed. Where had William found such a beautiful animal?

"Yes. Your horse. Have you had her long?"

Evelyn stepped up on the fence and let the breeze play at her ankles. Her feet felt so much better in her own boots. "Since a bit after . . . you know. She was an early gift. She's the only gift that didn't come with a sour taste in my mouth after I received it."

Austin hummed his assent, then headed inside the gate. "She's a fine animal. Come, you must go."

He saddled her horse for her and felt the mare's legs and haunches as he readied the animal for Evelyn's ride. He commented on her soundness but noted a defect in her coloring—a star on her fetlock under the hair there—which could render her unsuitable to be bred with a purebred stallion. It was a small detail that he noted to himself, not a little smugly, then helped Evelyn atop her mount. She was a perfect horse for his Evelyn though; that he knew.

He didn't speak of parting with her again but simply told Evelyn to take care of the horse and then sent her on her way.

The ride home was lonely, except for Ebony's company. The mare was tired but still alert after her long ride and playtime with Evan, who was older. Watching them together, she had felt as if she were watching herself and Austin. What they once were anyway.

Evelyn took care that her ride back to town was unnoticed. The small canyon bridge was eerily quiet as she passed over its wooden planks. Ebony's hooves echoed in the covered crossing, but no birds called from their nests underneath or from the trees that hugged the shorter sides of that end of the canyon.

She met no one on the bridge. She could not even hear the water trickling below, as she had when she rode out earlier. Cold air rushed about her ankles, tried to slip beneath her riding habit. She was chilled, as she had been before the mirror that showed her the shrinking, awful figure that William had become. She imagined the cold air at her ankles as the cold hands of the thing from the mirror. In that instant, she knew she had created it with her disobedience, with her sin.

A rational voice, one that sounded like Austin, told her that it was just her imagination. Yes, darkness abounded in the world, but it simply was. She had done nothing to cause it. That didn't help the feeling that something dark and cold came nearer, whether she had caused it or not.

Back at the estate, she got Ebony securely shut in her stall with an early dinner. By the time she had slipped back to the house, Evelyn had forgotten about the bridge, the strange cold, and the feeling of foreboding that had come with it.

40

Friday, October 16th

Olivia had expected the oldest cemetery in the area to be somewhere outside of town, but there it was, not more than ten blocks from campus, surrounded by a residential area. She must have passed it many times but hadn't spared it a thought. Simon's house wasn't far from it either, but whose house wasn't? The area was densely populated with the homes of many university professors. The house on Sunset she'd had her eye on wasn't three blocks away. She wasn't certain she still wanted it though. With everything going on, the permanence of a house that wasn't on the Weatherford estate seemed further away than ever, even with the ten grand from the showing.

Or she could move in with Simon. The thought hit her hard in the gut, and she felt herself turn red and hot. No. No, she couldn't think that. Get through the month first, spend some *normal* time with him.

She forced herself to focus. Perhaps this was where Austin's head had been stashed. Any burial site for the Monroes would have been claimed years before they were needed. And if that were the case, perhaps the site or the crypt had been built beforehand as well. What better, more secure place to hide something? It was as good of a lead as she had.

She imagined Evelyn was buried there too. Perhaps the woman didn't know because there was no comment on the subject. Olivia would just have to look for herself.

The cemetery was beautiful in the morning light. That was the photographer in her. Her subject was a beautiful one but a subject nonetheless. Cedars and cottonwoods towered over the limestone and wrought-iron fencing that marked the cemetery's boundaries. The entrance was an impressive limestone-and-iron archway. A plaque attached to one of the stone supports read "Our Union Soldiers, Our Heroes" and was dated at the turn of the century. Evelyn might have stood in that exact spot to watch the plaque be unveiled. No memory surfaced, but Olivia had a feeling it would visit her before too long.

The landscape breathes, is living, her companion said. *Some things do not change with time.*

Olivia rolled her eyes. Apparently, if it wasn't musical, it wasn't worth sharing.

A red Pontiac rolled up and parked next to her SUV. Olivia watched from her spot near the stone-and-iron fence as a guy she could only describe as "basically a baby" stepped out of his vehicle. Even from that distance, she recognized his face. It was one she had been seeing a lot of lately in old photographs and next to her for dinners and coffee. There was an eerie resemblance between the young man and the death photos of Ethan Weatherford. If she had happened upon one scrap of paper that pointed toward a cover-up, what else might be out there?

"Colton *Mun*roe," he said as he strolled toward her.

"Olivia Norwich," she replied as she held out her hand. Colton didn't take it. After an awkward moment, she dropped her hand.

"Sorry," he said in a voice that sounded anything but. "Just feeling cautious after the month I've had."

Olivia thought she understood. All the times Austin had taken her hand and pulled her away into the past. If Colton was what he claimed to be, then maybe he knew that.

Olivia pressed her sweating hand against her skirts, which she could feel but not see. She saw Colton's eyes follow, then dart to her face. Grey eyes that mirrored her own looked back questioningly.

"Do you see it?" she whispered, not wanting to disturb whatever was happening.

"Unfortunately, yes," Colton said as he took his phone from his pocket. It had some kind of lens installed on top of the camera port on the back of his phone.

"Watch this," he said. "Stand still."

She did, except for the hand that reflexively grabbed a handful of her cotton skirts. They felt soft, well-worn but well-maintained. Colton backed up a few paces, then stood with his phone pointed at her for a long moment. He gestured for her to stand beside him.

"What kind of lens is that?" she asked. "I'm a photographer, but I've never seen anything like it."

"It's my own," Colton said, not a little proudly. "I altered a cheap-o from a camera shop. Check this out."

There was the proof she had been looking for. Someone stood next to her watching a video of a girl with her brown hair in a halo about her head, hands clutching pale blue skirts. She could have been on *Little House on the Prairie*. Her face looked thinner in the video though, and Olivia remarked on it.

"Don't you recognize yourself?" he asked, looking at her.

Olivia's heart sank. Perhaps he didn't see. She didn't have to wait long for Colton to clarify himself. "I mean you a hundred years ago. Evelyn Weatherford-Monroe."

Olivia turned and walked into the cemetery, processing. A rush of dizziness came over her, then passed. She paused on the crushed limestone path just inside the gates and archway at the cemetery's entrance. "What does it mean?"

Colton looked up at the gates and archway. "You've heard about horseshoes over doors for luck, right? Well, in Ye Olde Days, dude named Saint Dunstan stuck an iron horseshoe on the devil, and Dunstan only agreed to take it off if the devil would agree to never enter anywhere that has one over the door. Guess it hurt pretty bad. This whole place is wrapped in iron and topped with a pretty iron horseshoe bow."

Olivia couldn't follow what he was talking about. Horseshoes? The devil? She shook her head. "I mean the Evelyn thing."

Colton caught up to her, rolling his eyes. "Thought you meant your return to your normal self. Guess it means you're haunted."

Olivia threw him a withering look. Annoying over explainer. "What am I supposed to do with it?"

They started walking at the same time, moving like the planchette of an Ouija board through the cemetery, slowing but not stopping, moving toward something. "If it doesn't bother you, nothing. It will pass with time."

They stopped before a set of old gravestones. Olivia didn't need to look down at them to know whose they were. "Would you be surprised if I told you that it's the furthest thing from not bothering me?"

"No," Colton replied, looking down at where they had stopped. Eva and Evette Weatherford. Nearby, Ethan Weatherford.

Olivia stared at the graves but felt no affinity with them. Evelyn had died long before her sisters. Evelyn was strangely quiet on the subject though. "Why didn't you want to talk to me when I called?"

Colton scoffed and toed at the soft dirt around the graves. "Because I had an idea who you were."

"How does everyone know that except me?"

The look Colton threw her was one she thought crossed his face often. "Surely you grew up hearing the legends. You live on their land, for Christ's sake."

"My mother never said anything about it."

"And no one said anything to you in school?"

"I went to Riley."

Colton rolled his eyes and sighed heavily. Olivia was about to ask him what frat house he'd been spending so much time in when Colton switched gears on her. For the better, she thought. He looked as young as her students but found a way to get on her nerves more quickly. She'd never had a brother, but she imagined they were just as annoying.

"What all have you seen so far?"

Olivia sighed, the tension of the last weeks coming out in the hard breath.

"Heavy sighing is a sign of stress," Colton said, smiling. He looked more like Simon than Ethan then. Olivia didn't think that was a coincidence.

"No shit?" Olivia shouldn't have given him credit for switching gears so quickly. She looked back at the graves before them. "And I've seen a ghost. Ghosts. Frequently. Something's living in the old Monroe house. Something's living with me too. Evelyn."

Colton absorbed her words silently. Olivia felt better and worse for telling him what she had seen, as if it were a secret that was eating away at her but which she was not meant to share.

"Something evil in the Monroe house? It is almost Halloween," Colton joked.

The sarcasm was annoying, but she had to admit she might be the uptight one. "I know. So many surprises. I wasn't certain I would get out of there with my life."

Something about what she said made Colton's face turn serious. "Yeah, yeah, if there is, you're lucky."

"I don't know what all is connected, but I think he . . . Simon . . . is possessed by the . . . a demon."

Colton nodded, businesslike. "Might be a strix, not a demon. And you did go into *his* house," he pointed out.

"What's a strix? And what does it matter? All it did was scare the shit out of me."

"How have you seen him? I mean, you know what a demon is. Classically, the term didn't mean a bad spirit. Christianity spun it that way. But it's a great general term for a bad spirit today. A strix is more complicated. Antoninus Liberalis, like two thousand years ago, wrote about people transformed into blood-and-flesh-hungry owls for their crimes against humanity—cannibalism in that case. It's a theory for where vampires come from, funny enough."

Olivia didn't think it was funny but conjured the image in her mind. She'd kept it sealed away in a nice box when she could. "He looked like a . . . gargoyle? I mean, I saw something that looked like a gargoyle, covered in tar, squashed face, that turned into someone who looked like Simon. He's a history professor at the—"

"William Monroe," Colton said. "And I know who Simon is."

"But he isn't related to—"

"Sure he is. If William Monroe was the super asshole I think he was, then for him to have morphed into something disgustingly otherworldly, I'd buy it. Demon or strix, take your pick on the label. His spirit got twisted either way."

Her phone rang. She silenced it. It rang again. And again. Each call sent her anxiety spiraling back upward.

"Do you need to answer that?" Colton asked. "I'm not the fuckin' etiquette police, but it seems like you should silence your phone when you're in a cemetery."

Olivia stared at her phone. It could be Simon, or it could be Not Simon. "He's been calling me a lot," she said around her thick tongue.

"Who?"

"Not Simon. Whatever he is."

"William Monroe has been calling you?"

"More than is probably appropriate."

The phone rang again, and this time they both stared at it. Colton reached over and silenced the call. The phone stayed silent this time.

"Block his number?"

Olivia waited for the phone to ring again, like waiting for a final hiccup that never came. "What good would that do?"

"Short of throwing your phone off the cliffs, I don't know what else to tell you."

"He'd just stop by," she replied, then looked around nervously.

"We don't want that."

Olivia's stomach jerked at the word "we." "The disappearances have stopped. If I'm . . . I don't want . . ."

"No, we don't want that," Colton said, gentler than before. A mature person might have been lurking in him after all.

The helpless feeling swept over her again. Just when she thought she had found footing, something else happened. "What do we do?"

Colton reached down and brushed leaves and dirt from the top of the Weatherford grave, then turned his grey eyes on her. "If you feel you can't ignore it, use your resources. Learn as much as you can about what and who you're dealing with. Find out why they're here. That's more of a movie joke though in my experience. Better to learn about them as people and discover their motives that way."

"What do you mean?"

"I mean things don't always happen for a reason. Or you open up a never-ending hole of arbitrary reasons until you forget why you're chasing it in the first place. Diversion tactics. They're here because they're here, and you want them gone. Research them, figure out what it takes to send them back where they came from. You have to figure out what they want. Even the good ones want something. In the meantime, text me, call, whatever. Let's meet back here in a few days to discuss things further, see what you come up with."

Olivia looked from Colton to the graves and back. It was a place to start. She could make a plan, come back and look for Austin's head when she could think more clearly.

"I'm not sure what Evelyn wants. She's been nothing but nice to me."

Colton's face was incredulous. "You're possessed. There's nothing 'nice' about that."

"But . . ." Olivia started, then stopped. Maybe Evelyn didn't want to leave because Austin was there. But she hadn't said anything of the sort, and she seemed keen on helping Olivia. Perhaps Olivia's implicit trust in the woman was misplaced. That thought settled like a stone in her belly.

"Be careful," Colton said as they parted, and Olivia heard Ethan's voice in his warning. He was a Weatherford; that was undeniable. But was he also a Monroe or a Hearth?

Back at her mother's house, she checked the locks on the windows and the front door every time she came back into the living room. Who knew if Not Simon might try and sneak in the way he was surely sneaking into the other women's homes, spiriting them away and doing God knew what with them?

The calls didn't stop, and Olivia's kneejerk feeling was to want Colton there after he had silenced the last round of calls in the cemetery.

Her phone rang again, though the number looked different. It was a campus number, unlike Simon's office phone. She silenced it the first two times but decided to answer the third. Perhaps it wasn't the imposter.

"Hello?"

"Olivia Norwich?" A female voice. Olivia felt her entire body relax.

"Yes, this is she." She only half listened as she scanned the documents before her. The puzzle didn't fit together nicely. Simon's version painted

William as off-kilter because of an old bullet, the historical society seemed to revere him, and Evelyn's journal hinted at something sinister. Olivia wasn't sure who to believe. And Austin himself? He seemed kind, level-headed. Not the sort of man who would haul off and kill a dozen people. Anything was possible though.

"Ms. Norwich, this is Martha Rogers."

The director of the College of Arts and Sciences. Olivia froze. "Yes?"

"I take it you didn't receive my email?" Martha asked coolly.

Olivia thought about all the notifications she may or may not have moved on her phone. "No, I didn't." Lie.

There was an uncomfortable silence on the line. "I'm very sorry to do this over the phone, Ms. Norwich, but myself, Dr. Wilson, and Dr. Cahara would like to have a short meeting with you."

Her tone suggested that Olivia knew what the meeting would be about. Olivia wracked her brain. "What day?" she asked. She could barely remember her teaching schedule at that point. She thought she had emailed her students for all the days she had missed, but she wasn't sure. She would be at every single class the next week though. Definitely would make sure.

"Sunday, Miss Norwich. Six p.m. sharp in the ESCS conference room. Please do not be late." Martha's voice had an edge that Olivia didn't like. They had been professional colleagues since Olivia's graduate school days, and Olivia hadn't known her to have a cranky side at all.

"Do I need to bring anything?" Olivia asked. She wanted to argue. A department meeting on a Sunday!

"Your lesson plans and syllabi. Your schedule. Any doctor's slips for missing teaching days. Anything else you feel you need. All of which I explained in the numerous emails myself, Dr. Wilson, and Dr. Cahara have sent to you. That you have been unavailable in person is also concerning. Students have waited outside your office on multiple occasions during your posted office hours."

"Oh." Olivia's stomach turned over. "Thank you. I'll see you Sunday."

She ended the call and sat heavily on the couch. She tried to calculate when she had last been in the classroom. She had been at least once the previous week, and surely she had sent out emails the other days letting her students know she wouldn't be making it to class that day. Surely she had let them know what homework to keep working on and what they needed to be prepared to do in the following class period. She'd been in and out of her office, but she didn't remember staying there for long. She'd been preoccupied.

She poured herself a large glass of wine and stashed the bottle in the cabinet above the fridge where she hoped her mother wouldn't poke around. It had been years since she had had alcohol in her mom's house. The woman took too many medications to even think about drinking on top of them.

Olivia popped a quarter of a Percocet in her mouth and took a long swallow of wine. The call from Martha wasn't good. It sounded like it was on the verge of we-might-terminate-you not good, but Olivia tried to keep herself from wandering down that path. If she could somehow put this off on the extreme stress of the festival project, she might be able to buy herself a mulligan and not get reamed too hard for her lapse.

She was about to give in to the panicky anxiety when the Percocet kicked in. Ah, yes. She stared out the kitchen window toward the dugout at the barely visible rise in the tall prairie grasses and the scrubby bushes that littered the far edge of the backyard.

Now that she was intimately familiar with where it was, it was unmistakable. Her eyes had been drawn to it every time she stood at the sink. Every time she looked off the back porch. Every time she looked out the window of the upstairs bathroom. A smallish tree near the entrance put out pinkish purple flowers in the spring. A young cottonwood stood near it. She had always been dissuaded from going inside, so she hadn't. Her father said it was his tool storage, so it was boring. Mom had said it was full of rats, and that was scary. And so, it had sat there, a cool, dry storage locker for the Weatherford's secrets. Evelyn's secrets.

Buzzed on wine and the Perc, it didn't take her as long as she thought it would to set up the back of the dugout as a darkroom. Once she cleared a path and got the room cleaned and organized (revealing the full extent of the hard-packed earth floor), she saw how large the space was. A few antiques in the back must have been original to the house, but she hadn't needed all of them. A small dresser held some of her equipment, and she had carefully boxed up the remainder of the papers and photographs she found in the room. She had been afraid to bring too much light into the room while the papers were still exposed, the same fear she felt about her photographic paper. She did it all by indirect flashlight, squinting at everything in the dim light. Sometimes the flashlight flickered like a candle, and she felt Evelyn's presence more clearly, slipping into the other woman's world without realizing it.

I played here as a little girl.

Olivia had been so immersed in the cleaning that Evelyn's voice sent chills through her. She no longer felt alone in the dugout, and the hall to the entrance once again seemed far away.

Mother and Father didn't live here very long before they were in the house. They preferred to stay in town, but even town was not much back then. It was not as it was when I grew older.

She'd dug her old equipment out of a hall closet stuffed from undergraduate days. What she didn't have at the house, she had extra at her studio, including chemicals. While it wasn't ideal, it seemed necessary at the time. Simon . . . well, not Simon but whatever Simon was carrying around with him now, might take advantage of knowing where she was most of the time. Dr. Cahara had apparently noticed that she'd been absent, but she wasn't married to making prints on campus. So long as she was getting them done, why should Cecelia care?

She found a set of sawhorses in the front of the dugout and another set in the garage (thank you, absent father). A large piece of plywood ensured she had a large worktable for nearly everything she needed.

While she worked in the dark, the feeling that she was not alone grew stronger. It was more than just Evelyn, but it wasn't sinister. It felt like curiosity.

Her safe light didn't reveal anything when she turned it on not long afterwards. It was only her, her equipment, and the dirt walls around her. A cool lick of a breeze reached her from under the canvas that covered the doorway. It felt like night air on the prairie. It made her expect Austin.

As she let her hands do their work, she thought about him and wondered what he might be up to. Evelyn only whispered quietly about what he did in the evenings when he was alive, her voice like listening to a radio on low at night. It was soothing, and Olivia absorbed the stories about checking the cattle, riding fences, taking trains out west, and sleeping under the prairie sky. To Evelyn it was hard work with a romantic edge. Did she know how hard life was then? How hard it was still?

It was late by the time Olivia rolled the print through its chemical baths. She accidentally grazed the ground with the print once before she was able to hang it to dry. Her first instinct was panic, worry about the print, but a little dirt wouldn't hurt. She hung the weights on the corners of the large photograph, which took up the entire far wall of the dugout, and stood back.

In the safe light, the white paper was red, and the greys looked black, but Olivia ached with joy for how the latest print had turned out. Her hands were stiff and slimy, her eyes tired, but the print was good. The stretch of the Flint Hills not far down the road from her mother's house had drawn her for years. Now it was immortalized.

The depth in the photograph was her best so far. The prairie stretched beyond the grasses and plants she had captured in the photograph's foreground. Trees grew tall in the distance, old cottonwoods that had stood sentinel for longer than even the pioneers who traveled those plains, wondering how far they stretched. Clouds rose in the sky, harbingers of fair weather. She had captured Canadian geese moving through the frame, and they formed their quintessential V shape just off center in the photograph, if one looked closely enough. In the grasses was the nose of a rabbit, who sat frozen while she was framing and taking each shot. She was happy he had stayed around long enough to be in the final frame she chose.

But there. Something moved in the photograph. It was a small black blob that swept through the grasses and toward the front of the frame. It was Evan again.

The anxiety didn't set in until Olivia realized it wasn't Evan this time. As the galloping animal came into view, Olivia saw that it was Evan's not-so-handsome counterpart.

As it moved closer in the frame, Olivia watched, frozen, as fire ignited the grass at its feet. Greyscale flames leapt at the horse but didn't touch it. Olivia could swear she heard a clicking sound as it jerked its head from side to side at anatomically impossible angles. When its eyes flashed toward her, they went from ghostly white to red, the only splash of brightness on the paper.

Olivia backed away from the image. The grass around the horse burned, and the flames spread outward. She smelled smoke.

In the red safelight on the nearly life-size photograph paper, the nightmare horse looked like something straight from hell. It opened and closed its mouth like it was chewing, and Olivia saw its unnaturally sharp teeth. The flames continued to spread, consuming the trees in the photograph. Black clouds rolled forward in the sky, overtaking the fair-weather clouds in Olivia's photograph. The geese burst into flame and went careening toward the earth. At any moment, the nightmare horse might burst from the photograph and overtake *her.*

Olivia fled from the dugout and out into the prairie night, where she gasped for breath in the cool air. She chanced a look at the dugout behind her and saw a flickering red light illuminating the front of the structure. It threw long shadows out into the beaten-down prairie grasses near the entrance.

She went beyond the light's reach and sat in the damp prairie grasses, trying to find her breath. Out there the last of the summer insects called to each other, and crickets chirped and hummed all around her. It was cool, but she lay back in the cradle of the prairie and stared up at the sky.

How long had she photographed the prairie and not known how much beauty it held? After what she had learned from Colton, how could she remain the same?

Slivers of clouds raced across the sky, made silver by the moon. Stars winked around the clouds. Far, far above, a satellite careened across the sky. For a time Olivia didn't understand what it was. It seemed like a strange shooting star.

There in the cradle of the prairie, everything else was washed away, and she returned to the earth. She stared at the moon's highway and the high clouds until her heart beat steadily, and the nightmare horse was only a distant fear.

41

WINTER 1899

THAT DAY, HE KNEW SHE WOULD COME.

He watched her glide across the fields, a ghostly sight to behold. The prairie grass moved like waves in the wind, curling over in a gust. glinting even in the overcast day. And her. Was she a wave too? Her hair moved like the grass. Her dress and shawl whipped around as if they longed to tear themselves from her body. And she was the color of the prairie, dressed in a pale-brown shawl and cloak and a grey dress. She moved in and out of sight in the grasses, camouflaged one moment and visible the next.

And what was underneath? A lamb? A wolf? Some other manner of creature that woman may become but always is?

He had seen it when he pleaded with the gypsy woman. Beneath her dark-eyed gaze, an animal waited. But Evelyn? What animal did she have inside that would not be tamed? Was she an animal, or was she one of her prairie flowers, rare and unique?

He knew the answer to that question. He also knew he would need to find the right words to apologize to her. He didn't believe he was wrong to be upset, but he was wrong to let it rot him away from the inside out. She was his Evelyn still, in his heart.

Their last meeting on the prairie, when they had gathered herbs for her hands, had reawakened something in him. Under the weight of the anger he manifested toward Monroe, toward himself, he had let so much become rotten. He remembered the walks with her on the prairie and the long hours spent musing on why this plant was this way and why the storms came in from the south in the spring and how much barb and wire he might sell that season.

Now it was all much more complicated. He knew where his heart lay, but he was concerned for Evelyn. He didn't want her in trouble, and with relations with Monroe already so strained, this might be what finally brought the tension to its inevitable breaking point. If somehow they could be a distance away by the time that happened, all the better.

He met her outside the gate, not far from where Evan grazed. The horse shone even in the dull winter day, and his winter coat was thick and warm. Austin had a difficult time catching him on some cold days when Evan wanted to run though the pasture instead of being led inside and shut in.

When he got close to her, he felt disappointment rise in him. He would never open his mouth and say it, but he could not believe how she had changed in so short a time. Her beautiful hair was shorn short and didn't shine with health. Her eyes were sunken, and her cheekbones protruded. Had she labored long as an invalid, unable to send word to him? But no, surely not. He had seen her within the season still.

"I expect you to send me away, but I wanted to see you one last time."

"Evelyn . . ." His anger toward her crumbled. This was his windswept woman, and he could take care of her where William Monroe could not. He would see to it.

"No, please. I just wanted to see you once more. I wanted to tell you . . . I wanted to tell you that I . . ." She broke down into tears, great sobs that hunched her over and sent her crying into her hands.

Austin reached out and gently touched her shoulders. "Evelyn, please. I cannot be mad any longer. I cannot."

Evelyn flinched from his touch, then stopped herself and apologized. Why couldn't she even look him in the eye?

A horrifying thought careened through his head. "My God, Evelyn, does he hit you?"

Evelyn shook her head emphatically. "No. No, William has never raised a hand to me."

"Then why do you flinch from me?"

"I don't know. I'm sorry. I'm so sorry."

Austin reached out for her. "May I hold you?"

Evelyn nodded through her tears and slid into his arms.

"What has he done to you?"

"I just . . . please, I don't want to talk about it any longer today."

He thawed at the sight of her. She had been his dearest friend. No matter how much she had hurt him, he believed she hadn't done it on purpose. She would not have. Could not have.

He pulled her into the crook of his arm the way he did with the young foals still wobbling on their new legs and guided her toward the house. It didn't seem like anyone else was about, but the theft of the filly had opened his eyes to the darker side of prairie life. And Evelyn. And his parents. He had always known that rattlesnakes were a hazard on the prairie, but what the world didn't tell a man was that sometimes prairie dog holes, invisible from the top of a horse or wagon seat, were often more dangerous.

He tried to still the anger that flashed. It was like smashing a large ant nest. Once the hill was disturbed, everything started to escape, and quickly, even though he had worked so hard to contain it.

Once inside, he had Ruth start tea, and he got Evelyn set up in the informal parlor with a blanket and a hot water bottle. Her fingers were blue at the tips.

"Has it gotten worse?" he asked quietly.

"What?" Evelyn's head snapped up. He saw animal fear there. "I'm sorry, I was off in my own world."

"Your fingers." He gestured at her hands, "Have they gotten worse?"

She curled her tiny hands into fists and shoved them into the folds of her dress. "Yes. I would wear gloves some at home, but William does not like them. He thinks they were what caused the whiteness to begin with."

"And what do you think?" He knew, but he wanted to hear her say it. It seemed her ability to converse had lapsed. The anger licked at him. He pushed back at it.

"I think my situation at William's has made them worse."

Austin pulled his chair closer to her and held out his hands. She set them in his with a little smile. "Just like the old days."

"Yes. It helped, did it not?"

Her smile spread as he clasped her hands inside his. His hands had always felt so hot, and now he knew why.

"Yes, very much."

Ruth brought the tea. For a time, they only drank tea and looked at each other. Evelyn nibbled on scone after scone, then started in on the sandwiches. Austin watched her eat, her appetite concerning.

"I don't suppose you have anything stronger than this?" Evelyn asked of the tea, a ghost of a smile on her face.

"I suppose the situation would merit it." Austin stood and pulled a small flask from where it was tucked over the hearth in the parlor, hidden away. Evelyn thanked him when he put a splash of it in her tea. He abstained himself. He'd had enough of a scare with his nearly uncontrollable anger outside.

She began to speak, haltingly at first, and then with gathering speed. Her voice grew hoarse after several minutes, telling him of strange situation after strange situation—how William liked their clothing to match, how he dictated what she ate and when, how he left her at home alone for long stretches of time without telling her when he would return and when she could eat again.

Austin heard her every word and stored it away. It was all fuel for his rage against William. It was more proof of his theory that the man was the devil incarnate. "That man is a regular curried wolf."

"Oh," she said, as if surprised. "No, I don't think he is so dangerous a devil. I think he's a man. I think he's ambitious. Particular."

"And was the devil himself not those things?"

"He was. Is. But he was not a man, and men, I think, are worse than fallen angels. We fell from God's grace long ago, and William has never known the touch of it."

He felt cold at her words. How long had she thought on these things under that man's roof? And look how long he had treated her thus, thinking she had merely made a poor choice. Of course William had snapped her up. He was ambitious, and Evelyn, besides her sisters, who were too young for William, was the most prized woman for a hundred miles. How Austin had not recognized that years earlier and made more of an effort with her parents, he didn't know.

"I want . . . you," Evelyn finished quietly, her tea with the extra courage hardly touched.

"It's not that simple, Evelyn."

"But it is."

He wanted to argue, to tell her it was for her safety, that she needed to go back to the place she now called home and stay there. But he was selfish too, and she was part of him. She was his.

"Come." He held out his hand for her. She took it as she had for so many years when they walked the prairie.

They walked together upstairs. Did his home look the same to her? The additions to the house had opened it up, showed off the latest styles in architecture while retaining the bones his father had intended for it.

Evelyn's eyes watched, but she didn't say what she thought. Then she turned to him and smiled.

He paused at the top of the stairs and kissed her as he had longed to do for many years. When he held her, she smelled of the prairie he loved so dearly. "I no longer wish to travel alone, Evelyn. I have wanted you as my companion these years."

A little hitch of breath was his response. Her hands on his back squeezed tightly. "Austin," she whispered.

He could feel how many things were unsaid. "Please," he said. "You don't need to say it."

"I'll say it for the rest of my life if I need to," Evelyn said and kissed him again. "I'm so sorry. And I will. I will come with you. Every moment in my dreams and every moment in between."

Austin held that in his heart and let his hands take in every part of her that he had wished to since he had known her.

She had on many layers beneath her dress. Three sets of underthings under her corset had given her body the illusion of shape. He stored the information away like so many of the other things that angered him. Evelyn didn't need his anger. She needed his love.

She had grown so slender. He missed the way her hips had sat nestled against him as Evan carried them across the prairie and the way she had looked in her prairie-wandering dresses, free from the corset that had changed her shape so drastically. Her shapely form had carried her on long walks with him, and her strong arms had helped when he pulled her astride Evan. God, he could still see her laughing face, thirteen and friends or seventeen in love.

She pressed his hands along her ribs, which stuck out grotesquely from her body. Her hipbones too. She was a ghost of herself.

"I wish I could will flesh onto your body," he said as he touched every part of her with the reverence that he knew she deserved.

She laughed, the first true laugh he had heard from her. "Am I that much diminished?"

He kissed her navel and hugged her to him. "Only your form, Miss Evelyn. The rest of you is as I remember."

She laughed again and swept her hands through his hair. "Then kiss me, and make me forget the rest."

And he did. But he didn't forget the anger that he added to his distaste for William Monroe. No, he would not forget all that the man had taken from him.

When they landed in his bed, she took him, sitting atop him, riding astride. She laughed. God, she laughed. It was music to his ears to hear it again.

She had laughed at everything before. Oddly shaped trees and flowers and plants. His herding dogs rolling in the late summer dust. Rolling hoops in the tall grass in the shade of cottonwood trees. Nothing was serious when they had been together. Now too much was serious, which meant they needed the laughter all the more.

"All of me, Austin, you have all of me," she whispered huskily, then laughed again. It was a sad woman's laugh. A woman who had seen too much but now had what she wanted.

In the setting sun, he made her his. She laughed and kissed him.

42

Saturday, October 17th

Simon couldn't focus enough to even think about what to bring to the next department staff meeting, let alone what to talk about. He was behind on readings for his graduate committees, and his teaching was suffering as a result. So was he. He just wanted to enjoy a quiet night with Olivia. Hell, he would have settled for sitting on the couch in silence with her.

That obviously wasn't what William Monroe III wanted, but Simon couldn't figure out why. He could understand the man's anger toward her—hell, he'd be angry too—but wouldn't he want to make amends after so long? Simon knew better than that though.

Olivia hadn't responded to his texts that day. He was worried about her, but he was more worried that his other side had done something to her. He knew better, but he drove by her apartment. Her car wasn't there. Maybe she was with her mother outside of town. He took his ass back home after checking her apartment. He wasn't going to go down the stalker path, especially if his counterpart was already harassing Olivia.

He'd woken up sore again that morning and felt as if he'd gotten hit upside the head by something. That was looking more likely, unfortunately. He got as close to the bathroom mirror as he could and pulled aside the hair on the side of his head. The skin looked discolored and bruised, and a scab would eventually form over part of it that still looked raw. It stung when he touched it. It also looked like he might need stitches, but he was afraid to go to the doctor. What if someone had reported being attacked, and he fit the description of the assailant?

Simon got the Ranitidine down from the medicine cabinet; the heartburn had been fierce lately. Stress and coffee and stress and scotch and stress. The perfect ulcer cocktail.

He read the reports of the missing women carefully. On a spreadsheet, he kept their locations last seen tagged, so he could access them easily. He attended the vigils when he could. He kept an eye on his credit card purchases, but nothing unusual had happened since the big charge. (And he still had yet to discover where the thing hid the larger purchase. Boots and socks alone wouldn't have been that much.) Anything to keep ahead of his cohabitant.

The vigils were awful. After the last one though, the one where the angry brother claimed the abductor was attending the vigil, he hadn't gone to another. A twisted guilt ate at him.

For all of it, he tried to stay away from Olivia when all he wanted was to run to her. He had lost control several times in her presence, and he was worried what that meant as time went on. So, he scheduled himself out of free time. How long that would last, he wasn't sure, but it should buy Olivia some time.

He volunteered at the department's annual donation drive that week and spent long afternoons sitting next to his colleagues and students, calling alumni and asking them for money. It was depressing. Calling alumni with their bachelor's degree in history never hit the donation jackpot. There was a cheer across the room as the engineering department secured another $5,000 donation. The event made him angry. His counterpart was silent. Plotting, no doubt.

After his Saturday shift, he had a few minutes to kill before his rescheduled Monday class. So, he checked out the bulletin board outside the department mailroom. There were readings he could attend, nearly one per evening. He jotted down their times in his planner, then paused to stare at his handwriting. Cursive. It had been since he had learned cursive, failed miserably at it, and opted for printing instead that he had used it. Something ferreted into his brain and suggested that perhaps this was William Monroe's handwriting. Simon sighed heavily and kept writing. He would to need to take great care the following week before the festival. Of everything.

His head throbbed mercilessly, and his students were restless. They knew he was a good teacher, but they weren't going to keep letting him slack off. Well, they would. That was the problem.

Just one more week. He could make it one more week before he could let himself fall apart. Olivia was constantly on his mind. That woman. She did things to his heart that he didn't know were possible. But it was wrenched so many ways with her. How could he ever make sense of it all? Everything with Evelyn, William, and Austin had to end first though. Anxiety shot through him. He was not equipped to handle such stress. But he could and had before. Not the same brand of stress but a lot of it. When his mom and dad had died, that had been a particularly awful brand of hellish stress. But he had made it through. Thank God for alcohol and Bridgette, he had made it through.

He'd slung a few straw bales for his grandfather before his parents passed. After that he did it to pay the rent. And then it was with the intention of carrying on his grandfather's trade. Business. Whatever one wanted to call it.

That's where Shep had come from. Not long before he left, his grandfather had given him the puppy. How Bridgette squealed over him. Shep was purebred, from an excellent line of herding dogs. That Simon took the dog was like a promise to his grandfather. He'd spent countless hours training the animal, running him with sheep, ducks, and geese and building obstacle courses for him in a small corner of the property. Then he left.

And now look where he was. He'd arrived in a whirlwind, settled, got to work, and now Shep was old. He'd been trained and brought up to herd, and then Simon had taken him to Nowhere, Kansas, with nothing to do but chase birds, squirrels, rabbits, and the occasional turkey. Simon alternated between guilt and relief that he had spared Shep from the possibility of being trampled to death but sentenced him to a lifetime of boredom.

Rescheduling his Monday class on a Saturday wasn't his brightest idea. How everyone had managed to make it was a miracle. At least it was a full class, but as for his full attention, they certainly didn't have it, but he made it through.

As he left the classroom and headed toward his office, two police officers approached from the opposite end of the hall. They stopped near his office. One looked vaguely familiar. Probably a former student. Oh God, which one of his students had they come in to ask him about? DUI charges, underage drinking, drinking in public, getting caught with marijuana, the list was endless on a college campus.

They were indeed waiting at his office when he approached. He greeted them with a smile. "How can I help you?"

"Simon Monroe?"

"That's me."

"We'd like to ask you a few questions."

His pulse accelerated. Something wasn't right. "Well, certainly. What can I help you with?"

The two officers looked like they were ready for him to bolt. He felt like he wanted to as he thought about what they must be after.

"We'd like to ask you some questions *back at the station.*" How subtle of them.

Simon felt another anger rise in him—not his own. His anger paled in comparison to this. That was what they wanted to question him about. Yes, of that he was certain.

He felt the other anger relax to a simmer. A palpable one but a simmer nonetheless. "I walked here today. I can go get my car or catch a ride with you."

"You can ride with us, no problem." The younger officer was definitely a former student. Stuart Kneidel.

"Great." Simon stared at the sign on his door. Not even office hours. Had they been waiting for this moment? Either way, it seemed he had no excuses. He hitched the strap of his leather satchel higher up on his shoulder. "Lead the way."

The ride to the station was uneventful and silent. Thankfully, Kneidel didn't get into their earlier student-teacher relationship. Perhaps he had forgotten. Or perhaps he hadn't, and this would be juicy gossip. Just what Simon needed.

He stared out the window at the changing leaves. It had gotten cooler, and the trees were in full turn. The wind helped them shed their leaves.

He hadn't ridden in the back seat of a car in years. He didn't particularly like the circumstances, but it did let him see Warren in a way he hadn't seen it since he had moved there. The old limestone fronts of Warren's historic houses watched him as he went by. He felt that as surely as if he had seen people standing on their front porches.

What had he been up to in the evenings and overnights when his memory failed him? The women had disappeared, but where had they gone? William Monroe hadn't had a recorded history of violence—Simon had researched that to death, looked at all the old papers the library had to offer. But there was Austin. No one disputed that William had a hand in that violent death. Crime of passion or simply a crime, Simon couldn't say.

The dirt he'd dragged in the other night wasn't a good sign.

He listened to the officers talk about their lunch as they pulled up to the station. Maybe they weren't too worried about him.

He felt a little different when he sat down with Officer Wells. The man offered him coffee but didn't smile. Simon's insides clenched up.

"Do you know why you're here?"

"No." And he didn't. Not consciously anyway.

The deputy sat across from him. "What do you know about Darlene Watkins?"

Relief washed over Simon. "I'm not familiar with that name."

"How about Patience Chambers, Riley Duvall, Anna Norlie, Bridgette Cunningham, Delilah Simone?"

Hearing the names strung together was eerie. It seemed like they must have similarities, but sitting in an uncomfortable chair in a room made of white cinderblocks, he couldn't seem to grasp it. "The last name I'm familiar with. She was a colleague on campus. I didn't know her well but saw her in passing."

"It's a college town. As you can imagine, there are people everywhere all the time. You were seen in the area at the approximate time of several of these incidents. We just wanted to know if you had seen anything strange in either the seven hundred block of South Laramie or the two hundred block of Southwest Street."

More relief. So, he wasn't a suspect, but the motherfucker doing the deeds hadn't been as careful as he should have been either. It didn't matter if he didn't remember the deed though. It was still his hands doing the dirty work.

"What day? What time? I live south of campus in one of the older neighborhoods. I have a dog. I take him on walks at all hours. I keep odd hours because I teach and am often awake grading late."

"This was three nights ago. Around midnight. You didn't have a *dog* with you." The man's emphasis on the word "dog" was strange.

He could barely remember that morning, let alone two days earlier. What had he been doing on a weekday night? Ahh, yes. Olivia had come by late, had walked home with him after they'd spoken at his office. She hadn't disappeared that night, thank God.

"I walked home from campus, but I had a . . . friend with me. But we weren't out long, and she came home with me," he added lamely. *Friend? Jesus.*

"Your friend will confirm this?" Officer Wells took meticulous notes on his fresh notepad. An inkling of anger trickled through Simon, but whether it was his own or the thing's, he couldn't say. Olivia would be ecstatic to be pulled into this. The sinking in his stomach was almost worse than the moment the officers had walked up to his office. But now he was all in.

"Yes, she could. She stayed the night."

"You understand I'll need her name and number." It wasn't a question.

"Yes, I understand." He gave Olivia's name and pulled out his phone to find her number. He wasn't worried about what Olivia would say, but he didn't exactly want to drag her into possession bullshit. More than she already was anyway. His stomach turned sour at the thought of how he had nearly lost control when she had been in his office. And the times he didn't remember? If anything, he should tell her to stay away for the time being. At least until he could figure out how to oust the thing. She had enough going on with her epic photography.

Wells continued to ask him questions until Simon was certain he'd spent two hours there. *What's your schedule like? Have you seen anything strange anywhere else on campus or in town? Who do you see frequently? Have any of your students been missing for more than three classes? Have any been missing on these specific dates?* And on and on it went.

"Mr. Monroe?"

"Yes?"

It seemed he had wandered off in his head again, answering the mundane questions automatically. The absentmindedness was too frequent these days, what with his preoccupation with the festival and Olivia and trying to figure out his alter ego.

"I'll ask again. Will you submit to being fingerprinted? Understand that this is a voluntary situation, and you are not being held for any crime. We do have a situation here in town though that's causing quite a panic for some people. And they want answers. Being in the clear would mean we wouldn't have to call you back for any . . . late-night walks that you're seen on." Wells drummed the table with his tobacco-stained fingers in a way that was meditative. Hypnotic. He watched each finger hit the table in rapid succession. One of the nails was split clear to the quick. The others were jagged.

For the first time, he heard a clear voice in his head. It sounded much like his own when he spoke aloud but deeper and with an edge to it. A hard edge.

Submit to it. I'll take care of this.

It made his skin crawl.

Submit to it. You have nothing to fear.

The hair on Simon's arms stood up, but he managed to get out that he would, indeed, let them fingerprint him. When he stood and shook the officer's hand, it didn't quite feel like he moved himself. William Monroe was making himself known.

Simon still felt nervous through the fingerprinting process. How would it not appear to be him doing those things? Whatever those deeds ended up being. Suppose his helpful alter ego didn't have his best interests in mind? Or perhaps he did, needing someone to carry him around and all.

The curious feeling that he was only half in control persisted.

I told you that you have nothing to fear. Just wait and see.

Simon didn't like this arrangement. He thought something laughed at that thought, but it didn't linger.

After the fingerprinting, they took him back into the nondescript room and left him there. He had only just thought to himself that they weren't supposed to do that when his counterpart said it aloud for him. He might've just sat there with his thumb up his ass forever if William hadn't said something. Simon had to give some credit to the man; he was driven and focused.

"I assume someone is listening," William said to the empty room. "What else do you need, or can I go?"

Moments later their uniformed friend came back into the room, full of fake apologies. Simon's anger flared along with William's.

William stood straighter than Simon was used to. His gut didn't stick out so bad when his posture was improved. Something to keep in mind, he supposed. "I understand you have a lot going on here, but I have classes to teach and meetings to attend."

"I'm very sorry, Mr. Monroe. There was a mistake up front, and they sent you back here instead of on your way. Please follow me."

He was strangely thankful that William spoke up. Feeling grateful toward such a man didn't sit right in his gut though. He thought he heard a chuckle at that as he walked out of the station.

43

Olivia parked in the little gravel lot next to the groundskeeper's building again and got out of her car. No other cars were parked nearby. She felt drawn back to the cemetery and not just because she had asked Colton to meet her there again. But what did she expect to find?

Evelyn's eyes saw the cemetery for what it was in her time, a new development from the day before. Nearly the same, though there had been fewer trees, fewer homes, and fewer graves. The groundskeeper's building was the same small limestone house it was in the present, only for Evelyn light was coming from under the door. Full-time watchdog. Outsourced to surveillance cameras in the modern day. She doubted Warren had anything like that in the cemetery.

Warren had finally become the quiet, sleepy, crime-free hollow it had always wanted to be since its turn-of-the-century upheaval. Until this October, that is.

Nothing from Simon all day, which worried her more than the repeated calls, but she slipped her phone in her pocket anyway (on vibrate this time). Then she grabbed the flashlight she'd never given back to Dr. Cahara and headed toward the cemetery's entrance. Colton could come find her when he arrived.

She stopped at the wrought-iron entrance when Evelyn hollered at her. Olivia sat down heavily on the limestone ledge and leaned against the iron fence, her head about to explode with the pain of Evelyn's screams. She fisted her hands in her hair.

The iron! Oh God, the iron! Please get away from the iron!

Olivia jumped away from the fence, and the screaming stopped, as did most of the pain in her head. "What the hell does iron have to do with anything?"

But as soon as she said it, she remembered Colton's rambling story from her last trip there and the dizziness that had just about brought her to her knees. Olivia looked up. Sure as shit, there was a giant horseshoe at the peak of the arch. What other superstitions would come to pass now? And what would happen to the talkative Evelyn if she did go through?

Just don't touch it. I don't know how you will enter the cemetery though. You must go under the iron archway.

Her head was a little clearer now. "God, can you get out of my head for five minutes then? I have to go in there."

I cannot leave. The musical voice had grown faint, almost tired.

Brilliant.

"Evelyn? You there?" No answer. It must be nice to just hide away whenever she felt like it. "I'm going in."

As Olivia passed under the iron archway that announced the Sunset Cemetery, she heard the faint sound of Evelyn crying, whimpering. Then the sound faded away, and her head cleared.

"Evelyn?" Olivia ventured.

No answer. That was interesting. The silence from the day before made sense now. Olivia tucked the information away for later. Would it keep the woman away permanently? For a short time? Only while she was in the cemetery?

Olivia walked slowly down the main path of the cemetery, looking left and right at the graves there. How was she going to find it? In the distance, she could make out groups of tall crypts. Surely that's where William Monroe's resting place was.

The ground sloped down slightly as she walked, and the homes in the distance faded from view. It was easy to see why the location had been chosen for a cemetery. It was a quiet place. The cottonwood trees sang their rushing, soothing song as she walked, and the maples rustled their changing leaves.

She read some of the headstones as she passed. They were so old. She didn't see anything later than the early twentieth century. Surely they were still using the cemetery.

At some point she ventured off the path and wandered among the headstones. She found the Weatherford graves again and stared at the engraved names. Ethan. Eva. The stone next to it was Evette. Evelyn's sisters, her brother. Bits of someone else's memory flitted through her mind, though Evelyn was still absent. The terror of those days after Ethan's accident and the help that came. Austin, steady as he always was, and William, who arrived with soothing words and kind gestures that she had not seen from him before. She let herself be taken in by those gestures. How could she not have seen?

Nearby headstones were also Weatherfords, quite a few of them in that small, inconspicuous part of the cemetery filled with trees.

She moved slowly back toward the center path and saw a circular gravel drive in the distance with a group of three large crypts at its center. Even from the swell above the back-center part of the cemetery, she could read the names on the giant black and pale stone crypts. "MONROE," they said, in bold chiseling. If that wasn't enough, each letter was inlaid with gold. She couldn't be surprised any longer by that family, surely.

The magnificence of the structures made her stop on the hill above them for a few minutes, so she could study them. They must've cost a fortune, but as wealthy as the Monroe family was, it would have been a necessary extravagance. She would have to get closer to see what they were made of, but they looked like black granite and limestone. Impressive was an understatement.

A chain-link fence that circled the three crypts had a poor lock that looked like it had been broken years ago. Probably kids having a good scare on Halloween.

Olivia stepped inside the fence. As she came upon the crypts, she realized their presence fully. Elaborate wrought-iron gates tipped in gold stood sentinel at each of the crypts. They shone despite their age. Olivia kept moving, slipped inside the largest of the gates.

She listened to the silence around her. No late-evening birds and no traffic. She couldn't see any homes from that deep part of the cemetery. A heaviness settled over her, thick deep summer air that stole her breath, though the day was cool. Evelyn was still silent. The sun was setting in the west, but that part of the cemetery was already dark.

She was pulled toward the crypt and away from it at the same time. She placed her hand on the limestone. It was still warm from the sun. The longer she stood there with her hand on the outside of the crypt, the longer she felt as if the crypts themselves were alive and watching her.

The heavy metal doors that led to William's grave were ajar. At the time, it didn't register as anything more than kids fucking around on Halloween. Later, she would think it was strange. But everything was strange that month. Everything.

Olivia slipped inside the crypt. She didn't want to be there anymore, but it was a reasonable place to look for Austin's head.

She was glad for the flashlight. A short hall led into the crypt, which was much larger on the inside. Like the dugout, it seemed to go on forever. A light shone from the back of the crypt. A trick of the setting sun. She walked on.

At the end of the cool limestone hall, the space opened up. Was she in a cave or what? But no, there was the resting place of William Monroe III.

Candles had been lit there. The realization made the hair on her arms stand up. The candles were placed on ledges around the large center room. On a tall granite or marble slab, a coffin rested. Fittingly, it was wedged open slightly, as if someone had been there recently. Or not so recently. Sick curiosity got the better of her.

She walked around the crypt, looking at all the nooks in the walls, ignoring the coffin for the moment. Items in the walls were kept in place, safe behind pieces of glass.

Horseshoes. A stack of decaying notes that looked like it might've been money at one time. Some old pieces of paper that looked like maps. Surveying tools. Bouquets of what once were flowers.

The maps drew her attention. She tried to study them through the glass while she kept one eye on the coffin.

She had never been a fan of zombie movies, preferring to skip them altogether (even the comedies), but this seemed like a prime time for something untoward to happen. She tried to ask Evelyn if she knew anything, but her head was empty of the woman's presence. That should have been welcoming, but it only frustrated her. There was no balance.

Olivia shone her flashlight over the part of the casket that was open. After what Simon had told her, she wanted to know: Had they put William back together after they discovered part of him strewn through and outside of town? Had all the king's horses and all the king's men been able to put Humpty Dumpty together again?

Peering into the casket, all she could see was part of a man's suit. That gave her the courage to push the lid open even farther.

She regretted that part.

The lid, off balance, pushed the casket toward her as the lid slid over the other side, crashing to the floor. The noise was tremendous. Two of the glass structures that held valuables shattered from the impact, which made more noise. Olivia jumped back out of the way, wishing she were anywhere but there.

When the noise settled and the dust cleared, she shone the flashlight around. Nothing jumped out at her. There was glass everywhere on the other side of the room, and two of the candles had sputtered out. She watched the wax drip slowly until it stopped and hardened.

She found some balls amid her racing heart and sudden urge to pee and shone her flashlight over the edge of the fully open casket. She squeezed one eye shut, unsure what she was going to see. It didn't frighten her as much as she imagined.

She stared at a skeleton in a black suit. A complete skeleton—or so it seemed. A faux rose was in his breast pocket. The suit looked old. Old fashioned. Leather shoes were on the bony feet.

The strange part was that one side of the suit jacket was open, as was the threadbare shirt underneath. The skeleton's ribs had been exposed, and one of them had been broken off. Splinters littered the dark jacket. Who would have done that? Kids practicing internet witchcraft might've lit the candles, but she couldn't believe they would desecrate a skeleton.

She needed to get out of there. If she stayed much longer, the authorities might show up. Or William Monroe III might wake in this form and decide he needed to get some fresh air. She didn't want either to happen.

Skirting the casket, Olivia went to the pile of paper. Maps—at least they looked like maps. She wasn't sure what they were of, but she took them anyway, sliding them carefully into the back pocket of her jeans. If anyone saw her in the cemetery, they wouldn't see her walk out with it. Not that it would help her if anyone did. She would be surprised if the noise didn't draw someone.

Wherever Colton was, she felt she should tell him what happened. He might be a frat boy asshole, but at least he would believe the crazy shit.

When she emerged from the crypt, it seemed like time had gone backwards. It seemed lighter than when she had gone in. Was it some trick of the light in that part of the cemetery?

Evelyn's silence still bothered her. And the thing about the iron. It had hurt Evelyn. She had screamed like it was awful.

"Evelyn?" she asked. Still nothing.

Outside the crypt, she pulled the heavy doors closed and twined the chain back through the handles. The padlock was rusted and broken, but she tried to make it look like the doors were locked. For a moment, she stood and admired the stonework on the doors. She shone her flashlight over them, following the pattern of vines to the little gargoyle faces at the center of each panel. Their similarity to the thing (*Strix*, Colton's voice interrupted) was unsettling.

Above it all, a name was chiseled though this was not inlaid with gold:

WILLIAM MONROE III.

She felt a chill.

The insides of the other two crypts were unremarkable. No odd long hallway back to an open room. Just concrete and dull gold plaques for William's father and grandfather. If Austin's head had been buried under the stone or concrete, there was no way she'd be able to get to it, much less know if it were there. But she knew now that William Monroe III was someone she didn't want to be around—in life or in his form after death. Something was very wrong with the man.

When she left the cemetery, she didn't take the center path. It felt exposed, like the rest of the cemetery watched and held its breath.

She walked along the far perimeter of the cemetery, the grass soft and damp beneath her feet. It had already begun to yellow and go dormant, and that part of the cemetery was littered with fallen leaves that had blown up against the limestone hedge. She idly touched the wrought-iron fence as she walked, thinking.

The tall trees above dripped on her occasionally, slowing her gait even more. It felt like a luxury to be able to think without another voice butting in with her opinion.

She was sheltered there, and the berms outside the cemetery gave her privacy to walk alone. No one else visited that place where the inhabitants and their ancestors were long dead. There was no one to celebrate the lineages there because they were all gone. Dust.

Except Olivia.

She wasn't sure where that thought had come from, but it gave her another chill. It was absurd though. Surely hundreds more people in Warren were related to people in that cemetery.

Olivia heard a whoosh of air and the sound of a horse chomping on a bit and turned to see Austin riding Evan just on the other side of the fence. Solid form and all. Even without Evelyn's influence, she was happy to see the pair. They were both so good.

"Hello there," she said softly.

She reached through the bars to pat Evan's warm nose. He pulled his head back quickly when it accidentally brushed the bars and released a burst of steam, but he reached back to her hand eagerly, wanting more pats. Olivia noted the movement, the steam. So, it wasn't just Evelyn who was affected by the iron.

Austin slid down from Evan's back, a graceful movement. She admired his skill as a horseman. She admired him as a man.

"Olivia." He smiled as he strode toward her.

Her senses were heightened there. Or perhaps it was the day. Austin was as real as she was. As he moved through the damp fallen leaves, the hem of his cloak caught the grass and leaves behind him. One yellow leaf stuck stubbornly to his leather boots, and the dampness shone on them.

There was a curious animal-at-the-zoo quality to it all, but she didn't know who the spectacle was and who was just passing through. But she wanted to photograph him there in that momentary sanctuary. Maybe he would let her someday.

She reached through the bars, and Austin reached toward her too. Their fingers twined, and Olivia made certain not to touch the iron. For once she was not transported, nor did memories filter into her head. She was alone with Austin.

A sadness filled her that she didn't quite understand. She might if she explored the feeling, as her mother's therapist would have said. She knew the exploration would tell her that she was lonely, desperately so. That she no longer wanted to travel this life alone. That she wanted a companion.

"Austin," she said quietly.

"Yes, my dear?" He watched her as quietly as she watched him, steady and unwavering. He was all man. But there was more. He was more than just a hardworking man. So was Simon.

That broke the spell.

She almost pulled her hand away, but Austin caught it and pulled her closer to the fence. She pressed her face against the bars and her lips to his. There was a hiss of steam, but Austin lingered over her lips.

Chapped lips. Warm lips. All man.

They pulled back mutually, and Olivia dropped her hands from his to wrap them around the bars, staring out from her cage. She knew this wasn't sustainable. But what was worse, dating asshole after asshole who could be seen with her in public or a perfect gentleman who was invisible to most of the waking world?

Her phone vibrated in her pocket and jolted her from the meditative state she'd been in. It startled something behind one of the great cottonwoods off to her left. Squirrels.

The caller ID read "Unknown." She almost didn't answer it—probably a robocall or Not Simon. But she answered anyway.

"Hello?"

"Olivia Norwich?"

The male voice was familiar but not in a spine-tingling way. That was welcome for once. "This is she."

"This is Officer Wells from the Warren PD. Are you available to come down to the station?"

Austin watched her, openly curious, but gave her privacy. He set to adjusting Evan's saddle, but Olivia couldn't keep her eyes off him.

"I'm so sorry. Is it my mom? Did you pick her up again?"

"Are you able to come now?"

Olivia looked at her wrist, but no watch looked back at her. How late was it? "Uh, yes, I can. I'll be there in about ten."

Austin watched her quietly. She appreciated that he didn't pry.

"I have to go," she said regretfully.

"Be careful," Austin said. His face was unreadable once more. Was that a ghost thing or a man thing? They might be one and the same. Men who couldn't say out loud what they were feeling or who had grown up not knowing the name became only ghosts of their potential selves.

"Thank you," Olivia whispered and then headed out of the cemetery.

Austin remounted Evan and turned him in the opposite direction, the horse's hooves making soft thuds across the open grass until she could see them no longer. Whether they had just disappeared from the view or from the waking world, she was not sure.

Olivia had no idea what to expect at the police station. Where had they picked up her mother now? How many officers had she talked to when her mother had started wandering away from home and out onto the prairie without telling anyone she had gone? Was it six or seven or a dozen times that she had to come to the station to pick her up? Once they got her meds right, most of the wandering had stopped. She'd found a level ground in the midst of whatever turbulence was her life. Olivia felt equal parts sad and exasperated by it.

Officer Wells, vaguely familiar, had the fine brown hair and grey eyes that she'd come to expect from anyone who'd lived in the area for their entire lives. Did no one else see it? She couldn't believe it was all a coincidence, as Ann had postulated. The mounting evidence suggested Olivia was not crazy for thinking it was odd. Not in Warren at least.

She quit staring at him and stared at her coffee instead. She took a sip. Bitter. She had always preferred tea. Evelyn, back once again, agreed. *Please be quiet while I talk to them.*

"This isn't about my mother?"

"I just want to ask you a few questions about where you were a few nights ago, Miss Norwich."

Oh.

"Yes, sir." She took another sip of her coffee. *I did just break into a crypt at the Sunset Cemetery though. Thought you should know.* She stifled the laughter that threatened. She'd almost forgotten to put the stolen maps in the back seat of her car when she rolled up to the station. She was so wrapped up in Austin and worrying about her mom. Evelyn had chastised her gently, and Olivia had slipped the maps under a pile of sweaters in her back seat. Perhaps . . . *Evelyn, you drive. I can't handle it.*

Evelyn was much more composed, and she sipped the bitter coffee at regular intervals through the initial pleasant conversation with affable Officer Wells.

"Can you tell me where you were this last Friday night, October twenty-third?"

Evelyn filtered through Olivia's memories. "Ah, hmm. Goodness, it's hard to even remember this morning at times, you know?" Her musical laugh earned a smile from the officer. A genuine one too. Olivia felt jealous of the woman's ease. Olivia had never been able to talk her way out of so much as a parking ticket.

Evelyn composed her thoughts from Olivia's scattered and frantic memories. That night stood out. "I was at the gallery on campus most of the evening to finish up with the second print I had brought in. I have a show for the festival, you see."

Officer Wells grunted. Whatever that meant. "And later that night? Did you go home and go to bed?"

She didn't like this turn of questioning. And she knew exactly where Olivia had gone. Straight to the bed of the one whom she detested. Olivia pleaded with her to tell the truth though, and Evelyn felt inclined to agree with her. Better to tell the truth, even if it was unpalatable.

"No, I didn't. I got a call from my . . ." What was the word she wanted to use? That this Monroe was Olivia's suitor made Evelyn's stomach turn. She forced it out anyway. "My boyfriend called late. I was still working at the gallery when he called at about eleven thirty or midnight. It was quite late. He asked me over."

"And you went?"

Evelyn felt her face burn. What awful questions these men had to ask. "Of course."

"When did you arrive?"

"I don't know. The gallery on campus isn't far from his place. Blocks. I walked. It would have taken us no more than fifteen minutes to reach his home."

"So, close to midnight."

"I suppose, yes."

"And Mr. Monroe was there when you arrived?"

Mr. Monroe. A wave of fear washed over her. Old fear. "We walked together. From the university campus."

"And how long did you stay?"

She was certain her face was flushed pink. That they could ask such questions was imprudent, investigation or no. It was no way to treat a lady. She looked down at her coffee, the cup warm between her hands. "I stayed the night."

"And you're certain he didn't leave at any point during the night?"

The night played for Evelyn as he asked the question. She certainly hadn't been able to leave that night, either. She could go away into the depths of Olivia's mind, but she always resurfaced. "I'm certain."

He seemed to have gathered whatever he wanted from her face. "Thank you, Miss Norwich. You've been a great help."

She couldn't look the man in the face. "You're welcome. May I go now?"

"Yes, certainly. Let me show you the way out."

They checked her contact information before she left, and then she was free to go. The cool air outside felt wonderful on her hot face. She was thankful for the darkness. It hid her shame.

Evelyn gave the reins back to Olivia. The arrangement was uncomfortable for both of them at times. Olivia thanked Evelyn awkwardly. She was more composed now at least.

With a jolt, she remembered she was supposed to have met with Colton in the cemetery earlier. That he hadn't shown and hadn't called shouldn't have made her belly ache like it did. Ghost hunter or not, the guy was probably just self-absorbed and had forgotten, but she needed him. She left the station texting him to reschedule, wanting to get home and in bed as quickly as possible.

44

Summer 1900

Evelyn was hurrying down the stairs to luncheon when the world went grey and her knees no longer held her. She stumbled over the carpeted stairs and slid down several, skinning the heels of her hands on the plush carpets. She must have cried out because Alyssa was there in a moment, helping her up.

"Missus, are you alright?"

Evelyn was so lightheaded that she didn't want to stand. "I'm fine, Alyssa. I'm sorry. I became faint and fell."

Alyssa helped her to her feet, but her knees buckled again. The world went hazy and soft around the edges. Evelyn grabbed for the banister as the room swam around her. She was not a woman prone to fainting or nausea unless she had eaten something off, but William had not yet said she could eat that day.

Alyssa called for help, and several servants came running. William's man was among them, and he lifted Evelyn with ease and carried her back to her room.

The sickness was violent but short once she reached her room, and there was only her washbasin to catch it. Alyssa rushed out for towels and was back shortly, pressing Evelyn into bed and wiping her face with a hot cloth.

"Please," Evelyn said. "Please, I'm fine. It must be the weather. I'm fine. Please." Alyssa shushed her and pushed her back against the pillows, hauling her feet up onto the bed and removing Evelyn's house shoes. Evelyn tried weakly to protest.

Not long after, William rushed into the room, pushing everyone aside, so he could reach Evelyn. "My dear, what is the matter?" She craved his concern when he was around others, for it felt real.

Tears sprang to Evelyn's eyes. She had not made it to luncheon. She was more frightened that she had disappointed William than she was about not having eaten, despite her growling and churning belly. "I'm so sorry. I became ill on the stairs. I don't know what came over me."

He wiped her forehead with the hot cloth. "What ails you now?"

"I'm dizzy still. My stomach aches, but I'm very hungry. I feel I could eat everything in this house."

Alyssa pulled William aside and spoke to him quietly in the doorway. Evelyn lay back on her pillow. She was fine. It was simply the heat of the day. The summer had been hot and sultry, and she had been uncomfortable for most of it. She had not been ready for the oppressiveness of it that year.

William sent Alyssa away to get a tray of food and told Evelyn she would eat in bed. Then he sat on the edge of the bed and took her cold hands in his. Her fingers, as they were most days at the Monroe residence, were mostly white. She had worn gloves at home to help, and Austin had warmed her hands even on the hot summer days when they should have been warm.

"My dear, Alyssa tells me you might be in a family way."

It was a good thing Evelyn was already lying down. She might have truly fainted if she hadn't been.

"I . . . oh," she said dumbly. Her ears rang as her mind flitted this way and that.

"How long has it been?" He left the end of the thought unsaid. She knew what he meant.

Evelyn didn't want to say she had lost track of time and could not remember. But, there. It should have been weeks ago. But she had not noticed. She had been busy searching for days and mornings and afternoons to ride out and see Austin. She was consumed with hiding her long rides out on Ebony, keeping up appearances, and making her days appear productive. Her monthly was no longer something over which she obsessed.

Happiness was the next emotion that filled her. The panic didn't set in until later.

"It has been weeks," she said finally and licked her dry lips.

William lit up. The smile that crawled across his face was terrifying. In her faint state, Evelyn thought she saw a red glint creep into his brown eyes and deep shadows grow on his face. She gasped, but then it was just William again, smiling and happy and not disappointed in her.

"What's wrong, dear? Are you feeling ill again?" He squeezed her hands in the way he once did that made her feel as if she were his only one in the world. She understood now how that had all been part of his game with her. She was his prize, and now that she was with child, she was doing something that would make him proud of her. She had been so naïve.

"Yes," she said, grateful she didn't have to lie. "I'm faint still. I need to eat."

William placed a hand on her stomach. "Yes, you do. I need a strong boy from you. Eat what Alyssa brings you today. I'll make a new menu for you going forward. Red meat and boiled potatoes with salted greens. I want a healthy boy."

Evelyn opened her mouth to say something. She didn't like meat. It felt heavy in her belly. She preferred bread and fruits and crisp vegetables. But she said nothing. It was more food, and she was hungry.

She began to devour the tray of food that Alyssa brought, and William left her to it while he went around to tell everyone in the house the good news. He told her to stay in bed for the remainder of the day.

Alyssa sat with Evelyn, keeping quiet company with her. Evelyn liked Alyssa, but she missed Maggie terribly. The two women were similar, though Alyssa was closer to Evelyn's age. Maggie had been more motherly.

Alyssa poked her head outside the bedroom door, then came back to sit in the chair by Evelyn's bedside. "He is away in the house somewhere. I can no longer hear him," she said, as if she expected Evelyn to speak.

Evelyn was busy pressing another biscuit into her mouth. Food felt good in her stomach. It made the pain, cramps, and dizziness go away. She took a long drink of tea and sat for a moment with her fullness. She wanted to eat more.

"My sister has told me some interesting tales of a woman from this house riding out at all hours during the day," Alyssa said. Her words drew a quick look from Evelyn, who felt her first desire to chastise an insubordinate. It was not like Alyssa to talk about the rumors that went around the house.

"And what do you make of those tales?"

Alyssa looked directly at Evelyn. "I think the lady is smart and kind and good and should be careful with herself in this dangerous house."

Evelyn nodded. "Yes, she should be careful, and she is. She only wants to be happy."

"As do we all, Missus," Alyssa replied. She removed a fat piece of cake wrapped in paper from the bundle of what Evelyn had thought were simply towels.

Evelyn thanked Alyssa with tears in her eyes and savored every bite of the cake until it was gone.

Over the ensuing weeks, William was doting and jovial. Evelyn had not seen him so smiling and animated since he had courted her. She didn't know what to do with the new attention. It made her wary.

Her mornings were difficult for a month, and she could not escape the house to see Austin. She gave Alyssa's sister a new coat, so she would ride a note to him though, and she daydreamed constantly about the next opportunity she would have to see him.

Alyssa continued to bring her confections from the kitchen to satisfy Evelyn's growing sweet tooth. William brought her concoctions that smelled awful and tasted worse.

"Drink this," he said one day, handing her a cup of something murky.

"What is it?" Evelyn asked. For all her knowledge of plants on the prairie, she could not identify the ingredients in the mixtures he brought her.

"A tonic to strengthen your womb." William seemed proud of himself.

Evelyn didn't say what she thought. She didn't want to drink it though. "What's in it?"

A shadow of the old William came over the man's face, something that twisted Evelyn's insides more than the thought of drinking the awful drink.

"Medicine. Drink. It will make you healthy," he said. The shadow lingered.

She drank it.

For days her stomach cramped, and she had spots of blood on her chemise and in her drawers. In her embarrassment, she hid the garments in her wardrobe and pressed a towel between her legs. Alyssa discovered them and found the truth out from Evelyn.

Feeling embarrassed but glad for Alyssa's continued pressure on the subject, Evelyn begged the woman to convince William that Alyssa should administer the tonic. Somehow, she did. The bleeding stopped.

She spent much time in her bedridden days thinking about Austin. She had no doubts that their time together had yielded the baby. She only hoped that William wouldn't suspect. Over and over in her mind, she traced her steps and William's. Had she done enough to hide her visits out of the house? The more she thought about it, the more nervous she felt. She put down her thoughts in her journal. The relief was only momentary.

She hadn't worried over the journal being found until she could not help but confess her secrets to it. She knew she had been doing it all along, but those early entries seemed so girlish now, so long gone. Brief entries about the weather as if that were the only important thing in the world or what Ethan was up to on an evening or what Evette had attempted to play on the piano that night. What silly concerns.

> I have counted too many far-off prairie sunsets outside my window with no blood for there to be any doubt that I'm in the family way. I don't really care what the doctor said. I know my own frame better than he. Is it not odd that they call it such a thing though? If I were able to choose, I know where I would like to be.
>
> I'm excited. Perhaps I should not be, but I am. I want to jump for joy, but I cannot. Or perhaps I will. William would only think me mad instead of happy. I do not think the man understands the range of the feeling of happiness. I should not say that. He has his own spectrum of happiness. Or his own lens through which he may determine his happiness. It is not a normal one, I do not think. I do not think anyone's is, but his degree of darkness is unusual. I do not think there is a woman in the world who could make him happy, for he craves his own miserable existence. What he wants for he will not find outside of himself.

When she was finally able to get out to see Austin, she rode Ebony much faster than she should have, anxious to reach him. The stout horse skirted the prairie dog holes deftly and leapt the creeks swollen from recent rains with ease. Evelyn didn't even slow her on the bridge, instead pressing her faster, so they would not be seen in such an open space.

Austin knew she was coming. She saw him open the gate at the far end of the pasture, and she whooped and pressed Ebony into a gallop. It felt so good to let her fly across the pasture. The summer air felt cool as it rushed past her face, loosening her hair and pulling at her skirts. The corset felt tight over her growing belly, but it didn't slow her. She didn't care if she shouldn't—it felt so good to have her horse running beneath her.

When she reached the gate, she slid from Ebony's back and ran the rest of the way to Austin, launching herself into his arms. Ebony tossed her head and trotted a few paces from her excited rider. Evan called to her from a nearby pasture, but she stuck by her mistress, catching her breath from the brief run.

Austin received Evelyn with a crushing hug and lifted her off her feet. When he set her down, his eyes were wet. She had never seen him cry in all her years of knowing him.

He knelt and hugged her to him again and pressed the side of his face against her corset. Her sister had written that some ladies no longer wore them, and Evelyn longed for that day to come for her.

She never forgot Austin's damp eyes when he looked up at her, nor did she forget how he worshipped her growing belly through that hard winter. Beside his hearth, Evelyn pretended that all was as she had thought of in her girlish daydreams. When the wind grew ugly, and the snow piled high, she held onto that dream all the more tightly.

45

6:00 p.m., Sunday, October 18th

The review started off as horribly as Olivia thought it would. She sat and sweated in her high-waisted wool slacks and lavender blouse as everyone came into the room. Dr. Rogers sat tightlipped in the corner, pen and notebook at the ready. Even Cecelia looked pissed.

The head of the department started after they all exchanged pleasantries, which Olivia wanted to get out of the way. She wanted it all out of the way, so she could move on.

"I'm not sure where to start, so we'll just jump into the middle of it," Dr. Wilson began. "We had a student email us to say that during part of the week of October fourth and over the beginning of the week of October eleventh, you didn't show up to the classroom for your Advanced Aesthetics and Portraiture course, nor did you email students to let them know you would be absent. Several other students emailed that you were absent from your Introduction to Photography course multiple times during this two-week period. Is this true?"

Olivia needed a calendar. But then again, it might not help her. The days blurred together. "I might have, unintentionally."

"You are aware, I'm sure, that one instance of no-show, no-contact could be excused, but this many together is the reason why we're here today." Dr. Wilson continued. Olivia had always liked the department head. He was no-nonsense and sometimes gruff, but he'd always been fair. She'd also picked up his habit of spreading student papers on the floor during flu season and spraying them with Lysol before she handled them for grading. It had seemed to mitigate some of the seasonal sniffles that she usually got.

"Yes, I'm aware, and I'm so sorry. I know that doesn't cut it, but this project I've been working on is—"

"Aren't you accustomed to the workload?" Dr. Thurston asked. "I seem to remember going to several of your showings and exhibitions that were presented during the in-session school year."

"Yes," Olivia said through gritted teeth. "But this project is exceptional, and I've been putting in extra hours for it. I think I've simply lost track of time working on it. This is the first time I've worked on such a large scale, and I've gotten a little . . . consumed by it."

"Would you consider that a good excuse for neglecting your teaching?" A fair but irritating question from Dr. Thurston. The man had a way of needling the point right under her skin.

"No," she replied honestly. "I don't think there's any excuse. I probably should have applied for a substitute, but I had no idea what this project would end up entailing. I think I started getting an idea when the fifty-six-inch, forty-pound roll of paper arrived that I would print on, but I thought I could handle it." She wanted to mention the stress of her mother's situation, but she'd been dealing with that for years, so it wasn't like it could get much more stressful.

Cecelia chuckled at the mention of the paper. "I've known you for, what, more than fifteen years now? I was a graduate student when she was an undergraduate in the program, and we've followed each other around since. I haven't had a single complaint or seen a poor teaching evaluation except for the normal disgruntled student type. 'Why am I getting a D, but I don't show up to class?' sort of thing. We all have those."

Dr. Wilson and Dr. Thurston nodded in agreement. Olivia felt a twinge of relief mingle with the nervousness. It didn't last long.

"That being said," Cecelia continued, "I don't think it's right to let you off without a stipulation. You're a tenure-track candidate, and I'd much rather keep that position in-house rather than give it to one of the fifty other eligible candidates who apply every semester. Sometimes more. I think John and Thomas agree, but they, of course, can't say that out loud."

Olivia waited in her puddle of sweat and nerves for what they were going to say next. At least the words "fired" or "dismissed" hadn't crossed anyone's lips yet. She wanted to scream what had been going on over the last three weeks. She wanted to yell that they needed to call the authorities, someone who was better equipped to handle all this instead of her. Hell, call someone else to handle the photographs while they were at it.

But, no.

No.

She realized with a rush that she wanted very badly for the photographs to turn out well. She wanted to produce good work. She had sweat and blood in it now, and she didn't want to quit. She hadn't had a creative rush like this in years, perhaps ever.

Dr. Wilson slid a piece of paper over to Olivia. "This is what we've outlined. We have taken your excellent track record into consideration, and this is what we came up with. Weekly check-ins for the rest of the semester, including your lesson plans, and a visit to one class of each of your three courses for monitoring."

"We're not babysitting," Dr. Thurston interjected, "just keeping you accountable."

Olivia felt her face burn. Nervous tears threatened. She was thirty-five, for fuck's sake. *Get your shit together, Olivia.* "I understand. I'm so sorry."

Cecelia softened somewhat. "We understand there's a lot of stress right now, but you have to ask for help if you're drowning in it. I know you were there for some of the stress-induced incidents that happened here a few years ago in the department, and we would like to keep those kinds of situations to a minimum, eliminate them altogether if possible."

"Are these conditions agreeable to you?" Dr. Wilson asked.

Olivia looked over the sheet he had given her. It was more than fair considering how much she had missed. "Yes, they are."

"Good," he said. "If you could email me your lesson plans for this week by the end of the evening, I would appreciate it. And we'll arrange for the first of the classroom visits in a few days. Please let us know if you have any questions or continue to have issues."

"I will. Thank you." Olivia couldn't even look at them as she stood and shook everyone's hand. Martha Rogers stood and left without saying a word.

Cecelia hung back when the others left and gave Olivia a hug. The tears threatened again, but Olivia held them back. It wasn't going to help her if she started blubbering.

"I tried to handle it on my end, but Thomas caught wind of it and couldn't help but get Dr. Wilson involved. I'm sorry, Olivia," Cecelia said quietly.

"I am too. Dr. Thurston was thrilled to get in on some inter-departmental drama, I'm sure," Olivia said.

"You know he was. I'm happy with the result though, and I hope you are too. I hope you come talk to me if you need help."

"I will. It was obviously asinine of me to let it snowball like it did, but I kept thinking—"

"You'll dig yourself out, or you'll catch up this weekend. I get it," Cecelia said. "Your work, by the way, is incredible. I didn't want to say it during the meeting, but I see why you've gotten caught up in it."

Olivia wasn't too upset that she couldn't feel proud of those words. "I'm really invested in this project."

Cecelia was someone Olivia needed to talk to more. As a friend and a colleague. She just had to get through the month.

"I can tell," Cecelia replied, then the two exchanged their goodbyes and went in opposite directions on campus.

Now that it was getting dark earlier, Olivia wished Simon—the real Simon—was there to walk her back to her car. A few other cars were in the parking lot—enough people were still on campus—but that didn't mean she felt any safer.

Her face was still hot from the meeting, but the sweat on the back of her blouse was cold. The interview back at the police station was still heavy on her mind too. What she had said would surely help Simon, but did they have to ask like that? Jesus. Evelyn agreed.

She'd just started back across the parking lot when she heard an odd sound. A clicking, like . . . like . . . like the game on the *Price is Right* . . . Plinko. It was the only thing she could relate it to. It was intermittent too, and between it was rhythmic plodding on the blacktop.

Ticktickticktick, clop-clop clop-clop, ticktickticktick, clop-clop clop.

She turned around to locate the sound, but it was almost impossible to hear where it was coming from with it bouncing off the nearby buildings. The sound came at her from every direction.

She needed to get out of the parking lot. She made a guess at the location of the sound and skirted through cars toward the far edge of the lot. It wasn't toward her car, but it was toward home and what she thought was away from the noise. She was going to sprint home if that was what she needed to do.

Ticktickticktick, clop-clop clop-clop, ticktickticktick, clop-clop clop.

She knew that sound.

Ticktickticktick, clop-clop clop-clop, tickticktickticktick, clop-clop clop.

The hair on her neck stood up. It sounded much closer.

Tick. Tick. Tick. Tick.

Oh, God.

She turned, and somehow it was right there behind her. Clopping up the final row of cars and gaining speed toward her. On its back was a figure that was clearly not Austin. The person was smaller in stature but handled a horse just as deftly. Of course that was the source of the sound. Their second meeting in a parking lot. God, she was an idiot. What a fucking idiot to be out alone when all of this was happening. Idiot, idiot, idiot.

The night with the horse coming out of the photograph was still fresh in her mind. She felt the heat of the fire again, saw the sickening angles that the thing's head took. Her imagination supplied the rest, watched the horse poke its snout from the large print, its teeth gnashing.

Olivia stumbled off the sidewalk as she stared at the large mass moving toward her, hoping that perhaps it was all a mistake, and he was going to run past her, "Ha-ha-ha Happy Halloween" and all that.

But no. Nightmare Horse was a giant beast of an animal that almost blended into the night except for its goddamn red demon eyes, supernatural beacons on the sides of its face. Its long tongue lolled out of its mouth like a happy foaming dog bounding toward its master. But its master rode on its back, all flying black cloak and headless distortion, and Olivia was the prey, to be chased down like a fox or a rabbit.

"Hey!" she yelled, a last desperate attempt at something, though she wasn't sure what.

Then the crooked-necked horse let out a screech that sounded decidedly inhuman.

That was it. Olivia turned and ran, pulling off the sidewalk and through the trees. The duo crashed onto the leaf-filled ground and headed into the trees after her.

She ran through the secluded area. She didn't care where she was headed so long as she could lose the thing. Thoughts came and went as her body pushed forward. She was briefly glad for all the conditioning she had done with Nathan before they'd broken up. All the races and obstacle courses. She was horrible at it, but for one second, she was grateful. She'd retained at least *some* of that endurance.

The duo crashed along behind her, dodging trees at a pace that was just slower than hers. God, how long had she been running? Where was she? She didn't have much wind left in her. She wasn't sure why she hadn't come across Laramie yet, to more people. Surely the thing wouldn't follow her around other people.

Time stretched on, and she realized she was running in the dark. She couldn't remember when she had left behind the lampposts that ran through the campus woods. Why hadn't she come across any streets yet? She should've reached her apartment already. There was no reason why she shouldn't have. Where was she? This wasn't campus any longer, and God, it looked like she had left Warren proper behind. That was impossible.

"Please!" she cried, but she heard no reply except the thundering of hooves behind her.

She chanced a look back. In the weak light, all she could see was the horse's hulking shadow, foam lathering its body, red eyes bright beacons, and the huge figure on its back.

The figure had no head. *He had no head!*

Olivia slipped on a wet patch of leaves and went down. Her elbow made contact first, and she felt the shattering pain all the way up into her head. Despite the pain, she tucked herself into a protective ball when she was pitched downhill. The leaves fell away beneath her, and she tried to grab onto anything. Sticks, the rounded edges of rocks, roots, all slid through her grip.

The cliffs! How had she run so far? Jesus Christ, he had herded her there! She hadn't run out of breath, running in front of a goddamn horse that could have trampled her anytime it wanted. Instead it just let her run until . . . until what? Until she exhausted herself? Until she fell?

She finally found footing on what felt like roots and pushed herself upward, grabbing at skinny trees above her. Her feet found and lost purchase on the slick rocks. Hooves plodded up above where she hung, and she felt the heat from the beast above her, smelled him.

Once on a drive back into Warren from her parents' house with the windows down, she came upon a dead cow in the road. When her headlights illuminated the thing just in front of her, she gasped, and her mouth and nose filled with the smell of death, blood, and decay. That was what the horse's hot breath smelled like.

The headless horseman leaned down from atop the devil beast. It looked like he was watching her.

"Please," she gasped, choking on the horse's horrible stench. "Why are you doing this?"

The headless horseman laughed. *He laughed.* Then he urged his steed forward, stutter stepping toward her. "Boo!"

Too surprised to have anything else in her head, Olivia lost her grip and felt only air.

She squeezed her eyes shut, but no air rushed past her face. Opening her eyes, her feet were on solid ground, but it was early evening. She collapsed to her knees in the leaves and looked around, shaken. She was at the bottom of a swell by the cliffs, nearly where she'd been the week before, taking photographs for the show.

But her hands! They and the rest of her were translucent, like when she'd seen Austin by the Daily Brew. Was she dead?

A shout nearby startled her. She stood on unsure legs and looked around.

"William! Please, you must stop!"

Hallucinating? Dead? But her feet crunched the leaves, and her mouth tasted like the Italian soda she'd grabbed on the way to the meeting. She swung around to locate the voice and saw a man lying steps closer to the cliff, the arm and shoulder of his shirt red and shining with fresh blood. Her stomach turned. She had never seen so much blood. Now she knew who it was, where she was.

A dark horse was tethered to a tree nearby, pulling frantically at its lead. Evan.

"Hey!" she cried, but the man and the horse ignored her. Austin. She knew it was Austin.

She called out again, and this time Evan stopped his pulling to turn and look at her. Olivia shrank away from his direct gaze. She was an intruder there.

A young woman ran up to the scene, horror on her face. Evelyn. Oh, God. Another man walked up from behind Olivia, a pistol in one hand and an axe in the other. Olivia tripped trying to get out of his way, but he walked *right through her*. Dead or hallucinating, she wasn't sure which.

The clean-shaven man with the axe was familiar. She had seen him in photographs, but she'd heard him on the phone much more recently. His gait was easy, relaxed, but still commanding. Whatever this was—hallucination or dream—her brain must've just been pulling on what it knew.

And Evelyn. A navy skirt with heavy gold embroidery looked like it weighed the slight woman down, and her white lace blouse was smeared with dirt, blood, and leaves.

To see them in real life instead of photographs was strange. They almost didn't register in Olivia's brain as the same people. Black-and-white to living color, like adding color to early photographs, it brought the images much closer, made them feel not quite so old, made her realize how similar everything was.

"You shut your mouth," William Monroe said as he pocketed the firearm. Then he walked over to the man on the ground and raised his axe.

Before Austin could protest, William struck his neck with the axe as if he were casually splitting a cord of wood behind the house.

Olivia and Evelyn screamed at the same time, eerily in stereo, and Evan bellowed and jerked at his tether. She had never heard an animal make such a sound. It sounded as pained and terrified as she felt.

Blood spattered across William Monroe's white button-up, and Olivia watched from her rooted spot as he drove the axe down again and again and again until Austin's head was severed from his body. Blood was everywhere. Austin's body flailed as if he were still alive, his hands reaching up and around as if searching for his head. Olivia couldn't look away, even as bile rose in her throat. This was too much. It was all too much. And what could she do but watch?

Evelyn cried and pleaded as she crawled through the grass and leaves toward the pair. The axe-wielding man turned and gestured to her, and she stopped short of them. She dropped her face in her hands and sobbed, crying Austin's name over and over again.

William spat on Austin's still form, then reached down to grab Austin's head. Olivia couldn't look away from the wide eyes and slack mouth or the dangling bits of flesh and tendon. The movies showed clean cuts in one fell swoop. This had been anything but.

William walked over to where Evelyn howled on the ground and tossed the head at her. "Here you go, dearest."

Evelyn recoiled, and the head landed solidly next to her. She cried Austin's name again. Briefly, the dead man's eyes flickered open and looked at Olivia.

Olivia froze. She felt the stare as surely as a touch. Deep-brown eyes bore into her before they rolled back, and his lids closed. But Olivia couldn't get past feeling touched, feeling as if he had *seen* her, seen what wasn't there. Just neurons firing or something. She had heard that somewhere. She didn't believe that now.

A little thought wiggled into her head. *Maybe that's why he's following you now. You were the last thing he saw, and once he came back, he wanted to find you.*

It was crazy. Simply crazy.

William tossed his axe a few yards away, then wiped his hands on a handkerchief in his back pocket. With a great sigh, he stuffed it back into his pocket, then began rolling and kicking Austin's body toward the cliff.

Evelyn stood, brushed leaves from her dress, and stumbled toward where he had left the axe. William turned when he heard her moving and reached for his pistol.

"Watch out!" Olivia cried.

Evelyn turned as if she'd heard Olivia and fell to her knees with her hands in the air when the man pointed the pistol at her.

"I'm saving you from him," William said. "You know that, right?"

Evelyn said something that Olivia couldn't hear.

"I saved you! You should be grateful!" he growled. "Now stay there! I don't have time for your hysterics."

He finished rolling the headless man to the edge of the cliff and pushed him off. Olivia heard the body slide for a moment, then the soft sound of flesh on dirt, then nothing.

A tremendous noise and movement in her periphery sent her stumbling back even though she wasn't in danger. Evan had torn himself from his tether and taken a large tree branch with him. He galloped with laser focus toward the edge of the cliff, one of the most beautiful animals Olivia had ever seen, and leapt off in a graceful dive. He seemed to hang in the air for a breath, silken hair and hoof feathers outstretched, before he disappeared. He let out a chilling neigh that echoed up the canyon before passing from hearing.

All three onlookers were still, riveted on the spot where the horse had made his leap. William was the first to make a sound, laughter rising out of him that escalated until he was bent over, holding his knees for support.

Evelyn sank to the ground and fisted her hands in the leaves, eyes as wide as Austin's had been.

William was still chuckling when he strode to the severed head and picked it up by the hair. He offered it to Evelyn. "Here you go, sweet! He'll never bother you again! Aren't you happy? Aren't you happy he won't ever bother you again? Tell me you're happy!"

Evelyn looked horrified, her mouth open, but no sound came out. "I'm happy. I'm happy," she whispered finally.

"Then take it!" He shoved the head into her hands.

She cried out and dropped it, sobbing Austin's name again.

"Pick it up! Don't you want to see him one last time? Pick it up!"

Evelyn finally obeyed, cradling the head against her stomach as she moaned. The hair on Olivia's arms and neck stood up at the sound, and she hugged herself. This was awful. It was too vivid to not be real. But how could it be?

Then Mr. William Monroe III looked at Olivia with a grin that revealed rows of sharp teeth that didn't look human. They were the teeth of the nightmare horse, the teeth of the gargoyle thing at the Monroe house. "And you," he said, snapping his fingers.

Olivia opened her eyes to the spinning sky, bright moonlight, and stars that winked through a zig-zagging gash far above. Cold rock was under her back, and her large bag was under one shoulder. Had she fallen on it?

Pale moonlight bounced down the sides of rock that rose up and away from where she lay. It illuminated the area around quite well, and the more her eyes adjusted to the light, the more she could make out from her prone position.

The cliffs!

She groaned and tried to wiggle her toes. They moved fine, as did her fingers. Her legs moved without issue too. She paused before she turned her neck. Hadn't she heard something about accident victims not knowing they'd broken their neck until they moved it, only to find themselves paralyzed after they tried?

But she had to move. A strong strange smell overwhelmed her as she lay there, testing her body parts. It was so strong she could taste it, and it was putrid. It was different from the nightmare horse but just as rank.

She turned her neck slowly to the right. Stiff but not painful. The left was the same. The moonlight shone on the boulders around her that she'd somehow missed landing on. She let out the breath she had been holding and tried to sit up.

Everything spun. She was going to have a hell of a headache later. But she was alive and breathing, and it appeared she hadn't broken anything. Digging into her bag, she found her flashlight, which, miraculously, was not broken. Her hand brushed some kind of shrub, and she instinctively batted at it. Pain shot through her wrist. She was certainly sore.

She looked up. She had no idea how far she had fallen. Or slid. Her hands felt skinned, and she was coated in dust and small rocks.

Olivia moaned and then stood. She fumbled with her flashlight until she managed to turn it on. She froze after one pass to her left. The sight was just enough to push her to the edge. She could choose if she went over it.

She hadn't landed among boulders. She had landed among bodies.

"Oh, my God," she whispered. "Oh, my fucking God."

She shifted away from the one she had illuminated and bumped into another one. She let out a strangled scream and apologized to the thing she had bumped into.

"Fucking God," she whispered.

It was the women who had disappeared. Or the one she couldn't stop staring at was. Fine brown hair was matted to her head, mouth open in a little sigh, skin mottled purple and grey. She had been more slender once. Before the warm days she had spent bloating and rotting in the canyon.

Olivia heaved several times. The bile from the beheading clawed up her throat and scraped her esophagus like steel wool. She dry heaved again but managed to keep her stomach from crawling out her mouth.

"Oh, Jesus," Olivia moaned. She wiped her mouth on a napkin she'd kept in her backpack for a time when she might have forgotten one for lunch. When would that ever happen again? Normal seemed so far away.

Then the woman's arm moved. Surely that was just a trick of her swimming head. But no, it moved again, and a low, awful sigh came from the body in front of her. That was just what bodies did after death, she told herself. The gasses trapped in them had to leave sometime.

Something behind her shifted on the loose dirt and rocks. She swung around with her light and saw one of the bodies that she had mistaken for a boulder attempt to rise to its knees. But its legs were splayed at such a strange angle that it was having trouble. The woman looked at her with a head that sagged to her shoulders.

Olivia backed away from the bodies as quickly as she could, shuffling across the canyon floor, so she didn't trip on anything she couldn't see. Her flashlight had left her nearly blind to anything outside its small circle. She couldn't even see the canyon walls.

Turning around, she held the flashlight above her head, so she could peer into the darkness. A scraping sound greeted her. Not for the first time that day or night, fear prickled over her skin.

How many women were making their way toward her? Six? Their state mesmerized here. She hadn't even seen anything in movies or on TV that she could compare it to. She occasionally came across autopsy and crime scene photographs during her research, but they had nothing on the real thing. Looking at something briefly on a screen or a piece of paper was another world entirely.

Another sound from the opposite end of the canyon gave pause to her near hysteria. After the evening she had just endured, the sound of hooves was too familiar. Jesus, was it the impostor again?

The memory of the demon horse rose in her mind as the hoofbeats closed in. What was worse, sticking around to see how the horror movie ended, or running the other way to see if the awful red-eyed beast was waiting for her?

Fuck it. She hobbled along toward the sound of the horse—surely the women would distract that thing for a minute, so she could get away.

As the horse pounded up to her, Olivia braced herself. No clicking or red eyes greeted her though. Shining her flashlight toward it, the thrill of recognition ran through her. Evan!

The animal was huge and intimidating but beautiful. Even in the insufficient light from her flashlight, she could see the muscles under his sleek black coat. He tossed his head and she stepped back, afraid of how big he was. The first morning she'd met him, she'd mistaken his beauty for meekness or softness. Whatever he was and wherever and whenever he was from, he was the realest thing she had seen all evening. Relief surged through her, and she rushed up to him and threw her arms around his neck. Warm, he was warm. She hadn't felt the cold until she felt how warm and alive he was.

Evan whickered and whuffed and pushed his soft nose against her hair. Then he sidestepped and dropped to his knees next to her.

She stared at him for a moment in the dim light, then approached carefully. "Do you want me to climb on your back?"

Evan tossed his head up and down. It was all the confirmation she needed. She awkwardly grabbed his mane and swung one leg over his back. Every sore muscle screamed. Her teeth rattled when Evan jerked to his feet. She was so far from the ground. Her stomach turned again, but there was nothing left for it to turn over, so it settled into aching instead.

Something pawed at her ankle. The contorted face of a woman younger than Olivia looked up at her. Even for the bloat and the eyes turned strangely yellow and bloodshot, she recognized the face. It was the face that her 8:30 class had mistaken for their teacher's, the one whom she'd first felt was her doppelganger.

The woman squeezed Olivia's leg once more, digging dirty nails into her skin, before Evan sidestepped the creature and took off for the end of the canyon. Trees whipped past her face, and Evan splashed through the creek, sometimes wading through water that touched her toes.

Olivia gripped Evan as tightly as she could. She wrapped her arms partway around his neck, then sat up and grabbed his mane. The reins flapped as Evan jogged, but she didn't know what to do with them. Exhausted, she was exhausted.

Where was Austin? Battling the imposter again?

At some point, Evan's gait became more ambling, and Olivia felt her body shift and move in rhythm with his steps. It was soothing, meditative. The soft leather saddle had warmed beneath her, and she felt herself relax a notch. Safe. She felt safe.

Perhaps she dozed for a time, somewhere deep and dark and dreamless. Once she thought she heard a male voice speak. He soothed her, and it felt like someone took the reins. Those kinds of dreams were OK.

She felt them move smoothly over the echoing boards of a bridge, which seemed to go on forever. But those old bridges were long gone. She had only seen them in pictures from early Warren.

The sound of hooves on gravel woke her. She lifted her head to see where they were and was jerked awake by the sight. They were coming up on her home, but it didn't look like her home, not like she knew it, anyway. It looked like the photograph from the historical society, except the trees were much larger, like they were in the present.

By the time they made it to the front walk where she could pretend the house looked just as she remembered it, she felt better, more distanced from the events that had just happened. She slid groggily from Evan's back when he stopped in the grass by the sidewalk that led to the front door. What a smart animal. A warm arm was around her shoulders, guiding her up the stairs. When she tried the doorknob, it was locked. Her mother must have forgotten Olivia was coming over for the night. She always forgot to lock the door when she was home. The arms that held her helped her unlock the door.

I'm so sorry, the voice said. *I should not have left you alone.*

The guiding presence disappeared when she walked inside, and some of the warmth left with it. Fear found its way through the cracks in her buoyancy. She moved around the main level, turning on lights and lamps, checking doors and windows. Finally, she locked herself in her bathroom and took a long look at herself in the mirror.

It wasn't a nice sight. Her hair was full of leaves and debris, and the rest of her was covered in a layer of dust. There was a smear of vomit on one sleeve. Other holes and tears had ruined her slacks and blouse. Her makeup looked more like a Halloween costume version of the walk of shame than the true crying, puking, stumbling night she'd just had. The dead might mistake her for one of their own.

She looked away and stripped off her clothes. Her outside looked how she felt inside. Somehow she must have slid down the canyon sides. That was the only logical way she hadn't died.

She looked at her naked body. It looked like she had a rug burn on her back and sides, and bruises had already appeared on her hips and arms. Had she tried to protect her face with her arms? She couldn't remember. There was a blank in her mind when she tried to think about sliding or falling into the canyon.

A bath. She wanted one desperately. She hadn't had a bath since she was a child. She had no memory of taking one as an adult. It seemed childish, a waste of time. But now all she wanted was to sink into hot water until she was warm to her core.

Calgon take me away, she thought wryly, and dumped whatever was left in the box into the tub and turned on the hot water. She found an ancient bottle of bubble bath under the sink. She added that too.

She sat in the tub for so long that it grew too cold to bear, so she drained the water and filled it again while she sat naked and shivering. The bath was safe, and it felt good. She might never leave it. She wanted the feeling back that she'd had while on the horse. Warmth. Safety. Security. Where was Austin now?

Could she call the authorities? God, what would she say? *Yes, I fell into the canyon, but I'm fine, and while I was down there, some dead bitches chased me for awhile. Then this horse saved me and took me home.* No, that wasn't insane.

She alternated thinking about it and holding her breath and trying not to think about it. When the night was on an endless loop though, it all came back around eventually.

She almost called Simon a dozen times, hovering over the call button, typing out a text and deleting it until finally she dropped the phone on the bathroom rug and slid farther into the bath until her chin touched the water. What could he do for her? She'd bugged him enough already. And there was a fifty-fifty chance he wasn't Simon at all that night.

Her eyes grew heavy, and she knew she should leave the tub, but it felt so good on her muscles. The cuts no longer stung so much, and if she didn't move, the rest of her felt somewhat normal.

That was stasis though, she supposed. That was what happened if one didn't move for the rest of his or her life. It was the rut she'd ended up in with Nathan. The rut she'd ended up in by keeping the apartment she'd had since her undergraduate years. The rut of her mother's illness. The rut of Warren.

She didn't mind the last part as much, but staring at the eight thousand bottles of Bath and Body Works scents she'd accumulated in that bathroom during her adolescence did bother her. They were the same bottles that littered her apartment bathroom. Physical markers of her stuck-ness.

She leaned over the side of the tub and woke up her phone. It was 12:30. Time no longer made sense. There was no way all that had happened in, what, four hours? Ann might still be out working at the library or her office. And what were those "dead" women doing? Were they still bumping around in the canyon? Did they return to their boulder positions when other people weren't around? Olivia wasn't sure which would be worse.

A poem from her childhood rose unbidden in her mind. *But then a great big rat will come, crawl in your mouth, and out your bum. Your skin will turn a sickly blue, your brains will melt and turn to goo.* Olivia giggled nervously. She didn't want to alarm her mother, so she stuffed the washcloth in her mouth and squeezed her eyes shut. She tasted dirt and blood, and behind her eyes, the sickly blue bodies of the decaying women stared at her, eyes wide and jaws wider. She giggled again and ground the washcloth between her teeth until all she could feel was the rough fabric in her mouth.

She eventually managed to drag herself from the tub, pruny and beaten. Too exhausted to do much else, she crawled naked and shaking under the blankets.

A stab of horror hit her when she realized she hadn't submitted her lesson plans to Dr. Wilson. She didn't know she'd had any of that terror left to give, but there it was.

She crawled over to her laptop, booted it up, and composed an email with sight blurred by whatever dust still lingered in her eyes. She'd be lucky if it was half-coherent.

When she was done, Olivia crawled back to her bed and curled in on herself under the blankets, unable to get warm. Simon was supposed to help her. If he had been the one atop the nightmare horse, whether he knew it or not, she could no longer go to him with any of this. Austin had done all that he could, had prevented this for as long as possible.

If the imposter came to her in the night, he could have her. She had nothing left. The bag that had saved her life contained the crushed remnants of her large-format cartridges and the undeveloped film that would have become her final photographs. That they were already final was not lost on her.

At the windows the old cottonwood scratched. It was the fingers of the women out in the rocky crevasse, which was their grave. It was the bones of the freakish horse, clattering as it came for her.

She closed her eyes and wished for it all to be over.

46

Monday, October 19th

It was Evelyn who coaxed her out of bed in the morning. All Olivia could do was lie there in the predawn hours and think about the pain and the horror she had seen and what she could do about it. Then she had lain there as the sun rose thinking about how her teacher evaluations were still going to be shit by the end of the semester. Then Cecelia would question whether she should have picked Olivia for a special project. Then at the next meeting, she was going to get fired for violating her agreement with the department. And it wasn't like her mother brought in much income, so she would have to give up the apartment and come back to live at her mother's house. The old Weatherford homestead. Wouldn't that be appropriate?

You are going to be just fine, dear. But if you cannot today, would you mind . . . allowing me?

Olivia's initial sigh of relief twisted into indecision. She couldn't control anything, not even her own body. She'd failed.

You are much too hard on yourself. This isn't forever. Think of it as a respite.

After an internal struggle that lasted another twenty minutes, she finally let Evelyn take the reins. The pain muted immediately, and her head cleared. She watched Evelyn go gracefully about her daily duties. She studied herself in the mirror and artfully arranged Olivia's hair in a way that was both old-fashioned and in style. She familiarized herself with the contents of Olivia's makeup drawer and perused Olivia's thoughts on application, then meticulously used each product. The result was subtle and feminine. Olivia was jealous of the apparent ease with which Evelyn could slip into her life.

She felt Evelyn's excitement when they arrived at campus, could feel the woman take everything in.

"I have wanted this for so long," Evelyn whispered.

Even her musical voice was not completely incompatible with the body she inhabited, Olivia thought.

What is it that you wanted?

"To be on the university campus. To take courses here," Evelyn murmured. "I visited once, but that was all."

Olivia tried to remember a time when she was so excited to step onto campus, but she wasn't certain she had ever been. She had known what she wanted, had gone about getting all the schooling necessary—or unnecessary, according to some—to be a photographer and teach photography, but she hadn't been joyful about photography since she was young. Until now. Until this project. Until last night.

Now she was learning how to be passionate about the campus and Warren too. It was a strange feeling that she spent most of the morning mulling over while Evelyn drove them through her early classes and a surprise visit from Dr. Thurston toward the middle of the second.

Olivia felt angry and embarrassed to be checked on, but Evelyn took it in stride. How was this woman the same as the meek one she had read about all month? This was not the cowering woman on the cliffs or the woman cowed by William Monroe. She shuddered at the thought of the cliffs.

What did you want to study?

"Botany. The plants and flowers of the prairie. To take cooking and baking classes. I know I have something to contribute," Evelyn said quietly as students filed out of class.

Olivia was not thrilled. Though her pain and anxiety were muted while Evelyn drove them around, the previous night ate at her.

When she finished teaching around noon and left campus to get food, she passed by a commotion at the gym. Anything extra going on in town couldn't be ruled out as connected now. Olivia forgot about food and directed Evelyn to the gym's side parking lot. The main area was cordoned off, but she had a decent view from there.

It seemed like the entirety of Warren's finest and the county sheriff were pulled up at the gym, but no lights flashed. The sheriff and several other cops returned to the building. Fifteen minutes later, two vans showed up.

Olivia called Ann. "Do you know anyone who would be working on what's going on at the gym?" she asked as she watched people walking around the back side of the building.

"No idea," Ann replied. "I think I know what's going on with you though."

Shock hit Olivia's belly like a stone. "You do?"

Ann laughed. "You're seeing Dr. Monroe. It's not exactly a secret."

The shock that hit her this time was of a different sort. Evelyn went silent, and Olivia felt the woman leave her immediate headspace. Unsurprising that this subject would drive her away. "Um. What?"

"Dr. Cahara saw y'all out at the Daily Brew and somewhere else, and I just *knew* that something had finally happened. I feel like I haven't seen you in weeks!"

Oh. That wasn't what she had been expecting. After the events of the last few days, Ann could have said she saw them in her crystal ball, and Olivia would have believed her. "I'm sorry. You've lost me."

"Don't play dumb. Come on! I want details!"

Olivia felt her face warm as she thought about those "details." "What do you want to know?"

"You're seeing him?"

Maybe she was, semi-unofficially. It had just happened, their time meshing organically. Thoughts of their nights together flowed through her mind. She had wanted everything he had done to her and more. Their interests meshed. Hell, they both worked for the university. She liked his dog and his house. She also liked the way she felt around him. She'd told the police about as much.

"I guess I am."

"You guess? What kind of answer is that?"

Olivia found her feet for the first time in the conversation. *Lighten up, Francis.* "It kind of sounds like you might have a bet going. I don't think I should satisfy you with a solid answer."

"Oh, come on! I need to know!"

"You'll just have to wait for the gallery opening to find out for sure."

"You're bringing him as your date?" Ann gushed.

Olivia wished she could be excited about it, like they were in college again. With everything going on, it seemed trite. "Come and see!" she said with a forced laugh.

Olivia felt worse after the conversation than before. Simon—no, Not Simon—was making it hard to know Simon anymore. All she wanted to do was pick his brain about what might be going on at the gym, but she didn't know who she would get when she called.

Regretfully, she texted Colton's number to see if he had any idea what might be happening. It had to be connected. Olivia logged onto the ancestry forums and scanned them. Who would say something first about what was going on? She compulsively refreshed the page, waiting for someone to make a conjecture. It didn't matter that the last post had been two days earlier. Surely someone was checking things out. It wasn't until later that she realized she was that person.

She sat there wondering long enough that her phone rang. The number wasn't familiar, but it was a campus number. Not Colton. She crossed her fingers that it wasn't Not Simon and answered.

"Hello?"

"Olivia?"

"Yes. Cecelia?" Good. It wasn't Not Simon. She did wonder what he was up to though.

"Yeah. Sorry, I'm calling from my office phone and not my cell. It died, and I've been avoiding plugging it in. One of those days, you know."

Oh, she knew. Maybe that was a tactic she could use. "Yeah, I get it. How's it going? I'm doing OK on timing for the photographs, surprisingly. I know we didn't have time to talk long during the meeting, but I—"

"That's not what I called about."

"Oh. What's up?"

"I'm sure you've heard by now what they discovered at the gym."

Olivia gripped the phone so tightly she thought she might break it. "Actually, I haven't. Been in the darkroom so much, you know. So . . . what's going on out there?"

"I can't believe you haven't heard. I don't think it's left the police department or the university yet, but I'm sure it will soon. This is juicy. So, you know the headless horseman thing?" Cecelia sounded almost breathless with excitement.

Olivia saw this going in two directions. Either way, she held her breath. "Yes."

"Well, they found something buried in the basement of the gym."

"What?" It was like when she touched one of the temperamental projectors, and it shocked her so hard she felt it all the way to her toes.

"I've heard a couple different stories already, but someone was doing maintenance down there, and they started hearing things. I don't know what—don't ask me—but they went to investigate and found some floor tiles had been disturbed. They pulled them up thinking they'd have to replace them, and bam!" Olivia jumped. She had been half listening to Cecelia while her mind raced around the possibilities. "Guess what they found?" Cecelia couldn't contain herself.

Olivia felt sick. "What did they find?"

"A headless skeleton. In the basement of the gym."

She wasn't sure what kind of reaction Cecelia was expecting from her, but silence was probably not it. Olivia was still trying to wrap her head around what Cecelia had said.

"Olivia?"

"Yep, I'm here." *Here trying to figure out what the fuck this means and what's going on. Holy shit.*

"They haven't unearthed it completely yet," Cecelia continued, "but they're trying to keep everything buttoned up as tightly as possible right now. They needed a photographer."

Oh, no. No, no. Her mind went to Austin in the cemetery. She could not marry the two warring pictures of the person she was learning to know.

"So, you're going to photograph it?"

"No. You are."

"Oh." Olivia sat in her odd shock. "Oh!"

"Yes, you."

She still couldn't make the two thoughts go together. Evelyn was still quiet.

"I would like to be there, yes," Olivia finally managed to say, "but I'm not qualified to take the photographs. And Cecelia . . . Dr. Cahara . . . I can't. My workload—"

"I personally recommended you," Cecelia said. "Your aerial work, your attention to detail. You're the best."

"I haven't done true aerial work in a year now, though I assume they want low-level aerial, which, yes, I have done. How do they normally handle this sort of thing? Doesn't Warren PD have a photographer? Because clearly they need that guy in there."

"I have no idea. They don't want to hire someone from out of town, so they called me to ask which of my people was the most qualified. And I said you are."

"I don't have the credentials for this job. I've never set foot on a crime scene. I'm not the right person for this. I'm drowning in my work. You were at the meeting." The memory of being chased after said meeting gripped her.

"It's not a crime scene. And I'm just asking for an hour of your time. Someone else will process the images."

"Oh." Olivia wasn't sure how to defend herself from there.

"Your attention to tone and neutrality are also what they're looking for, Olivia. You're their best choice. They're cataloguing and need a professional, someone who will pay attention to details and get an accurate scale. I can't think of anyone better."

"Thank you?" It was definitely a question. But she couldn't say no. She felt like a graduate student again, drowning in her workload. *Heap it on, Prof. Anything to get ahead of the pack.*

"I've got a list of equipment together for you. I know you've got some of it, but you're welcome to use what the department has too. Come after your classes today, please."

"I'm finished for the day, and I'm in the area." It was a tight-lipped response, but how was she supposed to feel after her colleague and boss had just agreed that her workload was unreasonable, then dumped something else on her?

"Oh, good! I'll meet you there with the equipment. Heads in the history department will be there too. You'll recognize a lot of faces, I'm sure."

Simon, whom Dr. Cahara had seen with her at the coffee place and told her roommate. What an incestuous, gossipy bunch they were. Olivia was suspicious that this was a setup for Cecelia to see her and Simon together. Granted, Olivia was the only one with true low-level aerial experience, but still. Olivia was more worried about what would happen when she saw him.

She had just wound herself up about the imposter at the cliffs after she hung up with Cecelia when her phone rang again.

"Colton?" There was a desperation in her voice that she didn't like.

"I saw your text." How such a simple statement could turn her desperation into annoyance was impressive.

"You blew me off this weekend."

He laughed. "You have that turned around. I got there just in time to see lover boy. Didn't realize he had materialized so fully. Also didn't want to interrupt. Figured I'd hear from you soon enough."

Austin. Olivia wiped a sweaty palm on her skirts. They were the beautiful navy velvet with gold beading that Evelyn had worn that day at the cliffs. She tried to focus on their softness instead of the terror that bubbled up. "They found Austin Hearth's skeleton at the gym."

"Ahhh, so that's what it is. I've been listening on my scanner, and they've been vague as shit. Detectives requested but no buses, and no fire. They kept talking about a 'subject,' then went quiet."

"I mean, they didn't say who it was. But they said headless skeleton. I've been asked to photograph it. Him," Olivia corrected.

Colton was quiet on the other end of the line.

"Would you be interested in coming by here?" Her voice cracked. Christ, she wished he was nicer. But she'd take whatever help she could get even if she had to beg.

"One chance in hell they'll let me in there."

Olivia thought quickly. "I need help. Please? I'll let you copy the memory card afterward."

"That's tempting. I imagine you'll want a copy too," Colton said. "I'll be there in ten."

Olivia spent the next ten minutes worrying over what she should do when she saw Simon. Outside, the day was dreary, the air heavy. It was almost storm weather, but there was a cool edge to it. She needed to get the final prints made, or she wouldn't make the deadline. She'd signed the paperwork for the showing without reading whether she would have to give up a portion of the compensation if she didn't produce the amount of work she signed on for.

Someone tapped on the passenger window, and she jumped, then cringed at how sore the sudden movement made her. But it was only Colton. Without asking, he slid into the passenger seat with a laptop and an Alpha Gamma Rho backpack and jacket.

Olivia looked at him and held back an insane urge to laugh. "You're in a frat?"

Colton had the nerve to look offended. "Order of the Sickle and Sheaf. How else do you think I found out about the Weatherfords and the ghosts in the area? I grew up on a damn farm outside of town."

For as much as they both knew about what was going on in town, she hadn't asked him any questions about himself, though this was the first time he'd offered, in any case. "I'm sorry, I—"

"Whatever," Colton said. "What's going down here?"

"Um, I guess I'm about to find out. I thought having the pictures might, I don't know, help us figure out where his head might be. And I feel like I owe you. I thought I was going crazy at first."

The Ethan Weatherford look was back again. There might be a brotherly bone in his body after all. There had to be if he was in Alpha Gamma Rho.

"It's the most materialized haunting I've ever seen."

Olivia saw Dr. Cahara park across from her and a few spots over. She waved. "How do you want me to get them to you? I don't know if they're going to let me leave with the card."

"Give me a minute out here. I've got some homework to do. Text me if you can get the camera back to me, and I'll copy the pics onto my computer, get you a card of your own." Colton opened his laptop and kicked back in her passenger seat. "If I don't hear from you, I'll figure out a Plan B." Apparently, he was going to wait in *her* car. She didn't argue or tell him to wait elsewhere. It was all she could do to not think about what she was about to see.

Nerves had her all wound up by the time Dr. Cahara came over and handed her a plastic tub of necessary equipment. Olivia shifted awkwardly to accommodate for her own camera bag and tripod. Colton's presence helped as he sat in the front seat "studying," but Cecelia's eyes lingered on him. Olivia didn't have to be a mind reader to understand that the woman wondered who he was but had enough tact not to ask. At least Colton had the wherewithal not to wave or make a fool of himself.

Olivia felt out of place as Dr. Cahara led her around behind the gym. Her festival work was landscapes, not close-up aerial photography. Cecelia reassured her that she was there to help, but all it did was strain her more. They entered a nondescript utility door and descended a set of metal stairs into the facility's basement.

They had gone down two flights when they ran into other people. Olivia wondered who had made the discovery and how it had come about in the first place. Who would start digging under some loose tiles?

Her imagination supplied more for her though. In her head she saw a fit-for-Halloween skeleton hand reaching up through the dirt. It scratched at the soil until it nearly reached the surface. Then it tapped at the tiles until they loosened enough for those bony fingers to breach the surface. She imagined someone going down there to get the heating system ready for colder weather. They saw the loose tiles and lifted one, revealing bony fingers sticking out of the ground, reaching up through the earth.

A shudder hit her as they walked. She was cold, and her fingers were white at the tips. She curled her fingers into her palms to warm them.

They reached another access door, and a cop (thankfully, no one Olivia recognized) let them through to another set of stairs. The light beyond was fairly brilliant, and Olivia saw a bustle at the bottom of the stairs. The sick feeling intensified.

The floor was dirt, which surprised Olivia, but she faintly heard Cecelia saying they had to pull up all the tiles in the room to be certain they'd found everything. She heard a low hum of many voices talking at once, but Olivia caught only some of the conversation. She squeezed her hands over the lip of the tub to bring herself back to the moment before she hyperventilated or passed out.

"Olivia?"

She turned toward the familiar voice and relaxed a notch. The humming in her ears stopped. "Simon, hey."

He looked awful. She wanted to say something, but too many people were around. Cecelia was talking to someone near where Olivia could see the ground had been dug up, but a tent over the exhumation blocked her from seeing down into it.

"I don't know if I can do this," she said in a low voice.

"I'm sorry you have to," he replied. He did sound sorry. She wanted to hug him.

"Have you seen him?"

"Yes."

"Have you seen him . . . elsewhere?"

"I hear *you* have." Was that jealousy in his voice? She couldn't tell over the din.

"I have," she replied.

"Be careful."

She knew what he meant. Careful of him, careful of Austin, careful of the entire situation. She didn't need him to tell her twice. Or at all. "I'm trying."

"Good. May I bring you over to it? I'll help however I can."

Professional but still personal. That was how she needed to be. She needed to think of it as a subject only. Get through it. Think about it later.

She let him, and he took her gently by the elbow and led her and Cecelia over to what Olivia could only consider a grave. He gave her elbow a gentle squeeze when she looked over the edge.

There was a cry in her head and then an emptying sensation, like the one in the cemetery. Olivia couldn't blame Evelyn. This wasn't Austin's best look.

Don't think of it as Austin, she told herself. *Pretend you're Indiana Jones, and Simon is your hunky sidekick.* She grinned at Simon, who gave her a confused look. She would have to tell him that gem later.

Being immersed in setting up the equipment with Cecelia helped. *Shift this light panel this way a bit, now back the other way a tick. Center this tripod, mark the spot. Adjust aperture. Check lighting. Focus, focus, focus.*

They're just bones, she reminded herself, but aside from biology class in high school and maybe an early undergraduate class, she hadn't seen bones up close like this. And not *like this* either.

The wild speculations going on around her also helped keep her mind off marrying the images of real Austin and long-dead Austin. Simon was at her arm often, and she appreciated the comfort, but she was also interested in what he thought was going on. To say she listened intently was an understatement.

Someone postulated that it was simply a prank for the upcoming festival, perfect timing and all that. Simon was quick with his response. "It's possible. We've had incidents nearly every year for as long as I've worked on these events and with Warren's early histories. It's a popular subject with teenagers."

It surprised Olivia at first, but the suggestion was tactful. There was a brief commotion at the top of the stairs, and Olivia lost focus on what Simon was saying.

A uniformed body on the stairs bent down until Olivia could see his face. "Olivia Norwich? This person says he's with the photographer."

Colton's friendly wave from his position behind the officer didn't help the openly curiously looks from both Dr. Cahara and Simon. Olivia thought she might die of embarrassment. So much for not making a fool of himself.

Olivia licked her lips. "He's with me. Colton Munroe. My assistant," she croaked. She felt Simon's eyes burning into her, but if she looked at him, she knew he'd see something in her face that would reveal her plan. She kept her eyes fixed on Colton, which wasn't difficult when she expected him to do something ridiculous at any moment.

Colton practically skipped down the stairs; he was either oblivious or didn't care that he was making a scene. He set his eyes on Olivia and held up his laptop like a trophy. "I got the laptop, Miz Norwich! I'm sorry I'm late!"

Dr. Cahara threw a questioning glance on her colleague. "Your assistant?"

Digging deep, Olivia reached for her professional side, scrambled to grab ahold of anything that was even half true. "He's my cousin. Interested in photography. I forgot my laptop, to check my focus on the first round of shots." She took a deep breath. *Settle yourself. You've got this.* "He's taking the same program at St. Mary's that I did, and I thought this would be a good opportunity for him. Besides, I forgot my laptop." She turned an honestly sheepish gaze at Dr. Cahara, hoping the lie about his college attendance wouldn't be questioned. Cecelia could check at this campus, but her range didn't extend to St. Mary's.

"You're studying photography at St. Mary's?"

Colton smiled, "Oh yeah!"

"What's your emphasis?"

Olivia's stomach dropped, but she shouldn't have worried. Colton had nearly as winning a smile as Simon did. "I'm just a freshman, ma'am. I won't narrow my focus until I get with my advisor at the end of the semester. I just do what the teacher tells me for now. Super enjoying the classes, though."

That seemed to satisfy Dr. Cahara, who laughed and turned to talk to someone whom Olivia guessed was another history department professor—he and Simon wore nearly the same sweater and slacks. Olivia released the breath she'd been holding, still careful not to look Simon in the eyes, and Colton got himself set up in the only empty corner of the room. The brightness of the laptop screen illuminated a sheen of sweat on his forehead. So he *was* nervous. Good. That made two of them.

Getting back to business, Olivia reached down and set her ruler next to the skeleton's left arm bone, the name of which escaped her. She still didn't feel qualified to be there, but if all they wanted was a good recording of the site, she supposed she could give them that.

When she set the identifying placard above the severed neck, where a skull should have been, she noticed more details in the site. In the dirt between his right hand and his hip were fibers of his clothing and the shiny side of a piece of metal. The desire to reach for it, to see what it was, was so strong that Olivia had to stop herself from getting closer. She could shift the camera though, and she slid it along its track, so she could get a closer look.

She brought the area into focus. Her heart clenched, and her hand went to the right pocket of her jeans to feel the small bump of the horseshoe cufflink there. She shifted the camera to the other side of the skeleton, snapping photographs in a daze as she went. Nothing was visible on the other side, but that didn't mean it wasn't still buried. Her mouth felt dry, her skin hot.

When she had taken a full round of photographs, she swapped out the memory card for a new one, then casually handed the card to Colton. After about ten minutes, she heard him say, "Focus looks good." She watched him close the laptop and hand over the card to Cecelia, who slid it into a protective case, then handed it over to what must've been a detective. She relaxed slightly.

Olivia continued to photograph in a haze as people bustled around her. Sometimes they had her stand back, so they could jump down into the excavation site. They seemed to do it so carelessly. She wanted to yell each time for them to be careful, to not hurt him. She felt the cufflink in her pocket almost obsessively, trying to reason it out. There was no way to, so she went about photographing the scene mechanically. Shift, lighting, shift, focus, snap.

Cecelia left at some point, said it was too crowded, and Olivia promised her in a haze that she'd leave the equipment and other memory card with one of the officers after they were done.

By the time she was finished, Olivia was exhausted and shaking. Her body was banged up all to hell too and was sorer by the hour. Another "Calgon Take Me Away" night was in order, and she felt nervous that someone might suspect what Colton had done. But she turned in the loaner equipment with the other memory card, and no one asked her or Colton any questions. She sent Colton out ahead of her with her own tripod and laptop, feeling protective of what they'd stolen. Dr. Cahara and the others might have been too busy to notice what had happened, but she wasn't going to take a chance that Simon—or Not Simon—had.

Simon walked her out to her car. They didn't speak as they walked, but Simon grabbed her hand and gave it a reassuring squeeze. She was thankful that the previous hour had passed without his alter-ego surfacing. Everything that had happened, everything that was in her head, wanted to spill out of her mouth, but she kept it closed. How could she confide in someone when he had a Jekyll-and-Hyde war going on inside? But perhaps there was a temporary solution.

"Would you come to the old cemetery with me sometime soon?" she asked when they neared her car. "There's some interesting finds there that I'd like to show you."

He gave her an odd look, as if he needed to process the request. Was William Monroe in there listening, wondering?

"I thought the architecture on the Monroe crypts was interesting. Photographically," she added. "I'd like to look at it with you." She hoped that wasn't a giveaway. She was still learning how to be sneaky.

"Yes, let's," he replied with a smile.

Olivia tensed. Was that a red glint in his eyes, or was it just a trick of the light? When he leaned in to kiss her, his hand gripped the strap for her camera bag. Evelyn sent off warning bells, but Olivia didn't need the woman to know what was about to happen.

His red eyes narrowed. Olivia swore she heard him hiss and caught an odor like the smell of the nightmare horse. She felt the animal's breath on her again before she fell from the cliffs, the stench, the heat. This was the imposter. She had no doubt.

A horn honked from the parking lot not three vehicles over. Simon jumped away from Olivia and released his hold on the camera bag. He looked over at her car, where Colton waved idiotically.

"Ethan Weatherford," he muttered, and Olivia knew it was no longer Simon next to her. Doubt kept falling away. She took his hesitation as an opportunity to step away from him.

"I've got to go."

He closed the distance between them. "Someday you won't have a spiritual bodyguard to keep you safe, my dear."

That didn't sound like something Simon would say. Perhaps not even William but whatever was also with William. And if Colton was her spiritual bodyguard, Lord help her.

"Goodbye," she said. He must have heard the finality in her tone because a look of panic that must've been pure Simon crossed his face before he was Not Simon once again. He stalked back to his car without a backward glance.

Olivia watched him go, her heart dancing in her throat. "Goodbye" wasn't what she had wanted to say, but it was much too late for anything else.

Colton's eyebrows said what he didn't about what had transpired. "Thought I might wait for you," he said.

Olivia nodded, shaken but bolstered by his presence. "He called you Ethan Weatherford. And my spiritual bodyguard."

That earned a short barking laugh from the young man. "I ought to put that on my next set of business cards."

Olivia watched the images of Austin's skeleton ghost by as Colton scrolled through them. He said nothing until he finished a minute later. "These look great. I got everything off the other card too. I'll make you a copy and get it to you tomorrow."

"Colton?"

"That's my name."

"Thank you."

He shifted uncomfortably. "Sure."

Olivia felt the last days of turmoil and torment behind her lips. It all wanted to rush out, but she didn't know where to start. So, she agreed to meet Colton the next day once he'd gotten her a card made and kept her mouth shut about the rest.

47

WINTER 1900

THEY SAT TOGETHER IN THE INFORMAL PARLOR WITH THE curtains drawn looking at Austin's books from his recent travels and pondering Evelyn's latest drawings. Evelyn loosened the strings of her corset and rested, enjoying the quiet and the company.

"Where have you been since I last saw you? You used to write to me, tell me where you were and what you saw. I felt I had been there myself; you told it so well."

Austin kissed the top of Evelyn's head as he brought over another set of postcards. "Colorado, mostly. And farther west than I have been before."

"Tell me of it. I wish to go with you."

"You have not seen the great Rocky Mountains, have you?"

"No, only as you have described them and the pictures I have seen."

And so he described his travels through them, the trains that ran along the sides of mountains, the tall passes where some wanted to mark their land boundaries with Austin's barb and wire, and the sights that could be seen at such elevations. Evelyn wanted to see them. He described the scenery in greater detail than he did the people. She had teased him about that before. "You're a great salesman," she had said, "but you dislike too much time with people." Austin had smiled and pinched her cheek.

"You'll understand when you're my age," he said, which made her giggle.

Evelyn rested a hand in Austin's and looked out at the room. There was much Austin could do with his place of solitude. She wanted to give the place some touches, as her mother had done in their home. She wanted to place a plant there and there. They could have her artwork framed and hung on that blank wall.

She searched Austin's face for a time. "Why does he hate you so?" she said. "I asked him once, and he said he tried to do business with you, but you refused."

Austin laughed "You are a brave woman to ask such a man about such a subject. His feud with my family has been long and arduous. It began with his father and our land and continued with myself and my horse—horses."

"Evan?"

"And father's stud, Ivanhoe. And a mare, Rowena."

"Please explain."

"Evan is a prize. You understand he is unique, yes?"

"He's beautiful. I've never seen another like him—not so strong or so agile or so impressive, and to work so hard for you."

Austin nodded and looked off across the room. "I do not advertise Evan's worth, nor do I care to for all the attention it would gather to me. There are only three other horses like Evan, fine studs who, with the right mare, produce technically flawless offspring."

"And William wants him?"

"He has for quite some time." The anger came upon him then the way twilight rushes over the prairie hills. He opened his mouth to speak of the stolen filly, but he closed it suddenly. That was his anger. Evelyn didn't need to be part of it. She needed only to enjoy the animal, which had been intended for her anyway.

"Why had you not told me this? I had no idea."

"Because it was so unimportant to me." His pride was unimportant. So was his anger. He felt it become sharp, like the blade his father had kept from the war. He kept it honed and polished, so he could never forget. "If we forget," he often said, "we drive ourselves into the same ruts over and over again." Austin had not forgotten that.

"But it would have been important to me. I feel it would have changed everything. How could I have wanted to be with a man who had wronged you and your family so?"

"That is a judgement you needed to make for yourself. I could not make it for you."

"He concealed himself from me. I might never have known!"

"And I cannot make decisions for you either, my love. I imagine I would have told you, and you would have laughed your lovely laugh and told me that I was mistaken, that he was more than what I had seen, and that nothing I could have said would have changed your mind."

Evelyn curled closer to him, and he could feel the shame radiating from her. "I don't know. He came into my life at such a strange time. You were gone so long, and Ethan died. It was a hard time at home."

"I'm sorry I was not there more."

"No, do not be. You were off doing what you thought was right. And I was here doing what I thought was right. It was not, but I understand that now."

Austin stroked her hair. He didn't know what to say.

"I do not have much solace there," Evelyn continued. "One of my only moments of pleasure has been Ebony."

The anger licked at his breast unexpectedly. No matter how happy he felt, a tendril of it was in everything he did. Evelyn's presence kept it the most at bay. Removing her from Monroe's grasp would remedy it entirely.

"Your mare," he said.

"Yes."

"She is beautiful."

Evelyn looked pleased. "Yes. I take care of her. Only since he gifted her to me have I been allowed outside by myself. Just to groom and walk her, I mean. I only ride her when William accompanies me in town. William says it has not been safe in town though. What has been going on? Even when I lived with Mother and Father, I didn't know so little of town and the wider world, but I never felt unsafe."

"He doesn't allow you out by yourself?"

She shook her head. "He said it isn't safe."

That prodded his anger. "I don't believe it has ever been safer here in Warren. Or in the world."

He watched Evelyn's face as she processed that. He saw anger and disbelief, even fear.

"It isn't," she finally breathed out.

Austin felt his heart clench for her. He reminded himself of the blade kept sharp.

There were tears in Evelyn's eyes, but she dabbed at them and put on a smile for Austin. "It is no matter. My happiness is not there. It's here, with you." She took his hand and placed it on her belly.

Austin looked up at her, happy shock on his face.

"Yes," Evelyn said, and she reached for Austin, pulled him toward her from his chair. She felt buoyant, jubilant. She felt she could do anything—tell William to fall off a horse, ride off into the sunset, any and everything.

"Evelyn, I—"

"Shush. I don't want to worry over it now."

They tried not to. Time passed regardless, and Evelyn found a kind of peace in the schedule she kept. The hardest times were when Austin left to ride south or west.

Sarah was born, and Evelyn's hours were filled with loving on the little girl. Though William was disappointed that Sarah was not a boy, Evelyn thought she was perfect, from her fine dark hair and caramel eyes down to her toes, which curled in just slightly, as Austin's did.

48

Tuesday, October 20th

The world looked different when Olivia woke the next morning. As she lay there, she thought it was only that she had slept interrupted for more than a few hours, but when she tried to move her body and couldn't, she understood. Fear and panic were still her first reactions, though not nearly as intense as they had been the first few times she hadn't given her consent to be taken over.

And what if she just gave in to it? Let Evelyn have the reins until at least the stress of the photographs dissipated? The event at the cliffs was physically and emotionally exhausting, and she just wanted to sleep for a while, to rest. The formal review had left her feeling insecure about her position at the university after years of positive evaluations from students and department heads. But she had clearly been unable to perform the responsibilities required of her for the past few weeks. Neglect of her duties snowballed quickly, and Evelyn had done such a good job for her the day before . . .

Olivia was tired. Her body hurt. Her photographs seemed so far away, but they still danced before her eyes in a slideshow. The prairie dips and swells. The trees at the cliffs. The cliffs themselves. The ever-varying grey tones that Olivia had labored over with love and care and strict attention to finishing details. Nightmare horse be damned. Her photographs were her best work.

But the photographs of Austin's skeleton weren't. Not that they weren't good, but they unsettled her. She couldn't reconcile the sight with him, with his flesh and blood. She had tried so hard to just look through the camera, to look at him only through the lens and not straight on.

Soon she would meet Colton to get a copy. Guilt coiled in her stomach. She could look at the photographs, then destroy the duplicate card. It would be worth it if any of the photographs offered clues about where Austin's head was.

What good will it do? Evelyn asked. *What do you think you will see that you haven't already?*

She had a point.

But no, Olivia could do this. Evelyn might be able to mine information from her head, and Olivia could guide her through things all she wanted, but Evelyn couldn't work on the photographs. They needed a meticulous eye, and it was Olivia's eyes and hands that needed to be on them.

But someone ought to look after your mother, Evelyn whispered.

Olivia got another hit of guilt from that. "I've been texting her. She's fine for now. I'm almost done with my photographs. And . . . and . . ." She couldn't finish the thought. She didn't know when Not Simon in his imposter getup would leave her alone.

Olivia caved, and together, they made breakfast for Olivia's mother. Olivia supplied the knowledge for blueberry muffins, and Evelyn finished them off and arranged them with a nice note in the kitchen for when

Olivia's mother woke. Evelyn gently reminded Olivia to check her mother's pill minder, then set it next to the breakfast offering.

Guilt stabbed her. She was thirty-five careening toward forty, and she'd never done anything like this for her mother before. All their bullshit had always been in the way.

She's still your mother, Evelyn said gently.

"Then why have I always felt like the matronly one?" Olivia asked.

Evelyn didn't have an answer for that.

Their drive into Warren to the Daily Brew was quiet. Olivia gritted her teeth as they drove through fog that blanketed everything. Trees, buildings, and streetlights appeared and disappeared, ships on the prairie ocean.

Evelyn liked Colton almost on principle because he was so like her brother. Olivia still became annoyed with every three words that came out of his mouth.

Olivia sat at the same couch at the Daily Brew where she and Simon had sat not long ago. She all but buried her face in a dark coffee with milk and sugar.

"You look like shit," Colton said when he plopped down a safe distance away from her on the couch. He was definitely the brother she never had.

"Thanks."

He held up a handful of crinkled papers. "By the way, you had a treasure trove in the front of your camera bag. You've been holding out on me and the, like, five hundred people who care about this"

Her eyes roved over the worn corners and nearly falling-apart folds. The papers she had pulled from the mess of books at her mom's house. She'd completely forgotten. And she'd left him in her car with her backup camera bag, several hundred photos with the nightmare horse, and who knew how many photos from the dugout and the archives. "You went through my stuff? How did you even have time before you came in the gym?"

"I was bored."

She was caught somewhere between incensed and thankful that he'd found them. "I had forgotten about them. I haven't even looked at them yet."

Colton handed over the stack. "Check them out. You're a minor celebrity now."

She unfolded the first few sheets of paper. Handwritten notes in neat cursive stared back at her.

> E,
>
> You understand, I'm sure, that this letter must be destroyed upon your reading. I regretfully came back too late, and for that I know I'll not rest easily for the remainder of my days.
>
> Please ensure the safety of the little ones by taking them into your charge as your own. The Vogts, save Jeremiah, can be trusted. So can William Prettyman, the photographer from Oklahoma. Gates will vouch for me, should you need another name. Time is of the essence, as you understand.
>
> A

Her mouth was dry. Her head buzzed.

She opened several of the envelopes and stared dumbly at the forms that legalized a name change for a young child named Ethan Weatherford Monroe. His new name was emblazoned at the bottom of the page: Theodore Colton Vogt. December 12, 1903.

"Well," Olivia began. "I suppose you know that name."

"My great-grandfather."

Olivia sifted through the rest of the paper. Bills of sale from 1919 for an acreage once used for small farming, 95 percent native prairie. Only remaining structures: limestone foundation, spring house, limestone fencing near road. Another form for a name change, this one from the 1960s. Everly Marie Norwich to Lydia Marie Norwich.

"That's my mom," Olivia breathed. "She had her name changed twice. Why would she do that?"

Colton peered over her shoulder. "I don't know. It was the sixties. Maybe she just wanted to."

Olivia didn't like that answer. She wanted to call her mom right then and ask her about it, but she knew all she'd get was stonewall silence and more trouble later.

"You sure look a lot like Evelyn," Colton said. He'd picked up some of the photographs that Olivia had finally put into protective sleeves. Should she be on the defensive?

"I know."

Colton stared at her, looking at her the way a woman might study a shirt for stains. "Yes, I think you do."

"Quit being a cryptic asshole." The words fell from Olivia's mouth before she could stop them.

Colton laughed. "I know! That's part of my problem. I know I'm an asshole, but I do nothing about it. What you see is what you get."

"Talk to me straight. I'm running out of time."

Colton rolled his eyes. "Sure you are. So, we know the kids survived, which makes us descendants, family. What else do you need? And how does that help anyway? You're better off finding where Austin's head is stashed."

"Of course, but all the proof we have here is circumstantial. Papers doctored, similar family names or name changes, piano lessons ordered for someone in someone else's name."

"Well, no shit. Of course it's circumstantial, stupid. They would have covered it up as best they could. Clearly your mom didn't cover it up super well or you wouldn't have found these." He shook the papers at her. "Why would anyone have thought that a few fucking pieces of paper would make it a hundred years into the future? They tossed that shit in your dugout and forgot about it. Then the place burned down, and no one wanted to go near it. Perfect scenario. Then something bubbled up out of the otherworld, and now you're about to go digging around in a place that's been in your backyard for thirty odd or forty years. However old you are."

"Don't call me stupid." He made her want to shove him off the couch.

"Is that really all you got from that? Come on."

"So, what?"

"I know who you are."

"Who am I?"

"Evelyn Weatherford, like we talked about in the cemetery."

"I'm her? I'm her descendant. I thought that's what you meant by it."

"That too, I think. But you also *are* her. Like a copy. A clone. A ripple from the past. I bet if you compared your DNA, it'd be the same."

"And you?"

"Whose name comes to your lips when you look at me? If it's Austin or Evelyn, I think you're right on the money. That he chose your Simon is pretty telling. *I'm* not submitting to a DNA test anytime soon; I can tell you that. But if this ever settles, sure. When I've left town and can't get involved anymore, I might."

Olivia fell into thought. Did that make her a descendant or a clone? Both? Did it matter? It did if she lingered too long on her thoughts about Austin. "I don't want to think about that."

Colton shrugged. "Suit yourself. I guess if you don't care, it doesn't matter."

Olivia didn't agree, but she didn't know how to express that in words. It still did matter somehow. She couldn't just wish everything away.

"Why'd you get into this in the first place?" Even a slight change in subject would be a relief.

"I saw things that other people didn't. Some felt them. Seemed a logical hobby."

Olivia gestured at the papers and photographs strewn out next to them. "And this business?"

"This is *your* investment," Colton said. "I ought to be charging you for our time together."

"And you're not because . . ."

"I haven't been sleeping much," he confessed. "These ghosts are more than restless. I don't even know if I want to call them ghosts anymore. This is way out of my league."

Olivia was chilled by his statement. It echoed feelings she hadn't put into words. In Evelyn's presence, Olivia felt ghostlike; her own wants paled in comparison to Evelyn's passions.

"Let's look at the photos," Olivia said. Something choked her as it threatened to climb out her throat. Probably her lifetime of uncertainty. She swallowed it down.

Colton sighed and handed Olivia a memory card. "Get your laptop out. Mine's fucked."

"Spill your cranberry vodka on it or something?"

He laughed. "Beer, actually, but thanks for thinking I'm that fancy."

Olivia shook her head but laughed anyway. It took ages for her computer to boot up, but at least the laughter took the edge off the strain.

They spent the next two hours poring over the photographs. For something she thought was so important, nothing was there. Nothing except bones and dust and rusted buckles and gold cufflinks. She wasn't a detective; she didn't know what to look for, how one patch of disturbed dirt might be different from another.

Austin had been buried with his holster still on, but no firearms or sword was in the grave. She had seen him with at least a pistol, and the stories said that sometimes he carried a sword. While those things were interesting, the pictures told her nothing new.

Olivia pulled the cufflink from her pocket and showed Colton. He raised his eyebrows at her. "I didn't realize you were the sort to steal something from a grave. Congratulations. You've risen in my esteem."

"He gave it to me. A week or so ago." When she went to hand it to him, he pulled his hands back in a dramatic gesture.

"Hell no! I don't want that ghost shit in my hand. You keep your talisman. I don't want anything to do with it."

Colton agreed to think on it all and then come to help her at the gallery when it was time. He didn't say why, and Olivia didn't ask.

By the day's end, she was run ragged again. No leads on Austin's head, no leads on what William might want next, and no leads on whether she would ever see "Just Simon" again. She was exposed and unprepared for whatever might happen next.

49

Circles. Simon was being run in circles. He tossed *Warren: The Early Years* onto his desk and pushed his chair away, so he could grab *Famous Feuding Families of Warren, Kansas* from the shelf. He knew the books by heart, but that didn't mean he might not glean something new from one of them.

And Olivia. Whatever she wanted to show him in the cemetery couldn't be anything he didn't already know. She hadn't returned any of his texts or calls from the night before or from that day. He knew he should leave her alone, knew William wasn't leaving her be as it was, but he had no one else to talk to. His own industriousness had turned up nothing. She had the answers; he knew it.

He hadn't felt forty when he saw her with the young guy at the gym. It was like being in high school again. The pangs of jealousy at seeing his crush with someone else sent him reeling back to his awkward teenage years when he was adrift and without focus or purpose.

Maybe he was just a student helping her out with the discovery at the gym. His cohabitator hadn't liked the man either. Those reasons though were infinitely clearer to him. He experienced fits and spurts of clarity in the blackouts now, and the name *Ethan Weatherford* had come through loud and clear that day. That would make the young man the third connection back to Evelyn and William and one who had clearly ended up with more of the Weatherford side. Olivia was the same way. But where was his own connection?

His phone rang and dragged him out of his circular musing about Weatherfords, Hearths, Monroes, and younger men who ignited a fierce jealousy in him.

"Simon?"

"This is he." Simon flipped through another book and tossed it aside. It wouldn't have anything new either. Every dead end he hit was more frustrating. Or was someone agitating him on purpose?

"Simon, it's Dr. Bourland. How are you doing?"

Simon paused. Why was the dean of the department calling him? And using his formal title instead of his first name? "Uh, I'm OK. Stressed about the festival, but I do that to myself every year, you know."

"Yeah. Listen, you missed the last two department meetings. I know it's not required, but poker night too. Wanted to make sure everything was good on your end."

Simon gave the phone his full attention. He must have been so busy keeping busy that he'd missed some required meetings. Shit. "John, I . . ."

"Dr. Bourland. I don't want our informal relationship to get in the way of professional duties. I don't know if my demeanor at the last poker night you were at gave that impression or not."

Simon was stung by the comment. "You didn't give that impression at all. I've just been rather focused on my festival duties this year."

"I hope so. Your midterm teaching evaluations weren't great. You've been spot on every semester for awhile now."

Be a good boy, Simon. You can't go mucking it all up now.

Creepy as the voice was, it was right.

"John—Dr. Bourland—what can I do for you, man? How can I make this right?" He had reverted to the Ohio bale slinger. He was twenty again and leaning on Bridgette and trying to figure out his place in the world one beer at a time before he found books and history.

Go play poker, have a drink, relax. Tell him you'll be at the next meeting. Help the gentleman wherever he needs. There's no need to act out of desperation.

William Monroe, teetotaler until the end, had another good point.

"Don't let me down, Monroe. You carry a fair amount of weight around here, and I've got to retire at some point."

Simon was glad he was sitting down. Now the man had his full attention, but he was already off talking about the next game and who would be there. Applying for dean of the department when John left hadn't really crossed Simon's mind. He was just over forty with enough teaching and some tenured years under his belt, but dean of the department? That seemed like a lot more work for not a lot more pay. It seemed more likely they would bring someone in from out of state before he applied for the position. He abandoned that train of thought; he didn't need it at the moment.

"I'll be at the next game; don't worry. And the next meeting. I'll chair it if you need me to." He hated that responsibility, but whatever needed to be done, he would do it.

"Good. I'll let you. Keep sharp, Monroe. There's a lot of year left still."

They said goodbye and hung up.

Simon added the department meeting and the poker game to his desk calendar and then sat back to think, rocking in his old wooden chair.

50

Late Winter, 1902

Little William came into the world blue and shriveled. He looked so like Evelyn's husband that she had to concede, in her heart of hearts, that William had finally succeeded with her. The thought was so strange but so powerful that she could not shake it even as she watched the midwife pull great strings of what looked like black saliva from the newborn's throat.

Fear skimmed over the top of Evelyn's pain. Visions of the thing from the mirror rose up in her mind. This was its fault. She knew it.

She was about to say something when there was a commotion outside the door. The doctor burst into the room with William on his heels, and Evelyn's midwife was pushed aside.

"What are you doing?" Evelyn cried, weak but lucid. She tried to prop herself up on the pillows, but the pain in her abdomen was too great.

William ordered the midwife leave. “This baby needs help breathing!” she protested. “I won’t leave until he cries.” William grabbed the woman and wrestled the baby from her arms.

“My God, William!” Evelyn sobbed.

“This child needs oxygen,” the physician said. Evelyn could not see from her vantage point what he did. Little William coughed, drew in air, and wailed. When the physician turned, Evelyn saw his skin grow rosy before her eyes.

The pain in her abdomen grew, waves of pressure like giving birth. She groaned and pushed back against the pillows. The physician rushed to her bedside and pressed on her swollen belly, feeling all around it. He wasn’t unkind, but Evelyn didn’t know him. To be seen in a such a state by a stranger, though he was a doctor, added to her distress.

“Mrs. Monroe, you are not carrying twins, are you?”

“Twins!” William exclaimed. “The X-ray showed nothing of the sort!”

The physician went beneath the sheet over her legs, and Evelyn felt the dizzying pressure of his hand inside her.

The midwife protested, but William grabbed her arm and dragged her from the room. Evelyn might have sworn she saw something move beyond the dark mirror on the other side of the room. She wanted to alert everyone, but the doctor pressed her back into the pillows with his other hand. “Please, madam, you mustn’t move. You have a second baby to deliver.”

In her panic, she didn’t understand. There was so much chaos. William was soon back at her side and had her swallow something vile.

“No, no, the mirror!” she tried to say, but darkness rushed up and swallowed her.

When she woke, she was in the hospital. It was much cleaner than she imagined, but the smell of something rotten reached her. She leaned over the side of her bed and retched. The movement flooded pain through her belly. One hand flew to her mouth to wipe it, the other to her belly to feel what ailed her so. Hot pain greeted her.

Evelyn pulled aside the white gown, which was not her own. Bloody bandages across her stomach greeted her. The skin there was stretched and bruised. She could not understand how they had cut her open and taken the child out without her knowledge. The feeling followed her home when Alyssa came to get her. William waited for her there, children in hand.

The curious feeling that she had given birth but not persisted. She felt that perhaps she carried within her a third child, one of her own creation. She knew it was shame, but she didn't think she should give birth to it unless she was well away from the household that had brought it upon her.

She loved young William, but she could not stand him, for he was so like his father. It created a war within her that she felt she could not win. She gave the child extra attention and showered him with gifts and toys, but she could not force herself to love him. He was plagued with mild sickness at least once a week. Milk soured in his stomach. The trim on his outfits scratched his thin skin.

She had no such aversion to little Ethan, who watched the world quietly with his caramel eyes. But Evelyn was terrified of the remarkable difference in their features, that somehow, though born at the same time, one looked more like William and the other like Austin.

A noise startled her out of her writing. William stood at the foot of the bed, watching her. She shrank into the bedcovers at the sight of his red eyes, taking the journal with her.

"I've been thinking, wife," he began. She listened but dared not say a word. "I think it will be more suitable if you only see the children during meals for the time being. Your health is of utmost importance." Evelyn opened her mouth to protest, but William spoke over her. "I'll have tasks for you to complete each day, so your hands and mind do not become idle. This is the manner in which you will recover. The wet nurse has agreed to my terms, as I knew she would."

"My children," Evelyn croaked.

William came to her side of the bed and stroked her hair with a gnarled hand. His last two fingers were normal, but his thumb, index, and middle fingers were claw-like and covered in black scabs. If it was from disease or injury or something else, Evelyn didn't know. She didn't want to be touched with the hand, but he continued to pet her.

"My children will be just fine," William said.

She felt she was watching herself from afar, helpless to slow the course of events.

51

THE CHASE NO LONGER THRILLED HIM AS IT HAD. HE HALF-heartedly shoved the latest Evelyn over the edge of the cliff with one booted heel. The woman, this one older and infinitely less interesting, slid unconscious all the way down. She scraped through brush and over crumbling shale and limestone, but the sound brought him no joy.

It had become a chore, this systemic eradication. And here he had been so excited about it. Even William was having his doubts.

Bored, that's the word he wanted. Such a modern notion, when one could have whatever one wanted with a click or a call.

Simon's utterly wholesome infatuation with the girl also wore on him. She seemed nice enough, as far as humans went, but much too pigheaded for his liking.

Fine. Truth be told, they'd both gone too far the other night with Olivia. As exciting as it had been at first, he regretted sending her off the cliff. She'd clearly not been much worse for wear when he'd seen her the next day, but the continued presence of a bodyguard was an ongoing annoyance.

He would have to find a way to separate them. All of them.

52

Noon, August 26, 1903

Evelyn studied the inside cover of her journal. It had been so good to her during that long last year with William. She would forever be grateful to Austin for the gift. She had needed it when Austin was away, and she was bored. She had needed it when William began his bizarre requests. And she had certainly needed a place to set her thoughts down since the twins' dramatic birth.

That day she got to see them. William had deemed her healthy enough to visit them once per day apart from mealtimes. Little William was a picture of the lordship himself. Little Ethan was quiet and good.

Her own words worried her at times though. She understood how the drama of the moment could be cause for sensation, but after every one of William's episodes, she would reread the passage days later and think that perhaps she was exaggerating how the scene had gone. Just as she had told Austin, the man was not truly the devil or a demon. He was only an overly ambitious man who stopped at nothing short of what he wanted. Something deep within her disagreed.

> I do not sleep much any longer. I have felt irreconcilably without mirth since my dear boy was born, and I cannot find my way out of it. All I wish for is Austin. Good, kind Austin. My desire is so great that these thoughts nearly spill from my mouth before William. William. William is angry. And not in the usual way. I have grown a callous over my heart to his usual way, but now he is different.
>
> God abandoned me when I married William, but I do not think the devil has. I think he began walking by William's side not long after we were wed. I didn't see it, and I didn't know, but now I see it in everything he does. He is so hateful, so vengeful. I worry
>
> I smelled smoke from a prairie fire late in the night when I could not sleep and could even see a faint orange glow out my window, but the smoke that drifted into town was white, which William tells me means a home is burning. He said there must have been lightning. There was a great rain overnight, but I didn't recall any lightning before it. William smelled of the prairie today, and smoke, so he must have gone to see what the ruckus was. I do not know why he will not tell me of the thing though. It is no great secret when anything happens to anyone around here, unless it is in the privacy of their homes. And even then we hear of much of it. Sometimes I wonder what is said of myself here in this house.
>
> William's hand is worse. It seemed to stagnate for quite some time, but since his last trip west, the dark scabs grow again.

Evelyn was writing in her journal next to baby William's bassinette when William strode in. Despite the shock that he had nearly caught her writing, she smoothly covered her journal with the embroidery she carried.

"Husband," she said more coolly than she intended.

"Wife," William replied lovingly as he approached the bassinette. She felt the word was meant for the baby though, not her. William leaned in to coo at the child and check on him. Even for the current state of things, Evelyn wished he would give her some modicum of affection. He had once, but that was before she had given him a son. Now all his hopes and dreams rested on the child. Little Ethan, born later, was second in his thoughts, and Sarah hardly saw his face.

William turned to her, his smile less loving now. "Wife, I found mud all up your mare's feathers. I thought to myself, 'My wife is good, and she would not go out without talking to me. She knows it is not safe out of the house. Besides, there is no reason for her to leave. She has everything she needs here.'"

"I . . ."

"Don't interrupt me. I'm still speaking. Were you not taught that you must wait until your spouse is finished speaking?"

"I'm sorry, I—"

"Do you know what is muddy now?"

She scrambled for an excuse. Her mouth felt dry. She no longer cared about the journal. All she wanted to do was run out of the room, down the stairs, and out the front door. Away. Forever. "Town, I imagine. Where I went."

William smiled, and the strange red tint she had come to know in his eyes appeared. They were his eyes, but they were not. He was anger manifested. Rage. "No, love. There is no mud on the streets in town. There is no mud on the prairie. There is no mud at the canyon crossings. There is mud on the cattle trails though. There is mud on the Hearth cattle trail."

Evelyn stopped breathing. Her head grew light. "I went riding. That is all."

William continued to smile, though the look had grown dangerous. "Riding. Where did you ride?"

She didn't know what to say or what to do with her hands. She knew she should look William in the eyes, but she couldn't. The red crept over his irises. "Just on the prairie. That's all. I may have taken an old cattle trail for part of the journey, but only for a time. I never saw anyone."

William said nothing for a time. He only watched her until she could no longer keep his gaze. "I told you not to leave the house."

Her anxiety went down a notch—but only just. "Please forgive me. For my entire life I have been used to roaming the prairie. I only wanted to go for a ride outside of town. I miss my home, my family."

William hummed around her response. Evelyn sat with her head down, staring at her hands and waiting for his reply. She pressed the long nail on her forefinger into her thumb, feeling the pain there. She focused on that. Back and forth she pressed the sharp nail. She turned it just slightly and pushed harder. A little well of blood came up in the cut. It brought a modicum of relief with it, but Almighty, was William going to take forever to respond?

"Well. I suppose you cannot be perfect. You must talk to me if you want to leave like that again though."

She wanted to say that she had, that she used to every time that she wanted to ride out, but he never let her go. He always said no. She had grown weary of asking and had stopped.

"Yes. Please forgive me." She curled her bleeding thumb into her fist and felt its little heartbeat there, focused on it.

"This time, yes." William placed a hand on the top of her head, as one might a child, and she froze.

"Thank you," she managed and then tried to change the subject. "Where have you been?"

William stroked her hair. "I have been working on our future, my dear. Warren is a fine place to settle, but why settle for Warren? There are other sites on the prairie that are prime for the railroad. Commerce moves west."

That sent her heart a flutter. Leave Warren? Be away from Austin? She couldn't imagine it.

William paused his petting, and Evelyn felt him slowly thread his fingers into her hair until he had a fistful of it. It was not painful, but Evelyn felt the danger. Felt it become dire.

She looked at him through the mirror next to her and saw his eyes shift from brown to red, then back to brown. His hand clenched her hair, then loosened. Without thinking, she tried to stand and run out of the room. William tightened his fist, and Evelyn's head and neck were dragged backward. Pain shot up her back and neck. She cried out.

At her cry, William let her go, a look of horror on his face. Tears sprang to Evelyn's eyes, and she held her neck with one hand. She saw two Williams, and the room wavered.

"Look what you did to yourself! If you hadn't moved, that wouldn't have happened!" William said. But the fear had her by then. She raced from the room, clutching her embroidery and journal to her chest.

As she reached the first step on the stairs, her slippered feet lost purchase on the carpet. She slid halfway down the stairs, and her dress and petticoats rode up painfully around her corset. More pain spread up her back and neck. She scrambled to her feet to see where William was.

At the top of the stairs sat something that only resembled William in the eyes and the shape of its skull. It sat hunched on the landing, its bulldogish face covered in the same tarry scabs that William had on his hands. When the creature took a step, it became William again.

He strode down the stairs, and she watched in horror as his form shifted back and forth. Hellish creature to devilish man. Hellish man to devilish creature.

Evelyn turned from the sight and crashed through the house, trying to get away from him. Her dress caught on the cabinet that held a pair of vases given to them as a wedding present, and when she pulled at the fabric, one of them crashed down. Shards of broken pottery went everywhere.

William flew into the dining room in a red-eyed rage. Evelyn hollered. Skirting the broken porcelain, she fled the room, her body pulling her toward the stables. William was close on her heels. She lost him briefly in the garden breezeway, and she tossed the journal into a pile of hay before William caught up with her.

53

3:00 P.M., AUGUST 26, 1903

EVELYN RUSHED INTO AUSTIN'S HOME, HAIR FLYING, HER dress half ripped at the sleeve. She wore no shoes. Had she ridden there without them?

"Austin! He has found us out! He will kill you!"

Ruth whipped around from where she had been walking down the hall with a tray of dishes. Her mouth snapped open at the sight of Evelyn, and the dishes became unbalanced. The topmost one fell to the floor and shattered.

Austin ran to Evelyn, shushing her and pulling her into the parlor. "My God, Evelyn, what happened?" He saw a madness in her eyes that had not been there before. "Evelyn, please. Ruth, please bring me some wine!"

Evelyn grabbed his arms. "I don't want wine, Austin, and I don't want to sit. Please! I rode here fast, the back way, but he left before me. William left before me, and he was heading this way with his gun. He's found out;

I know he has! He was yelling outside in the street about me to anyone who would listen!"

"Well, did you tell him?"

"No! I don't know what happened exactly, but it's . . . it's not him, you know. It's the other thing. He chased me outside, but I went back to the stables for Ebony, and I saw him with his gun. Austin, you have to get out of here! You have to go!"

"Evelyn, sit down and breathe. I understand you don't want to, but I need the entire story before I go rushing out of here."

"Austin, you have to go!"

"I have to go see what's going on. No matter what happens, I'll come find you. Do you understand?"

"He'll kill us both!"

He shushed her, trying not to let her hysteria pull him in. He felt as panicked as she sounded. "I'll come find you. Please hear that. You need to stay here."

"Austin!"

Austin guided Evelyn to her chair in the parlor and finally got her to sit. She was still speaking in circles when Austin rushed back a moment later with an old bottle of his mother's smelling salts. He opened the bottle and bade her breathe its contents. She finally calmed.

"I'm taking Evan to see what's going on. You stay here. Do you hear me?"

Evelyn nodded, her chest still heaving.

"I'll come back for you no matter what."

"What if—"

"No matter what."

He kissed her soundly and then raced out the door. He hollered for Patrick to get Evan saddled, but the boy moved too slowly.

Austin had to slow his movements so as not to spook Evan. The horse had a strong constitution, but it was still best not to let him see his master so agitated. If he did later, that was another thing. But to get him saddled, Austin needed to be calm.

"Evan, we have places to be, my friend." Austin checked and tightened buckles and gave Evan a thorough once-over. Everything needed to be in perfect alignment. They were to ride fast.

Austin slipped his gun into its harness at his chest. Then he slipped his grandfather's gun into his hip holster. One never knew what one would be up against. He had seen enough in the Wild West to last him lifetimes. One more man or demon didn't frighten him. He considered his shotgun. It might be necessary. He grabbed it and strapped it onto the pommel. He had ridden long and fast with more in tow.

The terrain flew by. Evan ate up the land with great strides of his long legs, and Austin tasted the barest lick of coolness in the heavy August air. Rain was imminent. The cicadas nearly drowned out the sound of Evan's hooves on the short canyon bridge. Summer still had an edge on the prairie, but not for long. The corn was ready for harvest, and the brown silks fluttered against the green husks as he and Evan rushed by.

He met William on the main thoroughfare as the man stepped from the sidewalk across the street near his residence. He didn't seem surprised at Austin's appearance, though he looked disdainfully at the dust that Austin had stirred up on his ride.

"What can I do for you today, Mr. Hearth?" William asked congenially.

"I think you know why I'm here."

William brushed at the dust that settled on his jacket. "So cryptic. So dramatic."

Austin dismounted and tied Evan to the ticket office's post. The pair strolled together toward the quiet end of the street as if they were simply discussing matters of business. In an arcane way, Austin believed William saw it that way.

"You're here because of my wife's tendency to wander away from home," William said, smiling easily.

Austin gritted his teeth at the statement. "I'm here because I've grown tired of your meddling in my affairs."

"Interesting choice of words."

"I could say the same of you."

"Tell me, what do you suggest, Mr. Hearth?" William spat the name, and Austin heard the jealousy in the man's voice.

The words came out before he could consider them. "A duel."

"A duel! Ha!" William was beside himself. "You show how outmoded and foolish you are, Hearth. You and I both could go to prison for such an inane endeavor."

Austin touched his piece, handed down from his grandfather. Despite the laws in some states, he had seen his fair share of disputes—political and personal—settled with pistols. More often in the night than not, but he had seen fair fights too. His father, lame in the foot after the atrocities of the wicked war of rebellion (as he was fond of calling the Civil War), had pushed the value of honor, saying how the world lacked it since the war.

"I think you can appreciate settling a matter with strategy and integrity, Mr. Monroe," Austin said. "You have served our great country, after all." He saw William's eyes on his pistol. Could that look have been jealousy too? Or simply anger from Austin's prod at his military history?

"Yes, that I can, outmoded though it may be."

"And we do it in the name of Miss Evelyn's honor." Austin could not help himself.

"*Miss* Evelyn! You forget, I think, that she has been mine these last years. Miss Evelyn's honor, indeed!"

"Her very own."

"Do you hear yourself?" William snapped. "What honor is there in what she has done, what you have participated in?"

"She would not have had you not mistreated her."

"Then she should petition for divorce like the progressive woman she longs to be."

"She is not—"

"Of course she is. Do you hear yourself?" William leaned in close to Austin, and Austin could see that something was wrong with the man's eyes. They were red where they ought to have been brown, and a shot of blood ran through the whites. What had happened to him? Something on his trips to the new town he was rumored to be surveying?

"Don't act like I don't know she's been fucking you behind my back," William growled, his voice low. "Don't act like I don't know what grew in her belly."

Austin jerked away from the laughing man. "What you claim is absurd."

William pointed to his eyes. "Would be, except I know, you see. I know."

"How?"

He was answered by something rotten in the air. Dead cattle in a pasture nearby, a dead horse that someone had not attended to for several days. It washed over the pair, and Austin felt it stick in his lungs.

"I'll meet you here tomorrow, Austin Hearth. With your pistol. That is my choice. It is an attractive and romantic notion for you westward traveling boys, isn't it?" William smiled, though Austin could not figure whether the man was putting him on or not.

"Are we not on the cusp of the West?" Austin asked, ignoring the slight. "Are we not forgotten out here among the prairie dog holes and the dust?"

That raised William's ire. "Warren is a rung above the West, my friend. You would do well to remember that. I'll see you on these streets tomorrow morning when the sun rises. We'll do it for *Miss Evelyn's honor*." William laughed at the last bit, and Austin felt his own ire rise.

Evelyn was gone when he returned to the house, and Austin wondered if it was only her spirit that had visited him, a specter of her torment come to warn him. He didn't ask Ruth whether she had seen her. He didn't need to. Shards of the dishes she had dropped at the sight still littered the floor. Spirit or not, Evelyn had visited, and Austin would not fail her.

54

Near midnight, August 26, 1903

Austin couldn't sleep. He slid from bed and slipped through the house, pulled on his long cloak, and went out to the stables. The spectral Evelyn didn't rest well with his mind. Portents of calamity.

He stopped when he saw his mother's spirit outside the door to the stables. She raised one arm and pointed toward town.

"I'm going," he said, and she faded into the clear night.

Evan was awake and ready for a ride.

That evening's cool rain, which had soaked the prairie and ushered out the August humidity, gave way to clear skies and crystal stars. Austin didn't hurry Evan through the dips and over the swells of the land. The open night sky was his place in the world. He had spent countless nights riding toward ranches and farms to talk barb and wire and post. Countless nights out in the fields with the cattle before that, watching the Kansas sky wheel and turn through the years.

Though the presence of the spirits unsettled him, he understood why his mother didn't rest well. On the trail, in the scrubby flatlands of western Kansas and eastern Colorado, many spirits didn't rest well. Whether they had perished on the way west or come that way to hide and die after the war, their hazy features had been a constant companion for himself and Evan. Sometimes they beckoned, like the ghost lights in the south, sure to bring him to ruin in a hidden creek bed or off a short cliff, but others simply pointed the way forward. Those were oddly reassuring signposts on his journey.

In town he discovered William's friends at the paper had printed out a short run of posters advertising their event the next morning. It had been framed as a performance, with Austin playing the part of the wandering outlaw looking to run away with the good mayor's wife.

He scoffed but understood the seriousness of the publication. Anyone from the outside would have no choice but to trust William's statement against Austin's own. He would need to tread carefully. He suspected that William's involvement in the Pine Ridge Campaign kept him from flirting too hard with the long arm of the law and would keep him from killing Austin in such a public situation. Keeping his nose clean in the dusty west under the thumb of his father was task enough. He didn't need more troubles.

Austin should not have let William goad him into the challenge though. He snagged one of the papers from the post in front of the ticket office. An antiquated answer to a nearly antiquated method of dealing with disagreements. Austin was impressed by the man's ingenuity, but the speed with which he'd turned the situation in his favor was concerning. Still, Austin was settled in his decision. His father's old gun would serve its purpose.

55

August 27, 1903

The next morning, the sun didn't rise, so dense was the fog that lay about the fields and near the streams and ponds. Austin rode his sorrel instead of Evan. That William would send someone to remove Evan from his property while he was otherwise occupied was not out of the question. He left Evan tethered at a cottonwood tree near the long canyon crossing in a secluded clearing and promised the horse he would return soon.

There were no words for everything that coursed through him. It worried him that William was so cool about Evelyn. It also worried him that the man wasn't worried about his own safety.

When Austin trotted into town, it was deserted, as he knew it would be. If Evelyn knew, Austin hoped she was kept sequestered. He was beginning to formulate a plan, one that involved a minor readjustment of his moral compass. It began with old bullets and ended with him taking Evelyn and the children from town during the ensuing weeks.

His sorrel's hooves kicked up little dust on that damp morning, and it was difficult to even see the storefronts on either side of him. The streets might be deserted, but eyes had to be watching from the storefronts and second-floor windows. Warren was usually bustling at that time of day, but the posters would have given fair warning.

"So, you came."

Austin heard William's voice before he saw him appear from the sheriff's door.

"Of course." Austin dismounted in front of the sheriff's walk and posted his sorrel there. "It seems to have turned into a spectacle overnight. I wouldn't miss it."

"The paper needed something to talk about." William looked different that morning, more unkempt than usual, and his eyes were shadowed. But Austin supposed getting half seas over and not sleeping the night before would do that to a man. William reeked of what Austin figured must be drink. The man boasted that he was a teetotaler, but he wasn't too young to start.

"And you needed to have your moment of glory," Austin replied. Now that he had arrived, he felt calm. The ball of anger sat nicely in his gut, ready to be used. His hands didn't shake, and his head didn't swim.

William nodded in assent.

They moved their paces off. One of the deputies, whom Austin could only just see on the sidewalk outside the sheriff's office, hollered for them to stop walking and turn.

As soon as he did, Austin took no time to think. He knew William would not wait for the count. Once they raised their pistols, he twitched his piece a hair to the right and fired. William fired at nearly the same moment.

A bullet whizzed by Austin's neck, close enough that he felt its heat, its burn. He smelled seared skin. He had been nicked closer than that on his travels west, but this was altogether too close.

The bullet hadn't come from William though but from the walk near the sheriff's office. He hurtled himself toward the opposite side of the street.

The rail in front of Jones' offered poor cover, but it was all he had. Bullets *shuck-shucked* into the wood post that protected his head. His sorrel squealed, and he stole a glance that direction. He could just see Monroe the Senior's hat above the horse's back. William wasn't in sight.

"I know we're having a little fuss here, Hearth, but William's been more than fair about your piece, about giving you a chance to settle this like a civilized man." Monroe the Senior's drawl was syrupy.

Austin wasn't an idiot. As much as he wanted to engage with the Monroe men across the street, that would land him in jail faster than he could shuck an ear of corn.

"Give in, Hearth!" William yelled.

His voice had come from somewhere to Austin's left. Austin shifted his hips just enough that he could see around the rail. William's booted foot shifted from view, heading north, back to where they'd begun. The man must've gone around the back way through the alley between stores.

Austin finally had a clear shot. He set the old gun just over the rail, blinked, steadied, and fired. A blink later, William was on the ground.

The dust cleared, and the street was silent save his sorrel's incensed huffs and someone groaning. Monroe the Senior was nowhere in sight.

Austin heard the man's cursing before he reached him, jogging up to see where his shot had landed. Just in William's shoulder, exactly aimed. The old bullets aimed true. Killing the man would leave Austin rotting in a prison cell, and he didn't want that. Monroe could have gotten away with it. Hell, he could've moved a bit farther west, but this was to prove a point, not kill the man. And the old bullet would do its own work on William in time. Austin had seen it plenty.

"Need a hand to the surgeon, Mr. Monroe?" Austin asked, more sarcastically than he intended. He didn't want to help him.

William laughed and shoved Austin away. "Goddamn, man! You certainly know how to show a person a good time."

"That was for Evelyn."

"Who is still mine, by the by," William said, a steely look in his eyes. He tried to sit up and finally managed to stumble to his feet, one hand clinging to his shoulder.

"She was never yours," Austin replied. "She is her own."

"You should have killed me," William sneered. "With this you prove nothing, and I go home to what is mine."

He shoved Austin out of the way and headed toward the sheriff's office. Austin collected his horse and watched William retreat inside. He hoped many eyes had been watching.

His father had warned him about old bullets. They were poison if aimed true. The wound would not take long to fester, even if William managed to dig out the bullet. And Austin didn't fool himself into thinking that William's father would not come for him, even for the old man's involvement that day. He needed to act quickly.

William hadn't been intimidated by the gunfight. Not that Austin had counted on it, but the man's disregard for his own life was a concern. What had simply been continuing the family legacy before William had gone off for his stint in the Army was now a festering wound at which William continued to scrape. He'd hit bone before long, and Austin needed to be ready for it.

56

Thursday, October 22nd

It would be the last morning Simon woke up with no knowledge of the events that transpired the night before. He was sure of it.

The unfinished basement had yielded nothing except painful memories of his parents. He'd forgotten that he'd put all the boxes of things he couldn't bear to sell or give away after they passed down there. His mom's old clocks and favorite knick-knacks. His dad's geodes and collection of wheat pennies. Scads of photographs.

Simon checked the rest of the basement, then booked it back upstairs. Shep followed loyally, tail wagging. Now it was time to check the place Shep had been spending most of his naptimes. The dog had even dragged some of Simon's dirty clothes to the corner alcove directly beneath the attic door and made a nest there. It wouldn't have been on Simon's radar had the dog not set up post there.

He opened the trapdoor to the attic and unfolded the built-in ladder. The light was already on in the attic, and a wave of familiar heat hit him from the room above.

Something else came with it too. A smell. He gagged with the first rush of it. If another racoon had gotten into the attic and died there, he didn't want to deal with it. But he knew that wasn't the source of the stench. It was something he'd only caught glimpses of in his nightmares, something he'd seen in Olivia's photographs, something he wanted to look away from but could not.

Memories of digging in his parents' attic with Bridgette mingled with his fear as he climbed the steps. Those papers and artifacts, the trunk, they were still up there, waiting. They'd traveled from Warren to Ohio and back again. Full circle. A clue was there that he had missed, but what it could be? He was at a loss. He'd pored over it all to the point of obsession.

The smell was worse at the top of the steps. Simon took a deep breath and poked his head through the opening into the attic. Nothing jumped out at him, but why would it? He was the most frightful entity up there. He poked about, avoiding the trunk, but nothing looked amiss.

The edge of a piece of black fabric stuck out of the side of the trunk, caught when it had been closed last. Horror spiderwebbed through his shoulders and over his head. That should've been a year ago or more, whenever he'd last been up there on the hunt for missing pieces. But he was certain that hadn't been the last time he was up there. It was the last time he remembered being up there, but no, not the last.

On auto-pilot, he reached out and unlatched the trunk. The rotten stench hit him, but other scents mingled with it. Coated cloth, smoke, horse, the outdoors. Not just the outdoors. The unique smell of the prairie outside Warren.

He pushed the lid open until it locked and then stared at the dark mass of fabric in the trunk. From his angle, he could see a stiff collar that must have been supported by something underneath. The extra piece of fabric that flowed over the shoulders of what was surely a cloak was what had gotten caught in the lid.

He reached out to touch it and then stopped, stilled by what had happened when he'd touched the other pieces of this fully customized getup, sent to his home and signed for by something that was not entirely him.

Shep whined at the bottom of the attic steps.

Without another thought, Simon shut the lid, climbed down the stairs, and shut the trapdoor.

57

OLIVIA LAY IN BED AND LISTENED TO THE SOUNDS OF THE REST of the family downstairs in the morning. The sound of Maggie's little shoes tapped down the hallway and then down the servant's stairs—no doubt with the previous night's bed warmers, to be readied for the next night—was music to her ears.

She lay there and listened and knew she had nothing to worry about. Mother and Father would take care of everything, would find her a comfortable place to land. The only thing she stood to gain from all that work was her name on a coffee table book someday, right? Not worth the heart attack or the stroke or losing her potential mate.

The sounds of the day passed her by. Luncheon and dinner and then the evening came on. Her sisters ran through the house. Music floated up from the piano. Feet came and went as the chores of the day also came and went.

Float into me, Evelyn's voice told her. *Your mind need never leave bed again. You can rest, dear. Rest as long as you need.*

Yes, that was an attractive thought.

Someone intruded on the moment. Olivia looked up from the bottom of the well, through the clear, cold water of Evelyn's memories. Someone splashed at the top, tried to reach her, to shake her. They had such long arms to reach to the bottom of the well, but the water was so heavy. It weighed down her eyelids, her arms, her legs.

Miss Olivia.

She swam through memories of sisters fighting and laughing and family meals where everyone was laughing and lessons with the governess, especially the ones about sketching and painting and long walks on the prairie and the ever-present companion . . .

Here, Miss Olivia.

Oh, Austin.

"Evelyn, dear, what you're doing isn't very fair to Miss Olivia."

Miss Olivia. She rather liked that he called her that. Miss. Little Miss. Miss Olivia. It made her feel cherished and protected but also respected. Fondness. That was the sensation it called upon.

"She no longer cares, Austin. And this way we can be together for as long as we want. Forever, even. We will never have to leave."

Olivia vaguely registered the idea but saw something cross Austin's face. Was it anger? Then she slid back into the deep pool of Evelyn's memories, diving deeper inside the woman, inside herself. But Austin kept talking, as if through water.

"I have not slept since all transpired. I'm tired, dearest Evelyn."

Then rest with me, the woman replied.

"I'm sorry, but I cannot. There is much work yet to be done. You need to let Olivia up, dear," Austin said gently.

Olivia felt an anger, a deep sadness from Evelyn that Olivia didn't understand, and then the well began to empty, and someone tugged at her heavy arms. She was almost angry herself. She had wanted to stay down there. It was cool and calm at the bottom of the well of Evelyn's memories.

There was no nightmare horse to run her down, no emotionally abusive ghost husband to harangue her, no mother who needed her attention daily because she couldn't be trusted not to burn the house down or take her medications on time.

But Olivia needed to finish what she had started. The committee meeting about her job had given her something to think about. She loved teaching, and she loved her art. She wanted to preserve the objects of the past. And here she was doing all that. She needed to get better at managing her time, but look at the beautiful thing she was doing, creating.

Hands reached down into the well for her as it emptied. She could swim, and she kicked her legs hard and rushed up to meet the hands reaching for her. Olivia broke the surface and drank in the cool fall air that came through the open windows at her mother's house. She had awoken from the strangest dream. The clock at her bedside read 5:30 p.m.

She sat up in bed and felt Austin's arms still on hers, pulling her up. But he was not there; the dream simply seemed that tangible.

"I need one last print," she said, mostly to herself. What didn't seem real was how close she was to finishing the project. Would everything else find a conclusion too? She had enough chemicals and supplies to make it happen in the dugout darkroom, and she would take it there, at her parents'—Evelyn's—home. One final shot looking out over the prairie.

She stood and stretched and shook the sleep and dream from her body. In her meditative state, she gathered her camera bag and tripod and went down the stairs. Her mother dozed in her chair in front of the television, a half-finished knitting project on her lap. Olivia drank in the momentary peace of the scene, then went outside.

She wasn't surprised when she found Austin waiting for her near the dugout as she lugged her equipment out into the cool day. He walked with her onto the prairie, and Olivia relaxed further. It wasn't that she couldn't take care of herself, but with these last weeks of being harassed by Not Simon, the imposter, it felt nice to have someone on her side, to be taken care of, protected. Besides, she was just a woman with no special supernatural traits to keep her from avoiding the thing and his nightmare horse, except perhaps leaving town.

They stopped at the swell of a hill and scanned the sky. Yes, she could wait there until the light was just right.

"My home was not far from here, over the hills," Austin said quietly. Was that sadness in his voice?

"Did the government knock it down or something? Or is the house still there?" Olivia began to set up her equipment, checking off each item methodically. When she could settle into her work, it was calming, soothing. Evelyn was strangely quiet. Perhaps she had been hushed by Austin's admonition.

"It burned down."

She didn't miss the sadness in his voice.

"What happened?" She stopped her process to watch him. He was immersed in looking toward the setting sun, toward his home, she supposed.

"Monroe did."

That struck her in the heart, as did everything new she learned about Warren's formative years.

"He hated you."

"He wanted everything I had. And in the end, he thought he had it and still was not happy. He wanted happiness, as all men do, but he didn't know how to go about getting it."

She imagined seeing Austin's home from that hill, looking west and thinking briefly that she would see smoke rising from a distant chimney. But no. Austin's home was gone, burned and buried with time and returned to the ground as Austin longed to be. Ashes to ashes, dust to dust.

And what of her family? She turned to see if her childhood home was visible. Only the tops of some cottonwoods beyond the rise of the hills to the north. Was she the end of them all? The last survivor of a string of tragic accidents and misfortunes?

If she waited any longer, the sun would set. She readied the large-format camera with more care than usual. Why should it feel so final? She should just be beginning her career, but these prints had taken something out of her.

She felt Austin watching her. "Your camera looks as if it could be from my time."

Olivia smiled and touched the side of the camera. "Yes. The bellows give it a look similar to the older cameras. This one is older than me, as it is."

Austin reached out to touch the frame around the camera, near enough to Olivia's hand that she could feel the warmth of him passing by. The light changed. Olivia knew it was time.

The wind up there had a life of its own, carving out the swells and shaping the hills as time passed. It spoke as she loaded her film and slipped under the light-blocking cloth.

The world turned upside down on the small viewing screen before her. Prairie grasses hung down at the top of her vision, and grey clouds soared where the land should have been. Inverted. That was how she felt. Did that mean she was seeing the world as it truly was? If she was already turned over, then was her reality different from everyone else's?

Austin handed her the cartridges without needing to be asked. He read from the light meter as if he had done it his entire adult life.

Developing the film was a blur. Austin stayed by her side, present for the entire process. They talked of weather on the prairie and how much snow they might see that winter and whether they would be snowed in as in years past. He had read Wordsworth and Longfellow. Olivia thought that as long as people were living on the Kansas prairie, they would speak of such things. Why hadn't she thought about that before? Had she been going through her life there without thinking that the world around her dictated how and when she did things? The thoughts came and went as she worked through the developing and printing process. She'd been so in the zone that she couldn't narrow her selection down past two shots.

Austin encouraged her to create both. Nothing within or without told her she couldn't. So, she did. Hours passed.

No nightmare horse visited the photographs, and Austin was properly complimentary about the images when they appeared. He was even more so after he helped her hang the pair for drying.

All the while, she—or Evelyn or both of them—was aware of his steps and movement in the room. Though the woman remained quiet, Evelyn's memories trickled down to mingle with Olivia's own. Images of an old four-poster bed and being helped quietly in the darkroom were stirred together until Olivia was not sure which had happened first. Was this what it felt like to be in love? Abject terror and bated breath coupled with a lust so searing, she felt it even now.

She wanted to touch Austin the way she touched film in the darkroom—carefully, meticulously. Something was so familiar about the man that she craved him, his company. It was a wholesome craving that she had not known.

What was it she got from the fields, the hills, the open expanses? She stared at the last print as it dried, feeling the landscape, watching it become more than just a subject.

Austin stood next to her, quietly observing the landscape with her. She didn't have the words for what the prairie made her feel. She had seen the photographic beauty of landscapes from behind her lens, but had she ever actually known their beauty? She knew cottonwoods. She could identify an acorn, but what else? It had drifted by without her noticing. Now she ached to know it all, every secret the prairie held.

She didn't remember how she came to find her bed that night, to fall awake dreaming. She only knew for certain that the west wind had breathed into her, had filled her the way it did the prairie sky on the hottest summer days. Olivia reached out and felt the tips of the tall grasses caress her palms as she moved through them. They spoke of things she was only just learning.

Austin touched her with questioning hands. He asked where she was going. *Where does your soul take you, grey-eyed one? And why?* He touched her hair, and she felt the prairie wind in her locks, the freshness of it married with the decay of fall, even the far-off wisps of cattle and woodsmoke. He became the wind, pressing about her as the wind wrapped around the hills, hugging its curves, every fiber caressed by the northwestern wind. He became fall on the prairie—hands cool as the wind, core as warm as the sun on limestone and the fine earth beneath the hills.

Where are you going? Austin's hands asked again.

"I don't know," she whispered.

"Where is the wind taking you?" he asked aloud.

"I don't know," she replied, for she still did not. The urge to surrender to it weighed on her, to let the wind take her where it would.

Where, Miss, where?

"Wherever," she breathed. *Wherever.*

She let the wind take her again, lifting her up and carrying her, a leaf. Cottonwood leaves, rustling, talking of all they had seen, their thirsty roots diving deep beneath the prairie to find water. Deep beneath the burrows of rabbits and moles and prairie dogs. Beneath the layers of limestone and sandstone and gypsum.

What we have seen, they said.

What have you seen? she asked as the wind caressed her face.

Death. Birth. Rebirth. The short, violent lives of men. More fickle than rivers, they.

"Austin," she breathed. Was she herself or Evelyn? She could no longer tell.

"Tell me where you are going, Miss," he said.

The possibilities tumbled through her. Austin, Evelyn, William, Simon. Prairie flowers, riding the range, a ghost unable to move forward or backward. Fixed. Fixated.

It could have been a dream, a hallucination, but it filled her. The question was a torment.

Where are you going?

She finally answered him, but was it true? At what point was she beginning? Where was she now? Her photographs so far, her miniscule accomplishments, had she even begun?

Was the beginning her birth, or was that moment the beginning? It became a spiral, threading backward and backward until it unraveled or turned in on itself and tangled. She had no beginning or end, so where could she go but nowhere if anywhere was nowhere?

Somewhere, I'm making myself, she replied, feeling it, not moving her lips.

Thoughts tumbled through her head, pulling her this way and that until she no longer knew which way was up. She only was and was only becoming.

58

Friday, October 23rd

The gallery coordinator opened the side door for Olivia, so she and Colton could bring in the photographs. Margaret looked sleep deprived and cranky, but Olivia didn't care. The woman had offered after-hours help from the gallery staff, had pushed it, in fact, but Olivia trusted no one save herself to handle the prints.

And apparently, Colton. When he'd said he wasn't sleeping, she didn't need to echo that she hadn't been either, just asked if he'd meet her at the gallery at 6:00 a.m. That he'd agreed to help her with the mural-size photographs surely meant things were nearing a head, but she bit back a comment. Speaking it would make it certain.

She had to get everything that she had finished up on the walls that day. Thankfully, the section relegated for her prints was roped off, and considering how early they had arrived, they would be finished before the gallery opened for the day at 11:00. She could return with the title placards over the weekend.

Olivia cursed as she dragged the large piece over to one wall. She was being careful, she told herself, and that movement wouldn't damage the photograph. She pulled the butcher paper from the print as if it were a Christmas present. The greyscale trees at the cliffs greeted her with enthusiasm. The depth she saw when she looked at the scene made her heart clench. The narrow aperture had worked well in the shot, and the sharpness of the cliffs and the trees was tantalizing to her eyes.

"Dodge and burn until you realize the scene," Olivia whispered to herself. "Evelyn, what do you think?" she asked as she scanned the first photograph, more to see if Evelyn still resided within it than anything. The woman had been hushed since the day before.

Finally, Evelyn spoke, though now she sounded farther away, perhaps at the bottom of Olivia's well. *They are haunting and lovely. I feel as if I could be standing there this instant.*

Olivia felt the thrill of fear at that. She *could* be standing there at the moment if she wanted to, and Evelyn's words felt like a push. She could go to the cliffs, to the prairie, walk away into them and never return. She had wanted to the day before, with Austin by her side. Those photographs were the most special. She should have hung those first.

"What does Evelyn think?" Colton asked.

She hadn't heard him come back in, but he carried one of the other wrapped prints as if the nearly six-by-nine-foot photograph weighed nothing. He took the protective paper off without being asked. Olivia was uncomfortable with her oddly implicit trust in him. Evelyn took it in stride.

"She says they are haunting and lonely. Lovely," she corrected, taking the print from him and maneuvering it toward the wall. He raised his eyebrows at her but said nothing.

Olivia leaned the photograph directly below where it was meant to be installed and stood back to look at it, resting her eyes on the sharp details. They were the most hauntingly beautiful landscapes she had ever photographed. And the clouds the way they were, had it stormed that night after or not? Three and a half weeks ago felt like an eternity. The previous night's dreams had followed her, clinging like the fog in the Flint Hills. Her questions swirled within the fog, the answers just beyond her reach.

"Why isn't he after the men? Aren't there male ancestors, relatives?"

Colton huffed as he hoisted the photograph with her. "I don't think your Simon would agree with that statement. And you probably ought to save the soul-searching questions for when we're not in the middle of something important."

Olivia shook her head at him. "It's not a soul-searching question. It's perfectly legitimate."

"OK, Professor," he retorted from where his face was pressed against the wall, looking for the wire to secure the print.

Olivia got in close too, the gallery wall cold against her flushed face. Ethan's eyes stared back at her from the other side of the photograph. A rush of brotherly affection flooded her at the same time as pure annoyance. He had Austin's hair and height but the Weatherford eyes and build.

"If this isn't fifty-seven inches from the floor at its focal point, I'm blaming you," Olivia huffed.

"It is."

She heard a noise somewhere near the main entrance to the horseshoe-shaped room, but she figured it was just Margaret coming to check their progress and to make sure they weren't putting more holes in the walls than they ought.

"Seems you already have a fan club." The voice sent a shock through Olivia. She whirled, bumping her side of the frame. Colton steadied the piece from his end, ensuring its stability. Hands in his pockets, Not Simon stood watching them from the main entryway into the gallery room. She was glad she didn't feel trapped in the horseshoe-shaped room and that she had Colton with her.

"Don't be rude," Olivia snapped. She sensed Colton's eyebrows shoot up before she saw them.

Not Simon grinned at her. "You know who this is by now, I take it? Of course you do. You're like a magnet for us."

Olivia rolled her eyes at him from her perch on the step stool, feeling more powerful than she knew she was. Colton's presence bolstered her though. "William, hand me the tape measure, please. I really need to get these hung before it's too late."

She had thrown him off balance, using his real name, but he handed her the tool, his fingers straying at her wrist. She could smell his warm breath, and she hoped Simon was OK, wherever he was. For a moment, it felt like him there with her, and she had to turn away. She couldn't keep the façade up forever.

Colton tilted one of the framed prints away from the wall, so he could peel its protective packaging off. Olivia hadn't asked him to do it, only thought it. "I know what he is too. He paid me a few visits about a month ago. It took him a few tries to get the message about fucking off."

"I see you've lingered here though. I seem to recall you saying you were going to leave town. Harder to do than you thought, yes?" William handed Olivia the other box of tools that she motioned for.

Colton watched with apparent fascination while he worked. "I agreed to help Olivia with her exhibition. I'll stay for the opening, wrap up my semester. Then I'm leaving."

"Good luck with that." Not Simon laughed. "Goodbye, Olivia, Mr. *Mun*roe. I'll see you soon."

He confused her—who he was and what he was really about and after. She balled up the sheet that had been protecting the sixth photograph and threw it across the room. Stupid. She'd just have to retrieve it in a minute anyway.

Olivia turned to Colton after Not Simon had stalked off. "You must have the largest balls on the planet. And thank you for being here. I imagine he dropped by to give me a difficult time. But I have my spiritual bodyguard here, so . . ."

Colton laughed hard enough that he had to set down his end of the photograph they'd lifted. "I'm just a good negotiator. And I think I'm too salty for him. Uncooperative. Too much of an asshole, like him."

Olivia didn't know what to say to that. She didn't know Colton very well, but she thought he probably had more Ethan Weatherford under his skin than he liked to admit. "Thank you for helping me with this. I had wanted Simon to help, but, you know."

They lifted the large photograph and set it against the wall where Olivia had marked. The Photoshop mockup she'd made looked fantastic, but it had nothing on the real thing.

"No problem," he replied. "And yeah, I know. Asshole came bugging me with that fucked-up horse of his, but I knocked his poltergeist ass out of my house. That's the last time I leave the house open to the great beyond for awhile, I think."

Olivia stepped back to look at the photograph. Evan galloped full out in it, and the nightmare horse wasn't far behind, its head swinging side to side so violently that she thought it might fly off. She wished they would stop for a moment, so she could remember which print it was.

"How can you stand that?"

Relief and anxiety. "You can see it too?"

"Yes. I didn't want to say anything about it last time, but now I can see your eyes following them. I can tell."

"I can't stand it. If I stare at it too long, it makes me crazy."

"I believe it," Colton murmured.

They worked the rest of the time in silence, handing each other the tools they needed or moving a piece a hair this way or that without saying a word.

59

September 5, 1903

Austin wasn't sure what woke him—the heavy smoke or the horses neighing outside. He pushed aside the curtains of the old bed and was met with smoke so thick he could not see to the door. He yanked the curtains shut and took several deep breaths. Wherever the fire was didn't matter. He just needed to get himself and the staff out. He had fallen asleep so early the previous evening after arriving home that he had no idea what time it was—everyone else in the house could have been awake for all he knew.

He took one more deep breath and held it, sliding out of bed and to the floor where the smoke wasn't so thick. Memories of the fire of his boyhood slithered through him as he made his way to the door and pressed his hand against it. Cool at the bottom. But as he slid his hand upward, the heat grew until he had to yank his hand away. Had the fire started in the attic?

There was no time to wonder. He grabbed what few affects he could, tied a handkerchief around his mouth and nose, and headed toward the window. The fire would soon be in there, or the smoke would get too thick and overcome him.

Outside the window, the fire spit burning pieces of house onto the roof, but he was able to clamber out and grab the top of the dormer for balance. The cool air was welcome to his irritated lungs. Smoke poured out of the window with him as he dodged the burning cinders that would soon set that part of the roof alight as well.

"Oh, Mr. Hearth!"

In the glow of the blaze, he saw Ruth and Patrick standing in the yard. Patrick held the bridles of several horses, which pulled and strained, nearly lifting the young man off his feet. They should have been let out into the pasture, stupid boy. And where was Evan? The horse was smart enough to get himself out. Austin needed to get off the roof before it collapsed. Then he could worry about his horse.

"Mr. Hearth, thank goodness!" Ruth called.

"Here, catch!" He tossed his boots, coat, and a small armful of books and papers stuffed into a pillowcase down to the waiting woman.

She gathered them up and then stepped back from the house again. Austin slid down a valley of the roof to the north—the south side of the house behind him was generating an impressive amount of heat. Once he reached the eaves, he assessed his exit down over the porch.

"I imagine all the ladders are in the barn, Pat?" Austin couldn't believe the tremendous noise the fire was making. It sounded like a train rushing into the station, except the train never arrived, only the sound of it repeating forever.

"They are, sir!"

"Thunderation," Austin grumbled. He got on his belly and scooted to the edge of the roof, looking over it to see if he could grab the edge and swing over to something. It looked like he could.

He swung down carefully, praying the goddamn shingles and edge of the roof would hold him. His wrists scraped along the sides of the shingles as he shimmied over a little farther to grab one of the porch's support pillars with his legs.

Christ Almighty, the heat was massive. Sweat and ash ran into his eyes. The shingles had torn through the hide of his wrists. He had thought himself invincible after years traveling across the prairie, only to have his own home be the thing that tried to kill him.

"Not just yet," he growled and swung his legs over to the pillar, grabbing hold with his thighs the way he would to break a wild yearling. Then he worked his arms to the pillar and slid down as quickly as he could. Flames licked at him from the front door. It looked like the door had been thrown wide open, whether from someone rushing out or someone rushing in, he could not tell.

Once he hit the ground, he stumbled backward, away from the house. He heard a great groaning and creaking of timbers inside the structure. He could do nothing but watch. The house, the barn, the outbuildings, they were all ablaze. Every last piece of furniture, every piece of tack in the barn. His mother's quilts. His photographs. His father's account books. Spools upon spools of wire. Everything.

Ruth, not one for tears, sobbed openly. "Sir, I could not get to your room! The fire was so thick! I thought you would perish in the blaze with none of us able to get to you!"

Austin settled the woman, then took the horses from Patrick and rushed them toward the pasture. They would be safe there. He untied their leads and let them loose once he had wrestled them inside the gate. They rushed away from the fire, their eyes wild with it. Austin wouldn't try to round them up until the following day at the earliest. Nothing lit the wild inside a horse like fire.

Relief filled him when he saw Evan's form not far off in the pasture. The orange flames reflected off the horse's silken coat. Evan appeared to be watching, standing still, pointed toward Austin and the house.

"What did you see?" Austin murmured. Evan had been safely closed in the barn for the night the last Austin had seen him. The horse was smart enough to let himself out of his stall but not the large doors of the barn. Surely Patrick had let him out first before the flames had taken the rest of the barn.

Heat lightning, unusual for that time of year, flickered in the southwest. If storms came up with it, it would not be there until long afterwards. Directly south, the sound of a wagon and a voice on the road somewhere in the distance reached him. They would have seen the fire from town and sent someone. It wouldn't make a difference. Everything was a total loss.

Austin wearily gathered the staff and tried to summon some reserves. His nerves were on edge. He instructed Ruth to gather her ladies and see if whomever was coming up the road would take them into town. They needed to be put up in a hotel. There were a few burns and some singed eyebrows but nothing worse than what could happen in the kitchen or around the house on the daily. Thank God for small miracles.

He and the men found some shovels that had escaped the flames and set about digging trenches. The house and barn were beyond being put out. They would need to burn until they were finished. But if the fire crept too near to the prairie, they would set the countryside aflame. That might be fine during burning season, but the way the wind was blowing, Warren didn't need to be set alight that night.

A wagon full of Vogts arrived not long later, followed by the Willemses and the Turners. They were his closest neighbors, and they arrived in force. One dropped their men and boys off, and the women in the household took Austin's female employees and headed toward town.

They worked tirelessly through the night and into the pre-dawn hours. Men grabbed whatever looked like it could be salvaged and hauled it down toward the long driveway and well away from the flames. Others shoveled dirt over any flames or embers that escaped the burning buildings. Austin wet a shirt from the well and tied it around his head and mouth. The cold water woke him and soothed the burns that peppered his exposed skin.

He turned toward the house to watch the flames in the still-creaking timbers. The roof and second floor had caved in hours earlier, and the framework of the first floor was black and covered in flames. Just beyond the house, he saw the spring house. The tree his mother had planted next to the door before he was born was bright with flame, its tender branches and green leaves burning like a torch.

It was then, standing there staring at the burning emblem of his mother's care and love, that he understood how the fire had begun. There had been no lightning and no storm, and he knew it was likely only because of Evan's good sense that he was still there in the pasture at all and not on his way to be safely ensconced at the Monroe estate. No, it had been done by a man who had everything and wanted more. It had been done by a man being driven mad by his own actions and now by the work of an old bullet. There was no doubt that William would have needed help, but Austin knew where the blame lay.

Austin let the anger radiate through him, then grabbed another shovel and started throwing dirt on the flames. He needed to get Evelyn and get out of town. This would end. Soon.

60

September 12, 1903

He had not been living in town long before he knew the state of his welcome. He felt them following, a pack of starving dogs waiting for the deer to stumble. Then they would be upon him.

With less need to ride Evan everywhere, he checked the hotel's stable obsessively. Sometimes only a quarter hour would pass before he felt the urge to check on the animal again. That he saw at least one Monroe but never more than two together at a time unnerved him.

He supervised the intense clean-up of his homestead when he could get away from messages at the ticket office from Gates down south and customers west. Late-season rains and winds had taken out some wood posts, and he had a handful of requests for the limestone. He could fill his days with endless messages to customers and meetings with manufacturers and the amicable old gentleman down at the limestone quarry, but the state of affairs wore on him. And not riding or walking down to the far end of the main thoroughfare where the Monroe estate began took a will that he was not certain he could sustain.

It was a dusty late-summer afternoon when he decided to take Evan through the wending animal trails that worked their way through the backside of the Monroe estate. Still an old-fashioned bunch, the Monroes had yet to install fencing at their property borders, so Austin's way was unfettered. And working out a strategy before he got Evelyn out was paramount.

He spied someone through the trees and chided himself for not being more careful. He bade Evan be still, observed for a few breaths, and calculated the threat.

It was a woman.

His heart skipped. Evan tossed his head at the friendly form, though Austin had asked him to be still. Something was at play that he didn't understand. Evelyn was waiting for him near the thick copse of trees out of the sightline of the Monroe house. When she saw him, she cried out and ran to him. She carried the journal he had given her what seemed a lifetime ago. He shushed her quickly, wary.

"Why are you here?" she asked, breathless as she held onto Evan's bridle. The horse bumped her with his nose. Evelyn's face was flushed and her hair loose. She looked like a wild thing. He wanted to ask her the same. He had not expected her, but he could not leave without her. Long gone was the time for building a plan. He could take her now, hide her, come back and take the children with whatever force necessary.

"I was looking for a safe route. It seems I have found it."

Evelyn looked back behind her, then extended a hand up to Austin. "Please!"

Once atop Evan, the pair embraced. Evelyn felt so slight to him.

"I want to take you from here this instant," Austin said.

"Truly?"

"Yes."

She clung to him. "Then go," she whispered, and Austin urged Evan forward.

"The children!" Evelyn said suddenly when they were near the canyon crossing, as if she had just remembered them. She clenched her hands so hard into Austin's shirt that she grabbed the flesh of his back.

"I'll come back for them," Austin said. He gently pried her hands from him. Evelyn was in no state to be left there again. He had money, resources. It was no great ordeal to start over somewhere westward.

He rearranged the plan in his head as they took the prairie way back to his old homestead. Monroe would soon realize Evelyn was gone. Time was of the essence. As much as his anger willed it, there was no place for revenge against Monroe at that juncture. Evelyn and his children's safety were more important.

They had cleared away much of the burned debris from his home. Great piles remained to be hauled away, but they had done so much already. He was grateful for his neighbors. He wouldn't have been able to take care of the clearing so quickly without them. Rebuilding would have been difficult, even with their help. Now it was no longer necessary. He would make his peace with that.

Evelyn was overcome at the sight of his former home. Even for a strong woman, he understood the shock of it. Had he not been in shock and a daze from the initial catastrophe, it might have hurt him more. As it was, he let the anger from it sustain him.

"Austin, your home," she said quietly as they rode quickly up the drive.

"I thank God it was only some timber and stone and a bit of wire. No lives were lost." Though he imagined that had been the intent.

He hurried Evelyn into the spring house. Its stone structure had escaped the flames, and the memory of the tree burning outside was seared into his memory. His childhood Bible lessons about Moses and the burning bush kept trying to creep into his mind, but where was God in any of this?

"God has abandoned us," Evelyn whispered once they were safely inside the spring house.

Austin eyed her. Had he spoken aloud? "I don't know where God is. I can only hope he keeps you safe here."

Evelyn settled into the back of the spring house, wrapping herself in the heavy blanket that Austin had stowed away. There was a light and what was left of his cold provisions, still stored in the spring waters. Evelyn would be fine there for a short time. Enough light came in from the skylight that she could burn the lantern for several nights if needed.

"Will you kill him?"

The question hung heavily between them, and Austin saw dark shadows under Evelyn's eyes. Something deep within him argued they were not just shadows. Bruises. Something more sinister. The anger licked at him. It wanted him to say *yes*. "I hope not. I only want to rescue the children and come back for you."

Evelyn nodded, staring at the whitewashed walls.

"This must end," Austin said. "Stay here. I'll be back once this is over. Then we will go."

Evelyn nodded and then settled down against the earthen floor. Austin knelt and gathered her to him. She pressed her face into the crook of his neck and wept as she told him what she had not wanted to wait until then to tell him. He kissed her tears.

"No matter what happens, I'll be back for you. No matter what. Do you understand?" he asked firmly.

She nodded.

Austin held her face in his hands and looked into her eyes. "I mean it. I'll come for you no matter what happens to me, to you, or to him. I'll make certain you're safe."

She hugged him hard once more, and then Austin was on his feet and out the door. He secured the door and then focused on what was before him. He made a final check of his guns and Evan's saddle and then swung up onto the horse.

They covered ground so quickly that he was certain to overtake William after he crossed the canyon bridge. There was no way Evelyn could have been missed long on the estate. He would be a fool to think William would think of anyone other than Austin when his wife went missing.

Thankfully, no one was on the crossing, so he could take the bridge as quickly as he needed. Evan pounded onto the planks, slowing slightly only to get better footing.

As the pair exited the bridge, Austin heard a tremendous sound that was followed by intense pain in his right shoulder and upper chest, and he was hurled from Evan. He hit the hard-packed ground so hard that the wind was knocked out of him. The world went grey for a moment. All he could feel were Evan's hooves nearby and the all-encompassing throbbing in his shoulder. The sound of another rider reached him, followed by another sound that was very familiar: a shotgun being reloaded.

He opened his eyes, rolled onto his left side, and gasped for breath. Evan stood protectively between him and the other rider. Austin made out the muscular black legs of Evelyn's mare and redoubled his efforts to stand. He was finally able to grab a stirrup with his left hand and haul himself to his feet. After a struggle, he released his own gun from the pommel.

The other rider must have seen it, for he cursed, and Austin heard clattering hooves on the bridge. Another shot rang out, and bits of splintered wood from the side of the bridge exploded around him. Evan squealed and danced sideways. Austin hoped he was only hit by falling wood pieces and not buckshot. The sounds of hooves grew distant on the bridge.

The world went grey again, and Austin dropped to his knees. He managed to get his coat off but regretted it once he did. His shoulder was shredded, as was a good part of his arm. Blood drip dripped onto the dusty ground as he sat there and watched it, swimming in and out of consciousness.

The devil had him in his sights. The thought consumed him as he sat there and tried to regain his sense of where he was. He was vulnerable on the road.

Austin wasn't sure how long he sat there, but it was long enough for Evan to worry after his master. The great horse butted his nose against Austin's back and lipped at his neck and hair.

"Aye, alright! Good God, man, give me a minute!" Austin stumbled to his feet and swiped for Evan's reins. The shock of his injury seemed to be wearing off, or perhaps was only setting in, but his worry for Evelyn rose every moment.

Evan slid down to his front knees, and Austin was finally able to swing a leg over the animal's back. He gripped his horse as hard as he could with his thighs and urged him back the way they had come. Every jarring step sent white-hot pain through his arm, radiating out through his chest. His hand was weak.

Austin pushed Evan, but Evan needed no help racing toward his old home. He knew the way as well as his master.

Even from a distance, Austin could tell that the door to the spring house had been removed from its frame. Good God. Whatever had gotten in there had been strong. Evelyn was strong, but Austin knew of no man or woman who could beat the devil in a wrestling match. Not without God's army behind them.

Austin didn't bother getting any closer. It was a waste of time. He and Evan had not passed them on the road, so William must have taken the back way and gone to the other canyon crossing.

Evan let out a long, trumpeting neigh, and after several seconds, Austin heard an answering whinny to the south and east. It had to be Evelyn's mare. Evan's daughter. They had gone to the other crossing. Evan spun on his heel, and off they went again.

Austin crossed the longer bridge more carefully, though he felt the urgency with which he needed to move. At the crossing, he passed more people, some of whom he knew. A wagon of Vogts heading back from town, Troy Stanford and his son. He hollered for them to stay clear, and they did. He was certain they wanted no part of this.

Not far ahead at the far end of the bridge was William. Evelyn's mare was strong but smaller than Evan, and she was slowed by the two-passenger load. William should have known better than to overload a horse like that. But desperate times . . .

"Evelyn!" Austin shouted.

At the sound of his voice, William veered off the road. Evelyn tried to turn and look at Austin, but William yanked her back toward him. He saw her struggle with him briefly. Evelyn cried out and tumbled from her steed and into the leaf-filled ditch near the side of the road. Austin saw her begin to rise, but he yelled for her to stay in place.

He followed William up the hills that ran alongside the canyon. No longer would this man get away with his torment of an innocent woman. No longer would he be able to squeeze the peace from Austin's life. No longer would he take the advantages he'd had for so long in that quiet town on the prairie.

Austin hooked the reins into his right elbow as the strength in his right hand failed him. Evan ran flat out, chest heaving with the effort of running uphill. As they neared the summit, Austin loosened his shotgun from its safe spot. He was confident he could still pull the trigger with his right hand if he could jerk his arm back quickly enough. This time he didn't need to aim precisely. He just needed to be close.

At the summit, he dropped Evan's reins and jumped from his horse's back. He clumsily tied Evan to a tree nearby. The horse would try to get involved, protect his master, and he didn't want that.

He heard a whinny down the hill, then the horrible sound of a horse screaming. Austin's stomach dropped, and he crept toward the edge of the hill. Ebony lay writhing in pain a hundred feet down the hill, one of her legs clearly broken.

He couldn't decide which way to go when it was decided for him. A twig snapped behind him.

"Drop the gun, Hearth."

"Don't listen to him, Austin!"

Austin spun around, and there was William, one hand fisted in Evelyn's hair and the other beckoning with his firearm for Austin to drop his. His stomach dropped. Why had Evelyn not stayed put?

"Don't listen to the girl, Austin," William mocked.

Austin dropped his gun. William moved in and kicked it out of the way, then pulled Evelyn back up the hill, toward where Evan was tethered, toward the edge of the cliffs. He pushed Evelyn down into the grass and bade her be still and shut her mouth.

Austin moved toward his gun when William was briefly occupied and tried to grab it. He must have been too focused on going for his gun because he saw the glint of a blade, but he didn't know where it had come from. It all seemed to move so slowly. How could William have concealed such a weapon on his person? Then there was pain. My God, the pain.

Time slowed. His next thought was a flash into his childhood, playing with his father's sword from the war, cutting his hand on the blade. He had been playing at soldier, vanquishing the enemy, when he nearly vanquished himself. The cut was not very deep, but it was a clean, a wicked cut that bled for some time before he could confess to his father what he had done.

His father had stitched the wound with his own hands and told Austin how many wounds he had sewn shut on the battlefield, even when he knew the men would die with or without his ministrations. It had been a comfort for them, had helped them pass more easily. There would be no such comfort now.

This pain radiated into Austin's head and down his back. Then he felt more pressure, and the ground leapt up to meet him. And then, curiously, the pain stopped, but he could no longer feel his hands or his feet. The pain from his hand and shoulder was gone too. His vision went red for a short time. Seconds or minutes or hours, he could not tell. Somewhere he thought he heard Evelyn calling his name.

Everything became dreamlike and slow. The world swung around in a great, slow circle. Curiously, he saw a girl standing not far from the scene, watching in horror. She wore strange clothes. He had only seen such clothing in the heat of the desert south, but even then it was odd. Her face looked like Evelyn's. Brown hair and wide grey eyes filled with concern. Thoughts came sporadically, then fired with points of light like shooting stars or sparks from his flint rock. He closed his eyes, unable to keep them open any longer. When he opened them again, he saw the blades of grass nearest him only in shades of grey.

Then another part of him was falling, feeling but not perceiving falling. He hit the ground. For a time he knew nothing. Distantly, as if he were hearing it from nearby and far off at once, Austin heard a tremendous pounding of hooves and Evan's deep resounding neigh.

Evelyn didn't know if she screamed or if it was Evan. The great horse had just plunged from sight, his beautiful mane and tail rushing out behind him as he went.

And Austin. Oh, sweet Lord. His head lay not far away from her, staring blankly out at the prairie. She was still in a daze as she watched William pick up the head and approach her with it.

He dropped it onto the ground in front of her. It hit the dirt with a sickening thud. "Here you go, sweet. He'll never bother you again! Aren't you happy? Aren't you happy he'll never bother you again? Tell me you're happy!"

She looked horrified, her mouth open, but no sound came out. "I'm happy. I'm happy," she whispered.

"Then take it!" He pushed the head toward her hands.

"No, no, no, no," she mumbled, tears spilling down her face. She wanted to retch.

"Pick it up! Don't you want to see him one last time? Pick it up!"

"Oh, God, Austin," Evelyn sobbed.

"Pick it up!" William nudged her with the barrel of his shotgun, and Evelyn finally scrambled to do as she was told. "You couldn't live without him, so we'll see how well you do with him."

When Evelyn looked up, she saw that the red had completely overtaken William's eyes. The irises were consumed, and the whites were bloodshot. He was no longer himself. Nor did she think he would ever be himself again. She wanted to say she didn't understand, but she was afraid, for the first time truly afraid what this man or beast might do in return.

William glared at her. "We're going to take a walk now and calm down. Stay right there for a moment." He trotted down the hill, back the way they came.

Too terrified to move, Evelyn stayed where she was. Blood from Austin's head dripped on the ground in front of her, forming a puddle in the dry dirt and grasses. A sudden gunshot and equine scream startled her, and she realized what had happened.

She jumped to her feet and ran to the edge of the hill, still carrying Austin's head. "No! No! She was not useless!"

William swung the shotgun toward her, but she knew it wasn't loaded. "A horse with a broken leg is useless, darling. You lived out here; you know that. Now, I told you to stay put, and you didn't. I imagine the gunshot startled you though, and I'm sorry for that. She wouldn't have had a good life any longer anyway."

Evelyn began crying again, overwhelmed and exhausted.

"Quit crying, or we'll be out here all night." William covered Austin's head in Evelyn's hands with part of Ebony's silken saddle padding.

"Now walk."

The walk was excruciating. It didn't take long for her arms to grow tired. They cramped and shook. Blood from Austin's head dripped down her arms, chilling her as the night came on. It caked there and pulled at the hair on her arms.

And his flesh cooled. Quickly. By the time they reached Warren proper, the wind-roughened skin of his face, which she had so loved to touch, was hard beneath her fingers. She could only thank God that she was not looking at it and that they were almost home. Just a few more minutes, and she would be able to put it down.

But once inside the kitchen entrance, when Evelyn tried to set her burden down, William chastised her. A lightning bolt of something went through her.

"I don't understand," she said.

William rummaged around in drawers. He finally returned to Evelyn's side with a spool of cooking string.

"You can't live without him, right?" His red eyes unnerved her, and the injury to his shoulder bled through his shirt.

"I . . . no . . . I mean, yes. He's . . . he's gone now, so I must." The horrible images that conjured up sent Evelyn into shaking tears.

"But he's right here with you," William continued. "And so he shall stay. Hold him out."

Evelyn did but squeezed her eyes shut. William removed the torn saddle pad from the head to reveal the already greying skin.

Alyssa and her sister came into the kitchen as Evelyn argued with William. Both girls cried out at the sight. William turned his red eyes on them. "You'll keep your mouths shut. Get the lady Evelyn anything she needs. Except a pair of scissors."

William wound the twine around Evelyn's hands, which still held Austin's cooling head. Alyssa and her sister stood in the doorway to the kitchen and stared until William snarled at them to get back to work and keep their heads down.

"William, please," Evelyn pleaded.

"What do you want?"

"When can I set this down?"

William laughed. "Oh, darling. Never. You can never set it down."

He continued to wrap the twine, securing Evelyn's hands to her lover's head. Her palms rested over his cheeks, and her fingers were just over his ears, in his blood-matted hair.

When William finished, he sent her to their room, bloodstained dress, new appendage, and all. She expected at any moment that he would cut the string and let her go free, lesson learned, so she simply sat at her mirror and looked at nothing.

It didn't happen. The gore from Austin's head seeped over her fine white linens, which protected the vanity. She hardly noticed.

William assigned Alyssa as Evelyn's personal handmaid to help her to the bathroom and for various other tasks. None of it seemed real. The shock of it all was still too new.

Alyssa wiped Evelyn's face with a warm cloth. She began to undress Evelyn, but it was impossible with Evelyn's hands tied as they were.

"Cut my dress from me," Evelyn said. She looked at anything that was not Austin's head.

"Missus, I don't think we could put you in anything after that. I would not know what to do."

"Cut the dress, Alyssa," Evelyn commanded. "Open the seams of a blouse, and sew me back into it. I'm still able to step into a skirt."

Alyssa did as she was told, though it took hours of painstaking work. Evelyn directed her to alter her favorite blouse—the one with the extra lace at the neck and décolletage—and her favorite walking skirt. It was done in a fine grey wool and had fanciful embroidery midway down and to her ankles. She chose a silver belt to bring it all together. Then her favorite pin at her neck.

The sewing and the dressing and wearing her favorite pieces did little to keep the horror much farther from her than her own two arms could reach. Her beautiful skirt was soon spattered with gore. Alyssa had taken the linens from the vanity and replaced them.

William commented on the fine job Alyssa did dressing his wife but didn't ask how she had done it. Evelyn heard Alyssa weeping quietly later that evening before she was to prepare Evelyn for bed. Evelyn told her she would simply stay in her day clothes.

Going to bed on the first night, Evelyn carefully set Austin's head on the pillow next to her, her right arm awkwardly beneath her. It ached in the morning, unaccustomed to being in such an attitude for so many hours. She continued to expect that William would release her.

On the second day, she mourned. Once William left for the day, great tears plagued Evelyn. She sobbed until she felt she could not any longer. Once Alyssa gave her some water, she sobbed again with her replenished tears. It felt as if she simply existed, living the emotions that ran through her and nothing more.

Time changed Austin—as did the flies. Evelyn blew them off or tipped her hands when she was awake, but she could do nothing about the flies while she slept. Thankfully, it was becoming cooler outside, but the flies still came, lured by the smell of rotting flesh.

In her desperation, she tried to hang a cloth over Austin's head by picking one up with her teeth and dropping it over him. She succeeded, but William didn't allow her to continue the behavior.

Austin's eyes drooped first, as if his lower eyelashes were far too heavy for his face. They dragged the skin down, revealing the yellowing whites of his eyes. They had become shrunken too, as if they no longer had anything to keep them moist.

Sleep became impossible. It was not so hard at first when she was exhausted and Austin didn't look so much different. The terror was different then, but she had hope that it would end. But when Austin began to change, to become a stranger, not human, she could no longer close her eyes at night.

It started to look as if his entire face was slipping sideways, and Evelyn realized it was because of the manner in which she was lying, with Austin as far away from William's side of the bed as possible. She tried to rotate the head, to no avail. William wanted the thing as far away from him as possible, so the drooping persisted.

William complained of the smell that began on the third day. Evelyn had perhaps become immune to it, for she didn't notice it. Or it had come on so slowly that she no longer recognized it.

She asked William what she might do for the smell, and he poured a bottle of her perfume on her hands and the flesh before her. It only mingled the scents and burned her hands.

Evelyn's hands became sore on the fifth day. When she tried to shift her hands, they would not separate from Austin's skin. Evelyn panicked, whimpering as she tried to move her hands this way and that. They would not budge.

"What's the fuss?" William asked from the top of the stairs. He had relegated her to the bedroom, saying she was unfit to see company in her current state. She had begged her way out of it, but William would not budge. She wanted to see the children. She wanted William to remove the burden from her hands.

Terror at being heard overtook her, and she froze. She didn't want to speak again unless William asked.

"I said, what's the fuss in there?"

"I cannot move my hands," Evelyn said quietly, afraid to raise her voice, afraid the children were listening, that one of them might run into the room and see her. Perhaps William had locked the door, but she could not try it, not with her hands the way they were.

"That's the point," he replied.

The panic didn't leave. She struggled against the twine hard enough that the rough string opened a gash on Austin's cheek. It began to ooze, grey and green. Evelyn's stomach churned, and she heaved, but nothing came up. William had spoon-fed her broth several times a day, but he had fed her nothing yet that day.

Evelyn began to simper. She desperately needed to use the facilities, but she didn't want to ask. She was on the verge of soiling herself when William came into the room.

"We can hear you from the family room. What ails you?"

"I need the facilities."

William rolled his eyes. "I think you're just saying that, so you may leave the room. We will have a chamber pot brought up from the cellar for you. You may use that if you truly need it."

Evelyn's face burned. When she tried to tell William that she had learned her lesson, he ignored her.

"What have you brought into this house?" she asked. Her voice had finally grown hoarse, and a feverish sweat had set in.

Red eyes looked back at her, an animal gaze. "Nothing that was not already here, my dear."

Evelyn didn't know whether she was addressing the man she had married or the thing in the mirror. She was thankful she had managed to throw a shawl over the repaired mirror.

At night the creature that was also William would crawl from the frame. Evelyn watched it emerge, then disappear near the foot of their bed. William, snoring, knew nothing.

The tar-covered thing slid under the covers on William's side of the bed. Evelyn watched with bated breath as the bump in the covers briefly became larger, then disappeared, and only the sleeping form of her husband was visible. As always, before sunrise, the shape under the quilts appeared again, slid off the edge of the bed, and returned to the mirror. Evelyn caught glimpses of it—a hulking shoulder, the side of a squashed face—but it didn't seem as interested in her anymore.

One night she didn't see the thing return to the mirror. It was then that William stopped coming to the room. Evelyn could no longer hear the children's laughter and footsteps echoing through the house. She didn't hear the staff admonish the children in hushed tones either. *Mother is sick.*

She cannot come out of the room. Mother is very ill. It is catching. Mother must rest. How many days did it go on?

She ventured out into the second-floor hall after a night alone when William didn't come to bed. Even then with Austin's visage unrecognizable, he had still come to bed every night. Until he didn't.

The house was quiet, and Evelyn was finally able to work her fingers around the doorknob to turn it and open the door. She thanked whoever might be watching that William hadn't locked the door. She would have surely starved and died in there if no one came to check on her.

She thought often of throwing herself out the window and ridding herself of the torment altogether. It was a thought that occupied much of her time once she accepted that Austin was gone. He could not help her now. He had promised to help her, had promised he would come for her no matter what. And now. Now look. He had broken his promise. Not on purpose. He had broken it because she had allowed William into her life.

But not today. Today it seemed that William had left. Today she felt giddy with possibility.

61

4:00 p.m., Saturday, October 24th

"Evelyn?"

Olivia felt anger, fear, and sadness spill over onto her. She was in the studio, unable to breathe, boxcutter in one hand and the other on the edge of the large print, frozen in the act of cutting it square.

I'm sorry, my dear.

The strange slimy sensation on her hands had grown to a new height during the day. They were cold, but they also felt like they had a layer of ooze on them, and she couldn't wash it off as she had been able to when it first started. They grew pruny as the day went on, even though Olivia had not showered or washed her hands more than once or twice.

She stared at her hands. Sores appeared on them. Her heart clenched. Was it real? Should she go to the hospital?

You need to find my journal. I do not want to speak of the things I saw, but I did write them down. They are still too near, still too painful.

Olivia clenched and unclenched her hands, and for a time, the sensation disappeared. "I don't know where the rest of your journal is."

Evelyn didn't answer, and not for the first time, Olivia felt anger at the woman.

Her hands hurt too much to continue cutting and framing, so she dropped the blade onto the table and stared at the large photograph in disgust. She had a brief thought that if she ran her hands through the circular saw instead of the pieces of frame, she wouldn't have to deal with the ooze on her hands any longer.

She kicked back in her chair to think about it for another moment before thoughts of where Evelyn's journal might be, where Austin's head was stashed, overpowered everything else.

62

Sunday, October 25th

Olivia hadn't slept. She wasn't sure of the time either. She stared at the aged wallpaper in her room until it began to move. The Victorian roses twirled while the vines around them twined. She pulled herself out of bed, still in her clothes from the day before.

Journal first, shower later. Priorities.

An hour later, Olivia dug through more piles of paper in the dugout looking for Evelyn's goddamn journal. Most of the paper was useless. Hoarder shit. There had been nothing in the basement. Literally nothing. She'd stood and stared at the blank walls and floor. Her memory was of it jammed full of stuff. Some of it had surely ended up in the dugout, but the rest? Her mother had been busy. It was concerning, one of those red-flag behaviors that Olivia was supposed to tell the therapist about, but her mother hadn't burned the house down yet, so that was a positive. She could talk to the therapist next week. Send her a text or something.

"What are you doing?" Austin asked gently when Olivia tossed aside a box of mason jars. They barely missed his boots, and the resulting crash of breaking glass startled her even though she had thrown them. She hadn't noticed they were glass, just that it wasn't the paper she needed.

Olivia snapped up, brought out of her deep thoughts. "Oh!"

Austin filled the doorway with his tall frame and broad shoulders. He wore a pair of what looked like denim jeans and a faded red button-up shirt. They looked strangely modern from across the room, but she would have bet they were circa 1899. In the late-afternoon light, she saw that the jeans had been lovingly patched several times, above his left knee and close to his right-front pocket where his hand rested. The sleeves of his faded red shirt with pearl snap buttons were rolled up to his elbows, showing off his muscular forearms.

Thoughts and images cascaded through her head. How much had he toiled to find his way there in the Great Plains? How much had he risked?

She recalled letters upon letters that Evelyn had sent and received, detailing his crisscrossing the Plains states and into the near west to do business with ranchers and farmers all over the backcountry. Except, what wasn't backcountry back then? She didn't know. Surely most of it was.

It was strange how near yet so far it seemed. She stood in a dugout pilfering through papers that hadn't seen the light of day in a century while a man who looked like he could blend into the twenty-first century but who spoke so politely that it was obvious he wasn't "from around here" stood staring at her in her Ugg boots, skinny jeans, and thin sweater. What in the world did she look like to him?

Then her dream from the other night came rushing back to her.

Where are you going, Miss? Where are you going?

She had answered him. What had she said?

"Are you all right?" Austin asked again as if he was addressing a spooked animal.

Olivia shook her head. The layer of slime on her hands would not wipe off. She felt Austin before she saw him, just as the trembling began. He pulled her into him and shushed her.

"There's so much!" Olivia wailed. It was all so heavy. So very heavy.

"I'm ready to rest more easily too," Austin replied, his lips against her hair.

Yes, yes, she was. She had flung herself into this the way she had flung herself into the impossible deadline project—all the way with no regard for herself. So, she cried against Austin's soft shirt until she was spent of tears.

"What are you searching for?"

Olivia tried to calm her breathing. His words echoed from her dreams. "My journal. Parts of it, anyway. A great section is missing."

Austin hummed against her. Olivia didn't know the last time she had felt that sensation. Some far-off memory from childhood flitted through her head.

"Yours or Evelyn's?" he asked.

Oliva thought on the question. "Evelyn's."

Another hum. "Evelyn used to tell me that William was fond of placing her things in his study under lock and key when she misbehaved. Like a child."

Why hadn't she asked him sooner? There was a buzz around her head, like faintness. She hadn't experienced much of that feeling until that month when the floor kept falling out underneath her.

"I see Evan in my photographs so much," she said, her mouth dry. "It terrified me at first, but now I want to know what it means. It has to mean something."

Austin looked at her strangely. "All you had to do was ask."

There was the crux of it. She hadn't asked. She had kept it all to herself and hadn't wanted help from anyone.

"Why is he there?" she asked, afraid of the answer, whatever it was.

"Is he leading you somewhere? He's a smart animal, you know. I trusted no others in my travels."

"I don't know." That possibility had sort of presented itself, but she hadn't been able to find a pattern to his incessant galloping yet. "I'm just ready to be done with it. I'm tired. And sore."

The look Austin gave her was hard to read. "How can I help?"

"I don't want to go into the old Monroe home alone."

I don't want to go there again!

"I need to check his desk though."

"I was wrong," Austin said suddenly. "To have done what I did."

Olivia didn't have to ask what he meant. "No, you weren't."

"According to some. Not according to my own conscience."

Olivia touched his hand but didn't say anything more on the subject. She didn't want to upset him. "Will you take me to the Monroe house?"

Austin nodded, catching on to whatever thoughts were forming in her mind. "I'll take you as far as I'm able. I could not enter last time. The way was barred to me."

The ride to campus was cold but uneventful. Olivia found a kind of happiness sitting astride the strong animal with Austin riding ahead of her. She thought as they rode, and it felt like a kind of meditation.

Maybe it wasn't such a bad thing if Simon had taken the pages from the journal. Not wanting to tarnish the already questionable reputation of the town's most influential people, Olivia understood, but she still wanted to know what had happened. She thought briefly that she could abandon the hunt altogether, but it would be easy to just . . . see if he had anything hidden that was useful.

The Monroe house was more difficult, but Evelyn knew of a hidden key that would allow Olivia in through the kitchen. She told her where to dig next to a decorative bit of limestone that had sat in the same place since it had been installed there more than a century past.

Evelyn directed her up the stairs and into William's office. Despite time's passing, it felt cold, hard. Olivia went to the desk situated under the windows. She needed to hurry.

She slid open a drawer. Nothing. Only the smell of old furniture greeted her. Drawer after drawer, nothing. Going there was a mistake.

She jumped when a shadow appeared in the doorway. Her heart sank. "What do you want?" she asked, but it came out as a squeak.

William strode into the room, all man. No shimmering golem now. "To see you. To see how you were doing. And you're in *my* office, by the way. But I went a little far the other night and wanted to apologize."

Olivia was tired, and she didn't have time for his games, but the statement sat oddly with her. "You hoped I was dead."

"No. You haven't been on campus except for brief stints at the gallery."

"I know."

"Don't you have things to do?"

"Of course. I've been doing them. I keep getting interrupted though, and it's awfully stressful."

"I'm sorry."

"You don't sound very sorry."

The look that crossed his face when she said that made her think he had heard that exact phrase before. She imagined it was an entirely different time though.

He managed to get inside the doorway, and Olivia backed away from the desk. She wanted to keep as much space between them as possible.

Not Simon closed the distance between them though and slid a hand around the back of her neck and rubbed gently there, like a massage. Olivia's body betrayed her by enjoying the sensation, and she relaxed into it for a moment, almost forgetting how dangerous it could be. Somewhere, he was still Simon. She believed that.

He pressed close to her, touching her in a way that was Simon but not quite. There was a purpose behind this touch, something that felt more wild animal than human. More like a hunt than a relationship.

Then he was fisting her hair, craning her neck back, so he could taste her. Part of her was lost to it, but the other part of her was figuring out how to get him the hell out when he gasped and jerked away from her. It sounded like a hiss, like steam escaping a kettle.

"What the fuck, woman?" he growled, holding out his hand.

There, in the meat of his palm, was a small gouge. It bled profusely for so small a cut. Olivia stared at it, confused.

As Not Simon squeezed his hand shut around the wound, blood poured from between his fingers. Olivia felt down her leg where his hand had been. She ran over something small and sharp protruding from her jeans.

She had forgotten about the cufflink in her pocket. There hadn't been any sharp parts on it though. She hadn't thought. She pulled it from her pocket, unthinking, and looked at it. Not Simon inhaled sharply, and Olivia snapped her head up to look at him.

His eyes, already red, flashed darker. Olivia liked the crimson-and-black look even less than the red. He hissed at her. "Where did you get that?"

Olivia clenched her fingers around the cufflink. It felt hot in her hand. It felt good, a talisman. "Um . . ."

"Where did you steal that from, woman?"

Olivia bristled, despite the warning from his eyes. "I didn't steal it."

Not Simon got a hand back around her neck again and squeezed. She felt the slickness of the blood from his hand on her neck. "You mean to tell me that you've been consorting with that ghost? Behind *my* back?"

Olivia struggled for breath and reached up to grasp his wrist. "Uh, please. It's not like that."

Not Simon narrowed his gaze and relaxed his grip. His wary eyes traced her face. "Then tell me. What is it *like*?"

When Olivia tried to reach up a hand to his face, he pushed it away. "None of that. Tell me about that spirit."

She didn't want to tell him about Austin. "Why don't you just kill me now?"

He squeezed his fingers, and her vision became fuzzy. "Because that wouldn't be any *fun*, would it? And I told you I don't *want* that. I want *more* than that. That's all in your power."

She gasped for air. When Simon had put his hands on her neck, it had felt erotic, sensual. Terrifying. "I don't understand!"

She scratched at his hands, and he released her neck. Olivia broke away, bumped into the desk, and sat down hard on its surface. She watched the open doorway. He would catch her before she managed to get into their room and climb out the window or the servants' door.

"You are much smarter than her, you know," Not Simon said.

"Who cares?" The room was no longer so fuzzy.

She regretted her careless words when Not Simon strode toward her again, his face contorted in a way that could only be described as supernatural, more like the golem thing that she had seen the first time there. Why had she returned? She tried to stand and run, but he was there to block her attempt and pushed her back against the wall next to the window.

"I said *tell me about that spirit,*" Not Simon growled.

"What the fuck do you want to know? He's the same goddamn man that you knew! What do you think he's up to?"

Not Simon slapped her hard enough that she saw stars, and her ears rang. "I want to know what he's doing here! Now tell me."

"He's protecting Evelyn!" Olivia cried, panicked. His hands were everywhere at once—on her throat, her face, her breasts, her hips, pulling her close. It was not the exciting rough night that she had had with Simon.

"And what else is he doing here? Looking for me?"

"I don't know!" Olivia hollered. The door was open, but she couldn't reach it. It was too far away.

"Olivia!" a voice yelled.

Austin! Where was he?

Not Simon dropped his hands from Olivia's neck and looked around for the source of the voice. Olivia's hands went to her neck. They came away smeared with blood. She thought arbitrarily of the Israelites marking their doorways with lamb's blood, so God would pass them over and not destroy their firstborn. She felt marked. It was the only thing she could think of in the moment. Then she did the only other thing she could think of in the moment after. She opened the hand that had clamped shut around the cufflink, then lashed out with it. Her ears buzzed, her sight wavering.

She caught Not Simon across one strong bicep with the small piece, and the effect was immediate. The metal cut through his clothing and skin at the same time, as if it were a knife. Blood poured from the wound, which should have been too small for so much blood. Black ooze followed.

Not Simon cried out in pain and stumbled away from Olivia and the door. She seized the opening and rushed out into the hall and down the stairs. She ran from the house and didn't look behind her until she had crashed out the front door and slammed it shut behind her. *Please let there be a security system.*

Austin waited at the drive with Evan, apparently unable to come any closer. Olivia flung herself into his arms.

"We have to get out of here!" she said, shivering as she clung to Austin.

Not Simon stood on the front porch, not having bothered with the door. He had a hand over his upper arm, and the look on his face, though far away, was clear. Anger. Vengeance.

"Miss Olivia, I'm so sorry. I'm so, so sorry. I cannot—"

"Please stop," she whispered into his coat. It was warm, and it smelled of horses, traveling dust, and gunpowder. "Just take me away."

Austin touched her neck, frantic. "You have blood on you."

"It isn't mine."

She heard a great rattling from somewhere around the side of the house.

Nightmare horse.

"We must be going," Austin said and gently helped her aboard Evan. He seemed so far away. The buzzing in her ears had not stopped. "I can get you to your destination before him, and I'll hold him off for as long as I can, but please hurry."

The ride was not so meditative. Olivia could only cling to Austin and focus on how good his coat smelled. She caught hints of woodsmoke, leather polish, and a dozen other scents. She tried to name them, to keep the other thoughts at bay. Lavender. Horse. But the thoughts continued to creep in.

She knew that Simon wouldn't have done such a thing, but Not Simon would. William Monroe would, to save his own skin. And she knew, intrinsically, that though Simon would not remember the incident, that didn't remove his culpability. The fact that he rode around on a black horse after the sun was down didn't make Olivia feel better either.

At the art building, Austin helped Olivia dismount, and she pressed herself inside the folds of his coat once more. Woodsmoke. Leather. Prairie grasses. Dirt. Horses. Evan.

Austin pressed a kiss to the top of her head. "Go now, Miss Olivia. There is much to be done."

She let herself into the building in a daze. The Schneider Art & History building was old, and most keys opened most doors. The few doors that had numeric locks had the same passcode, so teachers, administrators, and janitors could get into the rooms without much fuss. They were a trusted bunch, which Olivia appreciated greatly.

That made breaking into Simon's office easy. He had a personal passcode that she didn't know, but her key worked in the lock. She tried to carry the scent of Austin's person with her. How had she never noticed how comforting the smell of someone was?

Visions swam before her eyes when she opened the door to Simon's office. She shook from the event that had left her sweating in the freezing temperatures. It was William's office, then, all pristine surfaces and that awful metallic scent in the air. The spines of every book aligned just so. Cold, cold, cold. Then it was Simon's office again, the warm smell of old books and his little coffee press that he always forgot to empty. Yes, that was real. Then William's office again, a carriage approaching outside. Someone to pause the daily cycle. That was real too.

Olivia shook her head and stepped forward. She swung her hips to avoid a collision with William and Simon's desks. They sat askew to each other, no rhyme or reason to their relation, no yin and yang. Everything was twisted.

The bookcases held nothing interesting, and she gave up on flipping through books after the first handful. He would surely keep it closer, somewhere he could read through it again if he needed. Hell, maybe it was Simon, and he wanted it, so he could write a damn book about it. But she would've just given him the journal to borrow. No need to destroy it.

She sat at Simon's desk and tried the drawers. All locked. But they were the old 1970s desks that had master keys too, so she used her own key from her old grad school desk to open the big drawer on the left.

It was full of paper. Old paper.

Olivia sifted through the contents as quietly as possible. The scent of the journal wafted out at her. She was in the right place.

She found other things that looked like they might be useful—lots of photographs of William Monroe and many of his family, more ancient receipts, photocopied news articles. She wanted to take them, but she couldn't. She would take only what was hers.

But there, at the bottom of the drawer, was a small bundle of papers tied up like a scroll. The scent of the journal—earthy, dusty, prairie—hit her hard. She saw Austin hand her the journal again, as she had several times before, but this time she felt the moment in her heart. Joy at the gift coursed through her. Then, another scene. She took the journal from the table she had seen at the Monroe home and placed her needlework over it to hide it as someone entered the room.

She came out of the memory, sifted through the rest of the drawer. She drew back when she touched something cool and sticky. She turned on her flashlight and shone it into the drawer. Beneath all the papers was a piece of bone with twigs and herbs tied to it with what looked like kitchen twine. Memories of the Monroe crypt leapt out at her. What the hell was William Monroe's rib bone doing there? She took it. It had to mean something.

She clutched the papers close (what idiot didn't bring a bag or something to carry things in?), closed the drawer—no time to investigate what other goodies he might have kept in there—and tried to make sure that everything was as it was before.

Footsteps on the stairs.

He had followed her.

Old fear flooded her. She tasted the same metallic smell she had caught in William's office when he had cut his hand on the cufflink. New fear mingled with the old. The animal part of her said, *Run, hide, run, hide, run, hide.*

Focus.

She shut off her flashlight and peeked into the hallway. It was surely Simon (William) there for the grading (lecturing) that he did at night when he could concentrate (when most of the staff was away).

Dear God, he followed us. He'll find a way to make us suffer for it. Suffer for it.

"Please, don't," Olivia moaned. If she could just keep it together for a few more minutes, pretend it hadn't happened.

The footsteps were still in the stairwell. Taking a chance, she darted across the hall and down a few doors to her classroom. Surely she had left something in there during class that day. She flipped on the light and scanned the room. She must have left something. Someone must have left something. There had to be something.

Yes there, to our right. Evelyn spotted it before Olivia did. A lens cap.

"You don't even know what a lens cap is," Olivia whispered. No response. Her brain mate was borrowing memories and knowledge again.

Hurry! He's coming. At least they were both on the same page with that one.

Olivia ran to the window, swiping up the lens cap and someone's dropped homework (thank God for Susan) on the way. Standing on her tiptoes, she stuffed the papers on top of the AC unit where it met the window. She pushed them just far enough and arranged the drooping blinds over them, so they would be safe until she could leave the building.

Oh fuck. Where had Austin and Evan gone? They must have had enough sense to go somewhere else and not be seen. Lure the nightmare horse away, something.

Then she felt Austin's presence. Yes, he would come where he could. He had promised that.

The hairs on her neck prickled when he materialized behind her, and his heavy, warm hands settled on her shoulders. It was at once comforting and disconcerting. Olivia knew she could do this on her own, but it was good to have him there though he could do but little.

There was a knock on the door, and it opened slowly. Olivia braced herself and felt Austin's hands tighten on her shoulders. She was glad not to be alone—depending on who was coming into the classroom.

"Olivia?"

It sounded like Simon at least.

She relaxed a little, eased up the death grip she had on poor Susan's homework. "Yeah, just me."

When he came into the room, she wasn't so sure it was Simon. Something about the way he carried himself. He seemed a little straighter, taller, more imposing, but there was no blood on his arm. Or had he put a coat over it? Evelyn was silent, but Olivia tasted metal in her mouth. Blood. She wanted to spit.

"You're here late."

Olivia laughed and waved Susan's homework. *Quit acting deranged. Calm down.* "Yeah, sorry. Hope I didn't scare you. Was grading and realized I didn't have someone's essay. Was missing a lens cap anyway from the loaners everyone was using today."

Austin squeezed her shoulders again, and Olivia shut her mouth. She sounded out of her mind.

Simon's eyes flitted from her face to just over her shoulder. "My apologies. I didn't mean to scare you."

"No worries." Olivia hoped the smile looked genuine. She felt like she might pee her pants at any minute. That he hadn't said anything about the blood, that he wasn't concerned about how frightful she must look, set her on edge. It couldn't be Simon.

Get out, get out, get out, Evelyn chanted.

"I've gotta go," Olivia said and headed toward the door.

Simon stepped aside to let her by. Once she had made it a few steps down the hall, Olivia released the breath she had been holding.

"Evelyn," Simon called.

She froze, tension evident in her shoulders. Not Simon.

"Evelyn," he said again.

Her heart crawled up her throat. It was a miracle she didn't choke on it. "Yes?"

"Will you come to my office?"

She didn't turn. If she did, she wasn't sure she was prepared for whatever she would see there: the demonic red eyes, William's eyes, or Simon's golden-brown ones.

"Why?" Something caught in her throat, causing her voice to rasp.

"You know."

Who knew what?

Evelyn knew what William Monroe had for her. Olivia knew what demon-possessed Simon Monroe had for her. But the real Simon? What did he have for her in all of this?

"I want your hands on my throat," she said.

"I don't want to hurt you, but I want to hurt you," he replied.

"I want you to hurt me and make love to me after," she rejoined. She had to get out of the building before he realized she had the other pages. "I have to get home," she said. Rabbit heart beating in her throat. Ready to run from that place when she could not just an hour earlier.

A shuffle of feet but away from her. "Fine. But next time I won't be asking."

He didn't ask last time.

Olivia all but ran into the stairwell at the end of the hall. She waited a few beats before carefully opening the door and peering down the hall. A light peeked out from under Simon's office door.

Olivia slid back into the classroom and grabbed the papers from on top of the AC unit, then headed down toward the main level. She needed to get across the breezeway and into the Schneider building without being spotted by William or his steed.

She tried to stay quiet, but every time she brushed something in the hall that she could not see, she paused and looked back. No one followed.

Her heart hammered into her throat when she paused at the wooden door that opened onto the breezeway. She had gone back in time during her descent of the stairs, and the door, which should have been glass, was no longer.

Hearing nothing on the other side, she pushed it open and slid out into the cold. Night gathered around her, and no lights shone out from the mist in the common space beyond the breezeway. As there shouldn't have been. Not in 1900 anyway.

In the distance came the familiar clopping sound of the nightmare horse. Olivia gritted her teeth and ran for the other entrance. She counted the twenty limestone support pillars as she went.

One.

Two.

Three.

Four.

By the fifth one, the thing's hooves resounded on the cement walk leading up to the breezeway.

At the sixth, she swore she could smell its cloud of death and decay.

With the seventh, Evan, riderless, burst from nowhere and rammed into the side of the dark, foul animal. They clashed just on the other side of the pillars with a scream that sent the hairs on Olivia's arms and neck into frenzied, rolling shivers.

Nine.

Ten.

Eleven.

Twelve.

She caught a glimpse of Evan as he attempted to herd the other animal away from the breezeway. The nightmare horse snapped back with his sharp teeth, foam leaking from the corners of his mouth with each swipe.

Olivia crashed into the side door of the Schneider building. She hadn't realized she'd gotten all the way there. She shook her head, disoriented.

Evan paused as if to make certain Olivia had made it to her destination, then ran toward a common space, the other creature not far behind.

Once in the building, Olivia raced down the stairs to the basement. She clutched the papers and macabre bundle tightly against her heavy wool cloak.

She locked the archives door behind her and took steadying breaths. William didn't know about that place, and the nightmare horse was occupied with Evan. She would be safe there. Austin's presence had left her, but he was still around somewhere. She could feel it.

The archives room was not as silent as she would have liked. The sound of water dripping irregularly somewhere and the creak of the wood beams above made her cringe. She didn't mind the hum of the dehumidifiers. They kept her rooted in the modern world.

She had to read them though, and away from Austin. Whatever the pages held, she needed to read them first. Then she could go back to taking photographs with nothing more than what she saw through the lens. That would be a good day.

Olivia took a deep breath and let her eyes rest on the faded handwriting. It looked so familiar. This was the best course of action, she told herself, and began to read.

> October 20th, 1902
> William will not stop. He has begun, I believe, to suspect that I'm not always truthful with him, though he does not know how to force my mouth open and my brain to speak. I'm not scared of him any longer. Even if his rage may terrify me on this Earth, my soul is already in heaven. God may frown on my acts with Austin, though I'm married to William, but how could he with the way that William treats me? Austin is my true love, the man I should have married. Curse these stupid traditions! Women now, it seems, may marry who they wish, but only a handful of years ago, I felt I could not choose for myself! And women in the West are even asking for the right to vote! Imagine! I myself would not ask for that. I'm too much of my mother's generation, and I'm fine letting Austin take care of me. His vote is mine.
>
> But I'm wandering from where I began. I suppose that a journal will do that to a person. I'm certain that William is close to finding out about Austin and me. Perhaps he knows now. No one who knows would tell a

> soul, but William is a smart man. What lives within him is even smarter.

Other entries seemed normal, a strange contrast to the fear and paranoia that pervaded the woman's thoughts.

> Today the Schneiders dedicated a building on the university campus. Or so it has been related to me. I begged William that I might go, for I had heard in years long past of when their father built the structure. Seeing its limestone façade rise from the far end of Main Street was a thing of wonder when I was child and my happy memories of oft riding through with Austin still remain with me. William was not so impressed during our visit as I have said though he boasts enough about the building the Schneiders have built there. He says it will have nearly all electric lighting, the latest plumbing. He speaks of it in so much detail that I wonder if he had his hands in it. There is not much he doesn't in this town.

Olivia shifted through the pages to one toward the end.

> September 6th, 1903
> I cannot risk seeing A— this week. William is in a terrible temper, and I believe he has hurt himself. He will not say what, but his shoulder gives off so much heat, I think it must be infected. If he has fallen from a horse, it seems it wounds his pride too much to say. Little William was so shy around me today. I fear what his father tells him when I'm not there, when I'm kept in my room.

> September 12th, 1903
> I'm terrified of the creature that came from the mirror. I believe it is William and not William. I believe it will consume me if I cannot escape here. I see it on the stairs and on my way to the toilet. It impedes my path. It leaves great greasy traces along the carpet, which only I can see. I saw it at the children's door yesterday. I cried for it to stop, and it looked at me and smiled. And when William came to the sound of my cries, he looked right at the thing and then to me and asked me if I were well. He must have seen it. How could he not have? But I know he would not believe me.

After that the entries were no longer dated. Their author had written crossways over previous entries, so it was impossible to tell which happened first.

> I do not know what to do or who to tell. Dear God, please release me from this torment. I do not know who would even believe me, for the man has never struck me. I cannot believe I say it, but he is a flannel-mouth liar. He said the sweetest things to bring me here with no love in the depths of his soul.
>
> I have not slept, and I do not know what I truly see after seeing so much. Did the men of the warship Maine feel such terror after seeing their comrades taken down in cold blood by the Spaniards? Did they begin to see shadows and figures not truly there? I have been seeing things that are not there, hearing Austin though I know he is gone. I fear I have lost my sanity, for I cannot wash the gore from my hands.

> I still feel my palms pressed against his slick hair, against his ears. He heard enough though. I do not think he should be hearing seeing such things in death, so I was grateful for that small blessing at least.

"Evelyn, did he really?" Olivia asked breathlessly. Evelyn was silent. Olivia's imagination went into hyper drive. Her stomach clenched at the thought. "How long?" she asked.

Too long, was the quiet reply.

> My hands. They ache and burn, and I put salve on them or they too will rot and decay. I didn't know how the process went, but now I do. I thought of Austin and my brother every day of that torture. How they must be changing over time in the ground. Except I saw what was happening to Austin. Every day I saw how he changed. My hands, they shall never be the same. I made the salve that Austin used on his hands and mine so long ago, but it does not heal my wounds. They fester and rot no matter what I do for them. I fear I shall lose my hands before the year is done. I burn up with sweats in the night. The delirium takes me.

The coherence of the next entry chilled Olivia.

> Today I release myself. William says he believes I have learned my lesson, and he is right. I have not seen my children since that awful day, and I fear the worst. William will not say where they are. I'm frightened they are gone. My children are gone. He tore them from my arms and told me how unfit I am. How foolish I am. To think I could have made a life with a person who stirred nothing

in me. How foolish I was to make that choice over and over and over and over and over again.

Today I release myself. I had to chew through the twine with my own teeth before I could use a blade on them, but I freed Austin too. My poor love no longer looks himself. And my hands, I cannot scrub them enough. They are raw and covered with sores. I smell nothing but the stench of death.

Today I release myself to go where, I do not know, but anywhere from here is closer to Austin and further from those choices that bound me.

Olivia fell into Evelyn as she read the pages, memories surfacing that had been buried but not forgotten in the woman's mind.

Evelyn had cried through the first day, and William had let her. Once he had left on business or wherever he was, she felt hollow inside.

The day William didn't come, the day she released her hands, was a Sunday. When William didn't come, she ventured down the stairs. No one. She went into the kitchen. No one. Why was there no smell of food cooking, even for the staff? Her stomach snarled.

Despite her fear, Evelyn found a pair of shears and tried to work them with her useless hands. The shears didn't work. Desperate, she leaned her face in to pull at the twine with her teeth. The smell was thick in her nose, astringent. Tears welled in her eyes like when the staff at home prepared piles of onions while preparing for Christmas or Thanksgiving. Her cheek brushed Austin's, and she felt a smear of something move across her skin. Her empty stomach roiled.

She continued to chew through the string.

Once she had worked several fingers free, she found a knife and propped it up on a block of cheese in the kitchen. Slowly, she was able to saw through several layers of twine.

Austin's skin, so soft and pliable, fell off in great chunks while she tried to remove the twine. It hit the kitchen preparation area with soft thuds, like fat falling from smoked beef. She could nearly remove the twine without cutting it, but it was too painful to see Austin falling apart as he was. Bits of him were stuck to her hands too.

She finally cut through enough of the twine to pull her hands away and set Austin down. She could see bone through the torn and sagging flesh of Austin's face, and his hair had begun to fall out in great pieces. She wept when she finally set him down and removed her hands.

Rushing over to the sink, she tried to wash her hands of the filth that covered them. She felt ashamed. It was not filth; it was Austin, though she recognized him no longer.

The water was painful on her hands, and the extent of the open wounds was revealed to her under the water. She saw the bones of her hands. The flesh had been eaten clean through. She stared at it through the pain of the flowing water. How would that heal now that it was so exposed so?

The twine around her wrists had sunken into her skin, and bits of the it stuck in the skin as she peeled it away. The pain was distant but intense. It was as if her brain were wrapped in fluff, like the cotton fluff at the fair, as big as a cloud.

She wrapped her poor hands in white cloth soaked with salve, changing the bandages when they bled and oozed through. There might be medicine that would have helped her in the beginning, but nothing would help now. She knew that. She would lose her hands. They ached constantly. She no longer slept.

She knew her children were gone. Ghosts chased her through the house. Smoke drifted in the windows with the evening air. What was burning nearby, the prairie, a home, or her insides?

She knew she hadn't been the same since little William was born. Even around Austin, the light had seemed to go out of the world. Not as much with Austin though. Austin had given her the strength to see the joy in the world.

But now . . .

She couldn't remember where she had put the children. Jennie or Alyssa had been watching over them, but there was no sound in the house save what the wind did with the curtains. She had opened all the windows to let the smoke in.

Guilt, was this guilt? No, the children were gone. She had not seen them for so long. Who had taken them? William said she had, that what she had done had made them disappear. Once she lost her hands, she could no longer hold them. Even if she had not done what William said, she could not hold them anymore.

There was one final consolation. She brought the pretty bicycle inside from its safe spot by the garden door under the awning. It had been an impulse purchase on her last day in town with William. He had taken Ebony away from her after the incident with the mud, but he did take her to town in the carriage one final time. She had purchased the bicycle on a whim. It was new and fancy, and she had wanted it.

She practiced on it in the kitchen, getting good at riding it around and around the central preparation table, where Alyssa's sister worked.

Gathering up her skirts, she got herself settled on the tall seat and set to making circles in the large foyer. The black-and-white squares of marble seemed to swirl beneath her in a quick succession of shadows. Black, white, black, white, black, white. Faster and faster. The pain in her hands made her vision waver, but she daren't let go of the handlebars.

With each turn around the foyer, the silken curtains from the front room waved to her. She daren't lift her hands to wave back, but she hated to be rude, and her hands hurt so. The dark silk was a wave of dead grasses over the prairie. It was the waving trees that day in the hills overlooking the cliffs. It was the way Austin's neckerchief still waved merrily in the wind while blood soaked it. Oh, how his eyes had flitted in their last moments, away from her and back again. What had he tried to say?

Dizzy, she stopped the bicycle. The floor beneath her had finally become a spiral, tilting this way and that. Now she could properly wave to the curtains. She stepped off the bicycle, setting it upright on the little stand that William had custom made, so the machine would not fall over.

The curtains beckoned, whispering whatever it was that curtains whispered about. Her secrets, his secrets, the quiet violence that had been her life for the last four years.

She grabbed the fluttering fabric and yanked. The curtain came down, bringing the rod with it. She put her face in the fabric. It smelled like smoke, like rising panic. For a moment, she forgot the pain in her hands, forgot how they ached up her arms, nearly to her shoulders.

She had a pair of fabric shears in her hands. Where they had come from, she didn't know. But they worked beautifully to cut a long strip from the curtains. It was sturdy.

It took some doing to work it up into the chandelier, but once she managed it, sweating and sore from standing on the stool and reaching above her head, she stood back to admire it. The green velvet rope dangled tantalizingly from the chandelier—one of William's favorite possessions. He raved about its craftsmanship. She wanted to say, "I wish you would have raved over me that way, after you married me," but who would hear?

It swung slowly, throwing fragments of light across the black-and-white tiles. Young William would have loved it. But he was dead. That was what William had told her. The children didn't want to see her. She had killed them with her selfishness. That's what he had said, and she believed him. Why should she do otherwise? Everything else he had said had come to pass.

Perhaps people were moving around her, but all she could see was smoke from the prairie wafting in the open front windows. She called for Alyssa once or twice, but she could find her voice for no more than that.

She visited the kitchen a dozen times to see Austin. Now that she had set him down, she felt as if a piece of her own self were missing. She touched his hair, his forehead, spoke to him, then went out of the kitchen to wander parts of the house. It was a wonder that William had not found her out yet. Her stomach clenched with every quiet sound in the house, thinking it was William, that he would come in and tell her that she must pick up the head and continue her penance.

She returned to the soft rope that she had pulled through the chandelier. It was too far up. She went back to the kitchen to say hello one last time to Austin and left from the kitchen with a stool.

Evelyn stood on the stool and slipped on the velvet necklace. It felt warm against her face and neck. It reminded her of the velvet softness of her babies' heads after they were born. When they were cleaned off and dried and swaddled, and she pressed her face against their warm little heads while they slept in her arms. She couldn't get enough of the velvet fuzz of their hair. She touched it every chance she got.

Except now all she had was the velvet rope to remind her. She nuzzled against it, dreaming back in time.

When she stepped off the stool, the house was silent.

63

Monday, October 26th

Maybe it was strange, but Olivia understood why Evelyn had done what she had done.

Olivia stared at the large piles of laundry strewn across her floor and wondered if it would be OK to just turn a pair of underwear inside out and wear them again. No alarm bells went off, she so she absently grabbed a pair and pulled them on, followed by a blouse, skirt, and belt. There was no helping her hair, but she put some pins in it anyway to fight of the worst of the frizz.

Something tickled the back of her brain, like having the name of a flower on the tip of her tongue. Sometimes she would wake in the night and recall it. But she didn't have overnight now. Only precious minutes.

She dug into one of the boxes of Weatherford memorabilia that she kept by her bed. The maps from William's crypt were in some plastic sleeves at the bottom. She had put them away after she'd lifted them, not sure what they could do for her except that she'd taken them in the fear of the moment.

She unfolded the first one, turned it this way and that until she understood it. It was a surveyor's map. She was no expert, but knowing who William Monroe had been, it had to be of Warren. It showed the canyon running along north of town as well as several buildings that still existed.

She flipped to the next map. Warren with more buildings, all of them labeled. Olivia tried to understand how the roads ran. Some of them had to be the same as today. She read off their names, recognizing most and trying to put modern landmarks on them.

She spotted the corner where the credit union still stood. Next to that was a gas station, then a handful of restaurants. She kept going down Sedalia Street in her head until she was mentally at the gym. Looking down at the paper, she planted her finger firmly on the little building labeled "jail."

So, the gym was built over the old jail? That was pretty cool. Where they'd found Austin's skeleton made sense now. The ancestry forums had been shut down sometime the previous week by a moderator who said they had gotten off topic (surprise, surprise). The school paper had done a brief exposé on the discovery, but oddly, it hadn't been mentioned anywhere else that Olivia could find. Maybe such things took time.

She kept looking and found a map of the college buildings of William's day. They were spread apart, unlike the present. The buildings had filled in over the last 150 years, she understood, but William's pages told their early story.

There, off the quad that was present in the early college days, was the current art building.

There. That's the place I have been.

"Yes," Olivia muttered. "You've mentioned that several times now."

Olivia tried to think like William. Evelyn had left Austin's head sitting on the kitchen prep table. William had come home to a dead wife and a rotting head in the kitchen. He might have panicked, or maybe he didn't, if it wasn't William. But maybe he panicked and went around trying to find a place to hide the head that was out of the way. Maybe chance took him back to the campus. The only place he had been, according to Evelyn, was the Schneider building. Maybe he went in at night and found a place to stash the head.

There were other places where he could have put it, of course. William could have thrown the damn thing in a pond for all she knew, but she would have bet that he didn't. He would have taken it to the place to which the Monroes and Weatherfords were still drawn.

Evelyn whispered something that distracted Olivia. She needled until Olivia asked her what the hell she wanted.

This was not long after the Schneiders dedicated that building. A mere month. Just before everything.

Yes. Olivia remembered ghosting over that entry in Evelyn's journal.

She continued to go over the maps in her mind as she readied the final prints for the gallery. Another might need some adjusting, but she was nearly done.

Please don't tell Austin.

Olivia made an accidental cut off the straight edge for her photograph. "Goddammit it, Evelyn! You're not helping me."

The woman had said it many times since they had left campus in the middle of the night, interrupting her sleep, in the darkroom, when she was having a conversation with Cecelia, and when she was in the middle of a final meeting with the gallery curator.

Olivia finally gave up and let Evelyn have the reins for the rest of the afternoon. She was tired to fighting the woman for thought space in her own head. Since Austin had admonished Evelyn for taking too much of Olivia, the shared headspace had not been so restraining.

Doesn't Austin know already?

"I believe he still thinks William had a hand in my death."

Oh. OH.

She thought about that as Evelyn steered them toward the gallery. The woman kept herself moving much more than Olivia would; that was certain. But at least her terror felt distant when she rode in the back seat with Evelyn. And she could think in peace while Evelyn managed the mechanics of her currently stressful day-to-day life.

Evelyn stared at the photographs, looking at them along the length of the wall from a distance. Olivia hadn't viewed them from quite that spot yet, though Evelyn seemed drawn to it. She thought about what Austin had told her and tried to open herself to whatever possibility might present itself.

A large photograph of campus buildings was at one end of the gallery. Evan disappeared in a painting of flowers and reappeared in one with a squatty building that looked somewhat familiar.

Olivia hurried Evelyn over to get a closer look. The horse's appearance in other works of art was still unsettling. There it was. Evan ran toward what he knew, old Warren, and the only thing out that way back then was the jail. She'd stared at the maps long enough that it finally clicked.

"That's where his body was buried," she whispered.

Evan stopped abruptly and tossed his head up and down. Then he wheeled on his back legs and ran in another direction. He appeared in one of the photographs from the Monroe house, beginning as the odd "horse over photograph" that he did when he initially appeared until he blended into the scene and began moving down the street, taking the photograph with him.

Olivia followed him with her eyes, watching it head down toward campus. Then he appeared in another photograph nearby, a large print of the university's administrative building, built around 1860.

Evan took a sharp corner around the side of the building and galloped through an open field. That was strange. The journalism and mass comm buildings should have been there. And a parking lot and lots of sidewalks.

It disoriented Olivia as she tried to reconcile the images. But he wasn't running in the modern day; he was galloping through the past. The building that finally loomed up ahead of him was familiar though.

It's the Schneider building! My building! Olivia tried to scream.

"I know that place! But why would he have put it there?" Evelyn asked quietly. Olivia hurried back to the art building as Evelyn ruminated on the new knowledge.

The building was empty, but it should not have been. It should have been full of undergraduate students going into classes and graduate students filling up the studios. Cecelia should have been in her office, but the light was off.

Olivia drifted through the halls for an hour, wondering where William had stashed Austin's skull. Because that's all it must have been after Evelyn finally got her hands free.

The time capsule at the front end of the building was the first place she checked. But it was created in 1905, long after the events to which Olivia needed to connect.

She wandered toward the archives, wanting to see one more time what was down there and destined to dissolve into dust unless someone decided to care for them. She had the briefest thought that she could be that person. Cecelia was too busy. Olivia could take over the archives after this project, catalogue and organize them more efficiently, make them more accessible. If there was an project after this. Where would Austin go, and how would Simon be?

The thought was a lonely one. As she stood in the doorway to the archives room, she felt alone. Evelyn's voice in her head was a poor consolation. And if Evelyn left? She would be utterly alone.

Perhaps Evelyn had known the right way out. It was another horrible thought, one wrought of the loneliness. But it seemed she felt that all hope had been lost, that her children were gone, as was the one love of her life. All of it had vanished in the blink of an eye.

Once the project was over, what then? Would she go back to being her mother's full-time caregiver and teaching as many classes as possible, so she could pay the bills and afford her mother's medications? That was no life. As awful as the past month had been, it had been exciting. It had been something where there was nothing. Her mood, buoyed the other day by Colton and the thought that everything was nearly over, plunged. When it was over, nothing would be left.

The old stone walls looked back at her silently. They mocked her, she thought. But no, they didn't. They listened, soaked up her awful thoughts and gave them back to her.

She traced their lines with her eyes, memorized the shapes of the stones. Then her vision shifted. She was alone in William Monroe's house. Then she was alone in her old house, playing quietly by herself while her mother had a breakdown in the other room.

The vision became the Monroe house again. She turned down hallways and opened doors, ran downstairs, only to find herself back in the same place. Two hallways intersected, both dim, both lined with doors. At the end of the one on her left, a set of stairs led upward. Down the other hall was a door that took her back to the stairs. She could not make her way out.

Panic set in when she found herself at the door of her apartment, key in hand. She stood there, heart still seized up in terror at her hallucination. She rushed over to the second-floor railing that looked over the parking lot but didn't see her car. Had she walked all the way there, lost in the hallucination?

"Please, no," she said before sobs took her. She managed to let herself in the door and run to her room before Ann could question her. There she sat on her bed and cried, holding a pillow against her face, so Ann would not hear and ask if she was OK.

She wasn't OK. Not even remotely.

64

October 27, 1903

Austin spent most of his first days back roaming the prairie, searching. For what, he wasn't certain, but Evan seemed one with the dogged determination to seek out this elusive goal. It didn't occur to him at the time to wander farther than the prairie of his homestead and the areas around Warren.

Sunsets and sunrises offered consolation. He felt the cooling temperatures, but they only skimmed across the surface of his being. One morning he sat atop Evan near the summit of a hill he had walked often with Evelyn and watched the fog roll through the dips and swells of the prairie. He had not seen the ocean, but it reminded him of the foam that sometimes lapped the shore of a muddy prairie lake when the wind was up.

He sat there for most of the morning, just watching as the sun broke through the fog. His mind moved slowly, methodically. The fog revealed the land inch by inch, much as he had been taking back Warren inch by inch. Most of the lesser Monroes were ready to go, welcoming their passing with open arms, but he was not so certain that the eldest Monroe would see it that way.

Once the sun reached its zenith, he turned Evan toward town. They would amble there, he decided. The dead need not rush.

Austin watched Monroe Senior for several days. It seemed Austin had some modicum of control over whether someone could see him or not. Soon he would deliver the children to safety.

He slipped into the Monroe household on a breeze that sailed through an open window on the second floor. The smell of food greeted him. Somewhere distant, he felt hunger. Whether lingering instinct or true need, he didn't know. He followed the aroma down the stairs.

The opulent dining area was ready to receive the family. Purple-and-green damask wallpaper and dark velvet cushions on the fine dining chairs kept the light dim even for the gas lamps turned up.

He was like a gas lamp. If he turned himself all the way down, he was able to pass through doors and walls easily, float through windows on the wind. If he turned himself up, brighter, he was a solid form, able to touch things—and people, as he discovered.

The family was seated. Food was served. Austin was hungry.

Austin wandered behind Monroe Senior's wife, a woman whom he had never seen. She was dark of hair and fair of skin, though it was sallow that day, perhaps from being kept inside. Austin set his hands on the back of her chair and felt her tense. He turned his lamp up. The woman turned but didn't see him. Perhaps she was ignorant of the situation.

Monroe Senior dropped his fork, startled, his jowls quivering. Strange what a fine collar concealed. Austin stood and watched him, deep in thought as to whether he should help the eldest along in his gluttony.

No, not yet.

He left the dining room, only half conscious that Monroe Senior's eyes followed him from the room.

The feeling of righteous indignation persisted. Why would he be back if not to right the wrongs that had been done to him? It was a chance to set things right, to put Warren back on the right track.

He paced through the elder Monroe's home, lost in thought. He had not seen Evelyn since he had passed on. He wanted to see her, but he didn't want to frighten her. And there was so much still to be done. Everything needed to be in place first.

After dinner, Monroe Senior and his family prepared to go out. William was at his residence, but Katherine had decided to go out with her children and parents. William could and should be dealt with alone. His was a special case.

Austin watched as William Monroe Senior readied himself. He dropped his necktie several times before asking his wife to pick it up. She did so, commenting that he seemed not himself. She asked if she could have someone fetch the whisky.

William Senior's eyes flicked over to where Austin stood by the bedroom doorway. The man licked his lips and cast a glance back at his wife. He said he didn't know what she meant. It was simply indigestion from the rich meal they had just consumed. Would she say something to the cook about adding so much butter to every meal?

Austin faded through the wall and down toward the stables where the stable hands readied the team for the evening. When he passed through the barn doors, one of the stable boys crossed himself and hid in the nearest stall, though Austin knew he was invisible. Some were just more sensitive to the unearthly, as he had been when his mother appeared to him those years ago.

A general feeling of unease pervaded the stable after his arrival though. The horses stamped restlessly, and the barn cats and dogs ran away from his wake. Animals sensed far more than their human masters, though few could listen.

He watched them ready the carriage. He was poised, prepared for action.

The family ascended into the carriage, and then the driver ushered the team into the street. They would miss the show if they didn't hurry.

The horses didn't like Austin's presence. They pulled at their trappings, tails whipping, ears twitching, eyes rolling. Had his parents been given any signs that their carriage was doomed that day? Did their trusted Friesians give them any warnings? Perhaps they had been restless but unable to say that someone had gently placed sprigs of barbs from the honey locust under their chest straps, so the thorns pressed harder the more the horses moved. His father had used the durable wood in their home, crafting the railings and balusters from it, but the thorns were a beast to deal with. Monroe the Senior had used the wood himself in his home not long after, impressed with its quality. He had commented to Austin's father about the thorns.

Perhaps they had sensed it. His parents likely would have died anyway.

The Monroe horses snorted and shied as Austin and Evan danced by. They would be missing their show that night. And every eve after.

Austin pushed Evan just far enough ahead of the carriage that the driver spotted them and cried out. But even then, it was too late.

Austin grabbed one of the long lead lines and yanked. The driver lost his grip on it, crying out.

Austin's presence alone spooked the horses, but his cries and Evan's speed spurred them on. Faster and faster they went, out of town and toward the prairie.

As he drew back alongside the carriage, he caught a glimpse of himself in the vehicle's windows. How odd. There was no head on his shoulders. He reached up to pat his face and could touch it, but nothing was there in his reflection.

Evan's reflection also looked different. Bones protruded where they had not before. In life the great horse had been muscular and sleek. And his eyes, which had been dark and lively in life, shifted from ghostly white to red as Austin watched. Was that how they appeared to everyone else?

Spooks and haunts they were now, nothing else to these God-fearing people of the dirt. Austin feared God too but only if he didn't do what he knew he had been sent back to do. They needed fresh beginnings, all of them.

Monroe the Senior hollered something at Austin about damning him to hell again, but it didn't make sense. This was no hellish venture. This was righteous. Something he could only name as power rushed over him. Gone was the slow and steady, inch by inch. Now that his purpose was clear, action was swift.

Near the bridge, he urged the carriage horses faster. They were foaming at the mouth, and their hides were lathered with cold sweat. The carriage's axle groaned, and the wheels threatened to break apart at the next rut.

The driver lashed out with his whip and long crop, but it passed through Austin and Evan as if through dust. Austin clung to the long lead lines, focused only on getting to the crossing.

Austin urged Evan closer to the carriage horses, who wanted nothing to do with Evan's strange form. The great horse bumped into the hip of the lead horse and jarred the entire enterprise off the road at the crossing.

Instead of rushing onto the bridge, they crashed through the brush near the lip of the cliffs. An owl screeched and launched itself, its wide feathery wingspan stretching into the evening sky.

Austin heard the cries as momentum carried the team over the edge of the cliffs. He and Evan jumped with them.

The horses and carriage made a slow, graceful arc through the air. The horses treaded the air. The carriage fell. The entire show buckled in the middle, and then the carriage dragged the horses down, and the horses dragged the carriage down, and there was a great cacophony of animal screams and breaking trees. Dust and rock and dirt and trees and scrub were disturbed.

A flock of bluebirds were startled out of their late-fall dunk in the water at the bottom of the cliffs. They exploded upward in a blue cloud, through the torn trees and into the chilled air that echoed with what, to them, sounded like trees falling during a great storm.

Austin and Evan reappeared at the mouth of the bridge. Without looking back, Austin urged Evan toward town as dusk turned toward twilight, and the air turned purple, ready to burst.

65

Tuesday, October 27th

Olivia pored over the removed journal pages. She had missed something, and it was the perfect way to spend a day cloistered in the apartment after her early morning class, which Evelyn taught with ease again. If Olivia had another hallucination out in public, she might hurt herself or someone else. She and Evelyn had seemed to reach an accord for the moment. When Olivia told her to move aside, so she could handle a situation, she did. And when Evelyn suggested she take the reins, Olivia thought about it before she obliged.

The pages with crisscrossed entries were difficult to read, made more difficult by Evelyn's animated interruptions. Olivia was more in control again, annoyed once more by the immaturity the woman displayed.

"You wanted me to find the pages," Olivia hissed. She regretted it only because they hadn't given her any clues as to where Austin's head might be.

I did, yes. But, oh, I had forgotten the pain!

Olivia rolled her eyes and tried not to think unkind thoughts about the woman who shared her headspace. The woman could rest more easily (and quietly), once this business was taken care of.

> Today William took me out of the house into town.
>
> Today I ate the crumbs from William's plate after he had finished. He said I grew too round with child.
>
> Today William got me a bicycle!
>
> Today William's eyes were strange and red. I thought him mad at first, but he says it is only the smoke on the spring prairie. It so irritates his eyes.
>
> Today William droned on. More Schneider building construction and renovation. I grow weary of the talk. The great limestone "bricks" are such and such size, greater than any other building for 500 miles. They will not allow the building to be taller than the Practical Agriculture Building, which I cannot help but think would be where I should attend courses, should I be allowed. He goes on about these things so much I almost feel as if he boasts, so I may suffer to hear about what I cannot have. He is simply eager to see the completion of a project in which he has invested much money and time, but I cannot help but feel envious.
>
> William unaccounted for these three days.
>
> More talk of Schneider's building. William may soon talk me out of my desire to attend university with how he

> makes me hate him so for going there every day to supervise their renovations.
>
> William says he may take me to visit the construction!
>
> Out walking today. To stretch my legs, to feel the prairie alive beneath me is such a splendid thing! Many flowers to press.

The entries went on and on, some scribbled so quickly or pressed so hard with the pen that they were illegible. There were references in code that Olivia suspected were about Austin, some combination of French and another language she didn't recognize. With Evelyn's eyes like a pair of glasses behind her own, however, she saw the shadow of the words.

> My love, my heart. Rode Ebony today onto the prairie and felt so free. Fell into Austin's arms at his gate.

So many such words made Olivia's heart ache for the woman.

"He speaks of the Schneider building so often," Olivia said, afraid to say more about the Austin entries.

Yes, but why would he risk the journey there? I cannot see him doing more than simply dropping it into the compost.

Olivia wasn't so certain, especially after Evan went to such lengths to show her what he knew. How he knew, she could not put together yet, but she was thankful nonetheless.

After an unfruitful hour meditating on the entries and the various photographs strewn around her room, Evelyn suggested that Olivia go check on her mother—take the air, as it were. Olivia agreed that was wise. Perhaps the house would offer a fresh perspective. She had all the puzzle pieces now, but how they fit together needed finessing.

It was suspiciously quiet at the house.

"Mom?" Olivia called. Nothing.

The television in the den was on. Olivia poked her head in. Her mother was asleep in the recliner, her latest knitting project half-finished in her lap.

Olivia retrieved five mugs and a stack of plates from the side table next to her mother and carried them to the kitchen. The sink was overflowing with dishes. The fridge was ajar and emitted a smell that Olivia was afraid to investigate. At least there was water and food in the dog's bowl, but Olivia hadn't seen her mom's Yorkie yet.

Guilt stabbed her. She had been there in the last few days, hadn't she? Surely she would have done the dishes while she was there.

She tackled the dishes, the spoiled food in the fridge, and checked on her mother's pills and the dog. Satisfied that she'd made up for lost time at the house, Olivia settled onto the rag rug at the foot of her bed and spread the puzzle pieces out again.

A photograph had gotten stuck in the stack of pages Olivia had grabbed from Simon's desk. She couldn't imagine Simon not taking proper care of such an old piece of history, but he wasn't Simon.

It was a photograph of a group of men. Evelyn sneered at the photograph when she saw William in the group and set it aside, but Olivia picked it up and inspected it more closely. He was standing with a group of other men before a stone wall in a building. Tiny cursive writing said, "Finally complete! Auguste, Holtz, and John Schneider, David Vogt, Brady Flax, William Monroe III."

"I recognize that!" Olivia exclaimed. It had deteriorated without upkeep, but she knew about where the photograph had been taken. Which stone wall in the building was another question, but there weren't many to choose from.

Excitement overshadowed Evelyn's protest that they not go off too quickly and get themselves caught or put in a bad position. Olivia readied for bed and let the anticipation fuel her.

For the first time that month, she had something that looked like a plan, at least for the next day. As she passed into sleep, the sound of a fire crackling down to embers reached her. She smiled in her near sleep and pulled the heavy quilts around her, then snuggled closer to the snoring warmth next to her.

66

11:00 A.M., October 31, 1903

The Monroe household was empty. Austin wasn't surprised. William had holed himself up in the sheriff's office after the long funeral for his father. Austin was surprised the funeral still went on after his sojourn back to the gray country. Four days was unheard of. William wouldn't be there for long though. If he cared for his children at all, he would return home.

Austin ghosted through the front door and into the foyer. A dizzying pain told him that something wanted to prevent him from entering but didn't yet possess the power to do so. It reaffirmed his belief that Monroe carried a devil with him.

A group of people spilled out of a room off the kitchen. A young woman carried the two youngest. The eldest had a hand in the crook of her elbow.

The woman gasped and nearly dropped the two little ones when she crossed herself at the sight of Austin.

"Where is she?" Austin asked.

"Who, sir?" He saw fear in her but also curiosity. It had to be Alyssa, in whom Evelyn had confided.

"Evelyn. Miss Evelyn."

"She is gone from here. Did you not hear the bells?"

The pain heightened, but this time it came from within. "The bells were for Monroe Senior."

Alyssa shushed the smaller of the two children she carried. Her face grew flushed, and her voice wavered. "The bells were for Miss Evelyn."

"No," Austin said. "No, I don't believe they were."

"Sir," Alyssa protested. "You may go see for yourself in the cemetery."

"It is a sham."

Alyssa shook her head, her face red, the tears quick to come. "Sir, I found her. You must accept my deepest regrets . . ."

"It is a sham," Austin repeated. "I know it is. But I must move the children before I come for her."

"Where?" she asked.

"Maggie and Evette." Austin knew he probably looked imposing, but he didn't care. He needed to get the children to safety before he went to find William. And Evelyn. She was not gone; he could feel it in the depths of his soul. He had promised he would return for her, and he would make good on that promise.

Alyssa nodded, then bent down to talk to the eldest. How she had grown since Austin had seen the last photograph of her. He heard Alyssa tell her that she must be good for him and do as Austin said.

"Who are you?" the little girl asked. She had fine brown hair and looked up at him with her mother's eyes and his same slightly off-center nose. It would be endearing on her face as she grew older, not intimidating like it was on his. Sarah, after his mother's second name. Evelyn had wanted it to be her first name, but Austin hadn't wanted to take such a risk. His heart ached.

"I'm a friend," he said.

Young William watched him warily. The boy was young but observant. He had William's lean jawline, even for his youth. It made Austin's anger simmer again. It was not the boy's fault that his father was a monster, nor was it his mother's fault that she had birthed him.

"Papa gone," the child said, matter of fact.

"Yes," Austin replied. William didn't deserve these children, but it was no longer Austin's right to make that judgement. He had done nearly all he had come back to do, but above all, he must not harm the children, no matter whose they were. God or the devil would take care of them in their time.

"Mother was sad," Sarah said. The little girl reached up and let young Ethan squeeze her childlike fingers. It twisted Austin's heart. If Evelyn wasn't holed up in the house, Monroe would have taken her somewhere he knew she'd be safe. The sheriff's office, the surveyor's office, whichever building on campus he recently had a hand in. Austin would take the children to safety and then return for her. There were only so many places William could have hidden her.

"Yes, she can be," Austin said.

There was that twist again. And a spark of anger. The child had no inkling of the half of it. For William to do what he had done at the end . . . well, Austin would handle it now.

Alyssa herded the children out toward the yard where Evan waited. She kissed them and told them again to be good for Austin. Austin had to wonder how much she knew. She didn't say, only helped Austin with his wishes.

He was able to mount Evan with Sarah, then reached down for William and Ethan. He rode with the oldest in front of him and the other two securely in a woven papoose basket that lay over either side of Evan's withers.

"Be out of the house by nightfall," Austin warned.

"Sir . . ." Alyssa began.

"Be away from here by then. This cursed place must no longer stand."

Alyssa's reply was quiet assent. She watched him and the children go with hands clutched in her apron.

They could ride through the woods without being seen. The roads would be dangerous, watched. So would the canyon bridge, but he hoped he would be able to cross without being harassed.

The going was faster than he expected. Young William and Ethan were quiet for most of the ride, perhaps out of fear, though little Sarah exclaimed at every pretty flower and weed she saw. They had never seen the prairie. Austin would make certain they were allowed to see it whenever they wished.

It seemed he carried the prairie with him as they flew, but the season was changing to winter.

By the time he reached the Weatherford residence, Evan was galloping so fast that sparks flew from his iron shoes, and flames licked at the ground from the ends of his feathers.

Esther Weatherford cried out when she saw him. "Devil! Begone from this place!"

Johnathan was tight-lipped at the horseman's presence. His eyes saw the cargo that Austin carried.

Austin longed to tell them all that had transpired, but the time was long gone for that. He remained silent in the face of the curses they hurled at him.

Maggie met him in the prairie beyond the spring house with her own mount. She didn't recoil at his presence, but a shudder ran through her when she brushed against his cloak as he handed her the children. He gave her a sealed letter, which she accepted delicately, careful not to touch him. He wanted to ask where they would go, but he didn't need to know now that he, too, was going to other places. They could go where they willed.

"Maggie, I cannot thank you enough. If anyone found out, if anyone knew . . ." he trailed off when she shushed him.

"We are happy to help you. You have forever been a friend of the family."

Austin nodded, "Thank you. Please, I'll need you out of the house by nightfall."

Maggie must have known. "We will make sure the house is empty. I'm with Evette now anyway."

Austin turned Evan to leave and felt the very fabric of whatever held him there pull and sway. He didn't have much time.

"Oh, Mr. Hearth?"

"Yes?"

"Your mother stopped by today. I had thought . . . well, I had thought . . .. She said if I saw you to tell you that Olivia will help you. She seemed in a hurry, and I didn't question it." Maggie had to know how long ago his mother had died, but neither she nor Austin said a word in that direction.

He thanked Maggie again for her help and then took off across the prairie behind the Weatherford estate. His heart hurt with what needed done, but even the thought of it licked at the anger he held in check. He tightened his hands on the reins. He would not fail Evelyn or her children.

67

Wednesday, October 28th

When Olivia walked out the door that morning to drive to campus, she was excited and oblivious of her surroundings. Her step and her burdens felt light for once, and even Evelyn was quietly cheery.

A screech that her brain momentarily tried to identify as some kind of bird or a hawk split the silence. A flurry of black and red pounded up the driveway, and the nightmare horse uttered its screech again.

Olivia scrambled on the gravel drive back toward the house. She made it up onto the front porch just as the pair slammed into the corner of the garage behind her. The sound of splintering wood seemed a fitting addition to the cacophony the two made.

She slammed the front door, but they didn't follow her onto the porch. Anxious sweat soaked the top of her corset and the underarms of her blouse.

Once she caught her breath, she ran to the back door and out onto the deck. In the frantic haze, she thought she might trick the horse and rider as she had once tricked the mean chickens at Ann's grandparents' house. If she slammed the front door but left quietly out the back, she could trick the chickens into thinking she was still at the front door.

But the duo wasn't fooled. They came barreling around the side of the house. The nightmare horse kicked up great clods of dirt with its cracked black hooves. In the daylight, it looked even more terrifying. Great hunks of flesh hung from the places its bones had fully protruded from its hide. Its black hair was matted and stuck out from its red skin in all directions. Wounds on its haunches oozed. Flies buzzed about its face even though the temperature outside had cooled. Olivia realized with sick fascination that the animal had decayed over the course of the month.

It reared and planted its front hooves on the first step to the back deck, and Olivia shrank back inside the house. She didn't feel safe with only a sliding glass door between herself and that thing. But when he turned and made for the dugout, she couldn't stay still. Evelyn screamed inside her for the last place she wanted that thing to be. There were too many precious items inside that they both wanted safe.

Olivia wrenched open the door. "You stay the fuck away from here!"

Horse and rider turned back to her. Olivia stepped out onto the deck. She grabbed a brick from the stack that held down her mother's table on the back porch and heaved it at the horse, which had made headway back toward her. The brick glanced off the thing's hip and sent it staggering sideways several steps. It hadn't expected retaliation and didn't seem to know what to do about it.

With the second brick, the imposter raised a hand as if to shield his face from the blow. That brick missed him. The third missile hit him in the ribs. He uttered a very human cry of pain.

"Get out of here!" she yelled.

Her mother had appeared at the door without a word and watched the scene. Olivia was about to warn her away and continue her assault with the fourth brick when the woman whom Olivia had never seen move faster than an amble unless she was trying to get away from Olivia when she was found wandering darted out the door.

"Mom!" Olivia screamed, running after her. She watched in horror as her mother went straight up to the creature and grabbed its reins. It seemed she was without fear.

"Go!" she cried. She yanked on the reins with a strength that was not her own. The thing's head was drawn down as if bowing to her, unable to move or strike at anything. Perhaps Olivia's mother had Evelyn beside her, or Austin or someone else who had driven her mother to her mental breaking point so many years ago. In that moment of held breath, Olivia understood what had caused her mother's situation.

This had to end.

Olivia ran back inside, but a clattering outside the door froze her, and her breath caught in her throat. He couldn't come in there. He couldn't. He was out back being held by her mother.

She grabbed a large knife from the kitchen and headed to the door. When she looked through the peephole, it was only Evan who stared back at her. His horsy eyes were calm as he whuffed and chomped idly at his bit. Olivia tossed the knife onto the couch and opened the door, greeting the horse that she had once regarded with fear. Seeing him brought her more relief in that moment than Austin would have. Evan would not let them get her.

"Evan! Have you come to take me? Where's Austin?"

Evan whooshed out the air in his lungs as if he were exasperated and then sank to his knees, so Olivia could clamber onto his back. She clamped her fingers into his mane and clung to his sides with her thighs.

"Don't let me fall, OK, Evan?" Olivia could feel his huge muscles moving beneath her. The horse was as solid as a rock, and even though she knew she could trust the smart animal, he still frightened her. She had seen what he could do, what he was capable of at Austin's bidding.

Evan made another noise that sounded strangely like assent and then picked up the pace. He moved his head left and right as if checking his surroundings. Then he snorted and stretched his legs out as he ran faster.

Time shifted strangely as they rode, and Olivia felt the day and time wane even though Evan galloped effortlessly. Sunset came on. Perhaps the nightmare horse could not follow them that way. She didn't know.

Olivia held on tighter when they left the road and charged into the prairie. Evan took the cattle fences with a grace that didn't match the jarring landing Olivia felt. She was not a horse rider.

Finally, the nightmare horse appeared behind them. The dark duo slowly gained on them, but they were far enough behind that Olivia didn't feel worried yet. The elation from her brick throwing stayed with her. She'd peg them with her shoes if she had to.

Ahead, Olivia recognized the trees that ran along the sides of the canyon. There had been no bridge over the canyon since Evelyn's lifetime. For Olivia, there had always been the road that wended around where the canyon ended to the east. But now a covered bridge greeted them.

Olivia looked down. She had grown so used to the change that she hadn't noticed the pinch of the corset or the feeling of lace at her neck and wrists. Evelyn's pendant bounced against her breastbone with each of Evan's strides.

They glided onto the wooden bridge, the sudden change in the sound of Evan's hooves welcome to her ears. From the soft thudding of the prairie earth and the *shush-shush* of his legs in the grasses and low thickets to the loud clopping on wood and then back again.

Behind them the dark pair came to a shuddering halt at the entrance to the bridge. Olivia watched in fascination as the man whipped the animal, but the horse dug its heels in and would not go a step farther. The nightmare horse and his rider could not cross the canyon bridge with them. That would gain Olivia some time. She bent low over Evan's neck and thanked him.

Once in town, Evan took them through residential areas, over fences, and around pools covered up for the season. They ghosted through more stands of trees than Olivia could count. She didn't know there was so much dense growth between the north end of town and campus. They plowed through branches and bushes, but Olivia didn't care. At least they were out of sight of those who would be on the road. She clung to Evan's neck and closed her eyes, trying to hang on to the galloping horse.

The beat of his hooves beneath her vibrated through her chest, and she clamped her teeth together to stop their rattling. Evan's muscles worked hard as she felt him slow and speed up accordingly. When he turned and pivoted on a hind leg, he pushed forward with a force that surprised Olivia.

When Olivia feared that she couldn't hold on for much longer, she felt Evan slow, and she lifted her head to see where they were. They were certainly on campus, and the far side judging by the woods that were on Olivia's left. Evan stopped, frozen with his head erect and his ears perked forward as he listened to something that Olivia could not hear. She could see, however, that Evan had indeed spotted something in the distance.

It was hard to see at night when the only light was from the lampposts on campus, but she could make out a figure on a horse, and she felt her body seize up. Smart animal that he was, Evan had stopped in a patch of deep shadows, his head turned to see what the other figure was doing. Who would win the race if he saw them? Would he chase them off the cliffs, or would the bridge appear again for them? Poor Simon. Was it as terrifying for him to watch what was happening as it was for her to experience it?

Olivia imagined—no, fantasized—calling the police, as she had often dreamed of doing throughout October. She tried to imagine how they would respond to reports of a headless figure menacing girls on campus.

Laugh, probably. They surely received hundreds of prank calls during the Halloween season. But someone must have seen them before sunset

Finally, the figure on the horse moved away from them. Evan let out a great whoosh of air, and Olivia allowed herself a sigh of relief as well. She set her eyes down the path that led to the photography building.

"Let's go, please," she urged her charge. The cold hit her now that she wasn't simply being jostled on Evan's back.

The Schneider building loomed before them, and Olivia tensed, sure that Evan could feel it too. She felt helpless and helpful at the same time.

Her breath hung in the air, and Evan's formed a cloud about his face, so still was the night air. Olivia slid down from Evan's back, her legs feeling like wet photo paper. She petted the horse's soft face and placed a gentle kiss on his warm nose. "Thank you, Evan," she whispered. "If you'll wait for me, that would be wonderful. I won't be gone long. I promise."

She didn't want to be stranded with a skull in the middle of campus in the dead of night. It wouldn't look good to anyone—casual passersby or campus security. *Just brushing up on my Hamlet, officer.*

Moving quickly, she mounted the steps to the main doors of the photography building, pulling her keys out of her pocket as she went. She felt for the key with the straighter edges and was still slowing to a stop when she opened the door. She shut it behind her and locked it again, then paused to let her eyes adjust to the dark.

Shadows existed at night that weren't present during the day. Tricks of the light sent to terrorize her. The halls to her left and right were lit with the warm light from gas lamps outside, but the there was no light straight ahead of her where the tall staircase to the second floor stood. Without a fancy light on her phone like Ann had on her Nokia, she'd have to traipse up to her studio and then back down.

She felt her way over to the staircase and then ascended, clutching the banister, so she didn't trip and fall. What if he was there in the dark, watching her? What if he was a ghost like Austin and could manifest a physical form when needed? Oh, God, she was going to hyperventilate.

She closed her eyes when she reached the second floor and slid along the wall, knowing the way by heart. She reached her studio and let herself in. She felt around for the flashlight and, locating it, turned it on and let its light wash the hall. Then she locked up her studio and headed back to the stairwell, descending as quickly as she could.

Finally, she reached the lowest level: the basement and its winding maze back to the two doors that were the portal to her destination. She would start with what she knew was the oldest part of the building and work her way back up. The wall in the photograph was seared into her mind's eye, but she had slid the photo into her back pocket anyway.

She reached the doors that led to the archives in only a few minutes and fumbled with her keys until she opened the first door and then stood before the old door that led into the archives. Taking a deep breath, she unlocked the second door and stepped inside, darkness engulfing her.

The flashlight gave her trouble for a few moments, and she had a moment of panic before she got the thing to work. She found the light switch and flooded the room with light. She sighed and then began working her way around the room.

Halfway across the room, a noise stopped her in her tracks. The hair on her arms stood up. It sounded like . . . like clicking. Then the lights went out. Olivia felt the darkness close in on her. What was that noise? Where was it coming from? Was it getting closer? Did it know she was there?

Beneath the shimmer of fear that ran over her, she turned on her flashlight and forced herself to move toward the epicenter of the noise, somewhere on the far side of the room and close to the old stone walls. She couldn't see anything that was causing it but was cautious nonetheless.

Then she realized what the sound was. Teeth. Austin's teeth clicking in his one-hundred-year-old skull somewhere in the room. She had no words for the strange fear that she felt at that moment. She stopped a few steps from the last row of boxes of photographs and tried to locate the exact source of the sound. Moving to her left, it grew quieter, so she moved to her right, toward the other wall. When she had moved too far, it grew quieter again, so she moved closer toward the wall straight in front of her.

What had she noticed when she was first down in the archives? How decrepit it was. The plaster was falling off the walls. Some walls were limestone only, crumbling in the humidity. What an easy place to stash something. She pulled out the photograph. There, behind the men, was the same wall, covered with plaster decades into the future.

She leapt forward, listening along the wall until she thought she heard where the sound was the loudest. She stashed the photograph in her back pocket with a shaking hand.

She tried to peel away the stones that made up the wall, and some of the mortar came out in a shower of pebbly crumbles, but it wasn't fast enough for her. She grabbed a metal folding chair and, taking a deep breath, swung it at the wall.

A shower of rock exploded outward. The stones were loosened from their places, and more mortar fell out with the chunks of the stone. Olivia swung at the wall again and again, loosening more and more of the mortar and stones. The sound reverberated through the large room and probably throughout the basement as well. In her frenzy though, she didn't care how much noise she made.

Another hard swing brought an entire limestone brick tumbling onto the floor. It barely missed Olivia's foot, and she skipped out of its way, dropping the chair, so she could use her hands. She dug at the wall with her fingers, pulling stone after stone as a cloud of pulverized mortar rose around her in the dim light. The photographs, quiet in their boxes, listened to her tear at the wall. Those photographs had finally given up their secrets.

Stones came loose at an alarming rate, but Olivia didn't care if the entire wall came crashing down, as long as she could get to what she sought.

Sweat ran down her face in rivulets. She had been so cold not twenty minutes previous. She felt feverish now.

She let the dust settle and then scanned the hole in the wall with her flashlight, looking for some sign of white bone. She saw none, but she was sure she was close. The clicking had stopped, but that didn't mean anything. She would keep searching until she found Austin's head.

Moving down the wall, she pulled stones loose more carefully, examining the space behind each one with a methodical eye. Finally, she pulled away a stone that revealed the top portion of an open space in the wall. Her heart in her throat, she removed the stones around and below it. Five minutes later, she was staring at something round that was wrapped in decaying red fabric. She reached into the small chamber that had been cut out of the earth and grasped the decaying end of the cloth. Taking a deep breath, she slowly removed it, revealing what was underneath.

A bare, grayish skull stared back at her. Olivia noted the skull's fragility and obvious lack of skin or hair. It had been more than a decade since Olivia had taken any kind of science class that required she work with skulls or other human bones, but she knew what she was looking at.

Taking a deep breath, she reached into the chamber and carefully picked up the skull and several parts of human spine, cradling them in her shaking hands. The skull's jaw moved, and the teeth clicked together three times.

She left the archives with the skull cradled close to her body. She didn't bother to lock the doors, but she promised herself that she would return to do it later. She couldn't afford to waste time.

She took the stairs two at a time and then paused at the entrance to the photography building, looking out into the circle of lamplight outside. After a quiet moment, she slipped out the door.

"Evan!" she whispered. If the imposter saw her now, she would be dead.

The soft sounds of a horse's hooves greeted her ears, and she shrank back against the building until she saw the tall horse appear from one side of the building. He spotted her in the shadows and hurried toward her. Olivia went down the stairs to him, reminded of her second close encounter with Austin. How she had distrusted him. How Evan had scared her. What besides the impostor would frighten her now?

She hadn't thought things through though. How was she going to get the skull back to her apartment, so she could get her vehicle? She knew it was too far for Evan to carry her all the way to the gym and Austin's grave, but she was bound to either drop the skull or crush it if she attempted to carry it back with her while riding Evan. She stood there for a moment, unsure.

"Evan, how am I going to do this?" Her voice was a nervous whisper, and she looked around anxiously, searching for any sign of other people. She had been lucky thus far.

Evan snorted quietly and shook out his mane, then bent to his knees, an invitation for her to get onto his back. Still somewhat skeptical, she did as he suggested, holding the skull as close as she could to her body as she swung her leg over the giant horse's back. If she dropped the skull, and it shattered into a thousand pieces, well . . . she ought to just throw herself off the cliffs and be done with it all.

Evan stood slowly, giving Olivia time to situate herself and get a good grip on his mane with her free hand. When she whispered to him that she had a good grasp, he started off at a slow trot, taking the smoothest path while staying hidden. Olivia gripped him with her thighs as tightly as she dared, not caring that her muscles were already cramped from the previous ride.

Careful. No mistakes. Her voice or Evelyn's, it no longer mattered. On this they agreed.

They reached the apartment unmolested. Olivia had started to think of it as a halfway point to her mother's house. She could hide the skull there, where it was less likely to be disturbed, until she could come back for it and return it to Austin's shoulders.

She was ready to drop the lease though. Ann would be pissed, but she didn't care. It was just one more thing stressing her, and now that she was so tantalizingly close to getting the final payment from the city for the showing, she could drop that expense in exchange for a mortgage.

As she carefully set the skull inside an old running shoe box, wrapped in the softest cardigan she could find, she hoped she would live long enough that she *could* see Ann pissed at her again.

Still moving around in her frenzied excitement, she texted Simon. Tomorrow, she could show him what she had found.

But not that, Evelyn reminded her.

"Yes, not that," she murmured.

She could present her case no matter who might be listening, Simon or Not Simon. Then things would shake out as they would.

Her excitement and fear felt like a bubble around her, and she had found the calm center. She knew that itself was a kind of precipice, where one breath of wind off the prairie could send her one direction or the other into light or darkness or that strange place between that had no name.

68

5:00 P.M., October 31, 1903

William knew Austin would come. The entire town knew. They needn't have been afraid though. It was only William whom he was after now.

In the days before, Austin learned that Harry Whittaker was to become the acting sheriff. Jeremiah Vogt, one of the youngest sons of his closest neighbors, who had all come to help when his homestead was ablaze, had been named a deputy. Apparently, they had both helped bury his headless body. Where, he didn't know. They didn't say, but they spoke of it. Poor Jeremiah. He was only looking to do good, caught up in their politics. He should have known better. He would atone, just as Harry had.

After he had delivered the children to Evette, Austin watched, with anger consuming him, as William, half mad, eyes still shot through with red, had made an announcement in the dusty town square. That he had left the security of the sheriff's office was all Austin cared about.

The church bells still echoed in the streets. All this Austin had watched from a distance, knowing he was visible, a reminder of the power he held. They could not touch him, but he could touch them. Touch them, trample them, remove them from their seats of power. And finally, rescue Evelyn.

Evan cried out and rose onto his hind legs. He received an answering cry from the crowd, who turned as one to see him at the far end of the street. They were a sea of black, so many of them dressed in mourning. Austin wondered how much they had been able to find of Monroe Senior's family in the canyon. Among the bodies of horses and the twisted wood and metal of the carriage, not much would have been distinguishable.

William pointed at him, nonplussed by the display. "Look! The man who killed my wife is back for more!"

There was an angry cry from the crowd, but they did nothing, still wary of him.

Austin didn't believe William's words, so he ignored them, assuming William only wished to goad him into doing something foolish. William could not do it during Austin's life, and he would not get anywhere trying to do it after his death.

The crowd soon grew restless, perhaps tired by the long days of funerals. They dispersed in Austin's wake as he let Evan plod toward the far end of town.

In the late-afternoon light, the sun threw strange rays through the dust picked up by the wind. The day was warm for the end of the year, and the air had the taste of a spring storm in it. It tasted like a twister.

The closer he got to the Monroe home, the more urgency he felt. He would free Evelyn from her prison, and William would pay for his crimes.

He didn't intend to go in with so much speed, but the need to finish everything overcame him. He directed Evan toward the door and threw every ounce of his being toward it.

They both entered the Monroe household in a great crash and shower of splinters. William, disheveled and red eyed, stood at the far end of the foyer.

"I'm here for Evelyn," Austin announced.

William looked both dumbfounded and amused to find a dead man on a horse in his foyer.

"Where is Evelyn?"

The laugh that sprang from Monroe was bitter. "Don't you know? She's dead and buried! Dead and buried! See how well you saved her?"

"No," Austin said, not comprehending.

"Yes," William hissed, though the sound was not his. "Did you think she would live after what she went through? I did, stupidly. And look where we are now."

"You killed her."

Red was flooded with brown, then back to red. "I don't think you could call it that."

Anger flooded Austin. When William—or whatever looked like William—turned to run, Austin did the first thing he could think of: he grabbed the rope from his pommel. The rope snapped and sparked as he flicked it toward the man running down the hall. It caught William around his middle, and an unearthly scream was rent from the demon inside. Austin pulled the rope taut.

He would drag this thing to hell. Monroe was a sonofabitch, but he wasn't evil. No. The thing within him was, or as nearly as Austin could tell. And if it turned out to be the other way around, he would settle the matter for both of them.

He backed Evan out of the house, ignoring the unholy sounds that came from William as he was pulled from his home. The flames at Evan's feet licked at the rug, spread to the wall near the staircase.

Once outside, Evan turned on his heel toward the prairie hills. William and his demonic counterpart stumbled and fell to the ground. He growled and hissed and spat like a cat, inhuman sounds coming from him. The thing struggled to stand but could not with the heavy rope around him.

"Pull," Austin commanded, squeezing his legs and signaling Evan with his body. The horse obeyed. Through town they dragged their heavy load. Though Evan was not living, he struggled at first with the weight he towed. Further proof that their burden was not human. Austin urged Evan to go faster. They needed to reach the canyon crossing soon.

"Please, Mr. Hearth, stop! He is gone!" William cried.

When Austin spared him a look back, he was greeted with a grin too wide for a human to manage and a mouth full of teeth too sharp and long for any man. Austin cursed the thing for making him slow for even a moment.

Near the bridge, William's body separated from the thing within him, and then Austin only dragged a snarling creature covered in tar that left dark, sticky lines on the road. Austin gave the crumpled body only a glance. They needed more speed.

"Evan, come now!" Austin hollered into the wind. Austin dug his heels into his horse's side, asking for the last of his energy.

Flames burst forth from Evan's hooves again, and the great horse became a burning beacon, a harbinger of death. They galloped onto the bridge, igniting the wood in a great burst of heat. The demon screeched as the fire licked at him, and Austin wondered fleetingly why that was so. But this was the fire of God, not Lucifer.

So consuming was the fire that it reached to the other side before they were halfway across. It roared and swallowed everything in its path. Then the bridge gave a great groan, and Austin, Evan, and William Monroe's second skin disappeared in a great explosion of fire and smoke.

The papers and announcements in the days to come were sensational. Wichita, Dodge, and Kansas City all picked up on the story eventually. Most assumed it was all sensation. Or perhaps something had happened in the little town on the prairie, and it made for a good story, but it was of no concern to them at the end of the day.

"The man and his steed broke down the door of the Monroe home and proceeded to rope its only inhabitant, like a cowboy would a calf, and dragged the man from his house. The horseman pulled the man down the main thoroughfare, galloping his animal and dragging his victim behind. The mayor's body was found outside of town, unrecognizable. The skin had been all but stripped from his body."

"I watched the devil himself ride into town that day," one bystander said. "I watched a man and his steed, back from hell itself, try to send this town back to the prairie. But we would not be bested by the devil. We would not succumb to his evil."

There would be no one to tell them otherwise.

69

Thursday, October 29th

Going in to teach the next morning, the night before seemed but a dream. Olivia had woken in a daze on her bedroom floor next to the box in which she'd placed the skull. Her back and legs ached. The sky was growing lighter by the minute, but she felt as if she hadn't slept. The grey skull in the box near her head suggested she hadn't dreamt.

Had anyone seen her? She'd left a mess in the building's basement. Who else had a key? Would they know it was her? Yes, they would know it was her.

Olivia tried compulsively to wipe the soil from her hands. It would not budge. Her hands smelled almost sweet, like an apple that had fallen from the branch and taken up residence on the ground, determined to become one with the earth again.

Gloves, my dear.

"Yes, I should, I know," Olivia murmured. She couldn't touch anything without fear of getting dirt on it. No, it wasn't dirt. It wasn't from

Austin's skull, which she had found dry and safe in the walls of the art building. It was rot. She wiped her hands compulsively on her jeans. It wouldn't go away.

She managed through her early classes, only catching herself wiping her hands on her thighs a dozen times. She had to excuse herself in the middle of her 9:30 class to wash her hands, but she made it through after that with minimal anxiety. Dr. Thurston was not sitting in on the class that day, thank goodness. She had gotten through all that by the skin of her teeth.

She was feeling remarkably good (aside from her hands, which were bothering her constantly, but if she got into a good groove, she didn't notice them *as* much) when there was a knock on her office door. It had become a familiar knock over the last four weeks, one that had at first incited lust and pleasure but now elicited anxiety and worry.

"Olivia?"

She relaxed. It was just Simon, right on time for when he'd agreed to come to her office. Even their knock was different. William tried too hard to sound like a normal person. Simon just sounded like . . . Simon.

When she let him in, there was an awkward moment where she felt the pull to him so strongly that she almost reached out to him. She saw the same in him, but instead she took a step backward.

"Can I show you everything I've found?" Olivia asked, turning toward a great mess of papers, books, and photographs strewn over her desk. She kept her mouth shut about the skull and the journal pages, just as he kept his mouth shut about prowling about on campus looking for her the previous night—and assaulting her in the Monroe house the night before.

EXCITEMENT EVEN GREATER THAN THE DAY IN HIS FAMILY'S attic rushed through Simon and replaced the strange rejection he'd felt just a moment before. It was like she knew he'd found the costume and that he'd done nothing about it.

"There was a lot in the dugout," she said. "I don't know how it all survived the years. I think maybe my mom tossed a lot of it in there recently, but I have no way of knowing. She's been moving things around a lot lately."

Simon looked over the neat piles of old paper, books, and photographs. It was incredible. She had unearthed so much. Perhaps Evette had hidden things in there before the fire. It was unlikely they would ever understand that part at least.

"How is it that you found all of this so easily, and I've spent my entire life looking back at my family tree and poring over books and the internet and haven't gotten further than the turn of the century?"

Olivia shrugged. The gesture made him angry. "I don't know. All these things just seemed to land in my lap. I don't know if that's Evelyn or dumb luck."

"How did you find out that Evette had taken the children and given them to Maggie?"

Olivia shrugged again, and he wanted to shake her. The impulsive thought horrified him—why couldn't he just be patient with her, patient with his thoughts? It wasn't just the thing inside him. He felt it deeper than that. Somewhere lying not so dormant was a propensity toward violence. Or perhaps it was dormant. Perhaps a thing like that could be recognized but still lay sleeping.

"There were some papers in an old copy of Pilgrim's Progress that didn't make sense. So, I dug a little, and there was my mother and Colton, and . . . you know."

"Austin." He watched the flush sweep up her fair face when he said the name. Was Evelyn in there somewhere, listening, reacting?

"Yes," she replied softly and dropped her eyes to the floor, an Evelyn-like gesture. Would the Olivia of a month ago have cast her eyes down like that in apparent modesty? He couldn't remember. They were worlds away from that now.

The thing inside him—the demon, William, whatever—had been quiet that day, but his own anger still bubbled. "How do you know Austin isn't lying to you?"

"Why would he? Half of it is less than savory for him too. Not just William. Or, hell, Evelyn. All of them."

"Olivia." It was a statement. A warning.

"Austin wouldn't lie to me."

"Austin killed a dozen people. He tortured William Monroe."

"They deserved it."

"How can you say that?"

"Look at how they terrorized Austin, his family, his girlfriend, or whatever she was to him. Wouldn't you want revenge?"

"Look, I get that Austin took the law into his own hands because the law failed him. But that doesn't make what he did right."

"I don't care about what *you* think is right. It's not up to us anyway."

Olivia sifted through a pile and handed him a short stack of papers. Simon took them and read greedily. He forced himself to slow down, so he could catch everything. He had to know everything. How had this escaped his knowledge for so long? Had no one been in that dugout since it had all happened? He said as much to Olivia.

"I don't know," she replied. "My mother could have moved things out there, but I don't know that either. Not all of this could have been in the old Weatherford house. It had to have come from other places. I don't know. Austin wasn't there for it, and neither was Evelyn, so they couldn't contribute. I just kept . . . finding, unearthing things that put all the puzzle pieces together."

"It was well known that Evette was unable to have children," Simon whispered as he scanned the rest of the letter. It had no signature, but the telltale signs of the Weatherford girls' handwriting was all over the page—curlicues in each "s," the elaborate capital letters. Even the slight slant he knew was from the somewhat crooked writing desk they sat at.

"So, how do we know which children were Austin's and which were William's?" she asked, already knowing the answer. The woman inside her screamed it even though she had not been there.

My children lived! They lived! It no longer matters who! William made me think they were gone, dead, worse, but they lived! To know it instinctively is one thing, my dear child, but to see it confirmed is another!

"I can only assume they were Austin and Evelyn's," Simon said excitedly. "Maybe all three of them. With what we know now, we can say that with almost absolute certainty. But we would only know that without doubt if we compared your DNA to hers."

Olivia stared at him for a moment, her face unreadable. "I won't submit to DNA testing."

Simon didn't understand. "You have an obligation, a duty, to this town and its history. You have an obligation to yourself to know the truth."

The words seemed to sting her. "No, I don't. I'm done with all this. This has to end."

Simon felt the anger snaking through him. Why couldn't she see how important this was? "This means everything for this town! You should feel a duty to do this!"

"I owe this town nothing! They've done nothing for me these last one hundred years!"

The hair on Simon's neck stood up. Olivia's voice had taken on a curious double quality. He fought to find his own voice. "Then we'll never know, I suppose."

"But we do," Olivia said, her voice still strangely musical. "We do know. You're a Monroe. How is that a coincidence?"

"I have searched my entire adult life and never found a connection. How can you say something like that?"

Olivia pawed through another pile on the table and handed him two pieces of paper. Both were for name changes, but one had been altered. Simon looked them over and then sat down heavily. "Oh my God.

Westford. Weatherford. Not very creative but changed enough to make everything go away. And Monroe. Monroe must have just kept on, but they changed first names. My grandfather . . . my grandfather . . ." Simon's voice trailed off as he stared at the paper. He looked up at Olivia. "My grandfather would be William Monroe the Fourth. But where is that name change? Do you have more papers?"

Olivia was changed when he looked at her. She carried herself differently. Evelyn. Before him was Evelyn, not Olivia. There was a different quality about her skin, her hair, and her eyes. They were nearly identical except for a few of God's details. She shook her head.

"And you?" he continued.

"I'm not certain. Colton suggested I'm simply a . . ." Her voice trailed off as she looked at something he could not see.

Simon shook the papers in his hands. "Well, it's obvious that one of the kids is my ancestor. Probably the third one. Where did you find these?"

"Microfilm at the library. At the house in one of my mother's old books. I know she hid that. And her given name wasn't Lydia either. It was Everly, after her mother. That's what hung me up. I think names were changed twice to cover up more."

Simon had a driving-over-railroad-tracks stomach drop. "This is incredible. I can't believe after all this time, you didn't know. But you did."

Olivia . . . Evelyn . . . watched him coolly. He could understand why, as much as he looked like William. Was part William, as he understood it now. He just needed to find his proof. Here was Olivia's, and from what he could tell of the other papers strewn about, the Colton kid's as well.

"I need to keep these," Simon said, still looking at the papers in disbelief.

Evelyn glided close to him, and Simon saw her long skirts shimmer into being, her hair up in pins around her face. She plucked the papers from his hands. "No. You have no need. This needs to be finished, Simon Monroe."

The anger flared, and it no longer surprised him. "What are you going to do with all of this?"

Burn it, he could have sworn he heard someone say, but Olivia had not opened her mouth.

"I don't know yet." She clutched the papers to her breast, and Evelyn's holographic form solidified. Rich green fabric pleated and falling over supple leather walking boots. Lacy blouse tucked in and belted at the waist. Navy-blue ribbon at her neck. Hair pinned up in a halo about her face. Evelyn right before everything happened. The woman had seen so much change in her short life, but how much had she been privy to in that . . . this . . . isolated corner of the world?

Then he noticed other things. Items he had seen at the historical society not a week earlier. Simon pointed to the woolen shawl draped over her desk chair. "Isn't that . . ."

"Yes," she replied quietly.

"How—"

"I didn't steal it, if that's what you're wondering."

"No, I wouldn't—"

"I wondered it myself. If I'd, you know, gone wandering without knowing it. But I didn't. The one at the historical society is still there."

"How is that possible?"

Olivia shrugged. "The only thing I know is that I know nothing. I have no answer for it."

The sadness in her hit him in the same place that ached to know the truth of this entire business. "Evel . . . Olivia . . ."

"See, even you don't know." Olivia gave him a sad smile, then pushed out a bigger one. "Will you come with me somewhere? I just want to walk."

Evelyn wanted to walk, to wander the prairie as she had. They would have to settle for a jaunt around campus or just outside it.

She took Simon's hand and tugged. He looked like she felt, as if they both were walking through thick air, at once the dust of the past and the exhaust of the present.

"Where?" He was still tense. She couldn't blame him.

"Just a walk. I think the trees are nice south of campus."

He assented with a grunt.

They walked, their feet taking them toward the more heavily wooded and older section of homes south of the university, near Simon's home, near the place Olivia had once wished to put down roots.

Simon had calmed since their argument, though she had no doubt that the issue would present itself again soon. She could enjoy these moments of peace. Shells. They were both shells filled with the fog of the past, but what filled Simon's shell was infinitely darker than what had come to her.

The walk up the hill was quiet save for cars cruising by and the sound of squirrels busy in the trees above and digging it the dirt below, collecting forage for the coming winter. As always, Evelyn was in Olivia's mind, with warnings about the quiet man next to her. Olivia led them closer to the cemetery, angling toward it but not looking at it directly. Evelyn would know where they were headed, but Evelyn wasn't volatile in the way Simon's leech was.

Olivia's stomach clenched as they walked closer to the cemetery. She had tried so hard not to say where they were going directly. Simon had seemed content to be led, but Evelyn finally caught on to what Olivia was up to.

My dear, the iron! Then the warnings faded, and Evelyn's voice went silent.

Olivia watched Simon's face as they passed under the archway and into the cemetery. Whatever shadows were resting there seemed to drift away.

He turned to her. "What just happened?"

Olivia studied Simon's eyes. They looked clear, their normal soft brown. "Are you alone?"

He pulled away from her and took a few steps, looking around. "I think I am. Yes."

He came to her again and took her hands, pulled her close. For a moment, she relaxed against him. So much tension. So much pain.

"I came here searching for Monroe's grave, and when I touched the iron fence, Evelyn had a fit and nearly made my head explode. But when I went through the gate, she went away. Completely, I think. I'm sorry I couldn't get you here sooner."

"Well, we can't live here," Simon said. Olivia couldn't tell if he was joking or serious.

"We can talk at least. Come, let's walk."

They started down the center path. It seemed that no one frequented the cemetery. And why would they? Nothing more recent than the 1920s meant that anyone who would visit was likely already dead and buried, if not in that graveyard then somewhere else.

They paused at the Weatherford graves. "It's all so sad," Olivia said.

Simon laughed sardonically. "Sad is a romantic word for it. Warren's roots are rotten."

"I wouldn't go that far," she said softly.

"So, you suppose we could just ask nicely, and they'll leave?" Simon sounded bitter. How much had this changed him? Both of them?

Olivia threw him a withering glance. How could he have retained any good humor after everything that had happened? She didn't feel like laughing.

"I did some research," she said. "And I think we'll have to exorcise you. Or something like that."

Simon watched her with incredulous eyes. "Sounds so simple."

They stood there in silence, brushing against each other's hands, feeling the pull between them. Then he turned her to him and ran his hands through her hair. "We'd better go before they suspect," Simon murmured.

Olivia surrendered to the embrace. If it was their last, she wanted to remember him kindly. "Yes, we should. But about the . . ."

Simon drew back to look at her. "Do you have a plan?"

"Well kind of, but . . ." She didn't want to say that she thought it might hurt him. Possibly even kill him. The stone that had settled in her belly when she spoke with Colton turned over at the thought. But to be rid of this torment, was it worth it?

He shook his head. "What is it?"

She felt something crawl over her. It was his eyes. Though she had wanted to be near him a moment ago, now she saw the telltale redness creep across the whites of his handsome eyes. There was no need for Evelyn to be in her head to tell her to run. Now. Now it was just her own fool self wondering why she'd brought them there in the first place. Respite? Why had she thought they could have that so close to some kind of ending?

"We're safe here. You can tell me."

She thought quickly, tried to keep herself composed. Any leeway she'd gotten from Not Simon before was likely gone. And maybe he wasn't all the way there. Maybe he was stronger than Evelyn but still not strong enough to fully appear there. "I don't want you to remember it. I don't know what all he can see, so if you don't hear it, you can't give it away."

"But—"

"Please?" *God, please let Simon mostly still be here.*

"OK," Simon said. "OK. Yes, that's probably for the best."

"I'll see you at the festival?" She said it knowing she would see him before that. She had to.

Simon leaned in to kiss her and pressed her hands into his own. "Yes, tomorrow, at your gallery showing. I promise."

She left the cemetery before him, feeling an urgency as Evelyn appeared again. She could not tell him what she thought she might have to do.

70

Friday, October 30th

The gallery was mostly quiet as they readied for the night. Olivia let Margaret know she was making some final adjustments and wandered into the room with her prints. She stood in the doorway with a glass of wine, trying to comprehend their size. Had she really finished them on time? It seemed impossible with everything else going on.

Her prints looked back at her, scenes from the prairie leaping out at her on a grand scale. One frame (an express delivery from IKEA) seemed crooked from her angle, but she knew she'd put one together just a hair off when she was working with Colton. Or it came a hair off from the factory before she put it together. That was possible too.

Evan didn't appear in any of the photos, and neither did the nightmare horse. They had fulfilled their purpose. Olivia missed Evan's presence, even for all the anxiety it had caused her. He was good. She didn't miss the nightmare horse one iota.

"Going to start your own Group f/64?" a velvety voice asked.

She jumped and turned to see Simon at the main entry to the horseshoe-shaped room. How long had he been there? She had thought she was alone in the gallery. The doors didn't open until 6:00. But that he had found a way in didn't surprise her. Not Simon could likely track her scent like a bloodhound. It made her feel unnerved, wary. His charm and apparent interest in her photography project didn't help.

"I ought to," she said, "now that I can see my subject more clearly."

Not Simon took a long look down the wall. "That beast was annoying, wasn't he? Caused me a fair amount of trouble, you know." The demon's words always seemed to contain an inherent threat. Malice, anger, or sadism. But it was true. She wanted to say that the imposter's steed had caused her more anxiety, but that went without saying.

"What do you want?" She instantly regretted her careless words. The look in his eyes made her regret her words even more. He stepped up to her until they were standing chest to chest, and he was looking down at her. She felt like a child. She raised her hands and placed them on his chest, trying to create some distance between them. She didn't need a recap of earlier that week. "Please. People will be here soon. I want to enjoy my night."

He wrenched her head back and pressed a hard kiss to her neck, getting his teeth into her skin until she cried out, then released her forcefully. It sent her stumbling back several steps. She eyed him warily. If he tried to hurt her there, she couldn't do anything to stop him. And what could Austin really do against this thing?

"So, what's the difference between Simon and me? Hmm? What's the *real* difference? If you were mine, I'd do exactly the same things to you, my darling."

"No, it's not like that."

"Oh, shut up. It's exactly like that. He and I are one and the same, you know. Blood. History repeats itself. Don't you know that by now?"

She didn't want him to be angry. She didn't want to say it, but the words might soothe him. "I'm sorry," she said softly, voice lilting up. Evelyn bemoaned the words. She didn't understand.

He looked at her sideways, eyes red and narrow. "I don't believe you. No matter." He seemed subdued by the words for the moment though, and he turned back to the prints on the wall.

"What do you want?" she pressed. "I mean, what do you really *want*? I get that you want to kill me, but that's so trite."

Not Simon looked at her, a bewildered expression on his face that surprised her. "I want what I've always wanted. For you to be happy with me."

It was Olivia's turn to be stunned. "What?"

"I just want you to be happy with me."

"You're trying to kill me."

"I'm back in corporeal form for the first time in more than a century. Do you think I would squander it so quickly? If I must kill you because of that interfering and meddling Mr. Hearth, I will, but I would prefer not to."

The other women had been what to him, collateral damage? Weeding out the impure bloodline? Olivia was so stunned, she didn't know what to say.

"Is he causing you any trouble?" Colton asked.

Olivia and Simon turned. Colton was standing where Simon had been not moments before. Olivia was awash with feeling. Anger at the intrusion was higher on the list than relief that someone was nearby. She looked at her watch. Two minutes to six. Who had let him in? But she knew. Margaret. He'd been here helping the week before.

"I'm heading out," Colton said. "Just wanted to drop by here first. Glad I did."

Olivia extricated herself from Not Simon's bubble and followed Colton out to the parking lot. Her anger followed. She wished for another brick to throw at the calm man inside the gallery who had needled at her patience over the past few weeks.

She picked idly at a loose thread at the cuff of her blouse. The lace there had yellowed and would need to be bleached soon. She could feel Colton's eyes on her. If he saw her dress, he didn't say.

"How am I supposed to end this?" she asked.

"Who said you had to?"

"He'll kill me if I don't." His continued lack of concern angered her more. "My life is a wreck."

Colton reached inside his car and rooted around. "What does history tell you about demons, about breaking spells? I imagine the usual will do the trick no matter the evil. Whatever you do, I imagine you're also the one who has to do it—if you're set on ending it for good. That seems fitting."

She felt like a slim hope was sliding through her fingers. Why didn't he care at all?

"But *why* are they back?" she demanded. "There must be a reason. I have a difficult time believing that something else isn't going on."

Colton rolled his eyes at her. "Well, I did recently come into a souvenir. I didn't think there was anything to it, and I didn't have to pay much for it, but maybe it's connected."

He fished around in his pocket and presented a small squashed piece of metal. She took it from him, examined it in her hand. "What is it?"

"Kid I bought it from said it was a bullet. Said he got it in the cemetery."

Olivia's mouth was dry. "Did he say when?"

"Didn't ask, but I came into it about a month and a half ago."

"You know what this is, right?" Olivia felt faint, surely an Evelyn symptom. Her mind went in approximately ten thousand directions at once. Maybe the bullet had somehow been keeping William Monroe from coming back. Or it could just be a coincidence. But if it had, maybe if she returned it to its final resting place, they could extract the demon from Simon. Maybe with the bullet in its place, he could be saved.

Yes, remove the demon, said Evelyn's haunted voice. Goose bumps sprang up along Olivia's arms that had nothing to do with the cool evening.

"I know what you'd like it to be," Colton said.

"What it is!" Olivia countered, feeling rushed to action, both by herself and Evelyn. "You're the one who's supposed to believe in ghosts and spirits and all this bullshit anyway. And now you don't want anything to do with it? It makes no sense."

She felt an anger from him that reminded her of Simon. It was a simmer that they both seemed to have.

"I'm leaving town for the weekend. And maybe for good after finals," he said into the angry silence. He didn't entertain her question.

"But . . . you can't!" She squeezed her fist around the bullet.

"Sure I can. You can too."

"But . . . everything is happening," she blurted lamely.

"So? There are ghosts everywhere. Just because these are mine doesn't mean I need to stay here, attached to them."

She didn't know what to say to that. Leaving didn't seem like an option. She felt like she belonged there now, immersed in this.

I could never leave this place. It's home, Evelyn whispered somewhere inside her.

The breeze off the trees around the gallery sent her reeling into scent memory, of cool autumn winds blowing across the prairie, of the turning leaves of oaks and cottonwoods and maples and hedges. Her heart twinged with longing for something she had once not been fond of. Perhaps some things did change. Or maybe they were discovered as time went on.

"But they're your ghosts. Our ghosts. They won't leave us just because we leave here, will they?"

Colton's face said he didn't like that idea. "They can follow me if they want."

"I don't think we have a choice about things like that," Olivia replied. Something was buoyed within her. At least she was there. At least she wasn't running from what needed to be done.

"Whatever." Colton scuffed at the dusty lot where their ancestors had ridden when it was hard-packed dirt nearly every day not so long ago.

"So, what am I supposed to do?"

Colton threw up his hands. "Did you not hear me the first hundred times? I don't know!"

"Some people think the bullet is what drove William insane."

Colton laughed. "It may have driven him insane, but I wouldn't be the first to tell you that he had larger problems than a bullet lodged in his shoulder. He should've died. The demon or vengeful spirit or whatever you want to call it kept him alive at the end. Austin had to come back from the dead and obliterate the man's essence. How the hell you're supposed to do that, I don't know."

"But if I put the bullet back . . ." Olivia said, her voice barely above a whisper. Something about speaking the act aloud made it more ominous, more likely to fail.

Colton looked over his shoulder. Perhaps he felt it too. "Maybe it'll help. I couldn't tell you. The shit they tell you to do in the stories—they sometimes work and sometimes don't. I don't know why."

All he could really tell her was that he had checked out, but Olivia didn't open her mouth to say it. He probably understood that already.

"Well, thank you," she said. Alone. She was in this alone. Or nearly so.

He shrugged. "Sure, cuz. Good luck."

"Thanks," she replied.

She wanted to turn around and go back into the gallery, but Evelyn kept her watching until Colton's car was out of sight. Was that twinge in her heart a longing for family she had suddenly discovered and then lost or a longing for the ability to leave?

A few people had arrived while Olivia was occupied with Colton. Back in the gallery, William was waiting for her.

Olivia grabbed another glass of red wine and paused at each description tag as she approached him. She tried to relax, to finally soak in the showing. She'd been so busy half-distractedly writing the descriptions and putting them up that she hadn't realized what she'd done. She squeezed her wine glass and walked her photographs in the order she had chosen, the order she had put them up, the order in which they appeared in the program. How she had stressed over them in Photoshop, arranging and rearranging the photographs on the walls until she'd settled on the following.

- Out on the Prairie
- Homestead
- Westward
- Ambling Hills
- A Walk in Autumn Grasses
- Blue River Valley
- Town Living
- A Storm Approaches
- Respite
- Autumn Warfare
- Cliffs at Dawn
- Autumn Rebirth

No matter that she'd taken the photographs in a different order. *Autumn Warfare* was first, but it appeared near the end. She'd taken *Homestead*, *Westward*, and *Blue River Valley* on the same day with Austin. *Out on the Prairie* had been somewhere near the middle.

"I put them up in chronological order," she said, mostly to herself, but Not Simon heard. She saw him follow her eyes. Olivia looked at him with what was certainly horror on her face. All along she'd thought she'd been creating again, being the artistic being she had missed during all the stress with her mom and teaching and getting lost in mundane routine. But she'd fallen into another routine, at once familiar and foreign. What had been using her though? Or was she simply trapped in the spiral, following the footsteps of her ancestors to her doom?

She knew where she needed to be by dawn, and she knew she must return the bullet to its resting place. She took another long drink of wine. The buzz in her head wasn't from the alcohol though.

She wanted Simon there. Just Simon. But it wasn't doing her any good to want him there. He wasn't. That was it.

"What do you think of them?" she asked Not Simon. She didn't expect a serious answer.

"They defy definition," he replied, eyes scanning *Town Living*, one of the shots from inside the Monroe house. "I have this view in my mind's eye often," he continued quietly and reached out as if to touch the print. "The tree is smaller than the one in my own time. I imagine a storm finally knocked it down, and they replaced it. I was forever telling the staff that it would."

She hadn't been prepared for the thoughtful answer. "I need to get some air," she said. "Will you come outside with me?" The time-jumbled words tumbled out of her mouth before she could stop them. Evelyn screamed for her to stop, to reconsider, but Olivia wrestled with the woman in her head. She needed to be strong, capable, even for the whisper somewhere inside her.

Where are you going?

"What?" The man before her looked confused again. Good. That was better than angry.

"Come outside with me. I'm going to be here most of the evening, and I want some space before everyone else arrives."

He raised his eyebrows at her. "You want me to come with you?" She saw him feeling the words in his mouth. They had thrown him off balance.

"Yes," she said. She stepped away from him to swap her empty glass for a full one and to grab one for him. Evelyn's terror and Olivia's own memories of the past few weeks threatened to bubble up, but she wasn't helpless. And if she could keep him off kilter even for a bit, it would help. Breathing room.

Not Simon offered his arm as they headed toward the door. Olivia took it. Evelyn voiced her opinions in varying degrees of anger and despair.

"Please just trust me," Olivia said, then realized she had spoken aloud when Not Simon turned a questioning glance at her. "Uh, sorry." Olivia tapped her head with her free hand.

Not Simon nodded, then smiled his charming smile, the one Olivia had read about so frequently in Evelyn's journals. It was easy to see how Evelyn had fallen for him. The smile was disarming at the very least.

"I have a little voice too," he replied, that megawatt smile still aimed at her.

She tried to laugh.

Not Simon seemed to enjoy himself on their short stroll out to the gallery's concrete patio. The maples and cottonwoods clustered near the gallery leaned down close to them, showering them with leaves with each puff of wind.

"Do you like the wine?" Olivia asked, unsure where to go with the conversation now that they stood in relative peace. Like many things that month, she couldn't reconcile this calm man with the terror of the nightmare horse and the headless imposter getup.

He looked down at her, the confused expression back on his face again. "I didn't imbibe then. You must not remember. Your Simon enjoys it though, so I have taken a liking to it these days." She said nothing, and he stole little glances at her. "Do you like it?" he asked.

"Yes, I do. Don't tell anyone, but I like to take a glass into the darkroom with me when no one else is there. It's relaxing."

"You are more confident than she was."

Olivia heard a withering sigh in the back of her mind. "I don't know about that. A hundred years changes things. In the world, I mean."

"In some ways," Not Simon replied, then set his hand over the one she still had linked through his arm. "In most ways, nothing has changed."

Olivia didn't want to argue with him. He wanted to talk though, and she was prepared to listen until she had to get back.

"You're quiet," he said. "Tell me what you're thinking."

"I was thinking that you needed to talk after being silent for so long." More leaves danced through the parking lot and rustled in the great trees that lined the drive that headed off campus. They spoke in the voice she'd heard in her dreams, the one that asked her over and over, *Where are you going?* A tingle of that deep prairie magic was in the air, something that wanted to reply.

He hummed around her statement and leaned back, taking a sip of wine. Here was the suave William Monroe. Simon would lean forward over his wine, laughing and talking close to Olivia. She missed him.

"Warren has not changed. At its core it still wants to succeed, to progress, to withstand the wheel of time. I was surprised, then realized I should not be when I saw so many places still open from early Warren." She heard a note of pride in his voice.

"Any that you helped open?"

His eyes flashed to her, then out over the parking lot toward Main Street. "Yes. I supervised the building of many on the streets near us and some large buildings on the university campus. The signs have changed, but many storefronts have not. Stone and wood. Humans will build with them long after you are dead and gone."

He must have seen her face blanch or change because he laughed. "I don't mean by my hands. That is your choice. I mean William's soul, which is mine. I own him. I claimed him and his greed early on. Without me though, I imagine he would have done much worse to poor Evelyn. I tempered him, if you can imagine."

Olivia was holding her breath. She tried to let it out gently. "So you're . . . not William?"

Not Simon sipped his wine, watching her. His charming smile was laced with something more sinister now.

"I'm William, but I'm also what he invited in."

"And what is your name?"

He gave her a confused look again. It would have been endearing, like a puppy, if he had been anyone else. "I'm William."

"No, I mean your other name."

"That is my only name."

Greed, avarice, what? she wanted to say. But that only seemed like the answer to a riddle. *What is but has no proper name when it becomes part of you?*

William watched her intently. "I don't know if I would have liked you this way back then. I don't think I could have stopped my hand, William's hand. Hellfire has tempered me enough since."

Olivia had nothing to say to that. "You've got to let Simon finish getting ready for the festival too, you know."

Not Simon bristled, but Olivia was not afraid. For the moment. Her spirits had been raised the day before. "I don't have to do anything."

"I know you don't."

He watched her with the red eyes that had tormented Evelyn. Had tormented Olivia too. She took his arm again as they walked back to the gallery. Perhaps the terrible things that had happened were not as terrible as they seemed. Perhaps he truly only wanted to be happy with her.

In the doorway he bent and kissed her, long and lush. As he kissed her, she wasn't certain any longer if he was himself or William or the thing that inhabited the in-between space. The thing she understood resided in everyone but took time and honing to cultivate, just as goodness did. His kiss tasted of wine and regret. Bitter and hopeful. As he kissed her, she thought of Austin. Evelyn did not need to appear for her to know what kind of connection she wanted. She felt him tense against her. Then he released her and stood straight.

Olivia saw Austin from relatively far away. His tall form and black cowboy boots were not difficult to spot. He wore pants with long lines and a white collared shirt under a dark jacket. His hair was as perfectly arranged as Simon's usually was. Austin stood out and also fit in as he stood next to a modern man in similar trousers. Olivia watched with shock as

Ann approach the duo. Ann, who had no idea. Ann, whom Olivia had drifted so far from these last weeks. Together, they looked at one of Olivia's photographs. She watched, fascinated, as Austin discussed it with her friend and a stranger. She longed to hear what they said, to stand next to the man who had inspired some of her most treasured shots and a friend who had seen her photography develop over the years. Her instinct was to rush to them, but that was surely only Evelyn wishing to be away from the man next to her.

"What is *he* doing here?" Not Simon growled. Gone was his good mood.

"I didn't invite him." Olivia moved inside the doorway in the dream-like haze of wine and yearning. "I mean, he knew about the showing, but I didn't think to invite him."

Not Simon grabbed her arm and squeezed hard enough to draw a quiet gasp. The crowd in the gallery was loud enough that Austin couldn't have heard it, but he turned their way and caught William in the act. He excused himself from the conversation and strode toward them. Olivia prayed desperately that Ann wouldn't turn their way from her own conversation. She didn't need anyone else getting involved on her behalf.

"Let's take another walk, shall we?" William said. He guided her backward until they were standing outside again. Then several things happened at once.

Just outside the view of everyone in the gallery, Olivia, who had let herself be led quietly, wrenched her arm out of William's grasp. Their wine glasses went tumbling to the ground, shattering with that unique sound of breaking glass. Wine splattered her ankles. William was just swiping for her again when Austin appeared. A rustle in the grassy area nearby revealed Evan, ready and waiting.

William, outnumbered and without his steed, turned and ran. Olivia hadn't expected it, but she charged after him. She wanted to know where he was going. If they could corner him, she could end this!

"Miss Olivia!" Austin called.

"I just want to see where he goes!" she shouted back, but when she ran around the side of the building, he was gone.

Someone hollered from inside the gallery. Olivia, nearer to the front door now, walked briskly toward the entrance. She had thought she would just relax and enjoy her evening. She was delusional to have expected that. Perhaps she could salvage some of it if Not Simon stayed away.

Time slowed.

There was more yelling.

At first she thought a painting had fallen from the walls or someone had accidentally damaged a photograph. Then people started pouring out of the building, running out the front doors. Someone shoved the door open so hard that the frosted glass shattered and fell to the ground. Feet crunched over it. Olivia stood and stared at it. The cold wind was made colder by her ankles, still wet with wine.

The smell of smoke wafted to her moments later. She heard the sirens before she saw the fire.

Flames burst out of the front of the building, breaking several windows near the parking lot, near to where she had just walked. People screamed. Some of them had their phones out to take pictures and video. The heat was so intense that Olivia backed off until she was in the copse of trees at the back of the parking lot. She could still feel the heat of the fire from there. How people could stand so much closer, she didn't understand. She watched it in the same dreamlike haze that had followed her since her walk with William.

The sound of crunching leaves behind her made her stomach clench. She turned around. Nightmare horse in tow, the imposter strode toward her.

Whether out of pure fear or pure courage, she matched his stride and moved toward him. She avoided the nightmare animal's reach and held her arms up to the imposter in a gesture indicating surrender. When he slowed, she reached up and fisted her hands in the top of his cloak, then pulled as hard as she could.

The top portion of the outfit came away more easily than she thought it would. Where she expected to see William or Simon, the gargoyle thing gaped out at her, crunched up beneath the getup. He shrieked at her, revealing a mouth full of sharp teeth similar to his steed.

She hadn't expected that. Was Simon in there beneath the tar and gray skin, or was this something else altogether? And how had it escaped the Monroe house?

The thing shrieked at her again, and this time the nightmare horse reached out to try and take a piece of her. She turned and ran toward the sound of hoofbeats behind her. This would end, but she needed a few things first.

Austin loosed his foot from the stirrup and reached down, so Olivia could get a foothold and grab his arm to lift herself into the saddle behind him. She only had a breath to think of how fluid the motion had become, how much she enjoyed the simple teamwork it required.

"The cemetery! The skull! Oh, God," Olivia gasped as she clung to Austin.

As they raced from the parking lot, a speeding car peeled out into the entrance and nearly took Evan out at the legs, but the horse pivoted quickly and sidestepped the vehicle. Olivia was about to scream at the driver when she recognized the car. Colton! She looked behind her for William, but he was nowhere in sight.

"Colton!" she cried when he rolled down his window.

"I saw the fire engines coming this way, and I came back." His eyes raked over her, Austin, and Evan.

"Miss Olivia, we must go," Austin said impatiently.

"Colton! Can you run by my apartment and then meet us at the cemetery?" She dug around in the deep pocket of her skirts for her keys.

He knew what was there. "Yes!"

She leaned down as far as she dared from her perch on Evan's back. "I'm in the fourteen hundred building at the Warren Lamplighter. Apartment thirty-nine."

He caught the keyring that she tossed to him. "Where is it?"

"In my bedroom. In a shoebox. There's a bag next to it. I need that too." The incredulous look he threw her was all Colton. "What the hell was I supposed to do with it?" she hissed.

"Ethan?" Austin said in his commanding voice.

Colton's face grew serious. "Yes?"

"Please hurry. We'll meet you at the cemetery." With that, Austin pulled Evan up, and they took off toward the southwest.

It wasn't thirty seconds before William's hellish horse was behind them and gaining, whipped faster by the figure on his back. Olivia couldn't turn around long enough to see if it was the creature from the Monroe house or William himself.

Evan pulled up short. To avoid being stuck between a building and their foe, the horse leapt over the sidewalk and onto the street. No one was coming, but Olivia watched as a stoplight two blocks down turned green. Headlights grew larger as they rode toward them. Austin took the change in direction in stride and spurred Evan onward.

Olivia expected to pass through traffic as they approached it, but they didn't. People honked first, then the first cars swerved out of their way. She vacillated between elation and terror. Other people could see them!

Austin deftly navigated Evan through the oncoming traffic. Drivers swerved, flashed their headlights, honked. Someone leaned out his window to yell at them, only to be hit by William's steed. She watched the horse snap its teeth at other drivers bold enough to wave their middle finger out the window. Olivia heard crunching metal, breaking glass. More horns honked.

Finally, when there was a break in the traffic, they turned off to the south again. Olivia risked another look, but William was farther behind. It appeared he was having issues controlling the nightmare beast. Good.

Evan pounded up the cobbled road that led to the cemetery, his body slick with sweat. He tossed his head as they slowed, mane flying and eyes wild. Austin shushed him.

They both dismounted at the entrance to the cemetery. "I . . ." she began, still gulping air from their frantic ride.

"Catch your breath, my dear." Austin pushed the unruly waves of hair from her face.

Olivia wanted to throw herself into Austin's arms. Instead, she stood there, hands on his forearms, gazing up at eyes that held no judgement for her as her breathing returned to normal. Her heart still beat quickly, and she felt at once herself and Evelyn. "Time and experience have made me reserved, though my heart is bursting," she said, unsure of herself, her movements. His eyes missed nothing.

"Yet here you are," Austin replied.

Words that had no articulation caught in her throat. She said nothing.

"I see you," he whispered and squeezed her arms, acknowledging.

"How?" she asked. The arms beneath her hands felt as real as anyone else she knew. His words, his advice, they had all been sound, caring.

"Do you need an explanation for the way the world simply is?" Austin asked. Olivia didn't have anything to say to that. The look he gave her twisted her heart. "I'm a perfect shot, Miss Olivia. Don't forget."

"Austin!" Olivia hung on the look in his eyes.

"Go!" he commanded gently. "I'll keep Monroe busy while you wait for your friend."

Olivia slipped into the relative security of the cemetery as William clattered up the cobbled street and Austin mounted his trusted companion.

71

12:00 A.M., Saturday, October 31st

William rode his nightmare beast in manic lengths up and down the cemetery's iron fence. He had no outfit to conceal him now, and he shifted between William and the gargoyle thing nearly every time Olivia looked back at him. But he could not get at her. Bloody foam was at the horse's mouth, and it snapped at the bit as William yanked on the reins. It seemed even he could not always control the thing, and his control over it dwindled as time waned.

They both saw Colton at the same time when he popped the curb nearest the cemetery entrance in his red Pontiac. The car's bumper scraped the concrete so loudly that even the nightmare horse whipped its head toward the sound.

Colton shot out of his car and ran toward the fence. With surprising grace, he jumped onto the limestone wall and grabbed the iron fence with his free hand. He held the wrapped skull under his other arm like a football. Olivia met him there and climbed onto the wall. She reached for the bundle.

The ghastly duo exploded out of the darkness.

"Fucking shit!" Colton hollered and pressed the bundle so hard into Olivia's chest that she was knocked backward to the ground. Her right ankle groaned, and she went hard to one knee to protect it. A broken ankle was the last thing she needed. Bright spots danced in her vision from the pain.

William reached for Colton at the same time the nightmare horse reached out with its teeth. Colton turned and slid down the fence to avoid them. William's hand and the horse's nose connected with the fence where Colton had just stood. Steam burst from William and his mount. William cursed as the horse crow-hopped from what had hurt it. He struggled to regain control over the animal.

From so close, Olivia felt the heat of the pair, tasted their putrescence. She backed away as quickly as she could with her fragile burden. Despite Evelyn's silence inside the cemetery, she had an overwhelming urge to protect Colton.

She got behind one of the large cedars near the fence and moved to a portion of the fence that ran perpendicular to the section on which Colton was stranded. Olivia clambered onto the fence. She felt almost drunk on the adrenaline that ran through her.

"Do you want it?" Olivia cried, dangling the skull over the fence that ran away from where William waited for Colton.

The horse stopped. William turned his so-very-Simon-like frame toward her. William knew what Olivia was trying to do, but the nightmare horse didn't. It simply saw a target. Something it wanted badly. Though William shouted for it to stop and turn back toward Colton, the horse violently shook its head to have leeway with the reins and steered itself toward her.

As soon as the horse galloped toward Olivia, Colton slid from the fence and sprinted to his car. He got in and peeled out in reverse, distracting the nightmare horse again. It was enough. Olivia jumped down from the fence and ran for the crypts.

She stumbled over roots and low grave markers as she navigated in the dark. She heard the heavy breathing of William's steed trying to get at her through the fence and ran faster. When she came upon the crypt, she didn't hesitate. She wrenched open the door and slid inside.

The stale air sighed heavily. As the breeze crawled across Olivia's neck, she knew it must be midnight. Time to get the hell out of the cemetery. She couldn't assume it was safe any longer now that Monroe's power was at its height—or so Evelyn thought.

She took a final moment to check the contents of her satchel. Iron. Stolen items from the Catholic church down the street because she didn't know what she would need or how to use them. The cufflink. Austin's skull wrapped in a cardigan. It shifted in her vision between the two even though Evelyn was silent there. It was a hallucination. She squeezed her eyes shut and felt her cardigan between her fingers. Just a cardigan. Hers. Not Evelyn's. She hoped Colton had gotten out of town OK.

Then she stepped up close to the open casket in the center of the room. The terror she once felt at being there was lessened now, but her heart was still hammering. Gingerly, she pulled aside the disintegrating fabric. Even without the light, she would have been able to find the bullet's final resting place. Had this been what had driven William to insane lengths, or was it simply the fabric from which he had been cut?

The crypt didn't answer except to sigh again.

She fingered the bullet between her thumb and forefinger. It felt warm from her pocket, almost hot. It was squashed, and the sides were worn with time. Holding her breath, she slipped the bullet back into the bone. Outside she heard the scream of man and beast and hoofbeats fading into the distance. Olivia turned back to the task before her.

The bullet fit like a puzzle piece. How intense the man's pain must have been. How insane it must have driven him that his wife didn't love him, didn't choose him at the end. Or did he care that she chose death over him? Olivia didn't know what that was like, to have to choose between such things. But if Austin asked it of her, what would she say?

The skeleton beneath her hands had nothing to offer in response to her macabre thought except that someday she too would be buried and stripped of her flesh.

When she stepped out of the crypt and into the fresh air, she paused. In the distance near the Weatherford graves, several hazy figures stood watching her. Eva and Evette in their white frocks, always nearly children in Evelyn's memory. Evelyn didn't know how much Evette must have gone through to keep those children hidden away. How many papers forged, how many hushed words, how close her circle of trusted family.

Esther and Jonathon stood near them, even hazier than their children. Where had they gone in the wake of everything? Simon claimed they'd turned up in New York, but at the time, anyone could disappear and reappear with a new identity and blend into the crowd.

Olivia stood there watching them, listening to the slow drip of raindrops in the trees around her. The clouds were parting, and the moonlight was showing through, but the trees were still alive with the sounds of the rain.

"Thank you," she said to them.

Outside the iron fence, she heard a horse shuffling through the wet leaves. Everything had a particular sound, she had noticed, and it would be a long time before that sound left her memory, if it ever did. It belonged solely to Austin and Evan. William was nowhere in sight. That worried her.

Olivia walked out of the cemetery, barely acknowledging the dizzying rush that happened as she crossed under the iron boundary, the sudden weight of clothing now more familiar to her than leggings and sweaters. Lace hugged her throat and wrists. White skirts and petticoats didn't slow her as they once had. She hitched up the long pale skirts and hurried to Austin.

As she neared Evan and Austin, she reached a hand up. Austin caught it and hauled her aboard Evan. Was there such a thing as ancient muscle memory? She settled her skirts, laced one arm around Austin, and grabbed the leather strap at the back of Evan's saddle. She made certain the soft leather satchel with its fragile contents was secure on her person.

"Miss Olivia," Austin murmured. The smell of smoke was stronger on him than even a few hours earlier. She yearned to be the kind of person who did things outdoors and came home smelling of woodsmoke.

What's holding you back?

I don't know.

"Mr. Hearth," she said, another old reflex surfacing. Saying it that way twisted her heart again.

The town shifted as they rode. Olivia did a double take as they slipped across Main Street. The pavement turned to cobbles, then to dust beneath Evan's hooves. Streetlights winked out. Buildings faded into ether before her eyes. Prairie grasses took their place, as did clapboard buildings.

That is where I had my dresses made. That is where I bought my paper and pencils and watercolors. That is where they served the best ice cream.

Olivia took it all in with wide eyes. Shadowy figures of people came out of the dust. They didn't turn to watch the horse with its two riders heading out of town.

"Why are you both back at the same time? I still don't understand."

Austin was quiet as they rode, watching out over the trees and hills that were illuminated by moon and starlight bouncing from the clouds down to the earth. The trip back in time didn't seem to faze him. "I suppose you can't have one without the other," he said.

"I don't believe in that," Olivia replied.

Austin turned his deep eyes on her. They reflected the moonlight so brightly, and Olivia felt for a strange moment that he was more alive than she. "It doesn't matter. It exists whether you believe in it or not."

Olivia had to drop her gaze from his.

She didn't know how long they rode or to where, but the countryside looked so much like she had always known that she could not tell whether they were in or out of her time. It was all prairie vistas and several faraway lights of homesteads that winked through the trees and the rising fog.

A horrendous screech came from the thick stand of cedars and honey locust on their left. William atop his nightmare burst out of the woods and onto the road next to them.

"Simon!" Olivia screamed, and the man whipped his head around to look at her. There was a moment of recognition. Red eyes shifted to normal, angry face slackened. But in another blink, Simon was gone, consumed again by the thing inside him.

Evan put on a burst of speed, but it wasn't fast enough to get out of the other horse's reach. The animal snapped its mouth full of Evan's hide, and there was a cacophony of animal noises, man and beast crying out at each other.

Olivia was nearly unseated. She screamed as Evan did and grabbed more tightly onto Austin. The leather from the strap at the backside of the saddle dug into her hand despite its softness.

The two horses jostled each other as Evan tried to gain ground over the nightmare horse, and the other kept pace. It was dark, but Olivia could still see the dirt and dust they churned up on the road. It was in her nose and mouth and tasted like chalk.

Not Simon reached out a hand that looked only half himself and swiped at Olivia. She jerked the satchel away from his reach, but several long fingernails caught her across the face. On the second blow, the side of his hand caught her above one eye. Eyes watering, she reached out blindly and pushed away the long gargoyle arm that was stretched out for her. Olivia gasped in pain and tried to keep purchase in her seat.

Austin had a wild look in his eyes that Olivia had not seen before when he turned and saw what had happened to her. The man always seemed so in control.

"Miss Olivia, I need you safe," Austin said.

Olivia's head was still ringing from the blow from Not Simon. She heard Austin, but it took her a moment to comprehend him. She nearly lost her seat again when he pulled up on Evan's reins.

"I'm so sorry, Miss Olivia," Austin said. "I'll come for you when it is time."

Then he was pushing her from Evan's back, twisting her so that when she fell, she went down backside first. She didn't understand what was happening until she realized she was falling.

Olivia landed on her back and had the wind knocked from her lungs. Her bag landed with a clink on her chest. Her head flopped back and hit the ground hard. She was momentarily dazed, lying there watching the stars spin above her. Her breath hitched as she tried to recover, but it felt so much like the long slide down into the canyon that fear stole her breath again. The sound of pounding hooves and shouting moved away from her.

Jumbled memories cascaded through her head. Her mother—younger, grey eyed, and smiling as they played in the front yard. Then she was Mrs. Weatherford, and when Olivia looked down, she was a young child and wore a white frock that was much more suited to the 1890s than the 1980s. There was Austin, riding in from far off. She could have spotted him amongst the trees had they lived in the wood and not the prairie.

It's time to get up.

Olivia sat up, and nausea nearly overtook her. She hadn't fallen *that* hard. She got to her feet, found her balance, and checked her bag. Unbelievably, the skull was safe, intact. She adjusted her skirts and started up the hill toward the clash of animals, which didn't sound far away.

Predawn was a faint red light on the eastern horizon. Olivia stumbled up the hill just as the two figures approached each other. *Red sky at night, sailors' delight. Red sky at morn, sailors be warned.* From where she was, she could not tell who was who. Both men wore long black coats and carried silver pistols that flashed in the dawn light.

She heard words being exchanged but not what was being said. Visions of Evelyn's final jaunt up there swam before her.

As Olivia ran up, both men drew their pistols and fired. She saw the muzzle flashes just before she heard the concussion of the shots. Would it draw unwanted attention from the authorities? She didn't want to find out.

Then she saw Simon collapse, and he slid from the nightmare horse's back. The animal took off in the opposite direction, its legs jerking strangely. Austin's words sounded in her ears again. *I'm a perfect shot, Olivia.*

She believed him.

Olivia raced up the hill. She met Austin first, and he caught her into a hard embrace. "I hit him above the heart with a silver bullet. Hurry. You must finish him now." He pressed the ornate pistol into her hands. It was smooth and warm.

She approached the writhing demon warily. His red eyes bled, and he muttered in a language she didn't understand. Not Simon. No even William. Austin's words rang in her head. *I'm a perfect shot, Olivia. Know that.*

She trusted him. And now she had to finish it.

"Simon, can you hear me?" she asked as she readied herself. Iron will. God help her. Olivia expected a bloody open wound, but there wasn't much blood where Austin had shot the demon. She wanted to think it was promising, but she didn't know.

The demon cursed and spat at her. "Should have killed you when I had the chance, hoyden."

The horizon burned red.

She looked down at him, half Simon, half Not Simon. It was clear a struggle was going on, but Simon needed help. She set her knee in the center of his chest to hold him down. He eyed her suspiciously as she raised the pistol. Not Simon tried to flail away from her, but she held him down firmly. Austin had done the first part. Now she needed to finish it.

"No! No!" the man beneath her cried.

Olivia closed her eyes. It sounded too much like Simon. "I'm so sorry," she whispered hoarsely. Tears stung the gash on her face. She aimed for his heart, then pulled the trigger.

A roar that sounded like a train racing down the tracks came from the man beneath her. A great black cloud emerged from his chest, whirling like a tornado. Horrible dark faces spun around in the vortex, mouths open in a freight-train scream.

Olivia nearly stumbled back and away from it all, but Austin pressed her forward again. He seemed larger than life now, and Olivia thought for a strange moment that he was headless again, just another Halloween spook but ten feel tall.

"You must end this!" he shouted over the noise, and then he was Austin again, the man. "It's only a trick!"

A clunking and tinkling came to her over the din. The horse thing was back and had just breached the hill. Its legs buckled every few steps though, and its head swung disturbingly. Its bones chattered. It was doubly terrifying now. The bats in its ribcage finally escaped in a cloud, thousands of tiny shrieking creatures. They poured out around her, tore at her hair and her clothes, mingled with the dark tornado that sprouted from Simon.

She couldn't let the trick dissuade her. "I just want what's best for you, dearest," she whispered and then shot the creature on the ground again.

Her ears hummed with pain, but she quickly pressed the cufflink that Austin had given her into the wound. If it had done so much damage from simply brushing against him, surely it would do more now.

As the sound of the shot rang in the air, the horse thing's skin fell from its bones and pooled on the ground like discarded clothes, revealing the hodgepodge of bones that made up the animal's frame. What looked like mouse skulls bounced around inside the thing's skull. As the sound faded, the horse fell apart until it was just a pile of bones on the ground.

Silence. Then the birds in the trees near the canyon began to call again, their world returning to normal.

Olivia took the final piece from her pocket: the rib bone with the bundle of herbs. Not Simon's eyes flashed red, but he could not speak. How did she look to him? Did she seem just as broken and bloody as he looked to her?

"I just want what's best for you," she whispered one final time. While his furious eyes were on hers, she snapped the rib bone and the little bundle of herbs in half. It was like she had snapped him in half. Simon's back arched, and he screamed. The pile of bones near her burst into flames. She stumbled back away from him, right into Austin, who held her as they watched.

"Will it work?" she asked, more to herself than anyone else.

"I don't know."

"Then how did you know to use the gun?"

"I didn't. It was all I had."

After a few tense minutes, the bones were burned to ash, and Simon stilled. Austin nudged Olivia toward the scene, and she knelt beside Simon.

"Simon?"

The man groaned, then rolled on his side and threw up. Olivia helped him roll over farther, but he hollered and reached for his shoulder.

Austin knelt next to them and helped Simon sit up. Simon watched the man warily. "You've been shot," Austin said.

"No shit," Simon replied through clenched teeth.

Austin looked over at Olivia, and she felt the depth of his stare. "Go take care of the rest," he said.

She couldn't look away from him. She wanted to say what kept catching in her throat, but there was never a good time. "What about Simon?"

"He will be fine here."

Evan came trotting up the hill, head low but eyes clear.

Something ached in her chest. "What about . . ."

Austin smiled sadly. "I'll be fine as well, my dear. Now go."

She gratefully accepted Austin's help onto Evan's back, and then the horse took off toward the gym. She didn't look back. She felt stronger with every beat of the beast's hooves. Some kind of second wind. But Evan looked tired. His coat had dulled, and his leather trappings showed their age. There were great cracks in the leather, and his reins were soft and crumbling in her hands.

Evelyn whispered for her to hurry.

As they rode, Olivia saw the places she had photographed, how they connected, and the places that Evan had to supply for her. Then they galloped away from the photography building and toward the gym.

They raced across a covered bridge that spanned the canyon. Below them, a dark maw churned. Screams and moans reached Olivia. The women down in the canyon were restless again. But she and Evan left them behind too.

The air was sharp, and the trees danced eerily in the wind as it picked up. Olivia's hair whipped at her face, bringing tears to her eyes. The trees looked oddly dark in the light, as if they were not quite ready to give up the night.

The gym grounds were empty. At nearly dawn, it should have been open. Some patrons should have even left already. But no one was there, and no cars were in the parking lot. The tall, old trees looked strangely dark too, their long branches moving like reaching arms. The trees would have been old even when Warren was new, tall sentinels on the prairie.

As they got closer to the building, Olivia saw that it was only half modern. The modern face of the gym was translucent, and she could see the old face of the building, the smaller, squattier jail of more than century past. She pressed on.

The backside of the gym was darker than the front, as if scarred by fire. Everything looked like Old Warren back there. Instead of the little stand of trees that Olivia remembered looking at through the gym windows, there was stretching prairie. In the west, the sun and the sky were red and orange under dark clouds. Lightning flashed intermittently.

Evan snorted and shook his head, trotting around prairie dog holes. He seemed stronger there, though his form was less solid. Olivia thought for a moment that she could see his skeleton through his fur. It was a cartoonish and terrifying sight. She gripped the reins tightly.

Where the back door with access to the basement stairs was supposed to be, she saw an old Warren door instead. Evan stopped, and Olivia slid off his back with her package.

"Please don't leave without me," she said to the great horse. Evan whuffed in return and tossed his head up and down.

The wind took on a whistle, and a dust devil whirled up beside the building, pelting Olivia with dirt and dust. Coughing, she slipped inside the door to get away from it. Dirt crunched between her teeth. It tasted metallic.

She took the stairs down, down, down. They went on forever, shifting from steel grating to wood to earth as she went on and on and on.

She reached a trapdoor. Without thinking, she opened it. A ladder led down to the place she knew.

Olivia climbed down the ladder to the excavation site, carrying the skull carefully under her arm. Where the earth had been hard packed in the old basement room in modern Warren, now it was soft and pliable. It felt recently disturbed.

Olivia clicked on her flashlight and peered over the lip of the excavation site. She inhaled sharply and drew back, her heart hammering. The skeleton was no longer there. In its place was Austin's recently dead body, waiting for William and his family to bury it.

You don't know that.

Tell me what you think happened.

Silence.

A wooden ladder descended into the grave. Shovels sat next to a transparent hot water heater for the gym in modern Warren. Piles of soft earth sat around the site. She smelled the distinctive odor of tobacco and root vegetables.

Olivia held her breath and peered over the edge of the grave again. Austin lay there, covered in blood from his neck. His skin was grey, and his cloak was tattered and dull. It hurt her to look at him. Not just for the senselessness of it but for how diminished the man looked. To have seen him in so many forms, it had strangely not diminished her memory of him. She didn't know whether that thought belonged to her or Evelyn.

The skull chattered under her arm. It no longer sounded so hollow. Her stomach twisted. The head must match the body now too.

She tried to manage her fear as she climbed down the ladder into Austin's final resting place. She was disturbing it. Not that it had been very restful for Austin, but still. His fate in modern Warren was still up in the air. Where would they choose to inter him at the end of it all?

When she reached the earthen floor, she saw it was littered with footprints, the footprints of the men who had helped William Monroe remove Austin Hearth from history. Their boots had left distinct impressions in the soft soil. For a moment, a thrill of fear ran through Olivia. Suppose they returned while she was making things right?

Evelyn urged her to hurry.

She wasn't prepared for what the head looked like now. It was Austin, all right, but he looked nothing like his warm-bodied self. His skin was grey and gaunt and pulled away from his mouth and eyes in what looked like a half scream. It might have only been the way his head was resting, gravity taking its course. One eye was mostly open, the white shot through with blood.

And his neck.

Olivia didn't know that blood clotted after death, but she had seen so much in the last month that she knew she could handle that too. Hell or high water or something like that.

Old fear flashed through her as she handled the head. Evelyn's fear. It was fraught with the awful mixture of emotions that Evelyn had felt in those weeks. Disgust, fear, anxiety, love, hate, paranoia, and the torturous decline of her mind.

Olivia had to close her eyes to pick the head up after that. It was cold, and the flesh was hard. Her hands fit around the side of it in a manner that made other images rush through her mind. She didn't want to look at it, but she knew she must.

Cradling the head under her arm like a football—there didn't seem to be any good way to hold it, but she sure as hell wasn't going to hold it *that* way again—she jumped down into the grave, brushing Austin's booted feet in the process. Her stomach sank in fear, but his body didn't move.

She crept toward the top of his body and knelt. She still wasn't sure about this part. Evelyn guided her through it though, telling her how to carefully arrange the head, so it sat in its rightful place above Austin's shoulders.

She watched as tendrils of muscle reached out toward each other from the severed areas of Austin's neck, and his head slithered back to his body.

"It's time for you to go," she said to Evelyn. "I must create my own future now." The woman was gone with a warm breeze and the scent of the prairie hills in autumn. Olivia would never be able to taste the breeze the same after that.

At her feet, the body of Austin Hearth began to shake. Olivia scrambled up the ladder. Anything to get away from what might be another animated dead body. She didn't care if it was just Austin. She had had enough of the uneasy dead for many lifetimes. She pulled the ladder up and out of the grave for good measure.

She gave the room one last look and took a final long look at Austin's now-still body. The ghosts could come bury him now, and they would not know that he was whole while they did. Things could end instead of repeating over and over again.

"Rest easy," she whispered and then clambered out of the room. Feeling more tired than ever, she struggled onto Evan's back and let him carry her back to the present.

The same; it was all the same. They would go on as if nothing had happened, just as before. But perhaps now Austin would rest easily. Perhaps Evelyn would find her peace. Perhaps Olivia could find herself. Perhaps someday she could find Simon again, but not today. Not today and not tomorrow either.

They reached the bridge, and Evan's effortless canter slowed to a trot, his head hanging low. Something wasn't right. The wind howled louder still. A great whooshing sound to her right made her whip her head around. Flames, from where she didn't know, licked at the roof of the bridge and crept toward them.

"Evan! Please turn around!"

Evan broke into a weak canter, then slowed again. The bridge was burning, but Evan could not go any faster. Olivia screamed for him to move. She dug her heels into his sides and yanked on the reins, which disintegrated in her hands. The fire moved quickly. The heat was intense, all consuming.

She felt the bridge begin to give when they were only halfway across. Then they fell. Ash and heat and wood and horse and tree and rock all rushed by her. Evan neighed somewhere in the distance. She hit the ground for the second time that night.

When she opened her eyes, the fire was gone. She saw nothing around her except dark cliffs and stars wheeling above. Like the night when the imposter drove her into the ravine, she was mostly unharmed. Perhaps there was some disconnect between that world and her. Perhaps that had saved her, or perhaps it had hurt her.

Not knowing how far away the bodies of the other women were, she moved quickly to get off the canyon floor. She was at a place that wasn't so steep and had good footholds and handholds.

She scrambled over the side of the bank and was surprised to find herself just off the road where the cliffs took a bend. When she finally made it over the edge, scraping her forearms in the process, she scooted even farther from the drop and caught her breath.

Fatigue and hunger made her dizzy. When had she last eaten? All she wanted was a burger and fries and a milkshake from the Triangle Inn. She hadn't had that since college, but it was the only thing her hungry stomach desired.

She wasn't sure how long she sat there just thinking about food, daydreaming about its texture between her fingers, her lips, over her tongue. She could nearly taste it. Someone must have seen her from a distance in that early dawn light—maybe a hunter; she never knew. A wail from an emergency vehicle left no doubt in her mind that it was heading toward her. She looked up. There was no sign of Simon, Austin, or Evan.

She hardly remembered the firetruck that showed up first or the cruiser that arrived just after. The rest of the morning was a blur of questions that left her hazy mind twisted in directions that it didn't want to go. She refused medical treatment she didn't know how many times.

But the thread of the story remained the same. She and Simon had gone walking from campus, following the cliffs out into the country. They had lost track of time and distance. Eventually, they had gone far enough that Olivia was near home. She said she would walk the rest of the way. Simon said he would call a friend if he got tired of walking. They parted. She must have gotten disoriented in the dark, taken a wrong turn, though she knew the area well. She had slid into the ravine and must have been so tired she fell asleep there.

"No, there was no one to call."

"Yes, I know the house is in Lydia Norwich's name. I'm her legal guardian."

"There's no way she could get here."

"Yes, I'm fine."

"Yes, I was with Simon Monroe most of the night."

"Yes, I imagine I was with him that night too."

"No, thank you."

"No."

"No."

"No."

There was a fleeting moment where she wished Evelyn were there to help her through things as she once had. The thought dissipated almost as soon as it materialized though. Soon enough, she was free to go, pending a follow-up. She didn't expect that to happen.

As truly as she knew that William had gone, she knew Simon would tell the same story she had. It didn't surprise her now that they had found each other. She saw how they had tread in all the same circles, closer and closer until they collided. So, perhaps it had been they who had set the wheels in motion and not the world of restless ghosts. Perhaps they were the restless ones.

72

7:00 A.M., SATURDAY, OCTOBER 31ST

AUSTIN HAD TO HELP SIMON STAND. HE HAD NO WORDS FOR the pain.

"Where's Olivia?"

"Safe," Austin replied.

Simon tried to argue, but the deep breath he wanted to huff out got hitched up in the pain. "I need to see someone. Then I need to find her."

"You shouldn't," Austin replied. He didn't clarify to which statement he was referring.

"I've been shot."

"I'm under the impression that this gun is not ordinary. If you feel you should risk it, by all means, do so. But I'm not certain that is in your best interest."

Simon grunted in pain. "I have a vet friend who will take a look at it."

"Fine." Austin nodded. "May I help you get there?"

Simon was suspicious, but without the sensation of William Monroe crawling up his spine, there was no reason not to trust the man.

The landscape was strange as they walked. They were not in modern Warren, and the trees looked angry.

"Where are we?" Simon asked. He leaned on Austin far more than he would have liked, but something about the air and his shoulder made him feel weaker with each step. Austin moved without a problem.

The wind-worn man looked down slightly at him. Until then Simon hadn't realized how tall Austin was. "Warren still but somewhere between. It's hard to explain. I have lived here for so long that it's normal to me."

"Purgatory?"

"Perhaps. There is no one here save me."

Despite the pain, Simon wanted to pepper the man with questions. He eyed the gun in Austin's hip holster. "Where did you come across that?"

Austin looked down at it. "It was from my father. From his father. More of a family heirloom than something to be used. I carried it with me though. A talisman." He patted the gun in his chest holster. "This is what I normally use for protection."

"Where did your grandfather get it?"

"I never had an opportunity to ask him."

"Ah. I'm sorry." But Simon wasn't that sorry.

They walked in silence, and the landscape gradually became familiar.

Dennis was caring for a horse in the large-animal side of the facility when Simon arrived. Dennis's thin, grey hair stood up in tufts on his head. He looked like he'd been up all night. The animal lay on its side breathing heavily. Simon thought he had had enough of horses for awhile. Even in the back seat, being trampled by Austin's great steed wasn't pleasant. Nor was riding the giant nightmare beast, come to think of it.

He was about to ask Austin about that animal—just whose was it?—but when he turned around, the man was gone. He shook his head. Ghosts.

The pain had reduced to a fire that radiated through his shoulder. Still, it engulfed him. Yes, that was the right word.

Dennis didn't even have to ask what happened. His face asked for him.

"There was an accident."

"That you didn't report?"

"With an antique gun." It wasn't untrue.

Dennis opened his mouth to say something. Simon could have made a dozen guesses what it might be, but it seemed Dennis decided to keep his extra inquiries to himself. "Accident or not, you need to go to the hospital. I can't be responsible if you get an infection or something more serious. You might need surgery, especially if that 'antique gun' fired lead shot."

"It's embarrassing more than anything. I just wanted to see if you could do anything about it or whether I need to go to the hospital."

Dennis sighed. "Well, I'm not a people doctor, but I'll have a look." He stood and wiped his hands on a rag just outside the horse's stall. He didn't bother sliding the stall door shut. "How's that dog of yours? No more strokes, I take it?"

"No, none. He's been alright."

Dennis grunted his approval.

They walked through a breezeway into the facility's main veterinary area. Somewhere a dog whined while Simon heard the soft snoring of others. He cast a quick glance to his friend.

"I know you're not telling me everything," Dennis said.

"Can you get me some antibiotics? I can't afford to go to the hospital. That's the truth of it. University insurance is shit, and if I need surgery, I'm not going to be able to pay the bill."

Dennis's face was red, whether in sympathy or anger, Simon wasn't sure. "Fine," the older man replied. "I'll take an X-ray, poke around a bit, get it out if I can. I get hunting dogs in here all the time, and depending on where the buckshot is, we just leave it in them. If it's in soft tissue, your body might push the bit or bits out in time. Or maybe not. Your body might just heal around them. Or it'll get pissed that there's a foreign object lodged in you. But if I take a look, and sometime down the road you get a fever or the entry spot gets angry and festers, go to the hospital. You got it? And don't tell them you came here first."

"Got it."

Simon's mouth was dry as he prayed to anyone listening that he wouldn't have to do anything with the bullet. After what Olivia had told him, and knowing what he knew, he didn't think he would, but fuck, it hurt like a bitch.

The X-rays seemed to take a lifetime and involved Dennis poking at the wound more than Simon thought was necessary. Finally, Dennis slapped the image up onto the viewing screen. "The X-ray shows it's lodged in soft tissue."

Simon didn't think that was true. It had to be lodged in the bone. He didn't want to contradict his friend, but he was beginning to wonder if he should have gone there in the first place.

Dennis was gone quite awhile after he went over the X-ray with Simon. When he returned, he handed Simon an orange pill bottle. "I'm giving you an antibiotic. The pain isn't going to kill you, but an infection might cause you some trouble. You're an idiot, so I hope you're thankful you're alive."

Simon felt a flare of anger. However he had gotten involved instead of fleeing the damn state for a month, he could handle being called an idiot for it. "I deserve that, I suppose," he replied, tucking the bottle into his jacket pocket.

When he stepped outside, his favorite police officer was standing next to a cruiser, apparently waiting for him. Simon looked back at Dennis, who had a "What was I supposed to do?" look on his face.

Two hours later, all Simon wanted was a stiff drink that he wasn't sure he would ever have the chance to get.

"Lucky for you, your story checks out." Officer Wells tossed a clear plastic bag on the table. It landed with a thud that made Simon wince. What looked like one of Austin's guns sat before him—the one he'd seen strapped to Austin's hip as they walked through the grey morning to Dennis's place. Fucking Dennis. Simon stared at it, wondering how that had gotten to his home. He wondered what else they might have found, perhaps in the attic, but he remained silent.

"So, let me get this straight one last time. You went for a late-night walk with Miss Norwich. You went your separate ways, went home, started tinkering with the gun, and it went off, striking you in the shoulder. You went to Warren Rural Animal Services to have it looked at."

Miss Norwich. It sounded strange to hear her called that. He wasn't certain he could call her anything other than Miss Weatherford any longer.

"Yes, that's right."

"You didn't walk Miss Norwich home?"

"No."

"Why not?"

"Because she's fully capable of walking herself home."

"In the middle of the night with mur—disappearances going on? A walk of that distance?"

"She assured me that she was fine." Asshole. In all fairness, he would have headed straight back to where he had last seen her had Dennis not called the fucking cops on him.

"Why didn't you go to the hospital? A gunshot can be a serious wound."

"Because I was embarrassed. And I can't exactly afford the bill." That was only a half truth. Tenured pay was a notch above.

The officer sat and stared at him for much longer than Simon thought was necessary. What was he waiting for? A confession? Some fucking conversation? A lick of anger pressed at him. It felt comfortable to let it be there, waiting.

"So, I'm free to go, right? Like last time?"

The officer stared at him for another drawn-out moment, the bristly hairs that stuck out from his nose moving with each heavy breath. Simon could smell his coffee breath from across the table. "We'll be in touch."

"Sure." He hoped the officer didn't mean it.

Walking out with his hoodie in hand, he realized he should've cancelled his speech. There were at least a dozen good reasons why he should. One was Olivia. He had no idea where she was. Second, he'd been shot. Third, he hadn't slept. Fourth, he'd been shot. The pain was like nothing he'd ever experienced. Even accidentally slicing into his foot with a shovel when he was eight years old paled in comparison, and there'd been more blood then.

Even for all that, he went home, fed the dog, showered, changed his clothes, did his hair, combed his beard, and put on a suit. It felt right that that he should still go on. A fitting end, somehow.

Time forced him to drive down to Main and park on one of the side streets. The trees were strangely bare of their leaves. There had been quite a windstorm last night, though, and even in town, small branches, signs, anything not tethered well had been knocked down.

The events of the last month played through his mind as he watched the crowd gather. Why were they there? Had it all simply become a spectacle, a time to take their children to a carnival for the afternoon or evening, a way to pass the time? Time passed indeed, but everything circled back around. Everything. If a wound was deep enough, it festered forever.

William Monroe had stood in about that spot one hundred years earlier when he had proclaimed Austin Hearth to be Evelyn's murderer. What he knew now. What he carried with him now.

What pain was worse, the intense physical pain of his shoulder, which would abate over the next weeks, or the way his heart felt squeezed every time he thought about his ancestor, about Evelyn and Olivia? One was more intense in the present, and the other . . . the other dull squeezing ache might never quit. It was a permanent band around his heart.

And God, all the people there, waiting to hear him speak. Who of them had any idea? Who of them could even fathom?

He waited for his name and the beginning of the applause before he stood. His chest hurt with a pain that had nothing to do with his physical wound. Bridgette would commend him for growing such a large heart.

"Warren has had its share of struggles over the last century and a half," he began. Nods of assent from the first few rows where the town council was seated. Did they have any idea what had just transpired in Warren? Their faces gave nothing away, but it made Simon uncomfortable. He had a feeling they knew. How could he and Olivia have gotten away with so much otherwise?

"At the turn of the century, one hundred years ago, Warren was in the midst of tumultuous change that completely reshaped the town and altered the course of its history."

He heard murmurs from the front few rows. They had approved his speech beforehand, but he had altered the words a bit. He wouldn't push them though. He couldn't even push himself, for Christ's sake.

"But Warren made it through. And I think we can take a lesson or two from those days. I think we can learn about recovering from loss and keeping a positive outlook. The Monroe and Weatherford families built this town from the ground up, and their names are emblazoned across it. What we don't see are their spirits, which also linger still.

"The Monroes and the Weatherfords were diligent workers but in different ways. The Monroe family found opportunity, and they took whatever they could whenever they could. While there are those who may skew the Monroe family's morals one direction or another, I will call them what no one could argue: Opportunists. And the Weatherfords. Jonathan Weatherford was an astute businessman who found luck and good fortune wherever he went. His family suffered a great loss at the height of Warren's growth at the turn of the century, but they persevered nonetheless.

"The family we do not speak of much is the Hearth family. They came to Warren as lower-middle-class citizens who worked their way up society's ranks in a time when such a thing was just becoming possible. Their family also experienced tragedy at the turn of the century. I'm not here to speculate on any of that, but I would like us to consider the fortunes of each of these families and how they might mirror the different socio-economic standings of the many families that make up Warren today. Each family can teach us something.

"So, even though it is the past, it is still a part of us here in Warren. And while those families no longer have any ties to Warren, they are still very much part of the fabric of this town as we move forward, for they built us. We owe them a debt of gratitude for raising Warren from the dust."

Every word that came out of his mouth sounded trite after everything. After Olivia.

He choked out the rest of his speech. He said nothing about the fire because it wouldn't work with the positive bent of his speech. The crowd ate it up, and they would continue to eat it up long after he was gone.

He couldn't get off the stage quickly enough. Something that used to give him such joy and pride and a familiar feeling of belonging now made him sick. What William had done to Evelyn, and what she had done to him, didn't sound as romantic as it had before. And what Austin had done to the town . . .

Brutality had shaped Warren in those years. Brutality so raw it had resonated down to the present, to Simon and Olivia and who knew how many others who had escaped William's designs. Simon had wanted to say that, to drop the weighty truth on them and make them take it, but he knew that wouldn't do anything. Forcing someone to change their opinion, no matter how small, was an impossible task. He could take this new energy and keep digging though, keep uncovering the truth.

Where was Olivia? The pull toward her was as strong as before all the bullshit of that month, and he hoped they could move past it. Move on, move forward. He felt driven to get in touch with Colton Munroe, whom Olivia had apparently spoken to so much over the past few weeks. If the kid knew more about Warren, Simon needed to know about it too. Telling the truth would help them move forward, but he had to know Olivia was OK first.

He sat at the back of the crowd for a few minutes, only vaguely listening to the head librarian and quilting circle leader, Rose Westwurth, as she announced the winners of that year's quilt contest in various levels of skill and style and pattern, machine and hand stitching. Then, feeling compelled, he stood and made his way toward campus. He would start looking for her there.

73

Noon, Saturday, October 31st

Officer Wells dropped Olivia off at the end of long driveway. She never thought they'd be dropping her off instead of her mother, but here they were. She thanked him and started up the drive. The crunch of her shoes on the gravel was strange after riding a horse so often recently. The plod of hooves on gravel had been more soothing.

The house remained in the present, but Olivia could feel the ghost of its old bones. There, that would have been the spot where Ethan fell. And there, that was where the porch had once begun, where Austin sat with them on an evening.

And that brought her to Simon.

Oliva's heart gave that little gallop unique to thinking about someone close, but the images that rushed in afterward had her scrambling to shut down that train of thought.

She refocused. She would know on Monday whether he was OK. In the meantime, she had lesson planning to do. The mess in her campus studio also needed to be sorted. She would need to contact whoever would handle getting her ruined prints back to her. Laundry needed to be done, and she needed to check on her mother's med refills. Or get them completely reassessed. These were lists with items she could tick off. Normal things.

Her mother met her at the door. She asked none of the questions that had followed Olivia home from the station.

So Olivia stood at the threshold, mentally checking off boxes as she looked at her mother. Salt-and-pepper hair, which Olivia had seen brown and fine in her mother's wedding photographs. The tufts of baby hairs still grew that pale brown at her hairline though, as had Evelyn's. Her mother's grey eyes were alert and wondering.

Lydia held her hands out, palms up. Red lines like burns stared back at Olivia. Her stomach hitched. The dark though faded memories of Evelyn's days of torment with Austin's head in her hands seared through her. But they were only marks from the reins of the nightmare horse her mother had held back so Olivia could escape.

Olivia took her mother's hands. The older woman looked more lucid than Olivia had seen her in probably twenty-five years. "Something came for you yesterday," Lydia said. "It's on the table."

"Thank you." Olivia let go of her mother's hands to cross the threshold. Even without memories ghosting behind her eyes, she felt the past in the house. Its foundations in the Weatherfords still lived here through her mother, herself. The house held the echoes of Evelyn and her sisters—happy, laughing, artistically inclined—in Olivia's own photographs. Someday Olivia and her mother would talk at length about what happened, but for today, Olivia was simply glad to see the coherence in the woman's eyes.

She opened the envelope on the kitchen table. There was a check inside for the remainder of her commission for the gallery showing. She stared outside toward the dugout, check in her hand. The desire for the house on Sunset had vanished below the horizon. She would use the money here at the house. She saw with blazing clarity how it would happen. Preserve the dugout and its contents, donating to the historical society what was appropriate and storing the rest. The journal would stay with her now that it was complete again. She would spruce up her mom's bedroom and knitting area. Make over her own attic room into something more befitting a photographer in her late thirties. She'd have to negotiate ending her lease with Ann, but her friend would surely understand.

Olivia stepped out onto the back deck without thinking, still drawn to the space that remained just out of sight behind the scrubby cottonwood, which had lost all its leaves in the windstorm the night before. The cold seared straight to her bones, and she wished for her wool shawl.

She half saw and half felt Austin's presence as she stood on the back deck in the unexpected cold. That he was there did and didn't surprise her. His dark cloak whipped around in the chill air, his handsome face etched with concern, his companion close by as well. The horrible longing that was all her own welled up like a wave, an entire ocean waiting to engulf her. It could carry her away to a place from which she would never return. Her own grief, the unending grief of her ancestor.

Olivia slipped back inside and busied herself making tea for her mother. Surely he would go now, would take her longing and her pain with him. Tomorrow was November, finally. The wind was cold, and all the leaves had fallen. The scent of the prairie in autumn was gone.

THE END

CPSIA information can be obtained
at www.ICGtesting.com
Printed in the USA
JSHW030316030520
5417JS00003B/4

9 781734 560206